THE CINDERELLA
COUNTESS

Sophia James

This book is produced from independently certified FSC™ paper
to ensure responsible forest management.
For more information visit www.harpercollins.co.uk/green.

Printed and bound in Spain
by CPI, Barcelona

MILLS & BOON

First Published in Great Britain 2019
by Mills & Boon, an imprint of HarperCollins*Publishers*
1 London Bridge Street, London, SE1 9GF

© 2019 Sophia James

ISBN: 978-0-263-26891-1

This er

F

I'd like to thank all my lovely writing friends
from the RWNZ.

Your help and support have really been appreciated.

Chapter One

London—1815

'There is a man here to see you, Belle, but I warn you he is unlike any man I have ever seen before.'

'Is he disfigured?' Annabelle Smith asked from above her burner where a tincture of peppermint and camphor was coming to a boil nicely, the steam of it rising into the air. 'Or is he just very ill?'

Rosemary Greene laughed. 'Here is his calling card. His waistcoat is of pink shiny satin and he has ornate rings on every one of his fingers. His hair is styled in a way I have never seen the likes of before and there is a carriage outside in the roadway that looks like it comes from a fairy tale. A good one, with a happy ending.'

Annabelle glanced at the card. Lytton Staines, the Earl of Thornton. What could a man like this possibly want with her and why would he come here to her humble abode on the fraying edges of Whitechapel?

'Put him into the front room, Rose, and make certain the dog is not in there with him. I will be there in a moment.'

Rosemary hesitated. 'Do you want me to accompany you?'

'Why should I require that?'

'Our visitor is a young man from society and you are a young woman. Is not a chaperon needed in such circumstances?'

Belle laughed at the worry on her friend's face. 'Undoubtedly if this was society it would be needed, but it is not and he has probably come to purchase medicines. Give me five minutes with this brew and in the meanwhile offer him a cup of tea. If he asks for anything stronger than that, however, do not allow it for we need all the alcohol we have left for the patients.'

Rose nodded. 'He looks rather arrogant and

very rich. Shall I get your aunt to sit with him? I don't think I feel quite up to it myself.'

Belle smiled. 'If we are lucky, the Earl of Thornton might have second thoughts about staying and will depart before I finish this.'

Lytton Staines looked around the room he had been asked to wait in, which was small but very tidy. There was a rug on the floor that appeared as though it had been plaited with old and colourful rags and on the wall before him were a number of badly executed paintings of flowers. He wondered why he had come here himself and not sent a servant in his stead. But even as he thought this he knew the answer. This was his sister's last chance and he did not want another to mess up the possibility of Miss Smith's offering her help.

The woman who had shown him into the front parlour had disappeared, leaving him with an ancient lady and a small hairy dog who had poked its head up from beneath his chair. A sort of mongrel terrier, he determined, his teeth yellowed and his top lip drawn back. Not in a smile, either. He tried to nudge the animal away with his boot in a fashion that wasn't offensive and succeeded only in bringing the hound closer, its eyes fixed upon him.

In a room down a narrow passageway someone was singing. Lytton would have liked to have put his hands to his ears to cancel out the cacophony, but that did not seem quite polite either.

He should not have come. Nothing at all about this place was familiar to him and he felt suddenly out of his depth. A surprising admission, given that in the higher echelons of the *ton* he'd always felt more than adequate.

The cup of tea brought in by a servant a moment before sat on the table beside him, a plume of fragrant steam filling the air.

For a second a smile twitched as he imagined his friends Shay, Aurelian and Edward seeing him here like this. It was the first slight humour he had felt in weeks and he reached for the softness of the emotion with an ache.

Dying became no one, that was for certain, and sickness and all its accompanying messiness was not something he had ever had any dealings with before.

'Thank God,' he muttered under his breath and saw the old lady look up.

He tipped his head and she frowned at him,

the glasses she wore falling to the very end of a decent-sized nose and allowing him to see her properly.

Once she must have been a beauty, he thought, before the touch of time had ruined everything. His own thirty-five years suddenly seemed numerous, the down slide to old age horribly close.

With care he reached for the teacup only because it gave him something to do and took a sip.

'Tea was always my mother's favourite drink.' These words came unbidden as Lytton recognised the taste of the same black variety his mother favoured and the frown on the old woman opposite receded.

As he shifted a little to allow the material in his jacket some room, the dog before him suddenly leapt, its brown and white body hurtling through the air to connect with the cup first and his waistcoat second, the hot scald of liquid on his thighs shocking and the sound of thin bone china shattering loud upon the plain timber boards of the floor.

The dog's teeth were fastened on the stranger's clothing. Belle heard the tear of silk and breathed out hard, wondering why Tante Alicia had not reprimanded her pet for such poor behaviour.

'Stanley. Stop that.' She hurried into the front room with horror. 'I am so sorry, sir, but he loves the colour pink and your waistcoat is of the shade he is most attracted to.'

Her hands tried to dislodge the canine's teeth from their sharp hold, but she had no luck at all. If anything, the expensive silk ripped further and she was pulled over almost on top of the Earl of Thornton in the ensuing tangle, her hand coming across the warm wetness at his thighs before he snatched it away.

'Cease.' His voice cut through the chaos and for a moment Belle wondered momentarily if it was to her or to Stanley that he spoke.

Tante Alicia's terrier did just as he was told, slinking to the door and out of the room with his tail firmly between bowed legs, Alicia herself following.

Annabelle was left in a more compromising position, her balance precarious because of her desperate hope of allowing no more damage to a garment of clothing that looked as if it might be worth more than cost of this entire house put together.

'God, but he has torn it badly,' she said beneath her breath, further words dissolving into French and directed at her departing aunt.

She broke off this tirade when she realised its absolute inappropriateness and regained her feet, crossing to the cabinet by the window and proceeding to extract a pound note from her velvet purse in the drawer.

'I will certainly pay for any damage, sir. I'd hoped Stanley might have been outside in the garden, you see, but unfortunately, he was not.'

'He has a penchant for the colour pink because of a fluffy toy he had as a puppy?' the man asked.

'You speak French?'

'Fluently. I presume that you are Miss Annabelle Smith? The herbalist?'

When she nodded he carried on.

'I am Lord Thornton and I wish to employ your services in regards to my sister. She has been struck down with a wasting sickness and no physician in England has been able to find a cure for her.'

'But you are of the opinion that I might?'

'People talk of you with great respect.'

'People you know?' She could not stop the disbelief betrayed in her words.

'My valet, actually. You were instrumental in allowing his father a few more good years.'

'Yet more often I do not foil the plans of God.'

'You are a religious woman, then?'

'More of a practical one. If you imagine me as the answer to all your...prayers, you may be disappointed.' She faltered.

'I am not a man who puts much stock in prayers, Miss Smith.'

'What do you put stock in, then?'

For a second she thought she saw anger flint before he hid it.

'Brandy. Gaming. Horseflesh. Women.'

There was a wicked glimmer of danger in his gold eyes and Belle stepped back.

Miss Annabelle Smith looked shocked but he was not here to pretend. She had the most astonishing blue eyes Lytton had ever seen and when her fingers had run over his private parts in her haste to remove the dog from the hem of his waistcoat he'd felt an instantaneous connection of red-hot lust.

Hell.

Did the tea have something in it, some herbal aphrodisiac that befuddled his brain and bypassed sense? Because already he wanted her fingers back where they had only briefly rested.

He pushed the money she offered away and stood, his boot crunching the remnants of the teacup into even smaller parts, the roses once etched into the china now disembodied.

He could not imagine what had made him answer her query as to what he put stock in so rudely, but, he suddenly felt just like the dog—Stanley, had she called him?—all his hackles raised and a sense of fate eroding free will.

There was protection in the depravities of his true self and suddenly even his sister's need for Annabelle Smith's magical concoctions was secondary to his own need for escape.

But she was not letting him go so easily, the towel she had in her hand now dabbing again at his thigh.

Was she deranged? What female would think this acceptable? With horror he felt a renewed rising in his cursed appendage and knew that she had seen the betrayal of his body in her instant and fumbling withdrawal. The white towel was stained brown in tea.

'I thought…' She stopped and dimples that he had not known she had suddenly surfaced.

'I am sorry.' With determination she stuck the cloth out for him to take and turned her back. 'You may see to yourself, Lord Earl of Thornton. I should have understood that before.'

His title was wrong. She had no idea how to address a peer of the realm. He rubbed at his thighs with speed and was glad of the lessening hot wetness.

Taking in a breath, he realised how much he had needed air. She still had not turned around, her shapely bottom outlined beneath the thin day dress she wore. There were patches at a side pocket and the head of some straggly plant stuck out of the top.

She smelt of plants, too, the mist of them all around her. Not an unpleasant smell, but highly unusual. Most ladies of his acquaintance held scents of violets, or roses, or lavender.

'I have finished with the towel, Miss Smith.'

He was amused by her allowance of so much privacy.

'Thank you.' She snatched it back from him and the awkward maiden became once again a direct and determined woman, no air of humour visible.

'I would need to see your sister before I prescribed her anything. Proper medicine does not enjoy guesswork and a wasting sickness encompasses many maladies that are as different from each other as night is to day.'

'Very well. She is here in London for the next week, seeing specialists, so if you would have some time…'

'Pick me up here at nine tomorrow morning. I need to prepare some treatments but…' She hesitated and then carried on. 'I do not come cheap, my lord Earl. Each consultation would be in the vicinity of three pounds.'

Lytton thought she held her breath as she said this, but he could have been wrong. 'Done. I will be here at nine.'

'Good day, then.'

She put her hand out and shook his. He felt small hardened spots on her fingers and wondered what work might have brought those about.

Not the soft pliable hands of a lady. Not the grip of one either. The one ring she wore was small and gold. He felt the excess of his own jewellery with a rising distaste.

A moment later he was in his carriage, leaning his head back against fine brown leather. He needed a stiff drink and quickly.

'White's,' he said to the footman who was

closest, glad when the conveyance began to move away from the cloying poverty of Whitechapel and from the contrary, forceful and highly unusual Miss Annabelle Smith.

His club was busy when he arrived and he strode over to where Aurelian de la Tomber was sitting talking to Edward Tully.

'I thought you were still in Sussex with your beautiful wife, Lian?'

'I was until this morning. I am only up here for the day and will go home first thing tomorrow.'

'Wedded life suits you, then. You were always far more nomadic.'

'The philosophy of one woman and one home is addictive.'

'Then you are a lucky man.'

Lytton saw Edward looking at him strangely and hoped he'd kept the sting out of his reply. It was getting more and more difficult to be kind, he thought, and swallowed the brandy delivered by a passing servant, ordering another in its wake.

He was unsettled and distinctly out of sorts, his visit to the East End of London searing into any contentment he'd had.

'I've just had a meeting with a woman who concocts medicines in the dingy surroundings of Whitechapel. Someone needs to do something about the smell of the place, by the way, for it is more pungent than ever.'

'Was the herbalist hopeful of finding some remedy for your sister?'

Edward looked at him directly, sincerity in his eyes.

'She was.' Lytton said this because to imagine anything else was unthinkable and because right now he needed hope more than honesty.

'Who is she?' Aurelian asked.

'Miss Annabelle Smith. My valet recommended her services.'

'She cured him? Of what?'

'No. She prolonged the life of his father and the family were grateful. I can't quite imagine how he paid the costs, though.'

'The costs of her visits?'

'Three pounds a time feels steep.'

'Had you given her your card before she charged you?'

Lytton nodded. 'And I would have been willing to pay more if she had asked.'

'The mystery of supply and demand, then? How old is she?'

'Not young. She spoke French, too, which was surprising.'

That interested Aurelian. 'Smith is not a French name?'

'Neither is Annabelle. There was an older woman there who did appear to be from France, though. An aunt I think she called her after their dog attacked me.' He loosened the buttons of his jacket to show them the wreckage of his waistcoat.

'A colour like that needs tearing apart.' Edward's voice held humour, but Aurelian's was much more serious.

'I have never heard of this woman or of her French aunt. Perhaps it bears looking into?'

'No.' Lytton said this in a tone that had the others observing him. 'No investigations. She is meeting Lucy tomorrow.'

Edward was trying his hardest to look nonchalant, but he could tell his friend was curious.

'What does she look like?'

'Strong. Certain. Direct. She is nothing like the females of the *ton*. Her dress was at least ten years out of date and she favours scarves to tie her hair back. It is dark and curly and reaches to at least her waist. She was… uncommon.'

'It seems she made quite an impression on you then, Thorn? I saw Susan Castleton a few hours back and she said you were supposed to be meeting her tonight?'

'I am. We are going to the ballet.'

Susan had been his mistress for all of the last four months, but Lytton was becoming tired of her demands. She wanted a lot more than he could give her and despite her obvious beauty he was bored of the easy and constant sex. God, that admission had him sitting up straighter. It was Lucy, he supposed, and the ever-close presence of her sadness and ill health.

He wished life was as easy as it used to be, nothing in his way and everything to live for. One of his fingers threaded through the hole in his waistcoat and just for a second he questioned what ill-thought-out notion had ever convinced him to buy clothing in quite this colour.

It was Susan's doing, he supposed, and her love of fashion. Easier to just give in to her choice of fabric than fight for the more sombre hues. He wondered when that had happened, this surrender of his opinion, and frowned, re-solving to do away with both the excessive rings and the colour pink forthwith.

Miss Annabelle Smith was contrary and un-usual and more than different. He could never imagine her allowing another to tell her what to wear or what to do. Even with the mantle of poverty curtailing choices she seemed to have found her exact path in life and was rev-elling in it.

Belle awoke in the dark of night, sweating and struggling for breath. The dreams were back. She swallowed away panic and sat up, flinting the candle at her bedside so that it chased away some of the shadows.

The same people shouting, the same fear, the same numbness that had her standing in the room of a mansion she had never recognised. She thought she hated them, these people, though she was not supposed to. She knew she wanted to run away as fast as her legs could carry her and although she could never quite see them she understood that they looked like her. How she would know this eluded sense, but that certainty had been there ever since she had first had the nightmares when she was very young. Sometimes she even heard them speak her name.

The sound of the night noise from the street calmed her as did the snoring of her aunt in the room next door. At times like this she was thankful for the thin walls of their dwelling, for they gave her a reason to not feel so alone.

The visage of Lytton Staines, the Earl of Thornton, floated into her memory as well, his smile so very different from the clothes he wore.

She remembered the hardness of male flesh beneath the thin beige superfine when her fingers had run along his thighs by mistake. Her face flamed. God, she had never been near a man in quite such a compromising way and she knew he had seen her embarrassed withdrawal.

The incident with the spilled tea this afternoon began to attain gigantic proportions, a mistake she might relive again each time she saw him which would be in only a matter of hours as he was due to collect her in the morning at nine. She needed to go back to sleep. She needed to be at her best in the company of Lord Thornton because otherwise there were things about him that were unsettling.

He was beautiful for a start and a man well

used to the exalted title that sat on his shoulders. He was also watchful. She had seen how he'd glanced around her house, assessing her lack of fortune and understanding her more-than-dire straits.

She wondered what he might have thought of her paintings, the flowers she lovingly drew adorning most of one wall in the front room. Drawing was a way for her to relax and she enjoyed the art of constructing a picture.

In her early twenties she had drawn faces, eerie unfamiliar ones which she had thrown away, but now she stuck to plants, using bold thick lines. The memory of those early paintings summoned her dreams and she shook off the thought. She would be thirty-two next week and her small business of providing proper medicines for the sick around Whitechapel was growing. She grimaced at the charge per visit she had asked the Earl to pay, but, if a few consultations with the sister of a man who could patently afford any exorbitant fee allowed many others to collect their needs for nothing, then so be it. Not many could pay even a penny.

He'd looked just so absurdly rich. She wondered where he lived here in London. One of the beautiful squares in the centre of Mayfair, she supposed. Places into which she had seldom ventured.

Would it be to one of those town houses that he would take her in order to tend to his sister? Would his family be in attendance? Alicia had told her the Earl had mentioned a mother who enjoyed tea.

She had not addressed him properly. She had realised this soon after he had left because she had asked Milly, the kitchen maid, if she knew how one was supposed to speak to an earl. The girl had been a maid in the house of a highly born lord a few years before.

My lord Earl was definitely an error. According to Milly she could have used 'my lord' or 'your lordship', or 'Lord Thornton'. Belle had decided when she saw him next she would use the second.

At least that was cleared up and sleep felt a little nearer. She had prepared all the tinctures, medicines and ointment she would take with her to see Lord Thornton's sister so it was only a case of getting herself ready now.

What could she wear? The question both annoyed and worried her. She should not care about such shallow things, but she did. She wanted suddenly to look nice for the mother who enjoyed tea. That thought made her smile and she lay back down on her bed watching the moon through undrawn curtains.

It had rained yesterday, but tonight it was largely clear.

As she closed her eyes, the last image she saw before sleep was that of the Earl of Thornton observing her with angry shock as she had wiped away the hot tea from his skin-tight pantaloons.

Chapter Two

Miss Smith was sitting on the front doorstep of her Whitechapel house when his carriage pulled up to the corner on the dot of nine. She held a large wicker basket in front of her, covered almost entirely by a dark blue cloth.

The oddness of a woman waiting alone outside her home and completely on time had Lytton waving away the footman as he jumped down to the ground.

Miss Annabelle Smith appeared pleased to see him as she stood, her hand shading her face and the odd shape of her hat sending a shadow down one side of her cheek.

'I thought perhaps you might have decided not to come,' she said, her fingers keeping the cloth on her basket anchored in the growing breeze.

The heightened notice of her as a woman he'd felt yesterday returned this morning and Lytton shoved it away.

'My chaperon will be here in just a moment as Aunt Alicia would not settle until I agreed to have her with me. I hope that is all right with you, your lordship?'

She knew, now, how to address him. He found himself missing the 'my lord Earl'.

'Of course.' The words sounded more distant than he had meant them to be. She looked tired, dark circles under her eyes, and there was a cut on her thumb. He hoped the injury had not come about in the preparation of his sister's medicines.

Pulling the three pounds he had ready from his pocket, he offered them to her.

'If it is too much I quite understand,' she said, but he shook his head.

'I can afford it, Miss Smith, and I am grateful that you would consent to attending my sister at such short notice.'

The same velvet purse he had seen yesterday came out of her pocket, the notes carefully tucked within it.

'It will be useful to buy more supplies for

those who cannot pay. There are many such folk here.'

'You have lived in this house for a while?'

'We have, your lordship. It is rented, but it is home.'

'Yet you do not speak with the accent of the East End?'

She looked away, distracted as the same woman he had seen yesterday joined them, busy fingers tying the ribbons on her bonnet.

'This is my friend, Mrs Rosemary Greene.'

'We met briefly yesterday. Ma'am.' He tipped his head and the older woman blushed dark red, but was saved from answering as Annabelle Smith caught at her arm and shepherded her towards the conveyance. When the footman helped each of them up Miss Smith took a deep breath, giving Lytton the impression she did not much wish to get in. He took the seat opposite them as the door closed, listening to the horses being called on.

'Did you ever read the fairy tale *Cendrillon* by Charles Perrault, your lordship?' Her dimples were on display, picked out by the incoming sunshine.

'I did, Miss Smith.'

'Your carriage reminds me of that. Ornate and absurdly comfortable.'

'You read it in French?'

'When I was a child I lived in France for a time with my aunt.'

The traffic at this time of the morning was busy and they were travelling so slowly it seemed as if all of London was on the road.

The silence inside the carriage lengthened, their last exchange throwing up questions. She did not give the impression of one born abroad for her words held only the accent of English privilege and wealth. How could that be?

He hoped like hell that any of his extended family would not converge on his town house this morning, for he wanted to allow Miss Smith some time to talk with his sister by herself. His mother would be present, of course, but she was lost in her own sadness these days and appeared befuddled most of the time. Today such confusion would aid him.

It was as if Lucy's sickness had ripped the heart out of the Thorntons and trampled any happiness underfoot. It was probably why he had taken up with Susan Castleton to be honest, Lytton thought, her sense of devil-may-care just the attitude he had needed to counter the constant surge of melancholy.

Miss Smith was watching the passing streets with interest, her fingers laced together and still. When they went around a sharp corner, though, as their speed increased he saw her grasp at the seat beneath her, each knuckle white.

'It is perfectly safe. My driver is one of the most skilled in London.'

Blue eyes washed over him and then looked back to the outside vistas.

'People more usually come to see me, your lordship.'

'You don't use hackneys, then?'

'Never.'

This was stated in such a way that left little room for debate and Mrs Greene caught his eye as he frowned, an awkward worry across her face.

Portman Square was now coming into view, the façade of his town house standing on one corner. He hoped that Annabelle Smith would not be flustered by the wealth of it, for in comparison to her living quarters in Whitechapel it suddenly looked enormous.

As they alighted an expression unlike any

he had ever seen briefly crossed her face. Shock, he thought, and pure horror, her pallor white and the pulse at her throat fast. His hand reached out to take her arm as he imagined she might simply faint.

'Are you well, Miss Smith?'

He saw the comprehension of what she had shown him reach her eyes, her shoulders stiffening, but she did not let him go, her fingers grabbing at the material of his jacket.

Then the door opened and his mother stood there, black fury on her face.

'You cannot bring your doxies into this house, Thornton. I shall simply not allow it. Your valet has told me you were in the company of one of your mistresses, Mrs Castleton, last night and now you dare to bring in these two this morning. Your father, bless his soul, would be rolling in his grave and as for your sister...'

She stopped and twisted a large kerchief, dabbing at her nose as she left them, a discomfited silence all around.

'I am sorry. My mother is not herself.'

It was all he could think to say, the fury roiling inside him pressed down. He needed Annabelle Smith to see his sister, that was his overriding thought, and he would deal with his mother's unexpected accusations when he could.

The Earl of Thornton kept mistresses and his mother thought she and Rosemary were fallen woman? The haze of seeing the Thornton town house dispersed under such a ludicrous assassination of her character and if there had not been a patient inside awaiting she would have simply insisted upon being taken home.

This behaviour was so common with the very wealthy, this complete and utter disregard for others, and if the Earl had somehow inveigled her into thinking differently then the more fool she.

It was why Belle had always made it a policy to never do business with the aristocracy, her few very early forays into providing remedies for the wealthy ending in disaster. They either did not pay or they looked down their noses at her. However, she'd had none of the overt hatred shown by the Earl's mother.

Well, here at least she had already been paid, the three-pound fee tucked firmly into her purse.

The Earl looked furious, the muscles in his jaw working up and down and as they entered into the entrance proper he asked them if they might wait for just a moment.

'Yes of course, your lordship.' As Rosemary answered she drew Annabelle over to a set of comfortable-looking armchairs arranged around a table, a vase of pastel-shaded flowers upon it that were made of dyed silk.

Belle sat in a haze, the smell of polish and cleaning product in the air. Everything was as familiar as it was strange and she could not understand this at all. She had seen a house just like this one in her dreams: the winding staircase, the black and white tiles, the numerous doors that led off the entrance hall to elaborately dressed and furnished salons, portraits of the past arranged solemnly on the walls up and down the staircase.

'What on earth is wrong with you, Belle? You look like you have seen a ghost.'

'I think I have.'

'I cannot believe the Earl's mother would have thought we were doxies.' Rose looked horrified as she rearranged the red and green scarf draped about her neck into a more concealing style.

'She has probably never seen one before and I suppose we dress differently from the people who live around here.'

Belle hoped the woman would not return to find them again just as she prayed she could have asked for her coat and hat and left.

But she'd been paid well for a consultation and the carriage outside had rumbled on already down the street. Their only avenue of escape was the Earl. He suddenly came down the passageway to one side, another servant accompanying him.

'My sister's suite is this way. There is a sitting room just outside if Mrs Greene would feel comfortable waiting there.'

Rose nodded and so did Belle, this visit becoming more and more exhausting. She did not truly feel up to the task of reassuring a young, sick and aristocratic patient, but had no true way to relay that to the Earl of Thornton without appearing ridiculous. Still, if his awful mother was there with more of her accusations she would turn and go.

As they mounted the staircase the smell of camphor rose from her basket and Annabelle presumed the container in it had fallen over. Removing the fabric, she righted it and jammed it in more tightly against the wad of bandages at its side.

The light was dimmer now and the noises from the street and the house more distant. The scent of sickness was present, too, her nostrils flaring to pick up any undertones of disease. Surprisingly there were none, a fact that had her frowning.

'If you could wait here, Mrs Greene, it would be appreciated. My sister in her present state is not good at receiving strangers and one new face is probably enough for now.'

Seeing Rose settled Belle followed the Earl through a further anteroom, which opened into a large and beautiful bedchamber, full of the accoutrements of ill health and all the shades half-drawn. There were medicine bottles as well as basins and cloths on a long table. Vases full of flowers decorated every other flat surface.

At the side of the bed a maid sat, but she instantly stood and went from the room, though there had been no gesture from the Earl to ask her to leave.

'Lucy?' The Earl's voice was softer, a tenderness there that had been missing in every other conversation Belle had had with him.

'Miss Smith is come to see you. The herbalist I told you of.'

'I do not want another medical person here, Thorn. I've said that. I just want to be left alone.'

The tone of the voice was strong. A further oddness. If Lady Lucy had been in bed for this many weeks and deathly ill she would have sounded more fragile.

She had burrowed in under the blankets, only the top of her golden head seen. Her fingernails were bitten to the quick, every single one of them, but there was no discolouration of the nail beds.

'Miss Smith is well thought of in her parish of Whitechapel. She seldom visits outside her home area, so in this we are more than fortunate.'

'Where is Mother?'

'I asked her to stay in her room.'

'She is being impossible this morning. I wish she might return to Balmain and leave me here with you. How old is Miss Smith?'

'See for yourself. She is right here.'

The blanket stilled and then a face popped out from the rumpled wool. A gaunt face of wrecked beauty, the hair cut into slivers of ill-fashioned spikes.

Belle hoped she did not look surprised, the first impressions between a patient and a healer important ones.

'You are not too…old.' This came from Lucy.

'I am thirty-two next week. It seems inordinately old to me. But what is the alternative?'

Unexpectedly the young woman smiled. 'This.'

'Perhaps,' Belle said quietly. 'When did you last eat?'

'I am no longer hungry. I have broth sometimes.'

'Could I listen to your pulse?'

'No. I don't like to be touched.'

'Never?' Surprise threaded into her words. 'Who has examined you then?'

'No one. I do not allow it. It can be seen from a distance that my malady is taking the life from me. All sorts of medicines have been tried. And have failed. One doctor did touch me against all my will and bled me twice. Now I just wish to die. It will be easier for everyone.'

Belle heard the Earl draw in a breath and felt a huge sorrow for him.

'Could I sit with you for a moment, Miss Staines? Alone?'

'Without my brother, you mean. Without anyone here. I do not know if…'

But the Earl had already gone, walking like a ghost towards the door, his footsteps quiet.

Belle waited for a moment and closed her eyes. There was so much to be found in silence. The girl's breathing was fast and a little shallow, but there was no underlying disease in her passageways. She moved her feet a lot, indicating a nervous disposition. She could hear the sound of the sheets rustling and Lady Lucy sniffed twice. She was coming down with a cold, perhaps, though her constitution sounded robust.

Opening her eyes, Belle looked at her patient directly, the golden glance of the Earl's sister flecked with a darker yellow.

'Why do you lie, Miss Staines?'

'Pardon?' A shocked breath was drawn in with haste.

'There is no disease in your body. But what is there is something you need to speak of.'

'You cannot know this.' These words were small and sharp.

'Today I shall run camphor across your chest and peppermint under the soles of your feet. If I was you, I should then begin to take an interest in the world. Tomorrow I shall return with different medicines. A week should be enough for you to start getting up again and then we can face the problem that is the true reason why you have taken to your bed.'

'Problem?'

'Think about it. Your family is suffering from the charade you are putting them through and if the physicians they have dispatched to attend to your needs have never delved deeper into the truth of what ails you then that is their poor practice. But it is time now to face up to what has happened to you and live again in any way that you can.'

'Get out.'

Belle stood, her heart hammering. 'I am sorry, but I will not. Only with good sense can you face what must come next because, believe it or not, this is the way of life. A set back and then a triumph. Yours will be spectacular.'

'Are you a witch, Miss Smith? One of the occult?'

'Perhaps.' Her reply came with a fervour. This girl needed to believe in her words or otherwise she would be lost. 'Magic is something that you now require so I want you to unbutton your nightdress and I will find my camphor.'

Ten minutes later she was downstairs again and the Earl of Thornton had recalled his conveyance.

'I am sorry I cannot accompany you back to Whitechapel, Miss Smith, but I have other business in the city. You said that you'd told my sister that you would be back on the morrow so I shall make sure my conveyance is outside your house again at nine.'

'No. Tomorrow we shall find our own way. But have the maid bring up a plate of chicken broth with a small crust of bread for your sister. Tell her that such sustenance will do her good and I will be asking after how much she has eaten.'

'Very well. Thank you.'

The Earl did not believe that his sister would deign to eat anything. He was disappointed in her short visit, too, Belle could tell, the smell of camphor and peppermint the only tangible evidence of her doctoring. He imagined her a quack and a charlatan and an expensive one at that and would continue to do so unless his sister took her advice.

She tipped her head and turned for the pathway, unsurprised when the door was closed behind them.

Once home she sought out her aunt where she sat in the small alcove off the kitchen.

'I recognised the Earl of Thornton's house, Tante Alicia. I think I knew one just like it.'

Her aunt simply stared at her.

'It was similar to the house in my dreams. The one I told you about.'

'I always said that you were an auld one, Annabelle, a traveller who has been here before in another lifetime.'

'Who are they, Alicia? The people I remember who are dressed like those at the Thornton town house.'

'I have told you again and again that there are no ghosts who stalk you and that I do not know of these people you see.'

'Then who were my parents?'

'I never met them. I took you in when a nun from the convent in the village asked it of me.

A sick child from England who was placed in the hands of the lord when a servant brought her there, to the church of Notre-Dame de la Nativité. Maria, the nun, was English herself and spoke with you every day for years until your French was fluent and you could cope. That is all I know. I wish there had been more, but there was not. I'd imagined you would stay with me for only a matter of weeks, but when no one came back to claim you and the months went on...' She stopped, regathering herself. 'By then you were the child I had never had and I prayed to our lord every day that the situation would continue, that I would not have to give you up because that would have broken my heart.'

They had been through all this before so many times. It all made perfect sense and yet...

Today Lady Lucy had made perfect sense to her as well, hiding there in her bed in a darkened room where no one could get to her. She had stopped eating. She had ceased to want to live. The anger in Belle surfaced with a suddenness that she did not conceal.

Everyone was lying.

Her aunt.

Lady Lucy.

Even the handsome Earl of Thornton with his succession of mistresses and his bitter mother.

Taking leave of her aunt and walking to her own room, Belle lifted up a paintbrush, dipping it in oil and mixing it with red powder after finding a sheet of paper.

Nothing was real. Everything was false. She liked the banal deceiving strokes she drew as they ran across the truth and banished it. Lives built on falsity. Paintings borne on fury. Lady Lucy was young and well brought up. Belle wanted to kill the man who had left her the wreck that she was, but as yet there could be only the small and quiet steps of acceptance before the healing began.

Lytton spent the afternoon entwined in the arms of the beautiful widow Mrs Susan Castleton in the rooms he had provided for her in Kensington.

She had impeccable taste, he would give her that, but what had been wonderful, even as recent as last week, now was not.

His mother's words had stung and the look

on Miss Annabelle Smith's face had stung further.

Why did the healer have to be so damned unusual? His sister had gulped down the broth and the crust and asked for a cup of tea to finish her lunch with. She had not eaten properly in weeks and now after a ten-minute visit with the contrary Miss Smith she was suddenly pulling herself out of the mire. Lucy thought she was a witch and had told him so, a woman of fearful evil and unspeakable power. She did not wish for her to visit again.

Well, if a witch could cajole his sister into re-joining the real world then so be it, and her alchemy would certainly be welcome in his town house after the disappointing efforts of all the other renowned physicians. He would be asking her back.

'You are so very well formed, Thornton.' The whisper in his ear had him turning, Susan's chestnut curls trailing across his chest when she tweaked his nipple, her body nudging his own in further invitation.

God, she was insatiable. When he had first met her he could barely believe his luck, but now…now he wondered if she might squeeze all the life from him and leave him as much a wreck as his sister.

'I want to eat you up. All of you.'

Her words were so like what he had just been thinking that he pushed her from him and sat up.

He didn't want this any more, this salacious liaison so far away from what he knew to be right. Even a few weeks ago he would have found such passion exciting. Now all he wanted to do was escape.

'I need to go, Susan. I am not sure if I shall be back.'

If this was too brutal for her then he was sorry for it, but he disliked lying. To anyone.

'You joke, surely, Thornton. We have been here all afternoon feeding off one another.'

The further reference to food made him stand and find his clothes. Fumbling with the one ring he wore today, he twisted it from his finger.

'It is worth the price of the rent on this place for at least another year. I thank you for your patience with me, but now it is finished. I can't do this any more.'

Tears began to fall down her cheeks. 'You

cannot possibly be serious, Thornton. I love you, I love you with all my heart and—'

He stopped her by placing a finger across her generous reddened lips.

'You loved Derwent a year ago and you loved Marcus Merryweather before that. There will be another after me.'

As he walked away, garments in hand, she picked up a vase and threw it at him hard, the glass smashing against the side of his head and drawing blood as it shattered.

'You will regret this, I swear it. No one will ever make love to you in the way I have, especially one whom you might take as a wife. They are all cold and wooden and witless.'

Hell. Had Aurelian or Edward said something publicly of his plans to be married before the end of the Season? He hoped not. If that happened he would have a hundred mamas and their chicks upon him, courting him with guile and hope.

The day that had begun strangely just seemed to get stranger. He could feel warm blood running across one cheek and yet he couldn't go home because his mother was prowling through the corridors of his town house and Lucy had spent almost the entire morning crying.

His younger brother was in trouble again with his school and Prudence, his oldest sister, was in Rome seeing the sights with her new husband. He would have liked to talk with her, but she was not due back for at least a few months, skipping out of England with a haste that was unbecoming.

No one in his entire family was coping. His father's death the Christmas before last had seen to that and here he was, bogged down by the responsibility of a title he'd little reason to like and a mistress who had just tried to kill him.

Once he had been free and unburdened. Now every man and his dog wanted a piece of him. Once the most reading he had done was to glance at the IOUs from the gambling tables where his luck never seemed to run out. Now it was writing reports, filling out forms and doing all the myriad other things a large and complicated estate required.

He had barely come up for air in weeks save in the bed of Susan Castleton, but that was now also lost to him. He couldn't regret this even a bit, he thought, as he finished dressing and made his leave.

He'd spend the evening at White's and when the place closed he'd go to Edward Tully's town house. At least Derwent would understand his fading interest in a woman whom he, too, had once been intimate with.

'You need to go abroad, Thorn, and escape your family.' Edward's words were said with the edge of strong cognac upon them.

'Easy for you to say with your father still hale and hearty and an older brother who will take on the heavy mantle of the title.'

Edward laughed as he upended yet another glass of cognac and gestured to a servant going by to bring another bottle. 'How are the marriage plans going?'

Lytton swore.

He'd confided in Lian and Edward about his intention to marry as a result of Lucy's ill health, his own mortality staring him in the face. He now wished he hadn't.

'Wide hips and a passable face wasn't it?' Edward plainly saw a humour that Lytton himself did not. 'The first girl you saw with both qualifications?'

'I was drunk.'

'More drunk than you are tonight?'

At that Lytton laughed. 'More drunk and also happier, possibly.'

'Well, Lian is happy and so is Shay. Perhaps a wife is the answer. A woman of substance. No shallow-brained ingénue or experienced courtesan.'

'And where are those women?' Lytton asked. 'Shay found Celeste in the underbelly of Napoleon's Paris and Lian's Violet was thrown up from the greed of treason and lost gold.'

'Stuart Townsend said he saw you this morning in a carriage with a woman he did not recognise, Thorn. He said she looked interesting?'

Lytton shook his head. For some reason he did not want to talk of Annabelle Smith. His whole family must have disappointed her today and he did not wish to continue the trend. He stayed silent.

'And the fact that you will not speak of her makes it even more interesting.'

He stood. 'I think I need to go home, Edward, and sleep. For a hundred years, if I only could.'

'There's a masked ball at the Seymours' tomorrow evening. Come with me to that and blow away a few cobwebs.'

'Perhaps I might. I will send you word in the morning.'

Outside the sky was clearer and the stars were out. A vibrant endless heaven, Lytton thought, enjoying the fresh air. He had meant to stay at Edward's, but suddenly wanted to be home.

Annabelle Smith was due tomorrow again at the ungodly hour of nine and he did not want to miss seeing her. That thought worried him more than any other.

Chapter Three

This morning Belle did not take her basket. Instead she brought a book, tied in blue ribbon and inscribed. Rose stayed at home.

The Earl of Thornton was waiting for her in the entrance hall when she arrived at his town house. Today there was no other servant present and he took her coat and hat himself and hung them on the brass pegs to one side of the front door.

A gash across his temple was the first thing she noticed.

'You have been hurt?'

'Barely,' he answered and swiped at his untidy fringe.

'It looks like more than that to me, your lordship.'

'Your patient is upstairs, Miss Smith.'

She smiled at the rebuke. 'And your mother?'

'Is behaving in her room.'

'Did your sister eat anything yesterday?'

'More than she has in weeks. She imagines you to be of the occult. A blooded witch, I think it was she called you.'

'There is strength in such imagination.'

At that he laughed out loud and dipped into his pocket. A ten-pound note lay in his palm. 'For you. You have done more in fifteen minutes for my sister than all the other physicians put together.'

'Oh, I could hardly take that much, your lordship. Ten pounds is a fortune and more than many people in Whitechapel might make in a whole year.'

'It is not for you, per se. I thought you told me yesterday you use your exorbitant fees for good in your parish.'

'I would and I do, but…'

He simply leaned forward to extract the velvet purse from the pocket of her coat on the peg and slid it inside before returning it. She could do nothing but concur.

'Thank you. I shall send you receipts for exactly what I have spent each penny upon. Your lordship.' She added this after a few seconds.

They had reached his sister's sitting room now, the place where Rose had waited yesterday, and he stopped.

'I think you would do better to see my sister alone today.'

Taking a breath, Belle nodded and went in.

This morning Lady Lucy was not hiding from her, but sitting in her bed gazing out of the window. She looked small and thin and pale.

'I hear you ate both lunch and dinner?'

The girl turned to her, anger in her eyes.

'As I am not used to being threatened, I deduced it good sense to eat something, Miss Smith. Just in case.'

'Then you would not mind if I read to you, either?' Pulling the ribbons from the book, Belle sat unbidden on the seat at the side of the bed and opened the first page.

Mary, the heroine of this fiction, was the daughter of Edward, who married Eliza, a gentle fashionable girl, with a kind of indolence in her temper which might be termed negative good nature...

Half an hour later she stopped.

'Who wrote this?'

Belle was heartened by the question. 'Mary Wollstonecraft. The writer truly believed that feminine imagination could transport women from cruel circumstance.'

Silence abounded, the tick of a clock in the corner all that could be heard in the room.

'I want to gift this book to you, Miss Staines. I hope we might discuss its possibilities next time I meet with you.'

'When would that be?'

'On Wednesday. That should allow you some time to come up with an opinion. An opinion I would value,' she added, seeing the dark uncertainty in golden eyes.

'I am not sure.'

'Eat and read, that is all I ask of you. Food for the body and for the mind.'

'How do you know my brother, the Earl of Thornton?'

'I don't, really.'

'Where did you meet him?'

'He came to my house in Whitechapel and asked me to visit you.'

'He paid you?'

'Very well. More than I am worth, probably.'

'Are you always so honest?'

'I find facing life head on is the best possible way of escaping difficulty.'

'My mother would not think that way.'

'Sometimes one needs to find confidence inside without being swayed by the influence of others.'

'You talk like Thorn. Do you know that? He cajoles everyone to do his bidding and he is so clever he can always find the words. Mama says he is like our father, but I do not think this is true. He is a thousand times better.'

'You love him?'

'Everyone does. But he is as unhappy as I am.'

Lord, this conversation was going in ways she had no idea of and Annabelle hoped with all her heart that the Earl of Thornton was not outside listening.

'Why are you so unhappy?'

The least she could do was to bring the focus back on her patient.

'I have become a mere nothing.'

The heroine's words from the book. Lady Lucy had been listening after all.

Belle lowered her voice. 'Motherhood is the furthest thing from nothing that I know of.'

Her patient started at that and blanched noticeably. 'Have you told him? My brother?'

'No.'

'Please do not. I need to think…'

With care Belle placed her hand across thin fingers. 'I give you my solemn oath that I shan't speak of your condition to anyone.'

'Thank you.'

When she looked away Belle rose, tucking the book into the folds of cloth on the bed so that it would not fall.

'I will see you on Wednesday.'

Outside she found Lytton Staines where she had left him, a drink in hand.

'I hope this visit will be as successful as your last.'

'I shall see your sister again next week, your lordship. There will be no payment required.'

'Miss Smith,' he said, a sound of exasperation in the word.

'Yes, your lordship.'

'I am an earl. Ten pounds is nothing at all to me and I shall pay you exactly what I think you are worth.'

'Are you made of money, then?' For a second he stood so close she could feel the whisper of his breath against her cheek as he replied.

'Yes.'

She almost liked his certainty and his arrogance at that moment. He was a man who valued honesty just as his sister had said and he was kind. Of all the attributes in people, that, to Annabelle, was the most important.

'I will also accompany you home.'

'It is not necessary. I am quite capable of getting myself back to Whitechapel.'

'I know you are, but I would like to see you safe.'

'Very well.'

She stepped back and he led the way downstairs, the wound on his left temple beginning to discolour. She would have offered to tend it, but something told her that he would decline such an invitation.

A rich man, a brother, a son, an earl. A man with mistresses and with enemies. A man of generosity and cleverness, too. So many things that she now knew of him as well as so many things she did not. She wondered just what he might think of her?

'Is my sister going to recover, do you think?'

He asked her this as the carriage slid away from the curb. Today it travelled slowly and she thought the Earl had had some hand in that, for he had been speaking with the driver just before they left.

Instead of answering his question she found one of her own. 'How did your father die?'

Her words were bare and shock ripped across his face.

'Why do you wish to know that?'

'Your sister said something that made me wonder.'

'What did she say?'

'She said that you were a thousand times better than he was.'

'Hell and damnation.'

She could not believe that she had heard the Earl swear in front of her and thought he might apologise for it, but instead he turned to look out of the window as he spoke again.

'He killed himself.'

He had asked her if she was a religious woman once and said that he did not put much stock in prayers. But she could see it did mean something, after all, for shock was etched on his face. He believed his father consigned to hell just as his sister did. A permanent banishment. An unchangeable tragedy.

'When did this happen?'

'Two Christmases ago. He gambled, you see, and lost. At least when I sit at the tables, I win.'

'What did he lose?'

'Balmain, the Thornton family estate. I got it back for him by the luck of a full flush a week later and he was not thankful.'

'The sins of the father are to be laid upon the children.'

'Words from the Bible?'

'And from William Shakespeare's *The Merchant of Venice*.'

'You are a mine of information, Miss Smith. From witchery or just plain and constant reading?'

'What do you think?' She couldn't add his title, not even if her life had depended on it, for here in the carriage there was a sort of equality that simmered between them and an energy that she had never felt with another.

'I think you watch people and listen with your heart.'

'You do that, too, my lord.'

This time he only smiled.

Belle steeped medicines and pounded tinctures and she charged nothing to a hundred patients who could afford very little. She brought warm clothing and blankets for the babies and she found packs of cards and puzzles for those

with time to while away at the very endings
of their lives. She paid for shoes that were
not scuffed to within an inch of their existence and found oranges and fish fresh from
the stalls in the market on Whitechapel Road.
She noted down everything, every small and
tiny charge, and sent the Earl of Thornton her
reckoning two days before she was due to visit
next.

Within an hour she had a message back.

*That's the best ten pounds I have ever
spent.*

She was pleased for such an assurance. His
handwriting was strong and flowing, the *b*'s
and *p*'s were fluted in a way that made her
smile. She brought the paper to her nose and
breathed in, the scent of ink the only thing
discernible.

What had she wanted it to smell like? Him?

Swallowing, she placed the note down carefully on her desk and crossed to the mirror,
peering at herself once she was there.

She was not beautiful, nor perhaps even
mildly pretty. Her hair was unremarkable and
she had a tooth that did not sit at the same

angle as the others. Her eyes were also far too blue to be restful.

She spoke well, she read widely and she helped others. These were her attributes. Searching her mind, she probed for the other distant truth that lay hidden well away from sense.

She wanted the Earl to like her. With more than respect. More than esteem. She was enough of a woman to have read the books on filial love, and on lust and on sexual endeavour. She had devoured *Fanny Hill* by John Cleland and read the compendium of poetry by the Earl of Rochester, clandestinely, under her bed sheets at night. The novel *Justine* had come into her hands through a bookseller in London for whom she had made medicines and she knew the erotic works of the Greek poets Strato and Sappho. She was no prude even if she was still a virgin.

But she was lonely.

She was also thirty-one, almost destitute, nameless, without family, and inclined to strange dreams at night that made her question her sanity come the morning.

The sum of being abandoned sat on her like a weight, altering worth and condemning certainty. No man had ever come near her in the way of a suitor. Did she repel them or was she simply repellent?

These thoughts of wanting more and wanting it with a man like the Earl of Thornton were witless and unwise.

He had only ever looked at her in the way of an oddity, a woman who did not fit into any of the boxes the men of the *ton* needed their women to inhabit.

Appearance was not important to her and yet she was drawn to Lord Thornton's beautiful face with an ache. The wealth of a person was also a factor that had held no real weight. Yet the Earl's pounds had paid for things she would never have been able to procure otherwise, things that eased the wretched life of those struggling with very survival.

A conundrum and a puzzle.

She should take heed of his mother's warnings and make certain that she was soon gone from the lives of the Thorntons. Yet she couldn't. Lady Lucy needed her and, if truth be told, so perhaps did the Earl. To make him happier. To bring a smile across the sadness in his eyes.

They were right, these poets and novelists

of long ago. The erotic hopes of a body were hot and heady things. Her hands ran across her breasts, nipples standing hard and proud.

She was not immune after all to the charms of men. No, she shook her head and rephrased. Not men, but one man. The enigmatic and beautiful Earl of Thornton. She knew it was stupid. But there it was. Unarguable.

Lytton smiled at the letter Annabelle Smith had sent him. Fish and stockings, blankets and coats were not things he usually read of, but each item here had been qualified with the person who had received it and that was what made it fascinating reading.

A young child with a chest complaint that was ongoing, a housewife pregnant for the eighth time in one of the winding and narrow alleys off the Whitechapel Road. An old soldier without a leg who was nearing sixty and needed a pack of cards to fill in the hours of a lonely day.

Numbers had always been simple things for him and if his father had squandered the coffers of the Thorntons', then he had refilled them ten times over. Easily. But these pounds that he had accrued also lacked depth, no story behind them save that of an investment.

His mother's voice brought him from his thoughts and he watched as she came into the room, a book in hand.

'Have you seen what your healer has left Lucy?'

He looked up and shook his head as the small tome with blue ribbons was delivered with force to his desk.

'Mrs Mary Wollstonecraft writes that men and women need educational equality and is critical of conventional women. If one were to believe in her premises, where would society be? Washed up, I tell you, each wife and mother attending to her own needs and not to those of her husband and her children. Books like this are a disgrace, Thornton, and one you need to be aware of and forbid when the insidious opinion comes beneath your own roof, crawling into your sister's consciousness.'

For a moment he looked at Cecelia and wondered when it was his mother had changed from a gentle parent into this one? The death of his father, he supposed. It could not have been easy for a woman who would listen so carefully to gossip.

'Perhaps returning to Balmain would be a good thing for you? Lucy's sickness has not been easy for any of us.'

'You cannot think I might leave her? My God, she is still at death's door.'

'I think we both know that is not true. She is eating again and her countenance is rosier. Certainly, we have passed the point of no return and Miss Smith has done wonders for her.'

'Wonders?' The word was whispered. 'It is witchcraft she has employed and who knows how long such things truly last?'

'Being grateful might bolster hope, Mama. Miss Smith is a woman who is an accomplished healer and there is no more to it than that.'

'She knows things.'

'Pardon?' Lytton looked up.

'Lucy says that she can read her mind and find out exactly what she is thinking. She says it is unsettling.'

'Yet she still wishes to meet her. She told me so this morning, so it cannot be too uncomfortable.'

'Your father would not have allowed it. Such a one in the house. He would have told her to leave the moment she tried to inveigle herself in to our family affairs and sent her packing back to Whitechapel where she belongs.'

'He is dead, Mama. And has been for a good year and a half.'

'Someone shot him. Someone broke into Balmain and shot him. I know it.'

For a second horror slid down the back of his neck. His mother was going mad and he had not noticed. How long had she been like this? He had been so busy trying to save the estate he had given his mother's mental state little thought but Lucy must have known as well as David and Prudence. No wonder his oldest sister had disappeared off abroad and his brother was playing up at school.

A tumbling house of cards, he ruminated, and walked across to Cecelia, taking her hand as he led her to a seat by the window.

'I want you to go back to the country. I will bring Lucy up in a week or two and spend some weeks there as well. You need to rest, for this has all been more than trying for you.'

Unexpectedly his mother nodded. 'Perhaps you are right. I could garden and tend to my flowers and walk a little. The glade is always beautiful at this time of the year. When Lucy returns we can follow quiet pursuits.'

Patting her hand, he was glad as she calmed. 'The carriage will be readied in the early afternoon and the family physician will accompany you just to be certain. Everything will be arranged so that you will not have to worry again and your great friend Isabel will be thrilled to have you back.'

After his mother had gone Lytton did another hour's work to see to all the details of her journey before picking up the book and wandering into Lucy's room. He found her up in an armchair that was slanted towards the sun. She wore a thick nightdress tied at the waist and her feet were bare.

'It is fine to see you up again.'

Her smile brightened when she noticed him and brightened further when she glanced at the book he was carrying. 'Mama took it away.'

He handed it back to her. 'The stuff of treason, she thinks.'

'What do you think?'

'I have not read it, but there are movements afoot to cast more light on the inequalities of women. A lot of it makes sense.'

She undid the blue ribbons and found a dog ear on the top of one page.

'Listen to this.'

With exaggerated care she read a few pages to him, her voice trembling with the tale of the woman she spoke of. When she had finished she placed the opened book on her breast and looked over at him.

'It is saying that women need to have their own opinions and they are just as valuable as any a man might have. The story is a sad one and one of deceit and lies as the heroine and her friend try to come to terms with their life in a madhouse. Miss Smith says she wants to hear my opinion on the trials of women when I see her next.'

'Well, it seems that you certainly hold one. Do you like Miss Smith?'

'I think at first she frightened me. But she is strong. She does not take nonsense easily.'

'Nonsense like witchcraft?'

'You have been speaking with Mama? I made the mistake of telling her that perhaps Miss Smith was a witch when I first saw her and she took up this thought and would not stop speaking of it. I didn't realise how much anger she suddenly seems to be full of, though Prudence had warned me of it before she left.' She hesitated for a moment and then continued.

'I was wondering if I could ask Miss Smith to stay for morning tea when she comes. I know how busy she is, but the cook could make her famous scones and we have the raspberry jam from last year's crop at Balmain.'

'Of course. I won't need the carriage so she can be taken home in it afterwards.'

'Will you be here to join us?'

Lytton shrugged his shoulders. 'I have a meeting in the city which is important.'

'But if you can be here, would you?'

'I will try.'

In the afternoon Lytton visited the Thornton family banker and was reassured by the state of the finances. He knew the numbers himself, of course, but since attaining the Earldom he had been very careful to check every detail of his investments. He did not trust anyone.

He had a family to look after, thousands of acres of land to tend, servants and workers to provide for. The days of being careless were over, he had accepted that on the death of his father.

The keeping of a mistress was a lot less persuasive than it had once been as well. Susan Castleton had sent him copious notes trying to win back his favours, but he had replied to none of them.

He had heard from Edward how his name had been slandered by her in society, but that was the least of his worries. After the weeks of his sister being so sick, to have a glimmer of light in the future was gratifying and he did owe it to the unusual Miss Annabelle Smith.

Her vibrant blue eyes watched him in memory and for just a second he wondered what it would be like to have her beneath him tumbling into his bed.

The shock of that brought him to a standstill. There was no way in the world that he could enjoy her like that. The next woman he bedded would have to be his wife and she would need credentials and breeding that were incomparable to become a countess.

Still, the vision of Annabelle Smith naked with her dark curtain of hair falling around them was hard to shake off. Was she a virgin? Had she any experience with the pleasures of the flesh? God, even that thought had him hardening, here in the street with the daylight of London all about him and myriad shoppers walking past.

He could teach her everything he knew, every nuance of desire.

'Thorn.' The voice came through a haze and he turned to find Summerley Shayborne crossing the street to reach him.

'You look preoccupied.'

He smiled. 'I've just come from the bank.'

'Good news?' Shay knew of the trouble he'd been in last year with the estate when things had been turned upside down.

'Everything is fine and long may it stay that way.'

'You're the new and shining light of the financial world, I hear. An earl who seems to be able to pinpoint a lucrative investment without comparison? Most peers are holding on to the family plot by their fingernails, but it seems your latest project has just come through with flying colours.'

'The canning factory outside London? People need to eat and preserved fruit and vegetables are within the budget of most. Every large town in England by the end of the year will sport such a factory. Come in with me as a partner. I'll get Lian and Edward on board as well.'

'You're serious?'

'I am.'

'When can we draw up the contracts?' Shay looked excited.

'Next week. But keep it quiet for I don't want someone else beating me to the post.'

'Have a drink with us now, then. Celeste is at the town house and we would love your company.'

'Very well.' He hailed his carriage and they both piled in.

Lytton had always admired Shay's wife. She was tough in a way that intrigued him and beautiful enough to take his breath away every time he saw her.

She also was nothing like the bride that the *ton* had thought the lauded Summerley Shayborne, Viscount Luxford, would choose for himself.

'You said you would come to Luxford in the early summer, Thorn, but you didn't.' Celeste looked puzzled.

'I've been at Balmain for quite a few weeks because my sister has been sick. We have only just returned to town.'

'I've heard that just lately she is making some sort of a recovery?'

'I hope so. I have engaged a healer to try to coax her out of bed where she has been languishing. Miss Annabelle Smith from Whitechapel is her name and she seems to be making quite a difference.'

'The herbalist? She is the woman my lady's maid was speaking of so highly the other day, Summer. I should very much like to meet her. Is she at your town house this week seeing your sister?'

'Tomorrow she is, but only very early. At nine. She keeps unusual hours.'

'Could we call in? It might be my only chance to talk with the woman and she sounds more than fascinating.'

'Well, I don't see why not.'

Lytton had organised a meeting for the morning, but he supposed he could cancel it. His thoughts from earlier on had not left him and he felt…anxious. He could not quite imagine Annabelle Smith chatting about things with his sister and Celeste over jam scones and a cup of tea. He wondered, too, if Celeste had read any of the writings of Mary Wollstonecraft?

It was her birthday.

Well, her birthday as Tante Alicia had

deemed it given she was four when she had turned up in the French village without any past whatsoever.

The third of July. A hot morning in the village of Moret-sur-Loing when a nun had delivered a sick child to the house of the local healer and pleaded for the girl to be taken in.

This much she did know for Alicia had retold this story over and over and never a mention of the people who had abandoned her.

Annabelle had celebrated today with a new pair of stockings and a fresh orange. She had also fashioned her hair a little differently this morning, doing away with the heavy scarf and pinning it about her face. The curls escaped, of course, but rather than detracting from the whole picture she thought that they added to it. For some reason today she felt lighter and happier than she had in months and the sun above was a part of that, too.

She hoped Lady Lucy had read the book she had given her. She hoped she had kept eating, too. If she had, then the change in her from last week to this one should be more than noticeable.

A carriage standing before the Thornton town house had Belle frowning. She did not recognise it and hoped that there were not visitors who would take away time she would have with the Earl's sister. The horses were most handsome and the liveried driver on the box seat tipped his hat at her.

'Morning, miss. It's a fine day outside, to be sure.'

She smiled back at him and made her way up the steps, the door opened by a servant she had not met before.

'The master is expecting you, miss. He is in the blue salon. I will take you through.'

Dispensing with her coat and hat, she followed him and heard the conversation between a group of people getting louder by the moment.

She stopped and the servant looked around.

'I think there has been a mistake. I am here to see Miss Staines only. I have been attending to her medical needs.'

'You are Miss Smith, are you not?'

'Yes.'

'Well then, you are to come right this way.'

Belle straightened down her skirts as she went, a sort of dawning horror rising in her stomach. She did not wish to meet other guests of this house. She would not be accepted by anyone in society and surely the Earl of Thornton would know this.

The door opened. The Earl stood by the mantel with two strangers, a beautiful woman and a tall and handsome man. When the Earl saw her he excused himself and came to her side.

'I thought before you went upstairs to see my sister you may like to meet Lord and Lady Luxton.'

Belle took in a breath. This was a situation she had not come across before and she was silent as she watched for cues.

'Miss Smith.' The woman spoke first. 'I am Celeste Shayborne and I have heard much about your ministry in Whitechapel. My husband is most interested in hearing about it, too.'

As if to underline this as a truth the man beside her nodded.

'It seems your fame proceeds you, Miss Smith.' Lord Luxford spoke now for the first time, though Belle wondered at his tone. He did not sound quite as pleased as his wife. The social conventions worried her.

Should she curtsy before this lord as she spoke or was that unnecessary?

'Mine is a small clinic but in an area where there are many supplicants. I am quite perplexed that you have even heard of it.'

She used her voice like a weapon, Lytton thought, the low and husky tone surprising, but not as surprising as the King's English that she now spoke. Her voice had never held tones of the East End, though, and had always sounded quite refined.

If he had closed his eyes just then, it could have been any one of the titled and well-brought-up ladies of the *ton* talking. He saw the interest in Celeste's eyes and the curiosity in Shay's.

'Who are your parents, Miss Smith?' Celeste was never one to refrain from trying to decipher a puzzle and she asked the question baldly.

But Miss Annabelle Smith failed to answer, turning to him instead and finding a query all her own.

'I do hope your sister has recovered a little in the days since I have seen her, your lordship?

Now this was interesting, Lytton thought.

There were secrets here and he could tell that Celeste had determined it exactly the same.

'Miss Smith gave Lucy a copy of the Mary Wollstonecraft book, Celeste, and my sister has been most taken by the things the author wrote of.'

'Oh, I, too, have read her books and most heartily agree with the sentiments in them.'

Belle did not feel quite up to arguing for the rights of all women no matter what their station in life so she stayed quiet. She was feeling her way here and the truth of her being from Whitechapel's mean streets felt like an enormous stumbling block. She had not recognised this in the company of the Earl or even of his sister. But when society came crashing down upon her in a refined drawing room as it had here there was no getting away from it.

She did not fit.

A headache had begun to form behind her eyes and she prayed to God that the jagged lines of a worse malady did not reappear. Not until she could get home at least. She felt sweat run between her breasts and the fine beading of it on her top lip.

The Earl saved the day by asking her if she

wanted a drink, leading her across to a cabinet where an array of bottles stood on top of a polished mahogany counter.

She had never tasted true liquor in all of her life and searched for something non-alcoholic.

'The white wine is very good.' The Earl lent down and said this quietly.

'Only a small glass, please.'

He poured it with the sort of ease people used to heavy drinking must be wont to do. She did not really know, for her aunt was a teetotaller and any alcohol in the house was reserved for medicines. The devil's brew, her aunt had often said, and there was enough evidence around Whitechapel for them to believe in such a truth.

A cup of tea would have been welcome, but she felt she could not ask. The smile she sported hurt her cheeks and she wondered how much longer she could manage to keep it up. She wished she might excuse herself and go upstairs to see her patient.

'Celeste and Shay are friends of mine.'

'I see, your lordship.'

'Very good friends.'

She looked up and caught his glance. What

did he wish her to say? And what was he telling her?

The tumble of the unexpected was confusing, terrifying even, and she measured her breaths with a rigid count. These people knew of her and her clinic, they understood she was from poorer stock and they were still attempting to be friendly. She took a sip of the wine and then another, surprised by the strength of its taste.

Still, it was wet and it gave her something to do. In a moment she had finished the lot.

'Would you like more?' A frown dashed into golden eyes as she nodded.

'Thank you.'

This time she drank more slowly as he led her back into the room. It was relaxing her now, this white wine. For the first time in ten minutes she felt as if she might be coping.

'Where did you learn your healing skills, Miss Smith?'

Celeste Shayborne's voice had the lilt of another country in the words. French, perhaps. She recognised the cadence.

'My aunt is a herbalist. She taught me.'

'It must take a long time to learn?'

'Years and years. I am still learning now

and Tante Alicia is sixty-three and she says she does not know it all yet either. She has tried her hardest to teach me, though, in the hope that such knowledge will not be lost and I could be the one to hand it down to the next generation.'

Goodness. Had she said too much? She tried to remember every word she had uttered and found that she couldn't, a barrier between her and the world.

It was the wine. Placing her near-empty glass down on a table, she wished again that she could have asked for tea or coffee, anything to neutralise the rising warmth that was worrying.

Control was slipping and with it reserve.

'Your aunt is French?' Celeste Shayborne clapped her hands. 'Do you speak the language?'

'A little,' she said before she thought, for Lytton Staines had heard her using it on that very first day they had met after Stanley had torn his waistcoat. He would know that what she said was a lie, but she did not want the next questions that might rise with such an honesty.

The Earl's voice broke her panic and she was pleased for his words.

'I think something non-alcoholic might be

useful.' He poured a large glass of lemonade and handed it over.

Relief flooded into panic. She would be all right now. She would manage.

Exhaustion swamped gratitude and then sadness overcame that. So many emotions in so very few seconds she could hardly keep up. If she were at home she would lie down with a pillow across her head to keep out the daylight and she would sleep until the headache left her. Sometimes she took sulphate of quinine if it were severe, or cinchona bark or valerian. But there was nothing here that was remotely like anything she needed. She could see Celeste Shayborne looking at her with a frown in her eyes and even the Earl gave the impression of worry.

'I am quite all right. It's only a headache and I have them all the time. The wine was strong, too, and it's still early in the morning…'

A further glance from Thornton told her that her admission had been unexpected, inappropriate even, and her words tailed off. Shaking her head, she tried hard to find a balance.

'Perhaps on reflection I might be wise to leave. It seems that today is not a good day and I think I may need to go home and sleep.'

Another faux pas and had she just spoken completely in French?

'I think my headache is worsening and when that happens I am never good company.'

Goodness, now she was switching languages, the words blurring into each other, skipping over tenses and trailing into gibberish. She could not be quite sure she had pronounced any of them properly.

'So I bid you au revoir.' She had not seen Lady Lucy as she had promised, but did not feel at all up to it. She would come back tomorrow when she felt she might manage.

The Earl's arm was around her waist now and she allowed him to lead her to the door. Once in the entrance hall he found her hat and coat and then took her out to the carriage that he had asked to be brought around. Inside the conveyance, cocooned in silence and the comfort of the squashy leather seats, she breathed out.

'I am sorry.'

'For what.'

'For creating a spectacle. For being vulgar.'

'I hardly think you were that, Miss Smith. Entertaining is more the word that comes to mind.'

'You are kind.'

'Often in life I am not.'

She ignored that. 'Your friends were kind, too.'

'Have you ever drunk wine before?'

'No.'

'God.' His laughter was not quite what she expected.

'I hope as a consequence you don't want your ten pounds back now for I have spent it already.'

'I know of that. You sent me a note, remember. I did not realise that small sum of money could purchase so much. I commend you, Miss Smith.'

'Belle.'

'Pardon.'

'Belle. You can call me that. Everyone else does. It means beautiful in French, but I do not think she should have named me such for I am not.'

'Hell.'

'You are swearing again, my lord Earl. I'm not sure you should. It is more than rude and, while I am not a high-born lady, I am still a woman.'

He knocked on the window and the conveyance stopped. 'Take the long road around London for at least an hour, Barnes, and stop at the next shop that sells lemonade.'

'Lemonade, my lord?'

'In a very large bottle.'

Chapter Four

She had gone to sleep on his shoulder, her head pushed against him and one hand lying in his lap. His fine embroidered jacket was creased and the hat he had worn was on the floor beside him. Outside the day looked a lot later than it should have been.

'What time is it?' she asked, jerking away with horror. Her mouth felt furry and her stomach nauseous.

'Half past twelve.'

'We have stopped?'

'The horses needed a rest from walking.'

'Oh, my God.' She placed her head in her hands and said it again. 'You are telling me that we have been driving around London because I fell asleep? This is worse than Stanley, worse than the waistcoat, worse even than my trying to clean you up…' Trailing off, she groaned again before relapsing into silence.

'I think you exaggerate, Miss Smith. Nothing could ever be worse than a torn pink waistcoat.'

She laughed because there was nothing else for it and because she was grateful for his humour.

'I think it was the wine. Could you give your friends my apologies? I doubt that I shall ever see them again, but still…' She looked at him then and a new shame washed across her.

'Shay has worked as a spy in the war-torn countries of Europe and Celeste has been there along with him. They are not shrinking violets, Miss Smith, and I think a laugh is good for everybody.'

'You were reassuring me until the very last line, your lordship, and what of your sister's needs? As her healer I am supposed to be responsible and above reproach?'

He laughed again. 'And who is ever that in a whole lifetime?'

'Not me.'

'Put it behind you, Miss Smith, and decline the wine next time. Perhaps you are a lush?'

'A what?'

'A person for whom wine is intoxicating? I have never seen anyone get drunk quite so quickly before and on so little.'

'Oh, God.' Now remorse was back.

How awful had she been? How uncontrolled? She could recall pieces only in snatches. Large parts of the past few hours had gone, but the Earl's last memory of her would always be this.

He wore only one gold ring today and the wound at his temple was largely healed. She took in the small details of him piece by piece with an avid hope. The hope that every tiny shred of him might be recalled later to make her smile or wish for more, for so very much more.

Time. Words. Laughter. Life. As potent as any medicine she administered and as useful. That touch of truth had her turning towards him, the back of her hand resting against his all the way down the Whitechapel Road. She liked the warmth of it.

'My God, Thorn, who is Miss Smith and where the hell did you find her?'

Shay had arrived back at his town house

late that same evening, the moon slight and the night dark.

Lytton leant back in his chair, sending up a plume of smoke from the cheroot before him. Around him his house had settled. Lucy had recovered from her fury over Miss Smith leaving early, retiring on the promise that he would contact her come morning and arrange a further meeting. His mother had departed yesterday for Balmain so that distraction was gone and Susan Castleton had finally ceased to hound him hourly about reigniting the dead flame of their disastrous affair.

All in all it was good to sit and consider his day, quietly.

'Annabelle Smith is not as she seems,' he replied. 'There are secrets that she holds close, but I do not know of them. Yet.'

'Celeste loved her. She is sending Miss Smith an invite to spend some time with us at Luxford. Do you think she might come?'

'Probably not.' Lytton refilled both their glasses. 'By her own account she seldom leaves the borders of Whitechapel. Even Portman Square was a stretch.'

'A mystery, then, and one that refuses to unravel?'

'I think she unravelled completely this morning, don't you?'

'Did you accompany her back to White-chapel?'

'No, not for a while. I took her on a carriage ride around London until she sobered up. She went to sleep and I waited with her on the far side of Hyde Park. Three hours later we managed to return her home.'

'It just gets more and more interesting,' Shay said and began to laugh.

'What does?'

'That you should be protecting her as you do. Is she your mistress?'

'Hell. What do you think?'

'I don't know what to think, that is the trouble. She looks like a sultry angel, gets drunk like a sot and speaks two languages, both in the accents of the high born. And yet she resides in Whitechapel? There has to be a story there.'

'Don't dig, Shay. I want her to tell me of it herself.'

'There you go again. Who have you turned into, Thorn? I have never before known you to be so protective of a woman and one you imply you are not even sleeping with. Every unmarried female of the *ton* would like you to place a wedding ring on their finger and the unhappily married ones would settle for merely a turn in your bed. You have thrown off Mrs Castleton and made a fortune with every investment that you touch, yet here you are…shepherding a secretive seraph around London and keeping her well away from the wolves of society.'

'Perhaps there is still some slight bit of decency left in me then, after all?'

'Or perhaps you have finally met your match?'

'Enough, Shay. Let's have a drink and talk business. It seems at least then we might agree on the facts that are before us.'

Hours later when Shay had gone Lytton walked to the window and looked out over the streets of London. He turned towards the east. Miss Belle Smith would be there, stewing medicines and chopping plants, the dog Stanley watching her even as a hundred dangers hung around just outside her door. He wished she were here in Portman Square, safe and warm. He wished her hand still sat next to his own, the touch of her filling up his whole body with joy.

He wanted to gift her with as many pounds as she needed for her ragtag group of patients, but he did not dare to mention it for she didn't look like a woman who would take well to charity.

She was prickly and wise and innocent and unusual. She was also completely herself. He smiled, liking that assessment more than all the others put together.

He would call in tomorrow to see whether she would deign again to visit his sister, this time with the promise of only that. He sincerely hoped that she might say yes, not so much for Lucy's sake but for his own.

Rosemary Greene helped her to strip away the skin from the aloes and pulverise the green squashy middle of the plant for an ointment she had found very effective in the treatment of burns.

'You seem quiet, Belle?'

'I had a headache yesterday and I always feel slightly heavy afterwards.'

'The Earl brought you home in his carriage?

Alicia mentioned it and so did every other inhabitant living in this corner of Whitechapel.'

Annabelle decided to be honest. 'I think I got a little drunk, Rose. He poured me two glasses of wine and I swallowed them quickly. I should not have.'

'Goodness. Does your aunt know?'

She shook her head. 'Please don't tell her of it. It was my fault.'

'And the Earl, was he honourable?' A stillness fused into each word.

'He was. He sat with me in the carriage while I slept and then accompanied me home.'

'Did he touch you?'

'Only on the hand. He was by no means offensive.'

Rose returned to the task of wetting the aloe. 'Men can take advantage of innocence, Belle. They are not always principled. You have to be most careful, especially around gentlemen of wealth for they are the very worst.'

A sudden vision of Lady Lucy being pressured into something she did not want made Annabelle stand up. She needed to go back and talk with the Earl's sister.

She wondered how she might see her without having to go through the Earl of Thornton.

The idea of a letter was the most appealing, but she could not be such a coward.

Stanley was barking again at the front door, an incessant noise reverberating through the house. She loved the small terrier, but sometimes he was a handful and today she just did not feel like listening to such a ruckus.

'I will put him in with Alicia,' she told Rose, wiping her hands and then grabbing the dog by his collar. After seeing Stanley banished, she passed the front door again and noticed a shadow glimmering against the small window to one side. Someone was here? A patient? She was not expecting anyone this morning and hoped it was not an emergency.

Opening the door, she found the Earl of Thornton about to knock. He was dressed today in riding clothes and when she peered out she saw another man there holding two horses, his dress much the same.

'Good morning, Miss Smith. My sister has sent me to your doorstep on the express condition that I ask if there would be a possibility of spending some time just with her tomorrow. She is far better than she was, but is most distressed at missing you yesterday. If I sent the

Thornton carriage tomorrow afternoon at two, would that be suitable for you?'

Belle could barely believe he was here as she nodded her head. He had not sent her a written message or dispatched a servant to do his bidding, but had come himself and in full glory at half past ten in the morning?

'Lucy also bade me tell you that there will be tea and scones. The jam is raspberry from a particularly good batch in Balmain this past summer.'

'Then I can't see how I might refuse, your lordship.'

'You like raspberries?'

'I do.'

When he smiled the light danced in his eyes and the sun caught the gold of his hair and her breath hitched. There were a number of people on the street outside who watched him, but he did not seem to notice them as he tipped his hat and left. Shutting the door behind him, Belle leaned against it.

His formal visit held the same emotion as yesterday and, standing here in an old apron over an even older gown, she could not understand why. Her hands were still green from the aloe and her hair was roughly bundled into an untidy knot. The visage and clothes of the beautiful Lady Luxford shimmered in her memory, a woman of class and dignity. A woman who would not get drunk in a drawing room in the early hours of the morning and then virtually fall over on her face on the way to the door.

Everything had been simpler before she had met the Thorntons. Her business had been growing and she had felt a certain pride in what she had achieved. But now...now Lady Lucy's dreadful secret gnawed at her happiness and the Earl's very presence rattled her composure.

Thirty-two was not an age to be so very unsettled. She needed to see to the future of the Earl of Thornton's sister and then never visit either of them again. A loss bloomed at this thought, but she pushed it away quickly as she went inside to help Rose.

An invitation to the Derwent Ball was one of the most sought-after tickets of the Season. The Earl of Derwent, Patrick Tully, and his wife, Priscilla, always went to such extremes in decorating their salons and the food and music was renowned.

Lytton had come tonight because Edward Tully was a close friend and because he needed some distraction from all that was happening with Lucy. He also needed to stop thinking of Miss Annabelle Smith.

Everyone was there, the crush of success stopping him in his tracks as he filed through the front door in the company of Edward Tully.

'My God, it gets busier every year, Ed.'

'My brother will be pleased. He puts a lot into it.'

'And you?'

'I'm thinking of heading for the Americas, Thorn, to get away for a while.'

'And do what?'

'I could start up one of those canning factories you are always talking of. New York sounds like a big enough city and you've already asked me to be a partner.'

'If you are serious, I'd like you to be involved.' He turned to look at Edward and realised he looked a lot less than happy.

'I want more from life, Lytton. I want adventure and surprise. Come with me. We could both do with a break, I think.'

'I can't. Not now.'

'Because of Lucy?'

Lytton shook his head. Lucy was finally making a recovery, but the face of Miss Smith came to mind. He did not want her to be so alone.

'Hell.' He swore as he saw Susan Castleton bearing down upon him, forgetting everything except the overriding desperation to escape.

Edward comprehending his unease, shuffled him sideways into a group standing near the door. Albert Tennant-Smythe, Lord Huntington, was one of the men there and Lytton's ire rose. He had never liked Tennant-Smythe, his brash confidence founded on putting others down. Barely acknowledging him, he felt the anger reciprocated even as Huntington excused himself and left.

Odd that, he thought. Usually the fellow was so much more in your face and he also knew he was interested in becoming a part of his investment in the fruit and vegetable cannery production.

Lady Beatrice Mallory next to him had begun to talk and he leaned down to listen to what she said through all the noise.

'I saw Lady Luxford yesterday afternoon, my lord, and she said your sister was much recovered.'

'She is.'

'It seems you have inveigled the mysterious healer from Whitechapel to visit her and she has conjured up wonders. Lady Luxford was full of her praise. I remember seeing your sister at the Vauxhall Gardens a few months ago in the company of Huntington and his friends and she looked beautiful.'

The first niggle of something not being quite right took him by surprise. Why the hell would Lucy have been with that group, the wild arrogance of a set who took no care of others, concerning him. He had heard no word of such an excursion and he was certain his mother would not have encouraged it.

Nothing tonight was allowing him comfort. In honesty all he wanted was to be back in his carriage, ferrying a sleeping Miss Smith around the quieter roads of London and feeling the warmth of her hand against his own. That thought worried him, too. Was he going as mad as his mother? He took a glass of brandy offered by a passing footman and drank it quickly. He needed oblivion and he needed it fast. It had been a long time since he had been truly drunk, but tonight even the thought of it helped.

* * *

An hour later he found himself at the card tables, Albert Tennant-Smythe opposite him.

'The stakes are high, Thornton, but I hear you are well heeled these days so it should not bother you.'

'What are you putting on the table?'

'An Arabian thoroughbred.'

'Your horse?'

'My grandmother's.'

'She'll be happy to lose it?'

'Deal the cards, Thornton, and spit up the money if you are man enough.'

It was almost too easy to win and even with a good deal of brandy under his belt Lytton wondered at the method of the others' card counting.

Within twenty moments he had an IOU for the steed and there was a crowd of interested onlookers around them. Albert Tennant-Smythe looked furious and it was only the good sense of the Derwents to have provided hired muscle in the card rooms that saved a fight. Three burly boxers escorted Huntington from the house, his howls demanding another round drowned by the laughter of those in the room.

'You want to lose every other horse you don't own as well?'

'We will see what your grandmother might have to say about that.'

'This loss will be a thorn in Huntington's side, mark my words.'

Lady Huntington, the Dowager Countess, was known for her steel hand in trying to give guidance to progeny without moral integrity and Albert was the only grandchild still living.

Personally Lytton thought the ending of a family line with so little going for it might be a good thing and pitied any bride who would attach all her hopes to a man who'd probably never live up to them.

Lady Beatrice Mallory's words were also in the mix. Why the hell would Lucy have been in Tennant-Smythe's company? Tomorrow he would ask her and offer his advice to stay well away from a troublemaker for whom he held no liking.

He would see what else he could find out about Huntington in the meantime, who his friends were and what was the structure of his family ties. There was the grandmother, of course, but were there others, too, who it might be wise to understand more about.

Lytton had always trusted his instincts and he had a bad feeling about the Earl.

Belle took Lucy's hand and stroked her fingers, a plate of scones and a cup of tea beside her.

'You need to talk to your brother about your condition. You need his help.'

'Why? If I tell him everything, Thorn will insist on marriage and there is no way at all that I would ever want that.'

'Did he hurt you physically when…?' She could not go on.

'No. I went with him willingly because I thought he was dashing, I suppose, until I really knew what he was like and by then it was too late.'

'You said that he was years older than you are and as such he should have known better. Would you want me to talk to him?'

'I don't know. Would he listen?'

'I'd make him.'

Lucy began to laugh. 'How?'

'Let me think about that. I won't do anything at all until I speak to you. Would that be something you would be happy with?' Putting out her hand, Belle was glad when the young girl placed her own within it.

'Don't say anything to Thorn, though. I need to get a bit stronger before I can deal with all of this yet and the last year and a half has not been an easy one for our family.'

'What of your sister? Prudence, is it?'

'She is in Rome with her husband. She is also eight years older than I am and hasn't much time to listen to my opinions.'

'And your mother?'

'You saw what she is like. Papa's death has changed her and she is bitter now. Poor Thorn has had to deal with all of that as well as an errant younger brother and a bankrupt Earl-dom. He won back our country seat in a game of cards just before our father died. Did you know that?'

'From whom?'

'I am not certain as he has never talked of it and it would be poor form to mention it any-where else. My brother has the Midas touch in business though, and lately has been turning preserved food into gold.'

'Preserved food?'

'He has one big canning factory not far from

London with more popping up all across England. Most everyone can afford a can of preserves and that is where the money lies.'

Belle could hear those exact words coming from the Earl of Thornton's lips.

'He will marry soon, though, and I suppose to a wife who won't like us. She will be beautiful and cold and well born and then Thorn will become distant and we will all have to move out.'

'What makes you say that?'

'Because that is what happens in families of the *ton* and ours is falling apart at the seams. What bride would truly want to deal with us?' She straightened the bedcover as she said this, smoothing the quilt down. 'There are many in society who would vie for his hand. I've had to listen to small confessions from women about their penchant for my brother for months now. There is one woman, Lady Catherine Dromorne, whom people are touting as the next Countess. Our families are friends.'

Belle looked around Lucy's room. The decor was beautiful and tasteful and expensive. Every single bit of this house screamed money, from the manicured gardens to the tiled roof top. Nothing looked old or scuffed or mediocre. The Earl's Countess would presumably be exactly the same, a woman of refinement and breeding and pride.

The exact opposite of her.

'He left his mistress, Mrs Castleton, just recently, but she has been hounding him to come back.'

Annabelle hardly knew what to say to this.

'Lady Catherine has been a particular friend of his for a long while and Mama always imagined they might marry, but...'

When Lucy tailed off Belle felt regret. There was no one else in her world who could tell her anything of Lord Thornton's personal affairs and all Lucy's revelations were eye openers. When she had talked of her seduction by a man nearly twice her age it was all that Belle could do to hold in the anger she trembled with. Lord Huntington would get his dues, she promised, for there were many in Whitechapel who would jump at the chance to go with her to visit him. Big men, rough men. A threat would be enough, she was sure. Not to force him to marry Lucy, that was the last thing she wanted, but to get him to apologise. There was a healing in an apology and a properly felt and expressed one would go a long way in allowing

Lady Lucy to move on with her life. She hoped he might cry a little, this despicable Lord. A well-aimed punch to the stomach would probably elicit some tears, but it could be nothing that showed. Lady Lucy needed to believe in his repentance even if she herself never would.

Men like him did not change their spots. No, they went on to grimmer and grimmer crimes and she pitied anyone who had to weather that ride. She had seen this a number of times in Whitechapel. The desperate wives and mothers worrying if every day that their wayward son or husband lived might be their last. Happiness was not that golden easy glow that the stories talked of. It was the small satisfactions that came in tiny victories. A loaf of bread that was not mouldy. A shilling over at the end of a long hard week. A child who recovered quickly from a cough that had been worrying. A husband who returned home late after a fight, a little worse for wear, but still alive.

The Thorntons were immune in some ways to tragedy and exposed to it in other ways. Lady Lucy's innocence had counted against her just as her brother's success and arrogance had counted against him.

His sister would not take him into her confidence. Belle was pleased, at least, that the girl had spoken to her about what had happened for there was a release in confession.

Her pregnancy would be almost eight or nine weeks along. Soon it would show. Already there were times when she caught the red cheeks of expectancy and the curves that were softening. But Thornton was no fool. He would not be hoodwinked for much longer, either, and when he knew that Belle had not confided in him there would be hell to pay.

The Earl was the one doling out for her services and when he asked her for a diagnosis for his sister which she knew he would, she would have to lie.

'I think that Mrs Wollstonecraft's book has helped me, Miss Smith. There is a way I can get on with my life after all, for I would hope I am not about to be abandoned or become penniless like the heroine in the story. Perhaps I can become more like you and help in your clinic. You could teach me the rudiments of herbal medicines and I could feel useful again.'

'All those things are possible, Miss Staines, but not probable. Your family is wealthy and of good standing and I know for a fact that your brother would do anything in his power to see you happy.'

'But I cannot move in the circles I once did. Society will turn its back on me when they know.'

'Then turn your back upon them first. Lives can be lived with passion and joy in places away from the *ton*. You can certainly help in my clinic after the baby arrives, but for now with your compromised health you will need to be taken care of. Your brother can do that and will. It might be hard for you to tell him and even harder for him to hear, but he is a good man and a strong one. I know that he will want you to be in the best place you can be and I think you know this, too. Deep down.'

The small nod heartened her. 'But not yet. Not quite yet.'

'Very well.'

'You will come back to see me?'

Belle made herself smile. 'I promise it. Until you no longer need me at all.'

A small thin hand closed around her own and they sat in silence, the sunlight slanting through the curtains until Lucy fell asleep. With care Belle untangled her fingers and stood. Lady Lucy was so young and trusting.

A woman in Whitechapel would never have fallen for the drivel that Lucy had told her of nor would she have been lured into a quiet building and allowed him everything.

Once was enough to become pregnant. Every young girl of her acquaintance knew this as gospel.

The unfairness of life wrung deep. Was this what had happened to her all those years before? Had she been the product of such a union? A child without the strong ties of family that Lucy could at least lay claim to? A child of indifference and mistake? A child to be thrown away like rubbish? And then forgotten? For ever.

Oh, granted, she had loved Tante Alicia, but she had missed having a parent, one who might have played with her and laughed at all the things she'd seen young mothers and their children be amused by. She had seldom mingled with other children, never been taken to the places where they were. At first she had been ill, Alicia had said, and she did remember that. Then she had been confused. Her world had changed in a way she could not quite fathom and the memories of before had faded. Now it was just the ghosts of houses and the speech of people from long ago that remained.

She'd walked through life without being truly connected. That thought made her sit up, her heart beating louder, the truth of it disconcerting. But why should she think this now when last week she had been perfectly content doling out remedies and making potions?

It was because of the Earl of Thornton. He made her want things she would never have, things like permanence and a safe haven. He made her imagine that there could be another life just waiting around the corner. A life she would have had if...

My God, she was going crazy, but suddenly an inkling of what had been once for her flourished, the visits to the Thornton town house unleashing other memories. A grand house and servants and a garden that went on for ever into the distance, its edges surrounded by water. An old lady was there, too, with a kind face and a generous body, her eyes the exact same colour of her own.

But no one could tell her of that time and so these known things had slipped back into the hidden, crouching there in hope that the light would fall upon them and reveal the truth.

A knock at Lucy's bedroom door startled her.

'The Earl would like to speak with you in the library, miss, when you are finished here.' The young servant delivered his message and waited.

'Miss Staines is asleep. I will follow you down now.'

A moment later she was being shepherded through to a room towards the back of the house, one whole wall a set of doors that led out to the greenest garden Belle had ever seen. The Earl was there, standing on the lawn, a small snatch of sunlight on his hair as he turned.

'How is my sister today?' He asked this as he strode back into the room and latched the door. Shadows fell where sunlight had been only a moment before.

'She is sleeping.'

'What do you think ails her, Miss Smith?' There was a stillness in the words, a hesitation. Belle got the impression he had not truly wished to ask her this at all.

'It is complex, your lordship.' She struggled

for time, trying to conjure up some ailment that might have fitted Lucy's symptoms and failing.

'Try to make it simple, then.'

When she looked at him she understood that he had guessed far more than Lucy might have thought he would, but in this situation her professional loyalty had to lie with her patient.

'I think she needs time and tenderness. I think it may have been an infection that has resolved.'

A shutter crossed his golden eyes, an intensity replaced by indifference. She was sad to see it, but there was no other path for her to take. She had made a promise and she always kept her promises.

'Will you visit her again?'

'I shall, but I will not charge you, your lordship.'

This time he did not argue, but rang a bell that was on his desk and waited for the servant to come.

'Could you see that Miss Smith finds her way out, Harrison? If you need the carriage—' He stopped as she interrupted him.

'No. I am quite fine.'

'Then goodbye.'

So final. So emotionless. She was just another person supplying a service to an aristocratic family who must have countless need of things each and every week.

'Oh, and, Miss Smith…?'

She turned.

'Here is your book. Lucy said that she has finished with it.'

Belle stepped up to take it, making certain not to touch him inadvertently, and then she walked out.

Chapter Five

Damn. Damn. Damn. She had lied to him about his sister, for he understood that she knew far more than she let on. God, even he could now see that Lucy was with child and for a woman used to the various symptoms of a physical body such a knowledge must be staring Miss Smith right in the face.

When might others know of it? How many weeks did he have to find his sister a husband and make certain that she was safe? Had Lucy talked to Annabelle Smith and related the truth of how it had happened? That was another worry, the concern softening as he thought of her keeping Lucy's confidence when he had asked his questions.

She would not gossip. He knew that of her instinctively and was relieved. But she would lie to him, without a blink, bald lies that covered other mistruths. Her voice. Her past. Her fear of carriages and her confession that she thought herself plain. What was it she had said to him in her drunken state?

'Belle. You can call me that. Everyone else does. It means beautiful in French, but I do not think she should have named me such for I am not.'

Did she believe that, truly? And who was the 'she' who had named her, for this was not said in the way one might speak of a parent? Another person entirely, then?

He wanted to call her back and ask. He wanted to walk with her to the carriage and have one last ride in the manner of friends. More than friends? But he could not. He knew she would never flourish in society, a woman with no ties at all to the complex and convoluted world of the *ton*. It would be unfeasible and wrong to hope for it.

He should have kept the book with its fragile blue ribbons and its ridiculous ideas. No, not ridiculous, he corrected himself, but difficult. It would be a long time before the inequality that Mary Wollstonecraft spoke of between women and men was righted and these were

concepts that Lucy in her brittle state of mind
and body did not need to grapple with.

The day fell down upon him, a darkness
settling. Annabelle Smith was gone from him
with her mistruths and her lies.

The Earl of Dromorne had approached him
yesterday about a union between himself and
his eldest daughter. Lady Catherine was a
lovely girl, a friend, but he had no inclination
to follow up the proposal further. He could
do a lot worse, he knew that, for she was gracious and beautiful, competent and interesting. But he could not imagine her in his bed,
writhing beneath him, her face flushed with
sweat and desire.

Instead he saw Miss Annabelle Smith there,
her long dark hair around him and those dimples, which seldom showed, full blown upon
her face. He wondered what she would taste
like, feel like, smell like. They had barely
touched, but each time they had there had been
a shock of connection, a red-hot blaze of lust
and a surprising intimacy. Her fingers upon
his thighs in the drawing room, trying to wipe
off hot and scalding tea, her hand beside his in
the carriage, warm and small, her head against
his shoulder, the breath of her tickling his neck

as she lay asleep after her disastrous reaction to one and a half small glasses of white wine.

He smiled. He did not know one other person with that sort of intolerance to alcohol.

Perhaps he would instruct Shay or Aurelian to ask around about them, after all. They must have come to England quite a while ago, he deduced, given that their practice of making medicines would have taken a goodly time to establish.

Annabelle Smith and her Tante Alicia did not seem like outsiders in Whitechapel, a place that seldom took to strangers with any sense of pace or ease.

But Miss Smith held information that could ruin the reputation of the Thorntons and as such it behoved him to take precautions. If he found out things about her that were not salutary, could he use them as blackmail should she try the same with him? Would he want to? As she'd left today she had looked at him with a sense of betrayal in her sapphire-blue eyes, the light of them dimmed by comprehension. She knew she did not belong, every bit as much as he did, in the elevated world of the *ton*.

Lytton pushed a pile of work across in front of him and sat down at his desk. He was the guardian of a lot more than simply his life. He was not kind. He had already told Annabelle that when she had said he was. Business required a hardness and he was a highly successful businessman. It was just the way it was and the way it would have to be.

He opened his drawer and found her note listing all of the ways that she had spent her ten pounds. The difference between them was encapsulated in this little message. Annabelle Smith cared about everyone while he protected his family. While she saw ten pounds as a veritable fortune he could spend that in the blink of an eye. On a bottle of perfect wine or on a new pair of boots. Or simply by throwing it on to the gambling table and not really caring if he ever got it back. She'd written a thank-you note, something he doubted he'd ever do. Things came to him easily and without much effort. The horse from Huntington was one example. He could sell it at the Thursday auctions for a hundred pounds at Tattersall's or he could hold on to it to breed more colts and recover the money ten times over.

His world was bound by nothing and Miss Annabelle Smith's world was bound by everything.

He folded her note carefully and tucked it into the ornate wooden box where he kept things he did not want to lose, wondering about the connotations of such a choice even as he closed the lid.

'I think I lived somewhere else before coming to you, Tante Alicia. I saw a glimpse of a life I used to have when I was at the Thornton town house.'

Her aunt frowned heavily and shooed Stanley off her lap. When she stood Belle saw that her back must be sore again and that the knee she had hurt last summer falling over the front step was also playing up.

Part of her wanted to take back the words and allow her aunt some rest, but the other stronger part just could not.

'I saw a woman in my mind, too. An old woman who had eyes the same colour as my own. I need to know more, Tante Alicia. I need to know what these memories mean and who these people are.'

'Sometimes it is better just to leave the past alone, Annabelle. Things happen for a reason and to drag them all up again can be futile and hurtful. The future is there before you, to be met with enthusiasm and eagerness. I should concentrate on that if I was you.'

'Hurtful? For me, you mean?'

Her mind whirled at this new small piece of information and then seized on another bit of the puzzle. 'You said I was sick when I came to you? How sick?'

'Sick enough to die had you simply been left.'

'To die of what?'

'An injury.' Alicia said this loudly, but caught herself as her voice rose further. 'Someone had hit you, hurt you on numerous occasions. These are the truths that can wound, Belle, honesties that are pointless and avoidable.'

Belle stepped back, the summer air chilling as the possibilities of what had happened to her funnelled down. 'Did the nun who brought me to you say who had wounded me?'

'She did, but…' Her aunt stopped mid-sentence, indecision written across her face.

'Who was it? I have to know.'

'Your father. He was a violent man by all the accounts of those at the inn in which they had stayed.'

'They?'

'Your mother and him. It was your mother,

not a servant, who brought you to the Notre-Dame de la Nativité and implored the nuns to look after you. She had been hit herself, Sister Maria said, but she would not stay for any doctoring. It was you she wanted protected and safe.'

So much new information and so unexpected. So many facts that she hadn't had before. A picture of a family in turmoil. It was hard to take it in. No wonder her aunt had kept her silence.

'But you don't know their names?'

'I do not. I promise you.'

'Or any information as to where they went next? The mother and father?'

'None.'

'What of the innkeeper? Would he know?'

'There was a fire there the following winter. Both the innkeeper and his wife and any records they may have kept perished in it.'

A further untraceable end. Another way of finding out nothing.

'I have not told you this before, but your mother did leave a Bible with Sister Maria. There was no front-piece in it though, no signature. It was a simple clean copy like a thousand others of the same ilk.'

'Is it here still?'

'Yes.' Alicia walked across to the bookcase at the end of the room and drew out a small burgundy-covered tome, placing it into Belle's outstretched hands.

An Anglican Bible. The King James version. It felt so ordinary, but it wasn't. Her mother had touched this once, as she had handed over a broken daughter. Was it a message of hope or of religion or scripture? Looking through it, she saw there were no turned-down pages, no special places that had been made different. When she brought it up to her face there was only the smell of ink and age. Dust was there, too, the passing time gathered in leather.

'I've looked many times myself, Annabelle, for a clue. There are none.'

But there were, Belle thought. She was Anglican and she was loved. By a mother who had tried her best to save her and then disappeared. By a woman who could not protect herself, but would ensure her daughter's well-being.

The enormity of such a discovery had her sitting. If this message of love was the only thing she ever found out about her past, it would be enough. To know she was wanted.

To understand that even in violence devotion had won.

'Would Sister Maria still be alive, do you think?'

'I don't know. Perhaps?'

'Then I could send a letter to her at the church in Moret-sur-Loing?'

Alicia crossed the room to sit beside her. 'Now that you've remembered a few things, it is probable you will remember more. You are English so some members of your family might still be here.'

'Is that why we came to London?'

'No. France was in a turmoil and I thought you could be in danger if we stayed. You were still too young to be truly safe and I wanted to protect you.'

And here was another honourable guardian, a woman who would leave behind all she knew for the custody of a child who was not her own. Belle took her old aunt's hand and felt the crepe-thin skin, the sun from the fading day sending small last shards of light down upon them, dust motes swirling in the eddies.

Outside Whitechapel burst into night noises, the men coming home from the pubs, the merchandisers selling fish and bread for tea, the children running in dirty tumbling bundles home through the narrow and poverty-stricken alleys. The proper order of life had been turned upside down only for her and there was a reassurance in that as she sat clutching her mother's Bible.

Annabelle Smith came again to Portman Square the following Wednesday and Lytton was waiting for her.

'Could I have a word with you in the library, Miss Smith?'

Today she wore an old blue gown with a half-jacket in red. The hat she sported was too large for her head, the front of it falling down over her forehead in a way that looked almost comical. Why did she never look as he expected? She carried a bunch of white daisies, too, wrapped in newspaper.

'For your sister,' she explained when she saw him looking. 'They grow in one of my patients' garden and so I asked her if I could pick some.'

'I see. Could you sit down for a moment?' Already this meeting was veering off to some place he did not wish it to go and he was

pleased when they reached the library and
were alone.

With care she did as he asked, folding her
skirts across her legs so that not even the ti-
niest piece of skin showed above her boots or
below the hemline.

'I have reason to believe that my sister is
with child, Miss Smith.'

Lytton saw the shock of it on her face, the
darkening eyes, the way her tongue licked her
top lip. The utter stillness that was so unlike
her.

'I was hoping you might have some more
details to add to what I know.'

Her answer came very quietly. 'What is it
you do know?'

So she didn't deny it. The dark rush of sorrow made him swallow. 'Very little. My sister has always been secretive and as such it is
now difficult to see the way forward, to ensure the child has a father and she has a place
in society.'

'She will not marry him, your lordship.'

His heart thumped at this statement. Loudly.

'I told your sister that you would always be
protective of her and that she was safe here
with you.'

'Which, of course, she will be, but—'

She did not let him finish.

'He will not just get away with it. The man who did this to her. I promised her that, at least.'

Lytton was horrified and could not believe what he was hearing. 'It is not your problem to deal with, Miss Smith, it is mine. Who is he?' He tried to keep the fury from his tone, but failed.

'I am a healer, your lordship, and the things a patient relates to me in confidence are for my ears alone. If your sister wishes it different, she will tell you.'

'God. I want to kill him!' There was no kindness left in him now. If she had given him a name he would have primed his guns and left Annabelle there, revenge banishing reason and eliminating sense.

'I was thinking more in the line of a rough up.' Her voice came quietly.

'A rough up?' He stood. 'With a group of assorted strong men from Whitechapel? A measured punishment that was untraceable?'

She nodded.

'No. I will not let you do that. Nothing is untraceable and when you are caught...'

'The seething shifting population of White-chapel stays well out of the way of the law. Being caught, as you put it, is not something that happens often there. More normally the world just goes on a little different from the way it was before and the one who is at fault is punished.'

The Earl of Thornton was furious. Belle could see it on his face and in his stance and in the balled fists he held rigidly at his side. Men often struck out in anger in Whitechapel when they held the same look of violence and a new worry surfaced. Would he be like that?

Rising from her chair, she took a step back, bringing her reticule between them. If it was even possible, his eyes blackened further, one hand reaching out to take her arm.

'I would not hurt you. Ever. Believe at least that of me, Miss Smith.'

She did have faith in these ground-out words, impossible as they might seem, as she tipped her head to observe him. He was so beautiful up close, his eyes webbed in a lighter gold, a masculinity that was undeniable and worrying. She wanted to lose herself in such a glance and be taken to the point of no return, all logic melted.

Kiss me.

Had she said this? Relief welled when she realised she had not. But he must have seen the echo of it on her face as she turned away, this raw thought making her shake, shock scrawled in waves across her body. She wanted him, she did, wanted him to simply reach out and take her lips with his. She wanted to kiss him in the way women had kissed men all across the centuries, without barriers or reasons or explanation.

In her whole life she had been distant with men, detached and reserved. But with Lytton Staines, the Earl of Thornton, there was an awareness that was startling, almost discomforting, a sort of sentience that held no true understanding.

Stars hide your fires;
let not light see my black and deep de-
sires.

Shakespeare's words tumbled around and around in her head, the rhythm allowing her some equanimity. Others in history and literature had felt like her and they had managed, though Macbeth's dubious example was perhaps not quite what she was after. But the inclination to hide her feelings from both others and herself felt mildly honourable and so the words stayed. A protection to what lay beneath.

'Children are always a gift, your lordship, even ones that come unexpectedly. Your sister is young, but she is a survivor and the Thornton name can conceal much.'

She needed to bring the conversation back before she faltered, needed it to be about Lucy and her child and the future and not about the feelings that simmered between them or about the violence that hovered close.

'You truly believe this, that there is the propensity to recover from this?'

'A huge bulk of the population survives without having anything at all to do with society. Your sister can help out at the Whitechapel clinic, she can teach other younger girls how to read and write, she can...'

'Stop. You have no idea what is at stake here. With a child born out of wedlock my sister will never have a place to live safely, never be accepted by all the people she knows. Who would marry her now?'

'Maybe she is not after marriage.' Her own

ire had fired. 'Maybe she wants freedom and options and other possibilities.'

'Like the pathway you have chosen?'

'A husband is not always the way to lasting happiness, your lordship.'

'God.' The huge chasm that yawned between them widened further. Annabelle Smith had no idea of the life he lived, the conventions and expectations, the unspoken truths of privilege. And how could she? How could he even have supposed it? Her voice and her body and her startling eyes had mesmerised him, made him foolish, were still making him foolish, but it needed to stop. Now.

'How much could I pay you in order for you to keep quiet about this whole…situation, Miss Smith?'

'Pardon?' She looked puzzled.

'Blackmail, Miss Smith. I want to make certain that it never happens because of this. What sum would keep you from mentioning my sister's circumstances to anyone else…for ever?'

He felt her breathe out, felt the loss of her respect with an ache. 'The sum of honour, your lordship, and if you had to ask such a question then you have none.'

He smiled, though there was a tightness in

his throat. 'I have thousands of pounds to my name and a good number of them could be at your disposal if they allowed me to ascertain silence. Consider that.' Sometimes, thought Lytton, it took a few tries to get a person to reveal their true colours. How many times in the business world had he seen this? 'If you won't think of yourself, Miss Smith, then think of the difference such an amount might make in Whitechapel.'

'To sell my soul on the account of your deceit? To be devalued by standards that are repugnant to me? I think not.'

'You were the one who lied about my sister's malady.' He could not let it go, not just yet, not till he understood her purpose completely.

'I did not tell you of her condition because she asked me not to, as my patient.'

'And as the one paying the bills am I accorded no rights whatsoever? As a brother? As a guardian?'

'I cannot be the puppet of two masters, your lordship. It is neither feasible nor advisable.'

'Who are you then exactly, Miss Smith? No other soul from Whitechapel whom I have met speaks the King's English as you do and yet refuses the chance of a lucrative handout. If I asked around about your history, what might I find?'

The fear on her face made him falter.

'I do not wish to hurt you. I only wish to keep my family safe.'

'Then allow me to do my job, your lordship, and see to your sister's health needs. That is all. Afterwards I doubt we shall ever meet again.'

He nodded and summoned a servant, the relief he saw in her eyes as she left more than evident.

Perhaps she hated him, Belle thought. Perhaps it was easier. Perhaps in the full comprehension of the differences between them it would be a more sensible thing to feel. He had mistresses and a woman who had been handpicked for him in marriage by his parents. He had others, too, who were hopeful of a relationship according to his sister, for Lucy, by her own admission, had been beating off enquiries about him ever since arriving in society.

Annabelle sat down on her bed and put her head in her hands. The Earl thought she might blackmail him about his sister's pregnancy? What sort of a person would think such a thing? One with a huge estate to run and a family who was falling to pieces all around him, that was who.

He did not trust her. Perhaps he did not trust anyone as faith diminished under responsibility. What would it be like to live with a man like that, a man who imagined everyone his enemy, adversaries around every corner.

Reaching for her Bible, she held it close, wishing her mother were here to talk with, to ask advice from, to alleviate her utter loneliness. As she did this she noticed the stitching on the bottom back corner of the leather cover had unravelled, a small piece of paper tucked away inside suddenly seen.

With care she prised it out to find a single name written there. Annalena. The blue ink was faded and the writing was cursive, an old style of handwriting that was prevalent in the borrowed books from the printer in London.

Annalena.

She had no memory of this name, try as she might to find one, as she said it out aloud to herself in as many different ways that she thought it could be pronounced.

This little clue was enthralling and captivated her attention. Was it her mother's name? The woman with the beaten face who had thrust her at the nun at the Catholic church? Was it a place, somewhere denoting her origins? Or the name of the house in the green fields descending to a lake?

Annalena? Blue eyes were there. Eyes the same colour as her own. Piercing and sad. Saying goodbye to her. Holding her close. Crying.

'Come back to me, little one. Come back when you can.'

Belle felt her own tears pouring down her face here in her room years and years later. A mother. No. That did not quite seem right. An older woman. A grandmother?

Nannalena? Another remembered word. She had called her that, there in the green fields with the manor at her back, a winding moat across the front façade hiding a small river running to the sea.

She was lost from it. Lost from this and the woman. Annalena. Lost from sight and yet remembering. Abandoned, but loved. Once. Her own name was a part of this one. Anna. The whisper of history reached out and she heard them calling her, among the green of trees and flowers.

'Anna. Anna. Where are you?'

'Here,' she whispered. 'I am lost and waiting.'

How could she find them again, these people, with such a small and tiny clue? She could not ask for help from her aunt and she did not have the funds to leave London and search the rural countryside for a needle in a haystack.

She needed to remember more, but try as she might she could not. A headache was all she got for her trouble. That and a blinding realisation that she would need to be patient.

The Earl of Thornton's words today also reverberated around in her head.

'Who are you then exactly, Miss Smith? No other soul from Whitechapel whom I have met speaks the King's English...'

Her secrets were beginning to hunt her out, the small enclave she had lived in here widening with her recent visits to Portman Square.

There were answers close and possibilities which both frightened and excited her.

'Who are you, Miss Smith?'

It felt it would not be too much longer before she found her answers.

Chapter Six

Two days later she was back again at Portman Square and Lady Lucy looked so much better. It was youth, Belle supposed, for at twenty the body could bounce back from things that a decade later might only be managed with much more difficulty. The Earl of Thornton's sister made her feel old and after the interview with Lord Thornton in the library the other day she was already on guard, a melancholy assailing her that was unlike anything she'd ever known before. She hoped she would not see him almost as much as she hoped she would.

He was lost to her, the Earl. She could see it in his eyes and hear it in his voice. The end of regard. The beginning of distance. His sister, however, was more than animated.

'I am so glad you have come, Miss Smith,

for I have begun to take note of Mrs Wollstonecraft's words and such strength has been a considerable help. I feel now as though I can go on with my life in a renewed way.'

'And the child?'

'I shall retire to Balmain and live in the country with my mother until I decide what must be done next. London feels lessened for me now and exhausting and I need to recover.'

'Your brother knows you are with child. He has asked me for the name of the father.'

Lucy nodded her head. 'I thought he knew, for I could see it in his eyes when he spoke to me yesterday. If I tell him it was Huntington, I think he will kill him and then what will happen? The estate has only just recovered from my father's unwise excess and if Thorn is thrown into gaol for his act of revenge then where will it leave us all? My brother is a man who likes to be on top of things, you see, and one who dislikes any surprise. I think you are a great surprise to him, Miss Smith.'

Now this was new. 'How do you mean, Miss Staines?'

'Lucy. I wish you to call me that. Thorn is a man who is in control of every part of the Earldom. The finance, the family, the estates.

My sister, brother and I have probably all in our own ways been trials to him, but he has handled everything with aplomb. With you he has been knocked askew, for I think he cannot believe that a woman might choose her way in life without a man and enjoy it.'

Annabelle was astonished. In little more than a week the younger sister of the Earl of Thornton seemed to have grown up and blossomed. She was no longer downtrodden or sad and, although she was still very thin, she also looked healthy.

'I also want to ask something of you, Miss Smith, something personal.'

Annabelle nodded.

'I have decided to let go of my anger and, although I might have intimated to you that revenge was something I was after, I no longer feel that way at all. I want now to simply enjoy my baby without being held back by anything.'

'A wise choice, I think.'

'So the favour that I would ask of you is to forget all I told you and be happy for me.'

'I shall do that, Lucy. My aunt would applaud your choice, for there are things in my family that have been difficult and she is one who would look to the future with hope rather than to past regrets.'

'I knew you would understand. I hope you might be persuaded to visit me at Balmain. I could send the carriage down if you would deign to come. Perhaps when the baby is near time for I would feel far happier and safer if you were there.'

'I should like that.'

'I also want to give you something, Miss Smith. Something to remember me by.'

She walked across to a desk at one side of the room and extracted a small parcel wrapped in coloured paper and red ribbon.

'It is only a small token, I know, but it reminds me so much of you.'

When Annabelle opened it she saw it was a painting of flowers done in oil.

'It's a painting I bought last year in the Academy's Summer Exhibition. The fallen bloom is me and you, Miss Smith, are represented in the strength of the roses above.'

'It's beautiful.' And it was. How could have Lucy known she enjoyed images of flowers? Perhaps her brother had told her of the paintings in the front room at White Street. Her own attempts at mimicking nature seemed naive against the detail of this image.

'I shall hang it on my wall, Lucy, and think of you. I am sorry I have nothing to give in return...'

'Save courage, I think, and fortitude, things for a while I was badly lacking. I bought another copy of Mrs Wollstonecraft's book after my brother said he had returned the one you leant to me, just to keep. You were clever to think that it might be helpful.'

'You are not the first young woman to need advice, Lucy, and you certainly will not be the last.'

'See, that is what I mean, Miss Smith. Whenever you give advice it is with sense and vigour. I will miss you.'

'I will miss you, too, but if you talk with your brother you'll understand that he loves you with all his heart and that you are lucky to have such a protector.'

Lucy nodded. 'Most people are frightened of Thorn. His success scares them off, but he is also dangerous in a precise and measured way. He does not waste emotion, I suppose, or squander sentiment. He protects his family with all that he has and he does that well.'

Small fingers threaded around a lace hand-kerchief as she spoke, her nails still short and bitten.

The family. All the expectations of great wealth and history heaped on one man. It was no wonder the Earl of Thornton was sometimes taciturn. But he could be funny, too, and sweet. She remembered waking up in the carriage after her disastrous episode with the wine, her head having creased his linen shirt. She liked talking with him. She liked the sense of possibility edged with a danger that was fascinating. He was not a man who would bore her.

But she also knew her time with the Thorntons was coming to an end and that was as it should be. Lady Lucy would return to the country estate of Balmain and she would get on with her work in the poorer parts of London town, a few hundred miles away geographically, but a million miles apart in any other way that counted.

She clutched her beautiful oil painting and bade the Earl of Thornton's sister goodbye.

Lytton wondered what he was doing here. The Barretts' ball was well appointed, well attended and well thought of, but he was troubled.

Lady Catherine Dromorne stood with him, every piece of her in perfect place as she related to him details of the newest scandal of the *ton*. Not in a mean way, but in the way of a woman who could not countenance any behaviour that veered away from the narrow expectations of society, expectations she had been brought up with from the very cradle.

He felt restless and on edge. It had been three weeks since he had last seen Miss Annabelle Smith. She had left the house without a glance back, his sister's renewed health allowing no other necessary appointment in the future. Oh, granted, vague plans had been put in place to keep in touch, but her smile had been distant and forced.

She had been glad to get away from them all, that much was plain.

Lady Catherine's voice broke into his reveries. 'I can't understand how Lord Macmillan could have imagined he would not have been seen with Mrs Julia Chambers at that time of the day in a busy street. As my father said, the end of the world as we know it is coming sooner than we think if people insist upon liaisons with such unsuitable others.'

When had Catherine begun to parrot her father? he wondered. Lytton had never noticed this trait before. His mind returned to Annabelle Smith. Was it her circumstances that had softened his own attitude to those around him, allowing the person they were to triumph over the one everybody else thought them?

Mrs Julia Chambers had been married to a man who was a bully and a cheat, his wealth never quite hiding the lowly lineage he had been raised from. He had seen Gregory Macmillan with the beauteous widow on a number of occasions lately and never thought much of it, for she always appeared well mannered and demure. He held no idea of the circumstances of her background, but, from Catherine's words of warning, presumed that she certainly did.

The same ennui that had been building now for weeks suddenly assailed him. He felt jaded and tired, the weary task of pulling the Earldom from shambles suddenly heavy. He wanted to disappear, away from society, away from expectations, away from the constant badgering of those whose own straits were needing regeneration as much as his own. Even the canning factory tonight held no joy for him, the constant demands arising from it part of the reason he felt so damned tired.

The wreck of eighteen months of hard work, the sadness over the dreadful loss of his father, his sister's ruin and Annabelle Smith's lies fed into his defeat.

He wanted more. Aurelian and Violet de la Tomber danced together in the middle of the floor and the gaze they bestowed upon each other was beguiling. He imagined them going home after this to their town house and falling into a large soft bed full of promise. It would be a happy night.

He would sleep by himself.

Weeks ago after the Susan Castleton fiasco that realisation would have been exactly what he did want, but tonight all it felt was lonely.

'You are quiet, Thornton?' Catherine's voice was husky, one of the things he had liked about her right from the start.

'Tired, I think.' He tried to rally and asked her to dance even though it was the last thing that he wished to do. Once on the floor she gazed at him directly and his heart sank when he knew it was a waltz.

'I am sorry about my father's unexpected visit a few weeks ago. He took it on himself to organise my life and come to see you. Marriage is such an enormous step, do you not think?'

She said this in a way that made it sound completely the opposite and all of Lytton's defences were instantly raised.

'We know each other too well,' he countered, recognising that this was exactly the wrong thing to have said as soon as he had uttered it.

'And you think that a negative?' She watched him so closely that he changed tack.

'The Thornton estate is consuming my time, Catherine, and I cannot see it changing much for at least a year.' He saw her shaking her head and knew what she might say next, how she might try to cajole him into another option or of how she would be happy to wait. 'I will be in the Americas on business for a few months as well. Edward Tully is going over as my representative and will need a hand. I have promised him one.'

'I have heard differently. It is whispered by solid sources that you are after a bride.'

He swore under his breath as he almost lost his step. Who the hell had told her that? He'd made it very clear to her father that he was not interested in marriage and he knew instinctively that Edward, Aurelian or Shay would not have said anything of his ridiculous outburst about marrying the first girl he saw. Had someone else overheard it?

'Right now business keeps me frantic and so does the family.'

He was relieved when the music came to a stop and he was able to escort Catherine Dromorne back to her friends and make his own way to find a drink.

Aurelian waylaid him as he went.

'You look harried, Thorn. Is Catherine Dromorne still after your hand in Holy Matrimony?' There was humour in his tone.

'Her and half-a-dozen others. I shouldn't have come tonight, for I am not in the mood for flirtation and innuendo and definitely not for marriage.'

'Lady Thomasina Dutton was asking after you before. She has never seemed to me to be a girl who was vapid.'

Lytton drew his hand through his hair and swiped it back from his face. He had been smitten by Thomasina Dutton some while ago, but tonight even her beautiful face and endearing personality were undesirable. None of the women here appealed to him, none made his heart beat faster or his mind imagine things that were far more intimate.

He shut off the thoughts that lingered on a face with dimples and sapphire-blue eyes. *Not for me. Not ever for me.*

If he did not marry, then his younger brother's children could take over the title.

For a moment he felt displaced and dizzy, the room swirling around him in colour and movement and himself in the middle of it all, still and foreign and lost.

'Let's have a drink.' Lian's words came crashing into the silence and brought him back and he was grateful to be able to follow him to stand in the outside air on a balcony to one end of the room.

'What the hell is wrong with you, Thorn? You looked like you might fall over back there. Is the sickness Lucy has been afflicted with contagious?'

That question at least made him smile.

'No, and she is recovering daily.'

'The healer from Whitechapel did her job, then?'

'Seems to have.'

'Where is she now? Do you still see her?'

'Why should I? She was Lucy's physician, not mine.'

'A sore point, then? A raw nerve? Shay said he was much taken with the woman though she had no stomach for the drink. He said you took her home to Whitechapel by way of Hyde Park and spent three hours getting her there?'

'What are you saying, Lian?'

'The things that you are not, Thorn. I saw her this morning, by the way, in Regent Street, carrying a hefty basket. Lord Huntington was walking past and he looked most taken by her appearance. You might have competition, though he is the last man Miss Annabelle Smith needs to know at all. Remember him from school? He was a bully and a cheat.'

'He gave Edward a bloody nose the first time he met him and dragged all of us behind the sheds at one point or another. His uncle was some sort of boxing expert, if I remember rightly, and had taught him well.'

'Thank God we are no longer schoolboys.' Lian smiled and turned to look over the garden and the lights that had been placed on the small pathway.

'You looked happy tonight on the dance

floor, Lian. Being married suits you. It suits Shay as well.'

'It does. It's like finding a pot of gold at the end of the rainbow. Gold I was becoming less and less sure I'd find, I might add.'

'In what way?'

'I'd given up on thinking true love could ever be mine, but it can arrive on the single beat of the heart or an unexpected shaft of light and it can be unsettling.'

'You speak as if you think I should know this?'

'Catherine Dromorne looks like a rainbow tonight.'

'But she is not mine.'

'Then find your truth, Thorn, without compromise. Only you can know what is within here.'

His hand touched his chest, a small gesture with a large honesty attached to it.

Lytton finished his drink, refusing the next one from a passing footman.

'My life at the moment is busy, Lian. I haven't got time for further complications of the heart.

His friend's laughter was not comforting and he was about to say something when Edward Tully came out of the crowd, carrying a note.

'It's for you, Thorn. It's just been delivered.'

'Hell.' He could only think of one reason why a message would come to him here in the middle of the night and in the middle of the ball. Lucy had returned from Balmain two days ago to stay in the city for a week and she had not been feeling well.

Clutching the missive, he gave his leave to both Lian and Edward and made for the door.

Annabelle Smith had come in the carriage he had sent to Whitechapel arriving on the town-house doorstep after one in the morning, her hair bundled at her neck and her cheeks rosy from sleep. Her aunt accompanied her.

She barely gave him notice as she asked after his sister.

'How long has she been ill?'

'Since this morning. She had stomach cramps and felt unwell.'

'Why did you not call for me earlier?'

'Lucy was sure it was only something she had eaten. She did not want a fuss.'

'Well, she is about to get one now, your lordship.' There was a sort of fear in her eyes, a worry that immediately transferred itself to him.

'We will see her alone if you would like to wait. This is women's business.'

'Certainly.' He was almost glad for it.

Annabelle Smith tried to reassure him as he sat on the small sofa in the parlour attached to the bedchamber. 'It will be as it will be. No amount of worry will make it different. The child is in God's hands now.'

'But your own competence must count for something, surely.'

'It does, but it is early on in the pregnancy and sometimes a baby is simply not viable. I have seen this many times before.'

He was unsure how much a statement like that helped, but attempted to dredge up the rudiments of belief. 'Thank you.'

She simply looked at him then, a stillness settling between them.

'Should I call others as well, Miss Smith? The family physician?'

'No. We are enough and also we are very... discreet.'

He swallowed. He knew that was why he had called her, Miss Annabelle Smith with her healing skills and her independence. There would be no gossip after this, whatever happened. The chatter could be contained, isolated, and the reputation of his sister could be saved. Unless she died. That thought hit him hard and he stood even as Miss Smith and her aunt left him, the bag they carried between them large and full.

Perhaps it was a punishment, this, a penalty against a family whose patriarch had simply shot himself after gambling away the Thornton country estate. A retribution that came at a price: the price of the life of a bastard child and his mother.

He sat down again suddenly and weighed up the balance sheets. If he had been less honest, he might have kneeled to pray, but he was sure an omnipotent God would only see the falseness in such an action. It had been years since he'd truly believed in anything save the pursuit of money and to start beseeching a deity in a final hour of need seemed an empty hope and disingenuous to boot.

But he did whisper something under his breath. 'Please.' Whether it was directed at Miss Belle Smith or to the celestial power above he could not quite at that point fathom.

* * *

The clock struck five and Belle looked around the library, surprised by the time and its passing. Her aunt had been taken home in the Thornton carriage and Lucy was sleeping, tucked upstairs gently in a bed that was warm and safe and hers.

'There was no chance?' The Earl asked this from the seat opposite in his downstairs library.

'None. I tried.'

'I know.'

Silence resumed.

'Will my sister recover?'

'She will recover as well as any woman can after the loss of a child, no matter what its history.'

'Of course.'

He'd had lemonade brought up from the kitchens and slices of fruit bread. She was grateful for it.

It was almost companionable here, in the very early morning before the house began to move, books all around them and a muted dawn on the grass outside. Time between time. She often felt like this after the death of a patient, only a thin line separating the quick from the dead.

'No matter how much you think you know, it can never be enough to save them all.' The words slipped out, unbidden.

'But you tried and that is the difference.'

'One day, years and years on, there will be ways found to save them, these very little ones.'

She saw the leap of surprise in his eyes and she wondered why she might have told him this. Goodness, the Thorntons had thought her a witch when first she had come here and proclamations like this probably did her cause little good. But she needed to talk, too, needed to assuage the loss and find acceptance, the grief raw in her words.

'It's the young patients that stay with you, I think. The promise of what might have been and now will never be. The loss of all those years.'

She tried to keep the utter desolation from her voice, but failed.

'At least your work is honourable,' he said finally. 'At least you try to fashion a better world, a happier one, and if you can't then what is left is still enhanced because of your caring.'

She liked his explanation and smiled. 'I sometimes think that it takes pieces of me, little pieces that I can't recover. Tante Alicia says she deliberately does not let this happen, but I... I do not seem to be able to help it.'

Sipping on her lemonade, she looked at him directly. This morning she couldn't be bothered hiding from him, she needed to say what she said and he was the person here to listen. An earl or not, he was still a brother. A brother who had lost something as well.

He sat forward, his legs long and folded. His boots were of a shiny black leather and his buckles were silver, the metal embossed with a coat of arms. Small details that would for ever stick with her.

'My job takes pieces from me, too, and it is nowhere near as honourable. To save a life, even to try to save one seems to me to be unparalleled.'

The light had changed now, creeping in a more distinct form across the perimeter of the garden, changing shadows.

'If you would like to stay here at the town house, a room can be readied?'

'No. Thank you.'

'Then I almost hesitate to mention payment

for tonight's services, for what price does one place upon a life?'

'I did not save one.'

'But Lucy is safe. You made sure of that.'

The tears that she had held back all night suddenly began to fall and she swiped at them angrily, not wishing to give into the sorrow.

He did not move forward and for that she was grateful. Right then she did not need the physical.

'I cried for my father.' His words. A shared confession. She was certain he had told nobody else in all the world such a thing.

She looked up and into his soul, bared there before her.

'I hated him for doing it, for killing himself in the bed of a mistress after gambling away the family estate. How could that be tempered? How could I fix it?'

'The ruin of a family name? Like tonight? Again?'

'Exactly.' The word was harsh and sad. 'I am an earl, Miss Smith, a guardian of history and a minder of time and place, and while my sister's child would have caused a ruction in the fabric of the Thorntons, I still did not wish it away.'

'Then I am glad for it.'

'Just as I am glad you were here, too.'

She nodded and breathed out. Perhaps this was all that she had needed, a heartfelt thanks that encompassed his own secrets. A new beginning on an equal footing.

She was so tired she could barely move and she did not want to. There was something infinitely satisfying about sitting with a man who was strong enough to show his vulnerability after she had shown him hers. He did not seem to be in any hurry either as he leant back and watched her. The gleam in his eyes was brighter now.

'Your reputation is growing by the day, Miss Smith. I have had many enquiries about your services.'

'It is unusual for me to venture past Whitechapel, my lord. Generally, I feel happier there.'

'How long have you lived in White Street?'

'Almost twenty years now. Where does that time go? You look up and next thing years have past.'

'Why were you there? In France?'

'My parents were travellers.'

'They did not return home? Your mother and father?'

She shook her head. 'They died.'

She gave him the words like a truth even though she knew it was not one. But the alternative was too hard to say. *I was abandoned there. I was beaten up and left. Sick to death in a church.*

Now she was lying and the Miss Annabelle Smith he was more familiar with was back. Prickly. Independent. Unusual.

He did not want to ask her anything else because more falsehoods would wreck what was left of this one rare night and he liked that he had a memory of her that was honest and that the awkwardness of the other day seemed lessened.

'Will you return to see to my sister?'

'Yes. Tomorrow I shall come again, my lord. Sleep is what she needs now as well as good food and kind company.'

'Then I shall make sure that she receives both.'

She used his title at such random moments. Sometimes he thought she might have almost forgotten the distance in status between them. Sometimes he did, too.

His formal attire was so different from the clothes Annabelle had pulled on in the middle of the night and the fine bones in her face were drawn over sorrow, the flames of candles highlighting the startling blue in her eyes reddened with fatigue.

He would have liked to ask after the child that was gone but he didn't, reasoning that it would have been very small and she probably did not want such a reminder anyway. Her fingers were red, blisters running down the inside length of her forefinger, and when she noticed him looking she hurried in to explain.

'The hotter the water the better the outcome.'

He smiled at that. Such a concise and abridged medical statement with no pretence in any of it. He wished he could have leant over and taken her hand into his own, soothing pain, finding touch. But she gave no impression of wanting this, unlike all the women who had flirted outrageously with him in the Barrett's ballroom.

Two worlds separated distinctly.

Belle felt the connection between them, a sort of shared sorrow and common tie. The Earl was by far the most handsome man she had ever laid her eyes upon and yet it was not his appearance that riveted her. It was the pain in his eyes and the care he held for his sister. It was the sharing of his own fears and his unexpected openness.

His father's death had shocked her and yet he had told it to her without amendment. Why? Did he mean to frighten her off? Or was he trying to draw closer?

She knew nothing more of him other than what she had discovered in the half-dozen times they had met. She knew he was not married, but was there a woman with whom he had an understanding. His mother and sister had spoken of a mistress, but Belle guessed that was par for the course for the very wealthy. They did not give their hearts easily and when they did it was with a proviso. She had heard the stories after all many times around the fireplaces off the Whitechapel Road. The excesses of the very rich made them careless of feelings, it was said, and faithless. This certainly appeared to be the case with the Earl's father.

Thornton smelt of perfume and of women. His clothes tonight were nothing like she had seen him in before. They were dark, formal and well cut, the fabrics soft. He looked tired, too, his hair brushed back off his face in a quick sleight of hand, the colour of toffee and cinnamon and mid-brown autumn leaves.

Lucy had seemed more indifferent to the miscarriage of her child than he was. She had been quiet for nearly all of the doctoring until the very end when she had asked whether it was a boy or a girl.

'It is hard to tell this early.' Belle had said the words with kindness, but Lucy had simply turned away in her bed towards the wall and refused further conversation.

Perhaps it was for the best, this miscarriage, Annabelle thought. Perhaps there were things that in the elevated world of the *ton* were impossible to recover from.

She thought of all the young women in Whitechapel whose births she had attended. Many of these were products of violence or rape and yet the babies had been taken in and loved.

More differences. Further disparities.

With care she stood then, holding her bag before her and watching the Earl of Thornton rise, too.

'I should go for it is late.'

'Or early depending how one looks at it.' Already the birds were waking outside.

'Someone should stay with your sister at all

times for this day at least. It is just a precaution. If she begins to bleed again, call for me immediately.'

'I shall see that is done, Miss Smith, and thank you, for everything.'

He looked as if he might lean forward and take her hand. Indeed, she got the distinct impression that he started to before checking himself. The clock in the corner struck five thirty, a hollow sound in the oncoming dawn.

Chapter Seven

Her aunt was up when she arrived home.

'You stayed awake, Tante, and it is so very late?'

'I could not sleep. There is a difference. Who is the Earl of Thornton to you, Belle?'

'He is the brother of my patient. He is the one who has been paying the bills.'

'I think he is dangerous. I think you should stay well away from him, with his fine house and expensive clothes and eyes that look you over from top to bottom.'

For a second Annabelle was dumbfounded. 'You have it wrong, Tante Alicia. I doubt he even sees me for who I am. It's the way of those folk, don't you see?'

'No. He is a man who is used to getting exactly what he wants and right now that is you.

And as soon as it is difficult, which it would be given the differences between you, he will throw you over for the woman he should have been courting, the Countess he ought to have married, the one his family likes and who society welcomes.'

'My God.' Belle suddenly understood exactly what her aunt was saying. 'It happened to you, didn't it? In France when you were young? Someone just like the Earl?'

The fury in those dark eyes told her the truth even as Alicia tried to shake it away.

'It's why you did not marry? Why you had no children? Did you love him?'

But Alicia had gone back to her room, the door shutting hard. Death, betrayal and love. The day was full of pain and Belle knew there would be no simple remedy. With a sigh she dropped her bag on the floor before lying down fully dressed on the bed. The last thing she remembered before sleep came was the Earl of Thornton on the steps of his town house, watching her leave. Large and still and alone.

Dromorne arrived again the following afternoon at Portman Square and this time he was not to be fobbed off so easily for Catherine accompanied him.

'You have given the impression that you were more than interested in my daughter, Thornton, and because of it other suitors have held back on asking for permission to get to know her better. She is almost twenty-two now and three Seasons in your company have meant she is dangerously near to being left on the shelf. I need an agreement, Thornton, and I need it soon.'

Part of him just wanted to turf Lord Dromorne out on his ear, but the man was old and had been a family friend for many years. Besides that, he did not look particularly well, his face flushed red and bloated and his pulse racing. Catherine, next to Dromorne, looked so miserable she could barely meet his eyes.

'Say what you need to, Daughter, and do not hold back.'

Her brown eyes were full of embarrassment. 'I thought… I thought that we were… promised, my lord. I have not looked at another and I am old now.'

'Twenty-two is hardly old.' God, compared to his years it seemed damn young. The trap of it all blurred his future even as fire sprang into her words.

'It is when you are a female. It is as old as you can possibly be until you can no longer expect to find a suitable marriage. Everyone says so.'

This was far worse than he had thought. He had imagined Catherine being as rebellious as he was when he knew she was coming with her father to see him. He thought this whole mess would be sorted without fuss in a few moments, but he had miscalculated badly. His own words from a few months back were also a part of this mix up. He had intimated to his friends he would marry the next passably good-looking woman who could bear children. Well, here was one before him who was more than beautiful and who now professed to be ruined in making a fine marriage and all because of him. If he did not offer something Lord Dromorne would be sure to spread the gossip of the reckless Thorntons and all the memories of his father's stupidity would be back as the main topic of scandal yet again. None of this would be helpful to his newly expanding but fledgling businesses.

Annabelle Smith's face came to mind, but

he knew deep down that anything between them would be hopeless. They would both ruin each other. Still, he could not quite let it go.

'Give me twelve weeks, Catherine. If by then you have not found another whom you feel you might make a life with, then I will court you. I promise it. We have always been friends, but I had not imagined anything more. I am sorry.'

The frown on her forehead deepened, but her father looked happier. 'I will take your word as the unbreakable troth of a gentleman, Thornton.'

'You do that.' His words were angry and harsh and had Catherine not been standing there with her head bent and her hands working the material around and around in her fetching pink skirt he would have said more.

At best he could try to talk with her alone and reason with her. At worst he would be attached in twelve weeks to a woman of good birth whom his family liked and who would make an admirable countess.

The tangle of it all stuck in his throat.

Lytton visited Shay an hour later, pleased to see his friend at home and alone. In the library a few moments later and with a drink in hand he felt able to confess the exact reason as to why he had come. 'Dromorne came to see me today.' The words came quietly and Shay looked up.

'What about?'

'He thinks I have misled his daughter into an expectation of marriage for these past three years. He has now come with the express intention of collecting his debt.'

'What did you say?'

'What could I say?'

'Surely you did not consent?'

'I hedged. I told him that in twelve weeks if Catherine still had not found a man she loved, then I would court her properly. She was there so I could hardly say different.'

'I see.'

'Do you? I am thirty-five years old. I need an heir. I need a countess who can cope with all that the position entails. I need stability for my family, for Lucy and Prudence and David. And for Mama. I am the head of a family that is fragile and the only way to save it might be to sacrifice myself.'

'The speech of a martyr. *"Under love's heavy burden do I sink."* God. Leave England if you must on the pretence of business, but do not marry a woman whom you could never truly love.'

'It is not so black and white, Shay. I have a friendship with Catherine and I do respect her, but honour is all I have left at the end of the day and I can't just abandon that. My father did and I have hated him for it every day, ever since.'

'Your father was an ass, but you were always a good man, Thorn, under the wildness, so here's to you and happiness and a heartfelt warning that a whole life is a long time to live in the shadow of regret.'

Shay brought up his glass and Lytton smiled. 'I'll drink to that.'

Whitechapel Road was a long one and today a group of sheep and cattle were being driven through to the slaughterhouse a few streets away. Caught behind people and animals, Belle gazed around at the noise and the movement, a canvas of commerce and poverty and just plain hard living. Sometimes she loved this place, even despite its obvious problems. It was vital and busy and ever changing, the sedate and beautiful square of the Earl of Thornton's a far cry from here.

Here anything was possible, if not probable, and the folk who inhabited the lodgings were as diverse as the houses themselves. The milkmaids with their balance of buckets and their beautiful skin, the fish vendors, the children with their dirty faces and bare feet, the loose women, the clergy, the constabulary, the drunks. It was a tapestry of colour, form and shape, against a backdrop of violence and community.

Belle had walked these streets since she was twelve and newly come from France. She knew the alleyways to avoid and the taverns that harboured the worst of the thieves and felons. She understood the safety of daytime and the dangers of the night. There were so many faces here that were familiar now.

It was not often a stranger could traverse these streets without notice, but she was sure one had for she'd the uncanny feeling that someone had been following her for a few days now. Someone who did not belong here, someone who was an outsider. Someone who was watching her.

She had turned often and quickly, but had

never caught the perpetrator save for once on the very end of Whitechapel Road near Aldgate when a man at a distance dressed in the clothes of a gentleman had observed her and made to follow.

She had lost him easily, turning into Goulstone Street and then Wentworth, her increasingly fast flight putting an end to any continued surveillance. She had said nothing to Tante Alicia nor to Rose, not wanting to worry them with accusations that could be pointless, after all.

Who would follow her? Most people here were pleased for her expertise in medicines and ailments and would knock at her door if they had need of help. Everybody knew that she was as poor as they were. She did not pick or choose patients, but treated each one crossing the threshold of her lodging with the same courtesy as she had the one before. A fair and equal doctoring. She was therefore left alone to do as she willed in the parish and there had never once in all the years since arriving been an incident that had made her question the safety of walking here.

Until now.

She breathed a sigh of relief as she saw Rosemary crossing the street towards her.

'I heard you went back to the Earl of Thornton's house the day before yesterday in Portman Square, Belle?'

'I did. I was there briefly this morning, too. Miss Staines had sickened and needed medicines.'

Annabelle hated lying to her friend, but she could understand the Earl's point in respecting confidentiality. He had not been there this morning, but his sister had looked a lot brighter and was talking of going to the family estate in the country to recuperate. Perhaps she was relieved to have lost the child and to have a future that was largely untarnished before her once again. Belle had not mentioned the baby at all for the girl did not seem to encourage it, merely checking her stomach and pulse and temperature.

There was an awkwardness between them now, though. The end of one relationship and the beginning of another. Perhaps if she had been in Lady Lucy's shoes she might have felt the same, a reminder of an episode so terrible she wanted no more to recall it.

Belle had left quickly, knowing that she

might not be back again and knowing, too, that the young woman was on the road to a good recovery.

'Was the Earl present?' Rose looked more than interested as she asked this.

'He was not.'

'I liked him. I thought he was beautiful.'

Belle laughed. 'You barely met him.'

'But I can always tell if people's souls are good ones. It's my strength. His was pure.'

'I doubt if even he would tell you that was so, had you asked.'

'He's spoken of his character? With you? My goodness, tell me all about it.'

'Rose, stop. I will probably never see him again and that is just as it should be. People pass in and out of my life all the time, their need great until it is not.'

They were coming to the main road now on the edge of Whitechapel, the thoroughfare widening out. Belle had promised Tante Alicia that she would visit the markets for herbs as their supplies were running low and Rose was going the same way. She was glad for the company as they stood on the side of the road, ready to cross together.

The carriage came from nowhere, skidding

in the wet towards them and throwing them both to the ground. Belle felt her head whack against stone and knew a sharp pain in her right wrist where she had tried to shield her fall. Rosemary beneath her was lying very still.

Panic banished a lethargy that was becoming more appealing.

'Rose. Rose. Are you all right?'

Her friend's eyes fluttered. 'I think so. What happened?'

'A carriage hit us and it did not stop.' Already she could see the back of it turning a corner further off, nothing from this distance to distinguish it from the others that plied the road. She felt sick and shaking and, recognising shock, placed her hand at her neck to count her pulse. Fast and thready. Swallowing, she tried to take stock of her fright, but the tunnel about her was darkening and then the world was simply falling away.

She woke a few moments later propped up against a brick door well with many people about her. There was something tight around her head and she put her hand up to see what it was.

'Leave it there, Miss Smith, it's a bandage.' The man who brought them coal was kneeling before her, his brow furrowed. 'Your head was bleeding badly and the flow needed to be stopped.'

Rose was beside her now, her face white. 'You fainted, Belle. How do you feel?'

'Better. I am sure I will be fine.' She tried to come to her haunches, but the world swam dizzily and so she sat back. 'Give me ten minutes and we will start for home. Did you see the carriage who hit us, Mr Curtis?'

'Not really. It were a fine one, though, and the driver were in livery.'

That was new. And worrying.

Mrs Roberts from a few streets away had also come forward. 'Gracious me, Miss Smith, you were lucky you were not both killed. My son Harold is here with me as he is home for a few hours to see us. I will get him to help you.'

Belle wanted to say no because Mrs Roberts's son was a kitchen worker in a fine house in Portman Square. The woman had told her of it only last week in a voice filled with pride. Not the Thornton town house, for she had asked after the name of the man who employed him, but not far away either and surely folk of that ilk banded together socially.

However, when Harold came and lifted her,

his strength was gratifying. Testing her legs, she found everything to be in working order and noticed Rose to be doing the same.

'I'll see you both home, miss. You still look a bit wobbly.'

The bandage about her head throbbed and Annabelle tried to loosen it a little. She hoped it was clean and that the pressure from it would stem the blood loss until she could get back to White Street and deal with it herself. With thanks, she took Harold Roberts's offered arm, spots of colour dancing in her vision.

'The healer, Miss Smith, was in an accident today in Whitechapel, my lord. I thought you should know of it.'

'An accident?' Lytton stood very still as he waited for the answer.

'A carriage hit her. It came out of nowhere and threw her on to the road, according to Roberts. He works next door in the kitchens of Lord Stephens.'

Each of his valet's words came through a beating horror.

'Was she killed?' He could barely ask this question.

'Not killed, my lord, but hurt badly.'

'Where is she now?'

'At home with her aunt, Roberts said, my lord.'

Lytton looked at the time. Three o'clock in the afternoon. 'Tell the driver to have the carriage brought around and make sure it is ready to leave in fifteen minutes.'

'Yes, my lord.' Lytton could see questions in the eyes of his valet as he turned to find his coat. What the hell would happen now?

He had deliberately stayed away from his town house yesterday morning when Miss Annabelle Smith had come to see his sister. He hadn't wanted to meet her again, here, bounded by protocol. He had wanted a clean break and a certain ending and Lucy's improving state of health had been conducive to such a plan. She was recovering. The baby was no more. She had also stated an intention to retire to Balmain Hall and Lytton was all in favour of it. He knew his servants would not gossip, but he wanted to make sure that the man who had done this to his sister would not brag either. When Lucy could speak to him without looking as if she might shatter, he would pursue it further. But meanwhile he would make his own enquiries quietly so as not to incite question.

Right at this moment there was also the further problem of an accident. What did 'hurt badly' constitute? His mind raced across many possibilities but he batted them all away. He would go and see for himself. He would visit Miss Annabelle Smith openly. He would bestow a good sum upon her clinic for discreetness and for confidentiality and to help her through this dark time and then…then he would forget her, consign her to a mistake just as he had done with all the other women he had once admired.

It would be an end to the nonsense. Lady Catherine Dromorne and he would marry and produce heirs to take the Thornton name marching into the future. A continued line of Earls.

He swallowed away fury. It was ordained. He was only a vessel for such perpetuity, a slight figure in the descent of lords who had come before him and would come after him. The tapestry of history.

His first look at Miss Annabelle Smith drove each and every thought he had had in coming here away.

She looked beaten and scared and injured.

One eye was black, her head was bandaged and her wrist sported a sort of splint from the elbow to the tip of her fingers.

'What the hell happened?' He could not help the anger, roiling in without end.

'A carriage hit me. Rose was there, but she is recovered. We did not see it for it came on the end of Whitechapel Road where the street turns. Then it kept going.'

A tight corner by the sounds of it, Lytton thought. Had someone deliberately tried to hit them?

He sat when she gestured to a chair on the opposite side of the small room, three feet between them. He wanted to touch her, hold her tight in his arms against his chest to banish the demons so plain in her face. He wanted to tell her, too, that she should leave here and come to somewhere safe and beautiful. To rooms similar to those he had procured for Susan Castleton.

That thought had him flushing. He could not offer Miss Annabelle Smith that and she would never accept it.

They were caught here, in limbo, White-chapel throbbing outside her door and her aunt in the very next room. Caught by circumstance.

'Did you see who was driving, who was inside?'

'The driver wore livery.'

'Hell.' He saw her grimace. 'I promise it was not mine.'

For the first time a smile threatened. 'I did not ever think that.'

A new silence lay in the room as they both sought direction. Lytton could see that she was worried, he could see her lip quiver and that her wide blue eyes were bruised.

'I think…' She stopped.

'What?'

'I think someone has been following me. I have never really seen him, but I feel it. Someone dangerous. Someone who wants me gone.'

'Gone?'

'Dead, perhaps. Dealt with. Banished.'

At that he stood, being careful not to trespass upon their distance. Once breached, he was unsure exactly what might happen next.

'I will employ someone to walk with you. Someone large.'

She shook her head. 'I don't want to be a prisoner.'

'You also do not want to be dead.'

'Everyone will talk.'

'About what?'

'About you paying for a protector. There are woman here who have such men…'

'Annabelle.' It was the first time he had ever used her name.

'Yes.'

'There are two things that you can now do. Listen to gossip or feel safe. Which is it to be?'

'I want to be safe.'

'Good. There will be someone here for you in the morning. He will stay close until I have caught whoever it was who ran you down.'

'How could you do that? How could you find them?'

'Easily.'

She believed him for his troth was not lightly given. He looked tired today, the gold in his eyes clouded. He looked big, too, his strength easily seen and the power that sat on his shoulders well in evidence. She needed this strength even though she could not understand his promise.

'I would not be able to pay you for such a guard.'

'I would not expect you to.'

'And I won't use blackmail to get what I want. Ever.'

'I know that, too.'

This conversation was going everywhere, running across the threads of what bound them together. Lucy. Medicine. Respect. *Desire*.

That last realisation made Belle blush and she sought for pragmatism and logic. Why was Thornton here? She could not ask. She could only sit and wait until he left.

'I am sorry.' His words held echoes and it was as if he had read her mind. Again.

Then he was gone.

Chapter Eight

Lytton drove directly from Whitechapel to the home of Aurelian de la Tomber. His friend was more than interested in the story he told.

'So the driver wore livery?'

'Of gold and blue. And the horses were a grey pair. Roberts, a kitchen hand on the scene, had noticed them go past a few seconds before the accident. His mother, who was with him, said the curtains in the carriage were drawn.'

'The clues mount. We'll have this bastard in no time. What will you do with him.'

'Kill him with my bare hands the way I am feeling at the moment.'

'Is Miss Smith hurt badly?'

'She has a cut on the head, a black eye, two torn-off nails and a badly broken wrist. The skin across her cheek has been grazed and she is damned frightened.'

Lian whistled. 'This from a Boadicea who by public gossip is scared of nothing?'

'You have been asking after her?'

'Shay thought it wise. He said you were staring at her that morning as if she were the Holy Grail. He wondered at her story.'

'With friends like that who needs enemies?'

'Rumour also has it you will be marrying Lady Catherine Dromorne very soon.'

'I am.'

'While riding all over London in the hope of saving a woman who means nothing to you?'

Breathing out at that, Lytton laid one hand across the solidness of a mantel. 'Nothing is ever simple.'

'Try to explain it, then. I am here to listen.'

He took a breath and started. 'Annabelle Smith is brave and beautiful. She is also in need of a saviour.'

'Which is you?'

Nodding, he wondered at such honesty. 'There is something about her that is remarkable. Some sense of honesty and purpose and truth…'

'Shay says the opposite. He says all he could see in your healer was secrets.'

'She has those, too, but I think they are not hers. I think someone else has forced them upon her.'

'Merde,' Aurelian swore. 'I thought Violet and Celeste were mysterious and complex, but this woman…'

'I think someone from her past is now trying to kill her.'

'Why?' Lian suddenly focused.

'Because she is not as she seems. Because she is visible. Because she has escaped from the safe boundaries of Whitechapel and stumbled into my world.'

'So now you feel you are responsible?'

'Perhaps, for the one who wants her harmed is here, close.' Through the wide windows of Aurelian's study Lytton could see London town, the rooftops varied and the trees of summer green. It was raining again. Lately, he thought, it had scarcely stopped.

'Maybe you are right. They make sense, your deductions, the change of circumstance, the flighty darts of fate. Who are your enemies, Lytton?'

'There are many. Business fosters losers

who hate a winner. Gambling is the same and jealousy is a hard task master. The list is as long as your arm and as varied.'

'Then write the names down and I will cross each off as I look into their recent movements and the state of their stables. Surely a near miss would leave some sign upon the body of a chassis or in the paintwork and footmen and drivers can always do with an extra bob.'

'I'll ask at Tattersall's. They might recognise the description of livestock.'

'Do it carefully though, Thorn. If the bastard knows you are enquiring after him he will use the time to hide his trail and if the driver was indeed liveried he will have the means to do it.'

'I appreciate this help, Lian. Could you keep all this confidential for now?'

'When can I meet her? Miss Annabelle Smith?'

'You never will. She is not for me.'

'If you say so, Thorn. Have a drink then and tell me more about Lady Catherine Dromorne.'

Lytton lay in bed that night, wondering about Annabelle Smith's safety. He had hired a man recommended to him by Lian under the instructions to be there at White Street in the early morning. He could not think after the near miss today that the perpetrator would be up to trying anything more tonight.

He needed to sleep because he had hardly had any rest since this whole thing with Lucy had begun weeks before. Yet he couldn't seem to relax as images of Annabelle with her damaged face and head and hand came to mind.

God, he'd plighted to courting Catherine Dromorne in twelve weeks' time and he had hardly given her a thought. That worried him, as did the fact that he could have somehow been the catalyst for the attack on Annabelle Smith.

Had someone seen him at her house or her at Portman Square and put two and two together to make five? Did they think there was more to their relationship than simply paying for her services as a herbalist? He frowned at this. He had found himself calculating the same possibility and yet she had hardly given him any sort of carte blanche on her affections.

Rather the opposite. Today she'd looked as though she had wanted him gone for all the minutes he was there, though the same sort of spark between them had ignited as it had each and every other time they had met, the warmth of it curling into his blood.

He would not let her be hurt. He would protect her to the very last farthing of his more-then-substantial fortune and even that thought was worrying. She was an enigma, sometimes this and sometimes that and then something else entirely. His reactions to her were topsy-turvy and disquieting.

He'd gone to Whitechapel to offer money in order to have her out of his life and instead? Now she was more inveigled in it than she had ever been before and he did not want that changed.

Lian had caught on to his ambiguity and had known that Annabelle Smith held more than his mere respect. If he carried on in this way, others soon would, too.

The moon was out tonight, almost full. He wondered if she saw it from her room in Whitechapel as it hung high above London, shining on all the various facets of it. Did she find sleep in her pain or was she lying there as he was, sleepless with thought?

Could he ever regain the sort of life he had had before he had met her? The life where he had barely glanced at another in terms of for ever.

God. That truth had him sitting and reaching for the brandy bottle by the side of his bed. Business was brisk and required all his attention. Lucy was in need of him with her loss of the child and in her bid for freedom. His brother had been sent down from school and was due at Balmain come the morrow and God knew where Prudence was, running from it all in the far-flung parts of southern Europe.

He could not be thinking of a healer from Whitechapel who should mean nothing to him and could only cause trouble. Yet he was and there wasn't a thing he could do about changing it.

He slept fitfully and in small bursts and was glad when the dawn came and he could finally get up.

Belle looked at her face the next morning and grimaced.

Her left cheek was red raw from scraping the road and the eye that had blackened was now swollen and sporting other colours of purple, red and a dark crimson. Her hair was still matted from the blood she had lost and the bandage had left deep ridges in her forehead when she unwound it. At least it had stopped bleeding and the pounding headache of yesterday had subsided to a lesser ache.

She could not believe the Earl of Thornton had come again. She was astounded by his offer of a guard and his direct and honest manner with her. They had not touched. She was glad of that because in her shock and fright she knew if they had she might have simply clung on to him and held there, like a limpet to a rock in the face of a storm-filled sea that was sweeping her away.

Thornton made her less and more all at the same time. Less careful, more trusting, less certain, more aware. He stripped back the façade and found her core, trembling against circumstance and soft inside the hard shell she had wound about herself for all the years of her life.

Surviving.

Soon there would be nothing left to fight the foolish hopes that were rising each time she met him and then what might happen?

A guard was in place when she opened the curtains, a tall bulky man who stood still like a sentry, highly visible in the moving tableau all about him. People looked, of course they did, but they moved on as well because of the menacing and ominous stance. He meant business. He wanted violence. A man like that in Whitechapel was a known quantity. People stayed well away.

'Have you seen him, Belle?' Her aunt came through the doorway, her glance upon him through the glass. 'He says he will remain at your side until he is told not to. He does not expect that to happen any time soon. His name is Mr McFaddyen. A Scot, I would guess, and a Highland one to boot. Milly says he could probably snap a man in two with his bare hands if he wanted and he has the look of one that does.'

'Is this supposed to be reassuring, Tante?'

'It depends if it is the man who went out of his way to make certain his carriage hit you and Rose yesterday. If it were he, I should be at Mr McFaddyen's side, cheering him on.'

'How is Rose this morning? Have you heard?'

'Her sister came to visit a little while ago and she is doing fine. She came to enquire after your well-being.'

'Did you tell her I was much better?'

Her aunt shook her head. 'Are you, Anna-belle?' Those words came with an underlying sorrow and as a direct challenge.

'As well as a person can be when someone has just tried to kill them, I suppose.'

'There were no problems before we met the Earl of Thornton. None of this kind anyway.' Her aunt's words were tinged with accusation.

'What are you saying?'

'We should leave and go somewhere else. To the north of England, perhaps. Away from these people with money and power.'

'Why? What aren't you telling me?'

'I think your parents were of the same class as Thornton. I heard gossip in the village after they had travelled through.'

Shock and pain were a poor mix. Belle felt her heart beat so fast she thought she might fall.

'So you think this has something to do with…before? This threat?'

'I do not know, but if it is it could be peril-ous to all of us.'

And then she understood more. Tante Ali-cia had never reported her missing in the tiny French village. The church had dispatched her and Alicia had kept her, not allowing a word

to go to the authorities or to the law. There
would be no trail to follow if anyone happened
to be looking, no true identity that could be
argued. She had become Annabelle Smith at
the turn of fate and stayed that way. Such actions would have placed her aunt in jeopardy
should a proper search have been made. But it
hadn't and surely after all these years it would
never be.

Could someone have recognised her because
of her visits with the Thorntons? Would that be
even possible? A child of four or five looked
very different from a woman of thirty-two. Her
hair had darkened, for one thing.

But Tante Alicia believed she had been
recognised and that was what was important.
Belle now needed to reassure her that she
would stay out of harm's way and remain res-
olutely in this crowded part of Whitechapel
where strangers were noted and danger would
be lessened by familiarity. No more strolls to
the far end of the Whitechapel Road, no more
sojourns towards the city markets and beyond.

'If anything happens again, we will leave
immediately, I promise it, but I do not want to
be chased away after we have made a life for

ourselves here. To begin all again anywhere would be hard.'

'But not impossible.' Her aunt's voice was strained.

'No, you are right. Not impossible.'

'And you will stay here inside today?'

'Yes. I hardly feel up to anything else, but at least the bleeding has stopped and my wrist feels less painful.'

'I don't think it's a break. It holds more of the feel of a bad sprain. In a week we will remove the splint and the hair at your temple will grow back in the patch that I have shaved.'

Belle smiled and moving forward, wrapping her arms about her aunt in the best fashion that she could.

'It will all be fine, Tante Alicia. Perhaps it was just some terrible mistake…'

She stopped as a shout echoed from outside, the neighbour in the adjoining lodgings hailing them from the doorway.

'I have fresh milk and herrings for you, Miss Smith, and Mrs Drayton from down the road managed to procure farm eggs from the market in the Old Spitalfields. She said the Pauls, from across the street, will send over hot bread at noon and that the child's mother who you helped with the boils last week is promising you a mutton stew. A veritable feast, if I say so myself.'

When Belle looked across at her aunt there were tears in her eyes. Perhaps it would be all right, after all. She accepted a cup of tea from Milly with a smile.

In the morning Lytton was again in Whitechapel and was pleased to see Mr Angus McFaddyen standing outside the front door of the downstairs lodging in White Street.

He had meant to simply send a message to state the sort of hours and conditions he wanted the guard to adhere to, but had found himself fretful of the passing time and so had called a carriage instead.

'Has it been quiet?'

'It has, my lord. Many have passed, but none have come close to the house at all. The women inside have insisted on feeding me every hour and the sun is about to shine.'

'Stay here until another comes. I have found a night guard to relieve you so that you can sleep and be back every morning at five.'

'Very good, my lord.'

Thus satisfied, Lytton knocked and the door

was opened almost instantly by the same maid who had handed him the cup of tea on his very first visit here. She was wiping doughy hands on her apron.

'Your lordship,' she said, bobbing in a quick curtsy. 'I shall take you through to Miss Smith.'

Annabelle's eye this morning was all the hues of red, dark and light. It was also so swollen the blue in her eye only showed through a small slit of skin. Catherine Dromorne's perfect sort of beauty was once all he had liked and admired. Now he was even starting to question that. Her hair was down, which was unexpected, and fell in long, dark, curling swathes to her waist. She did not look even slightly bothered by the fact that it was unbound in his company, something every other woman of his acquaintance would have.

'I hope I find you well, Miss Smith?'

He had used her first name yesterday, the informality of it rolling off his tongue. Today he didn't.

She nodded and placed the bowl she'd had in her hands beside her on the sofa, a sharp knife and a cloth joining it.

'I am much recovered.' She made no effort at all either to conceal her bruises and he liked the fact that she did not. *Take me as I am*, such an action seemed to shout. *This is me.*

'How is your broken wrist?'

'I do not think it is broken, after all, which is a relief. My aunt is certain I have been left with only a bad sprain.'

'And your head?'

'Is fine.'

The catalogue of her wounds was not something she looked like she wanted to speak about further.

'How is Lady Lucy? Is she up and about yet?'

'She is, indeed. My sister will retire to Balmain, our country estate, next week. Mama will no doubt nurse her to death and she will be scurrying back to London as soon as she is able. So life goes on, different but still possible.'

Word of his mother brought a darkness to her eyes, but he had no inclination to try to explain his complex family life, so he left that topic alone altogether.

'I have instructed people to begin the search for the carriage that hit you. I hope to have an answer back in a few days.'

'So quick?'

'The guard outside will be here until I have found the person responsible. At night there will be another just as competent to replace him.'

'Thank you. Mr McFaddyen's presence has indeed offered us some support.'

He could see she had slept badly, for the ring beneath her uninjured eye was dark. He could also see she had been pummelling medicine with a pestle and mortar, a dark red paste sticking to the side of the bowl.

'It is turmeric mixed with castor oil. For boils,' she explained when she saw him looking.

She had not stopped work, then? She had not lain down on her bed and allowed others to wait on her. It was a lack of money, probably, and the need to make a living. If he imagined she would accept it he would have laid all the pounds he carried in his pocket on the small table beside her. But he knew that she would not and he didn't want another argument over money. How were she and her aunt paying the rent on this place then without work? Did they have savings put away to cope with situations like this one?

The ridiculousness of that thought made him

frown. How did one take steps to prepare for a killer? There was so damned much he wanted to offer her and so little he could. Catherine Dromorne's face hovered on the edges of his worry, too.

'I have instructed the kitchen staff in Portman Square to put together a box of food for you. A boy will deliver it this afternoon.'

She shook her head. 'When there is trouble in places such as this people band together. Already this morning we have been brought more food than we can store.'

'Then what of the rent? How can I help with that?'

Instead of answering, she began to speak again. 'This is not your fault we have come to such a pass, your lordship. We will not refuse the guard, but any other assistance is unwarranted. You have already overpaid dearly for my services to your sister.'

'Do you have a sweetheart, Miss Smith?' Lytton asked the question before he had thought, carelessly. Usually he was never that, but there was something about her that made him unwise. Some desperation to know.

She shook her head. 'Have you?'

He hadn't been able to talk with any woman

as he did with her, in such an easy comradeship and a shared respect. Awareness was there, too, simmering under every single polite word like a hidden furnace, the heat around them undeniable.

'No. The Earldom was thrust upon me at a time I was not sure I wanted it. It came with scandal, bankruptcy and death. A baptism by fire, if you like, and one that has taken up all of my time ever since.'

'But you survived?'

He laughed out loud. 'I did.'

'When I came to Tante Alicia at first it was like that for me. Not on the scale of yours, of course, but I was sick and alone and in a land I did not recognise. I wasn't sure I wanted to be there, either.'

'What were you sick with?'

Lytton knew the instant her glance fell that she would not answer him, but he wasn't going to leave it there. He reached deep into his jacket pocket.

'I have brought you a gift, Miss Smith, for your recovery and for protection. I am assured by my research that turquoise also allows healing and promotes calmness. A stone of many qualities.'

* * *

The box was small and of dark green velvet with an ornate clasp of engraved gold. Belle could barely believe he had brought a present of this magnitude for her and she held back in reaching out.

'I am not sure that I should…'

He flipped the lid and a bracelet sat inside on baize, the beads of a colour of pure green-blue, but veined in smoke. She had never seen anything quite so beautiful before. She almost wished she had not liked it so that she could have shaken her head with feeling and insisted he took it back.

As it was the words of refusal just would not come.

'Its true value lies in history. It was worn by the second Countess of Thornton when her husband the Earl took her to London to visit the Queen.'

'Like the cat in the nursery rhyme?'

He smiled.

It was expensive, then, perhaps even priceless. 'If you ever want it back…'

'I shan't.'

She was now in a quandary, the danger of touching him felt in each part of her body should she reach over and take it from his hand. She was pleased, therefore, when he leaned over and put the box on the sofa beside her.

The bracelet fitted perfectly, an amulet alive with beauty. Even with her two torn-off nails and rough grazed skin her hand looked prettier, more feminine.

'I will always wear it.'

'Good. Let's hope the healing properties begin to work their magic, for you look like you are in need of it.'

'I have nothing to give you in return.'

'You saved my sister's life.'

'Does she speak of it much? The baby?'

'Not yet.'

'Don't push her, then. Let her tell you all of it in her own time. People need to think about things sometimes before they can work out exactly what it is they want to say to others.'

'I do not imagine she will say anything to me knowing that I'll want to kill the man who hurt her.'

'To throw away your own life for someone who is not worth it seems impossibly futile.'

Her new bracelet was warming against her skin, the day outside was finally clearing and the Earl had visited her now for two days in a row. She'd wanted life to be easy and safe and for this minute it was, a guard in place and the promise of another tonight, her aunt having a nap and Milly in the kitchen making pies.

But it was Lord Thornton who made her feel the safest, for he was shelter from a world that had turned upside down. He was a good man and strong, like those fairy-tale heroes she'd read of in books.

He stood now, hat in hand, but did not move closer.

'If you ever have need of me tell McFaddyen or send a note to Portman Square and I will come. When information arrives to hand about the carriage and its occupant, I will let you know. I promise it, no matter who is behind this.'

'Thank you.'

He looked as if he wanted to say more, but had thought against it, merely tipping his head before he left, the doorframe too low for his height so that he needed to duck down.

Belle smiled. Nothing fitted him here in Whitechapel and yet he was not out of place. She could see his danger as much as she could see the refined and elevated lord and was glad for it.

The Earl of Thornton had no sweetheart. That small information brightened her day and she brought her good arm up so that she was able to look more closely at the gemstones in her bracelet.

Why had he given her this? It seemed an excessive gift for attending to his sister. It had also been well chosen, the fit perfect and the colours exactly her own. She had never before had any jewellery and the delight of it warmed her.

Her mother had worn jewellery. For just a second through time she remembered a finger with an ornate blue setting and a chain of gold around a thin white neck. Closing her eyes, she tried to bring the vision back, conjure her up, this mother who had passed through the small village of Moret-sur-Loing and left her there. But there was nothing. She had gone.

She could not believe she had spoken to Thornton of her sickness and of her displacement in a new and foreign land. She could see him storing each new fact learnt about her past and building a picture. Would that be dangerous? Her aunt had intimated it might well be and she might not be wrong.

If the man who had tried to kill her was close and watching, then it stood to reason the Earl could also be a target. For helping her. For placing guards. For being so very visible.

Perhaps this was why he had come today, to try to lure this other away? But he had brought the bracelet, too, in its velvet box on a bed of green baize, the catch decorated with a gold mark. An expensive piece denoting worth and from the hallmarks of history.

The woman who had worn this had gone up to London to visit the Queen. Elizabeth the First, perhaps? Had her missing parents' relatives been among those received at court? So many questions and so few answers. But they were coming, she knew they were, and this bracelet was only a part of the knitted fabric of memory.

Lytton could not settle.

He had tried to read, tried to write, tried to beat out a tune on the piano in his bedchamber, but none of it was working. He felt wound up and furious, all the clues to the carriage that had tried to knock down Annabelle leading to nothing. Tattersall's had no knowledge of the livestock, the stables close by had not rented a carriage to any liveried riders and no one had remembered seeing the conveyance pass through Whitechapel Road or Aldgate or further afield at the time of the accident.

He was still out there, the bastard, untouched, laughing probably at his cleverness in covering up his tracks. Even Aurelian hadn't been able to find out anything and as one of the greatest spies of all time that was saying a lot.

Lytton had left the brandy alone tonight. He didn't want to drink. He needed his wits sharp and his intellect ready. He wished he was still there with Annabelle Smith in Whitechapel, sitting right next to her to make sure that she was safe.

The bracelet had suited her. It was part of a small set of jewellery that had been passed down to him from his grandfather when he had turned twenty-one. Special valuable pieces. Pieces more likely destined to be given to a wife, perhaps? He swore under his breath, castigating himself for the hundredth time that he had ever given his ridiculous promise of courtship to Catherine Dromorne. He knew he should not have.

The future skewered into different pathways and he could find no road to take that might lead to the sort of life he wanted.

Chapter Nine

He saw Catherine Dromorne and her family at the soirée of the Shaybornes three days later. It was a small gathering and as soon as he saw Shay he understood why they were there.

'My wife says it is better to know the reasons for the choices you have made. We want to see you happy.'

'And who would say I am not?' Suddenly the anger in him rose.

'You do not look happy, Thorn. Lately it seems as though you have the world upon your shoulders, but here is Lady Catherine Dromorne and I know she is waiting to talk to you.' He looked over at her pointedly and smiled.

With no other option Lytton joined the Dromorne group and Catherine fastened on to him.

'I am sorry the rumours are abounding about our promise to marry, Thorn. My father let it slip and so…' She stopped, her face a picture of innocence.

'There are always rumours, Catherine, but I am presuming no one save the parties concerned has the full story. It might be difficult otherwise.' He tried to moderate his tone, but wondered if he had done a good enough job when he saw her frown. A dainty frown in a heart-shaped face that would make any other man melt.

'I do not wish for difficulty. Mama and Papa have enough of those—'

Their conversation was cut short as her mother joined them. The Countess of Dromorne was an arresting woman and Lytton had heard all the stories of her first Season in society. She had been incomparable and her daughters had taken after her, though he doubted that they had quite reached the heights she so obviously had.

The blonde perfection of mother and daughter was striking and Lytton found himself looking for flaws that must after all be present, though he found none.

'My husband and I are pleased for the

commitment you are showing to Catherine, my lord. I know your mother must have been thrilled as well, as this union was something we had spoken of together when our daughter was first born.'

Lytton had not told Cecelia anything at all about the understanding between them, preferring to push it under the carpet until he had to face it or at least until he saw his mother next and could try to explain.

'My younger daughter Jane is due out this next Season, so it is always a pleasure to get one child well seen to before the other arrives.'

Relief rather than pleasure was evident in her voice and Lytton was grateful when refreshments came and she turned to help herself.

Catherine, however, hurried on to another topic. 'I hear that your sister is so much better for although she was a few years behind me at school I always liked her. Mama is a friend of Lady Isabel Franklin, who lives near Balmain, so we receive the gossip about your family.'

Not all of it, Lytton hoped, and accepted a glass of white wine from the passing footman. Visions of Annabelle Smith in the carriage came with force, her hand in his, her smile uncertain, the dimples in her cheeks so deep that they contained shadows.

He could see Aurelian watching him from over in the corner, but there was nothing else he could do but concur that he had lost the battle and that unless something extraordinary happened he would have a wife in tow by the end of the year. A wife that he liked, but would never love. A wife that would suit the Earldom admirably, but would never hold his heart.

Catherine herself looked less worried as he continued to bide at her side, talking to him of her latest foray into the world of fashion and of a horse she had recently procured.

'I heard you had won a beauty yourself, Thorn, and from Lord Huntington. I imagine he would not have been happy. He has gone back to Highwick Manor to face his grandmother, by all accounts, for it was her steed. She is a woman of opinion and steel, the Dowager Countess, and not one I would like to cross. Do you know her?'

He didn't. He had no real knowledge of Huntington's family at all.

'Oh, well, enough of them. Mama feels we should have a party in three weeks at our town house. An invite will be coming your way and

I hope you might stand with me in the receiving line.'

To announce his intentions to everyone present, Lytton thought, vowing to be out of London for that occasion. He was not ready for this, for any of it. All he wanted was to go home and try to work out when and where his direction in life had gone so terribly wrong.

'I hope, Catherine, that you do realise I see you as a friend. I have never held stronger feelings.' He knew this was hardly the place to have this sort of conversation, but time was running out and he needed her to understand.

Catherine shook her head and waved the words away. 'Well, who has really, Thorn? Look around you. This love that people speak of is a myth, I think. If one can get on in a marriage and enjoy friendship, surely that should be enough?'

'The Shaybornes have more, I think, and the de la Tombers.'

'Two couples out of a hundred and who really is to say it will last? Please, Thorn, we have never once had a disagreement. We laugh at a lot of the same things. Our parents are friends and we have had a most similar upbringing.'

He could not dispute that and yet in all the sentiment he understood a loss.

When a friend of Catherine's came over to join her he made an excuse and was able to extricate himself from further talk. Celeste Shayborne took his arm as he passed her by.

'You seem to be spreading yourself thinly of late, Thorn. I seldom see you any more.'

'The curse of being busy, I am afraid. The cannery business is time consuming.'

'So are women, I should imagine? Annabelle Smith was certainly interesting. And beautiful, too. I have heard you have been a regular visitor in Whitechapel ever since?'

'A carriage knocked Miss Smith over. I was seeing if she needed help.'

'My God. I had not heard of that? Is she all right? Does Summer know?'

'No, he doesn't, for it just happened and, yes, she lived, but with bruises and scratches.'

'Who wanted her hurt?' Lytton could see her mind working. Celeste Fournier had once been a spy in Paris and for her nothing extraordinary was ever simply chance.

'I am trying to find out. Lian is helping me.'

'I can't imagine someone like Annabelle Smith having enemies unless...'

'Unless what?'

'Could he have materialised from the time she does not wish to talk about?'

'I am certain he has.'

'Then what has changed lately? You? You have come into her life? Could he know you?'

'That is a good point, Celeste, and I will think about it.'

'If Annabelle Smith wants to talk to me about her past, I would be very happy to listen. God knows my own was hardly exemplary.'

'She barely talks to me of it, Celeste, so I doubt she will want that.'

'But she will talk when you earn her trust. Besides, when we met her I saw her watching you with something more than mere interest in her startling blue eyes, something more akin to worship.'

'I doubt she would agree with your assessment of her feelings.'

'I knew in a moment that Summer was the one for me, the one I would love for ever. A good union is like that, Thorn. A poor one only emphasises what is missing.'

'Thank you for your advice, Lady Shayborne.'

Celeste laughed at his tone and finished her drink.

* * *

Lytton returned home in a worse mood than he had ventured out with. He'd hardly wanted to spend any time with Catherine and her family, skirted around the best intentions of his friends and allowed Celeste to plant the hope that perhaps Miss Annabelle Smith really did think more of him than she was showing.

And a foolish hope it was. Miss Smith had not uttered anything that could be construed as vaguely personal and she had always looked thankful as he had left her company.

Even the bracelet had been a poor idea. In Whitechapel it would probably be stolen and then pawned, no one having the slightest idea of what the thing was really worth. Or she might wear it only once or twice because she had promised it. Miss Smith gave the impression of a woman who would keep promises no matter how irksome they might become to her.

All in all, he had sold his soul to pragmatism and reaped the reward of compromise. He was miserable.

He noticed the rapping bang on the front door just before midnight and tipped his head to listen. The butler was saying something loudly and the visitor was shouting back in a voice that was louder still.

Fire was one of the first words Lytton heard and he stood. Where? Here? He sniffed at the air and could detect no scent of smoke. Feet were running now towards the library and he crossed the floor to open the door before the knock came.

'There is someone here from Whitechapel, your lordship. Mr McFaddyen I think he said his name was and…'

Lytton was out of the door before his man was even finished speaking, striding towards the front lobby and the dishevelled and ash-covered giant who stood within it.

'What's happened?'

'The house went up, my lord, in a flash. It were started under the front door and spread like wildfire.'

'Did she get out? Miss Smith and her aunt? Are they safe?' He felt as though time was suspended, the ticks of the grandfather clock to one side slowing and the roar in his ears muffling any sound left. Like running through water, but on land. Drowning.

'They are, Sir, but only by a whisper and there is nothing left of their possessions. They are in the carriage outside. I brought them here 'cos I didn't know what else to do.'

The world refocused and Lytton walked out into the night to find Annabelle sitting on the carriage seat with the door open and watching the sky. Her aunt was fast asleep beside her, wrapped in the only blanket between them.

'Hell.' He could say nothing else as the tears she had held on to suddenly flowed down her cheeks at the sight of him, clean runnels of skin showing where soot had just been.

'I did not want to come, but…'

Lytton looked back at the house and made up his mind.

'Stay inside the carriage and I will be right back.'

Thornton House would be too much of everything for two women ripped from Whitechapel by fire and standing in the dirty rags of what was left of their clothes. The servants would talk and Annabelle would hear all of what he wanted her not to. The ravages of snobbery would destroy her as would the blow to her reputation should he deem to invite her in with only her aunt as chaperon. And that was notwithstanding any gossip about

his peculiar arrangement with Lady Catherine
Dromorne.

No. It had to be somewhere else and the
rooms that he had learnt Susan Castleton had
vacated last week in Kensington would be the
bolthole he needed. He was still paying the
rent, after all, and the place was the peak of
discretion when it came to the ever-changing
residents. His mind whirled as he catalogued
the furniture within. Was there anything un-
toward or plainly crude about the decor? He
thought not, even though it was slightly on the
wrong side of being respectable. He did not
imagine Annabelle and her aunt would know
enough about the more usual interior decoration of the great houses in London to be surprised by this one, so he left that there.

After retrieving the keys from his library,
he returned outside. Tomorrow he would hire
servants and get the place in order. Tonight
Annabelle and her aunt looked only as if they
needed a bath and a bed.

Annabelle watched him intently, the splint
missing from her hand now and the black
eye much less swollen. He could not tell if
the bruising was still present, but thought

not given the whiteness of her skin showing through the line of tears.

Three days since he had seen her last. It seemed like for ever.

He took the seat opposite to the women, Aunt Alicia having wakened now and sitting in a miserable bundle against the door. McFaddyen climbed in beside him.

'What can you tell me about the fire?'

'It were lit, my lord, but we saw nothing at all.'

'You were not out front?'

If it was possible for a large and ornery man to look embarrassed, McFaddyen did.

'I were inside sitting down to dinner, your lordship. The maid Milly had just left to visit her mother and Miss Smith had invited me in, for it were the last of the mutton stew I had been smelling for days and so...'

'I see.' And he did. Kind manners had undone them. Sharing the last of their meagre amount of food with the guard had allowed an opportunity for whoever it was that wanted them dead.

'How did you get out?'

'I grabbed them both and charged through the front door. The dog is missing.'

Lytton breathed in hard. Stanley. Even a hound who had ripped his pink waistcoat and barked outrageously every time he had visited did not deserve to die that way.

'We will look for him again tomorrow. Dogs have a way of escaping such things.'

Aunt Alicia looked at him directly as he said this and he saw an aching hope in her old eyes.

In Annabelle's he saw nothing. She sat there as if she were made of stone, her expression dead and her chin quivering.

'Her Bible is burnt,' the old aunt murmured in her best English by way of explanation and Lytton frowned. He had not thought Annabelle Smith was so religious.

'I can buy you another one, Miss Smith.'

She simply shook her head at that and looked away. As she moved Lytton saw the beads of blue and green around her wrist under the tattered remains of her patched-up shirt and he swallowed.

It was all gone. Stanley. The house. Her paintings. Lucy's gift. The medicines. The furniture. Their lives. Gone up in smoke in the time it might take to make a cup of tea. Her Bible was the thing she regretted the most after Stanley, a link to her mother that had only just been forged. She had slept with it beside her ever since her aunt had retrieved it from the top shelf and told her the truth of where it had come from.

And now here they were, washed up again into the care of the Earl of Thornton in the late evening and smelling like burnt logs. At least she had been wearing her bracelet when Mr McFaddyen had seized them around the waist and dragged them out. It was safe. She tucked the treasure up under her sleeve so that it would not be damaged further by the soot.

This time she could not pay him. This time, if he were to have turned them away, they would have been on the street, trying to fathom where on earth they might go next.

Oh, the nuisance of it for him, she thought. No wonder the Earl would not take them into his house, but had brought them further afield. She had not wanted to meet his glance for fear of the disgust she might see there. She wanted to be apart from it all, somewhere else, somewhere clean and free. But most of all she wanted to lie down and just sleep.

Her wrist was sore and her head ached and the cut received on her leg as she was dragged through the house would need to be tended. She looked down at the soft leather of the carriage seat and saw that the soot from their clothes had left rivers of darkness upon it. There was blood there, too.

When the conveyance drew to a halt the Earl alighted first and held out his hand and Belle could do nothing but place her fingers into his. His palm curled up, the warmth of him scalding, and she might have tripped with the shock had he not steadied her.

'Careful.'

He was close now, almost against her, his big body shielding hers from the cold of night. Her aunt was watching as was the guard, Mr McFaddyen, but even with the onlookers Belle found it impossible to let go as she began to shake.

'You are safe now. No one will hurt you here.'

But they would, she wanted to say to him, and they will, because you are who you are and I am who I am. In this one small second after disaster they had a place, hung between realities and compassion. In another moment even that would be gone and common sense would prevail.

Tears resurfaced with the grief of it and then all contact was gone as he reached for her aunt.

She stood in the street, watching the building until the others stood beside her. This area of London looked nothing like Whitechapel with its dirtied bricks and its filthy streets. Here everything was clean and there was no one around. An empty place. With trees and greenery and a park just yards away. The steps were shining and the door was made of gold.

Large bunches of real flowers were displayed in vases as they walked inside and a few scattered armchairs were carved with angels and cherubs in a style she had never seen before.

Taking a candleholder that sat on a table, the Earl ushered them up a circular ironwork staircase at one end of the hall. He looked completely at home in such a place and amid the paintings decorating the wall almost from top to bottom. Once on the landing she saw the rugs on the floor were thick, burgundy interwoven with orange and blue and cream.

Then there was a door and a key turned and they were inside a space that was twenty times bigger than their dwellings in Whitechapel. A room that went on for ever.

'I hope this will do?' The Earl's voice was an echo as he glanced around quickly. Was he looking for something? Annabelle thought.

'It is like a palace,' Belle whispered before she realised she had, drawing herself in so that the dirt would not spoil anything here. Her aunt seemed to be doing the same. McFaddyen had stopped by the door as if he understood that his sooty bulk wouldn't be conducive at all in a place like this.

'There is a bath this way. I will have hot water sent up. The bedrooms are in there.'

One room had angels on the ceiling that had the look of a picture Belle had seen in the church at Moret-sur-Loing. They were all naked. Lamps on each side of the bed had the same general look except these were of women displaying bounteous charms.

The married couple who once lived here must have enjoyed each other, Belle thought, and smiled. Thornton for his part did not look happy at all.

'I will have the rooms looked over tomorrow and some of the pieces in it replaced.'

'It is beautiful, but if we make it dirty—'

He didn't let her finish.

'I'll pay to have it cleaned.'

It was his, this place, for people owned many more houses than they could ever live in when they were wealthy. It was a knowledge on the streets.

'We won't be here long. Friends will help...' She tailed off. Places were small and crowded in Whitechapel, but Rose would have them, she was sure of it, at least until they could get on their feet.

A knock on the door brought a wave of servants in, all carrying clothes and food and other necessities and before she knew it Alicia and she were whisked off into a bath chamber. When she returned to the main room in a borrowed nightdress and slippers both the Earl and Mr McFaddyen were gone.

The letter came first thing in the morning, by special mail.

Lytton had not been to bed, the events of the night leaving him tensed up and furious, and he knew that today would be a busy one trying to piece together exactly what had happened in White Street.

The address at the top of the page was Highwick Manor in Essex and the stamp at the bottom was from the Dowager Countess of Huntington.

I put pen to paper to ask you, Lord Thornton, if I could purchase back from you the horse you won on a game of dice at the Derwents' ball.

My grandson, Albert Tennant-Smythe, Earl of Huntington, held no true right to place this steed as surety on the gambling table for the animal was my own personal property and one bred from the line of horses my late husband brought from France.

As you might have gathered this mount was a favourite of mine and I dearly wish for it to come home. I will pay well for that privilege if you would name a sum.

I realise this request is unusual, but as the ageing chatelaine of a family who has had their share of battles and disappointments I pray for some resolution.
Yours sincerely,
Dowager Countess Annalena Tennant-Smythe

The woman was rumoured to have a backbone of steel, but in these words all Lytton could see was a woman at the end of her tether because of the poor actions of her family. In that, he felt a strong and shared understanding.

Taking a fresh sheet of paper, he quickly scribbled out a message.

Returned with my compliments
Thornton

He called in his butler.

'Could you see that that horse I won at the gambling tables from Lord Huntington is sent back to Highwick Manor in Essex, Larkin? It seems that the animal did not belong to him in the first place and his grandmother would like it back.'

'I shall speak with the stable master and manage that today, my lord.'

'Could you also find out from the house-keeper how the women from Whitechapel are faring this morning and report back to me?'

'I can answer that right away, my lord. Apparently they both slept very well by the account of the maid who was stationed there overnight. However, Miss Smith had a sizeable gash on her leg and the older woman has awoken with a cough. This morning Miss Smith, accompanied by Mr McFaddyen, has returned to Whitechapel to see a friend and to look for a lost dog. A Mrs Rosemary Greene is the name of the friend by all accounts.'

God, did Annabelle Smith ever stay just where she would be safe? Did she not think that one day of rest might not be enough after the fright they had had yesterday?

'Could you call the carriage around, Larkin.'

Belle saw the carriage from a distance and knew it to be the Earl's. The borrowed dress she had on was of a brighter shade than she usually wore and her hair had been placed up by one of the Thornton maids into a style emulating the wealthy. The differences had left her on edge, her life from before gone and this new one confusing.

When the conveyance stopped the Earl strode towards her with pace and she excused herself from the company of Mrs Hammond, an older woman who lived three doors up.

'I had not thought you would have been here so early, Miss Smith?' His glance took in her clothes and hair and he frowned. The housekeeper had brought them from Portman Square for her and she wondered if perhaps the woman should not have.

'I came to see if Stanley was about, your lordship. My aunt is fretting over his loss.'

He ignored that and asked his own question. 'How is your leg? The one hurt in the fire?'

So he knew about that, too. The Earl did not miss much.

'Much better.'

'Yet you are limping?'

He looked towards what was left of the house, the downstairs room fire blackened and smoke damaged. No one would live there for a long while and, apart from a few pewter bowls and some cutlery in the ashes, nothing else had survived.

'You could salvage only this?'

'We might find more. When we came from France we had almost as little.'

'You told me you came to England because it was dangerous there?'

'Moret-sur-Loing was close to Paris. Tante Alicia thought I should be safer away from it all and, at twelve I thought so, too. I am thirty-two now. Ancient.' She smiled to soften the point.

'Hardly that. You must know you are beautiful.'

With her un-straight tooth and her wide

eyes? But he was not joking, she also realised, the compliment given with meaning.

He did not touch her, but something changed right then in the space of a second. An acknowledgment of regard. A proclamation of intent. His golden glance bored into her own without looking away, the force in them magnetic.

'Why was the Bible you lost yesterday so important?'

A different query from what she expected. 'It was my mother's and I don't have much else to remember her by.'

'Were her eyes the same colour as your own?'

Suddenly Belle knew that they had been and it was like receiving an unexpected gift. 'They were. I had forgotten that.'

'Sapphire-blue with a hint of grey.' His words were said softly, almost as a caress, out here in the open of White Street, out here under the regard of others about them.

Her heart tripped fast, beating in her throat. 'Thank you for all you have done for us, your lordship. I am trying to find other accommodation here, though, so you can have your rooms back.'

'Thorn. My friends call me that. As I don't use this place you can stay for as long as you wish.'

She shook her head. 'If you could put up with us for just a few days longer I am certain we will be able to find other lodgings, your lordship.'

'Thorn,' he said again and she smiled.

Chapter Ten

Even in hand-me-downs and with the bruising
to one eye still apparent, Annabelle Smith was
breathtaking. Her beauty was not just external
either. It was also in her voice and in the way
that, with the odds against her, she could still
see the possibilities in life.

He would never be bored in her company.

He would never lack conversation.

He would never be able to take her to his
bed and make her his wife.

The grief in that realisation nearly brought
him to his knees and he imagined simply taking her by the hand and running away, from
England, from the Earldom, from everyone
who knew them.

The sound of barking broke the spell as a
small wiry terrier ran towards them, part of
his back almost hairless and one ear singed.

'Stanley?' Annabelle's voice was choked up as she knelt down to put her arms about the wildly excited dog. 'Not all is lost, then.' When she picked him up his squirming body made her borrowed gown dirty and his tongue ran across her face.

If he forgot everything else in life, Lytton vowed he would never forget this one particular moment, out in the sun, after a fire, when life began to beat again in the face of tragedy. This was what he was missing, what he had always been missing: joy, honesty and laughter, wealth even in poverty.

'Would you ride with me in my carriage, Miss Smith, and I will take you and the dog back to your aunt?'

She looked at him for a few seconds as though deciding what to do.

'First I need to get these things.' Her hand gestured towards the meagre pile of reclaimed possessions.

'Mr McFaddyen will watch over the house and try to find more. He will bring them to you later.'

'Very well.' She followed him over to his conveyance and placed Stanley on the seat before getting in. After speaking to his guard, the Earl got in, too and closed the door, this time taking the seat next to her.

Silence shrieked around them, only the noise of the dog licking itself breaking the tension. He could feel the line of her thigh against his own and took in a breath. He was running out of time to be cautious and to be careful. Catherine Dromorne's promised twelve weeks were being eaten up day by day and the amount of minutes he might have alone with Annabelle Smith was limited. He did not know whether he should be honest with a confession as to how he regarded her or to lead with actions.

He chose the second and took her hand in his, a small hand with two broken nails and the turquoise bracelet above it on her wrist.

He did not speak. He merely looked at her and she looked back. It was not surprise on her face he saw, but something much more intense. An ordained purpose, perhaps, or simply acceptance. Her tongue licked the dryness of her lips and she tipped her head back against the cushioned leather of the seat.

In invitation and in knowledge.

Carefully he ran one finger across her cheekbone, high and delicate, before lowering it on to her lips, tracing the outline and knowing the shape. He needed to be careful, to slow down, to not frighten her.

'Can I kiss you, Annabelle?'

Question sat in her sapphire eyes.

'I will not hurt you, I promise.'

A foot became six inches and then there was nothing between them save warmth. She still had her eyes open, the blue in them threaded with caution.

'This is just for us,' he whispered, claiming her mouth under his own and as soft as he could make it.

He had meant to barely kiss her, to see what she would allow, to settle nerves and find the boundaries. But he couldn't. One touch had released a desperation for he wanted things he'd never had before, things like honesty and trust. Grace was there, too, and decency and charm, unfamiliar and strange.

He adjusted his angle and came in deeper, the quiet kiss becoming more fierce. And then she kissed him back, leaning closer, volatile, mercurial and surprising.

She was not the timid and restrained woman he might have expected. No, she was brave, her hand entwining around his arm and holding him there. The breath she took was shaky, but her eyes were bold, slashed in blue directness. The slam of connection intensified, his body hardening under promise.

God, he was in a carriage careening through the busy streets of London and none of the curtains were drawn. He broke off the kiss and pulled back, panic building as he realised how close he had come to losing control.

Miss Annabelle Smith was a witch after all and, closing his eyes for a moment, he tried to regain composure. When he opened them he saw she was watching him intently with a heavy frown on her brow. She gave the impression of being as astonished as he was by what had just happened.

'I am sorry.' Her words.

Laughing out loud, he laid his head back against the seat and felt relief settle.

He saw humour in what had just occurred? How could he possibly think her wantonness and her lack of restraint was funny?

'The very last thing you need to be, Annabelle, is sorry.'

She could not understand what he meant by that, but the conveyance was slowing and the building she and her aunt were currently staying in was just around the corner. Her lips felt swollen and warm, the possibility of a world opening to her that she had never before glimpsed apart from in her illicit books.

They were right, those authors, about the heat of blood and the rising of desire, each emotion tempered with a loss of self that was shocking. If the Earl had not pulled back and broken the kiss, where would it have led? Belle knew that she would have had no way of calling a halt. Even now she twisted her hands into each other to stop her reaching out, glad when Stanley crawled into her lap and caused a distraction.

What would happen next?

He had not sounded angry, but then again he could hardly be pleased, either? When the carriage stopped he reached out for the door to open it.

'I hope your aunt is pleased to see the return of her dog,' he said and picked up Stanley, waiting till she had alighted before handing the animal back to her.

He would not come in? He would say goodbye here? Would she see him again tomorrow? She could not ask. With a forced smile she simply tilted her head.

'Thank you for the ride home, your lordship.'

His golden eyes darkened as she gave him her formal goodbye. 'It was my pleasure, Miss Smith,' he answered and watched her as she went through the golden doors of the Bishop Building.

Once she was inside Tante Alicia was delighted to see Stanley.

'I think it is a sign, Belle, a sign that from now on things will get markedly better.'

Annabelle tried to enjoy her happy premonition, but then excused herself to wash up after the labour of sifting through the ashes of their former home. She needed time to try to understand the way her body had responded to the Earl's, for a distance that hadn't been there before was suddenly, a detachment and reserve that felt worrying.

Would he say anything of her behaviour to his friends? Would they laugh together about the sheer absurdity of such an exchange, feeling sorry for a woman so patently unsuitable?

Tante Alicia had seen Stanley's return as a sign that things from here could only improve, but the Earl had hightailed away with an unseemly haste and she had no idea when or even if he would be back.

* * *

Edward Tully turned up at Portman Square about twenty minutes after Lytton had returned home.

'I come bearing gifts.' He handed over a parcel.

'What is this?'

'I have purchased a ticket to go to the Americas at the end of next week and, as I am going to be away for a while, I thought you might like to have this.'

Opening the present, Lytton smiled. He had always admired a small statue that Edward had commissioned three years ago, a bronze of a horse on its hind legs whickering into the wind.

'I thought it denoted freedom, Thorn, and was keen for you to have it. You seem shackled lately by your life and this is a reminder of what it could also be.'

The muscles on the stallion were well defined and the mane of hair running down his back was magnificent.

'I'd heard you sent your winnings at the gambling table from my brother's ball back to the Huntingtons'. The gossip is that Albert Tennant-Smythe is more than furious at the gesture for it has painted him in a bad light. Be careful of him, Thorn, for he is a man of limitless anger as well as a spiteful temper. By the way, I was speaking with someone the other day and they said that Lucy had been seen in his company a few times. Did you know that?'

This was the second time he had heard this and a sharp shock reverberated down his backbone. Why had he not followed this up before when Beatrice Mallory had informed him of it?

He knew the answer.

Annabelle Smith had taken up all his thoughts of late and was continuing to do so. He wondered if he should speak to Edward about his feelings, but decided not to. The kiss from today still burnt into his conscience and it had taken a will of steel not to follow her into her accommodation and try to discover if she felt the same.

If she did, what could he truly do about it and, if she didn't… God, it would break him. He gulped down more brandy and put one hand on the shiny surface of the bronze.

'I will look after it until you get back, Ed. It's too much of a gift to just give me.'

Edward Tully laughed. 'You have always

been one of my best friends, Thorn, ever since those first early years when we were consigned off to school together. For me the statue has been a guide to a new and braver direction. I hope it might work the same for you. I also want you to take the keys of my house in case you have need of some…privacy.'

'Privacy?'

'Privacy to find out exactly what it is you do seek in a bride. A bolt hole, if you like, away from the strident gaze of society and family.'

'Thank you.' He took the set of keys and laid them down next to the statue of the stallion.

After Edward had gone Lytton collected the bronze and placed it at the front of his desk in his library. He could look at it there. Everything was changing. Ed was off to America, Aurelian and Shay were married happily and he seemed stuck.

He would visit Lady Catherine Dromorne tomorrow and talk to her. He couldn't believe she'd still want to marry him if he told her that he didn't love her in the way she deserved. He would also agree to any condition of breaking their understanding as long as it left him free.

Then he would go up to Balmain and try to find out exactly how well his sister had known the despicable Lord Huntington. If the answer was what he thought it might be, he would leave for Highwick and have it out with the bastard. Then he would return to London and offer Miss Annabelle Smith the best possibility he could. Not marriage, obviously, but a form of something semi-permanent that might do just as well. Not a mistress, for that was too uncertain, but a long-term consort with provisions for financial redress if anything at all went wrong. Provisions to look after her aunt. Provisions to fund a clinic. Provisions to allow her independence. Provisions for children if they were to have any.

Calculated. Logical. Eminently generous.

Lytton nodded. Perhaps the bronze of Edward's was clarifying his thoughts after all and he was pleased for it. The offer of the use of his house might also come in handy.

When he went to see Annabelle Smith the next day he found her alone.

'Your aunt is not here?'

'She went with Rose and Stanley for an excursion to the park. For some sunshine, I gather.'

My God, he could not believe his luck. He

thought he might have had to ask her for another carriage ride in order to find some time alone and here they were, undisturbed.

Shutting the door behind him, he leaned back against it, trying to think of just where to begin. Her eyes were of endless blue.

'Annabelle.' She frowned a little at his use of her Christian name. 'I know yesterday you must have been surprised when I kissed you, frightened even, but—'

She interrupted him. 'I wanted to kiss you. I wanted to kiss you as much as you wanted to kiss me.'

Such an open confession made him smile. Could it be this easy? He crossed the room to stand beside her, but didn't touch.

'Would there be any chance of me kissing you again? Today?'

'There would, your lordship. I thought you were very good at it.'

'Thorn.' Why wouldn't she use his name? 'You have had some practice, then?'

When she smiled her dimples showed. 'None at all, but I can recognise competence when I am confronted with it.'

No one had ever said such a thing to him. Oh, granted, he often had praise from his lovers in bed, but it had never before been couched in quite such an endearing way.

'I have read books on such things, your lordship. I know the works of John Cleland and the Earl of Rochester among others. I also provide medicines to a man in London and he often exchanges books as payment.'

The last words were said with a tremble.

'A voyeur, Miss Smith?'

He ran his hand down her good arm, lacing her fingers into his own. The pulse in her throat was beating fast and hard. 'Then allow me to show you more than the printed pages ever could.'

Pulling her to him, he placed one arm around her so that they were chest to chest, the feel of her breasts against his own all rounded flesh and softness. God, she made him frantic and desperate without even a word.

His lips rested gently on hers and he ran his tongue across them before leaning back. 'When will your aunt be home?'

'In an hour or so.' Her voice shook, but she did not look away.

Did he mean to ravish her right here and now between the servants lingering somewhere outside and an aunt who would be home as soon as the clouds darkened the day?

She had told him an hour, but a glance out of the window said it would be more likely half that time and she would not throw her virginity away on the chance of it.

Was he asking that? Surely not?

She faltered and tried to win back confidence, but when his hand cradled the back of her head and he slanted a kiss so that he covered her mouth completely, she held no chance of refusal.

Her fingers came up to his hair, threading through the thick of cinnamon and gold and brown, an aching need building as she kissed him, finding her own pressure in the truth of what was offered. No small desire this, but the galloping heat of lust.

His tongue came against hers and she opened further, allowing an entrance, the rest of her body feeling fluid in a shift of bone and blood. The room faded as did the day along with time and inhibition.

She wanted more. She wanted what she had read of in her books at night when her aunt was asleep and she could imagine two people cleaved as one in the arms of passion.

The strike of pure want left her breathless, a feeling of warmth and desire spreading to every part of her body so that the room fell away and good sense went with it. She curled into him without restraint, his hardening masculinity egging her on. She was no longer part of this world as her breath hitched and her head fell back.

The column of her throat was thin and pale as he nuzzled in, his other hand falling to one breast, feeling the nipple firm up against his touch. She was like liquid heat, the breath of her on his face, her fingers clenched around his arms so that her nails almost stung through the cloth of his jacket.

Lifting his head, he took her mouth again, harder this time with a force that was undeniable. God, he was losing control, her thighs against his own, the thin layer of silk all that stopped him from finding her centre. He wanted to reach in and take, stamp her as his own and never let go. He wanted to lead her to her bed and make love to her till the morning in all the ways he knew how. He wanted to wrap her in his arms and place her in his carriage and make for his hunting lodge in Scotland, far away from anyone and anything.

A knock at the door brought them back and away from each other. Lytton noticed how her fingers curled around the back of the sofa reinstating balance. She looked at him as if she was in a trance, as if she had no idea of what had just happened, her chest heaving and her lips swollen.

Who the hell would be here right now? When the door opened the servant announced the arrival of Aurelian de la Tomber, his hat removed as he came into the room.

Annabelle's lips were reddened as she stood there and he knew his own arousal would be plainly evident behind the fabric of his trousers. Lian was a man who never missed a thing and his first words told him exactly that.

'I passed two women at the front of the building who seemed to be heading this way. They should be here in a moment.'

Annabelle tipped her head and left the room, her chamber lying through a small passageway behind them. Her absence left an awkward void.

'That was Miss Smith, I presume? I hope you are being careful with her, for she does not quite seem the sort who might weather a dalliance. Weren't these Susan Castleton's rooms?'

Lytton swore, caught in limbo between deceit and lies. He no longer knew quite what was the truth—a casual dalliance, an impermanent union, or a troth that might last a lifetime and beyond. For the first time in a long while he could not speak.

She had floored him with her response. No woman before had ever made him lose control so quickly or warmed his soul with only a kiss. He felt confused.

'I think I shall go.'

'I will come with you.'

Lian looked worried, but Lytton was too muddled to even stop him.

A moment later they were outside after descending by way of the stairs, missing Annabelle's aunt and her friend.

'What the hell just happened in there, Thorn?'

'I don't know. I kissed her and the world shifted.'

A hoot of laughter was disturbing. 'When I first met Violet all I could see was her light. What do you feel when you kiss Catherine Dromorne?'

'I haven't.'

'What? Never?'

'I haven't wanted to.'

'Well, there is your answer, Thorn.'

All the parts of him were beginning to settle again now that he was out in the fresh air. 'I don't know what you are saying, Lian?'

'Don't you? Think about it more then, Thorn, until you can understand the truth. Meanwhile I have news for you which is why I sought you out. I have heard that Susan Castleton is Lord Huntington's new mistress.'

That news had Lytton frowning. 'God, I hope she knows just what she is getting into.'

'Maybe there is some history there, for word is she has known him for quite some time. The Tennant-Smythe family are an odd mix of good and evil. The old grandmother seems a woman of character, but her two children were far from it according to all that is said of them.'

'Huntington's father was handy with his fists, I recall?'

'His name was Albert, as well, and he was a violent man. Young Albert probably felt the back edge of his hand many a time which could account for the deficiencies of his son.'

'And the other child?'

'I have not been able to find out anything of her although I do know she was a daughter called Elizabeth who seems to have disappeared off the face of the earth. The family were always quite isolated up in Highwick after the old Earl passed away and, apart from Albert Tennant-Smythe, Lord Huntington, they do not mix in society much.'

'I had a letter from the grandmother about the horse her grandson lost to me in a game of cards at the Derwent Ball. She wished to buy the steed back and implied that it was not his to give away in the first place.'

'What did you do?'

'I've sent the stallion back to her. Without payment.'

'That was generous of you though it will probably encourage talk in the *ton* about the foolishness of her grandson.'

The webs had begun to spin, Lytton thought, faster and faster and he felt a sort of sideways shift. God, his whole life of late was turning upside down and Annabelle Smith seemed to be always in the very middle of the chaos. Something Aurelian had said was niggling at him, too, and he swallowed.

'You were saying when you saw Violet the

first time all you could see was her light. How did you mean that?'

Aurelian stopped walking and turned towards him. 'I knew there was something about her that drew me in, something stronger than anything I had ever known before. Something that could not be ignored. I was struck down by her in the first seconds of meeting her. It was indescribable.'

'Hell.'

'You felt the same thing, then? With Annabelle Smith?'

Lytton did not want to answer that, did not want to even contemplate it as the truth.

'Let's just keep looking for the bastard who is trying to hurt her.'

He was glad when the other nodded and they walked on.

Belle smiled as her aunt and Rosemary came through the door, though her heart was racing for she felt the shawl she had fastened around her shoulders might not hide all that she needed hidden.

The Earl was gone with his friend, away from the house and yet all she wanted was for him to come back. To kiss her again, to lay his hands upon her body and make her understand the truth of passion. She did not care that it would not be for ever. He would never marry her, but perhaps just one night of lust would be enough. She was thirty-two, after all, and she would be careful to make certain nothing would come of a union in the way of a pregnancy.

To go to her grave as a woman without once experiencing the delights of sexual intercourse suddenly seemed tragic. This could be her last chance. Her first and last, she thought next, but did not dwell on that.

Could she offer? Would he accept? And where would she be able to lie with him undisturbed?

Her aunt looked exhausted and grey. From the fire, Annabelle thought. Shepherding her into her bedchamber, she bade her lie down while she found some tea. Rosemary hovered at her side when she returned to the main room.

'Your aunt seems out of sorts, Belle. She worries about you. She feels you are in danger and that she is holding you back.'

'Holding me back from what?'

'I don't know. She never mentioned any specific thing. She just said that you need to bloom and that this is the year you will do so.'

'Losing all our earthly goods does not feel much like blooming to me, Rose.'

Rosemary laughed. 'I was speaking to Mrs Roberts about your predicament and she said she has rooms you could rent now that her son has left home. I think they are quite small, though, and the kitchen would need to be shared. Milly dropped in to see me, by the way, and sends her love. She has been offered a job in the tannery in Stepney and says she will take it now that your home is gone.'

The everyday crept into the extraordinary even as Belle tried to call it back.

She had no idea as to what to do next, which direction to take. She felt uneasy here in these rooms in the middle of London, but Mrs Roberts's rented space did not feel right either. She wanted her house back and her life back. She wanted to walk the streets of Whitechapel and see familiar faces and yet even that was lost to her now given the carriage accident and the fire. She also wondered if both events could be related and what that meant for her.

Three hours later another visitor knocked on their door and Lady Lucy, accompanied by her maid, was shown in.

'I hope it is all right to visit you, Miss Smith. I am back from Balmain for a few days and after hearing about the fire I just wanted to see for myself that you were…safe.'

'I am. Your brother has been most kind and allowed me the use of these rooms until others more suitable can be found.'

'Then I am glad for it. I will be returning to the country on the morrow, but I wanted to thank you for all you have helped me with. I thought last time we met I was rather… occupied and I hoped to set things right between us.'

She smiled and glanced at her maid standing to one side of her.

'Well, I see you are much recovered now and you certainly look to be in fine health.'

'The country air does wonders for the spirit and you should join me one day, Miss Smith. A small sojourn away from the city might be just what you need, too.'

'Perhaps.' Belle left it at that. She did not want to travel to Balmain to find the Earl there given his most inappropriate behaviour. She also did not wish to be anywhere near his mother.

As if Lucy had read her mind she began to

speak of her brother. 'Thorn has news, too. He will be married to Lady Catherine Dromorne before the end of the year so we now have a wedding to plan which should take my mind off things. Thornton and Lady Catherine have been promised to each other for years, according to Mama, and she is more than happy with the union.'

The shock of such words had Annabelle swallowing. The Earl had caressed her when he had known he was promised elsewhere in Holy Matrimony? He had stood there and asked to kiss her, taking her words of consent without any attempt at honesty.

He was exactly the man she had first thought he might be in her drawing room, wearing his pink waistcoat and his fingers full of rings. Shallow. Disloyal. A rake. Looking around the room, she saw other things that had not made sense before, but now did. The removal of the intimate paintings and statues had left a discoloration of the walls beneath them that was still visible.

'Is this where your brother kept his mistresses, Lady Lucy?'

She knew it was rude to ask such a question and saw Lucy's eyes widen. The maid behind looked away, trying her hardest no doubt to simply blend in with the wallpaper.

'I do believe that it might have been, Miss Smith.'

There was a knowledge in her gold eyes that told Belle other things as well. The Earl's sister had come with a warning and with her particular donation of truth. Take it as you will, she might have said, but understand the consequences. The consequences that I had to deal with. Make your decision while knowing all the facts.

'Mrs Wollstonecraft's book has allowed me a new outlook on life, Miss Smith. The independence you spoke of is indeed a gift. Lady Luxford sends you her warm wishes, too, for I saw her yesterday at the town house. They had just had Lady Catherine and her family for afternoon tea, I believe, to welcome them into the fold.'

An intertwining *ton*, all the pieces fitting and the promises kept. How foolish she had been to think she could have ever been a part of that.

'But I have also brought you something, Miss Smith.' She turned to the maid behind her and the woman handed over a small package wrapped in brown paper. 'Thorn said most of your possessions were lost in the fire at White Street and I remembered the painting I gave you and assumed that it, too, was gone. Would you accept the twin of that one as a replacement? It would mean a lot to me if you did.'

The wrapping fell away easily, this painting done in blues and greens rather than with the reds and purples.

'It's by the very same artist, but whereas the original's title was "Autumn", this one is "Spring".'

'Thank you. It is beautiful and I shall treasure it.'

The rebirth. The rebuild. A regeneration.

Perhaps it was applicable to her situation. Perhaps now she had to find the courage to rise from the ashes of her life like a phoenix. Like Lucy herself had with the sort of bravery that Mary Wollstonecraft advocated?

Belle felt shattered and broken, the question of what happened next hanging like a sword across her head. She could not stay here, that much was for certain.

When Lucy stood and made to leave, she decided to accompany her down to the carriage, just to have a moment away from these rooms and to be out in the open air of the day. But as they came on to the street Lucy gasped and turned to grab her hand and Belle saw a man standing there a few feet away watching them. He looked vaguely familiar.

'Lord Huntington?' Lucy's voice was small and frightened and Belle's heart began to beat fast. So this was Albert Tennant-Smythe, the trickster who had stolen Lucy's virginity and left her compromised in every way.

She stepped in front of Lucy, sheltering her. 'You are not to come anywhere near Lady Lucy, Lord Huntington, for your behaviour towards my friend was appalling and heinous and, believe me, you shall be punished for it.'

He smiled at that and moved forward.

'I mean it,' she said in a louder voice now, her good hand coming up to push him back. Mr McFaddyen had gone to find medicine for her aunt after eliciting a promise that Belle would not open the front door. Now that she had she was alone in this. Still, she was hardly defenceless and if the foolish Earl wanted to create a scene on the street, then she was more than willing to give him one.

She screamed as loud as she could, a piercing desperate cry that would bring people running. But before she could utter more than a few seconds' worth of sound Huntington had stepped forward, his hand across her mouth.

She bit down hard. Years in the tenements of Whitechapel had honed her reaction to danger and he leapt back, blood running down his fingers and ill-mannered words in the air.

'You slut. You stupid ugly pretender.'

He raised his fist and Belle pushed Lucy backwards, expecting the force of his anger to land on her as she did so. But then everything changed. The Earl of Thornton came from nowhere, barrelling into Huntington with force and sending them both sprawling on to the street beside her, arms and legs flailing and in virulent fury.

Chapter Eleven

Albert Tennant-Smythe was about to hit Annabelle. Lytton could not believe it.

He charged, but the Earl had his forearm raised, blocking his fist, an elbow ramming into Lytton's side and, as he rolled away, Huntington's hand reached under his shirt and a knife glinted in the dullness of the day. Lytton felt the stab of it in his forearm and dimly heard a scream before his other arm deflected steel so that the wicked point hit stone and the weapon skittered away.

Grabbing his hair, he slammed the Earl's head down on to the cobbles, but if he thought the bastard was finished he was wrong.

Strong legs wrapped around his own, toppling him to one side and then it was his turn to feel the thud of knuckles against the flesh of his mouth and eyes. He was blinded for a moment by blood or by the force, he knew not which, but fury held strength as well and he smashed the other in the side of the head, feeling the crunch of skin and bone. Huntington went down, his nose bleeding, his eyes closed and his body curled up around the pain. Groaning.

'Thorn?' His name said softly. 'Thorn?'

And then he was back, back in a street in Kensington in the middle of a London day, his sister crying, Annabelle looking shocked.

He let his body relax into stillness, as he took in breath.

'Thorn?' His name again. Annabelle's voice. She'd never called him that before, never used his family name in any of their many conversations.

He closed his eyes momentarily. His arm ached and he was sure one of his bottom teeth had been loosened, but his focus had been re-gathered by the strong sense of her.

'Take my sister home.' His first words were directed at the Thornton driver and he was glad when the man took them as an order. Within a few seconds Lucy and her maid were in the awaiting carriage and then she was gone.

The law was there even as he turned, the large group of bystanders multiplying by the moment as four Runners descended on them. Without thought Lytton stepped across to Annabelle and took her hand, bringing her to his side where she would be safe.

'You will all need to come with us, sir, to the Public Office, for we cannot allow such lawlessness on London streets.' An unfamiliar carriage had now drawn up beside them and two Runners got in. Albert Tennant-Smythe was being shepherded into his conveyance by the other two, blood dripping down his face and on to his clothes.

Lytton did not want the law involved, especially if Lucy's name was to be bandied about because of it, but there was nothing else to do but accompany the men to the station.

'I hope he dies.' He could not help the bleak desolation in his words and did not even try to temper vehemence even as the two law men opposite looked over at him.

'You found out?' Annabelle's query was quiet.

'Yes.'

The silence between them lengthened, the blood in his mouth pooling and a nausea rising. He was glad Annabelle was with him despite everything, safe for this moment from a world that had fallen to bits. He saw blood on the cream in her skirt.

'God. He didn't hurt you?'

'No. I bit him. I think it is from that.'

He laughed and was surprised by the sound of it.

Lytton Staines looked battered and hurt, the flesh around his eye blackening and his top lip split. Blood stained his fingers and his shirt was torn where a knife had ripped through the fabric to slide into the forearm below.

Belle had meant never to speak to him again, yet here she was pushing back his sleeve to peer at the wound.

'It's deep.' Her fingers pressed down and he grimaced. 'An inch or so to the left and he'd have sliced your radial artery here.'

'Then I was fortunate.'

His flat tone suggested anything but. She wondered what might happen when they reached the Public Office, but didn't dare to enquire. At least for the moment they were away from Lord Huntington. Her fingers fisted in her lap and they sat there in silence, the two men opposite them tight-lipped and frowning.

Half an hour later they were in a room, a magistrate before them.

'What the hell were you thinking, Thornton? Attacking Huntington like that out on the street in broad daylight and in front of at least three dozen bystanders?'

'The man is an ass, Wilton.'

So they knew each other these two, Belle thought, and was comforted by the fact.

'Then why not find him in some dark corner and deal with him? Somewhere where nobody else could observe you? Somewhere the law would not have had to be involved? Somewhere justice could have taken place quietly?'

'He was going to hit Miss Smith with his big bloody fist.'

'Yes, I heard that.'

'He had a knife as well.'

'Which we have confiscated. Huntington does not seem to be talking at all. He has called for his lawyer. He does not wish to take this further. Do you?'

'No.'

'Good. I hoped you would say that. There

are a number of newspaper reporters at the front door ready to pounce on you for a statement. I have arranged for a carriage to collect you at the back.'

'Thank you.'

'I should also imagine there will be unwanted talk in society, but I am certain you can handle that?'

'I can.'

'If you need any help with this privately from me, Thorn—'

The Earl did not let him finish.

'I don't, but I am thankful for the offer.'

'Very well. On my behalf the case is closed then.' He handed over a sheaf of papers. 'On your part you might like to keep the statements and names of those who supported your side of the argument. In case the Earl has other plans, you understand.'

When the door opened behind them both men shook hands, the file tucked under the Earl's arm as they followed the one who had come to show them the way out. As they turned a corner into a further passageway a woman stepped out before them, an older woman with bright white hair, two servants by her side.

Annabelle caught only a quick glimpse of

her before she stepped back against the wall and shaded her face with her hand as if she was feeling unwell. The older woman's maids crowded around her in consternation as they passed. The Earl gave no sign at all of knowing the woman. Perhaps she had come for Huntington? A grandmother or a great-aunt? Or perhaps she was here on other business altogether.

Annabelle was glad when the carriage was suddenly before them and there was no sign of others anywhere.

'Where do you wish to be taken, my lord?' The driver stood at the doorway, hat in hand.

'Number Twenty-Nine Bromfit Place in Kensington.'

'Very well, your lordship.'

In a few seconds the conveyance was moving and ten moments later it stopped in front of a tall stately town house.

'This belongs to a friend of mine. He has gone up north to see his family before leaving for the Americas.'

As Belle stood she thought the Earl looked wobbly. The footman hurried forward, knocking on the door, and when a servant answered they were soon inside. Lytton made straight for a sitting room of sorts, the shelves behind full of small models of planes, ships, buildings and other inventions that she had never seen the likes of before.

'Ed's passion is to invent things,' he said by way of explanation and then sat down in a leather chair by a small cabinet, helping himself to a drink.

'I would offer you one, but after last time…?'

He left the rest as a question and waited until she shook her head.

'I hope you do not mind me bringing you here. We need to talk and I thought it the most private of all the places I know.'

'The magistrate will not question you further?'

'No. Wilton is a friend of mine and can be trusted. If Huntington does not talk, then neither shall I.'

'Because it will be better for Lucy that way?'

'Yes.' His eyes were burning gold, no tenderness within them. 'Once that secret is uncovered publicly there will be nothing I can do to stop it hurting my sister. As it is Tennant-Smythe knows I know and for the moment until all this dies down I need to imagine that to be enough.'

'And after?'

He ignored that and asked her another question entirely.

'Can you sew?'

'As in clothing?' Belle could not understand just what he meant. Did he wish for her to mend his shirt?

'My skin. I think it might need a stitch or two.'

Relief bloomed. 'Yes, of course. Is there a needle?'

'Probably in the drawers of that desk over there.'

He waited till she found one, threading up the cotton and knotting one end.

'Take off your shirt.'

She saw his smile.

'I'll need hot water, too.'

The same servant as before came on the pull of a cord and the Earl asked him to bring water, flannels and bandages.

When he placed the bottle he'd held down on the table between them she picked it up. 'This will keep things clean.'

Overturning the liquor into a kerchief from her pocket, she waited until it was soaked in and pulled the needle and strands of thread through the damp material.

With his shirt off she saw that he was not a man prone to indolence. His body was well muscled, an aged scar of considerable proportion slicing down the top of the same arm that he had hurt.

He didn't look inclined to talk of it, though.

'How did you find out about Lord Huntington?' She needed to keep his mind off the pain that was to follow.

'I'd had word of my sister seeing Huntington from a few people, but then I read a letter my sister had written to him but had never sent. It was jammed into the Wollstonecraft book in her room. Huntington did not rape her, by the sound of her confessions, but he pushed her much further than he should have.'

'The familiar and unsettling entitlement of a lord.'

Belle pricked through his skin, but he did not move an inch. Knotting the stitch before taking another, she blotted away the dribble of blood. She should mention that she knew about the purpose of her accommodation in Kensington and the name of his unmentioned bride-to-be, but just for this moment he was her patient and she would leave confronting him until she had finished stitching at least.

'The Earl has always been a troublemaker. I knew him at school.'

'Your sister made a lucky escape, then.' She finished a sixth stitch and then a seventh, finally knotting the last one off and placing her linen handkerchief across the gash.

'Luck is a word that can hold many shades.'

'As does truth, my lord.'

Reaching for the roll of fabric the servant had delivered, she wound the length of it around his arm, tying it off with a divided end. He replaced his shirt immediately, buttoning the garment up to the neck with difficulty. There was sweat on his brow.

She did not help him. She would fashion a sling for him when she could, but for now…

'Your sister mentioned that you are to be married before the end of the year.'

He stilled, though the pulse in his throat quickened.

'So I was wondering how you thought it appropriate to…kiss me in the light of such a troth?'

Holding the wounded arm into his side, he stood. His eye was swelling, his lip was bleeding and there was a graze right down the side of his cheek. Yet he looked beautiful, his eyes fastened upon her, a sadness there edged in despair.

'I could not help myself and Lady Catherine Dromorne is, in truth, no more than a friend.'

'Who you have asked to marry?'

'Not exactly…'

Now anger did surface.

'How does one become promised to another in a "not exactly" way?'

'I am an earl and the position, while having many advantages, also has its drawbacks.'

'Drawbacks.'

'I cannot marry just anyone. Catherine and I have been promised from birth and it is my duty to make certain the Earldom leaves my hands in better shape than I found it in.'

'Then what am I doing here? With you? Why did you bring me here to this place?'

'Because I cannot ever get time alone with you and because there is something between us that is inexplicable. I want to know what that is. Understand it.'

'And then what? Will you proceed to ruin me and then scurry back to your suitable bride-to-be. Like Lord Huntington? Or did you mean to establish me as a mistress in your grand rooms in Kensington? A little bit on the side when you had the time or the inclination. A visit now and then when you felt like it?'

'No. It was not like that.' He stopped, giving the impression that he wanted to say more, but couldn't. 'I wanted to protect you, keep you safe...'

The weight of his words felt heavy inside her. He had done that. Time after time. After the carriage accident, after the fire, after the Earl had brought his big heavy fist down through the air in her direction.

He had protected Lucy, too, and her Aunt Alicia. He had employed McFaddyen to stand guard on the apartment and brought Stanley home from the ashes in Whitechapel.

He'd been a buffer to absolute poverty, a bulwark against homelessness and starvation. He was still being that, even now, with his damaged hand and face. But his destiny lay elsewhere, not by his command, but by the forces of history.

The anger left her in a rush and all that was left was tiredness.

'I think we shall never understand what this

is between us, my lord, but we need to have the sense to leave it alone.'

He sat at that on the chair by the window and leant back against the leather headrest. His exhaustion was palpable. The blood loss, she supposed, for the cobbles had been running with redness. Quietly she took her place opposite him, in a deep burgundy armchair, positioned at an angle to include his own.

'I will order us something to eat, Annabelle.'

He waited until she nodded before calling the servant back.

It had begun to rain outside. Belle could hear it dripping against the window. But her own world was encapsulated in here, the sense of dislocation heightened by the strangeness of the room and all the small inventions around her. The Earl waited till the servant was gone before he began to speak again.

'You pushed my sister behind you when Tennant-Smythe was about to strike. I do not know one other woman who might have done the same.'

'I am from Whitechapel, my lord. There is nothing soft there.'

'You used my name when you called to me in the fight?'

'I thought he might kill you with the knife.'

He smiled at that. 'Hardly. Shay and Aurelian taught me much about the art of defence.'

'Yet there is a large scar at the top of your injured arm?'

'That came from a mistake. I trusted the man who did it, you see.'

'Who?' A single word dragged from horror.

'My father. I had just won Balmain back in a game of cards and he was not thankful. He shot himself a few hours later. I have never told anyone those exact details before.'

'He hated you?'

'He hated himself. At least for me I have tried to behave honourably. The rooms in Kensington were all I had at such short notice and I had my staff take away anything even vaguely offensive the day after you arrived.'

'The statues and the paintings. I wondered where those had gone.'

'I have been seeking something else more suitable in the meantime, but…'

'But?'

'You do not accept help easily and it seemed such a gift might be construed as charity and as such rejected. So we are at an impasse, you and I, caught by circumstance and perhaps by lies.'

'Your lies?'

'Ours, Annabelle. Can you not feel what is here in this room between us?'

Shock held her still. He felt it, too, this connection, quivering and desperate? 'What is it?'

'Desire,' he whispered. 'Yearning. Need. There are a hundred other words I could say and all them together might still not explain it.'

'But it is there none the less.' Her words rolled into the silence as the lump in her throat made tears pool in her eyes.

Neither of them moved, the fragility of such a confession too new and too wondrous. With only a tiny mistake it might shatter, these troths of hope and faith. Such a brittle truth. Everything was too precarious with Lady Catherine Dromorne in the mix and her own lack of family. It was too soon for honesty. She stayed quiet.

The food came on a tray. There was cheese and figs and crusty bread as well as a cake and biscuits. He had asked for tea as well, the steaming aroma of it filling the air around them.

As the maid bent to pour the Earl stopped her. 'We will manage. Thank you.'

When she was gone Belle leaned to pick up the teapot, glad for something to do. He took milk and two teaspoons of sugar. She handed over the cup with care, making certain that she did not touch him, and then she poured one for herself.

She looked frightened and uncertain. She looked as if she might leap from the chair and run out the door. But the teacup at least momentarily anchored her. Lytton sipped at his own drink with distaste. He seldom drank the stuff, but she had poured it for him and he needed harmony. The sugar at least steadied him.

He wished he might simply have reached over and taken her hand, but he did not dare to. The ground he stood on was shaky and the next move had to be hers if there was to be any hope in it.

'I have had no luck with identifying the carriage that hit you and your friend on the Whitechapel Road despite an exhaustive search. Whoever it was went to great measures to avoid being caught.'

'Which implies either wealth or luck?'

'My pick is probably both.'

She nodded and sat back, her feet square on the floor, her boots scuffed with age and use.

'But I will find him,' he continued. 'At least believe that.'

'Thank you.'

A silence again. Ignoring the awkward tension that swirled around them, he breathed out. When she looked up the light caught her eyes, surprising him as they did each time with the pure blueness.

'Where do we go from here?'

Her question was brave for it tackled their dilemma head on and he decided to answer in kind. 'Either you leave, Annabelle, and we never see each other again, or you stay.'

'Stay?'

'Here.'

'I cannot…'

'I promise I will do nothing you don't want me to.'

For the first time he saw her dimples.

'I won't press you for anything.'

He couldn't believe he had said that. But he meant it. If there was nothing more than the promise of a simple touch, he would accept the offer. All he wanted was for her to be there, by him.

When she nodded he felt his heart beat faster in his throat. He hoped Annabelle did not see the power she held over him.

'I have sent word to your aunt to say you are with me so that she will not worry.'

Her glance met his. 'Or she will be more worried than she was before.'

'Why?'

'She thinks you are dangerous to me in ways that I cannot fathom. She thinks all that has happened with the carriage accident and the fire has come about because of my association with you.'

'And what do you think?'

'That she is probably right. Before meeting you my life was centred around Whitechapel and healing. No one there wished for my demise. More usually they were glad for my help.'

'And then everything began to happen after you came to Portman Square to aid my sister? God, you don't think it was any of us, do you? My mother might be a bitter woman and inclined to depression and delusion, but I am certain she would not flout the law.'

Was it himself who had put her in danger by asking for her services? Had someone seen her with him and decided that in Annabelle Smith there lay a pathway to revenge? He had enemies, he knew he did, but still he could not think of one who would take things to the extent of trying to kill an innocent.

'I want to see you safe, Annabelle, in any way that I can.' The light was falling and inside the shadows gathered.

He stood then and crossed to the window, looking out over the city, at the rooftops and at the road below which was almost empty at this time of the late afternoon.

He felt at a crossroads. Take one step in any direction and his life would change for ever. He needed these next moments to count.

'Whenever I touch you I feel that I have come home.'

One tear traced its way down her cheek, falling to her gown, wetting the silk so that the yellow of it turned darker. Almost gold.

'But I am not a saint, Annabelle. Barely even a ghost of one and I confess that I have known lovers in the carnal way many a time.' Turning, he made himself say more. 'But I also swear I have never wanted a woman as I want you, never burned as I do for your touch.'

He stopped as she walked across to him,

holding her fingers against his cheek in the way of a caress. He closed his eyes and he felt her warmth across his mouth and around the shape of his lips.

'I don't want to hurt you,' she whispered and for a moment he did not understand what she was saying. Break his heart? Slice away any hope?

'Your lip. It is cut.'

He smiled.

'What would happen, if I said yes? That I would stay tonight with you, here in the house of your friend?'

'Then I would have to ask you to marry me, Annabelle.' He tried to make the words sound kinder, but the shock of them arced through him, a troth he had never once before given in all the years of his life, but words torn from need and hope.

She shook her head, the dark of her curls falling across the yellow in her gown. There was a deep frown on her forehead. 'It would ruin us both and I will not be the cause of that.'

He brought her fingers to his lips, kissing them along the healing wounds on her skin. His broken lady, brave and true.

'So if I will not marry you and I cannot be your mistress, where does that leave us?'

'Here,' he answered and his lips came across her mouth, tasting and seeking, finding acquiescence, her body speaking with the words she could never say. Accepting.

His kiss this time was nothing like the others. Instead it was slow and soft and gentle. There was a sadness there, too, as if this would be the very last time he held her close. With it came an intimacy that was staggering.

Neither of them closed their eyes, the gold of his own saturated with desire as their bodies began to move together. Opening her mouth further, she felt his tongue tasting, felt his hands on her face drawing her in, felt the beat of his heart speed up to match her own. Cleaved into one. Hers. Her man. Thorn with his honour and his beauty and his braveness. Thorn with his Earldom and his family and his responsibilities.

She would not tell him she loved him, not now and not like this. But she did love him. To the very bottom of her heart and soul. She wanted the best for him. She wanted him to be happy. She wanted him to have a place in the world, in his world, the world of the *ton*.

Breaking off the kiss, she dropped her forehead against his chest. She needed to leave before she could not. Removing the bracelet he had given her, she handed it over to him.

'I cannot keep this.'

He nodded and let her go, one step between them and then two.

'You are sure?'

'We live in different worlds, my lord, and what might work at first would eventually not. Could you live in Whitechapel, with all its customs and idiosyncrasies, in a two-bedroom house with the street at your doorstep and a thousand things that are unfamiliar and frightening and dangerous?'

'A different world from the one I'm used to, you mean? One I was not conversant with?'

She nodded. 'Portman Square is as foreign to me as is society with all its many and intricate expectations and unwritten rules and there would be so many things I would do wrong. I would be as lost there as you would be in Whitechapel, no touchstone to simply be. Then afterwards, after it all failed, to be left with regret and hatred...' She stopped. 'It would be impossible to survive such a thing. I know it.'

'I always thought you were brave, Annabelle, brave enough at least to try?'

'Brave enough to let you go, too. To wish you well in your new ventures and to hope that your life should be exactly as it was determined when you were born an earl.'

She hated how her voice had begun to shake. Another moment and he might hear it. Just one more to get through to appear to be in control. She saw him swallow and the emptiness in his eyes broke her heart.

'The carriage shall be brought around then to take you home, Miss Smith.'

'Thank you, my lord.'

He did not put the bracelet down, but kept it in his fingers, turning the stones. Belle could feel his eyes on every part of her body. A farewell. A valediction. The tightness in her chest made it hard to take in breath.

Once back in the apartment in Kensington she went in to see Alicia in her bedchamber. Her aunt was reading.

'I received the message and did not expect

you back so soon. Are you all right, Belle? You look pale.'

'What happened with the man in your life, Tante Alicia. The one you loved when you were young?'

Her aunt sat up and carefully smoothed out all the creases on her sheet before speaking. 'He married another and they lived happily ever after. When he left my heart was shattered and it was a long time before it began to mend. I could not suffer that twice, so I made it my mission to never cross his path. My family had lost its place in the world, you see, any lands and houses we once owned were gone and we were largely shunned by society. I had no position left to be in his life, no way of becoming the woman he needed.'

'Yet you were well brought up? You were hardly a poor match for him? Did he ever try to see you?'

'Many times. It was, in truth, part of the reason that we came to England.'

Breathing out, Belle put her head in her hands.

'The Earl of Thornton almost asked me to marry him today.'

Alicia's concern was obvious. 'What answer did you give him?'

'That I could not. That I would never fit. That I would ruin him if I was to ever say yes.'

Old hands came to cover her own, the age spots easily seen. 'I think that was the right decision, Annabelle.'

'Do you?'

'Yes. You did just as I did. You are allowing the Earl to live his life as it ought to be lived. The life he was born to. The life he would miss for ever if you had only thought of yourself.'

'But it hurts. Here.' She placed her hand across her heart.

'It would hurt more to see the Earl's possibilities dissolve before your eyes. He would say it did not matter, but in the end it would. Then there would only be blame and hurt. You would see it in his eyes when he could no longer hide it and hate yourself for it. Just as I would have done had I followed my heart.'

'I think we should leave here tomorrow early in the morning. Mrs Roberts has offered us a room. Just for now it would be a good start and then who knows where we might go.'

'I will get up and pack our things. At least after the fire we do not have much.'

Alicia's voice shook as she said this. Another move at her age difficult and unwanted and Belle felt a further arrow dart into guilt. If she were not to survive this…

'None of this is your fault, my love, and I will be perfectly fine, so stop worrying.'

The ghost of relief was there as she turned to her own room to find her things. Thorn had not asked her to marry him from love, she thought. Lust was more of a reason and the sheer want to keep her with him, two people from completely different worlds who somehow had been drawn together.

Then I would have to ask you to marry me, Annabelle.

Those were his words when he had realised she might stay. A duty. The honourable thing to do. There was nothing of adoration in such words, nothing of the things she felt at all. The Earl of Thornton had uttered them only because it was the right thing to do.

She folded the few clothes she had in a bag along with the painting Lady Lucy had insisted she take and then she sat down on the large bed and closed her eyes.

'Help me,' she whispered whether to God, her mother or the world in general she knew not which. Then she breathed in deeply three times and stood. Whatever happened next she would survive it because the worst of all possibilities had just taken place. No one and nothing could ever hurt her again as badly as Thorn just had.

Chapter Twelve

Lytton did not go straight home, but made a diversion to White's to sit for a while in the quiet of the place and simply be. When Aurelian came over he almost thought to leave but decided against it, his friend's smile full of concern.

'You look exhausted, Thorn. From business or from love?'

'Love?'

'It is becoming known around town that you have installed a new mistress in the rooms vacated by your last one.'

'Who is saying that?'

'One can barely move in the *ton* without eyes watching and as Miss Annabelle Smith is more than beauteous she is a worthy target.'

'She is not my mistress. I tried to ask her to marry me, but she refused.'

Lian began to smile. '*Mon Dieu*, Thorn. You have what?'

'You heard?'

'*Mon Dieu*, but how the mighty have fallen. I thought you always said that you would only marry for convenience? This situation is hardly that.'

'Which is the problem. Miss Smith feels our worlds would never fit. She turned me down because of it.'

'To protect you? She sounds like an angel.'

'I think she is.'

'I can't believe this is you speaking? Wait until I tell Violet. Does Shay know?'

'No. You are the first person I have seen since her refusal.'

'So what now?'

'I need to talk with Catherine to break off any agreement between us. I also need to talk to the old aunt of Annabelle's, for I think she does not trust me and I can't quite understand why. After that I will go to Rundell's and purchase the most beautiful sapphire ring that I can find. Perhaps that will convince her of my sincerity.'

'Women want the words, Thorn. I don't

think a priceless bauble is quite what the un-usual Miss Smith would desire.'

'What words?'

'Talk to Violet or Celeste before you make your next assault. They will let you know ex-actly.'

'I might just do that. Is your wife at home tonight?'

Aurelian's laughter worried him.

The Dowager Countess of Huntington, An-nalena Tennant-Smythe, graced Lytton with a visit two days later. As a woman who seldom left her home in Essex he was astonished to find her calling card in his hand.

'Put her in the blue salon, Larkin. I will come immediately.'

She was far smaller than he imagined and when she looked up at him Lytton felt a shock of astonishment. This was the same woman who they had passed outside Wilton's office as they'd left and she had Annabelle's eyes. The same colour and shape. The same star-tling blueness with grey just at the very edges.

Was he going to see Annabelle in everyone now that she had disappeared, packing up her things from his apartment and gone to God only knew where?

Whitechapel, if he could guess but unless she wanted him to find her he knew that he would not be able to locate her for all the looking in the world. The place had its own sense of loyalty and in the alleys and the small joined narrow roadways people could be hiding for ever.

'My lady. It is a pleasure to welcome you here.'

The woman turned directly towards him, her prim figure outlined against the large window behind. 'My grandson by all accounts tried to kill you, Lord Thornton, and I have come to apologise for his foolish and dreadful behaviour. He almost struck a woman in public, too, it is being said and I presume she was the woman I saw you with at the Magistrates Office? There are whispers he hates you for returning my steed to me at Highwick, which was a kindness that I cannot thank you enough for.'

'You do not need to apologise for the Earl. It is his shame.'

'No. It is also a family shame and, believe

me, the Huntingtons have had more than their share of scandal.'

'My family is much the same.'

At that she laughed and deep dimples graced each cheek. Another reminder of Annabelle. He reached for the brandy and offered her a drink.

'Oh, I never drink alcohol, Thornton, for it does not agree with me. I get drunk on a drop of the stuff.'

'Perhaps you would rather some tea?'

'No, for I shall only stay a few moments.'

Lytton was quite charmed by her forthright honesty. Her hair was snow white and the plain navy gown she wore sat well upon her. She balanced on the very edge of the leather wingchair nearest the fire. Her knuckles were white as she screwed her hands together, fingers full of substantial rings.

'My grandson will return to Highwick within the week to lick his wounds, I suspect. His father was a bully and he is turning out just the same. Don't have offspring, Thornton. They can only be a disappointment.'

'You have other children?'

'No. My only daughter was killed years ago with her family while journeying in Europe.'

She did not continue and there was a shake in her voice that had not been there before.

'But enough of all that. I have come with a gift for you. A swap if you like for the stallion you sent back to me. This one is a mare. I have named her Countess, a personal vanity, I suppose, but I find it difficult to imagine her being called anything else.'

'I did not expect repayment.'

'No one has ever done such a kindness for me before. More normally I am out of sorts with the world, but you have restored my hope. I will tell my grandson that if there are any more outbursts like the one you encountered I shall cut him off entirely from the largesse of my own personal fortune. He was a difficult sullen boy who has turned into the same sort of man. My son's son. Two peas in a pod.'

She stood at that and collected herself. 'Before I go, though, I should like to ask you one question. You have been seen in the company of an unusual healer, a Miss Annabelle Smith by all accounts. I am presuming she was the woman I briefly encountered the other day as you walked to your carriage and I should very much like to meet with her.'

'I am afraid she is rather reclusive, my lady.'

'It is said she resides in one of your apartments?'

'She did, but she left with her aunt and gave no forwarding address.'

'Could you give her a message from me?'

Bringing out a sealed envelope from her reticule, she handed it over. 'It is a private correspondence, Thornton, so if time passes and you truly do not see her then I trust you will burn it. But I sincerely hope she may be contacted in some way.'

The day just got stranger. Did the Countess wish for some medical advice? he wondered. She looked quite hale and healthy, the tone of her skin radiant and her eyes clear.

Everything that concerned Annabelle Smith always had that edge of mystery and here it was again.

'I shall do my best.'

When she stood Lytton saw desperation in her eyes, an emotion so strong that he almost stopped her to ask what is was she wanted from Annabelle. But manners prevented such a direct and inappropriate enquiry.

A few moments later when her carriage pulled away from Portman Square the bright livery caught his eyes, gold against blue. Had not Roberts mentioned something of the same colours on the conveyance that had knocked Annabelle down on the Whitechapel Road?

Coincidence was often not the quirk of fate it purported to be. He had learnt that fact over his life many a time. Summoning his valet, he asked him to find Harold Roberts, the kitchen hand serving at the Stephens's residence, and bring him to the town house.

Energy suddenly filled him and he felt a shift in his world as he walked back inside, the small thin missive in his hand with its red wax seal, monogrammed and beribboned. Taking a book from his library which depicted the seals and crests of all the great families of the *ton*, he finally found the Huntington seal.

Apart from the colours there had been some talk at the scene of the shape of a ship on the top of the crest. This family crest contained all the elements spoken of. Fury began to fill him and this was followed by pure and utter worry. If Huntington was behind all this, Lytton knew he would not stop trying to hurt Annabelle.

But why would he? Tennant-Smythe's connections to his sister had thrown him off track, but he suddenly saw that the truth in the Earl's attempts on Annabelle's life lay in another direction entirely.

She had told him she felt someone had been following her and Shay had once mentioned seeing Huntington watching her in Regent Street. The Dowager Countess's visit and letter was another clue in the correlation of a link between Annabelle and the family as was her own admission of travelling in France and of her parents never returning home. They died there, she had told him, and he had known she was not telling him everything.

Annalena Tennant-Smythe had said her daughter had been killed along with her family while journeying in Europe and there had been more than a shake in her voice, too, hidden things as apparent as what she admitted.

A granddaughter. A blue-eyed dimpled granddaughter in much the same mould as she herself must once have been.

Swearing he stood, helping himself to a brandy and downing the lot. Did Annabelle know any of this?

Other clues began to fall through the air. The family name was Tennant-Smythe and hers was Smith.

My God, if she was the lost heiress, then

Huntington might have a great deal of motivation to see her gone, especially given his grandmother's lack of knowledge of her being here in England. How had he found out? How could have he known?

From seeing her at Portman Square probably while attempting to get in to see his sister, for Larkin had spoken of a gentleman who failed to leave a card but who had come calling twice.

That particular realisation had him thumping his glass down hard on the table. It was his fault Annabelle had been recognised. If he had never asked her to call on his sister, she might have simply stayed hidden in the streets of Whitechapel, just one of the thousands of poor who plied the area with their trade.

Yet she deserved a place, a family, an awareness of who she was and how she had disappeared. She needed to be given the choice as to where she would turn next, options in a life that was at present becoming more and more difficult.

But first he needed to find her. Money brought opportunity and he had a lot of it. He also had a reason now to make her listen and to tell her the truth of her past. It was not just for his sake now, this need to see her again, but for her own. He would begin with Mrs Rosemary

Greene and then work his way through all of Annabelle's acquaintances that he knew of.

He was glad when Larkin announced that Roberts was waiting outside. Here was another source of information, another way of swaying this matter in his favour.

When the lad was shown in Lytton asked him to sit. He did so with a look of concern on his face.

'Don't be alarmed, Roberts. You are here because I need to find Annabelle Smith and quickly. She is in danger and she does not know of it.'

'Like the carriage accident and the fire, my lord. I said to my mother it did not look like coincidence to be hit twice like that and so quickly.'

'Precisely. I think I know the man who is behind these attacks and I need to keep her safe.'

Harold Roberts nodded. 'She has left London for Oxford, my lord, and is currently residing in the house of my mother's sister with her aunt. I will write you out the address.'

'I won't forget this, Roberts, and I promise I shall do everything in my power to make sure that she is not harmed.'

'I know you will, your lordship. She needs a friend.'

* * *

An hour later Lytton was in Hyde Park near the Serpentine. He knew Lady Catherine Dromorne would be walking here as she did each Tuesday at about three o'clock in the afternoon and he needed to see her before he departed for Oxford.

Spotting her standing over by the lake, he was relieved when she asked her accompanying maid to drop back and allow them some sense of private conversation.

'I have been thinking of what you said, Thorn, about us being friends. Perhaps on my side there has been the want for more, but on yours—'

He butted in. He had neither the time nor the inclination to make this any other than it was. 'For me you were always just a friend, Catherine. A woman whom I enjoyed talking with.'

'The thing is that now I find myself thinking that perhaps I should want more than only friendship.'

God, Lytton thought, was she saying what he hoped she might be? Was she realising the lack in their relationship would never sustain them over years of union?

'So I wondered if perhaps we might meet

quietly somewhere, perhaps at your house, and we could…do more than kiss.'

The shock of her suggestion coming hard on the heels of an easy road to freedom hit him.

'Perhaps if we took our relationship to the next level we might discover important things, things we would both be thrilled with. I do not wish to lose you, Thorn, but I have heard rumours…'

She stopped, colouring a little and turning her gaze away.

'Rumours?'

'That the Whitechapel healer has taken your fancy and you have installed her as your new mistress in your apartments in Kensington.'

'I haven't. That is an untruth.'

'She is apparently very beautiful and clever. You were seen fighting for her honour on the streets not long ago. It seems that Lord Huntington came off much the worse for your intervention?'

He could say nothing of Lucy and her relationship with Tennant-Smythe and so he had to allow Catherine to believe that it was for Annabelle's sake that he had gone into battle.

'It got me thinking, you see. I would not wish for a milksop husband who could not protect me. I found your behaviour quite arousing, Thorn, arousing enough to want to have this conversation with you.'

God. He did not quite know how to go on from here.

Nothing was progressing as it should. His intentions. His future. His hope for a simple way out of a relationship that was becoming increasingly fraught.

He wanted Annabelle. He wanted to sit and talk with her and take her in his arms and kiss her. He wanted her blue eyes and her dimples and her softness and the way she managed people, with care and with kindness.

'I admire Miss Smith greatly.'

'I imagine that most people do. She is, after all, skilled at the arts of healing and is a herbalist of some note.' A coldness crept into her voice and Lytton brought the matter to hand.

'Whatever it takes for you to release me from my promise of a marriage I will do it. I do not love you like that, Catherine, and I never will. One day you might be thankful for my honesty.'

'But not this day, Thornton. I think you have played me as a fool.'

'It was not my intention to do that and I am sorry.'

'I am, too. Mama has advised me that I should hang on to you no matter what. She does not think I shall ever receive a better offer.'

'What do you think?'

'I do not know any more. There is no handsome rich suitor waiting for me to turn you down and my options are dwindling.'

My God, he suddenly thought. *This is what I would be stuck with for ever were I to marry Catherine. Compromise and disappointment.* And just like that he could no longer do it, no longer pretend anything.

'I will not marry you, Catherine, on any grounds at all and we need to find a way forward that allows us both some dignity.'

'My father will be furious.'

'But it is not his life he is ruining. It is ours. What would you want to do most in the world if anything were possible?'

'Travel. Get away from my parents. I would like to go to Europe like your sister, see the sights, learn about the world.'

'I would pay for you to do that if you would break off the betrothal. I could make it possible for you to join Prudence and her husband in Italy.'

'How much would you pay?'

He should be frowning at her about-turn, but he wasn't. Instead he understood just how narrow was his miss with disaster and how close he had come to allowing responsibilities to dictate his happiness.

His mother and father had hated each other and so had his grandparents. Every single generation of Thorntons that he could remember were tarred with the same brush of disappointment and this was the tragedy in his blood, the true curse of the Earldom.

'Send me a receipt, Catherine.'

'My withdrawal from being linked to your name will be on the grounds that I no longer found you suitable. Perhaps you began to bore me and I felt a lifetime in your company would be unsustainable.'

'I'd agree to anything.'

'I will say you were simply not the man I hoped you to be and that I made a lucky escape.'

'I should not refute it.'

Lytton in truth did not care what she said as long as it allowed him his freedom.

'Then this is goodbye.' Tears were sliding down her cheeks.

He nodded and left her in the park in the sunshine before sending messages to both Aurelian and Shay.

They came quickly and were both curious.

'I am no longer promised in any way to Lady Catherine Dromorne and the relief is so great I have been walking on air. She will go travelling and no doubt slander my name across the *ton*, but I do not care. All I can see is freedom.'

'We didn't think you would go through with it, Thorn, for your heart was so plainly not in it.' Shay's words were quietly said.

'And that is what brings me to the reason for this meeting. I think Huntington was the one who was trying to get rid of Miss Smith. His grandmother, the Dowager Countess, came to see me yesterday and there were things she said that got me thinking.'

'And the point of all this?' Shay looked puzzled.

'I think he is dangerous to Annabelle. He has tried to kill her twice and something tells me he will try again.'

'Why?'

'Annabelle Smith is somehow entwined with the Tennant-Smythe family. After doing some research I discovered that the Dowager Countess's daughter was lost with her husband in a carriage accident on the coast in the south of France. The thing is there was a young daughter travelling with them and she was never heard of again.'

Aurelian helped himself to a drink. 'But you think you may know what happened to her, Thorn?'

'At a guess I would say it is Annabelle Smith, but she has gone to ground. Before she disappeared I intimated that I wanted to marry her, Shay, and she refused.'

A whoop of delight was not what he expected.

'Finally. Right from the first moment of seeing her Celeste and I knew she was the one for you. So where is she now?'

'In Oxford. I got her address today and am leaving London in two hours.'

'To bring her back here?'

'No. To reunite her with her grandmother. I sent the Dowager Countess a message just before you came.'

'And Huntington?'

'Is in London with a broken nose and arm. For this moment he will be going nowhere.'

'Giving you a clean slate to fashion a reunion?'

'And to make sure that Annabelle has her rightful place again. The grandmother is a fierce woman. I doubt when Annalena Tennant-Smythe knows the whole story of his attempts on her granddaughter's life that a broken nose and arm are all the Earl will be left with. I have sent her a letter telling her of my plans to see Annabelle and I hope she might join me on the journey north.'

Two hours later he drove north with all haste, the horses his finest and the promise of more on the road to Oxford. The Dowager Countess sat beside him and in his hand was the bracelet of turquoise that he had given to Annabelle a week before.

Belle sat down against the south side of the wall beyond the garden to find some shade and leaned against it.

Here for a moment she was alone and unwatched. Here the sadness that had accompanied her since leaving London could be allowed some release as the thickness of sorrow choked away breath and pretence.

He was lost to her now, the Earl of Thornton, gone perhaps to marry a woman he had been long promised to. The tears came quietly, rolling down her cheeks in a stream of bewilderment. One finger covered her lips and she felt him there, real and warm, his breath against hers and his golden eyes watching closely.

It seemed as if the air she took no longer was enough and that she might die of the sadness and of her empty unending future. Her hand closed across her mouth to stop sound. This is what aloneness felt like. She huddled around its pain until there was no feeling left and the spent emotions had run their course.

Then she stood and wiped her eyes and her face on the material of her skirt, replacing agony with a tight smile. The world would see only this. She had been abandoned once and she could weather it twice, she swore it under the grey summer skies.

She returned half an hour later to the house of Mrs Roberts's sister where two rooms had been set aside for herself and her aunt. Mary

Humphries was kind and hospitable, and although the dwelling was small it was scrupulously clean and very central to the town.

They could stay here for a little while or at least until the cough her aunt had been afflicted with had lessened. Then they would travel further north. Away from London and from Lytton Staines, the Earl of Thornton. Away from the possibility of her ever seeing him again.

The knock on the door came at around six o'clock just as they were sitting down for some soup and bread.

'I am not expecting anyone at all,' Mary said as she got up to answer it. 'Though sometimes Mr Browne from up the street pops in for a quick conversation. He has been lonely since his wife died so perhaps I could ask him in to join us.'

Annabelle smiled and thought again what a good person Mary Humphries was. Alicia simply frowned and resumed drinking her soup. Her aunt had closed in on herself after the fire in Whitechapel and had not welcomed human discourse of any sort ever since. Another worry. Her world was falling to pieces and she had no way of stopping it.

Lytton's voice at the doorway made Belle stand, shock running across her body in small tremors, her heart almost jumping from her chest. In a house this size he looked huge and important and vital. The travelling clothes he wore underlined his intent and when he removed his hat his hair fell in all the shades of gold and brown across the whiteness of his collar and an artfully arranged neckcloth.

'Ladies.' A lord of manners and charm. 'I am very pleased to find you here.' He looked directly at her.

She could not speak, any reply frozen in her throat. The last time they had met he had discussed marriage. Today he was all business and formality. Her hand gripped the back of the chair so that she would not fall.

'I wonder, Mrs Humphries, if you allow me a few minutes alone with Miss Smith and her aunt? My carriage is available outside to take you to any eating establishment in Oxford that you might name and partake in a meal with the compliments of myself, the Earl of Thornton?'

'Of c-course, your lordship.' Mary Humphries was flustered, allowing the Thornton manservant to lead her out of her own dining room and closing the door snugly behind them.

Then there was only silence and disbelief and that same longing that had been present in every single meeting between them so far.

Swatting it away, she took a step towards him.

'Why are you here, my lord? What could you possibly want with us here in Oxford?'

Alicia stood beside her, jarred out of mental ennui. It was like those hour glasses with the sand sifting through time, one second empty and the next completely full, turned into the new position, brought back in to life.

'She will not marry you, Lord Thornton. She cannot.'

'Tante.' God, this was going far worse than even she could have imagined it, Thornton's glance hardening at her aunt's words, the line of his mouth tighter.

'I have brought a visitor with me, Annabelle. I think she is someone who you need to meet.'

An old woman then came in to the room before she could say yes or no, helped in by one of Thornton's servants.

'This is the Dowager Countess of Huntington, Annalena Tennant-Smythe.'

Annalena? The name in her mother's Bible?

The newcomer was beautiful, her eyes blue

and clear. Her hair was silver white and tied beneath a small hat into a chignon, the strands catching the light so that they glinted.

'Hello, my dear. You may not recognise me, but I think… I think I would always know you.' Tears had pooled in her eyes and her voice shook. 'When you were little you used to call me Nannalena.'

Nannalena? The echoes of the name were there from long ago and Belle strained for more of the memory.

Come back to me, little one, come back when you can.

This was the woman who had said that to her, all that time before. The hands, the rings with the sapphires upon them, the eyes that were the same as her own. She breathed in. Even the smell was the same. Lost. To her. A lifetime ago.

The room began to swirl around, upending balance and sense. Belle tried to find a place to cling to and then the Earl's arms were around her, lifting her up, his jacket beneath her cheek, binding her to him. The sofa came under her and a blanket was found, warm and thick to take away her shakes. Her fingers threaded into Thorn's and she held on for all she was worth, the only centre in her out-of-control world.

'Don't go. Please.' She whispered the words and he smiled.

'I won't.'

The older woman sat now in a chair next to the sofa. 'I am sorry to give you a fright, Anna, but I have had rather a big one myself.' A handkerchief was in her grasp now and she dabbed at her eyes.

Anna? Her name? Anna Buchanan. She remembered that, too. Lady Anna Elizabeth Tennant-Buchanan.

'Who are you?' Her voice was working again, but even as she asked the question she understood exactly who this was.

'I am your grandmother. Your mother Elizabeth was my daughter and I have never been able to find you though I have searched and searched.'

'Where?'

Thorn balanced on the arm of the sofa and she looked up at him as though she needed confirmation on all that was being said. He nodded, allowing her belief.

'In Europe. Your parents died in a carriage accident near Marseilles in France twenty-seven years ago and there was never any sign of you, but I always prayed and hoped. And now…well… Thornton has brought you home to me and I cannot thank him enough.'

'How did you know?' This query was for the Earl.

'Your cousin was responsible for both the carriage accident and the fire. He wanted you gone, I suspect, before his grandmother got word of you. It seems that to divide even a little of your grandmother's wealth was untenable to him.'

The Dowager Countess frowned and was about to speak when Aunt Alicia moved forward to stand in front of her.

'Anna was delivered to me by a nun from the Notre-Dame de la Nativité in the village of Moret-sur-Loing. She said your daughter had brought the child in to be safe from her violent husband, for they had both been hurt by his fury.'

'I warned her. I warned Elizabeth so many times, but she would not listen.' Annalena Tennant-Smythe's voice was shaky and Annabelle reached out at the pain she could hear, her fingers cupping the small fragile hand. Her skin felt like crinkled paper but warm.

'Your father was a handsome man and my daughter was head over heels in love before he'd said his first words. I had my reservations about such a whirlwind romance, but he was charming and well born and so...' She tailed off. 'George Buchanan hit her once at Highwick, but Elizabeth would not hear a word against him. He was a Scottish earl and the family held extensive lands in the hills to the north of Edinburgh and after they left with you late one night I never saw them again. My husband was a violent man, too, so perhaps she was drawn to someone of a similar character to her father. I never forgave myself for the loss of a daughter and a granddaughter and then to have you back, alive after all these years...' She could not carry on.

Annabelle took a breath and began to explain. 'My mother saved me, I am sure of it, for when she delivered me to the small village outside of Paris she made the nuns promise that they would look after me until she could come back. Tante Alicia has done her very best to keep me safe ever since.'

'Then I have you to thank, too, Alicia. There are no words to say what I feel, but...'

Reaching out, Annalena hugged her aunt.

Alicia's own arms came around the Countess's back and they clung on to each other, two older women caught in the storm of family disappointment, violence, greed and love.

'I did listen out for strangers who might have come to Moret-sur-Loing to find Annabelle, but they never arrived. I only wanted the very best for her.' Her aunt sounded exhausted, but she also sounded relieved.

The circle of life and lies had come fully around. She was no longer Annabelle Smith but Anna Elizabeth Tennant-Buchanan, the granddaughter of a countess, this old woman whose quiet bravery was astonishing.

Thorn was a huge part of it, too, for without him this would not be happening. It was his cleverness that had placed all the pieces of the puzzle together after making the connections.

She was a lady now, a woman of the *ton* with titles from the peerage on both sides of her family; all the reasons she had rejected the idea of being married to the Earl of Thornton in the first place. Yet there was a sadness in his eyes as she felt him unlink her fingers and stand back.

'I shall leave you in the hands of your family, Annabelle. Your grandmother can protect you now. Alicia will travel with you also back to the Huntington seat in Essex and this is how it should be.'

'You won't come with us?' Terror struck her.

'No, but I shall be there in London when you are introduced to society. Shayborne and Celeste shall stand with you as will Aurelian and Violet and you will be a sensation. No one will equal you and this is your birthright.'

He said the words in the way that made it certain he wanted no argument. He stated it as a goodbye, too.

Her grandmother was nodding, as was her aunt, the two of them a formidable pair.

Had her new circumstances made him waver, the reality of being aligned with a woman who was the cousin of the man who had mistreated his sister too onerous to contemplate?

She felt marooned by Thorn's indifference and by his willingness to leave, to simply walk out and desert her here while he returned to London.

She could understand none of it and the initial warmth of finding family began to fade under the realisation that she was losing the only man she would ever love.

He had never said he loved her, however, and he did not now. She went to stand, but her grandmother held her back.

'I asked Thornton for some time, Anna, and he promised it.'

Chapter Thirteen

Once back in London Lytton went straight to the town house of the Huntingtons in Grosvenor Square and demanded to see Albert Tennant-Smythe.

'He is indisposed, my lord. The doctor has just left.'

'Tell the Earl it would be worth his while to get up. Tell him I will wait ten minutes.' He handed across his card.

'Yes, your lordship.'

His name was noted and uncertainty flared, but the servant strode up the stairs to relate the message none the less as Lytton waited.

Four minutes later Tennant-Smythe was before him, sporting two black eyes, an arm in a thick bandage and a broken nose.

'If you are here to finish the job on me,

Thornton, then you'd best be getting on with
it. As you can see I am in no condition to re-
sist and—'

Lytton interrupted him. 'I am not going to
gaol because of the sorry likes of you, Huntington. Your attacks on Annabelle Smith are
repugnant and vile. While I would love to wrap
my hands around your neck and squeeze the
life from you, I also realise the sheer stupidity of such an action. I want you gone. From
England. For ever. I have first-hand accounts
of your part in the carriage accident in Whitechapel and I believe that it was you who set
the fire in White Street. I have enough evidence to have you flung into gaol for a good
many years, yet to drag you through the mire
of your misdeeds would impinge upon your
grandmother and cousin who are innocents in
the face of all the crimes you have committed.'

The other swallowed at that and real fear
crossed in to his eyes.

'Your cousin has been reunited with her
grandmother and they have retired to Highwick together. Annalena Tennant-Smythe
knows in intimate detail all that has taken
place and to say she is ill pleased is putting
it mildly. However much I would like to see

you rot in gaol personally, I am of the opinion that complete ruin often promotes a misguided and unwelcome notion of revenge and so I am here to offer you an alternative. Leave England within the next few days accompanied by two servants of your choice and I shall provide you with enough money to start again. In America, perhaps. Or somewhere else as equally far-flung. Your choice.'

'Why would you do that?' His sneer did not look nearly as pronounced now.

'I told you. I want you gone. I do not want the Huntington family to be caught up in a scandal just as much as I wish my own not to be. If you do return, everything I hold on the choices you have made shall be offered to the magistrate here in London, immediately, and I shall be baying for your blood.'

He looked at his watch. 'You have ten seconds to decide your next course of action, Huntington. Starting now.'

In three seconds his answer came.

'I accept.'

'My man shall visit you tomorrow with a substantial bank draft. He shall want the name of the ship you have decided to take and the destination you will travel to before he hands it over to you.'

'I am sorry…'

'I do not want your apologies, Huntington, I just want you gone.'

In his carriage a few moments later Lytton leant back against the leather and looked out across the London streets. Part of him shook with the need to simply plunge a sharp knife through the chest of the Earl, but the other more sane part warned against it.

He must do everything he could now to safeguard Annabelle's name. She did not need scandal or foolishness or shame. Gossip would be rife about her past and her unexpected return to London society and he wanted her to have a place here, a home and a family.

He had promised the Dowager Countess on the way to Oxford that he would allow her to show her granddaughter her birthright before seeing her again. An introduction into a society ready to pick a stranger to pieces, no matter how illustrious their family, needed to be handled carefully and with exactly the right set of circumstances and he did not want his relationship with Lady Catherine Dromorne to be part of the equation. Setting Annabelle up in his old apartment had been a mistake, too, he knew that now and by withdrawing from her life completely until she came out any rumours might be allayed.

But he felt alone and desolate and his interview with Huntington had left him edgy and furious.

When Annabelle had taken his hand he had wanted to simply pick her up and take her home, for after days of not seeing her he was anxious to know that she was safe and well. The shock of her grandmother's reappearance had taken its toll on her, too, he could see that it had, but he could also decipher a sense of excitement and belonging that had not been there before.

With the Earl gone Lytton had made sure that she would stay safe and for now that was all he could do. He needed to let Annabelle go in order to find her again and allow her time to know who she truly was.

Would she still choose him? This query wound around in his head like a curse, for he knew that she would be fêted and admired by every unmarried red-blooded man of the *ton*.

But a promise was a promise and he meant to keep his word. In six weeks the Dowager

Countess Annalena Tennant-Smythe would bring out her granddaughter at a splendid ball in the family town house in Grosvenor Square and he would then make it clear to her exactly how he felt.

Chapter Fourteen

The European silk gown she wore had been primped and fussed with for hours, so that the floating sleeves sat just right and the organza top skirt embellished with embroidered leaves fell in a draped and classic fashion. Peach suited her, she decided, the soft shade picking up the darkness of her hair and the whiteness of her skin. Ribbons of the same shade were threaded through the high waist and the neckline sat off her shoulders, plunging in both the back and the front.

Annabelle tried to pull it up a little so that it did not seem quite so low, but the dressmaker was having none of it, instantly taking it back to where it had been and admonishing her gently.

'With skin like yours, my lady, and a bosom

worth looking at, there should be no reason why one would not show it off. So often I dress girls with far less charm and a lot more un-called-for arrogance. You will be the belle of the ball and your grandmother will be thrilled, for even in Paris at this moment I doubt one would find a more beautiful gown or a more beautiful woman to fill it.'

Belle thought she would have to take the word of Madame Hervé, for she had no true idea at all of the latest trends in ball gowns and neither did she have much interest in finding out. But the whole idea of being such a centre of attention filled her with anxiety.

She just wanted this first foray into society over so that life as she had known it might return even in a small measure. She could not believe the time it had taken across the past weeks to learn the steps of the dances under-taken at the great balls or the complex eating habits and the rules and manners associated with being a lady that were so ludicrously nu-merous and unfailingly exact.

Would Thorn be here tonight? Would he ask her to dance? Would he like the new and improved Lady Anna Elizabeth Tennant-

Buchanan? There was not much left of the woman he had known in Whitechapel.

He had not come to Highwick. He had not arrived at the doorstep of the Hall to see her. It was only this week that her grandmother had explained she had asked the Earl of Thornton for a promise not to visit so that the life she had lost all those years ago might be able to be fully realised again. Had he let her go? Had he moved on? He had not mentioned love when he had tossed out his words on marriage in the house of his inventor friend and the fact that he had installed her in the rooms of his former mistress didn't bear great witness to any higher order of intention.

He had wanted her, she knew that, and wanted her badly. Badly enough to even propose his idea of a union?

Her grandmother had come into her room now and she had a long burgundy case in her hands.

'These were my mother's, Anna, and her mother's before her. Would you wear them tonight?'

She flicked open the catch and the necklace and matching earrings of sapphires and diamonds inside were astonishing. Belle had never owned any jewellery apart from the bracelet that she had returned to Thorn.

'They are beautiful.'

'They will show the world that you are sponsored by me and in the *ton* that is not a small thing.'

The last six weeks had been eye opening. Her grandmother was a woman of culture and pride and passion. But as well as all those things she had taken her and her aunt beneath her wings and made sure that they had wanted for nothing.

Alicia had flourished, the chesty cough that had plagued her in Whitechapel for years and years had all but disappeared in Highwick. It was one of the reasons her aunt had not journeyed down to London to see her out in society. She simply could not bear the thought of the London air aggravating her lungs again, the purity of that in the countryside much more to her liking.

Annabelle could scarcely believe her change of circumstances. Now instead of sharing a small rented dwelling in Whitechapel, her grandmother had allotted each of them luxurious suites in Highwick Manor and dressed them both as befitted their station.

She had not seen the Earl of Huntington once and neither had her grandmother and for that they were both actually extremely grateful. She prayed to God that she would not come across him at the ball tonight, for he was one of the few people in the *ton* who would know that Miss Annabelle Smith and Lady Anna Buchanan were one of the same. Thorn's friends, of course, held that same knowledge, but she did not imagine them to be a threat at all.

She was nervous. Nervous of making a mistake. Nervous of not being all her grandmother hoped she could be. Nervous of seeing Thorn's indifference or even dislike.

'We will go downstairs in fifteen minutes, my dear,' Annalena said as she fastened the necklace and turned her to the mirror.

She looked so very different. She looked like a lady. She looked as if she was born to be in the peach-silk gown with her hair pulled up at the back and a series of ringlets curling around her face. Fastening the earrings with shaking hands, Belle turned to pick up her reticule. It held a handkerchief, lavender salts and a dance card and was embroidered with peach-coloured ribbons to match her dress.

Like the fairy tales in the books she had read

in the Tennant-Smythe library of princesses and godmothers and cruel circumstances that had been altered for the better on a trick of magic.

Like Cinderella going to the ball.

She had heard the carriages drawing into Grosvenor Square across the past half an hour and knew the Countess had invited above two hundred guests to her grand and formal evening. The sound of conversation and music could be heard here upstairs, laughter punctuating the hum every now and again.

After this there would be no turning back.

A knock at the door brought the maid in with a calling card.

'The Honourable Percy Rawlings is in the room outside, my lady.'

'Oh, good, send him in. My brother has offered to be our escort tonight and he is always very good at these large occasions.'

Belle had met Percy a number of times already, the affable man a firm favourite of the household. She was glad they would have him to lead them down and said so as he appeared.

'Well my love,' he returned quickly, 'your rediscovery has been one of the nicest things to have happened in my life and I know you will be a huge success. It can seem daunting, but Annalena and I shall chase away any wolves.'

Her grandmother brought them each a chilled drink of lemonade and they clinked the crystal glasses together.

'To family,' her grandmother said, 'and to happiness. To Elizabeth, too, wherever she is for making certain in the only way she could that her daughter should return to Highwick.'

The poignant reminder of her mother made Belle smile gently. 'I wish Mama could have been here.'

'She is,' her grandmother returned. 'She is here in you.'

Lytton had come to the Tennant-Smythe ball with Aurelian, Violet, Shay and Celeste. He had come early and found a spot at the end of the room by some pillars. He had refused every drink offered for he needed to be at his best tonight with all his wits about him.

Violet next to him noticed his latest refusal and smiled. The hope he could see on Violet's face made him even more nervous and he wished like hell he had not taken Aurelian's advice and asked for help on the words Annabelle might most want to hear.

Violet had been kind, he would give her that, but her instruction to him to allow Annabelle to see all his fears and worry held a sort of hopeless impossibility here at a very public ball. Celeste had been just as confusing. Her counsel had consisted of using the sort of prose he'd never felt comfortable with and at the end of the conversation he even wondered if she might be jesting. He could not ask Aurelian or Shay to clarify things, either, for he was so far out of his depth with the raw emotions it was almost like drowning.

But he had taken his own steps to convince Annabelle to favour him, the deed in his pocket holding the sort of weightiness he knew she might well understand, though even that thought held its complications.

Pray to God she had not changed. The mantle of being a lady would be a heavy one and there would be so many possibilities now open to her. Had Miss Annabelle Smith from Whitechapel been supplanted entirely by this new version? He had not felt this nervy since he was a youth and he swallowed away the frantic beat of his heart.

The music began suddenly heralding the arrival of the guest of honour and all eyes looked upwards to a grand staircase at the end of the room upon which three figures were now descending.

Annabelle stood on the right, a shimmering beauty in a gown of a colour he had rarely seen before. Her hair was up, but the length of it hung around her face in curls before reaching down her back. She looked nothing like the woman he had known in London, dressed in her ill-fitting hand-me-downs and her unusual scarves. Yet though the outward trimmings might be different, there was still that calm centred sureness that had always attracted him and a good sense that was so very beguiling. Others felt it, too, and a hush covered the room.

When people moved in for introductions he saw that she was enjoying it, her hand raised in just the right way, words tripping from her lips to make them laugh and lean forward and listen. It was easy to see the conquests and the triumphs as those she spoke with kept returning to her side.

The victory of beauty and grace and something else far less definable.

Inclusion was the nearest he could come to the meaning of what he sought. She did not have airs and arrogance, but kindness and acumen.

Suddenly Lytton could no longer bear it and, excusing himself from his friends, he walked towards the French doors to one side of the room and out on to a wide balcony. His fingers grasped on to the stone balustrade. He felt nauseous and hot. If this went badly…?

Others had come out now for some respite from the packed and noisy salons and he could not help but hear what they were saying.

'Lady Anna is the most beautiful woman I have ever laid eyes on and she is also so very substantial. Her conversation is nothing like the inane exchanges we have forever been subjected to.'

'Thank God, I say. Did you see Frederick Alley? He was smitten by her and so was Aleric Carswell.'

'As was every other unmarried male of the *ton* and a good few of the married ones besides. Where the hell has she been hiding, do you think?'

'In France, according to the Dowager Countess's brother. Near Paris, by all accounts.'

'She will be married before the month is

out, that much I will say. I can see every eligible male formulating their troths as we speak.'

Lytton walked further away so that he would not hear them. She had been in the cold for so many years he needed her to enjoy the heat, to know what a success she was and to revel in it. Annalena Tennant-Smythe had done a sterling job with her granddaughter; her hair, her gown and her demeanour could not be faulted. She was the embodiment of a woman whom both males and females could warm to, the whole package with nothing at all missing.

He should leave now and allow her the choice of love. He had, after all, placed down his hand and failed and he wanted her to be happy. He should simply walk out and return home. She knew where he lived, after all, but had never come. There had been no contact between them whatsoever.

Annabelle saw the Earl of Thornton's friends approach her and looked around for him, disappointment rising. She had not seen him anywhere and she had been looking. With a sigh she took Celeste Shayborne's offered hand and thanked her for coming.

'I should have guessed you were a lost heiress, Lady Anna, the moment I met you. There were so many clues, after all.'

'Call me Anna and I am so pleased to see you all here.'

'Thorn didn't come up with us.'

'Oh, he is away from London, then?' Belle tried to keep the regret out of her words, but knew she had failed as Celeste shook her head.

'No. I mean he is here somewhere in this enormous room, but we seem to have lost him.'

'He has gone for a drink. A fortifying one, I imagine.' Aurelian now took up the conversation and there was laughter in his words. 'Though I am sure he will seek you out when the masses have fallen back a little.'

'It is rather a crush, isn't it?' Annabelle replied, wishing she might simply roam about the room in search of the elusive Earl.

'The sign of a successful debut, I would say. Shay imagines you will have myriad marriage proposals on the table by the morrow and whoever you choose would be undeniably lucky.'

'I sincerely hope that does not happen.' The words fell out of her mouth even though she knew honesty was not a particularly valued commodity here in the heartland of the *ton*.

Celeste began to laugh. 'I remember feeling

exactly the same as did Violet. Have you met Aurelian's wife yet, Annabelle?'

The name made her smile and she turned to the newcomer, a beautiful woman with the reddest hair she had ever seen.

'No, I have not had the pleasure.'

'Oh, it is all mine, Lady Anna. I am so glad that your family found you and brought you home.'

No one else had quite said it like that all night and Annabelle instantly felt a connection with Violet de la Tomber. In the eyes of both these women she saw a vein of humour and irreverence, and a sort of half-hearted acceptance of the ways and oddities of the *ton*.

She wished she might have friends like them, friends who were honest and forthright and not at all bound by convention. She wanted to hold their hands and keep them both with her, human shields against the arrogance and snobbery that was so prevalent here.

'I hope Thorn will find me,' she suddenly said. It was far to familiar, she knew it was, and much too honest, but the hours were running down to midnight and she imagined that he might leave without even seeing her.

'He will.' Celeste spoke firmly. 'He is a

good man who thinks you need the chance to shine in your own light without being shaded by his. But he will come when he understands the truth of what he feels, I know it.'

Her grandmother had joined the group now and asked if Annabelle would come to meet some old friends of hers. With nothing else to do but acquiesce, Annabelle followed her.

The clock had struck two before Thorn approached her. She was standing with Violet over to one side of the room and looked even more beautiful close up than she had at a distance.

When Violet saw him she quickly excused herself, giving him the chance of a moment of aloneness with Annabelle.

'You look beautiful.' Ridiculous words, but true.

'Thank you.' There was a half-smile on her lips.

'Would you like to dance?'

A waltz was just warming up and people all around them were taking to the floor. Dancing would give him some distraction and promised a few moments of uninterrupted closeness.

'I am still not particularly proficient at the

steps so I hope you will not mind if I tread upon your feet.'

'I won't.'

He took the hand that she held out and she walked beside him. There were sapphires and diamonds around her neck and on her ears, the largesse of the Huntington family on display.

All the words he had practised to say fell away and he was left with silence, the music all around them, the lights above and the warmth of her body so close against his own.

They could have been dancing alone in a glade set in a far-off enchanted forest, bare of people. For a second he closed his eyes and just felt the shape of her fingers under the long white gloves as he breathed in a pervading scent of lavender. Opening them again, he saw that her hair shone dark beneath the lamps, the colour of wood under water or winter leaves underfoot.

Annabelle was matchless and original and completely herself. Her dimples showed up as deep shadows on each cheek.

'I thought you might not come, my lord. I imagined the night ending and still not seeing you...'

'I'm sorry. You were busy.'

'Not so busy that I could not thank the one man who has rescued me again and again, without recompense or reward.'

'It's been a lot quieter on that front lately.' The start of a smile surprised him, but then Annabelle had always had the ability to make him laugh. 'McFaddyen sends you his greetings.'

Her step was out of beat and they stumbled slightly, the movement bringing their bodies closer. He could feel the shape of her breasts under thin silk and drew in a breath. She had filled out and he had thinned down. There seemed to be no end to the comparison of differences.

'I brought you a gift.' He unlinked one hand and dug an envelope out from his pocket. 'Perhaps you might open it later?'

'Thank you.' The frown across her forehead made him want to lift his fingers and rub it away. He was pleased when she deposited the deed in her reticule, the peach ribbons adorning it twinkling in the light.

He wished that this dance might continue all night, the feel of her in his arms, the warmth of the summer evening, the way she allowed him to lead her around the room. The sheer closeness.

'You are a far better dancer than I am, my lord.'

'I've had years of practice.'

'I heard that Lady Catherine Dromorne has broken off your engagement. It seems she discovered you were not the man she thought you to be.'

'A fortunate detection. I think she is in Italy now with my sister Prudence, who has decided to stay on with her husband. I hope Catherine finds what she is looking for there.'

'Which is what?'

'Love. A soulmate. Someone to make life bearable. Someone to love her back.' He tried to keep the words light, but could not, and his fingers closed tighter around her own.

'You did not come and see me at Highwick? Not once?'

'Your grandmother asked it of me. She wanted a new start for you and all the possibilities that such a thing might entail.'

'Possibilities?'

'Choices, I should imagine, and options. A selection of husbands to settle down with, a man who might suit your station and your inclination. It seems there are many here tonight who would like to show their hand.'

'I have already had one offer.'

His heart sank.

'Which I've decided to accept.'

God, he had lost her then and there was no way he could save what had been between them.

'Then I give you my congratulations, Lady Anna. I hope he deserves you.'

'Oh, I think he does.' Her voice held amusement.

'And I hope he knows how to make you happy.'

'That, too.'

She was smiling, which did not quite seem right. Annabelle had never been unkind before.

'He understands me, you see, as no other ever has and he protects me to the very core of his being. I could not imagine my life with anyone else. He is my perfect match and I think he knows that I am his as well.'

The small clues clicked into place and pleasure made his blood run hot.

'Annabelle?'

'Yes, Thorn.'

'Will you marry me as soon as I can procure a licence?'

She moved in closer. 'Why do you ask me?'

'Because I love you. Because there will never be anyone else for me. Because we belong together and without you I am only half a person.'

The music had stopped now but they stood there still, oblivious of what was happening around them, of the stares and the conjectures, of the growing puzzlement and the speculation.

'I love you, too, Thorn, and I have done since first Stanley tore your pink waistcoat in the front room at White Street.' She could see him swallow and take in breath and his hand shook beneath hers. 'I want children and a home with you and a family and for ever.'

'God.' The word sounded torn from the depths of hope.

'I think it's yes you are supposed to say and then you kiss me.'

He grabbed at her hand and, taking no care of the stares of all those around her, he pulled her from the room and into a small salon that sat on the other side of the doors they had just exited.

'Yes,' he said before his lips came down in ownership and tenure and Annabelle saw then all he had kept harnessed, the need and the want and even the fear.

The thin peach gown held no hope against his fervour as his hands clutched her to him, a grasp that gave the promise of never again letting her go.

Love.

Desperate. Shaking. Disbelieving. Unguarded.

She felt the tears on her cheeks even as he wiped them up with his finger.

'I will never leave you again, Annabelle. I thought…' He stopped. 'I thought after last time that you might not want to see me again.'

'Love me, Thorn.'

'I do. Desperately.'

This time she kissed him, bringing his head down and taking his mouth. The thrall that snaked through her was indescribable. He was hers and she was his and everything that came before now was as nothing. This day, this moment, this night was the beginning of the life she wanted, with a man whom she trusted and understood. An honourable man who would always protect her and always love her.

She took in breath as he pressed her against him, feeling the rustle of paper in her reticule.

'What is in your envelope?'

'Something I purchased for you. Something I think you will like.'

He let her go as she brought the paper from her bag. It was a deed for a property in Whitechapel, a place on the Whitechapel Road. Her name was the sole one written upon it.

'I thought you would suffer if you were unable to keep practising your particular kind of medicine and I wanted you to be independent and self-reliant even if it was not me you chose.'

She burst into tears and he looked surprised.

'You do not like it?'

'I love it. I love that you would think to do this for me, Thorn. It is simply perfect, the best wedding present I could ever imagine. But I want the deed changed. I want your name to be there, too, together.'

'Together,' he echoed and a new desperation assailed them. She could feel a growing hardness between his thighs and his breathing had changed.

'I want you.' This was said as a hoarse and raw troth, no question in it, though when the door unexpectedly opened they broke away from each other, their fingers still entwined.

'Anna?'

Her grandmother stood there with her great-uncle at her shoulder. Both looked more than surprised even as Thorn took charge of the situation and began to speak.

'I have asked your granddaughter for her hand in marriage and she has said yes. The ceremony will take place as soon as possible.'

Annalena came forward, an enormous smile on her face. 'I never imagined that this could be so wonderful, my dear. The Earl of Thornton as your husband is a perfect choice because he is kind as well as powerful and you will need that.'

Annabelle hugged her grandmother and then she hugged Percy. There were tears in his eyes as he let her go.

'When will the wedding take place?'

'As soon as I can get a licence.' Thorn spoke, his voice filled with pride.

'I don't want it huge, Thorn. I want a small and intimate ceremony with just the family and a few friends and I would very much like it to take place at Highwick.'

Her grandmother looked delighted. 'Huntington has written to me from America and he said he will not return to England for a long while. I think it is for the best that he stays away. A recompense for the way he has behaved, perhaps?'

'A new beginning,' Thorn added as Rawlings shook his hand in congratulations.

'Shall we announce your intentions tonight with everyone present?' her grandmother asked.

'Yes.' Both she and Thorn said this at once.

Chapter Fifteen

Three weeks later

'You are the most beautiful bride that any man could hope for.'

Annabelle stood before him in her white-silk under-gown with flowers woven through her hair, the curls of which moulded around her waistline.

'When I am old and infirm and I cannot remember one other thing, I pray to God that I will remember this.'

They had been married three hours ago in the chapel at Highwick and had now retired to the suite in the east wing of the hall which had been reserved especially for them.

Aurelian had been his best man and Shay had been the groomsman. Annabelle had asked

Lucy to attend her and Mrs Rosemary Greene had journeyed especially from Whitechapel to be her other bridesmaid. Lytton's brother David had come up from the school he'd recently returned to and had enjoyed the celebration, but Prudence his sister had not been able to make the trip from Italy under such short notice.

Belle held her marriage ring up to her new husband now, one finger turning the gold and sapphires so that they glinted in the light.

'I don't think that I could possibly be any happier.' Her voice was quiet and filled with a shyness that was new. 'But I need to tell you something before…' She stopped and blushed, an action so unlike her that he frowned.

'Tell me what?'

'I know I am ancient, but the thing is that I am still a virgin. I don't comprehend quite what you might want me to do though, as I've told you, I have read books and so I am not entirely unsullied…'

He brought his hand forward and ran a finger across her lower lip to stop the unending torrent of apprehension. She was nervous, for the skin on her arm had raised in to goosebumps.

'There is no right or wrong in making love, Annabelle. There is only truth.'

The air had changed around them now, from delight and joy to desire and need. Lytton could feel the blood thrum through his veins as he ran his finger down further across her chin and the long lines of her throat to rest on the rise of one breast covered in white silk.

The round firmness of it filled his palm and he flicked at her nipple, her head tilting back so that she closed her eyes, breathing with surprise and shock.

'It feels…hot.'

'And this?'

His hand pulled back the flimsy fabric and came in to the nakedness beneath. The hard bud of her grazed his skin and he took the firmness between one finger. 'Do you feel this?'

She only groaned in response.

'Or this?'

He had slipped the strap of her gown across her shoulders so that her breast was now visible and his mouth came around her, sucking gently.

Bright blue eyes flew open and her fingers came to rest upon his head.

'This is allowed?'

He laughed. 'This and so much more, my darling. Trust me.'

'I do.'

The sweetness of her answer tugged at him, her innocence and her purity. He had never once before made love to a virgin, for every woman he had bedded was well attuned in the ways of the joining of flesh.

This was different. Annabelle drove him wild even while he harnessed such a desperate need. She was soft and pliant and open and real. When his mouth fastened back on her lips he revelled in her.

His. The one word had his member standing firm against his thighs. He ached with the desire to possess her and he trembled with the necessity to take it slowly.

Drawing in breath, he pushed down the other strap so that the silken sheath fell in a pool to the ground. On her feet were silken slippers and in her hair were white gardenia buds, their scent beguiling and fragrant.

Fragrant like Annabelle with her dimples and her long dark hair, her swollen lips and the ivory of her skin whorled into redness by his mouth.

'Hell.' He couldn't keep his emotion in, the word surprising her.

* * *

Thorn was swearing again. Was there something wrong? Was there a flaw that she had never considered in her body, a defect that she had not understood before?

He looked heated and he was breathing quickly, his eyes darkened to a bruised brown and standing there before him, virtually unclothed while he was fully dressed, she suddenly felt…wicked.

Not wrong, no, not that, but revealing in a way that let him see right into her. Opening her legs, she tipped back her head, liking the feel of her hair heavy against the round of her bottom. A temptress. A siren. As far away from the careful and sensible Miss Annabelle Smith as she could have possibly come.

The sensuality of what was happening kept her still, her breath shallow even as all the parts inside her melted into feeling, sharp in one way and muted in another.

Take me, she wanted to say. Take me to the places I have only read about and let me know the magic between a man and a woman, between a husband and a wife.

The candles on the sideboard flickered, the scent of them heady. The grandfather clock in the corner struck the hour of six and a curtain billowed against the incoming breeze from an opened window letting in a slight but welcome breeze.

It slid across her body and Thorn laughed, his head coming down as he licked a trail where the zephyr had lingered, from navel to breast. The coldness left was almost painful and her breath banked. He would hurt her soon because all the books spoke of that. Ripped asunder and plundered. It was the way of men when they took. Her teeth began to chatter.

'Don't hurt me too much. Please.'

'Ah, sweetheart,' he replied and stood, unbuttoning the small garment that was left on her and peeling it away so that only nakedness remained, a single lacy garter at her thigh and a gold bracelet from her grandmother at her wrist.

With a soft, reassuring movement he opened her legs, her thighs spread against his hands, his fingers coming into the centre of her, a quiet intrusion, a small but determined assault. Then one was in her, up inside and joined with another. She felt the thickness of them and the stretching as they arched up deeper, his own body beginning to move against hers with the rhythm of his hand.

Not gentle now, but seeking. Her grasp came down to hold him there, her feelings growing wilder as he quickened. She could not breathe, could not move, could not escape from the plundering hardness, her heart thumping and the sweat building until there was nowhere left to go but up, up into trembling release, up into heaven and sweetness and relief. She could not stop her sounds, short guttural groans that made her breath swell and her stomach clench, hard inside, almost falling.

He simply picked her up then and took her to the bed, laying her down unresisting, the wetness on his fingers staining her skin with the musky smell of passion. Her own hand came to the place his had just been and the surprising wet made her gasp.

'It is your body welcoming mine, Annabelle. It is beautiful.'

He had taken off his shirt and his trousers followed, the fall unbuttoned and then gone. She had never seen a man before unclothed save in books, and flesh and blood was a lot more immediate than the marbled statues of ancient gods.

Scrambling up, she sat and he came in beside her, placing her hand upon him, so that she could feel the softness among the hard, familiarising her.

'It is just me, my love, ready for you. It might hurt a little at first, but then…' He stopped and she saw him swallow. 'But then we will fit. I promise it.'

Crossing his heart, he lifted her so that she sat astride him on his knee, a careful gentle lift. The tip of him rested in the place his fingers had been and then ventured deeper, stopping when the pain began.

'I love you.' His words were whispered against her cheek and he held her still, filling her, feeling her, helping her to understand the small and powerful questions of the flesh and waiting for a sign.

The throb of blood, the quickening beat of their hearts and this time when she moved he moved with her, in and out, deep and then deeper, the rush of lust, the answer to fear, the understanding of a reciprocal pleasure that bloomed deep between them.

Tipping her head, he looked straight into her eyes, their joining complete. 'Come with me, sweetheart. Come now.'

Another feeling rose. Not quiet. Not gentle. Not waiting. She rode him with her own need, pushing into fervour and intensity as waves of consummation crashed all around them, beaching on to the sands of love.

Complete. She felt as if her life had just begun in this second and as if every other moment before it had been leading to exactly this. She was spent and elated, she was exhausted and energised. She wanted to keep him inside her for all the hours of the night, beating in her, quenching the fire. There was no world around them save the one that was here and she never wanted to leave it.

'You are everything to me, Thorn.' The words were whispered as she kissed his neck. She wanted him again, violently. She wanted the feelings back, the power and the beauty.

He seemed to understand what it was she asked of him because he laid her down and then his mouth was there, his tongue, his breath, the softness of flesh and the urgency. Filled up with him her hand threaded through his hair and she moved, no rhythm now, but broken strokes and uneven.

When she climaxed this time she wondered

if she might lose consciousness altogether as she stopped breathing and simply felt.

He was a magician and she was his assistant, a lover of such prowess that she could not grasp the consequence. When he sat up he kissed her mouth and she could taste herself on him.

'I feel like a king,' he finally said. 'The king of happiness.'

She laughed and stretched. 'The king of lovers, too.'

'A king with a queen who takes my breath away. Thank you, Annabelle, for everything.'

'Will it always be like this? Making love?'

'I hope so. Perhaps it is particular just to us, this elation, because I have never felt it before.'

'Then I am glad.'

She felt the shake of his humour. Joy in the marriage bed, complete and perfect.

'Others will know what is between us because it will be impossible to hide.'

'And when they guess they will be happy for us. We have both been lonely for so long. Besides, Aurelian and Shay both have women who complete them and perhaps we might help Edward find the same when he returns to England next year.'

'Your inventor friend?'

'You will like him. He has the same sort of enquiring mind as you have.'

'My aunt would say the same of you, Thorn.'

'Alicia seems a lot happier now and healthier, too.'

'She wants to run the clinic in Whitechapel. Rose is going to help her and Milly, our kitchen maid in White Street, will be a part of it, for she has not enjoyed her new job at the tannery. I also want to be involved as much as I can be.'

'I never doubted it.' His smile was kind.

'That's another reason why I married you. You believe in me and support me. I don't know what might have happened if I had never met you. I might have been sad for ever.'

'We would have met, Annabelle. I'd have made sure of it.'

Epilogue

One and a half years later

They sat by the fire on a cold January evening, the snow thick outside and the sky stormy. Aurelian, Violet, Shay, Celeste and all their children had left that very afternoon, having spent the Christmas holidays up at Balmain. Edward Tully was still here, though he was often out in the evenings.

'Where does Ed go at night?' she asked Thorn dreamily, sitting in his arms on the thick rug in their bedchamber and watching the flames.

'To drown his sorrows, I think, down at the village tavern. He is lonely and lonelier still in the company of all of us. I remember feeling exactly the same before I met you and for some time after. Happiness seems so elusive when you do not have it.'

A noise to one side of the room had her turning. 'Sleep is elusive, too, my darling,' she replied very softly so that Harry did not waken. At eight months their son was full of energy, but a very light sleeper. They had taken to having his cot in their room much against everyone's wishes, but for them it felt right.

Thorn's hand cupped around her stomach, easily accessed under the nightdress she was wearing.

'And this new little one? I wonder who this will be?'

'Ours,' she replied and leaned back to kiss him, surprised as always by the passion his small touches engendered. One and a half years together and the magic just kept on growing so that she felt the luckiest woman in all the world.

His family had come to Balmain this year and though she had always been close to Lucy, his mother, too, was beginning to thaw. Alicia had had her part in that, too, and Annalena as well, for the three of them had formed a close friendship and were often seen together talking.

A family.

All the pieces of it disparate, but forming a whole that was comforting and strong.

'Annalena had a letter from Huntington the other day.'

She felt him tense.

'He asks if perhaps he might visit us in the summer. He regrets all the things that he has done and wishes to make amends.'

'Is your grandmother happy with him coming?'

'She is. He has not been well and I think she worries for him.'

'And how do you feel, Annabelle?'

'He is my cousin. He should have a second chance.'

His arms folded around her, bringing her in closer, and she smiled. This was how life was supposed to be lived, with joy, hope and forgiveness. Passion, too, was a part of it and, turning, she slipped the nightgown from her shoulders and watched his eyes as the fire played over her breasts.

'My beautiful Countess,' he said as his mouth came upon her.

* * * * *

MILLS & BOON

Coming next month

HIS CONVENIENT HIGHLAND BRIDE
Janice Preston

Lachlan McNeill couldn't quite believe his good fortune when he first saw his bride, Lady Flora McCrieff, walking up the aisle towards him on her father's arm. Her posture was upright and correct and her figure was... delectable. The tight bodice and sleeves of her wedding gown—her figure tightly laced in accordance with fashion—accentuated her full breasts, slender arms and tiny waist above the wide bell of her skirt. She was tiny, dwarfed by her father's solid, powerful frame, and she barely reached Lachlan's shoulder when they stood side by side in front of the minister. True, he had not yet seen his new bride's face—her figure might be all he could wish for, but was there a nasty surprise lurking yet? Maybe her features were somehow disfigured? Or maybe she was a shrew? Why else had her father refused to let them meet before their wedding day? He'd instead insisted on riding over to Lochmore Castle, Lachlan's new home, to agree the marriage settlements.

Their vows exchanged, Lachlan raised Flora's veil, bracing himself for some kind of abomination. His chest loosened with relief as she stared up at him, her green eyes huge and wary under auburn brows, the freckles that speckled her nose and cheeks stark against the pallor of her skin. His finger caught a loose, silken tendril of coppery-red hair and her face flooded pink, her lower lip trembling, drawing his gaze as the scent of orange blossom wreathed his senses.

She is gorgeous.

Heat sizzled through him, sending blood surging to his loins as he found himself drawn into the green depths of her eyes, his senses in disarray. Then he took her hand to place it on his arm and its delicacy, its softness, its fragility sent waves of doubt crashing through him, sluicing him clean of lustful thoughts as he sucked air into his lungs.

He had never imagined he'd be faced with one so young…so dainty…so captivating…and her beauty and her purity brought into sharp focus his own dirty, sordid past. Next to her he felt a clumsy, uncultured oaf.

What could he and this pampered young lady ever have in common? She might accept his fortune, but could she ever truly accept the man behind the façade? He'd faced rejection over his past before and he'd already decided that the less his wife ever learned about that past, the better.

Continue reading
HIS CONVENIENT HIGHLAND BRIDE
Janice Preston

Available next month
www.millsandboon.co.uk

COMING SOON!

We really hope you enjoyed reading this book. If you're looking for more romance, be sure to head to the shops when new books are available on

Thursday 21st March

To see which titles are coming soon, please visit
millsandboon.co.uk/nextmonth

PATRICK O'BRIAN

The Far Side of the World

HarperCollins*Publishers*

HarperCollins*Publishers*,
77–85 Fulham Palace Road,
Hammersmith, London W6 8JB

This paperback edition 1994
3 5 7 9 8 6 4

Previously published in paperback by Fontana 1985
Reprinted six times

First published in Great Britain by
Collins 1984

Copyright © Patrick O'Brian 1984

Patrick O'Brian asserts the moral right to
be identified as the author of this work

ISBN 0 00 617017 X

Set in Imprint

Printed in Great Britain by
HarperCollinsManufacturing Glasgow

AUTHOR'S NOTE

Perhaps few authors are wholly original as far as their plots are concerned; indeed Shakespeare seems to have invented almost nothing, while Chaucer borrowed from both the living and the dead. And to come down to a somewhat different plane, the present writer is even more derivative, since for these books he has in general kept most doggedly to recorded actions, nourishing his fancy with log-books, dispatches, letters, memoirs, and contemporary reports. But general appropriation is not quite the same thing as downright plagiary, and in passing it must be confessed that the description of a storm's first aspect on p. 308 is taken straight from William Hickey, whose words did not seem capable of improvement.

If these tales are to continue, however, it is clear that the writer will soon have originality thrust upon him, for he is running short of history. Some ten or eleven years ago a respectable American publisher suggested that he should write a book about the Royal Navy of Nelson's time; he was happy to agree, since both the period and the subject were congenial, and he quickly produced the first of this series, a novel based upon Lord Cochrane's early days in command of the *Speedy*, which provided him with one of the most spectacular single-ship actions of the war as well as a mass of authentic detail. But had the writer known how much pleasure he was to take in this kind of writing, and how many books were to follow the first, he would certainly have started the sequence much earlier. For the 14-gun *Speedy* did not capture the 32-gun *Gamo* until 1801 and this was followed by the ill-judged

Peace of Amiens, which left enterprising sailors less time to distinguish themselves than they could have wished and deprived later writers of a great deal of raw material. Historical time has not yet run out for these tales, and in the present book the naval historian will detect an echo of HMS *Phoebe*'s pursuit of the USN *Essex*; but even in the early nineteenth century the year contained only twelve months, and it is possible that in the near future the author (if his readers will bear with him) may be led to make use of hypothetical years, rather like those hypothetical moons used in the calculation of Easter: an 1812a as it were or even an 1812b.

Yet if he should do so it will be strict chronology alone that is affected; he will continue to respect historical accuracy and speak of the Royal Navy as it was, making use of contemporary documents: the reader will meet no basilisks that destroy with their eyes, no Hottentots without religion, polity, or articulate language, no Chinese perfectly polite, and completely skilled in all sciences, no wholly virtuous, ever-victorious or necessarily immortal heroes; and should any crocodiles appear, he undertakes that they shall devour their prey without tears.

CHAPTER ONE

'Pass the word for Captain Aubrey, pass the word for Captain Aubrey,' cried a sequence of voices, at first dim and muffled far aft on the flagship's maindeck, then growing louder and more distinct as the call wafted up to the quarterdeck and so along the gangway to the forecastle, where Captain Aubrey stood by the starboard thirty-two-pounder carronade contemplating the Emperor of Morocco's purple galley as it lay off Jumper's Bastion with the vast grey and tawny Rock of Gibraltar soaring behind it, while Mr Blake, once a puny member of his midshipman's berth but now a tall, stout lieutenant almost as massive as his former captain, explained the new carriage he had invented, a carriage that should enable carronades to fire twice as fast, with no fear of oversetting, twice as far, and with perfect accuracy, thus virtually putting an end to war.

Only a flag-officer could 'pass the word' for a post-captain, and Jack Aubrey had been dreading the summons ever since the *Caledonia* came in, a little after dawn: within minutes of receiving it he would have to tell the Commander-in-Chief how it came about that his orders had not been obeyed. Seeing that Aubrey's small, elderly, but sweet-sailing frigate *Surprise* was to return from Malta to England, there to be laid up or sold out of the service or even sent to the breaker's yard, Admiral Sir Francis Ives, the Commander-in-Chief, Mediterranean, had directed him to go by way of Zambra on the Barbary Coast, there to reason with the Dey of Mascara, the ruler of those parts, who showed a tendency to side with the French and who had uttered threats of hostile action if he were not given an enormous sum of money: if the Dey proved stubborn, Aubrey was

9

to embark the British consul and to tell his Highness that the instant any of these threats were carried into action, all ships bearing the Mascarene flag should be seized, burnt, sunk, or otherwise destroyed, and the Dey's ports blocked up. Aubrey was to sail in company with the *Pollux*, an even older sixty-gun ship that was carrying Rear-Admiral Harte back to England as a passenger, but the mission to the Dey was his alone; and having accomplished it he was to report to the Commander-in-Chief at Gibraltar. It seemed to him a fairly straightforward assignment, particularly as he had an unusually well qualified political adviser in his surgeon, Dr Maturin, and off the mouth of Zambra Bay he left the *Pollux* with an easy mind, or at least with a mind as easy as was right in one who had spent most of his life on the sea, that dangerous, utterly unreliable element, with nothing but a plank between him and eternity.

But they had been betrayed. At some point the Commander-in-Chief's plan had become known to the enemy and a French ship of the line together with two frigates appeared from the windward, in evident collusion with the Mascarenes; the Dey's forts had fired on the *Surprise*; and in the subsequent activity Aubrey had neither had an interview with the ruler nor embarked Mr Consul Eliot. The *Pollux*, closely engaged by the French eighty-gun ship, had blown up with the loss of all hands, and although by her brilliant sailing qualities the *Surprise* had run clear, Jack Aubrey had in fact accomplished nothing of what he had been sent to do. To be sure, he could represent that in the course of the manoeuvres he had wrecked a heavy French frigate by luring her over a reef, and that the *Pollux* had so mauled her adversary in the fight and had so shattered her in blowing up that there was little likelihood of her ever regaining Toulon; but he had nothing tangible to show, and although he was satisfied in his own mind that materially the Royal Navy had gained rather than lost by the encounter he was by no means sure that the Commander-in-Chief would see it in the same light. And he was all the more uneasy since adverse winds had delayed his run from Zambra Bay to Gibraltar, where he had expected to find the Commander-in-Chief, and since he could not tell whether the boats he had sent off to Malta and Port Mahon had reached the Admiral in time for him to deal with the crippled Frenchman. Sir Francis had an alarming reputation, not only as a rigid disciplinarian and a right Tartar, but also as one who would break an erring subordinate without compunction. It was also known that Sir Francis longed for victory even more than most commanders-in-chief: for evident, positive victory that would please public opinion and even more the present ministry, the effective source of honours. How the Zambra action would appear in this respect Jack could not decide. 'Another couple of minutes will tell me, however,' he said to himself as he hurried aft in the wake of a nervous, inaudible youngster, keeping his best white tights and silk stockings well clear of the buckets of pitch that were carrying forward.

But he was mistaken: the call had originated in the other flag-officer aboard, the Captain of the Fleet, who was confined to his cabin by the present bout of influenza but who wished Jack to know that his wife had taken a house no great way from Ashgrove Cottage, and that she should be very happy in Mrs Aubrey's acquaintance. Their children were much of the same age, he said; and then, they being fond parents and long, long from home, each gave the other a pretty detailed account of his brood, while the Captain of the Fleet showed his daughters' birthday letters, received some two months ago, and a little scrubby rat-gnawn pen-wiper, the work of his eldest's unaided hand.

During this time the Commander-in-Chief himself carried on with what was left of his paper-work, a task that he had begun just after sunrise. 'This to Captain Lewis, and his damn-fool words about an enquiry,' he said. ' "Sir, Your letter has not contributed in the

11

smallest degree to alter the opinion I had formed of your having determined to avail yourself of this influenza to get the *Gloucester* again into port. The most serious charge made against you is the savage rudeness offered to Dr Harrington on the quarterdeck of the *Gloucester*, wholly unbecoming the character of her commander and particularly reprehensible in the desponding state in which your improper conduct has placed the crew of His Majesty's ship under your command. If you continue to court enquiry in the style of the letter I am replying to, it will come sooner than you are aware of. I am, Sir, your most obedient servant." Damned rogue, to try to bully me.' The two clerks made no reply to this, but kept their pens plying fast, the one on a fair copy of the previous letter, the other on a rough of this, though the other inhabitants of the great cabin, Mr Yarrow, the Admiral's secretary, and Mr Pocock, his political adviser, responded with a 'Tut, tut, tut'.

'To Captain Bates,' said Sir Francis, as soon as one pen had stopped squeaking. ' "Sir, The very disorderly state of His Majesty's ship under your command, obliges me to require that neither yourself nor any of your officers are to go on shore on what is called pleasure. I am, Sir, etc." And now a memorandum. "There being reason to apprehend that a number of women have been clandestinely brought from England in several ships, more particularly so in those which have arrived in the Mediterranean in this last and the present year, the respective captains are required by the Admiral to admonish those ladies upon the waste of water, and other disorders committed by them, and to make known to all, that on the first proof of water being obtained for washing from the scuttle-butt or otherwise, under false pretences, every woman in the fleet who had not been admitted under the authority of the Admiralty or the Commander-in-Chief, will be shipped for England by the first convoy, and the officers are strictly enjoined to watch vigilantly their behaviour, and to see that no

12

waste or improper consumption of water happen in the future." ' He turned to the second clerk, now ready to write. 'To the respective captains: "The Admiral having observed a flippancy in the behaviour of officers when coming upon the *Caledonia*'s quarterdeck, and sometimes in receiving orders from a superior officer, and that they do not pull off their hats, and some not even touch them: it is his positive direction, that any officer who shall in future so forget this essential duty of respect and subordination, be admonished publicly; and he expects the officers of the *Caledonia* will set the example by taking off their hats, and not touch them with an air of negligence." ' To Mr Pocock he observed, 'The young people now coming up are for the most part frippery and gimcrack. I wish we could revive the old school,' and then continued, ' "To the respective captains: the Commander-in-Chief having seen several officers of the fleet on shore dressed like shop-keepers, in coloured clothes, and others wearing round hats, with their uniforms, in violation of the late order from the Right Honourable the Lords Commissioners of the Admiralty, does positively direct, that any officer offending against this wholesome and necessary regulation in future, is put under arrest, and reported to the Admiral, and, let the sentence of a court-martial upon such offenders be what it may, that he is never permitted to go ashore while under the command of Sir Francis Ives." '

While the pens flew on he picked up a letter and said to Mr Pocock, 'Here is J.S. begging me to intercede with the Royal Bird again. I wonder at it: and I cannot but think that this form of application must end ill. I wonder at it, I say; for surely, with such a high mind and unrivalled pretensions, a peerage is an object beneath him.'

Mr Pocock was a little embarrassed to reply, particularly as he knew that the clerks, in spite of their busy pens, were listening intently; for it was common knowledge throughout the fleet that Sir Francis longed to be a

13

lord, thus rivalling his brothers, and that he had fought with unparalleled fury for the Mediterranean command, as the most likely means to that end. 'Perhaps . . .' he began, but he was interrupted by a scream of barbarous trumpets close at hand, and stepping over to the stern-gallery he said, 'Bless me, the Emperor's envoy has put off already.'

'God damn and blast the man,' cried the Admiral, looking angrily at the clock. 'Let him go and . . . no: we must not offend the Moors. I shall not have time for Aubrey. Pray tell him so, Mr Yarrow – make my excuses – force majeure – do the civil thing – bid him to dinner and let him bring Dr Maturin; or let them come tomorrow morning, if that don't suit.'

It did not suit. Aubrey was infinitely concerned, but it was not in his power to dine with the Commander-in-Chief today; he was already engaged, engaged to a lady. At Jack's first words to Mr Yarrow the Captain of the Fleet's eyebrows shot up under his nightcap; at his last, the only excuse that in a naval context could acquit him of being a wicked contumelious discontented froward mutinous dog, the eyebrows reappeared in their usual place and the Captain of the Fleet said, 'I wish I were engaged to dine with a lady. I may draw a rear-admiral's pay, but I have not seen one, apart from the bosun's wife, since Malta; and what with this damned influenza and having to give an example I do not suppose I shall see another until we drop anchor in the Grand Harbour again, alas. There is something wonderfully comfortable about having a lady's legs under one's table, Aubrey.'

In principle Aubrey was all agreement: by land he was quite devoted to women – indeed, his devotion had very nearly been his undoing before this – and he dearly loved to have their legs under his table. But in the case of these particular legs (an uncommonly elegant pair) and of this particular dinner, his mind was far from easy: in fact uneasiness of one sort or another fairly crammed his mind today, leaving little room for its usual cheerfulness.

14

He had given Laura Fielding, the lady in question, a lift from Valletta to Gibraltar, and in ordinary circumstances it was a perfectly usual thing to carry a fellow-officer's wife from one port to another. These circumstances however were very far from ordinary: Mrs Fielding, an Italian lady with dark red hair, had appeared in the middle of a midnight downpour with no baggage, under the protection of Stephen Maturin, who offered no explanation of her presence, only observing that in Captain Aubrey's name he had promised her a passage to Gibraltar. Jack knew very well that his intimate friend Maturin was deeply concerned with naval and political intelligence and he asked no questions, accepting the situation as a necessary evil. But as a very considerable evil, since rumour had connected Jack's name with Laura's at a time when her husband was a prisoner of war in the hands of the French: yet in this instance rumour was mistaken, for although Jack was at one point very willing to give it consistency Laura was not. Nevertheless the rumour had reached the Adriatic, and there the escaping husband, Lieutenant Charles Fielding of the Navy, had met it aboard HMS *Nymphe*; and being of an intensely jealous nature had believed it at once. He had followed the *Surprise* to Gibraltar, landing from the *Hecla* bomb the night before. On hearing the news Jack had at once sent the pair an invitation to dinner the next day; but in spite of Laura's kind note of acceptance he was by no means convinced that he might not have an exceedingly awkward situation on his hands at half past two o'clock, when he was to receive his guests at Reid's hotel.

Landing at the Ragged Staff a little before noon he sent his barge back to the *Surprise*, with very unnecessarily repeated instructions to his coxswain about the rig, the cleanliness and the promptitude of those hands who were to assist at the dinner; for the Navy, though often reduced to salt horse and hard tack, ate it in style, every officer and guest having a servant behind

15

his chair, a style that few hotels could equal. Then, observing that the Parade was almost empty, he walked along towards the Alameda gardens, meaning to sit on the bench under the dragon-tree; he did not choose to return to his ship at present, for not only was it painful to him to see her, knowing that she was condemned, but in spite of his efforts the news of her fate had spread and sadness with it, so that the *Joyful Surprise*, as she was known in the service, was now but a dismal place. The tight, well-knit community of some two hundred men was about to fall apart, and he reflected upon the pity of it, the waste – a hand-picked crew of able seamen, many of whom had sailed with him for years and some, like his coxswain, his steward, and four of his bargemen, ever since his first command – they were used to one another, used to their officers – a ship's company in which punishment was extremely rare and where discipline did not have to be imposed since it came naturally – while for gunnery and seamanship he did not know their equal – and this invaluable body of men was to be dispersed among a score of ships or even, in the case of the officers, thrown on shore, unemployed, simply because the five-hundred-ton, twenty-eight-gun *Surprise* was too small a frigate for modern requirements. Instead of being reinforced and moved as a whole to a larger ship, such as the thousand-ton, thirty-eight-gun *Blackwater* that Jack had been promised, the crew was to be scattered; while the promise had gone the way of so many promises. The influential Captain Irby had been given the *Blackwater*, and Jack, whose affairs were in a state of horrible confusion, had no certainty whatsoever of another ship, no certainty of anything at all but half-pay of half a guinea a day and a mountain of debt. Just how high a mountain he could not tell, for all his skill in navigation and astronomy, since several lawyers were concerned, each with a different notion of the case or rather cases. These thoughts were interrupted by a cough and a diffident 'Captain Aubrey, sir. Good day to you.' Looking up he saw a tall thin man of between thirty and forty with his hat raised from his head. He was wearing naval uniform, the threadbare uniform of a midshipman, its white patches yellow in the sun. 'You do not remember me, sir: my name is Hollom, and I had the honour of serving under you in *Lively*.'

Of course. Jack had been acting-captain of the *Lively* for a few months at the beginning of the war, and in the early days of his command he had seen something of a not very efficient, not very enterprising midshipman of that name, a passed midshipman with the rating of master's mate: not a great deal, since Hollom, falling sick, had soon removed to the hospital ship, not particularly regretted by anyone except perhaps the schoolmaster, another elderly passed midshipman, and the grey-haired captain's clerk, who formed a little mess of their own, well away from the more usual and more turbulent midshipmen in their teens. As far as Jack could remember there was no vice in Hollom, but there was no obvious merit either; he was the kind of midshipman who had not improved in his profession, who had no evident zeal for seamanship or gunnery or navigation and no gift for dealing with men, the kind of midshipman that captains were happy to pass on. Long before Jack first met him, a good-humoured board had passed Hollom as fit for a lieutenant's commission; but the commission itself had never appeared. This happened often enough to young men with no particular abilities, or no patron or family to speak for them, but whereas most of these unfortunates bore up after a few years and either applied for a master's warrant if their mathematics and navigation were good enough, or left the service altogether, Hollom and a good many others like him went on hoping until it was too late to make any change, so that they remained perpetual mids, perpetual young gentlemen, with an income of about thirty pounds a year when they could find a captain to admit them to his quarterdeck and nothing at all if they could not, midshipmen having no half-pay. Theirs was perhaps the most unenviable position in the whole service and Jack pitied them extremely: nevertheless he hardened his heart against the request that was sure to come – a forty-year-old could not possibly fit into his midshipman's berth. Besides, it was evident that Hollom was an unlucky man, one that would bring bad luck to the ship; the crew, an intensely superstitious set of men, would dislike him and perhaps treat him with disrespect, which would mean starting the hateful round of punishment and resentment all over again.

It was clear from Hollom's account of himself that he was finding more and more captains of this opinion: his last ship, *Leviathan*, had paid off seven months ago, and he had come out to Gibraltar in the hope either of a death-vacancy or a meeting with one of his many former commanders who might be in need of an experienced master's mate. Neither had occurred and now Hollom was at his last extremity.

'I am very sorry to say so, but I am afraid it is quite impossible for me to find room for you on my quarterdeck,' said Jack. 'In any case, there would be no point in it, since the ship will be paying off in the next few weeks.'

'Even a few weeks would be infinitely welcome, sir,' cried Hollom with a ghastly sprightliness: then, clutching at a straw he added, 'I should be happy to sling my hammock before the mast, sir, if you would enter me as able.'

'No, no, Hollom, it would not do,' said Jack, shaking his head. 'But here is a fi'pun note, to be repaid out of your next prize-money, if it would prove useful to you.'

'You are very good, sir,' said Hollom, clasping his hands behind his back, 'but I am not . . .' What he was not never appeared; his face, still retaining something of its artificial sprightly expression, twitched oddly, and Jack dreaded a burst of tears. 'However, I am obliged for your kind intention. Good day to you, sir.'

'God damn it, God damn it,' said Jack to himself

18

as Hollom walked away, looking unnaturally stiff. 'This is infernal goddam blackmail.' And then aloud, 'Mr Hollom, Mr Hollom, there.' He wrote in his pocket-book, tore out the page, and said, 'Report aboard the *Surprise* for duty before noon and show this to the officer of the watch.'

A hundred yards farther on he met Captain Sutton of the *Namur*, Billy Sutton, a very old friend, since they had been youngsters together in HMS *Resolution*. 'Lord, Billy,' cried Jack, 'I never thought to see you here – I never saw *Namur* come in. Where is she?'

'She is blockading Toulon, poor old soul, and Ponsonby is looking after her for me. I was returned for Rye in the by-election. Stopford is running me home in his yacht.'

Jack congratulated him, and after some words about Parliament, yachts, and acting-captains Sutton said, 'You look most uncommon hipped, Jack; like a cat that has lost its kittens.'

'I dare say I do. *Surprise* is ordered home, you know, to be laid up or broke, and I have spent some truly miserable weeks, making preparations, fobbing off whole boatloads of people who want a lift for themselves or their families or friends. And not five minutes ago I did a very foolish thing, clean against my principles: I took a middle-aged master's mate off the shore because he looked so goddam thin, poor devil. It was mere senti-mentality, mere silly indulgence. It will do him no good in the end; he will be neither grateful nor useful, and he will corrupt my youngsters and upset the hands. He has Jonah written all over his face. Thank Heaven the *Caledonia* is in at last. I can make my report and be away as soon as my launch returns from Mahon, before anyone else comes aboard. The port-admiral has tried to foist a number of horrible creatures on to me, and to take away all my best men by one dirty trick or another. I have resisted pretty well so far; after all, the ship may come into action between this and the Channel, and I should like her to do herself credit; but even so . . .'

'That was a sad business in Zambra Bay, Jack,' said Sutton, who had not been attending.

'It was, indeed,' said Jack, shaking his head; then after a moment, 'You know about it, then?'

'Of course I do. Your launch found the vice-admiral at Port Mahon, and he sent *Alacrity* away for the C-in-C off Toulon directly.'

'How I hope she reached him in time. With any luck he should be able to snap up the big Frenchman. There was something very dirty about that affair, you know, Billy. We sailed straight into a trap.'

'So everyone says. And a returning victualler spoke of a great turmoil in Valletta – some high civilian cutting his throat and half a dozen people shot. But it was all at second or third hand.'

'There was no news of my cutter, I suppose? I sent it off for Malta with my second lieutenant as soon as the wind came right round into her teeth, so there was no hope of fetching Gibraltar for a great while.'

'Not that I have heard. But I do know your launch was put aboard the *Berwick*, since she was to rendezvous with the C-in-C here. We sailed in company until yesterday evening, when she carried away her foretopmast in a squall, and as Bennet dared not face the Admiral until everything was perfectly shipshape, he signalled to us to go ahead. But with the wind veering like this,' said Sutton, glancing at the high ridge of Gibraltar, 'he will be backstrapped, if he don't mend his pace.'

'Billy,' said Jack, 'you know the Admiral far better than I do. Is he indeed still so very savage?'

'Pretty savage,' said Sutton. 'Have you heard what he did to the midshipman that looted the privateer?'

'Not I.'

'Well, some boats from the squadron boarded a Gibraltar privateer, found her papers all in order, and left her in peace. Some time later a midshipman belonging to the *Cambridge*, a big hairy sixteen-year-old who loved to be popular with the hands, went back and made them give him and his boat's crew porter, and then, having lost his wits entirely I suppose, he put on the master's blue jacket with a silver watch in its pocket and walked off laughing. The master complained and it was found in his hammock. I sat on the court-martial.'

'Dismissed the service, I suppose?'

'No, no: not so lucky. The sentence was "to be degraded from the rank of midshipman in the most ignominious manner, by having his uniform stripped from his back on the quarterdeck of the *Cambridge*, and to be mulcted of the pay now due to him,' and it was to be read out aboard every ship in the command – you would have come in for it if you had not been in Zambra. But that was not enough. Sir Francis wrote to Scott of the *Cambridge*, and I saw the letter: "Sir, You are hereby required and directed to carry out the sentence of the court-martial on Albert Tompkins. And you are to cause his head to be shaved, and a label affixed to his back, expressive of the disgraceful crime he has committed. And he is to be employed as the constant scavenger for cleaning the head, until my further orders." '

'Good God,' cried Jack, reflecting upon the head of an eighty-gun ship of the line, a common jakes or privy for more than five hundred men. 'Was the wretched boy of any family, any education?'

'The son of a lawyer in Malta, Tompkins of the Admiralty court.'

They took some steps in silence, and then Sutton said, 'I should have told you that the *Berwick* has your former premier aboard, too, the one who was promoted for your action with the Turk, going home to try to find himself a ship, poor fellow.'

'Pullings,' said Jack. 'How happy I shall be to see him – never was such a first lieutenant. But as for a ship . . .' They both shook their heads, knowing that the Navy had more than six hundred commanders and not half that number of sloops, the only vessels they could command. 'I hope she has her chaplain aboard as well,' said Jack. 'A one-eyed parson by the name of Martin, a very fine fellow and a great friend of my surgeon.' He hesitated for a moment and then said, 'Billy, would you do me the kindness of dining with me? I have rather a difficult party this afternoon and a witty cove like you rattling away would be a great advantage. I am no great fist at conversation, as you know, and Maturin has an awkward way of turning as mum as an oyster if the subject don't interest him.'

'What kind of party is it?' asked Sutton.

'Did you ever meet Mrs Fielding in Valletta?'

'The beautiful Mrs Fielding that gives Italian lessons?' asked Sutton, cocking an eye at Jack. 'Yes, of course.'

'Well, I gave her a lift to Gibraltar: but because of some silly rumours – false, Billy, false upon my honour, completely false – it seems that her husband conceived some suspicion of me. It is the Fieldings that are coming to dinner, and although her note assured me they should be delighted to come, yet I still feel that a source of sparkling repartee would not come amiss. Lord, Billy, I have heard you address the electors of Hampshire in the most fearless way – jokes, badinage, anecdotes, topics – why, it was almost eloquence.'

Captain Aubrey's fears were unfounded. Between her husband's arrival yesterday evening and the hour of dinner, Laura Fielding had found means of convincing him of her perfect fidelity and unvarying attachment, and he came forward with an open smiling expression on his face to shake Jack's hand and to thank him again for his kindness to Laura. Yet even so Captain Sutton's presence was by no means unwelcome. Both Jack and Stephen, who were very fond of Mrs Fielding, felt uneasy in her husband's presence; neither could understand what she saw in him – a heavy, dark man with a thick forehead and small deep-set eyes – and they both resented her obvious fondness. It somewhat diminished her in their opinion,

22

and neither felt so strong an inclination for social effort as they had before; while for his part Fielding, once he had given a bald account of his escape from a French prison, had no more to say, but sat there smiling and fondling his wife under the table-cloth.

It was now that Sutton proved his worth. His chief qualification as a Member of Parliament was an ability to speak at great length in a smiling, cheerful way upon almost any subject, urging universally admitted truths with the utmost candour and good nature; he was also capable of reciting bills and other Members' speeches by heart with perfect accuracy; and he was of course a defender of the Navy in the House and out of it, whenever the service was adversely criticized in any way.

At the first remove Laura Fielding, who was perfectly aware of her husband's limits and of her admirers' feelings, tried to revive the conversation (now grown monstrously insipid) by crying out against the Commander-in-Chief for his treatment of the wretched Albert Tompkins, who was the son of an acquaintance of hers in Valletta, a lady whose heart would be broken when she heard of her boy's hair, 'which fell in such lovely curls, scarcely needing the tongs at all.' Sir Francis was worse than Attila; he was a bear, a worthless.

'Oh come, ma'am,' said Sutton. 'He may be a little strict at times, but where should we be if all midshipmen wore their hair like Absalom and spent all their leisure stealing silver watches? In the first place they could scarcely go aloft without danger, and in the second the service would fall into sad disrepute. And in any event, Sir Francis is capable of great kindness, astonishing magnanimity, Jovian lenience. You remember my cousin Cumby, Jack?'

'Cumby of the *Bellerophon*, that was posted after Trafalgar?'

'The very man. Now, ma'am, some years ago, when Sir Francis was C-in-C before Cadiz and when there was a great deal of murmuring and discontent in the fleet, with undisciplined and even half-mutinous ships coming out from the Channel, Sir Francis ordered the Marines to parade at ten every morning aboard every line of battle ship – anthem played – arms presented – everyone present – all hats off – and he always attended himself in full-dress uniform, blue and gold: all this to promote discipline and a sense of order, which it did effectually. Once, I remember, the captain of the maintop forgot himself and kept his hat on after the anthem had begun: Sir Francis had him flogged out of hand, and after that all heads were as bare as the palm of my hand. But young men are sometimes thoughtless ma'am; for as Friar Bacon said, you cannot expect *old* heads on *young* shoulders; and my cousin wrote an irreverent skit on the C-in-C and the ceremony.'

'So he did, the dog,' said Jack, laughing with pleasurable anticipation.

'And somebody took a copy of the skit and conveyed it to the Admiral, who invited my cousin to dinner. Cumby had not the least notion of what was afoot until the end of the meal, when a tall chair was brought in and the Admiral bade him sit in it and read *that* to the assembled company, all of 'em flag-officers or post-captains. Poor Cumby was dumb-founded, as you may imagine; but however there was no help for it, and when the Admiral said "Sing out" again in a stern voice, he began. Shall I repeat it, Jack?'

'Aye, do. That is to say, if it would not be disagreeable to Mrs Fielding.'

'Not at all, sir,' said Laura. 'I should very much like to hear it.'

Sutton took a draught of wine, straightened himself in his chair, and adopting a pulpit voice he began, 'The First Lesson for the morning's service is part of the third chapter of Discipline.

1. Sir Francis Ives, the Commander-in-Chief, made an image of blue and gold, whose height was about

24

five feet seven inches, and the breadth thereof was about twenty inches. He set it up every ten o'clock, on the quarterdeck of the *Queen Charlotte*, before Cadiz.

2. Then Sir Francis Ives, the Commander-in-Chief, sent to call together the Captain, the officers, the parson, the seamen, and the Marines, to come to the dedication of the image which Sir Francis Ives, the Commander-in-Chief, had set up.

3. Then the Captain, the officers, the parson, the seamen, and the Marines, were gathered together, unto the dedication of the image which Sir Francis Ives had set up; and they stood before the image which Sir Francis Ives had set up.

4. Then the Captain cried aloud, To you it is commanded, O officers, parson, seamen, and Marines, that at what time ye hear the sound of the trumpet, the flute, the horn, the clarionet, the drum, the fife, and all kinds of music, ye take off your hats, and worship the blue and golden image that Sir Francis Ives, the Commander-in-Chief, hath set up; and whoso taketh not off his hat and worshippeth, shall be surely visited with the Commander-in-Chief's displeasure.

5. Therefore, at that time, when all the people heard the sound of the trumpet, the flute, the horn, the clarionet, the drum, the fife, and all kinds of music, they took their hats off and worshipped the blue and golden image which Sir Francis Ives, the Commander-in-Chief, had set up.

6. Wherefore, one morning after that time, a certain officer drew near, and accused a thoughtless thoroughbred seaman.

7. He spake, and said to Sir Francis Ives, O, Commander-in-Chief, live for ever!

8. Thou, O Commander-in-Chief, hast made a decree that every man that shall hear the sound of the trumpet, the flute, the horn, the clarionet, the drum, the fife, and all kinds of music, shall take his hat off and worship the blue and golden image; and whoso taketh not off his

hat and worshippeth, shall be surely visited with thy displeasure.

9. There is a certain seaman whom thou hast made a petty officer, and hast set over the affairs of the maintop: this man, O Commander-in-Chief, regarded not thee this morning: he took not off his hat and worshipped the image thou settest up.

10. Sir Francis Ives, in his rage, commanded to bring the captain of the maintop. Then they brought this man before the Commander-in-Chief.

11. Then was Sir Francis Ives full of fury, and the form of his visage was changed, against the poor captain of the maintop.

12. Therefore he spake, and commanded that they should rig the grating, read the Articles of War, and call the boatswain's mates; and commanded the boatswain's mates to take their thief's cat-o'-nine-tails.

13. And he commanded the most mighty men that were in his ship to seize up and bind the captain of the maintop, and that he should be punished with one dozen lashes.

14. Then the captain of the maintop, in his trousers, his hosen, and his shoes, but without his jacket and his shirt, was bound up to the grating, and was flogged with one dozen lashes.

15. Then was the captain of the maintop sore at the displeasure of Sir Francis Ives, the Commander-in-Chief.

Here endeth the First Lesson. And now, ma'am,' said Sutton, speaking more like a human being again, 'I come to my point, because when Cumby reached the last piece, the Admiral, who had been as grim as a hanging judge all this time, and all the other officers too, burst out in a roar of laughter, told my cousin to take three months' leave in England, and ordered him to dine aboard the flagship the day he returned. That is my point, do you see – Sir Francis can be savage or he can be kind, and there is no telling which.'

* * *

26

'There is no telling which,' said Jack Aubrey to himself as the barge carried him over the water to the flagship fairly early the next morning. His signal had not been thrown out at the Commander-in-Chief's usual unearthly hour, for the *Avon* had come in at dawn with dispatches: and with mail, including a well-filled sack for the *Surprise*. Her captain's share of the letters, or to be more exact the share that dealt with business, made it clear that it was essential that he should get a ship – preferably a frigate with a chance of prize-money – to be able to cope with the situation at home; so Sir Francis' opinion of him was now even more important than it had been before. The other letters, those from Sophie and the children, he had in his pocket, to read again while he was waiting for the Admiral.

Bonden, steering the barge, gave a significant cough, and Jack, following his eye, saw the *Edinburgh* standing in, a ship commanded by Heneage Dundas, Jack's particular friend. He glanced at Stephen, but Stephen was deep in his own thoughts, grave and withdrawn. He too had letters in his pocket for further reading. One was from his wife, Diana, who had heard an absurd story of his having a very public affair with a red-haired Italian woman: it must be absurd, she said, because Stephen could not but know that if he publicly humiliated her before people of their own world, then she would resent it very bitterly indeed. She did not set up as a moralist of any kind, she said, but she would not stomach an open affront from anyone on earth, man, woman, or freemartin. 'I shall have to deal with this directly,' said Stephen, who knew that his wife, though uncommonly good-looking, was also uncommonly passionate and determined.

Other letters were from Sir Joseph Blaine, the chief of naval intelligence, and the first, written officially, congratulated 'his dear Maturin' upon what he described as 'this brilliant coup', hoping that it would lead to the complete elimination of French agents in Malta. For a long while English moves in the Mediterranean and on its African and Asian shores had been countered by the French almost before they were made and it was clear that secret information was being sent from Malta to France. The position was so serious that the Admiralty had sent its acting Second Secretary, Mr Wray, to look into it; but the coup in question was Maturin's independent discovery of the chief French agent in Valletta and his principal colleague or accomplice, a senior official in the British administration, a Channel Islander by the name of Boulay, a man very well placed for learning facts, plans and movements of the first importance to the enemy. This discovery followed a long and complex operation carried out by Maturin with Laura Fielding's unwitting help; but it had occurred only a few hours before he was obliged to leave Valletta, and he had therefore been compelled to send his information to Mr Wray and to the Commander-in-Chief for action, Wray being in Sicily for a few days and the Admiral off Toulon. He had done so reluctantly, because the letters necessarily disclosed his status as one of Sir Joseph's colleagues, a status that he preferred to keep secret – so much so in fact that he had declined collaborating with Wray or the Admiral's counsellor and oriental secretary, Mr Pocock. Wray was a newcomer to the world of naval intelligence, coming from the Treasury, and Maturin had thought the affair too delicate for inexperienced hands; furthermore, he understood that Wray did not enjoy Sir Joseph's fullest confidence, which was not surprising, since although Wray was certainly able and intelligent he was also a fashionable, expensive man, much given to high play and not at all remarkable for his discretion. The same objection of inexperience applied to Pocock, though in other ways he made a very good head of the Admiral's local intelligence service. Yet even if both Wray and Pocock had been far more objectionable, even if they had been downright fools, Maturin would still have written: his was a very important discovery, and the first of the two men to reach Valletta had only to make use of his exact, detailed information to wipe out the French organization in half an hour, with the help of no more than a corporal's guard. Even if it had meant revealing his true identity ten times over he would certainly have written, above all to Wray, who must in all probability return to Malta well before the Admiral; for although Maturin had a very considerable experience of intelligence-work, and although he was wary, percipient, and acute enough to have survived several campaigns in which many of his colleagues had died, some under torture, he was by no means omniscient; he was capable of making mistakes and he had no suspicion of the fact that Wray was a French agent, a man who admired Buonaparte as much as Maturin detested him. Stephen saw Wray as a somewhat flashy, unsound, over-clever fellow; he did not know that he was a traitor, nor did he even suspect it.

Ever since leaving Valletta Stephen had been passionately eager to learn the result of his letters, and he would certainly have been aboard the flagship the moment she appeared, had it not been for naval etiquette and because any untimely, unusual visit on the part of a surgeon to Mr Pocock must necessarily excite comment, to some degree lessening his obscurity and with it his usefulness as an agent, to say nothing of his own personal safety.

But there were also other letters from Sir Joseph, personal letters, some parts of which would require both literal and figurative decoding – letters in which Sir Joseph spoke in veiled terms of rivalries in Whitehall and even within the department, occult influences acting on the Board, underhand dealings, his friends and followers being displaced or denied promotion; and at present Sir Joseph seemed discouraged. Yet the most recent note was dashed off in quite another tone: it spoke with keen approval of the work of a person in the United States who had sent news that a plan often put forward in the American Navy Department was now to be carried into execution, a project that for brevity's sake was called Happiness and that dealt

29

with American activities in the Pacific. 'I shall not trouble you with the details, since you will hear them aboard the flag,' wrote Sir Joseph, 'but it appears to me that at this juncture there is a great deal to be said for viewing the coleoptera of the far side of the world, until the storm blows over; a great deal to be said for the pursuit of Happiness.'

'The vainest chase that ever was,' reflected Stephen, but with no more than a fragment of his mind, the rest of it being taken up with an intense desire to know what had happened in Malta and with wondering how to justify himself to Diana in the shortest possible time, before she should make one of those rash passionate moves so characteristic of her.

'The boat ahoy,' hailed *Caledonia*.

'*Surprise*,' replied Bonden, and the flagship instantly began preparing for the ceremony of receiving a post-captain.

Although he had spent many years at sea Dr Maturin had not gained the slightest tincture of seamanship. At one time or another he had contrived to fall between the boat that was carrying him and almost every class of ship and vessel in the Royal Navy; he had also fallen between a Maltese dghaisa and the solid stone-built quay, and between Wapping Old Stairs and a Thames wherry, to say nothing of less stable craft; and now, although the *Caledonia* had shipped a broad accommodation-ladder, a kind of elegant staircase with rails and entering-ropes covered with red baize, and although the sea was perfectly calm, he very nearly managed to plunge through the narrow gap between the lowest step and the next, and so under the flagship's side. But Bonden and Doudle at stroke oar were used to his vagaries: they seized him directly and set him cursing on the steps again with no more than a torn stocking and a slightly barked shin.

On the quarterdeck, where Jack was already talking to the captain of the *Caledonia*, he saw Dr Harrington, the physician of the fleet, who hurried over, and after the most cordial greetings and a few words about the present influenza invited him to come and look at two cases of military fever as curious as he had ever seen, occurring in twins and perfectly symmetrical.

They were still contemplating the finely-spotted patients when the message came: could Dr Maturin spare Mr Pocock a few moments, when he was disengaged?

The moment Stephen's eager eye caught sight of Mr Pocock's face he knew someone had blundered. 'Do not tell me Lesueur was not taken,' he said in a low voice, laying his hand on Pocock's sleeve.

'I am afraid he had wind of Mr Wray's approach,' said Pocock. 'He vanished without a trace. But five Italian or Maltese accomplices were taken up, and Boulay killed himself before he could be arrested: or so they say.'

'Did the Maltese and Italians yield anything upon being questioned?'

'It seems that with the best will in the world they had nothing to yield. They were fellows of no importance, messengers and second murderers working under men whose names were meaningless. Mr Wray was satisfied that they could not tell him anything before he resigned them to the firing-squad.'

'Did he give you any message for me?'

'He sent his heartiest congratulations on your success, infinitely regretting your absence, but begged you would forgive him if he did not write for the moment, he being so very much out of order, particularly as I should be able to give you an account of his proceedings. He deplored the escape of André Lesueur more than he could say, but was confident that he should soon be taken, Government having put five thousand pounds upon his head. He was also confident that with the death of Boulay all treacherous communications between Malta and France would come to an end.'

After a short silence Maturin said, 'You seemed to express some doubt about Boulay's death.'

'Yes,' said Pocock, making a pistol of his fingers

and holding it to his temple. 'He was found with his brains blown out. But Boulay was a left-handed man, left-handed in all he did; and the pistol had been put to the right-hand side of his head.'

Stephen nodded: ambiguous deaths were commonplace in the rougher levels of intelligence. 'At least I hope I may assume that Mrs Fielding's free pardon has passed the seal – that she is quite safe from any importunity of any kind?'

'Oh yes,' said Pocock. 'Mr Wray attended to that at once. He said it was the least he could do, after your extraordinary efforts. He also charged me to say that he was going home overland, and would be happy to be of any service. A courier goes off to him tonight.'

'Most obliging in Mr Wray,' said Stephen. 'And perhaps I may avail myself of his kindness. Yes. I shall entrust him with a letter that I should like my wife to receive as soon as possible.'

They both of them meditated for a while and then moved on to the next subject. Stephen said, 'You have seen Captain Aubrey's official account of the Zambra affair, of course? It would be improper in me to speak of the naval side, but since I was concerned with the political aspects, I should very much like to know how the Dey is to be handled now.'

'Ah, there I am on much safer ground,' said Pocock. 'With the French agents in Valletta I dare say I should have done no better than Mr Wray, but the Oriental world is my province, and in Mascara . . .' He drew his chair a little nearer, and contorting his hairy, ill-favoured face into an arch and even roguish look he said, 'Mr Consul Eliot and I arranged the neatest little parricide you can imagine, and I think I may promise a new and better-disposed Dey at present.'

'No doubt parricide is more readily brought about when a man has many wives, many concubines, and a numerous progeny,' observed Stephen.

'Just so. It is a usual factor in Eastern politics. Yet in the West there is still a certain prejudice against its

32

employment, and perhaps you would be so kind as not to mention it specifically when speaking to the Admiral. "A sudden dynastic change" is the term I have employed.'

Stephen sniffed and said, 'Mr Wray stated that he was much out of order. Was this also just a form of speech, merely describing an unwillingness to write the whole thing out again, or had it a basis in fact? Was he perhaps deeply affected by Admiral Harte's death in the *Pollux*? Conceivably there was more attachment between them than appeared to the casual observer.'

'Oh, as to that,' said Pocock, 'he put on the mourning proper for a father-in-law, of course; but I do not believe he was much more affected than a poor man who suddenly inherits three or four hundred thousand pounds may be expected to be. He *was* out of order, very much out of order, but it seemed to me the effect of extreme nervous tension and exhaustion of spirits, and perhaps of the oppressive heat; between ourselves, colleague, I do not believe he has a great deal of bottom.'

'I am glad he has a great deal of money however,' said Stephen smiling, for Wray had lost a preposterous sum to him when they played piquet day after day in Malta. 'Do you suppose the Admiral will want to see me, at all? I am extremely anxious to get to the top of the Rock the moment the east wind stops.'

'Oh, I am sure he will. There is a question to do with a certain American plan that he wishes to discuss with you. Indeed, I wonder he has not called us in well before this. He is a little strange today.'

They looked at one another. Apart from the 'American plan', which was certainly that of Sir Joseph's letter, Stephen very much wanted to know the Admiral's opinion of Jack's conduct in Zambra Bay; Pocock very much wanted to know what Stephen would be at on the heights of Gibraltar at midday. Both questions were improper, but Pocock's was far less important and after a moment he said, 'Perhaps you have an appointment high on the Rock?'

'So I have too, in a manner of speaking,' said Stephen. 'For at this time of the year, unless there is a levanter blowing, prodigious vast great quantities of birds pass the Strait. Most of them are raptores, which, as I am sure you know, generally choose the shortest passage over water; so you may have thousands and thousands of honey-buzzards, kites, vultures, the smaller eagles, falcons, harriers, and hawks crossing in a single day. But they are not only raptores: other birds join them. Myriads of white storks, of course, but also, as I am credibly informed, the occasional black stork too, God bless her, a bird that I have never yet beheld, a dweller in the plashy forests of the remotest north.'

'Black storks, sir?' said Pocock with a suspicious look. 'Black swans I have heard of, but . . . Perhaps, as the time is getting on, I should give you an outline of this American plan.'

'Captain Aubrey, sir,' said Mr Yarrow, 'the Admiral will see you now.'

Jack's first impression, as he walked into the great cabin, was that the Commander-in-Chief was drunk. The little man's pale leathery face had a pink flush, his bowed back was straight, his usually cold, hooded old eyes shone with a youthful gleam. 'Aubrey, I am delighted to see you,' he said, standing up and reaching over his paper-covered desk to shake hands.

'Come, that's civil,' thought Jack, somewhat relaxing his noncommittal expression and sitting on the chair the Admiral pointed out.

'I am delighted to see you,' said Sir Francis again, 'and I congratulate you on what I reckon a thumping victory. Yes, a thumping victory, when you compare the respective losses. A victory, though no one would think so from your official letter. The trouble with you, Aubrey,' said the Admiral, looking at him kindly, 'is that you are no goddam good at blowing your own trumpet; nor, by consequence, at blowing mine. Your letter,' – nodding at the laborious pages Jack had left the day

34

before – 'is downright apologetic instead of triumphant; it is *concerned to say* and *regrets to have to report*. Yarrow will have to recast it. He used to write speeches for Mr Addington, and he knows how to make the best of a case. It ain't a question of lying, nor of showing away or puffing yourself neither, but just of refraining from crying out stinking fish at the top of your voice. By the time he has finished with your letter it will be clear even to the ordinary land-borne public that we have won a victory, clear even to the ordinary newspaper-reading cheesemongers, and not only professional men. Will you join me in a glass of sillery?'

Jack said he would be very happy – exactly the thing for such a hot morning – and while the bottle was fetching the Admiral said, 'Never think I don't grieve for poor Harte and the *Pollux*, but in practical politics any C-in-C will always give an old worn-out ship for a new one half as powerful again. The French two-decker was the *Mars*, you know, fresh off the stocks. They managed to warp her under the guns of Zambra – *Zealous* and *Spitfire* saw her there, together with your big frigate burnt to the waterline on her reef – but they will never warp her out again – *Mars* my arse, hey? Hey? – even if her back weren't broke, which it is, because our politicoes have nobbled the Dey.' The steward, a very much smoother soul than Jack's Killick, though still a seaman with gold rings in his ears, drew the cork with a London butler's gravity and Sir Francis said, 'Aubrey, here's to your health and happiness.'

'And to yours, sir,' said Jack, savouring the fresh, flowerly, grateful wine. 'Lord, how well it does go down.'

'Don't it?' said the Admiral. 'Well, there you are, you see: on balance we are up by at least half a ship of the line and of course by your whole frigate; and the contumelious Dey is knocked on the head. Yarrow's rephrasing will make all this perfectly clear to the meanest understanding, and your letter will look extremely well when my dispatch appears in the Gazette. Letters . . . Lord above,' said the Admiral, pouring out another glass and waving his hand at the mass of correspondence, 'sometimes I wish no one had ever found out the art of writing. Tubal Cain, was it not?'

'So I have always understood, sir.'

'And yet sometimes they can be tolerably welcome. This one came this morning.' Sir Francis picked it up, hesitated, and then, saying, 'I had not the smallest expectation of it. I have not mentioned it to anyone. I should like people I respect in the service to be the first to know – it is after all a service matter,' he passed the letter over.

Jack read

Dear Sir

The great exertions, ability, and zeal, which you have displayed during your command in the Mediterranean, not only in the active operation of the fleet under your orders, but in the internal arrangements and discipline which you have established and maintained, with such effect to His Majesty's service, have been noticed by His Royal Highness with so much approbation, that he has been graciously pleased to declare His intention of honouring you by a distinguishing mark of the royal favour; I am accordingly commanded to acquaint you that His Royal Highness will confer on you the dignity of a Peer of Great Britain, as soon as it shall be known what title you would desire to bear . . .

Without finishing he sprang up, and shaking the Admiral's hand he cried, 'Give you joy with all my heart, sir, or rather my lord as I should say now – eminently well-deserved – it does honour to the whole service. I am so happy.' And indeed his face shone with such honest pleasure as he stood there beaming at the Admiral that Sir Francis looked at him with more affection than his hard old face had shown for many years. 'It is perhaps a vanity,' he said, 'but I confess it pleases me very much indeed. An honour to the service, as you so rightly say.

And you are part of it: if you read farther on, you will see he mentions our turning the French out of Marga. God knows I had no share of it – it was your doing entirely – though legally it was just within my time of command: so, you see, you have earned me at least one of the balls in my coronet, ha, ha, ha!'

They finished their bottle, talking of crowns, imperial and otherwise, strawberry leaves, for whom reserved, titles that descended in the female line, and the awkwardness of being married to a peeress in her own right. 'That reminds me,' said the Admiral, 'you could not dine aboard yesterday because you were engaged to a lady.'

'Yes, sir,' said Jack, 'to Mrs Fielding. I had given her a lift from Valletta. Her husband joined her here, coming in *Hecla*, so I asked 'em both.'

Sir Francis looked very knowing indeed, but he only said, 'Yes, I had heard she went aboard *Surprise*. I am glad it ended happy, but in general women in a ship are a very bad thing. A gunner's wife to look after your youngsters, by all means, and perhaps one or two other warrant officers', but no more. Quite apart from the moral effect, you would not believe the amount of water they waste. Fresh water for washing their smalls they will have, and they will go to any lengths to get it, corrupting sentries, ship's corporals, even officers – the whole ship's company, indeed. However, I hope you will be able to come tomorrow. I mean to indulge in a little private celebration and then I am away, back to the Toulon blockade.'

Jack said that nothing would give him greater pleasure than celebrating such news, and the Admiral continued, 'Now I must turn to a completely different subject. We have certain intelligence that the Americans are sending a frigate into the Pacific to attack our whalers: the *Norfolk*, thirty-two. She is comparatively light, as I dare say you know, and although she has a much heavier broadside than *Surprise* she carries only four long guns, all the rest being carronades; so that at anything of a distance the two could be considered a match. The question is, would a man of your seniority accept such a command?'

Jack mastered the delighted smile that did all it could to spread over his face, and bidding his heart beat quieter he said, 'Well, sir, as you know I was promised the *Blackwater* on the North American station; but rather than sit idle at home while their lordships find me an equivalent, I should be happy to protect our whalers.'

'Good. Very good. I thought you would say that: I hate a man that refuses an active command in time of war. Well, now,' – picking a sheaf of papers from his desk – 'the *Norfolk* was to weigh from Boston on the twelfth of last month, but she has to convey some merchantmen to San Martin, Oropesa, San Salvador and Buenos Aires, so it is to be hoped that you will have time to cut her off before the Horn. But if not, clearly you must follow her round, and that means six months' provisions. Relations with the Spanish authorities, such as they are, are likely to be difficult, and it is very fortunate that you will have Dr Maturin. We will ask him for his views on the opportunity of putting in, but before he comes tell me if you have any particularly deserving men in the *Surprise*. I am in a promoting frame of mind, inclined to spread happiness, and although there can be no question of commissions, a few warrants or removals to a higher rate may prove possible.'

'Why, sir, that is very kind in you, most benevolent,' said Jack, horribly torn between a sense of justice to his shipmates and a very strong disinclination to weaken his crew. 'My master and gunner are both of them fit for a ship of the line; and I have two or three very promising young petty officers, perfectly qualified for a bosun's warrant in an unrated vessel.'

'Very well,' said the Admiral. 'Let my flag-lieutenant have their names this afternoon and I shall see what can be done.'

'And, sir,' said Jack, 'although there is no question

38

of commissions at present you will allow me to mention William Honey, a master's mate, who brought the news from Zambra to Mahon in the launch, and Mr Rowan, my second lieutenant, who went away for Malta in the cutter.'

'I shall not forget them,' said the Admiral. He rang the bell, and when Pocock brought Stephen in he said, 'Good morning to you, Doctor. I dare say you and Mr Pocock have been considering this American plan?'

'In part, sir. We have traced the path of the *Norfolk* down the Atlantic coast of South America, but we have not entered the Pacific. We have not yet reached Chile or Peru.'

'No,' said the Admiral. 'Nor does our intelligence reach so far. We have a reasonably detailed course as far as the Horn, and after that nothing at all. That is why it is so important to intercept her before say the height of Falkland's Islands: there is not a moment to be lost. But first I should like your opinion of the political situation in the various ports she is to call at – whether it would be advisable to put in for information or whether we might meet with obstruction or even downright hostility.'

'As you are aware, sir, the Spanish possessions are in a state of extreme confusion; but I am confident that we may put into San Martin, and Oropesa, and of course the Brazilian San Salvador. I am far less sanguine about Buenos Aires and the River Plate, however. From the very beginning the region was colonized by the offscourings of the worst parts of Andalusia, slightly relieved by a few shiploads of criminals; and of recent years the mongrel descendants of these half-Moorish ruffians have been under the tyrannical rule of a series of low demagogues, disreputable even by South American standards. There is already a great deal of ill-will towards us, because of the recent action and their humiliating defeat; and since a tyrant's position is a little less insecure if the discontent can be directed at a foreigner, who knows what imaginary crimes may not be fastened upon our people? What lies

39

invented to mislead us, what delays contrived to hinder our progress, and what information conveyed by all possible means to our enemies? Unless we have a singularly devoted correspondent there I cannot recommend a visit to Buenos Aires.'

'I am entirely of your opinion,' cried the Admiral. 'My brother was there when we took the town in the year six, and a nastier, dirtier place he had never seen, nor nastier, dirtier people; and he was a prisoner of war there when a French officer assumed command and took it back again – they used him barbarously, barbarously. But I will not dwell upon that.' He reached for his pen and wrote energetically. 'Aubrey, here is my direct rescript for your six months' stores; and don't you let those mumping villains at the cooperage-wharf keep you standing off and on. As I said, there is not a moment to lose.'

CHAPTER TWO

It was profoundly true that not a moment was to be lost, since even the space between breakfast and dinner might see the *Norfolk* a full degree farther south if she had any luck with the north-east trades, and by so much nearer the vast expanse of the Pacific, where she might so easily never be found at all. Yet from the very beginning of this state of emergency Captain Aubrey was compelled to lose a great many of them: moments, minutes, hours and even days that fled away into the past, never to be recovered.

In the first place common decency required him to receive the ceremonial visits of Mr Gill, the frigate's master, and of Mr Borrell, her gunner, come to take their leave on being promoted into the *Burford*, 74, and to utter particularly laborious speeches, returning thanks for his kind recommendation. Then came Abel Hames and Amos Day, formerly his captains of the maintop and the foretop respectively, the first now bosun of the *Fly* gun-brig and the second of the *Eclair*, who found great difficulty in beginning to express their gratitude, but who having begun, were sadly puzzled to leave off. And when he had at last got all four over the side, heartily cheered by their shipmates, the *Berwick* came in, instantly sending the *Surprise*'s launch across, commanded by William Honey, the master's mate Jack had dispatched from off the coast of Africa to carry word of the disabled French two-decker a tolerably perilous four hundred miles to Port Mahon; and Honey was so justifiably pleased with his success that it would have been inhuman not to attend to his account of the voyage. Honey had barely finished before another boat from the *Berwick* brought the Reverend Mr Martin, her chaplain, a naturalist and a great friend of Stephen's, and

Captain Pullings, formerly Jack's very able first lieutenant but now promoted – a captain without a ship or any real prospect of a ship, and a captain only by courtesy at that, since his official rank (and of course his meagre half-pay) was that of a commander. They were both very cheerful and both in their best clothes, come to pay their respects to Captain Aubrey, who had to be called from the stowing of the hold, and to talk at large about earlier commissions in a variety of ships. Captain Aubrey greeted them with a singularly artificial smile, and as soon as Martin had gone off to show Stephen a paper nautilus, a *female* paper nautilus, he said to Pullings, 'Tom, forgive me if I seem inhospitable, but I have just been ordered to take in six months' stores with the utmost dispatch. Gill is removed to *Burford* and no new master has been appointed – Borell is gone too – Rowan is somewhere between this and Malta – Maitland is having a tooth drawn at the hospital – we are twenty-eight men short of complement – and unless I go and stir up those wicked dogs at the cooperage we shall be here until we ground on our own beef bones.'

'Oh, sir,' cried Pullings, to whom the significance of an urgent six months' stores was instantly apparent, 'is that indeed the case?'

'Now, sir,' said Jack's steward, walking in without any ceremony, 'I must have that there shirt.' Then seeing Pullings his acid, housewifely face broke into a smile; he put a knuckle to his forehead and said, 'My kind duty, sir, and hope I see you well?'

'Blooming, Killick, blooming,' said Pullings, shaking hands and then taking off his fine blue coat with its golden epaulettes. 'Be a good fellow and fold that carefully and find me a frock.' And to Jack, 'If you do not think it would upset Mowett, sir, I should be happy to take over the hold, or the watering party, or the gunner's stores: I am quite at leisure, you know.'

'He would rise up and call you blessed,' said Jack, 'and so should I, if you would relieve me in the hold while I run to that infernal – while I run to the port-admiral's and

42

the cooperage. Never was such a Behemoth of vice as that master cooper. Lucifer ain't in it.'

Leaving Behemoth's lair, poorer by five guineas but with his heart eased by the promise of diligence, Jack hurried towards the Waterport gate, clasping a sheaf of papers that he consulted from time to time, commenting upon them to the short-legged midshipman who trotted at his side. Even a sixth-rate man-of-war needed an astonishing amount in the way of naval stores, while each of the warriors she carried was allowed seven pounds of biscuits a week, seven gallons of beer, four pounds of beef and two of pork, a quart of peas, a pint and a half of oatmeal, six ounces of sugar and the same of butter, twelve ounces of cheese and half a pint of vinegar, to say nothing of the limejuice, the necessarily enormous quantity of fresh water for steeping the salt meat, and the two pounds of tobacco a lunar month, for which however he had to pay at the rate of one and sevenpence a pound – an enormous bulk when multiplied by two hundred. Seamen were, furthermore, intensely conservative and most passionately attached to their rights, and although they would compromise over their beer, their very, very small beer, cheerfully and indeed eagerly accepting a pint of wine instead if they were in the Mediterranean or half a pint of rum, made into grog, in all far foreign waters, and agree that duff might be considered the equivalent of meat on stated occasions, almost any other change was sure to lead to trouble, and wise captains avoided innovation at all costs. Fortunately Jack had an efficient purser in Mr Adams, but even Mr Adams could not make the Victualling Board's local minions spread more canvas than they chose; and in any case Jack suspected that the purser, like the bosun, might be feeling a little out of humour, a little less willing to run himself into the ground, since Jack had recommended the master and the gunner for promotion, but neither Mr Adams nor Mr Hollar. The truth was that the *Surprise* had been brought to such a degree of excellence with their great guns and carronades that the ship could almost dispense with a gunner, except for minding his stores; and Jack himself could perfectly well see to the navigational side of the master's duties (in fact, he could do them rather better than Mr Gill); but at this stage a skilled and relatively honest purser was of the first importance, while an excellent bosun was essential at all times, particularly now that Jack had lost those splendid seamen, the captains of the main and foretops. In Captain Aubrey's mind there had been a conflict between loyalty to his shipmates and loyalty to his ship; the ship had won, of course, but a certain guilt haunted his conscience, still tender for these things if for little else.

Just opposite the Convent he met Jenkinson, Sir Francis' flag-lieutenant. Until this point he had only nodded or waved to his various acquaintances as he hurried along but now he stopped and after the briefest interchange of civilities he said, 'As you know, Mr Jenkinson, the C-in-C was very kind to me yesterday, so kind that I hardly liked to mention that *Surprise* was twenty-eight men short of complement. Do you think it would be possible to raise the subject today, before he sails?'

'I very much doubt it, sir,' said Jenkinson, without any hesitation. 'I very much doubt it would be opportune.' In respectful terms he said that was a matter Jack must fight out for himself with the port-admiral; and having made that plan clear he said, 'It is understood, is it not, that Dr Maturin too dines aboard the flag today? I believe there is some farther point that Mr Pocock wishes to raise, and the Admiral was afraid that his invitation was not quite clear. I had intended to come aboard you on my way back.'

'I had not understood the Doctor to be invited, I must confess,' said Jack. 'But I will make sure that he waits on Sir Francis.' He wrote in his pocket-book, tore out the sheet and gave it to the midshipman, saying, 'Calamy, run back to the ship and give this to the Doctor, will you? If he is not aboard you must find him, even if it

44

means running up to O'Hara's tower; but I dare say the hospital is more likely.'

A hundred yards farther on Jack came face to face with his old friend Dundas of the *Edinburgh*, a friend who certainly could not be waved or nodded to.

'Why, Jack,' said Dundas, 'you look distracted. What's afoot? And why are you running about in a round hat and those vile pantaloons? If the Admiral sees you he will put you under arrest for topping it the shopkeeper.'

'Walk along with me, Hen, and I will tell you,' said Jack. 'The fact of the matter is, I *am* distracted. I was ordered to take in six months' stores yesterday and I have been hurrying to and fro among these slow sly circumspect creatures ever since, without getting any forrarder at all – I have lost my master and gunner and two petty officers – I have only one lieutenant aboard – I am twenty-eight men short. As for these clothes, they are all I have. Killick has taken everything else away, to be washed by the Gibraltar laundrywomen in fresh water, every stitch bar my square rig for dinner with the Admiral this afternoon, God help us – hours wasted, stuffing food I do not want at a time when I cannot afford five minutes and should be glad to eat a cold piece of beef and bread and butter in my hand.'

'Still,' said Dundas, 'how glad I am that you are not going home to lay the poor *Surprise* up in ordinary, or worse. May I ask where you are bound, or would that be indiscreet?'

'I do not mind telling you,' said Jack in a low tone, 'but I would not have it generally known. We are to protect whalers. And that reminds me. You always sailed with a fine ballast of books: have you anything on whaling? I am sadly ignorant about the whole subject.'

'Northern or southern?'

'Southern.'

'I had Colnett's book until I was fool enough to lend it. But I can do better than that – by God, Jack, I can do much better than that. There is a man here on the Rock called Allen, Michael Allen, that was master of

45

the *Tiger* till he invalided from her a few months ago: a thoroughbred seaman. We were shipmates once, and we said how d'ye do on the Parade not half an hour ago. He is quite well now, and eager for a ship. And he sailed with Colnett!'

'Who was Colnett?'

'Do you not know who Colnett was, Jack, for Heaven's sake?'

'Would I ask if I knew?'

'But surely even you must know of Colnett; everybody knows of Colnett.'

'What an entertaining witty rattle you are to be sure, Hen,' said Jack in a dissatisfied tone.

'Not to know about Colnett. Lord! Only think. But of course you must remember Colnett. Just before the last war, in ninety-two I think, some merchants asked the Admiralty for a vessel to go looking for places where the southern whalers might wood, water and refit. The Admiralty let them have the *Rattler* sloop and gave Colnett long leave of absence to command her. He had been a midshipman with Cook and he took her round the Horn into the Pacific . . .'

'Forgive me, Heneage,' said Jack. 'But I must just look into the port-admiral's office. Be a good fellow and step into Richardson's' – nodding towards the open door of a cool shaded tavern – 'and wait for me over a bottle. I shall not be long, I promise you.'

He was not long. He came into the big sanded room, bowing under the lintel, his naturally florid face some-what redder than usual and his bright blue eyes brighter still with anger. He sat down, drank a glass of pale ale, and whistled a stave. 'Do you know the words they sing to that?' he asked, and Dundas replied,

'We'll give you a bit of our mind, old hound,
Port-admiral, you be damned.'

'That's right,' said Jack.

At much the same time Stephen said to Martin, 'That

makes eight more black storks: seventeen in all, I believe.'

'Seventeen it is,' said Martin, checking the list upon his knee. 'What was that smaller bird low down on the left?'

'It was only a bar-tailed godwit,' said Stephen.

'Only a bar-tailed godwit,' repeated Martin, laughing with delight. 'Paradise must be very like this.'

'Perhaps a little less harsh and angular,' said Stephen, whose meagre hams rested on a sharp limestone edge. 'Mandeville reports that it has mossy walls. But let it not be supposed that I complain,' he added, and indeed his face, usually withdrawn and reserved, fairly shone with pleasure.

The two of them were sitting high-perched on the very chine or ridge of Gibraltar under an immense, cloudless, gentle blue sky, with the grey cliffs falling almost sheer to the Mediterranean on the left hand: on the right lay the distant bay with all its shipping, and straight ahead the dim peaks of Africa rose from a blueish haze. A soft south-west breeze cooled their cheeks, and across the strait there passed a long loose train of birds in an unhurried easy glide, sometimes single lines, sometimes much thicker troops, but always passing, the sky never empty. Some, like the black vultures and the storks, were huge; others, like the tired hobby that sat preening his red breeches on a rock not ten yards away, quite small; yet large or small they all glided on together without the least sign of animosity, sometimes wheeling in close-packed spirals to gain height but most passing quite low overhead, so low on occasion that they had seen the crimson eye of the bearded vulture, the orange of the goshawk's.

'There is another imperial eagle,' observed Martin.

'So there is too,' said Stephen. 'God bless him.'

They had long since given up counting the white storks and the various kinds of buzzard and harrier, the smaller eagles, the kites and commoner vultures, and now they concentrated upon the rarest of the rare. On the left hand, beyond the hobby, in a cleft overhanging the sea, a peregrine kept up a strong harsh hacking cry, presumably expressive of desire; and on the right hand, lower down, Barbary partridges could be heard: the air was filled with the scent of lavender and lentiscus and a hundred other aromatic shrubs hot in the sun.

'There, there!' cried Stephen. 'Below the storks – to the right – that is a lappet-faced vulture, my dear sir. My lappet-faced vulture at last. You can see her pale, well-rounded thighs, almost white.'

'What a satisfaction,' said Martin, following the bird with his single, carefully shaded eye, and some minutes after it had vanished, 'There is an odd creature almost exactly over your ship.'

Stephen fixed it with his pocket spyglass and said, 'I believe it must be a crane, a solitary crane. How curious.' He also fixed Jack Aubrey on the quarterdeck of the *Surprise*, stalking to and fro like Ajax and waving his arms about. 'Why, he looks as though he were in quite a passion,' he murmured indulgently: he was used to passion in the executive officers at these times of preparation for a voyage.

But he was not used to quite this degree of passion. Captain Aubrey had just received the message, delivered by a frightened, breathless, purple-faced Calamy, that Dr Maturin sent his compliments, but 'did not choose to come'.

'Does not choose to come,' cried Captain Aubrey. 'Red Hell and bloody death.'

'He said he thought he might not dine today at all,' quavered Calamy.

'And you bring me this message, wretched boy? Do you not know that in such a case you must insist, you must explain?'

'I am very sorry, sir,' said Calamy, who at twelve was quite wise enough not to protest that he *had* insisted, he *had* explained, until he had been positively cuffed and threatened with worse if he did not go away and stop frightening the birds – his unnecessary, vehement gesticulations had already startled three Andalusian hemipodes

48

that were just about to land – where was he brought up, to be prating so to his elders? Did he not know shame or decency at all? He now bowed his head, and his Captain asked him whether he did not know that an officer-like fellow must not be put off with answers like that from persons who, however great their learning and virtues, were essentially civilians?

But Jack was never one for prolonged moralizing, still less now, when every minute counted: he broke off, glanced fore and aft, trying to remember who was in the ship and who was not. 'Pass the word for Sergeant James,' he said, and to the sergeant, 'Pick four of your quickest-moving Marines and follow Bonden up to the top of the Rock at the double: Mr Calamy will point out the way. Bonden, go ahead and make the situation clear even to civilians, if you can: in any event I expect to see the Doctor here at two. Killick will have his number one rig ready to be put on.'

At four bells in the afternoon watch, or two by the clocks in the town, Jack was sitting in front of a small looking-glass in his sleeping cabin with a freshly-laundered cravat the size of a topgallant studdingsail spread out ready to be folded about his neck when he heard a confused thumping, bundling sound on deck, followed by Killick's shrill, indignant, shrewish voice, a cross between that of a much-tried long-soured nursemaid and of an uncommonly rough tarpaulin-hatted tobacco-chewing foremast-hand, and by some indistinct oaths.

A little before five bells he came on deck in all the glory of full dress, with the Nile medal in his button-hole, his Turkish decoration, a diamond chelengk, blazing in his gold-laced hat, and his hundred-guinea Patriotic Fund sword at his side; and there he found Stephen, looking stuffed and sullen in his rarely-worn good coat, a comparatively subfusc garment. The frigate's barge lay at the starboard mainchains, the bargemen in gleaming white trousers and frocks and broad straw hats, the Captain's coxswain standing at the tiller, with Mr Midshipman

Williamson and the sideboys waiting at the rail, while the bosun and his mates held their calls ready poised: it was all a shocking waste of time; but high ceremonial waste, like blazing away for King Charles' restoration and Gunpowder Plot, was no doubt necessary for the good of the service. Jack glanced about the harbour and saw boats converging upon the *Caledonia* from all the King's ships; and the port-admiral's barge had already put off from the shore. He smiled at Stephen, who gave him a bitter look, and said, 'Lead on, Macbeth.' Macbeth instantly sprang from the larboard gangway, where he had been standing by a tackle-fall, ready to get on with the ship's urgent business the moment the ceremony was over. Standing before his Captain with his huge bare red bony splay feet brought neatly together he plucked off his blue bonnet and asked, 'Wheer tu, sirr?'

'No, no, Macbeth,' said Jack, 'I did not mean you; and in any case I should have said Macduff . . .'

'Macduff, Macduff,' the cry went through the ship. 'Sawny Macduff to the quarterdeck at the double.'

'Belay there,' cried Jack. 'Scrub it. No, no. My meaning is, the officers may go over the side as soon as they please.'

Quite unmollified by this, Stephen was handed muttering down into the boat after the midshipman, and Jack followed him to the howl of silver pipes.

The Commander-in-Chief's sudden flush of benevolence had called together a surprising number of guests, and Stephen found himself tight-wedged at the bottom of the table between the *Caledonia*'s chaplain and a black-coated gentleman who had come out to act as deputy judge-advocate in some particularly delicate courts martial. Yet this party, though a little too numerous for comfort, had its advantages: the humbler people were removed from the admirals by so solid a phalanx of post-captains that they could talk away at their ease, almost as though there were no Olympians present; and presently they were making a fine convivial din.

The lawyer seemed a knowledgable man, willing to converse, and Stephen asked him how, in naval courts, a suit for tyranny and oppression might be instituted in cases of extreme disparity of rank: whether, to take an entirely hypothetical example, a froward commander-in-chief and his accomplice of post rank who persecuted an innocent subordinate might be brought before officers on the same station or whether the matter would have to be referred to the High Court of Admiralty, the Privy Council, or the Regent himself.

'Why, sir,' said the lawyer, 'if the persecution were tortious, and if it happened at sea, or even on fresh water or reasonably damp land, the Admiralty court would no doubt have cognizance.'

'Pray, sir,' said Stephen, 'just how damp would the land have to be?'

'Oh, pretty damp, pretty damp, I believe. The judge's patent gives him power to deal with matters in, upon, or by the sea, or public streams, or freshwater ports, rivers, nooks and places between the ebb and flow of the tide, and upon the shores and banks adjacent – all tolerably humid.'

At this point Stephen became aware that Dr Harrington some places higher up the table and on the other side, was smiling at him and holding up a glass. 'A glass of wine with you, Dr Maturin,' he said, with a civil bow.

Stephen returned the smile and the bow with a very good will, and drank the wine that a heavily-breathing Marine poured into his glass, his brimming glass. It was the same sillery that Jack had drunk the day before and it went down even more gratefully. 'What delightful wine,' observed Stephen to nobody in particular. 'But it is by no means innocent,' he added, slowly drinking the rest of the glass. Because of the total confusion in the frigate he had had no breakfast apart from a cup of coffee; the packet of sandwiches and the flask of cold negus that he had forgotten to take up the Rock lay in his cabin still, attended by a growing crowd of rats and cockroaches;

51

his usual dinner time was two hours earlier than this; the latter part of his morning had been intensely frustrating, hot, dusty and hurried; and so far he had eaten nothing but a crumb of bread: he felt the effect of the wine well before his glass was emptied – a very slight swimming in his head, the faint birth of a certain benignity, a willingness to be pleased with his company. 'Quo me rapis?' he murmured. 'Sure it destroys one's sense of free will. Jove made Hector bold and timid, timid and bold by turn, so there was no personal merit in his heroism, no shame in his running away. From a misanthrope Bacchus makes me sociable . . . Yet on the other hand I had already bowed and smiled; I had performed at least the motions of complaisancy; and how often have I not observed that the imitation begets the reality.'

His neighbour, he found, had for some time been telling him about the nice distinctions to be found in English law. '. . . it is much the same with deodands,' he continued. 'If a man leap on to a cart in motion, however slight that motion may be, and miss his footing so that he break his neck, then the cart and all it contains is a deodand, forfeit to the King. But in the case of a cart that is standing still, while the man climbs up by the wheel, and climbing falls to his death, the wheel alone is deodand. In the same way, if a moored ship is the cause of a man's death, only the hull is deodand, whereas if she is under sail the cargo too is forfeited, so long as it is within the domain of the common law: for on the high seas, my dear sir, a very different set of rules applies.'

'Deodands,' said the chaplain on Stephen's right. 'The patron of my brother's living in Kent has the grant of all the deodands in the manor of Dodham. He showed me a brick that had fallen on a mason's head, a gun that had exploded in firing off, and a very furious bull that its owner did not choose to redeem with a payment of money; and he told me of yet another fine point of law – that if a child fall off a ladder and kill itself, the ladder is not forfeit; whereas if its father do so, then it is. I mean, that the ladder becomes a deodand in the second case, but not in the first.'

'Very true,' said the lawyer. 'And Blackstone explains this by the fact that in the times of Popish superstition it was held that infants, being incapable of sin, had no need of the propitiatory Masses purchased with the deodand, or rather its redemption. Yet other authorities . . .'

Stephen's attention drifted away until the parson touched his sleeve and said, 'Dr Harrington is speaking to you, sir.'

'You will support me, colleague, I am sure,' called Harrington down the table, 'when I say that barely one in ten of our people is directly killed by the enemy, or dies from wounds received in battle. Disease or accident account for nearly all of them.'

'Certainly I will,' said Stephen. 'And perhaps it may be said that these figures suggest the relative importance of the combatant and the non-combatant officers.'

'Or perhaps it may be said,' cried a very witty, very red-faced Marine officer, 'that for every man the enemy kills, the medicoes kill nine, ha, ha, ha!'

'Come, Bowers, recollect yourself,' said the Admiral. 'Dr Harrington, Dr Maturin, a glass of wine with you.'

By this time they had moved on to a noble Hermitage (for to honour the occasion the Admiral had fairly stripped his cellar on the Rock) and as he savoured it Stephen said to himself, 'I must remember to pin Harrington for a mate.'

This he did in the rosy full-fed cheerful crowd that stood about the quarterdeck and poop with little coffee-cups in their hands during the interval between the end of dinner and the arrival of the boats, saying, 'Dear colleague, may I beg you to help me to an assistant? In general, as you know, I prefer to sail without one unless I am in a two-decker, most surgeon's mates being sad ignorant bouncing rapparees. But with the prospect of a long voyage before me, I feel I must have some strong young man skilled in drawing teeth. I have rarely been happy in my tooth-drawing. In my youth it was considered far below a physician's dignity; I never learnt the knack, and recently I have had some most unfortunate experiences. I can do it, given time, of course; but often enough the tooth comes out more slowly than the patient might wish, and in little pieces. If we have a ship's barber with a turn that way I usually leave it to him, or when I can I send the case to hospital.'

'That is odd,' said Dr Harrington, 'because I have seen you carry out all the greater amputations with extraordinary speed and apparent ease.'

'Yet there it is,' said Stephen. 'Who is capable of the more is not necessarily capable of the less, as my old nurse used to say; and I should be most grateful for a young man unusually clever with his hands.'

'As for mere extraction,' said Dr Harrington, 'I know a fellow whose performance would astonish you. Look,' – opening his mouth wide, tilting it to the sun and pointing. 'Look,' he said, pointing to a gap and speaking in a strangled, inarticulate open-mouthed voice, 'second molar, right maxilla.' Then, more like himself, 'Only five days ago and yet almost no wound, as you see. He did it with his fingers alone: remarkable. But he is not a young man, and to tell you the truth, Maturin,' said Dr Harrington, bending close and shading his mouth, 'he is something of a quacksalver. How the Board ever came to pass him, I do not know. He seems to possess almost no Latin at all.'

'If he can draw teeth like that, he may do it in plain English for me,' said Stephen. 'Pray, where is he to be found?'

'At the hospital, and his name is Higgins. But I speak for nothing but his dexterity; he may be a mere empiric, or even worse.'

'Dr Maturin, if you please, sir,' said a messenger, and Stephen was led away to the secretary's cabin, where both Mr Yarrow and Mr Pocock were waiting for him. Mr Pocock said that he had received Dr Maturin's

54

letter for the courier to carry to Mr Wray and that it had already left. Stephen thanked him, observing that in all likelihood much time would be saved, a point of real importance to him. Then there was a short silence. 'I am somewhat embarrassed to begin,' said Pocock 'since the information I am to pass on has been communicated to me in a deliberately obscure form, so that I am obliged to speak as though I were withholding many of the facts, which must seem strange and perhaps even offensive to Dr Maturin.'

'On the contrary,' said Dr Maturin. 'If, as I presume, confidential matters are concerned, I had far rather know only the details that concern me: it is then materially impossible for any blunder or inadvertence of mine to disclose the rest.'

'Very well,' said Mr Pocock. 'It appears, then, that Government has sent a gentleman to one or more of the Spanish South American colonies with a large sum of money: he is travelling under the name of Cunningham in the packet *Danaë* from the Cape, a swift-sailing brig. But the minister is now much concerned at the possibility of the *Danaë*'s being taken by the *Norfolk*, and if the *Surprise* should meet with the packet she is to warn her of the danger and, if it can be done with little loss of time, escort her into a South American port. But should this not be possible, or should the port be on the eastern, or Atlantic coast, then other measures must be taken. The gentleman has two chests of specie, and these will be left in his charge; but his cabin also contains a far larger sum in bills, obligations and so on. He is unaware of the fact, though I presume the person to whom this larger sum is consigned must have been supplied with directions for finding it. In any event, here are the directions,' – passing a slip of paper – 'and they will enable you to remove the package. And here is a note that will ensure that the gentleman understands the position. There: I have said all I was required to say.'

For some time the *Caledonia* had been filled with

familiar sounds, the stamp and go of some hundreds of men at the capstans, and various pipes and cries usual in unmooring ship. Now there was a pause, and Yarrow said, 'I dare say they are hauling away the cat before hooking on the fish.'

Pocock said, 'Perhaps they will stopper with a dog.'

Stephen said, 'It is my belief that they have raised a mouse, and that having seized it with a fox they will clap on a lizard.'

'Lord, what a jargon the honest creatures have invented, upon my word,' said Pocock, laughing heartily for the first time in Stephen's acquaintance with him. 'Were your terms authentic?'

'They were indeed,' said Stephen. 'And there are hounds too, somewhere about the masts.'

'So were my cat and fish,' said Yarrow. 'The master explained them to me only yesterday; and he mentioned horses, dolphins, flies, bees, a positive ark, ha, ha, ha!'

'If you please, gentlemen,' said the tall stern flag-lieutenant at the door, and all three civilians at once stopped smiling, 'the Admiral awaits your pleasure.'

The *Surprise*'s boat had long since borne her captain and his bargemen back to their labours, and the flagship's accommodation-ladder had vanished too. From the middle deck Stephen contemplated the steep and dangerous descent, the peevish sea worked up by the freshening south-westerly breeze, and the little harbour tub, manned by two amphibious strangers, bobbing like a cork down there. He hesitated, and Pocock, who understood his hesitation only too well, said, 'If you will take one step down, holding on to me, while Mr Yarrow holds my other hand, at the same time grasping this ring, I believe we may all advance together, in a kind of human chain, without too much peril.'

It was perhaps a ludicrous sight, but it served its purpose, and as the flagship, close-hauled on the starboard tack, swept nobly down towards Europa Point, packing on sail after sail, the harbour tub delivered Dr Maturin to the extremely busy *Surprise*, quite dry from head to foot, his watch still going (it often suffered when he plunged into the sea) and the curious, close-written documents he had just received unblurred by the action of salt water. He crept aboard by way of the stern ladder and found himself in the midst of a most intense activity. Jack had already thrown off his fine clothes and he was standing on the capstan calling out directions to those who were about to warp the ship two cables lengths to windward, while grave, concentrated men hurried by on either side of him, and along the gangways, and down in the waist, and all over the forecastle. 'There you are, Doctor,' he cried on seeing Stephen. 'I am sorry I had to desert you, but we must gather rosebuds while we may, you know. We are just warping up to Dirty Dick's – tallow, coals, pitch, and Stockholm tar – so if you have anything to do on shore, now is the time. No doubt you have already thought of your medicine-chest, portable soup, splints and so on?'

'I shall go to the hospital directly,' said Stephen, and this he did, as soon as the frigate touched the quay.

'Pray, Dr Edwardes,' said he to the head physician, 'do you know Mr Higgins?'

'I am acquainted with a Mr Higgins, who attends from time to time in an unofficial capacity, in case we have anything for him to do. Mr Oakes not infrequently sets him to drawing teeth, which has put our barber's nose finely out of joint, I can tell you: but it does appear that he has a real gift that way. And no doubt he can cut corns, too,' – laughing scornfully. 'If you are in need of his services – and he performed an extraction on Dr Harrington, no less – I will send for him. He is working in the wash-house at this moment.'

'I should prefer to see him in action. Do not stir, I beg: I know the way.'

Even if Stephen had not known the way, the sound of the drum would have guided him. He opened the wash-house door as the beat began to quicken and he saw Mr Higgins in his shirt-sleeves leaning over a seaman, while a benchful of other patients watched with extreme and anxious attention. The drumbeat grew faster, louder, louder still; the seaman uttered a shrill, strangled, involuntary shriek and Higgins straightened, the tooth in his hand. All the patients gave a sigh of relief, and as he turned Higgins saw Stephen standing there. 'What may I have the honour, sir?' he asked with a very respectful bow, for he had at once recognized Stephen's uniform: a surgeon's coat was by no means as gorgeous as a captain's, but to an unemployed surgeon's mate it was infinitely more interesting, since its wearer might require an assistant.

'Pray carry on, sir,' said Stephen. 'I should like to watch.'

'I beg pardon for the fair-ground noise, sir,' said Higgins with an uneasy laugh, placing a chair for Dr Maturin. He was a small wiry middle-aged man with short cropped hair and his present look of genteel complaisance sat oddly on his unwashed, unshaved face.

'Not at all, at all,' said Stephen. 'Any din that is in the patient's interest is legitimate, nay laudable. I have used gunfire before now.'

Higgins was nervous and perhaps it cramped his style, but even so his was a remarkable performance: once he was sure of his tooth he would give the drummer a nod – there was an excellent understanding between the two – and as the beat began he hung low over his patient, talking loud into his ear, pulling his hair or pinching his cheek with one hand while he manipulated the gum and tooth with the other: then at another nod the drum grew furious and at the height of the crescendo, with the patient's senses all aswim, he would exert just the necessary force, sometimes with forceps, sometimes with his bare fingers alone, in a very smooth, efficient, practised gesture.

'I am the surgeon of the *Surprise*,' began Stephen, when the patients had left, all beaming now, each with a clean handkerchief held ritually to his face.

'Oh, sir, everybody here in the medical line knows Dr Maturin,' cried Higgins, 'and Dr Maturin's valuable

58

publications,' he added with a certain hesitation.

Stephen bowed and went on, 'And I am looking for an assistant skilled in dental surgery. Dr Harrington and my shipmate Mr Maitland speak highly of your talents, and I have seen you operating. If you wish I will ask Captain Aubrey to apply for your appointment to the ship.'

'I should be only too happy to sail under your orders, sir,' said Higgins. 'May I ask where the *Surprise* is bound?'

'That has not yet been publicly given out,' said Stephen. 'But I understand it to be the far side of the world: I have heard mention of Batavia.'

'Oh,' said Higgins, his exultation momentarily checked, for Batavia was most notoriously unhealthy, even worse than the West Indies, where whole ship's companies might die of the yellow jack. 'Yet even so I should be delighted at the prospect of repairing my fortunes in a ship commanded by such a famous prize-taker.'

It was true. In his time Jack Aubrey had taken a very great many prizes, so many indeed that he was called Lucky Jack Aubrey in the service. As a young commander in the awkward little fourteen-gun brig *Sophie* he had filled Port Mahon harbour with French and Spanish merchantmen, harrying the enemy trade in the most desperate fashion; and when a thirty-two gun xebec-frigate called the *Cacafuego* was sent out especially to put an end to his capers he captured her too and added her to the rest. Then as a frigate-captain he had taken a Spanish treasure-ship among other things, and he had had a large share in the spoils of the Mauritius, together with its recaptured Indiamen, among the richest prizes in the sea. To be sure, the Admiralty had taken the Spanish treasure away from him on the pretext that war had not been legally declared, while in his simplicity he had allowed various dishonest landsmen to cheat him out of much of the Mauritius wealth and so involve his remaining fortune that neither he nor his lawyers could tell whether he would be able to retain any of it at all; but in spite of this he still had much of the aura of Lucky Jack Aubrey as well as the nickname.

Mr Higgins was not alone in wishing to become rich, and as the news of the *Surprise*'s prospect of a long voyage spread a great many people applied to go with her; for at this stage of the war it was only frigates that could hope for those glorious encounters in which a man might earn a hundred years' pay in an afternoon. At the same time a number of parents and other relations showed a strong inclination to place their boys on the quarterdeck of one of the outstanding frigate-captains, a man with a remarkable fighting-record and one known for his care in bringing up his midshipmen – a strong desire to send them aboard the *Surprise* even if she were going to the fetid, fever-ridden swamps of Java.

When Jack had commanded the ship in the Mediterranean he had hardly been importuned at all, since it was known to be nothing more than a temporary command for one or two specific missions; but even now that the case was altered (at least to some degree) this was still not one of those long commissions in which he could settle down to the forming of young gentlemen. With reasonable luck he should intercept the *Norfolk* well before the Horn, and even if he did not he hoped to be back in a few months' time: he would therefore have refused all youngsters but for the fact that he had a son himself, young George, whose future he had ensured by making various captains promise to take him aboard when the time was ripe; and now, when these captains or their near kin asked him to do the same he could not very well refuse. Nor could he in decency dwell on the unhealthiness of Batavia, since he knew very well that he was not going there – the whole thing was a mild ruse on Stephen's part, aimed at disguising their movements from the probable foreign agents on or near the Rock and the certain neutrals who passed up and down the Strait, often calling in for stores and gossip. The result was that he now had four little boys in addition to Calamy and Williamson, four squeakers, pleasant, reasonably clean, well-mannered sons of naval families, but still a sad trial to him. 'I tell you what it is,' he said to Stephen at one of their rare meetings in the town, when they were both buying strings, rosin and sheet-music, 'I shall have to ship a schoolmaster. With Calamy and Williamson, that makes six of the little beasts, and although I can teach them navigation when things are quiet and beat them whenever they need it, it seems a poor shabby thing to send them out into the world without a notion of history or French or hic haec hoc. Seamanship is a very fine thing, but it is not the only quality, particularly by land, and I have often felt my own want of education – I have often envied those fellows who can dash off an official letter that reads handsome and rattle away in French and throw out quotations in Latin or even God help us in Greek – fellows who know who Demosthenes was, and John o' Groats. You can cut me down directly with a Latin tag. And it is no good telling an ordinary healthy boy to sit down with his Gregory's *Polite Education* or Robinson's *Abridgment of Ancient History*: without he is a phoenix like St Vincent or Collingwood he needs a schoolmaster to keep him to it.'

'I wonder whether you sea-officers may not rate literature too high,' said Stephen. 'Though to be sure I have known some sea-going boobies who can conduct their ships to the Antipodes and back with nicely-adjusted sails but who are incapable of giving a coherent account of their proceedings even by word of mouth, let alone in writing, shame on them.'

'Just so: and that is what I want to avoid. But both the schoolmasters I have seen are mere mathematicians, and drunken brutes into the bargain.'

'Have you thought of asking Mr Martin, at all? He is not very strong in the mathematics, though I believe he now understands the elements of navigation; but he speaks very fair French, his Latin and Greek are what you would expect in a parson, and he is a man of wide reading. He is unhappy in his present ship, and when I told him that we were going to the far side of the world – for I was no more exact than that – he said he would give his ears to go with us. Yes: "would give both my ears" was his expression.'

'He is a parson, of course, and the hands reckon parsons unlucky,' said Jack, considering. 'And most sea-going parsons are a pretty rum lot. But then they are used to Mr Martin; they like him as a man – and so of course do I, a most gentlemanlike companion – and they do like to have church rigged regularly . . . I have never shipped a parson of my own free will: but Martin is different. Yes, Martin is quite different: he may be holier than thou, but he never thrusts it down thy throat; and I have never seen him drunk. If he was speaking seriously, Stephen, pray tell him that should the transfer be possible, I should be very happy to have his company to the far side of the world.'

'To the far side of the world,' he repeated to himself, smiling, as he walked towards the old mole: and on the far side of the street he saw an uncommonly handsome young woman. Jack had always had a quick eye for a pretty face but she had seen him even sooner and she was looking at him with particular insistence. She was certainly not one of the many Gibraltar whores (though she brought carnal thoughts to mind) and when their eyes met she modestly dropped her own, though not without a kind of discreet inward smile. Had that first insistent look been a signal that he would not be too fiercely repelled if he boarded her? He could not be sure, though she was certainly no bread-and-butter miss. At an earlier age, when he accepted any challenge going and some that were not going at all, he would have crossed over to find out; but now, as a post-captain with an appointment to be kept, he remained on his own pavement, only giving her a keen, appreciative glance as they passed. A fine black-eyed young person, and there was something distinctive about her walk, as though she were a little stiff from riding. 'Perhaps I shall see her again,' he thought, and at that moment he was hailed by another young woman, not quite so handsome, but very plump and jolly: she was Miss Perkins, who usually sailed with Captain Bennet in the *Berwick* when the *Berwick*'s chaplain was not on board. They shook hands, and she told him 'that Harry was hoping to get his grum old parson to take a long, long leave, and then they would escort the Smyrna trade up the Med again among all those delicious islands how lovely'. But when she asked him to dine with them he was obliged to refuse: alas, it was not in his power, for he was already bespoke, and must in fact run like a hare this very minute.

Heneage Dundas was the bespeaker, and they dined very comfortably together in a small upstairs room at Reid's, looking down into Waterport Street and passing remarks about their friends and acquaintances as they went by below.

'There is that ass Baker,' said Dundas, nodding in the direction of the captain of the *Iris*. 'He came aboard me yesterday, trying to get one of my hands, a forecastleman called Blew.'

'Why did he do that?' asked Jack.

'Because he dresses his bargemen in all colours of the rainbow, and likes them to have answerable names. He has a Green, a Brown, a Black, a White, a Gray and even a Scarlet, and he fairly longed for my John Blew: offered me a brass nine-pounder he had taken from a French privateer. Somebody must have told him that Iris meant rainbow in Greek,' added Dundas, seeing that Jack still looked puzzled, if not downright stupid.

'Really?' said Jack. 'I had no idea. Yet perhaps he knew it before. He is quite a learned cove, and stayed at school till he was fifteen. What would he do if he had *Amazon*, I wonder?' – laughing heartily – 'But I do hate that way of making monkeys out of the men, you know. He is kissing his hand to someone this side of the street.'

'It is Mrs Chapel,' said Dundas, 'the master-attendant's wife.' And after a pause he cried 'Look! There is the man I was telling you about, Allen, who knows so much about whaling. But I dare say you have already had a word with him.'

'Not I,' said Jack. 'I sent round to his lodgings, but he was not in the way. The people of the house said he was gone to Cadiz for a couple of days.' As he spoke he looked intently at Allen, a tall, upright, middle-aged man with a fine strong face, wearing the plain uniform of a master in the Royal Navy, and as he took off his hat to a superior officer, a lieutenant of barely twenty, Jack saw that his hair was grey. 'I like the look of him,' he said. 'Lord, how important it is to have a well-assorted set of officers, men that understand their calling and that do not quarrel.'

'Of course,' said Dundas. 'It makes all the difference between a happy commission and a wretched one. Have you managed to do anything about your lieutenants?'

'Yes, I have,' said Jack 'and I think I have solved the problem. Tom Pullings has very handsomely suggested coming along as a volunteer, as I thought he would; and even if Rowan don't join from Malta before we sail, I can give Honey or Maitland an acting order: after all, both you and I were acting lieutenants, taking a watch, before their age.'

'What about the port-admiral and his young man?'

'I utterly refuse to have that niminy-piminy blackguard on my quarterdeck,' said Jack. 'The port-admiral may be damned.'

'I should like to see you telling him so, ha, ha, ha!' said Dundas.

Happily the need did not arise. As soon as Jack walked into his office Admiral Hughes cried, 'Oh Aubrey, I am afraid I must disappoint you of young Metcalf. His mother has found him a place in the Sea Fencibles. But sit down, sit down; you look quite fagged.' So he did: Jack Aubrey was a tall, burly man, and the labour of propelling his sixteen stone about the reverberating sun-baked Rock from dawn till dusk and beyond, trying to urge slow officials into equally brisk motion, was telling on him. 'On the other hand,' continued the Admiral, 'I have just the master you need. He sailed with Colnett – you know about Colnett, Aubrey?'

'Why, sir, I believe most officers that attend to their profession are tolerably well acquainted with Captain Colnett and his book,' said Jack.

'Sailed with Colnett,' said the Admiral, nodding, 'and is a thorough-going seaman, according to all accounts.' He rang the bell. 'Desire Mr Allen to walk in,' he said to the clerk.

It was just as well that Dundas had spoken highly of Mr Allen, for otherwise Jack would have made little of him: Allen did not do himself justice at all. From his boyhood Jack had been an open, friendly creature, expecting to like and to be liked, and although he was by no means forward or over-confident he was not at all given to shyness, and he found it difficult to conceive that the emotion could still paralyse a man of fifty or more, filling him with a repulsive reserve, so that he responded to no civil advance, never smiled, nor spoke except in reply to direct questions.

'Very well. There you are,' said the Admiral, who seemed equally disappointed. 'Mr Allen will join as soon as his order is made out. Your new gunner should have reported already. That is all, I believe: I will not detain you any longer.' He touched the bell.

'Forgive me, sir,' said Jack, rising, 'but there is still the question of hands: I am short, very far short, of my complement. And then of course there is the chaplain.'

'Hands?' exclaimed the Admiral, as though this were the first he had ever heard of the matter. 'What do you expect me to do about them? I can't bring men out of the ground, you know. I am not a goddam Cadmus.'

'Oh no, sir,' cried Jack with the utmost sincerity, 'I never thought you were.'

'Well,' said the Admiral, somewhat mollified, 'come and see me tomorrow. No. Not tomorrow. Tomorrow I am taking physic. The day after.'

Allen and his new captain walked out into the street.

'I shall see you tomorrow, then, Mr Allen?' said Jack, pausing on the pavement. 'Let it be early, if you please. I am very anxious to put to sea as soon as possible.'

'With your permission, sir,' said Allen, 'I had rather go aboard directly. If I do not attend to the stowing of the hold from the ground-tier up, I shall never know where we are.'

'Very true, Mr Allen,' cried Jack, 'and the forepeak calls for a mort of care. *Surprise* is a very fine ship – no better sailer on a bowline in the service – can give even *Druid* or *Amethyst* maintopgallantsails close-hauled – but she has to be trimmed just so to give of her best. Half a strake by the stern, and nothing pressing on her forefoot.'

'So I understand, sir,' said Allen. 'I had a word with Mr Gill in the *Burford*, and he told me he could not rest easy in his cot, thinking about that old forepeak.'

Now that they were out in the open, surrounded by quantities of people and talking about subjects of great importance to them both, such as the ship's tendency to gripe and the probable effects of doubling her, Allen's constraint wore off, and as they walked along towards the ship he said, 'Sir, may I ask what a Cadmus might be?'

'Why, as to that, Mr Allen,' said Jack, 'it might not be quite right for me to give you a definition in such a public place, with ladies about. Perhaps you had better look into Buchan's *Domestic Medicine*.'

They were received aboard by a more than usually distracted Mowett: the purser had refused to accept a large number of casks of beef that had twice made the voyage to the West Indies and back; he said they were short in weight and far, far too old for human consumption, and Pullings had gone to the Victualling Office to see what could be done; Dr Maturin had flung his slabs of portable soup into the sea, on the grounds that they were nothing but common glue, an imposture and a vile job; and the Captain's cook, having rashly and falsely accused the Captain's steward of selling Jack's wine over the side and being terrified of what Killick might do to him once they were out at sea, had deserted, getting into an outward-bound Guineaman. 'But at least, sir, the new gunner has joined, and I think you will be pleased with him. His name is Horner, late of the *Belette*, and he served under Sir Philip. He has all the right notions about gunnery: I mean, he has our notions, sir. He is in the magazine at present; shall I send for him?'

'No, no, Mowett, let us not delay him for a moment,' said the Captain of the *Surprise*, looking along the deck of his ship, which might have come out of a particularly disruptive battle, with stores, cordage, spars, rumbowline and sailcloth lying about here and there in heaps. Yet the disorder was more apparent than real, and with an efficient master already busy in the hold (for Mr Allen had disappeared almost at once) and a gunner trained by Broke already busy in the magazine it was not impossible that she might put to sea in time, above all if he could induce Admiral Hughes to give him some more hands. As he looked he saw a familiar figure come over the forward gangway, the broad and comfortable Mrs Lamb, the carpenter's wife, carrying a basket and a couple of hens, attached by their feet and intended to form part of the Lambs' private store for the voyage. But she was accompanied by another figure, familiar in a way, but neither broad nor comfortable, the young person Jack had seen in Waterport Street. She was perfectly aware of the Captain's eye upon her, and as she came aboard she dropped a little curtsy, before following Mrs Lamb down the fore hatchway, holding her basket in a particularly demure and dutiful manner.

'Who is that?' asked Jack.

'Mrs Horner, sir, the gunner's wife. That is her young hog, just abaft the new hen-coops.'

'Good God! You do not mean to say she is sailing with us?'

'Why, yes, sir. When Horner asked I gave permission right away, remembering you had said we must have someone to look after all these youngsters. But if I have done wrong . . .'

'No, no,' said Jack, shaking his head. He could not disavow his first lieutenant, and in any case Mrs Horner's presence was perfectly in accordance with the customs of the service, though her shape was not; it would be tyranny and oppression to turn her ashore now that she had installed herself, and it would mean sailing with a thoroughly discontented gunner.

Captain Aubrey and Dr Maturin, in their private capacities, never discussed the other officers, Maturin's companions in the wardroom or gunroom as the case might be; but when Stephen came into Jack's cabin late that evening for their usual supper of toasted cheese and an hour or two of music – they were both devoted though not very highly accomplished players, and indeed their friendship had begun at a concert in Minorca, during the last war – the rule did not prevent Jack from telling him that their common friend Tom Pullings was to sail with them once again as a volunteer. Jack had not proposed it, nor even thrown out any hint, although it was such a capital thing from the ship's point of view; but in fact it was a thoroughly sound move, approved by all Pullings' friends on shore. There was not the least likelihood of his being given a ship in the immediate future, and rather than sit mumchance on the beach for the next year or so, he was very sensibly going on a voyage that would give him a much stronger claim for employment when he returned, above all if the voyage was successful. 'They love zeal in Whitehall,' observed Jack, 'particularly when it don't cost them anything. I remember when Philip Broke was made post out of the horrible old *Shark* and turned on shore, he made a kind of militia of his father's tenants and drilled 'em day and night; and presently the Admiralty gave him the *Druid*, thirty-two, a wonderful sailer. Now Tom has no peasants to drill, but protecting our whalers shows just as much zeal, or even more.'

'You do not anticipate any inconvenience from there being two first lieutenants?'

'I should, in any other ship and with any other men; but Pullings and Mowett have sailed together since they were youngsters – they are very close friends. They arranged it between themselves.'

'I believe I have heard the first lieutenant spoken of as one who is wedded to his ship; so this will be an example of polyandry.'

'Anan, brother?'

'I mean a plurality of husbands. In Thibet, we read, one woman will marry several brothers; whereas in certain parts of India it is considered infamous if the husbands are related in any degree.'

'A precious rum go in either event,' said Jack, considering, 'and I don't know that I should much care for it myself.' As he tuned his fiddle a vision of Mrs Horner came before his mind's eye, and he added, 'I do most sincerely hope it will be the only case of polyandry we ever see in this commission.'

'I am no great advocate for it,' said Stephen, reaching for his 'cello. 'Nor even for a plurality of wives. Indeed, there are moments when I wonder whether any satisfactory relation is possible between men and . . .' He checked himself and went on, 'Did you remind the post-admiral about Mr Martin at all?'

'Yes, I did. And about our missing hands, for God's sake. I am to see him again the day after tomorrow.' He raised his bow, beat the deck three times with his foot, and at the third they dashed away into their often-played yet ever-fresh Corelli in C major.

'Well, Aubrey,' said the post-admiral, when a hot and weary Captain Jack came into his office at the appointed hour, having run all the way from the rope-walk and its singularly dogged superintendent, 'I believe I have solved your problem: and at the same time we have decided to pay you a great compliment.'

69

Jack had been deceived by many a land-shark in his time, and parted from his perilously hard-earned prize-money with pitiful ease; but in matters to do with the sea he was much more wary and now he gave the Admiral's look of smiling good will no credit whatsoever.

'As you may know,' the Admiral went on, 'there has been a certain amount of trouble in *Defender*.' Jack knew it very well indeed: the *Defender*, a badly commanded and thoroughly unhappy ship, had very nearly mutinied off Cadiz. 'And it was in contemplation to bring the troublemakers before a court-martial here: they are all in the *Venus* hulk. But it was represented that the trial must be long and time-consuming, and that the ministry was most unwilling to see still more newspaper paragraphs about disorders in the Navy; so one of the gentlemen present cried, "Send 'em to Captain Aubrey. Aubrey is the man for situations of this kind. There is nothing like a ship in first-rate order for reclaiming your scabbed sheep, as St Vincent used to say when he sent difficult hands to Collingwood." Here is a list of them.'

Jack took it with a cold, suspicious air; and after a moment he exclaimed, 'But they are nearly all landsmen, sir!'

'I dare say,' said the Admiral carelessly. '*Defender* had a recent draft from home. But any man can push on a capstan-bar and swab a deck: every ship needs some waisters.'

'And there are nothing like enough to make up *Surprise*'s complement,' said Jack.

'No. But we have several hands about to be discharged from the hospital, and you may have them too. There is nothing like sea-air for setting a man up, and long before you reach the Line they will be as brisk as bees in a bottle. Anyhow, there it is. Either take them or wait a month before another draft comes out. In my day any young captain would have seized the offer with both hands. Aye, and he would have looked grateful, too, instead of chuff and sullen.'

'Oh sir,' said Jack, 'believe me, I am fully conscious of your goodness, and am duly grateful for it. I was only wondering whether the hands about to be discharged from hospital were those my surgeon saw in the – how shall I put it? – in the rigorous confinement ward.'

'Yes,' said the Admiral, 'they are. But it don't really signify, you know. Most lunatics are only shamming Abraham to get out of work; and these are not the dangerous raving kind. They don't bite: they would not be discharged else. It stands to reason. All you have to do is put 'em in chains and flog 'em hearty in their fits, just as they do at Bedlam. Was you ever at Bedlam, Aubrey?'

'No, sir.'

'My father often used to take us. It was better than a play.' The Admiral chuckled at the recollection and then went on, 'And there is another thing you have to thank me for, Aubrey. I have managed to persuade Captain Bennet to part with this chaplain for you.'

'Thank you, sir: I am most grateful, and will send my midshipman for him at once. He is sure to be up on the top of the Rock with Dr Maturin, and we have no time to spare.'

Emerging from the office into the heat of the day he found his midshipman, the youngster who had been with him since breakfast, tagging along to carry messages if need be and half running to keep up with Jack's long stride – found him sitting on the steps with his shoes off. 'Williamson,' he said, 'the Doctor and Mr Martin will be somewhere up by Mount Misery; the sentries on the upper battery will show you where. Tell them with my compliments that by making great haste we may get to sea sooner than I had thought, so Mr Martin should stand by to come aboard with all his dunnage; and I should be glad of the Doctor's assistance with some new hands.'

'Yes, sir,' said Williamson.

'Why, what's amiss?' asked Jack, looking at his pale, dusty face.

'Nothing, sir,' said Williamson. 'The skin has rubbed

quite off both my heels, but I shall be perfectly all right if I may go in stockinged feet.'

Jack saw that the inside of his shoes was red with blood: the last miles must have been exceedingly painful. 'Well,' he said kindly, 'that shows a proper spirit. Stay here. I shall pass by Anselmo's on my way to the ship and I shall send you back an ass. You can ride an ass, Williamson?'

'Oh yes, sir. We had one at home, a dickey.'

'You may gallop if you wish. We have hurried so much already that it would be a pity to spoil the ship with a ha'porth of tar at this stage. Remember: my compliments and I should like to see the Doctor within the hour, while the chaplain should be ready to come aboard at very short notice. And don't you let them put you off with going on about their birds. You must be respectful, of course, but firm.'

'Respectful but firm it is, sir,' said Williamson.

Jack had two long, important calls to make before returning to the ship, and for the first time since the beginning of his furious drive to get to sea both were encouraging: the ordnance people, who instead of changing two of his slightly honeycombed twelve-pounders for new ones had hitherto showed a strong inclination to keep all four, were now all compliance, and even offered him a pair of handsome brass gunner's quadrants as well; while the rope-walk, having recovered from its ill-humour, showed him two new fifteen-inch cables that he might have whenever he chose to send a boat for them.

He reached the *Surprise* in a more sanguine mood, far more inclined to look cheerfully upon the prospect of admitting a score of mutineers into his ship. Pullings and Mowett accepted the situation philosophically too, for although most of the pressed hands they had known had been pretty decent, upon the whole, the quota system sometimes resembled an emptying of the inland gaols and on occasion they had had to deal with some very sinful characters indeed. 'Collingwood used to say that a mutiny was always the fault of the captain or the officers,' said Jack, 'so perhaps we shall find them as innocent as so many lambs unhung, and merely maligned. But as for the men from the hospital, I had rather the Doctor looked at them first. I do hope he will come down presently. If we can get one more thing settled, we are by so much the nearer to sailing.'

'But sir,' said Pullings, 'the Doctor is here already. They both of them came racing along the quay an hour ago, gasping and covered with dust and calling out to us not to pluck up the anchor, nor to spread the sails abroad, because they were there. They are below, now, lying in hammocks on the orlop and drinking white wine and seltzer-water. It seems they did not quite understand your message.'

'We will let them lie until we have seen the new draft. Then we will ask the Doctor to look at the hospital offering, for it seems that they are all madmen. I should be happy to have almost any pair of hands that can haul on a rope, but there are limits, even in the Navy.'

'I have heard of maniacs so devilishly cunning,' said Pullings, 'that they pretend to be sane, so they can creep into the magazine and blow up the whole ship and themselves with it.'

The draft from the hulk arrived, pale for want of sun and air, unshaved, and with red marks on their wrists and ankles from the irons; few had much in the way of bags or chests, for the *Defender*, a very badly officered ship, was also a thievish one, and most of their property had vanished as soon as they were put in the bilboes. They did not look like innocent lambs unhung. A few were striped Guernsey-frocked tarpaulin-hatted kinky-faced red-throated long-swinging-pigtailed men-of-war's men, and judging by their answers as they were entered in the ship's books some of these were right sea-lawyers too; a few were lowering, resentful sailors recently pressed out of merchant ships; but most were landsmen. They seemed to fall into two classes, the one being what the Navy called bricklayer's clerks, men with a certain amount of education who said they had seen better days and whose talk impressed the simple foremast jacks, and the other made up of strong-minded independent characters, probably given to poaching and deer-stealing or their urban equivalents, who found any discipline hard to bear, let along the *Defender*'s alternate slackness and tyranny. And then of course there were a few silly, weak-headed fellows. They were not a draft anyone would have chosen, and the Surprises looked at them with pursed lips and cold disapproval; but all the officers had seen far worse.

'Nagel served with me for a while in the *Ramillies*,' said Pullings, when they had been sent forward for slops. 'He was rated quartermaster until he answered once too often. No great harm in him, but obstinate and argumentative.'

'And I saw Compton, the barber, once,' said Mowett. 'I went to a party, an entertainment, aboard *Defender* when Captain Ashton had her, and he did a turn as a ventriloquist. They had some capital dancers, I recall, as good as Sadler's Wells.'

'Now let us see the hospital men,' said Jack. 'Mr Pullings, pray see whether the Doctor has recovered his breath.'

Stephen was breathing easily enough, but from the smouldering fire in his eye it was clear that he had not quite recovered his equanimity. 'I have been practised upon,' was his only reply to Jack's kind enquiries. 'Let the discharged patients be brought forward.'

Those few Surprises who had no immediate urgent task in hand gathered for the fun, and all those who could paused in their work to see them come aboard; but the general look of pleased anticipation vanished as the first stumbled across the gangway, an ordinary-looking seaman, but weeping bitterly, his grey face turned to the sky and the tears coursing down. No one could possibly doubt his extreme unhappiness. The others were not much amusing, either. Stephen retained one whose only trouble was a limited knowledge of English and an extreme difficulty in speaking, because of a cleft palate, which made his answers very strange, a very big, diffident, gentle man from the County Clare; three head injuries from falling blocks or spars; and one genuine Abraham-man. 'The big fellow I will keep for my servant, with your leave,' he said privately to Jack. 'He is perfectly illiterate and will suit me very well. The three others might just as well be at sea as on land: I anticipate no great danger from them. Matthews is certainly feigning madness and will recover his senses when we sink the land. But the rest should never have been discharged, and must go back.'

Back they went, and as they reached the quay a message arrived from the port-admiral. 'Upon my sacred word,' said Jack, having read it, 'I am fit to go with them. All our break-neck hurry, all our stowing the hold by lantern-light, all my hellfire fagging up and down this Sodom and Gomorrah of a town, has been quite unnecessary. I need never have crammed the ship with mutineers and maniacs: I need never have taken them off his hands. The *Norfolk* has been detained a month in port – we had all the time in the world – and that wicked old hound knew it days ago.'

CHAPTER THREE

For once in her long, long naval life HMS *Surprise* had time to spare, and Jack was heartily glad of it. He would not have to drive her as he had so often driven her before, flashing out topgallants and royals as soon as she could possibly bear them and then whipping them in again a moment before they split; he would be able to husband his spars, cordage and sailcloth, a great comfort to a sailor's mind at any time but even more so when there was a possibility of the ship's having to double Cape Horn and sail westward into the great South Sea, where there was no chance of finding a spare topmast for thousands upon thousands of miles.

The possibility was slight with the *Norfolk* delayed for a full month, particularly as the *Surprise*, in Gibraltar, was much more favourably placed for reaching the south Atlantic than her quarry, and Jack thought it most probable that by making Cape St Roque and there standing off and on he would either find her on her way south or at least have news of her. It was here that the coast of Brazil tended far out to the east and Jack had raised the headland many a time on his way to the Cape of Good Hope; and many a time had he seen the trade bound for the River Plate and points south shaving St Roque close and hugging the land for the sake of the leading winds inshore: sometimes there had been as many as twenty sail of merchantmen in sight at one time, all following the same familiar tract. Yet Jack had been at sea long enough to know that the only thing about it he could rely upon was its total unreliability: he did not trust in Cape St Roque nor any other cape, but was fully prepared to carry on to Van Diemen's Land or Borneo if need be.

Still, he was glad of this respite. It would not only

give all hands time to breathe after their furious activity in preparing for sea, but it would also enable him to do something towards turning his new hands into the kind of seamen the ship would need on coming to grips with the *Norfolk*. When he was a prisoner in Boston he had seen her as well as several other American men-of-war, and although the *Norfolk* could scarcely be compared with frigates like the *President* or the *United States* with their twenty-four-pounders and their line-of-battle-ship scantlings she would be a tough nut to crack. She would certainly be manned by a full crew of uncommonly able seamen and she would be officered by men who had learnt their profession in the unforgiving waters of the north Atlantic, men whose colleagues had beaten the Royal Navy in their first three frigate-actions. One after another the *Guerrière*, the *Macedonian* and the *Java* had struck to the Americans.

Seeing that Captain Aubrey had been a passenger in the last of these, it was little wonder that he had a high opinion of the United States navy: to be sure, HMS *Shannon*'s victory over the USN *Chesapeake* had shown that the American sailors were not invincible, but even so the respect in which Jack held them could be measured by the zeal with which the new hands were now being put through the great-gun exercise and small-arms drill. Most of them seemed to have been taught nothing aboard the *Defender* apart from swabbing decks and polishing brass, and as soon as the *Surprise* had cleared the Strait, with Cape Trafalgar looming to starboard and Moorish Spartel to larboard, a troop of cheerful spotted dolphins playing across her bows and a topgallant breeze in the north-north-west urging her on her way, her officers took them in hand.

Now, on the third day out, their backs were bent, their hands were blistered and even raw from heaving on gun-tackles, and in some cases their fingers and toes were pinched by the recoiling pieces; but even so Mr Honey, the acting third lieutenant, had just led a party of them to one of the quarterdeck carronades, and the shriek of its slide just over his head caused Captain Aubrey to raise his voice to an uncommon pitch in summoning his steward. Or rather in trying to summon his steward: for Killick was nattering with a friend on the other side of the bulkhead, and being an obstinate, stupid man he neither would nor could attend to two things at once – he had started an anecdote about an Irish member of the afterguard called Teague Reilly and the ancedote he was going to finish. "Well, Killick," he say to me in that old-fashioned way they have of speaking in the Cove of Cork, scarcely like Christians at all, poor souls, "you being only a bleeding Proddy, you won't understand what I mean, but as soon as we touch at the Grand Canary I am going straight up to the Franciscans and I am going to make a good confession." "Why so, mate?" says I. "Because why?" says he . . .'

'Killick,' cried Jack in a voice that made the bulkhead vibrate.

Killick waved his hand impatiently towards the cabin and went on, ' "Because why?" says he, "Because the barky's shipped a Jonah for one, and a parson for two, and for three the bosun's girl put a cat in his cabin; which crowns all." '

The third summons Killick obeyed, bursting into the cabin with the air of one who had just run from the forecastle. 'What luck?' asked Jack.

'Well, sir,' said Killick, 'Joe Plaice says he would venture upon a lobscouse, and Jemmy Ducks believes he could manage a goose-pie.'

'What about pudding? Did you ask Mrs Lamb about pudding? About her frumenty?'

'Which she is belching so and throwing up you can hardly hear yourself speak,' said Killick, laughing merri-ly. 'And has been ever since we left Gib. Shall I ask the gunner's wife?'

'No, no,' said Jack. No one the shape of the gunner's wife could make frumenty, or spotted dog, or syllabub, and he did not wish to have anything to do with her. 'No, no. The rest of the Gibraltar cake will do. And toasted cheese. Break out the Strasburg pie and the wild-boar ham and anything else that will do for side-dishes. Tent to begin with, and then the port with the yellow seal.'

In his drive to get to sea Jack had not troubled about replacing his cook until the very last minute; and at the very last minute the wretched man had failed him. Rather than lose a favourable wind Jack had given the word to weigh cookless, relying on picking up another at Teneriffe. But there was this serious disadvantage: on the one hand he particularly wished to invite his officers early in the voyage, partly to tell them of their real destination and partly to hear what Mr Allen had to say about whaling, about rounding the Horn, and about the far waters beyond it; yet on the other there was a very old naval tradition that required a captain to give his guests a meal unlike that which they would eat in the gunroom, thus making his entertainment something of a holiday, at least in respect of food. Even in very long voyages, when private stores were no more than memories and all hands were down to ship's provisions, the captain's cook would make a great effort to prepare the salt horse, dog's-body and hard tack rather differently from the gunroom cook; and Jack Aubrey, a Tory, a man who liked old ways and old wine, one of the comparatively few officers of his seniority who still wore his hair long, clubbed at the back of his neck, and his cocked hat athwartships in the Nelson manner rather than fore and aft, was the last to fly in the face of tradition. He could not therefore borrow the services of Tibbets, the officers' cook, but was obliged to scout about for what talent the ship might contain, since Killick's genius extended no farther than toasted cheese, coffee and breakfast dishes, and Orrage, the *Surprise*'s official ship's cook, was a negligible quantity in the epicurean line. Indeed he was not a cook at all in the landsman's sense, being confined to steeping the salt meat in tubs of fresh water and then boiling it in vast coppers, while one member of each seamen's mess attended to all the fine work. In any case he had no sense of taste or smell – he had been given his warrant not because he made any claim to knowing how to cook but because he had lost an arm at Camperdown – yet he was much loved aboard, being a good-natured creature with an endless variety of ballads and songs, and uncommonly generous with his slush, the fat that rose to the surface of his coppers from the seething meat. Apart from what was needed to grease mast and yards, the slush was the cook's perquisite; yet Orrage was of so liberal a disposition that he would often let his shipmates have a mugful to fry their crumbled biscuit in, or chance-caught fish, though tallow-chandlers would give him two pounds ten a barrel in almost any port.

As the sun climbed over a light blue and sparkling sea, so the diminishing breeze hauled into the north-east, coming right aft. Ordinarily Jack would have set royals and probably skysails; now he contended himself with hauling down his driver and jib, hauling up his maincourse, scandalizing the foretopsail yard, and carrying on with spritsail, forecourse, foretopmast and lower studdingsails, maintopsail and maintopgallant with its studdingsails on either side. The frigate ran sweetly before the wind, in almost total silence – little more than the song of the water down her side and the rhythmic creak of the masts, yards and countless blocks as she shouldered the remnants of the long western swell with that living rise and turn her captain knew so well. But she also sailed through the strangest little local blizzard, sparse but persistent enough to make Maitland, who had the watch, call for sweepers again and again. It was Jemmy Ducks, plucking geese in the head: the down flew from him for the first few yards, since the *Surprise* did not in fact outstrip the wind (though she certainly gave the impression of doing so), but then it was caught in the eddies of the spritsail, whirled up, spinning again and again in the currents created by the other sails and settling all along the deck, falling as silently as snow. And all the while Jemmy Ducks muttered to himself,

'Never be ready in time. Oh, oh, all this God-damned down!'

In the silence Jack stood watching with his hands behind his back, swaying automatically to the rise and fall, watching these patterns with the keenest attention, they being a direct reflection of the true thrust of the sails, a set of variables exceedingly difficult to define mathematically. At the same time he could hear Joe Plaice fussing about in the galley. Plaice, an elderly forecastle hand who had sailed with Jack time out of mind, had begun to regret his offer of making a lobscouse almost as soon as it was accepted; he had grown horribly anxious as time wore on, and in his anxiety he was now cursing his cousin, Barret Bonden, his mate for this occasion, with a shocking vehemency and (he having become somewhat deaf) in a very loud voice.

'Easy, Joe, easy,' said Bonden, jerking him in the side and pointing forward over his shoulder with his thumb to where Mrs James, the Marine sergeant's wife, and Mrs Horner had brought their knitting. 'Ladies present.'

'Damn you and your ladies,' said Plaice, though rather less loud. 'If there's one thing I hate more than another, it's a woman. A woman aboard the hooker.'

Every half hour the ship's bell spoke; the forenoon watch wore away; the ceremony of noon approached. The sun reached its height; the officers and young gentlemen either took its altitude or went through the motions of doing so; and the hands were piped to dinner. Yet through the bellowing of mess numbers and the banging of mess kids, Plaice and Jemmy Ducks stuck doggedly to their tasks in the galley, standing there in the midst of the tide, blocking the fairway fore and aft. They were still there an hour later, angering Tibbets as he cooked and served up dinner for the gunroom – a much diminished gunroom, with only the two acting lieutenants, Howard the Marine officer, and the purser, all the other members walking hungrily about on deck in their best uniforms, they being invited to dine in the cabin.

The two seamen were still there, looking pale by now,

at four bells in the afternoon watch, when at the first stroke the officers, headed by Pullings, walked into the cabin, while in the galley Killick and the stout black boy who helped him clapped on to the tray bearing the massive lobscouse.

Captain Aubrey had a great respect for the cloth, and he seated the chaplain on his right hand, with Stephen beyond him and Pullings at the far end of the table, Mowett being on Pullings' right and then Allen, between Mowett and the Captain.

'Mr Martin,' said Jack, after the chaplain had said grace, 'it occurred to me that perhaps you might not yet have seen lobscouse. It is one of the oldest of the forecastle dishes, and eats very savoury when it is well made: I used to enjoy it prodigiously when I was young. Allow me to help you to a little.'

Alas, when Jack was young he was also poor, often penniless; and this was a rich man's lobscouse, a Lord Mayor's lobscouse. Orrage had been wonderfully generous with his slush, and the liquid fat stood half an inch deep over the whole surface, while the potatoes and pounded biscuit that ordinarily made up the bulk of the dish could scarcely be detected at all, being quite overpowered by the fat meat, fried onions and powerful spices.

'God help us,' said Jack to himself after a few mouthfuls. 'It is too rich, too rich for me. I must be getting old. I wish I had invited some midshipmen.' He looked anxiously round the table, but nearly all the men there had been brought up to a very hard service; they had endured the extremes of heat and cold, wet and dry, shipwreck, wounds, hunger and thirst, the fury of the elements and the malice of the King's enemies; they had borne all that and they could bear this – they knew what was expected of them as their Captain's guests – while Mr Martin, when he was an unbeneficed clergyman, had worked for the booksellers of London, an apprenticeship in many ways harsher still. All of them were eating away, and not only eating but looking as though they enjoyed it.

'Perhaps they really do,' thought Jack: he was even more unwilling to stint his guests than to force food down their gullets. 'Perhaps I have been eating too high, taking too little exercise – have grown squeamish.'

'A very interesting dish, sir,' said the heroic Martin. 'I believe I will trouble you for a trifle more, if I may.'

At least there was not the slightest doubt that they thoroughly appreciated their wine. This was partly because drinking it spaced out the viscous gobbets and partly because both Plaice and Bonden had salted the dish, which bred an unnatural thirst, but also because the wine was thoroughly agreeable in itself.

'So this is tent,' said Martin, holding his purple glass up to the light. 'It is not unlike our altar-wine at home, but rounder, fuller, more . . .'

It occurred to Jack that there might be something pretty good to be said about Bacchus, wine, sacrifice, and altars, but he was too much taken up with finding small objects of conversation to work it out (wit rarely flashed spontaneously upon him, which was a pity, since no man took more delight in it, even at infinitesimal doses, either in himself or others). Small things he had to find, since by convention all the sailors sat like so many ghosts, never speaking until they were spoken to, this being a formal occasion, with a comparative stranger present: fortunately, if he ran out of topics he could always fall back on drinking to them.

'Mr Allen, a glass of wine with you,' he said, smiling at the master and thinking, as he bowed, 'Perhaps the goose-pie will be better.'

But there are days when hopes are formed only to be dashed. The towering pie came in, yet even as he was explaining the principles of the dish to Martin Jack's knife felt not the firm resistance of the inner layers of pastry but a yielding as of dough; and from the incision flowed thin blood rather than gravy. 'Pies at sea,' he said, 'are made on nautical lines, of course. They are quite unlike pies by land. First you lay down a stratum of pastry, then a layer of meat, then a layer of pastry, then another layer of meat, and so on, according to the number of decks required. This is a three-decker, as you can see: spar-deck, main-deck, middle-deck, lower deck.'

'But that makes four decks, my dear sir,' said Martin.

'Oh, yes,' said Jack. 'All first-rate ships of the line, all three-deckers have four. And by counting the orlop you could make it five; or even six, with the poop. We only *call* them three-deckers, you understand. Though now I come to think of it, perhaps when we say deck we really mean the space between two of them. I am very much afraid it ain't quite done,' – hesitating over Martin's place.

'Not at all, not at all,' cried Martin. 'Goose is far better rare. I remember translating a book from the French that stated, on great authority, that duck must always be bloody; and what is true for the duck is truer still for the goose.'

'What is sauce for the duck . . .' began Jack; but he was too depressed to go on.

However, in time the Strasburg pie, the smoked tongue, the other side-dishes, a noble Minorcan cheese, dessert and a capital port overlaid the unfortunate, even vulturine memory of the geese. They drank the King, wives and sweethearts, and confusion to Buonaparte, and then Jack, pushing back his chair and easing his waistcoat, said, 'Now, gentlemen, you will forgive me if I speak of matters to do with the ship. I am happy to tell you that we are not bound for Java. Our orders are to deal with a frigate the Americans are sending to harry our whalers in the South Sea: *Norfolk*, thirty-two, all carronades apart from four long twelves. She has been delayed a month in port and I hope we may intercept her on her way, south of Cape St Roque, or if not there then at some other point off the Atlantic coast. But it is always possible that we may have to follow her into the Pacific, and since we have none of us rounded the Horn, whereas I understand that Mr Allen knows those waters well, having sailed with Captain Colnett, I should be obliged if he would let us know what to expect. And I dare say he could tell us a great deal about whaling too, a subject I for one am shamefully ignorant of, could you not, Mr Allen?'

'Well, sir,' said Allen, with scarcely a blush, his shyness having worn off with use and an unusual amount of port, 'my father and two uncles were whalers out of Whitby; I was brought up on blubber, as you might say, and I went a number of voyages with them before I took to the Navy. But that was in Greenland fishery, as we call it, off Spitzbergen or in the Davis Strait, going after the Greenland right whale and the nordcaper, with the odd white whales, walruses and sea-unicorns thrown in; I learnt a great deal more when I went with Captain Colnett to the southern fishery, which as I am sure you know, sir, is chiefly for the spermaceti whale. The spermaceti whale: and all the ships are out of London.'

'Yes,' said Jack, and seeing that Allen was straying from his course he added, 'Perhaps it would be best if you were to give us an account of your voyage with Captain Colnett: that would deal with the navigation and the whaling all in due order. But talking is thirsty work, so let us take our coffee here.'

A pause, in which the scent of coffee filled the cabin and Stephen's whole being yearned for tobacco; but it could be smoked only in the open air of the quarterdeck – some ships were so severe as to insist upon the galley – and that would mean missing Allen's discourse. Stephen was passionately interested in whales; he was also fairly eager to hear about their possible rounding of the Horn, that cape notorious above all others for danger, for endless beating into enormous westerly gales, for hope long deferred, scurvy, and ultimate discomfiture; he repressed his longing, and willed the master to begin.

'Well, sir,' said Allen, 'the Americans out of Nantucket had been taking sperm-whales off their own coast and southwards a great while, and before the last war they and some Englishmen took to going farther south by far, to the Gulf of Guinea and off Brazil and even right down to Falkland's Islands. But it was we who first went round the Horn for spermaceti. Mr Shields it was, a friend of my father's, who took the *Amelia* out in eighty-eight and came back in the year ninety with a hundred and thirty-nine tons of oil. A hundred and thirty-nine tons of sperm oil, gentlemen! With the bounty on top that was close on seven thousand pound. So of course other whalers hurried after him, fishing along the coast of Chile and Peru and northwards. But you know how jealous the Spaniards have always been of anyone sailing in those waters, and they were even worse then, if possible – you remember Nootka Sound.'

'Indeed I do,' said Jack who owed all his present happiness to that remote, dank, uncomfortable inlet on Vancouver Island, far to the north of the last Spanish settlement on the west coast of America, where some English ships, trading for furs with the Indians, had been seized by the Spaniards in 1791, a time of profound peace, thus bringing about the great rearming of the Navy known as the Spanish disturbance, which in its turn caused the first of his splendid metamorphoses, that which changed him from a mere (though perhaps deserving) master's mate to a lieutenant with His Majesty's commission and a gold-laced hat for Sundays.

'So, sir,' said Allen, 'the whalers were most unwilling to put into any port on the Pacific side, not only because the Spaniards were proud and injurious any gate, but because, being so far from home, they could never be sure whether it was war or peace, and they might not only lose their ship and their catch, but be knocked on the head too, or be kept in a Spanish prison till they died of starvation or the yellow jack. Yet when you stay out in all weathers two or three years, it stands to reason you need to refresh and refit.' All the officers nodded, and Killick said, 'That's right,' covering his remark with a cough.

'So Mr Enderby, the same as sent Shields out in *Amelia*, and some other owners applied to Government, asking for an expedition to be fitted out to discover safe harbours and sources of supply, so that the southern fishery might carry on and do better than before. Government was agreeable, but what with one thing and another it turned into what I might call a hermaphrodite voyage, half whaling and half exploring, the one to pay for the other. The Admiralty first said they would lend the *Rattler*, a good sound ship-rigged sloop of 374 tons, but then changed their minds and sold her to the owners, who turned her into a whaler with a whaling-master and a crew of twenty-five all told, as against her complement of a hundred and thirty as a man-of-war; yet the Admiralty did appoint Mr Colnett, who had gone round the world with Cook in *Resolution* and who had sailed the Pacific in merchantmen when he was on half-pay between the wars – in fact he was at Nootka Sound itself, and his ships it was that were seized! So he went commander of the expedition; and he very kindly took me along with him.'

'Just when was that, Mr Allen?' asked Jack.

'At the very beginning of the Spanish Armament, sir, in the winter of ninety-two. It fell unlucky for us, because the bounty was already out for seamen in the Navy, and we lost some of our people and could only get landsmen or boys in their place; and that delayed us till January of ninety-three, so we lost our whaler's bounty too, and our fine weather. Howsoever, we did get away at last, and we raised the Island, if my memory do not lie, eighteen days out.'

'What island?' asked Martin.

'Why, Madeira, of course,' said all the sea-officers.

'We always call Madeira the Island, in the Navy,' said Stephen with great complacency.

'Then Ferro nine days later. And we were lucky with our winds; when we lost the north-east trades a breeze slanted us right across the variables – very narrow that year – until we picked up the south-east trades in 4°North, and they rolled us down to 19°South, crossing the Line in 25°30'West. No. I tell a lie. In 24°30'West. We ran into

Rio a fortnight later and laid there a while to set up our rigging and caulk; and I remember Mr Colnett harpooned a five hundredweight turtle in the harbour. After that we sailed to look for an island called Grand, said to be in 45°South, but what longitude no one knew. We found plenty of black fish – that is what we call the small right whale, sir,' – this in an aside to Martin – 'but no island, Grand or Petty, so we bore away south and west until we struck soundings in sixty-fathom water off the west end of the Falklands. The weather was too thick for any observation for some days, so we gave them a wide berth and stood away for Staten Island.'

'Meaning to pass through the Straits Lemaire?' asked Jack.

'No, sir,' said Allen. 'Mr Colnett always said the tides and currents there worked up such lumpish seas it was not worth it. Then coming into soundings again in ninety fathoms at midnight – Mr Colnett always kept the deep-sea lead going, even with so small a crew – he thought we were too near, so we hauled on a wind and in the morning we had no bottom with a hundred and fifty fathom; so we bore up for the Horn, doubled it with more offing than Mr Colnett would have chosen – he liked to keep fairly well in with the land for the sake of the more variable winds – and the next day we saw the Diego Ramirez islands north by east three or four leagues. And what will interest you, sir,' – to Stephen – 'we saw some white crows. They were just the size and shape of those the northcountrymen call hoodies, only white. Then we had some very thick weather with the wind at west and south-west and most uncommon heavy seas; but however we fairly beat round Tierra del Fuego, and then off the coast of Chile we had fine weather and a southerly breeze. In about 40°South we began to see sperm whales, and off Mocha Island we killed eight.'

'Pray how did you do that, sir?' asked Stephen.

'Why, it is much the same as with the right whale,' said Allen.

'That is as though you should ask me how we take off a leg and I replied that it was not unlike the ablation of an arm. I for one should like a more detailed account,' said Stephen, and there was a general murmur of agreement. Allen looked quickly round. It was hard to believe that so many grown men – seamen and in their right senses too – had never seen a whale killed or at least heard how it was done, but their interested, attentive faces showed him that this was indeed the case, and he began, 'Well, sir, we always have men in the crow's nests, and when they see a whale spout they sing out, "There she blows". Everyone lays aloft as though his life depended on it – for, you know, whaling hands go not for wages but for shares – and if the next spout is right, I mean in this case if it is the sperm whale's thick low spout directed forwards, the boats are lowered down, whale-boats, of course, sharp at each end – lowered down double-quick and the men jump into them and the gear is passed after them, two hundred fathoms of whale-line in a tub, harpoons, lances, drogues, and they pull off, as fast as ever they can at first, then when they are near slow and very quiet, because if he is not a travelling whale he will usually come up again within a hundred yards of the same place if he dives and if you have not startled him.'

'How long is he likely to stay down?' asked Stephen.

'About a glass and a half – three quarters of an hour: some more, some less. Then he comes up and breathes for maybe ten minutes, and if you take care and paddle quiet you can come right close to him as he lies a-blowing. Then the boat-steerer, who has been in the bows all this time, sends the harpoon home – whale sounds at once, sometimes stoving the boat as he throws up his tail, or peaks his flukes as we say, and goes down and down, the line running out so fast it smokes against the bollard and you have to sluice it – boatsteerer and headsman change places, and when the whale comes up again at last the headsman lances him – a six-foot blade behind the flipper if he can manage it. I have known an old experienced headsman kill a whale almost at once, with him going into his flurry, as we say, when he can very easily stove you, lashing so wild. But generally it takes a long time: lance and sound, lance and sound, before he is killed. The young forty-barrel bulls are the worst, being so nimble: I do not suppose we succeed with one in three, and sometimes they tow you ten miles to windward, and even then they may carry all away. The big old eighty-barrel fish are far less trouble, and it was one of them I saw killed with the first stroke. But you are not sure of your whale till he is tried out. Shall I tell how we do that, sir?' he asked, looking at Jack.

'If you please, Mr Allen.'

'Well, we tow the whale alongside the ship and start cutting-in: we make him fast and then we either cut off the fore part, the upper part of his head that we call the case because it has the spermaceti in it, and hoist it on deck if he is a small one or veer it astern if it is not, to wait till we have done flinching, or flensing as some say. And that we do by making a cut above his fin, lifting the blubber and slipping a toggle through it, fast to a purchase from the maintop; then hands go on to the carcass with long sharp spades and cut a spiral band in the blubber about three feet wide. It is close on a foot thick on a good fish, and it comes easy away from the flesh; the purchase raises it, canting and turning the whale at the same time, do you see – indeed, we call it the cant-purchase. On deck they cut the blubber up and toss it into the try-works, which is cauldrons amidships with a fire underneath that fries the oil out: and the fritters that are left serve for fuel after the first firing. Then when all the blubber is aboard we attend to the head, opening up the case and ladling out the spermaceti, the head-matter: it is liquid at first, but it solidifies in the barrel.'

'It is a true wax, is it not?' asked Martin.

'Yes, sir, a true pure white wax when it is separated from the oil, as pretty as you could wish.'

'What can its function be?'

No one had any suggestions to offer and Allen went on, 'But as I was saying, you are not sure of your whale until he is tried out, barrelled and safe in the hold. Of the eight we killed off Mocha Island we only profited by three and one head, because the weather turned dirty and they broke away either towing or from the side. After Mocha we sailed along the Chile coast until about 26°South, when we bore away for St Felix and St Ambrose Islands, which lie a hundred and fifty leagues to the west. Miserable places, no more than five miles across: no water, no wood, almost nothing growing, and almost impossible to land: we lost a good man in the surf. Then back to the main and along the coast of Peru in sweet weather, lying to at night and looking for English ships by day. But we saw none, and reaching Point St Helena in 2°South with the wind westering on us we took our departure for the Galapagos Islands . . .'

Mr Allen carried the *Rattler* to the islands, looked at two of them, Chatham and Hood, without much enthusiasm, returned to the mainland with a westerly breeze, in steady drizzle, and so moved north of the equator, losing the seals and penguins that had been with them so long, and suffering cruelly from the oppressive heat. On to the well-watered, tree-covered Cocos Island, inhabited by boobies and man-of-war birds, a wonderfully welcome refreshment in spite of blinding rain and even fog – on to the shores of Guatemala, to the inhospitable island of Socorro, to Roca Partida, where the sharks were so fierce bold and ravenous that fishing was very nearly impossible – they took almost everything that was hooked, and the tackle too, and one rose to seize a man's hand over the gunwhale. On to the Gulf of California, aswim with turtles; and here Cape St Lucas was their northernmost point. They cruised for some weeks off the Tres Marias, but although they saw many whales they killed only two; then, the ship's people being sickly, they turned her head south, returning much the same way they had come, except that they spent much more time in the Galapagos, where they met with an English ship ready to perish for want of water – only seven barrels left.

Allen spoke of the noble tortoises of James's Island with something close to rhapsody – no better meat in the world – and he gave an exact, detailed, seamanlike description of the curious powerful currents, the set of the tides, the nature of the few indifferent anchorages, the sparse watering places, and the best way of cooking an iguana; and then of the measures that had to be taken to deal with the hood-ends that sprang after a heavy blow in 24°South, not far from St Ambrose and St Felix once more. He spoke of a few more whales sighted and pursued – usually with little success and once with the loss of two boats – and then, having carried the *Rattler* round the Horn again, in much better weather this time, and up to St Helena, he brought his account to an abrupt end: 'We made the Eddystone, then Portland in the course of the night, stood off and on till morning, and so ran up and anchored in Cowes Road, Isle of Wight.'

'Thank you, Mr Allen,' said Jack. 'Now I have a much clearer notion of what lies ahead. Captain Colnett's report was made known to the whalers, I imagine?'

'Oh yes, sir; and they follow his recommendations for most of the islands, particularly James's in the Galapagos, Socorro and Cocos. But nowadays when the sun has crossed the Line bringing dirty weather off the coast of Mexico, they tend to bear away westward for the Society Islands or even farther to New Zealand.'

There were a good many other questions, especially about the hood-ends, cheeks of the head and wash-boards, which quite fascinated the sailors, and then Stephen asked, 'And how did your people fare in their health, during all this long voyage?'

'Oh, sir, we had a most capital surgeon aboard, a joy to us all, Mr Leadbetter; and except for James Bowden who was killed when a boat overset in the surf he brought them all home hale and strong, though sometimes they were inclined to grow down-hearted and pine because we had so many disappointments with the whales, and those that were saddest went sick of the scurvy between the Horn and St Helena: but Mr Leadbetter recovered them with James's powder.'

After some remarks about low spirits and scurvy, mind and matter, and the influence of a general fleet-action upon constipation, the common cold and even chicken-pox, Stephen said, 'Pray, sir, can you tell us anything of the anatomy of the sperm whale?'

'Why, yes, sir,' said Allen, 'it so happens that I can tell you a little. Mr Leadbetter was a man very eager after knowledge, and since we always rummaged the whales' guts for ambergris – '

'Ambergris?' cried Pullings. 'I always thought it was found floating in the sea.'

'Or lying on the beach,' said Mowett. *'Who does not know,/That happy island where huge lemons grow,/Where shining pearl, coral, and many a pound,/On the rich shore, of ambergris is found?'*

'Our first lieutenant is a poet,' said Jack, seeing Allen's startled look. 'And if only Rowan had been able to join from Malta we should have had two of them. Rowan composes in the modern style.'

Allen said that that would have been very gratifying indeed, and continued, 'Certainly you find it on the shore, if you are lucky – there was John Robarts of the *Thurlow* East-Indiaman walking by the sea in St Jago while his ship was watering who found a lump weighing two hundred and seven pounds and went straight home, sold it in Mincing Lane, bought an estate the other side of Sevenoaks and set up his carriage directly – but it passes through the whale first.'

'In that case,' said Pullings, 'how does it come about that ambergris is never found in the high latitudes, where there are whales as thick as hasty pudding?'

'Because it is only sperms that are concerned with ambergris,' said Allen, 'and they do not go up into the northern waters. The whales you see there are a few right

93

whales and all the rest are those wicked old finners.'

'Perhaps the sperms find the ambergris on the sea-bed and eat it,' said Jack. 'The right whales or the finners could never manage such a thing, with all that whalebone in the way.'

'Perhaps so, sir,' said Allen. 'Our surgeon rather fancied it originated in the whales themselves, but he could not really make it out. The fact that it was waxy and as he said un-animal puzzled him to the end.'

'And did you find any, when you inspected the whale's intestines?' asked Stephen.

'Only a little, I am afraid,' said Allen, 'and that only in one fish. It was rare that we could search thoroughly, since we flensed 'em all, or nearly all, at sea.'

'I have never seen ambergris,' said Mowett. 'What is it like?'

'A smooth rounded mass of no particular shape,' said Allen. 'Dark mottled or marbled grey when first you take it out, rather waxy and strong smelling, not very heavy: then after a while it grows lighter-coloured and much harder and takes to smelling sweet.'

'Eggs and ambergris was Charles II's favourite dish,' observed Martin, and Pullings said, 'I believe it is worth its weight in gold.' They reflected upon this for a while, slowly passing the brandy-decanter round, and then Allen went on. 'So since we opened the whales in any case when the weather allowed it Mr Leadbetter took the opportunity of looking into their anatomies.'

'Excellent. Very good,' said Stephen.

'And as he and I were particular friends I used to help him: I wish I could remember a tenth part of the things he explained to me, but it was all a great while ago. Teeth in the lower jaw only, I recall; the two nostrils uniting to make a single valved blow hole and therefore an asymmetrical skull; scarcely more than a trace of pelvis, no clavicles, no gall-bladder, no caecum – '

'No caecum?' cried Stephen.

'No, sir, none at all! I remember how on one calm

day with the whale floating easy by the ship we passed the whole length of the intestine through our hands, a hundred and six fathoms in all – '

'Oh no,' murmured Jack, pushing his glass from him.

' – without finding even a hint of one. No caecum: but on the other hand an enormous heart, a yard long. I remember how we put one in a net and hoisted it aboard; he measured and calculated that it pumped ten or eleven gallons of blood a stroke – the aorta was a foot across. And I remember how soon we got used to standing there among the huge warm guts, and how one day we opened one that had a calf in her and he showed me the umbilicus, placenta, and . . .'

Jack abstracted his mind from Allen's account. He had seen more blood shed in anger than most men and he was not unduly squeamish; but placid butchery he could not bear. Pullings and Mowett were of much the same frame of mind and presently Allen became aware that upon the whole the cabin did not relish his discourse and he changed the subject.

Jack came out of his reverie, hearing the word Jonah; and for a confused moment he thought they were speaking of Hollom. But then he realized that Allen had just said that in view of their anatomy it was no doubt a sperm whale that had swallowed the prophet – they were sometimes to be found in the Mediterranean.

The sailors, happy to be released from Fallopian tubes and biliary concretions, spoke of sperms they had seen within the Straits, Jonahs they had known, the horrible fate of ships in which Jonahs had sailed, and Jack's party ended in an even more civilized way, moving from the sea to the land – plays seen, balls attended, and a furlong by furlong account of a fox-chase in which Mowett and Mr Ferney's hounds would certainly have come up with their quarry if he had not plunged into a field-drain as darkness came on.

But although the cabin escaped more grisly details, the gunroom did not: here the master, unawed by the

Captain's presence and supported – indeed spurred on – by the surgeon and chaplain against the disapproval of his messmates, might deliver all the anatomy his powerful memory had retained; and in any case Mr Adams the purser, who was of a hypochondriacal cast, liked to hear; while anything that even remotely touched upon sexual matters fascinated Howard of the Marines.

Not all the details were grisly, however, nor even anatomical. 'I have read accounts of northern voyages, and of the pursuit of the whale,' said Martin, 'but I have never been able to form any clear notion of the economy of whaling. From that point of view, how would you compare the northern and southern fisheries?'

'When I was young,' said Allen, 'before the Greenland waters fell off, we used to reckon that five good fish would pay the voyage. On the average we might take thirteen ton of oil from each, and close on a ton of whalebone; and in those days a ton of whalebone fetched about five hundred pound. The oil was twenty pound a ton or a little better, and then there was the bounty of two pound a ton for the ship, so you would end up with perhaps four thousand five hundred. It had to be divided among some fifty people, and of course the ship had to have her share; yet even so it was a reasonable voyage. But now although the oil has risen to thirty-two pound the bone has dropped to no more than ninety, and the whales are smaller and fewer and farther off, so you need nearer twenty fish not to lose by the trip.'

'I had no idea whalebone could be so costly,' said the purser. 'What is it used for?'

'Fripperies,' said Allen. 'Milliners' and dressmakers' fripperies: and umbrellas.'

'And how does that compare with the southern fishery?' asked Martin. 'For if the only quarry is the sperm, there can be no question of whalebone in the south. The voyage must be made for the oil alone.'

'So it is,' said the master. 'And when you consider that taken one with another sperms give no more than two tons of oil, whereas a good Greenlander gives ten times as much and prime bone too, it seems a foolish venture; for although sperm whale oil fetches something like twice as much as ordinary oil and the head-matter, the spermaceti, fifty pound a ton, that does not compensate for the lack of bone. Oh damn my – that is to say, oh dear me, no.'

'Please to explain the apparent contradiction,' said Stephen.

'Why, Doctor,' said Allen, smiling on him with all the benevolence of superior knowledge – nay, superior wisdom, 'don't you see it lies in the time available? In the Arctic Ocean – in the Greenland fishery – we set out in early April to reach the edge of the ice a month later: in the middle of May the whales arrive and in the middle of June they are away, leaving nothing but those wicked finners behind them, and a few bottle-noses that are neither here nor there. If you have not filled half your barrels you may steer westward for the Greenland coast and try your luck along the drift-ice for what it's worth until August; but by then 'tis getting so cold and dark you must go home. It is much the same in Davis Strait, though you may stay a little longer in the sounds if you don't mind the risk of being frozen in till next year, your ship being crushed maybe and you eaten up by the ice-bears. Whereas the sperm lives in the temperate and tropical waters, do you see, and you may hunt him as long as you please. Nowadays most southern whalers reckon on staying out three years, killing perhaps two hundred fish and coming home with a full ship.'

'Of course, of course,' cried Stephen, clapping his hand to his forehead. 'How foolish of me.' He turned to the servant behind his chair, saying, 'Will you fetch me my cigar-case, now, Padeen?' and to the master, 'Mr Allen, do you choose to take a turn upon the deck? You have twice mentioned the finner with strong disapprobation, and Mr Martin and I would be most grateful, were you to develop your views at greater length.'

'I will be with you in five minutes,' said the master,

'as soon as I have clean-copied my noon observation and pricked the chart.'

They waited for him by the starboard hances, and after a while Stephen said, 'Were there so much as a blade of grass in view or a sheep, you might call this a pastoral scene.' He exhaled a waft of smoke that drifted forward, a coherent body, over the waist of the ship, for the breeze was still right aft, blowing with so even a breath that the countless shirts, trousers, jackets and handkerchiefs hanging on the complex system of lines rigged fore and aft all leaned southward together in an orderly manner, like soldiers on parade – no wanton flapping, no irregularity. With much the same sobriety their owners sat here and there upon the forecastle and among the maindeck guns: this was a make-and-mend afternoon, and for the new hands at least it meant turning the yards and yards of duck they had been given that morning into hot-weather clothes. It was not only the foremast jacks who were busy with their needles, either: on the larboard gangway one of the new youngsters, William Blakeney, Lord Garron's son, was learning how to darn his stockings under the eye of the lady of the gunroom, a bearded hand who had served under his father and who in the natural course of events was now acting as his sea-daddy, a capital darner who had attended to the Admiral's table-cloths in his time; while Hollom sat on the larboard ladder, showing yet another squeaker the best way of sewing on a pocket, singing quietly to himself as he did so.

'What a beautiful voice that young man has,' said Martin.

'So he has, too,' said Stephen, listening more intently: it was indeed wonderfully melodious and true, and the tired old ballad sounded fresh, new and moving. Stephen leant over and identified the singer. 'If he goes on improving like this,' he reflected, 'the men will soon stop calling him Jonah.' For the first days Hollom had eaten wolfishly, filling out with remarkable speed; he no longer looked graveyard-thin nor absurdly old for a master's mate – in fact he might have been called handsome by those who did not require a great deal of masculine determination and energy – and poverty and ill-luck no longer stared from his clothes. He had obtained an advance on his pay, enough to unpawn his sextant and to buy a fairly good coat, and since these were duck pantaloon and round jacket latitudes – no officers wearing uniform except for visits to the cabin or taking the watch – he looked as well as any of them, being exceptionally clever with his needle. He messed with Ward, Jack's conscientious, quiet, somewhat colourless clerk, a man who had been saving for years to put down the surety required before he could become a purser, his highest ambition, and with Higgins, Stephen's new assistant. He had not distinguished himself by any extraordinary display of skill or effectual drive during the furious days of fitting out, but on the other hand he had done nothing to make Jack regret taking him aboard. 'All in the lowland sea ho,' he sang, bringing the verse and the seam both to an end. 'There,' he said to the youngster, 'you finish it off by running it through half a dozen times and casting a round knot in the last turn.' He cut the thread and handed the boy the spool and scissors, saying, 'Run down to the gunner's and give these back to Mrs Horner with my best compliments and thanks.'

Stephen felt a gentle nuzzling at his hand, and looking down he saw that it was Aspasia, the gunroom goat, come to remind him of his duty. 'Very well, very well,' he said testily, taking a final draught from his cigar: he quenched the glowing end on a belaying-pin, wiped the pin over the side, and gave Aspasia the stub. She walked quietly back to the shade of the hen-coops by the wheel, chewing it, her eyes half-closed, and as she went she crossed the path of the master hurrying forward. 'I am sorry to have kept you waiting,' he said. 'I was obliged to mend my pen.' 'Not at all,' they said, and he went on, 'Well now, as for these old finners, gentlemen, you have four main kinds, and there is nothing to be said for any of 'em.'

'Why is this, Mr Allen?' asked Martin in a disapproving

tone: he did not like to hear so large a branch of creation condemned.

'Because if you plant your harpoon in a finner he is apt to knock your boat to matchwood or sound so deep and run so fast he either tows you under or takes out all your line; never was a creature so huge and fast – I have seen one run at thirty-five knots, gentlemen! A hundred foot long and God knows how many tons running at thirty-five knots, twice as fast as a galloping horse! It is unbelievable, was you not to see it with your own eyes. And if by any wild chance you do kill him or far more likely if you come upon him stranded, his whalebone is so short and coarse and mostly black the merchants will not always make an offer; nor will he yield you much above fifty barrels of indifferent oil.'

'He can scarcely be blamed for resenting the harpoon,' said Martin.

'I remember my third voyage,' Allen went on, not attending. 'We were over by the Greenland shore, late in the year, since we had not filled even half our hold. Thick weather, a northern swell making the ice creak loud, a bitter cold evening coming on, and one of our boats got fast to a finwhale. How they came to do it I cannot conceive. Edward Norris, the harpooner, was an experienced whaler and even a first-voyager can tell a finner by his spout – quite unlike a right whale's. And you can see his back fin as he rolls over and goes down again. Any gate, you see him plain when you are close enough to plant your iron. But however it happened, with fog or waves, or wind in the harpooner's eyes, there they were, fast to a finner. Up went their flag for more whale-lines and they clapped 'em on one after another: a tricky job, with the line running out so fast that it makes the bollard char and hiss as you keep pouring water on it. He carried out four full tubs and part of a fifth, close on a mile of line; and he stayed down a great while, maybe half an hour. When he came up old Bingham, the headsman, lanced him directly, and that was the end. He spouted red, threw up his flukes, and

100

set off south by west like a racehorse. They all screeched out for help – we saw the boat tearing along, throwing white water far on either side, going fast away into the murk – what they had done we could not tell – maybe a kink in the line round a man's leg and him half over the side so they dared not cut, or maybe a hitch round a sprung plank – but anyhow a moment later down they went, towed under among the ice, six men and we never found trace of them, not so much as a fur hat floating.'

'The sperm whale is not quite so swift or so formidable, I collect?' said Stephen after a pause.

'No. He could be, with that terrible great jaw. He could snap you a whale-boat in two and scarcely notice it. But he hardly ever does. Sometimes he beats you to pieces with nis flukes, sounding or lashing in his death-agony; but he does not go for to do it. There is no vice in him. Why, in those early days, when no whalers had ever been in the great South Sea almost, he would lie there awash looking at you quite kind and inquisitive with his little eye. I've touched him before now, touched him with my hand.'

'Do any whales attack, unprovoked?' asked Martin.

'No. They may bump into you, and start your backstays; but that is because they are asleep.'

'What are your feelings, when you kill so huge a creature – when you take so vast a life?'

'Why, I feel a richer man,' said Allen laughing: then after a moment, 'No, but I see what you mean; and I have sometimes thought – '

'Land ho,' called the lookout from on high. 'On deck there. High land one point on the starboard bow.'

'That will be the Peak,' observed the master.

'Where? Oh where?' cried Martin. He leapt on to the fife-rail, but insecurely, falling back with his heel and much of his weight on the first and second toes of Stephen's left foot.

'Follow the line of the bowsprit,' said the master, pointing, 'and a little to the right, between the two layers of cloud, you can see the middle of the Peak, shining white.'

'I have seen the Grand Canary!' said Martin, his one eye gleaming with brilliance enough for two. 'My dear Maturin,' – with a most solicitous look – 'how I hope I did not hurt you.'

'Not at all, not at all. There is nothing in life I like better. But allow me to tell you, that it is not the Grand Canary but Teneriffe, and that it is of no use your springing about like that. If I know anything of the service, you will not be allowed to land. You will not see the canary-bird, grand or small, upon her native heath.'

Prophets of doom are nearly always right, and Martin saw no more of the island than could be made out from the maintop as the *Surprise* stood off and on while the launch ran in, coming back through the crowded shipping with a cheerful fat brown man hung about with his own copper saucepans and warranted capable of Christmas pudding and mince pies by Captain Aubrey's very old acquaintance the present governor of the town.

'Never mind,' said Stephen. 'The great likelihood is that we shall water at some one of the Cape Verdes. How I wish it may be St Nicolas or St Lucy. There is a little small uninhabited island between them called Branco, and it has a puffin peculiar to itself, a puffin distinct from all other puffins, and one that I have never seen alive.'

Martin brightened. 'How long do you suppose it will take us to get there?' he asked.

'Oh, not above a week or so, once we pick up the trade wind. Sometimes I have known it begin to blow north of the Canaries and so waft us down with a flowing sheet past the tropic line and on almost to the equator itself: something in the nature of two thousand miles with a flowing sheet!'

'What is a flowing sheet?'

'What indeed? I seem to recall Johnson defining a sheet as the largest rope in the ship, and perhaps it is desirable that such a rope should flow. Or perhaps it is no more than one of the poetical expressions the seamen use: at all events they employ it to give the general impression of a fine free effortless progress. Their language is often highly figurative. When they reach the broad zone of calms and variable winds that lies somewhat north of the equator, between the north-east and the south-east trades, the zone that the French mariner so emphatically calls the *pot au noir*, the pitch-pot, they say that the ship is in the doldrums, as though she were low-spirited, profoundly melancholy, and she lying there with idly flapping sails in the damp oppressive heat, under a cloudy sky.'

At this point however the sky was perfectly clear, and the *Surprise*, although not yet quite her joyful self again, having too many right awkward bastards to deal with, was far from sad or despondent. In 28°15'N. she picked up the trade wind, and despite the fact that it was by no means wholehearted, all hands began to look forward to the modest delights of the Cape Verdes, those parched blackened intolerably hot and sterile islands. The ship had settled down to the steady routine of blue-water sailing: the sun, rising a little abaft the larboard beam and a little hotter every day, dried the newly-cleaned decks the moment it appeared and then beheld the ordered sequence of events – hammocks piped up, hands piped to breakfast, berth-deck cleaned and aired, the new hands piped to the great-gun exercise or reefing topsails, the others to beautifying the ship, the altitude observed, the ship's latitude and her progress determined, noon proclaimed, hands piped to dinner, the ceremony of the mixing of the grog by the master's mate – three of water, one of rum, and the due proportions of lemon-juice and sugar – the drum-beat one hour later for the gunroom meal, then the quieter afternoon, with supper and more grog at six bells, and quarters somewhat later, the ship cleared for action and all hands at their fighting stations. This rarely passed off without at least some gunfire, for although the usual drill of running the great guns in and out had great value, Jack was convinced that nothing could possibly equal the living bang and leap of the genuine discharge in preparing men for battle, to say nothing of teaching them to point the muzzle in the right direction. He was a great believer in gunnery: he had laid in a personal store of powder (the official allowance being far too meagre for real training) to keep his gun-crews in practice; and since few of the ex-Defenders knew anything of the matter at all, much of this private powder went to them, so that often as the first dogwatch drew to an end the evening would be lit by fierce stabbing flames, the ship a little private storm lost on the vast face of the smooth calm lovely ocean, a little storm that emitted clouds, thunder and orange lightning.

An ocean too smooth for Captain Aubrey's liking. He would have preferred two or three almighty northern blows early in the voyage – blows of a violence just short of carrying away any important spars, of course – and this for many reasons: first, because although he had at least a month and more probably something like six weeks in hand, he would have liked even more, being persuaded that you could never have too much time in hand at sea; secondly, because of his simple-minded love of foul weather, of the roaring wind, the monstrous seas, and the ship racing through them with only a scrap of close-reefed storm-canvas; and thirdly because a thundering great blow with topmasts struck down on deck and lifelines rigged fore and aft, lasting two or three days, was almost as good as an action for pulling a heterogeneous crew together.

And they needed pulling together, he reflected: this was the last dog-watch, and as the great-gun exercise had been exceptionally good the hands had been turned up to dance and skylark. They were now playing King Arthur on the forecastle, one man wearing a mess-kid hoop by way of a crown while a set number of others flung buckets of water over him until by antic gestures, grimaces or witticisms he should make one of them smile, the smiler then being obliged to take his place. It was a very old and very popular hot-weather game, and it caused infinite mirth among those who were not penalized for laughing; but as Jack, followed by Pullings, moved a few steps along the gangway, partly to watch the fun and partly to scratch a backstay in the hope of increasing the feeble breeze (a heathen gesture as old or older than the game) he noticed that almost none of the ex-Defenders were taking part, even in the laughter. In a pause between buckets King Arthur caught sight of the Captain near at hand and stood up straight, knuckling his crown, a sprightly young topman named Andrews whom Jack had known ever since he was a Marine Society boy. 'Carry on, carry on,' said Jack. 'I must get my breath first, sir,' said Andrews pleasantly. 'I've been blowing the grampus this last glass and more.'

In the momentary silence a very curious shrill and inhuman voice, not unlike that of Punch or Judy, called out, 'I'll tell you what's wrong with this here ship. The people ain't micable. And the Defenders are picked on perpetual. Extra duty, extra drill, work double tides: always picked on, day and night. Tom Pipes cuts capers over us: and the people ain't micable.'

The tradition of not informing was so strong that all except the stupidest foremast hands instantly looked down or over the gunwhale or into the twilit sky with studiously blank faces, and even the stupidest, having stared openmouthed at the speaker for a brief moment, followed suit. The speaker was perfectly obvious, Compton, once the *Defender*'s barber: his mouth hardly moved and he was looking over the bows with an abstracted expression, but the sound came directly from him: and almost at once Jack recalled that he was a ventriloquist – the extraordinary tone was no doubt part of the act. The words were meant to be anonymous, impersonal; the occasion was as unofficial as anything aboard could well be; and in spite of Pullings' obvious desire to collar the man the incident was best left alone. 'Carry on,' he said to those around King Arthur, and he watched for half a dozen buckets before walking back to the quarterdeck in the gathering darkness.

In the cabin that night, as they tuned their strings, Jack said, 'Did you ever hear a ventriloquist, Stephen?'

'I did too. It was in Rome. He made the statue of Jupiter Ammon speak, the creature, so that you would have sworn the words came from the god, if only the Latin had been a little better. The small dark room – the prophetic deep-voiced solemnity – it was very fine.'

'Perhaps the place has to be enclosed; perhaps the principles of the whispering gallery apply. At all events it don't answer on deck. But the fellow thought it did. It was the strangest experience: there he was, telling me things to my face as though he were invisible, while I could see him as plain as . . .'

'The ace of spades?'

'No. Not quite that. As plain as a . . . God damn it. As plain as the palm of my hand? A turnpike?'

'As Salisbury sphere? As a red herring?'

'Perhaps so. At all events the Defenders gave me to understand they were unhappy.'

The bosun's cat dropped through the open skylight: it was a lean young cat of indifferent character, somewhat whorish, and it at once began rubbing itself against their legs, purring.

'That reminds me,' said Jack, absently pulling its tail, 'Hollar is going to ask you for a really good name, a classical name that will reflect credit on the ship. He thinks Puss or Tib is low.'

'The only possible name for a bosun's cat is Scourge,' said Stephen.

Understanding dawned on Captain Aubrey quite fast, and his great fruity laugh boomed out, setting the larboard watch on the grin as far forward as the break of the forecastle. 'Oh Lord,' he said, wiping his bright blue eyes at last, 'how I wish I had said that. Get away, you silly beast,' – this to the cat, which had now crawled up his breast and was rubbing its whiskers against his face, its eyes closed in a foolish ecstasy. 'Killick, Killick there.

Remove the bosun's cat: take it back to his cabin. Killick, do you know its name?'

Killick detected the slight tremble in his Captain's voice, and since for once he was feeling relatively benign he said No, he did not.

'Its name is Scourge,' said Jack, bursting out again. 'Scourge is the name of the bosun's cat, oh ha, ha, ha, ha!'

'It is very well,' said Stephen, 'but the instrument itself is a vile thing in all conscience, and no laughing matter at all.'

'Martin says much the same,' said Jack. 'If you two had your way, nobody would be flogged and nobody would be killed from one year to the next, and a pretty bear-garden that would be. Oh dear me, my belly hurts. But even you cannot say that this is a flogging ship: we have not rigged the grating once since Gib. I dislike the cat as much as any man, only sometimes I have to order it.'

'Bah,' said Stephen. 'In anything but a servile constitution it would never be countenanced. Are we ever going to play our music now? It is the busy day I have tomorrow.'

Tomorrow was the day when in all probability the *Surprise*, even at her present staid pace, would cut the tropic line, a point at which Stephen liked to bleed all those under his care as a precaution against calentures and the effects of eating far too much meat and drinking far too much grog under the almost perpendicular sun: had he been the captain, all hands would have been kept to a diet of pap and water-gruel between the latitudes of 23°28'N. and 23°28'S. The bleeding was to take place on the quarterdeck, where the people would be assembled as for a muster and cross over one by one, so that none might escape by skulking about the cable-tiers or even hiding in the enormous coils themselves: for there were some, who though willing enough to shed blood in battle or even to lose their own, could not bear the notion or the sight of the deliberate incision. The afternoon was the time for it, but quite early in the morning both surgeons were busy putting a fine edge to their fleams and lancets. Higgins was still exceedingly shy of his chief, as though he were afraid that the Doctor might address him in Latin at any minute. Higgins' stock of that language and indeed of a good many English medical terms was so very slight that Stephen thought it not unlikely that he had borrowed the name and certificates of some qualified man, probably a former employer. Yet he did not regret having brought him: Higgins had already exercised his undeniable, however qualified, dental skill on two occasions when Stephen would have been unwilling to operate. The men looked upon him as something of a phoenix, and several of the *Surprise*'s steady old hypochondriacs, powerful healthy seamen who reported sick once a week and had to be comforted with pills made of chalk, pink dye and sugar, had deserted Stephen. They consulted Higgins privately, and although Stephen did not mind this at all, he was slightly disturbed by some stories that had come through to him: the live eel said to have been removed from John Hales' bowels, for example, did not sound quite orthodox, and perhaps in time the tendency would have to be checked. For the moment however he had nothing much to say to Higgins, and Higgins had nothing whatsoever to say to him: they ground on in silence.

Three decks above their heads (for absurdly enough they were working by lamplight, next to the medicine-chest, far under the waterline) Captain Aubrey was pacing up and down in the bright sunshine with Pullings at his side. Although the wind was still so faint, fainter than he had ever known the north-east trades, there was a pleasant contended look upon his face. The beautifully clean decks stretched away before him, and they were filled with mild, sensible activity as the ex-Defenders were shown how to reeve gun-tackles and house their pieces just so. From the fore-cabin came the youngsters' chorus of hic haec hoc and their mirth, mildly checked by Mr Martin, at the final his his his, his his his: after their dinner but before his own he would go through their day's workings with them, that is to say their separate statements of the ship's position at midday, determined by the height of the sun and the difference between local noon and the Greenwich noon shown by the chronometers, the whole checked by dead-reckoning. The answers were sometimes very wild: some of the boys seemed incapable of grasping the basic principles and they tried to fudge their workings by mistaken rule of thumb or plain cribbing; and Boyle at least (though from a naval family) had never learnt his multiplication table beyond five times. Yet on the whole they were a pleasant set of boys, and although Calamy and Williamson rather disliked being put to their books again after having sailed so long without a schoolmaster, and although they tended to boast and show away before the first-voyagers he did not think they were tyrannical: it seemed a cheerful midshipmen's berth, and the gunner and his wife looked after them well. Certainly Mrs Horner got up their shirts for ceremonial occasions such as dining in the cabin better than Killick: he suspected her of using fresh water.

The young gentlemen's chorus changed. They were now chanting autos autee auto, and Jack's smile broadened. 'That's what I like to hear,' he said. 'They won't be brought by the lee as we are brought by the lee when someone flashes out a Greek remark at us. They will instantly reply, "Autos, autee, auto to you, old cock: Kyrie eleison". And a classical education is good for discipline too; the hands respect it amazingly.'

Pullings did not seem wholly convinced, but he was saying that Mowett certainly thought the world of Homer when the cat, which had not yet learnt the sanctity of the quarterdeck, crossed their bows, evidently meaning to caress and be caressed. 'Mr Hollar,' called Jack, his voice carrying easily to the forecastle, where the bosun was turning in a dead-eye, 'Mr Hollar, there: be so good as to take your Scourge forward and place him under cabin-arrest: or put him in a bag.'

Stephen's witticism had long since passed through the ship, growing even wittier with repetition, explanation to the dull, and elaboration, and the animal was carried along the gangway with many a cry of 'Scourge, ho!' and many a grin, for the *Surprise* was not one of those stern dismal ships where a man might not speak on deck without being spoken to by a superior.

Jack was still smiling when he observed that this was the ship's usual punishment day: was there anything serious? 'Oh no, sir,' said Pullings. 'Only a couple of squabbles, one drunk and incapable – it was his birthday, sir – and one reproachful words. Nothing that six-water grog won't cover. I had thought of leaving it out, since we are to be bled this afternoon.'

'I was about to suggest the same thing,' said Jack, and he was going on to some changes in the watch-list that would integrate the new hands more thoroughly with the old Surprises and make their life somewhat easier when he saw a sight so ugly that it checked the words in his gullet. Hollom was going forward along the larboard gangway: Nagel, an able seaman but one of the most sullen, bloody-minded and argumentative of the Defenders, was coming aft on the same narrow passage. They were abreast of one another; and Nagel walked straight on without the slightest acknowledgement other than a look of elaborate unconcern.

'Master-at-arms,' cried Jack. 'Master-at-arms. Take that man Nagel below. Clap him into bilboes on the half-deck.' He was exceedingly angry. He would do a great deal for a happy ship, but not for a moment would he put up with deliberate indiscipline: not for a moment, even if it meant running the frigate like a prison-hulk for the whole commission. He had heard St Vincent's passionate cry, uttered at a time of incipient mutiny throughout the fleet, 'I'll make them salute a midshipman's uniform on a hand-spike,' and he wholeheartedly agreed with the principle.

To Pullings he said, 'We shall take defaulters at six bells as usual,' and the look on his face positively shocked Howard of the Marines, who had never seen him anything but cheerful or at the worst impatient at the dockyard's delay.

While this was going on a messenger came below to ask when it would be convenient for the gunner to wait on Dr Maturin. 'At once, if he chooses,' said Stephen, wiping the oil from the last of his fleams. 'Mr Higgins, perhaps you will attend to the sick-bay.' It was the commissioned and warrant officers' privilege to consult the surgeon in privacy, and Stephen had little doubt that although the gunner was a heavy, broad-shouldered, dark, fierce-looking man, and battle-scarred, he was one of those who disliked being bled, and meant to beg off.

In a way he was right, since Horner's visit was indeed connected with the bleeding. But even before he had sat the man down Stephen realized that there was more to it than mere reluctance. For one thing, Horner's voice had nothing of the soft, gasping, self-pitying quality which seamen felt was owing to themselves, to the Doctor and to the situation when they came to see him as patients. Not at all. Horner's voice was gruff and it had a strong underlying ferocity in it. Crossing him would not answer and so far no one in the ship had ever done so. After a few general remarks and an awkward pause he said he did not wish to be bled if loss of blood would stop him doing it. He had come very near to doing it these last nights, he thought, and if losing even half a pint was to throw all aback once more, why . . . But if bleeding made no odds, why, the Doctor was welcome to take a gallon if he pleased.

Stephen had not practised so long among men who were both modest and inarticulate without coming to know what a number of meanings 'it' might assume, and a very few questions confirmed his first intuitive understanding. Horner was impotent. But what disturbed Maturin, making him fear that it was most unlikely he should be able to help his patient, was the fact that he

111

was impotent only where his wife was concerned. Horner had already done great violence to his feelings in making this disclosure and Stephen did not like to press him on the exact nature of their relations, but he gathered that Mrs Horner was not particularly understanding; she said nothing – they never spoke about it at all – but she seemed contrarified and gave short answers. Horner was almost certain that someone had put a spell on him and he had been to two different cunning-men to have it taken off immediately after their marriage; had paid four pound ten; but they had done no good, the buggers. 'God love us,' he said, breaking off, 'they are piping hands witness punishment. I thought there was no defaulters today. I must run and put on my good coat. So must you, Doctor.'

It was in their good coats that they slipped into their places on the quarterdeck, a quarterdeck all blue and gold with formal uniforms, while abaft the mizen and along either rail the Marines stood in scarlet lines, the sun blazing on their white cross-belts and fixed bayonets. Jack had already dismissed the squabblers, the birthday drunkard and the reproachful words with the sentence 'Sixes until this time next week'; for although over a course of many years Stephen had assured him again and again that it was the amount of alcohol that counted, not the water, he (like everybody else aboard) still privately believed that grog, doubly diluted to a thin, unpalatable wash, was far less intoxicating – it stood to reason. He was now dealing with Nagel. 'What have you done? You know damned well what you have done,' said Jack with cold, concentrated and absolutely unaffected anger. 'You passed Mr Hollom on the gangway without making your obedience. You, an old man-of-war's man: it was not ignorance. Disrespect, wilful disrespect is within a hair's breadth of mutiny, and mutiny is hanging without a shadow of a doubt. It will not do in this ship, Nagel: you knew what you were about. Have his officers anything to say for him?' They had not. Hollom, the only one who could in decency have spoken up, did not see fit to do so. 'Very well,' said Jack. 'Rig the grating. Ship's corporal, order the women below.' White aprons vanished down the fore hatchway and Nagel slowly took off his shirt with a sullen, lowering, dangerous air. 'Seize him up,' said Jack.

'Seized up, sir,' said the quartermaster a moment later.

'Mr Ward,' said Jack to his clerk, 'read the thirty-sixth Article of War.'

As the clerk opened the book all present took off their hats. 'Thirty-six,' he read in a high, official tone, 'All other crimes not capital, committed by any person or persons in the fleet, which are not mentioned in this act, or for which no punishment is hereby directed to be inflicted, shall be punished according to the laws and customs in such cases used at sea.'

'Two dozen,' said Jack, clapping his hat back on to his head. 'Bosun's mate, do your duty.'

Harris, the senior bosun's mate, received the cat from Hollar and did his duty: objectively, without ill-will, yet with all the shocking force usual in the Navy. The first stroke jerked an 'Oh my God' out of Nagel but after that the only sound, apart from the solemn count, was the hiss and the impact.

'I must remember to try Mullins' Patent Balm,' reflected Stephen. Near him those youngsters who had never seen a serious flogging before were looking frightened and uneasy, and over the way, amongst the hands, he saw big Padeen Colman weeping openly, tears of pity coursing down his simple kindly face. Yet upon the whole the people were unmoved; for Captain Aubrey this was a very heavy sentence indeed, but in most ships it would have been more severe, and the general opinion that two dozen was fair enough – if a cove liked to sail so near the wind as not to pay his duty to an officer, even if it was only an unlucky master's mate without a penny to his name, probably a Jonah too and certainly no seaman, why, he could not complain if he was took aback. This seemed to be Nagel's opinion too. When his wrists and ankles were cast loose he picked up his shirt and went

113

forward to the head-pump so that his mates could wash the blood off his back before he put it on again, the look on his face, though sombre, was by no means that of a man who had just suffered an intolerable outrage, or an injustice.

'How I hate this beating,' said Martin a little later, as they stood at the taffrail together, watching the two sharks that had joined the ship some days before and that cruised steadily along in her wake or under her keel: experienced cunning old sharks that ate up all the filth that was offered but that utterly disdained all baited hooks, that provokingly kept just too deep for the exact identification of their species, just too deep for the musket-balls that were showered on them every evening at small-arms drill to have any effect, and that spoilt Captain Aubrey's early-morning swim. One he would have tolerated, but he had grown timid with advancing years and two he found excessive, particularly as a very disagreeable incident with the tiger-sharks of the Red Sea had recently changed his ideas about the whole race.

'So do I,' said Stephen. 'But you are to consider that it accords with the laws and customs of the sea, a tolerably brutal place. I believe that if we have our singing this evening you will find it as cheerful as though the grating had never been rigged.'

The grating in question had been unrigged and the deck well swabbed at least half an hour before this, for eight bells was within a few grains of sand ahead, and all across the deck just abaft the mainmast the officers and young gentlemen had the sun firmly in their quadrants and sextants, waiting for the moment when it should cross the meridian. The moment came: everyone was aware of it, but following the ancient ritual the master first told Mowett, and Mowett, stepping across to Captain Aubrey, took off his hat and reported to him that the local time appeared to be noon. 'Make it so,' said Jack, and noon it therefore became by law. Immediately after this the ship echoed to the striking of eight bells and the piping of the hands to dinner, but Stephen made his way through the uproar to the master, asked for the position, and hurried back to Martin. 'Give you joy of the day, my dear,' he said. 'We have just crossed the tropic line.'

'Have we indeed?' cried Martin, flushing with pleasure. 'Ha, ha! So we are in the tropics at last; and one of my life's ambitions has been fulfilled.' He looked eagerly about the sea and sky, as though everything were quite different now; and by one of those happy coincidences that reward naturalists perhaps more often than other men, a tropic-bird came clipping fast across the breeze and circled above the ship, a satiny-white bird with a pearly pink flush and two immensely long tail feathers trailing far behind.

It was still there – still watched by Martin, who had refused his dinner in order not to lose a moment of its presence – sometimes taking wide sweeps round the ship, sometimes hovering overhead, and sometimes even sitting on the mainmast truck, when Stephen and Higgins began bleeding all hands. They only took eight ounces from each, but this, bowl after bowl, amounted to nine good buckets with foam of an extraordinary beauty: but they had rather more than their fair share of fools who would be fainting, because as the breeze declined and the heat increased a sickly slaughterhouse reek spread about the deck; and one of them (a young Marine) actually pitched into a brimming bucket as he fell and caused three more to lurch, so angering Dr Maturin that the next half dozen patients were drained almost white, like veal, while guards were placed over the buckets that remained.

However, it was all over in an hour and fifteen minutes, both surgeons being brisk hands with a fleam; the corpses were dragged away by their friends to be recovered with sea-water or vinegar, according to taste; and finally, seeing that fair was fair, each surgeon bled the other. Then Stephen turned to Martin, whose bird had flown by now, though not without having showed him its yellow bill and its totipalmate feet, and said, 'Now, sir, I believe I may

115

show you something that will gratify a speculative mind and perhaps determine the species.'

He asked Honey, who had the watch, for half a dozen keen anglers, and the bosun for two parcels of junk, each the size of a moderate baby. Up until this time all hands, including the Captain and his officers, had been clasping their wounded arms, looking rather grave and self-concerned, but now Jack stepped forward with much more life in his eye and said, 'Why, Doctor, what would you be at?'

'I hope the biter may be bit,' said Stephen, reaching for the mizentopsail halliards, to which the shark-hooks and their chains were attached. 'And above all I hope that the species may be determined; Carcharias is the genus, sure, but the species . . . Where is that black thief Padeen? Now, Padeen, thread the babies on the hooks – handle them as though you loved them – and let them soak up the good red blood till I have circumvented those villains behind – abaft – astern.'

He took a bucket and poured it slowly through the aftermost starboard scupper; both Mowett and Pullings uttered a dismal cry as they saw their holy paintwork defiled, but the hands who would have to clean it came flocking aft with pleased expectant looks. Nor were they disappointed: as soon as the blood-taint (though almost infinitely diluted) reached the fish they came to the surface, casting rapidly to and fro across the frigate's wake, their black fins high over the white water. Two more buckets, going astern in a pink cloud, excited them to a frenzy. They raced in, running up the ship's side, all caution gone, crossing under her keel, flashing through the wake and back again with frightening speed and agility, now half out of the water, now just under the surface, making it boil and froth.

'Drop the first baby,' said Stephen, 'and let him hook himself. Do not pluck it out of his mouth, on your souls.'

The tail man had barely time to whip a turn round

116

the gallows-bitts before the stout line was twanging taut, the hook well home, and the shark threshing madly under the starboard quarter while the other, in a blind fury, tore great pieces out of its belly and tail.

'Next baby,' cried Stephen, and poured in the rest of the blood. The strike of the second shark was even stronger than the first, and the two of them together heaved the *Surprise* three points off her course.

'Now what are we to do?' asked Martin, looking at their monstrous and quite shockingly dangerous catch. 'Must we let go? If we pull them in their lashing will certainly destroy the ship.'

'Sure, I cannot tell at all,' said Stephen. 'But I dare say Mr Aubrey will know.'

'Steer small,' said Jack to the helmsman, who had been watching the fun rather than his card, and to the bosun, 'Mr Hollar, a couple of running bowlines to the crossjack yardarm, and don't you wish you may get 'em aboard without ruining your shrouds.'

In the event, such was the wholehearted zeal of every-one in the ship that the enormously powerful, very heavy, very furious creatures came over the side with no damage at all, lying there on the deck looking larger than life and more savage by far, snapping their terrible jaws with a sound like a trunk-lid slamming. All the sailors Stephen had ever known had an ancient deep-seated hatred for sharks, and these were no exception. They exulted over the dying monsters and abused them; yet even so he was surprised to see a man so recently flogged as Nagel kicking the larger one, and apostrophizing it with all the wit at his command. And later, after the forecastlemen had borne off the one intact tail to decorate the frigate's stem and bring her luck and when he and Martin were busy with their dissection, Nagel came back and asked very diffidently whether he might have a piece, a small piece, of the backbone, just the scrag end, like; he had promised a morsel to his little girl. 'By all means,' said Stephen. 'And you may give her these too,' – taking three frightful triangular teeth (necessary for the identification of the species) from his pocket.

'Oh sir,' cried Nagel, at once wrapping them in a handkerchief, 'I thank you very kindly.' He thrust them into his bosom, wincing as he did so, knuckled his forehead and lumbered off forward, moving stiffly. Half way along the gangway he turned and called back, 'She'll be main delighted, your honour.'

On this day at least, Stephen was an accurate prophet. By the time of the evening singing, after a purely formal beating to quarters, the massive blood-letting and the excitement of the sharks had quite overlaid that morning's punishment. The cook obliged them with a ballad of eighty-one stanzas about Barton, the Scotch pirate, accompanied by three Jew's harps, and Mr Martin's nascent choir went creditably through part of the oratorio he hoped to perform before they returned to home waters. As a passenger in an earlier command of Captain Aubrey's, a ship of the line, he had brought the more musical section of the crew to be word-perfect and often note-perfect in the *Messiah*, and there were many of his former singers now in the *Surprise*. He had an indifferent voice himself, and he played no instrument well, but he was an excellent teacher, and the hands liked him. And when the concert proper was over many people stayed on deck for the pleasure of the evening air. Hollom was one of them: he sat on the larboard gangway with his legs dangling over the waist, and from time to time he played a few notes on Honey's Spanish guitar. He was searching for a tune and when he found it he chanted the words over twice, quite softly, then struck a chord and sang out clear and sweet, as pure a tenor as could be wished. Stephen took no notice of the words until Hollom came to the burden, *Come it late or come it soon/I shall enjoy my rose in June*, which he sang three or four times with some subtle variations and in a curious tone that might have been called an amused confidence. 'A golden voice,' thought Stephen, looking at him. He observed that although Hollom was facing the opposite

118

rail his eyes were in fact discreetly turned forward, and following their direction he saw Mrs Horner fold up her sewing and rise at the third repetition with a displeased, rebellious expression and go below.

CHAPTER FOUR

The Indiamen were seen quite early in the morning while Jack was in the pure green sea, with nothing below him for a thousand fathoms and nothing on either hand but the African shore some hundreds of miles away on the left and the far remoter Americas on the right. He swam and dived, swam and dived, delighting in the coolness and the living run of water along his naked body and through his long streaming hair; he felt extremely well, aware of his strength and taking joy in it. And for this brief spell while he was not in the ship he did not have to think about the innumerable problems to do with her people, her hull, rigging and progress, and the wisest course for her to take, problems that perpetually waited on his mind aboard; he loved the *Surprise* more than any ship he had known, but even so half an hour's holiday from her had a certain charm. 'Come on,' he called to Stephen, standing on the cathead, looking pinched and mean. 'The water is like champagne.'

'You always say that,' muttered Stephen.

'Go on, sir,' said Calamy. 'It's soon over. You will like it once you are in.'

Stephen crossed himself, drew a deep breath, grasped his nose with one hand, blocked an ear with the other, closed his eyes and leapt, striking the sea with his buttocks. Because of his curious lack of buoyancy he remained under the surface for a considerable time, but he came up eventually and Jack said to him, 'Now the *Surprise* has no one to direct her worldly or her physical or even her spiritual affairs, ha, ha, ha!' This was true, for the *Surprise*'s boats were all towing astern so that the heat should not open their seams, and in the last sat Mr Martin: they were on the edge of the Sargasso Sea, and he had already taken up a fine collection of weeds, as well as three sea-horses and seven species of pelagic crab.

'Sail ho,' cried the lookout as the far haze cleared with the rising sun. 'On deck, there: a sail two points on the starboard bow . . . two sail. Three sail of ships, topgallants up.'

'Stephen,' said Jack, 'I must go back at once. You can reach the boats, can you not?' They had been swimming (if that was the word for Stephen's laborious, jerking progress, mostly just under the surface) away from the ship, and with her easy motion added to theirs something in the nature of twenty-five or even thirty yards now separated the Captain from his command, a distance not far from Stephen's limit.

'Oh,' said he, but a ripple filled his mouth. He coughed, swallowed more, submerged and began to drown. As usual Jack dived under him, seized his sparse hair and drew him up to the surface; and as usual Stephen folded his hands, closed his eyes, and let himself be towed, floating on his back. Jack abandoned him at Martin's boat, swam fast to the stern-ladder, ran straight up the side and so, pausing only for his shoes, to the masthead. After a moment he called for a glass and confirmed his first impression that they were homeward-bound Indiamen; then, hearing the shrill metallic voice of Mrs Sergeant James, he called for his breeches to be sent into the maintop.

On deck he laid a course to intercept them – it would take the *Surprise* only a trifle out of her way – and hurried below to join the smell of coffee, toast, and things frying, bacon among them. Stephen was already there, taking an unfair advantage with the sausages; and as soon as Jack sat down his other guests appeared, Mowett and the younger Boyle. From time to time young gentlemen were sent down to report the strangers' appearance and behaviour, and before the feast was over a disconsolate Calamy came to say 'that they were only Indiamen, sir; and Captain Pullings said that the nearest was the *Lushington*.'

'I am delighted to hear it,' said Jack. 'Killick, pray

tell my cook to make a special effort today: we shall have three Company's captains to dinner. And you may rouse out a case of champagne in case we meet early. Sling in half a dozen in a wet blanket from the crossjack yard, just under the windward side of the awning.'

Early they came and late they left, pink and jolly, after a dinner that ended with the Christmas pudding for which Jack's new cook was so justly famous, and measureless wine. A cheerful dinner, since two of the captains, Muffit and M'Quaid, had been embroiled with a French squadron in the Indian Ocean, together with Jack Aubrey, Pullings and Mowett in this very same ship, and they had a great deal to say, reminding one another just how the wind had veered, and how, at a given moment, M. de Linois had paid off round and put before it.

Cheerful, but as the ships slowly drew apart Jack paced up and down on his quarterdeck with a grave, considering look on his face. Muffit, an immensely experienced East India sailor, had told him that never in all his time had he known the belt of calms and variable breezes between the south-east and the north-east trades so wide. He and his companions had lost the south-easters in two degrees north and it had taken them more than five hundred miles of creeping and towing before they picked up the first true north-easter, and that no more than indifferent strong. The question that he was weighing in his mind was whether, in view of the *Surprise*'s mediocre progress, he should now bear away westwards, abandoning the Cape Verde islands and their water and relying upon the torrential rain that so often fell in storms between nine and three degrees north of the Line. The water collected in sails and awnings had a villainous taste of hemp and tar and at first it was scarcely drinkable; but the saving of several days might prove to be of the first importance, since it was by no means sure that the *Norfolk* would have had the same paltry breezes. Yet it was by no means sure that the *Surprise* would be rained on, either. The rainstorms in that belt, though sometimes almost unbelievably heavy, were limited in size: before now he had passed through the variables without once being wetted, though he had seen black masses of cloud on either horizon, or little isolated storms here and there, in three or four places at once with miles of clear water in between; and the fate of the waterless ship in the calms was horrible to contemplate. On the other hand the atmosphere of that region, though hellfire hot, was always intensely humid; you did not feel very thirsty, and much more fresh water was used for steeping the salt meat than for drinking.

His mind so ran on these things that when he and Stephen were playing that night his fingers, which should have been providing a mild deedly-deedly-deedly background to the 'cello's long statement in a slow (and perhaps rather dull) movement they both knew perfectly well, wandered off at a point of easy transition to another slow movement by the same composer, and were only pulled up by a shocking discord and by Stephen's indignant cries. Where did Jack think he was going to? What would he be at?

'I beg your pardon a thousand times,' said Jack. 'I am in the D minor piece – I have been gathering moss – but I have just made up my mind. Forgive me a moment.' He went on deck, altered the dear ship's course to south-west by south, and coming back he said with a contented look, 'There: we may die of thirst in the next few weeks if it don't rain, but at least we shall not miss the *Norfolk*. I mean,' he added, clapping his hand to the wood of his chair, 'we are somewhat less likely to miss her now. Yet on the other hand I am afraid you will have to tell poor Mr Martin that he will not see the Cape Verdes after all.'

'The poor soul will be sadly disappointed. He knows far more about beetles than I do, and it appears that the Cape Verdes rejoice in a wonderful variety of tetramerae, forbidding though they may appear to a shallow, superficial mind. I shall break it to him gently. But will I tell you something, Jack? Our hearts are not in the music tonight.

I know mine is not, and I believe I shall take a turn in the air and then go to bed.'

'You are not offended by my moss, Stephen, are you?' asked Jack.

'Never in life, soul,' said Stephen. 'I was uneasy in my mind before ever we sat down; and for once music has not answered.'

It was quite true. That afternoon Stephen had gone through the papers that had accumulated in his cabin, throwing most away and reducing the others to some kind of order; and among those he discarded was the most recent of a series of letters from a Wellwisher who regularly sent to let him know that his wife was unfaithful to him. Usually these letters only aroused a mild wonder in him, a mild desire to know who it was who took so much trouble; but now, partly because of a dream and partly because he knew that appearances were against him – that he certainly *appeared* to have been traipsing about with Laura Fielding – it reinforced an anxiety that had been with him ever since the mail first reached the *Surprise* in Gibraltar. Although by most standards their marriage would hardly have been called successful he was very deeply attached to her and the thought of her being angry with him, together with the frustration of being unable to communicate with her, overcame both the usual steadiness of his mind and his persuasion that the letter carried by Wray would convince her of his unaltered regard in spite of the fact that his explanation of Mrs Fielding's presence was necessarily incomplete and in some respects quite false. For now, in his present low state, it was borne in upon him that falsity sometimes had the same penetrating quality as truth: both were perceived intuitively, and Diana was intuition's favourite child.

He paused in the waist of the ship with the strong breeze eddying about him before he groped his way up the ladder to the quarterdeck. The night was as black as a night could be, warm velvet black with no stars at all; he could detect the ship's motion by her urgent heave and thrust, and living vibration of the wood under his hand, and the creak of the blocks, cordage and canvas overhead, but never a sail nor a rope could he see, nor even the steps in front of his nose as he crept up. He might have been entirely deprived of the sense of sight and it was only when he brought his nose above the break of the quarterdeck that his eyes returned to him, with the glow of the quartermaster at the con, a greyhaired man named Richardson, and of Walsh, the much younger timoneer. Quite close at hand he made out the hint of a darker form looming this side of the mainmast; and to this form he said, 'Good night, now, Mr Honey: would the chaplain be aboard at all?'

'It's me, sir,' said Mowett, chuckling. 'I swapped with Honey. Yes, Mr Martin is still up. He's in the launch, towing astern; and I doubt he comes in till sunrise, it being so uncommon dark and awkward. You can just make him out, if you look over the side.' Stephen looked: there was not much phosphorescence on the sea, although it was so warm, but there was enough for the troubled wake to show as it swirled about the towing boats, and in the farthest he could just distinguish the rise and fall of Martin's little net. 'Perhaps you would like to join him?' suggested Mowett. 'I will give you a hand over the taffrail, if you choose.'

'I do not choose,' said Stephen, contemplating the length of faintly luminous water and the increasing perturbation of the train of boats – barge, gig, jolly-boat, and both the cutters, all quite far apart – that would have to be traversed before the launch was reached. 'Bad news will always keep. But listen, James Mowett, are they not tossing about in a very dreadful manner? Is there not some danger of their being drawn below the surface, engulfed in the mill-stream of the wake, and of Mr Martin's being lost?'

'Oh dear me no, sir,' said Mowett. 'No danger at all: and was it to come on to blow, to really as one might say blow, why, I should back a topsail, hale him alongside and so pass him a line. Ain't it agreeable to be moving at last? This is the first time we have done better than five knots since we laid the Rock: the barky began to speak at the beginning of the watch, and now she must be throwing a fine bow-wave, if only we could see it. *She plies her course yet, nor her winged speed/The falcon could for pace exceed.*'

'Are those your lines, Mr Mowett?'

'No, no, alas; they are Homer's. Lord, what a fellow he was! Ever since I began reading in him, I have quite lost any notion of writing myself, he being such a . . .' Mowett's voice trailed away in admiration and Stephen said, 'I had no idea you were a Grecian.'

'No more I am, sir,' replied Mowett. 'I read him in a translation, a book a young lady gave me for a keepsake in Gibraltar, by a cove named Chapman, a very splendid cove. I began because I esteemed the giver, and because I hoped to be able to knock poor Rowan on the head with some pretty good images and rhymes when he rejoined, but I went on because I could not stop. Do you know him?'

'Not I,' said Stephen. 'Though I did look into Mr Pope's version once, and Madame Dacier's. I hope your Mr Chapman is better.'

'Oh, it is magnificent – a great booming, sometimes, like a heavy sea, the *Iliad* being in fourteeners; and I am sure it is very like the Greek. I must show it to you. But then I dare say you have read him in the original.'

'I had no choice. When I was a boy it was Homer and Virgil, Homer and Virgil entirely and many a stripe and many a tear between. But I came to love him for all that, and I quite agree with you – he is the very prince of poets. The *Odyssey* is a fine tale, sure, though I never could cordially like Ulysses: he lied excessively, it seems to me; and if a man lies beyond a certain point a sad falseness enters into him and he is no longer amiable.' Stephen spoke with some feeling: his work in intelligence had called for a great deal of duplicity – perhaps too much. '. . . no longer amiable. And I should not quarrel with those who say that

Homer had no great hand in the poem. But the *Iliad*, of God love his soul, never was such a book as the *Iliad*!'

Mowett cried that the Doctor was in the right of it, and began to recite a particularly valued piece: soon losing himself, however. But Stephen scarcely heard; his mind glowed with recollection and he exclaimed, 'And the truly heroic scale, that makes us all look so mean and pallid; and the infinite art from the beginning to the noble end with Achilles and Priam talking quietly together in the night, both doomed and both known to be doomed – the noble end and its full close, for I do not count the funeral rites as anything but a necessary form, almost an appendix. The book is full of death, but oh so living.'

Four bells interrupted them, and clear round the ship came the cry of the lookouts and the sentinels: 'Lifebuoy, all's well.' 'Starboard gangway, all's well.' 'Starboard bow, all's well,' followed by all the rest. The carpenter's mate, bringing a lantern with him, reported eleven inches in the well – half an hour's pumping at dawn – and the midshipman of the watch, having fussed some little time with the lantern and the sand-glass, said, 'Seven knots one fathom, sir, if you please.' Mowett wrote this on the log-board: the lantern vanished down a hatchway, the darkness returned, even thicker than before, and Stephen said, 'There was a foolish man of Lampsacus, Metrodorus by name, that explained away the gods and the heroes as personifications of this and that, of fire and water, the sky and the sun, and so on – Agamemnon was the upper air, as I recall – and then there were a great many busy fellows who found out hidden meanings in Homer by the score: and some would have it that the *Odyssey* in particular was an enormous great bloated metaphor, the way the writer of it would have seen a superior acrosticmonger. But as far as I know not one of the inky boobies ever saw what is as clear as the sun at midday – that as well as being the great epic of the world, the *Iliad* is a continued outcry against adultery. Hundreds, nay thousands of heroical young men killed, Troy town in blood and flames, Andromache's child dashed from the battlements and she led away to carry water for Greek women, the great city razed and depopulated, all, all from mere adultery. And she did not even like the worthless fellow at the end. James Mowett, there is nothing to be said for adultery.'

'No, sir,' said Mowett, smiling in the darkness, partly from recollections of his own, and partly like everybody else aboard – all the old Surprises, that is to say – he was as certain of Dr Maturin's criminal conversation with Mrs Fielding as if he had seen them kiss and clip in naked bed. 'No, sir: nothing at all. And I have sometimes thought of giving him a hint; but these things are too delicate, and I doubt it would answer. Yes, Boyle, what is it?'

'Who is this *him*?' said Maturin to himself.

'I beg your pardon, sir,' said Boyle, 'but I believe there is a hail from the launch.'

'Then lay aft and see what is afoot. Take my speaking-trumpet, and sing out loud and clear.'

Boyle sang out loud and clear, and coming back he said, 'As far as I could make out, sir, the chaplain wishes to know whether we apprehend any worsening of the tempest.'

'It is what we have been praying for this last age, after all,' said Mowett. 'But perhaps we had better bring the launch under the counter; he may be a little uneasy in his mind. Jump down and help him up the stern-ladder; there will be plenty of light from the cabin.'

'How very kind of you,' said Martin, sitting on the capstan to recover his breath after his climb. 'The boat was plunging up and down in a most alarming fashion, and I could make no observations at all this last half hour.'

'What were you observing, sir?'

'Luminous organisms, mostly minute pelagic crustaceans, copepods; but I need calmer water for it, the good calm water we have had almost all the way. How I pray it may grow quiet again before we leave the sargasso quite behind.'

'I don't know about the sargasso,' said Mowett, 'but I think you may be pretty sure of calm weather before we cross the Line.'

And indeed long, long before they crossed the Line the trade wind died in the frigate's wake and left her with her towering canvas limp, all the noble expanse she had spread to catch the lightest airs hanging there discouraged and the ship rolling horribly on the great smooth swell.

'So these are the doldrums,' said Martin, coming on deck in his best coat, the coat worn for invitations to the cabin, and looking about the hot, lowering sky and the glassy sea with great satisfaction. 'I have always wanted to see them. Yet even so, I believe I shall take off my coat until dinner-time.'

'It will make no odds,' said Stephen, whose spirit of contradiction was more lively than usual, because of a sleepless night, much of it filled with longing for his private vice, the alcoholic tincture of laudanum, a form of liquid opium that had consoled him in anxiety, unhappiness, privation, pain and insomnia for many a year but which he had given up (except medicinally) on his marriage with Diana. 'Your coat protects you from the radiant heat of the sun, and the mechanism of your body maintains it at a constant temperature: as you know, the Arab of the desert goes covered from head to foot. The apparent relief is a mere illusion, a vulgar error.'

Martin was not a man to be overborne, however; he took off his coat, folded it carefully on the hammock-cloth, and said, 'The vulgar error is wonderfully refreshing, nevertheless.'

'And as for the doldrums,' Stephen went on, 'I believe you may perhaps misuse the term. As I understand it, in nautical language the doldrums are a condition, a state; not a region. They are analogous to tantrums. A child, and God help us a grown man alas, can be in the tantrums anywhere at all. Similarly a ship may be in the doldrums wherever she is long becalmed. I may be mistaken, but Captain Aubrey will certainly know.'

Captain Aubrey knew, but since they were his guests he contrived to agree with both, though inclining somewhat in the chaplain's favour: he conceived that from seamen's slang or cant doldrums was become a general word by land, used in Mr Martin's sense of what used to be called the variables. He had a great esteem for Mr Martin; he valued him; but he did not invite him as often as he felt he should; and now by way of making amends he not only filled his glass very often and helped him to the best cuts of the leg of mutton but also strained the truth in his direction. The fact of the matter was that he felt a constraint in Martin's presence. He had known few parsons, and his respect for the cloth made him feel that a grave face and a sober discourse, preferably on topics of a moral nature, were called for in their presence; and although he did not much delight in bawdy – indeed never talked it except in bawdy company where the reverse would have seemed offensively pious – the compulsory decorum weighed upon him. Then again, although Mr Martin loved music he was an indifferent performer and after one or two sadly discordant evenings full of apology he had not been asked to play in the cabin again. Jack was therefore more than usually attentive to his guest, not only congratulating him (quite sincerely) upon his sermon that morning, not only feeding and wining him to a pitch that few men could have withstood in a temperature of a hundred and four with a humidity of eighty-five, but telling him in some detail of the sail that was to be put over the side that afternoon for the hands to swim in: those hands, that was to say, who could not take to the sea itself, for fear of drowning. This led on to observations about seamen's, particularly fishermen's, reluctance to be taught to swim; and at the far end of the table Pullings, who as a captain by courtesy was allowed to pipe up of his own accord, said, 'It is a great while since you have saved anyone, sir.'

'I suppose it is,' said Jack.

'Does the Captain often save people?' asked Martin.

'Oh dear me, yes. One or two every commission: or

more. I dare say you could man the barge with hands you have saved, could you not, sir?'

'Perhaps I could,' said Jack absently, and then, feeling that he was not doing his duty by his other guest, he said, 'I hope we shall see you over the side this afternoon, Mr Hollom. Do you swim?'

'Not a stroke, sir,' said Hollom, speaking for the first time; and he added, after a slight pause, 'But I shall join the others in splashing about in the sail; it would be a rare treat to feel cool.'

A rare treat indeed. Even at night heat seemed to emanate from the bloody moon, and during the oppressive, stifling days the sun, even from behind its frequent low cloud, made the pitch bubble in the seams of the deck and the tar melt so that it dripped from the upper rigging, while resin oozed from under the paint and drooled down the sides as the ship towed slowly south and west, all boats out ahead and the pullers relieved each glass. Sometimes a hot, capricious breeze would ruffle the oily sea and all hands would dart to brace the yards to take advantage of it; but rarely did the *Surprise* travel more than a mile or so before the breeze came foul or died away altogether, leaving her lifeless on the swell, rolling to such a degree that in spite of their strengthened and new-swifted shrouds and doubled backstays her masts were in danger of going by the board, even with the topgallants struck down on deck; and not only Mrs Lamb but also some of the *Defender*'s landsmen took to their beds again with utterly prostrating sickness.

It was a wearisome time, and it seemed to last for ever. One day's noon observation could be distinguished from the last only by the finest instruments used with the greatest skill; the heat worked right down into the lowest depths of the ship, making the bilgewater stink most vilely, so that those whose cabins lay far below, Stephen and the chaplain among them, had but little sleep. And when they came on deck in the night watches, carrying rolls of sailcloth against the soft pitch of the seams, they were

131

cruelly chivvied from place to place as the hands, usually under their Captain's immediate command, raced to catch the last waft of air. It was a time when theories crumbled: although he was as impervious to heat as a salamander – revelled in it, indeed – Stephen shed his stuff coat, his cloth breeches, his good wool stockings, and appeared in a white banyan jacket, usually open on his meagre chest, airy nankeen pantaloons, and a broad-brimmed sennit hat, plaited for him by Bonden, whom he had taught to read many years before in these same waters: far, far kinder waters then, and a very much quicker passage, incalculably cheaper as far as expense of spirit was concerned. In the same way Jack's views on humidity did not prevent him from drinking up his whole private store of East India pale ale, nor from going over their supplies of water with the master again and again, adding up what was left in the 159 gallon leaguers of the ground tier, the 108 gallon butts, the hogsheads and half hogsheads, laid bung up and bilge free in the wings, and coming to a most discouraging sum total. Even at no more than a purser's quart a head – a far cry from the gallon of beer of home waters – the store diminished by nearly half a ton each day; and that took no account of the great quantity absolutely required for making the salt meat edible.

They did come in for the skirt of a rainstorm in 6°25′N., but it did little more than prepare their spread-out awnings and sails, cleaning them for the next hypothetical downpour. The few butts of water they collected were so brackish and tarry and full of maker's dressing from the new sailcloth that it could not be drunk in their present moderate state of need. Jack had it barrelled, however. If this went on they would give ten years' pay for a cup of a far worse brew.

He was worried: first by the lack of water, of course; but also by his lack of progress. He knew the *Norfolk*, and he knew that if she was commanded by any of the American officers he had met about the *Constitution* or as a prisoner of war in Boston she would be running south as fast as ever she could go with due regard to her masts and rigging: she might even make up her month's delay and pass Cape St Roque before him. The ship's people worried him, too. The Surprises had accepted and absorbed the Gibraltar lunatics, treating them kindly, cutting up their meat for them and bawling into their ears when they could not quite understand; but in spite of the heavy shared labour of towing ship and of the changes he had introduced into the watch-bill, most of the Defenders they could not bear. Almost all the punishment inflicted was brought about by fighting between the two sides, and Jack looked forward to the eventual crossing of the Line with real anxiety; in the traditional rough fun ill-will could take an ugly shape. He had known unpopular men maimed before this, and one actually drowned during the horse-play: that was when Jack was a master's mate in the *Formidable*. And his anxiety was increased by the fact that tempers were wearing precious thin with continual toil in the great oppressive heat, and the short commons. Of course, being sole master after God, he could forbid the ceremony; but he would be ashamed to command a ship ruled in such a manner.

Then again there was something in the air, something he could not yet define. Jack had been lucky in the matter of employment, spending most of his life afloat, and this had given him more experience of ships' companies than most officers of his seniority; and his experience had also been more extensive, since an irascible captain had disrated Mr Midshipman Aubrey at the Cape, turning him before the mast as a common hand, there to live, eat, sleep and work with the rest of the men. This had brought him intimately acquainted with seamen's ways and moods, the significance of their looks, gestures and silences; and now he was certain that something was afoot, something concealed but generally understood. It was quite certainly not a hatching mutiny and it was certainly not the heavy gambling he had known in a few ships rich in prize-money, since the Surprises now had barely a groat between them;

but there was a certain excitement and there was a certain secrecy that might have belonged to either.

He was quite right; and this something was understood throughout the ship by everybody except her Captain, her chaplain and of course her gunner. In a crowded man-of-war it was very difficult to carry out anything privately and all hands knew that Mr Hollom was having to do with Mrs Horner. He was ideally placed for such an enterprise, since he slung his hammock in the midshipmen's berth, and the gunner's realm, where Mrs Horner looked after the youngsters, was just at hand. Very few other men in the ship could be in those parts without exciting comment and now that he was reasonably well fed Hollom made full use of his opportunities.

It was generally thought that he made too full use of them; that after a discreet beginning he had grown over-confident; and that presently he would cop it, mate, cop it something cruel. Hollom was not a man to bully the hands or bring them up for punishment, so he was not at all actively disliked, but since he was not much of a seaman he was not respected either; and then in spite of his good luck for the moment, his much-envied good luck, there was always the possibility of his being a Jonah. He remained a stranger to the ship. Much the same applied to Horner, whose sullen temper and underlying ferocity made him no friends aboard, though for his part he was respected as an efficient gunner and feared as a right awkward bastard, if crossed.

So there were these two strangers to be watched, watched with the liveliest interest, in the intervals of trying to draw the ship out of the variables; and as the couple's caution grew less, so it seemed to the fascinated spectators that the explosion must be coming near. But these conjectures, though freely exchanged, never reached the cabin; and in the gunroom they were repressed when the chaplain was present.

Jack therefore remained ignorant of the specific reason for the knowing looks that he observed from his usual post by the windward hances; but even if he had known he would still have ordered the boats away when the bonitoes appeared. At dawn flying-fish had been found on deck by the score, and as the sun rose their persecutors could be seen skimming about in schools just under the surface. The boats, plying net and line with prodigious zeal, brought in several loads of fish, fish that did not have to be steeped in precious fresh water; and as Stephen remarked to Martin, the bonito, like his cousin the great tunny, was not only a warm-blooded fish but also a great promoter of Venus.

All hands, except Mrs Lamb, ate as much bonito as they could hold, and after the feast Hollom's lovely *Rose in June* could be heard coming from below, he now being off duty. The gunner came on deck to attend to one of the forecastle carronades: the song stopped abruptly. On the forecastle the gunner clapped his hand to his pocket, missed his handkerchief, and began walking back to his cabin.

The couple were saved only by the pipe of all hands as Jack decided that the patch of dark purple cloud with lightning flickering beneath it on the far north-east might possibly bring the edge of a turning squall down to them, and that it would be as well to strike the topgallantmasts, although they had been swayed up only a few hours before, to catch the last gasp of the flying-fish breeze.

It was as well that he did so, for the squall turned more sharply than he or Pullings or the master had expected; after various evolutions it came hissing across the calm sea on the larboard quarter, a line of white advancing at thirty-five miles an hour, backed by impenetrable darkness and preceded by three small pale birds racing across its front. It struck the ship with a mounting howl, laying her right over and shooting Stephen and Martin, who had incautiously let go their hold in an attempt at identifying the pale birds with their spy-glasses, into the lee-scuppers. Even before kindly hands had plucked them out the whole air was one roaring mass of rain, warm and so thick with great drops and with finely-divided water-dust that they could hardly breathe as they crept up the sloping deck, and the scuppers were already spouting wide. 'I beg your pardon?' shouted Martin through the almighty, omnipresent din.

'I was only calling out "Butcher" to the Doctor,' roared Jack into his ear. 'That is what we say at sea when somebody falls down. Here, clap on to the fife-rail.'

For ten minutes the *Surprise* raced along under a close-reefed foretopsail, and as soon as the wind had moderated a little they began to spread various cloths for the rain and to rouse out barrels: but unhappily the downpour had almost spent itself in the useless flooding of the deck, and part of what was collected in the mainroyal, stretched between the stanchions of the forecastle and weighted with roundshot, was lost when Mr Hollom cast off the wrong hitch, being somewhat bemused in his intellects.

Still, in the short time it lasted they gathered water for eight days, very pure water; and the women aboard, even the almost paralytic Mrs Lamb, had filled all possible tubs and buckets – their smalls were already put to soak. And what was even better, the squall was followed by a steady breeze, perhaps the first breath of the south-east trades.

Yet these things had to be paid for, of course. The sun-baked decks leaked abominably and the *Surprise* (though bowling along so cheerfully) echoed with the sound of drips right down to the orlop and the hold itself, wetting all the storerooms, except the tin-lined bread-room, all the cabins, and all the hanging beds within these cabins; and even before the evening sun went down in its abrupt, tropical fashion, the hot imprisoned air was filled with the smell of mould: mould, blue or green or sometimes a mottled grey, growing on books, clothes, shoes, marine specimens, portable soup, and of course the great beams under which everybody slept and against which everybody except the Captain banged his head from time to time. This was not because Jack Aubrey was more dwarfish than the rest – indeed he stood rather

136

more than six feet tall – but because his cabin had more clearance. Or rather his cabins, since he had three: the coach, to larboard, which included the lower part of the mizenmast and a thirty-two pounder carronade and in which he had his meals unless there were more than four or five guests; his sleeping-place to starboard; and then right aft the noble great cabin, stretching clean across the ship and lit by the splendid, curved, inward-sloping, seven-light stern-window, the airiest, lightest, most desirable place in the ship, Killick's kingdom, perpetually scoured, swabbed, scraped and polished, smelling of beeswax, fresh sea-water, and clean paint.

'Perhaps we might have some music tonight?' suggested Stephen, coming up from his fetid dog-hole.

'Oh Lord no,' cried Jack at once. 'So long as this charming zephyr lasts, I must sail the ship: I must stay on deck.'

'Sure it will sail whether you are on deck or not: you have capable officers, for all love, and they must sit up in any case, their watches coming in due succession.'

'That is eminently true,' said Jack. 'But in a near-run thing it is a captain's duty to be on deck, urging his ship through the water by the combined effort of his will and his belly-muscles: you may say it is buying a dog and barking at the stable door yourself – '

'The stable door after it is locked,' said Stephen, holding up his hand.

'Just so: the stable door after it is locked, yourself. But there are more things than heaven and earth, you know. Stephen, will you not sit in the cabin and play by yourself, or invite Martin, or transcribe the Scarlatti for fiddle and 'cello?'

'I will not,' said Stephen, who hated any appearance of favouritism, and he vanished into the smelly gunroom, there to play halfpenny whist with Martin, Mr Adams, and the master, a game in which concentration was rather harder than usual, since Howard the Marine was learning to play the German flute according to a method which, though said to be adapted to the meanest understanding, puzzled him extremely, while Mowett was reading pieces of the *Iliad* to Honey in a low voice but with immense relish, so that Dr Maturin was not altogether sorry when the loblolly boy called him away to make his evening rounds with Mr Higgins.

On deck Captain Aubrey, eating a piece of cold or at least luke-warm pease pudding with one hand and holding on to the aftermost maintopgallant standing backstay with the other, did indeed urge his ship on with contractions of his belly-muscles and a continuous effort of his will; but he also did a great deal more than that. It was quite true that he had competent officers, and Pullings and Mowett in particular knew the dear frigate very well; yet he had known her longer by far – his initials on her foretopmast-cap had been carved there when he was an unruly mastheaded boy – and not to put too fine a point on it, he sailed her better.

He might almost have been riding a high-mettled horse whose moods and paces were as familiar to him as his own, for although he never hauled on a rope nor laid a hand on the wheel (except now and then, to feel the vibration of her rudder and the precise degree of its bite) he had a highly responsive crew, men with whom he had sailed the ship in pursuit of splendid prizes or in flight from hopelessly superior force, and through them he was in the closest touch with her. He had long since abandoned the cautious show of canvas, the snugging-down with reefed topsails of the early days of the voyage, and now the *Surprise* ran through the night with studdingsails aloft and alow as long as they would stand. As for the hands, most of them were perfectly aware that this was another occasion on which the ship was flying from a hopelessly superior force: they had observed the Captain's retention of the first barrels of noisome rainwater; through the ever-present servants they had heard all the conversations in the cabin and the gunroom on the subject; and, by plain eavesdropping, all those on the quarterdeck. And those few contrary-minded or heavy-arsed dullards who were not convinced by their shipmates' rhetoric were wholly persuaded by the succession of prime helmsmen being called to the wheel out of their turn, by the continuous presence of the skipper, watch after watch, and by his insistence that they should flash out jibs and staysails with supernatural speed.

He was still there at dawn, taking advantage of every heave of the ocean or thrust of the wind to drive the ship a little farther, a little faster. The breeze had veered southerly and at this point the *Surprise* was as close-hauled as she could be, her weather-leeches shaking; it grew much stronger with the rising sun, and now she really showed what she could do on a bowline – her lee forechains under the splendid foam of her bow-wave, a white line racing down her side in a curve so deep that her copper showed amidships, and a broad wake that fled out straight behind her, a sea-mile every five minutes. With the idlers called and both watches on deck he packed them along the weather rail to make her stiffer still, set his mainroyal and stood there, braced against the slope of the deck, soaked with flying spray, his face drawn and covered with the bright yellow bristles of unshaven beard, looking perfectly delighted.

He was still there at noon, when the breeze, somewhat more moderate but now blowing with beautiful steadiness from the east-south-east, had declared itself to be the true trade wind; and with infinite satisfaction he, the master and all the other officers found, when the sun crossed the meridian, that between this observation and the last the *Surprise* had covered 192 miles, running clean out of the zone of calms and variables.

After an early dinner he spent the afternoon in his cot, lying on his back and snoring with such a volume and persistence that men as far forward as the belfry winked at one another, grinning, and Mrs Lamb, speaking in a low voice and shaking her head, told the wife of the sergeant of Marines that she pitied poor Mrs Aubrey from the bottom of her heart. But he was up and about for quarters; and since both watches had been called in the night he let the evening go with no more than the very popular and unlaborious form of small-arms exercise in which all hands, including the Marines, fired at a bottle hanging from the foreyardarm. And when at last the drum beat the retreat he astonished Pullings and Mowett by observing that perhaps tomorrow they might start painting the ship: there was not much point in scraping the decks yet, the pitch being so soft, but they would be very sorry to have any merchantman or Portuguese man-of-war see the *Surprise* in her present state of abysmal squalor.

What he said was perfectly true. Although a boat had pulled round her every morning when it was practicable, with the captain of the head and his mates swabbing all that could be swabbed, resin, tar, pitch and oily sea-borne filth had dimmed the frigate's brilliant Nelson chequer, and her gingerbread work was not at all what a loving first lieutenant's eye could have wished. But these things were generally attended to late in a voyage, when there was some likelihood that the freshness of the effect would strike all beholders dumb with admiration; and at present the *Surprise* was well over five hundred miles from the nearest point of Brazil. Furthermore painting ship almost always meant slower progress, and although of course it would have to be done before they reached soundings, Pullings would have expected Jack not to delay this side of the Line for anything but a rainstorm to fill their rows and rows of empty barrels. Yet both he and Mowett had been brought up from boyhood in a service that did not encourage the questioning of orders, and their 'Yes, sir,' came with no more than a barely measurable hesitation.

Dr Maturin had no such inhibitions. When he came into the cabin that evening he waited until Jack had finished a charming little rondo and then said, 'And are we not to make haste and cut the Line tomorrow, so?'

'No,' said Jack, smiling at him. 'If this wind holds, and it is almost certain to mind its duty as a true trade wind, I hope to cross in a little more than twenty-nine degrees of west latitude on Sunday. So tomorrow you should be quite near your old friends the St Paul's rocks.'

'Is that right? What joy: I must tell poor Martin. Tell, what was the rondo you were playing?'

'Molter.'

'Molter?'

'Yes. You know, Molter Vivace. You must have heard of Molter Vivace. Oh ha, ha, ha!' When at last he had had his laugh out, he wiped his eyes and wheezed, 'It came to me in a flash, a brilliant illumination, like when you fire off blue lights. Lord, ain't I a rattle? I shall set up for a wit yet, and make my fortune. Molter Vivace . . . I must tell Sophie. I am writing her a letter, to be put aboard some homeward-bound merchantman, if we meet one off Brazil next week, which is probable. Molter Vivace, oh dear me.'

'He that would make a pun would pick a pocket,' said Stephen, 'and that miserable quibble is not even a pun, but a vile clench. Who is this Molter?' he asked, picking up the neatly-written score.

'Johann Melchior Molter, a German of the last age,' said Jack. 'Our parson at home thinks the world of him. I copied this piece, mislaid it, and found it ten minutes ago tucked behind our Corelli in C major. Shall we attempt the Corelli now, it being such a triumphal day?'

Nobody could have called the next day triumphal. The *Surprise* had stages rigged out over her sides and all hands turned to scraping her wood and hammering the rust off her ironwork, and then laying on paint and various kinds of blacking. Early in the morning Stephen had told Martin of their approach to St Paul's rocks, which, in the right season of the year, harboured not only a large variety of terns but also two steganopodes, the brown and far more rarely the blue-faced booby; this was not the right season, but there was some hope of stragglers and as soon as their duties permitted they took chairs to various vantage points from which they might lean their telescopes to look for boobies and even perhaps to view the rocks themselves, rearing lonely from the ocean.

But rarely had they settled for ten minutes before they were desired to move – to mind the paintwork, sir – for God's sake to mind the paintwork: and when they hovered near the taffrail and the elegant gilded carving they were told that they might stay a little while, so long as they touched nothing; but they were not on any account to breathe on the gold leaf until the egg-white had dried and they must certainly not lean their glasses on the rail at any time. Even the boats were better than this, although at sea-level the horizon was brought in to a mere three miles: yet presently the boats too were hauled in for scraping and painting, and when they showed a certain restiveness they were told that 'they would not like to have the barky mistaken for a Newcastle collier, by a parcel of Portuguees, nor her boats for mud-scows.'

It was Calamy who suggested that they should go into the foretop, from which (the foretopsail being clewed up) they could see almost the whole ring of the world, and that for an immense distance too: he helped them to climb up, settling them comfortably on the studdingsails that were kept there, and brought them their telescopes, a broad-brimmed straw hat apiece to preserve their brains from the now almost vertical furnace of the enormous sun, and a pocketful of those broken ends of biscuit known as midshipmen's nuts, against hunger, since dinner was likely to be late.

And it was from this lofty platform that they first saw an undoubted frigate petrel and then, following the cry of the lookout on the maintopgallantyard, the white nick on the horizon as St Paul's rocks heaved up in the south-west. 'Oh, oh,' said Martin, putting his glass to his single eye and focusing carefully, 'Can it be . . . ?' A line of heavy, purposeful birds came flying towards the ship, quite fast, not very high: a hundred yards out on the starboard beam they checked their run, poised, and plunged one after another like gannets, a headlong dive that sent water jetting up. They rose, circled, dived for some few minutes more and then flew off with equal purpose to the north-east.

Martin relaxed, lowered his glass and turned a radiant face to Stephen. 'I have beheld the blue-faced booby,' he said, shaking him by the hand.

Long before this the seven-bell men had gone to their turpentine-tasting dinner, followed one glass later by the rest of the hands, with their customary bellowing. Now *Heart of Oak* was beating for the gunroom feast, and presently a messenger came up to tell them that the gentlemen were waiting.

'My best compliments to Captain Pullings,' said Stephen, 'and beg to be excused.'

Martin said much the same, and they returned to their contemplation of these barren islands, now quite near. 'Never a herb, never a blade of grass,' observed Stephen. 'Nor yet a drop of water but what falls from the sky. The birds to the left are only noddies, I am afraid: but then, on the topmost round, there is a booby, my dear sir, a brown booby. He is in a sad state of moult, poor fellow, but he is still a true brown booby. All that white is the droppings of the birds, of course, many feet thick in places; and it has so strong an ammoniac reek that it catches you by the throat. I was ashore there once when the birds were breeding: barely a foot of ground without an egg and the fowl so tame you could pick them up.'

'Do you think the Captain would stop for just half an hour?' asked Martin. 'Think what beetles might be there. Could it not be represented to him . . .'

'My poor friend,' said Stephen, 'if anything could exceed the sea-officer's brutish indifference to birds it would be his brutish indifference to beetles: and do but look at the boats in their new wet paint. I was able to go only because we were becalmed, whereas now we are running at five knots, because it was a Sunday, and because an officer very kindly rowed me over in a boat. James Nicolls was his name.' His mind went back to that deeply unhappy

143

man, who had almost certainly let himself be drowned off this very rock that was now going gently astern a short mile away: he had disagreed with his wife, had tried to make peace, and no peace came. Stephen's thoughts moved on from James Nicolls to marriage in general, that difficult state. He had heard of a race of lizards in the Caucasus that reproduced themselves parthenogenetically, with no sexual congress of any kind, no sexual complications: Lacerta saxicola was their name. Marriage, its sorrow and woe, its fragile joys, filled his mind and he was not altogether surprised when Martin, speaking in a low, confidential tone, told him that he had long been attached to the daughter of a parson, a young lady whose brother he used to botanize with when they were at the university together. She was considerably above him in the worldly consequence and her friends looked upon him with disapproval; nevertheless, in view of his now very much greater affluence, his income of £211. 8. 0 a year, he thought of asking her to be his wife. Yet there were many things that troubled him: one was that her friends might not regard even £211. 8. 0 as wealth; another was his appearance – Maturin had no doubt noticed that he had only one eye – which must necessarily tell against him; and still another was the difficulty of setting out his mind in a letter. Martin was not unaccustomed to composition, but he had been able to do no better than this: he hoped Maturin would be so good as to glance over it and give him his candid opinion.

The sun beat down upon the foretop; the paper curled in Stephen's hand; his heart sank steadily. Martin was a thoroughly amiable man, a man of wide reading, but when he came to write he mounted upon a pair of stilts, unusually lofty stilts, and staggered along at a most ungracious pace, with an occasional awkward lurch into colloquialism, giving a strikingly false impression of himself. Stephen handed the letter back and said, 'It is very elegantly put indeed, with some uncommon pretty figures; and I am sure it would touch any lady's heart;

but my dear Martin, you must allow me to say that I believe your whole approach to be mistaken. You apologize from beginning to end; from start to finish you are exceedingly humble. There is a quotation that hovers just beyond the reach of my recollection together with the name of its author, to the effect that even the most virtuous woman despises an impotent man; and surely all self-depreciation runs along the same unhappy road? I am convinced that the best way of making an offer of marriage is the shortest: a plain, perfectly legible letter reading *My dear Madam, I beg you will do me the honour of marrying me: I remain, dear Madam, with the utmost respect, your humble obedient servant*. That goes straight to the heart of the matter. On a separate half-sheet one could perhaps add a statement of one's income, for the consideration of the lady's friends, together with an expression of willingness to make any settlements they may think fit.'

'Perhaps so,' said Martin, folding his paper away. 'Perhaps so. I am very much obliged to you for the suggestion.' But it required no very great penetration to see that he was not convinced, that he still clung to his carefully balanced periods, his similes, his metaphors and his peroration. He had shown his letter to Maturin partly as a mark of confidence and esteem, being sincerely attached to him, and partly so that Maturin might praise it, possibly adding a few well-turned phrases; for like most normally constituted writers Martin had no use for any candid opinion that was not wholly favourable. 'What a wonderfully true voice Mr Hollom does possess, to be sure,' he said, cocking his ear towards the deck after a silent pause. 'A great blessing to any choir.' From this they went on to speak of the life of chaplains afloat, of naval surgeons, and of the *Surprise*. Martin: 'She is quite unlike any of the ships I have been in. There is none of that running at the men with canes and knotted ropes, no kicking, few really harsh words; and if it were not for those unfortunate Defenders and their fighting with the Surprises there would be almost no punishment days. Or at least there would be none of this distressing and I think inhuman flogging. Quite a different ship from one that I was lent to last, where the grating was rigged almost every day.'

Maturin: 'Just so: but then you are to consider that the men of the *Surprise* have served together for years. They are all man-of-war's men, with no recently-pressed landlubbers, no Lord Mayor's men among them; all tolerably expert sailors who work together and who need no running at. Nor any of the starting, reviling and threats so usual in less happy ships. But the *Surprise* cannot be taken as at all typical of the Navy, alas.'

Martin: 'No, indeed. Yet even here there is sometimes a vehemency of rebuke that I for one should find hard to bear if it were addressed to me.'

Maturin: 'You are thinking of the "Oh you wicked mutinous dogs, sons of everlasting whores." ' At a particularly busy moment Awkward Davis and his mates, eluding their young gentleman, tried to pass a light hawser aft for the painters' stages not as they were ordered but according to their own lights, and this passionate cry from the quarterdeck had greeted the parting of an entangled lower studdingsail boom. 'Harsh words, sure: but God love you, they would bear infinitely harsher from Mr Aubrey and still give no more than a tolerant smile and a droll wag of their head. He is one of the most resolute of fighting captains, and that is a quality they prize above anything. They would still value him extremely if he were severe unjust tyrannical sombre revengeful malice-bearing; and he is none of these things.'

'Certainly not: a most gentlemanlike, estimable character indeed,' said Martin, leaning over the top-rim to see the last of the rocks, now far astern, almost lost in the shimmering heat. 'Yet even so, such inflexibility . . . five thousand miles of ocean and not five minutes' stay to be contemplated. But do not think I complain – that would be wicked ingratitude after the sight of the blue-faced booby, of six blue-faced boobies. I perfectly remember your

146

warning me that for a naturalist the naval life was one of nine hundred and ninety-nine opportunities lost and one that might perhaps be seized. Yet the Evil One will be reminding me that tomorrow we are to heave to and lie motionless Heaven knows how long for the ceremony of crossing the Line.'

A muted ceremony however, for most exceptionally it took place on a Sunday when church was rigged, and even more exceptionally it took place in a newly-painted ship, with all hands acutely aware of their best clothes on the one hand and of the wet paint, the freshly laid-on pitch tar, and the still-moist blackstrake just above the wales on the other. Furthermore Mr Martin had read a grave sermon by Dean Donne, and the choir had sung some particularly moving hymns and psalms. There were Africans, Poles, Dutchmen (a broad category), Letts, Malays, and even a mute solitary Finn on the *Surprise*'s books, but most of her people were English, and Anglican at that, and the service brought home very much to mind. In general the mood remained serious even after Sunday duff and grog, and those few volatile spirits who would be fooling were perpetually reminded to 'watch out for the paintwork, mate; mind your bleeding step,' by those who would have to make all good if anything were smeared.

The *Surprise* did back her foretopsail and lie to almost on the very Line itself; Badger-Bag did come aboard with his train, exchanging the customary greetings and witticisms with the Captain of the ship and calling for those who had not crossed the equator before to redeem themselves or be shaved. Martin and the youngsters paid their forfeit, and the others, all of them former Defenders, were brought to the tub; but there was not much zeal in the shaving – again and again Badger-Bag's style was cramped by cries of 'Mind the paintwork, Joe', and his usual obscene merriment could not really flow free on a Sunday in the presence of a parson – and presently it was over, with no harm done, only a certain feeling of flatness. And even that was remedied by a concert in the evening, the ship's first in the southern hemisphere, with all hands singing and Orrage the cook coming out very strong with *The British Tars* –

> *Come all you thoughtless young men, a warning take by me*
> *And never leave your happy homes to sail the raging sea.*

Mr Martin had not visited the Canaries, nor the Cape Verdes, nor yet St Paul's rocks, and presently it seemed that he was to be done out of the New World too. Five days later, the *Surprise* raised Cape St Roque at dawn, a dim, remote headland, and then bore away to cruise in the most frequented shipping-lanes, where the currents and the local winds brought most vessels from North America and the West Indies quite close inshore south of Recife, off the broad estuary of the São Francisco river. Quite close inshore, that is to say, from a sailor's point of view, since the land could actually be seen if one ascended to the masthead, a faint line, rather harder and a little more irregular than cloud. Here Jack meant to stand off and on, with the barge just in sight in the offing and the launch beyond it, waiting for the *Norfolk*. He had not been on his chosen station more than a few hours when the morning sun showed him the *Amiable Catherine* of London, homeward-bound from the River Plate. The *Catherine* had not the slightest wish to speak the *Surprise*, knowing very well that the frigate might press several of her best hands, but she had no choice: Jack had the weather-gage, a much faster ship, and ten times the number of men to spread her canvas. Her master came aboard with a glum face and the *Catherine*'s papers: he left looking pleased and somewhat drunken, since Jack, both from natural choice and policy, always treated merchant-captains civilly. The *Catherine* had not seen or heard of the *Norfolk*, nor of any other American man-of-war in southern waters: no talk of any such thing in Montevideo, St Catherine's, Rio or Bahia. She would take great care of *Surprise*'s letters and put them straight into the post; and she wished her a very happy return.

Four more ships or barques gave the same news in the course of the day; so did a pilot-boat that came out to ask whether they wanted to go up the river to Penedo. On coming aboard the pilot startled the quarterdeck by uttering a delighted screech and kissing Mr Allen on both cheeks – the master had once spent a considerable time in the pilot's father's house in the port of Penedo, recovering from the dry gripes – but he then won the good opinion of all within earshot by assuring the Captain that no man-of-war could possibly have passed the headlands without his knowledge. The anxiety that had been growing so in Jack Aubrey's mind dissolved, leaving a delicious feeling of pure relief; although he had taken such an unconscionable time in getting there he was still ahead of the American.

'This is capital,' he said to Pullings and Mowett. 'I do not think we shall have to cruise here for so long as a week, even if *Norfolk* has had very indifferent breezes. If we stand well off, keeping the double-headed hill on our beam, she should pass inshore, which gives us the advantage of the current and the weather-gage, and then hey for Saffron Walden. Not that I think that she would decline an engagement, even if she were to windward of us.'

'The water . . .' began Pullings.

'Yes, yes, there is the water,' said Jack. 'But we have enough for nearly a week on short allowance, and in these latitudes, at this time of the year, I have rarely known a week go by without rain pouring down: we must have our casks and awnings ready at the first drop. And if it don't rain, why, we can run in – the master knows a good watering-place no great way up the river – leaving the boats to keep watch. Even if she does slip by she will not have any very great start, and we can make it up by cracking on, before she is aware.'

The long days passed, furiously hot, horribly thirsty. The heat pleased some, Stephen among them, and the

Finn, who silently took off his fur hat for the first time since Gibraltar; but Mr Adams on the other hand was all agasp and aswim, obliged to be sponged in a hammock under the weather-awnings, and Mrs Horner lost her looks entirely, going yellow and thin. It was also observed that her song-bird lost his voice: no more Gathering Flowers in May, no more Rose in June, nor no more flaming Spanish guitar on the gangway neither. But the guilty pair no longer excited any very considerable interest, partly because they seemed to have grown much more cautious, partly because their liaison had lasted so many thousands of miles that it was now almost respectable, but very much more because all hands were engaged in such strenuous gunnery practice in such heat that they had little energy left for adultery, the contemplation of adultery.

It was now that Captain Aubrey's private powder came into its own. Horner and his mates filled cartridge by the hour, and every evening at quarters the *Surprise* erupted in deadly earnest, the long savage flames and the smoke jetting from her sides in rippling broadsides running from the bow-guns aft, fired at empty beef-casks towed out five hundred yards, very often with shattering effect and with something close to the old *Surprise*'s speed of one minute ten seconds between two discharges of each gun, although almost every crew contained a Defender or a Gibraltar lunatic.

In the afternoon of the fifth day the wind came off the land, bringing with it the smell of tropical river mud and green forest, but no rain, alas, only a single chrysomelid beetle on the wing, the first true South American that Martin had ever seen. He hurried below to show Stephen, but Higgins told him that the Doctor was engaged: would Mr Martin sit down and take one of the invalids' thin captain biscuits and a trifle of the sick-bay brandy? Martin had barely time to decline – a biscuit in such arid heat was a physical impossibility unless it was accompanied by something far wetter, far more voluminous than brandy – before the gunner walked out, looking black and grim.

'It may be nondescript,' said Stephen, peering at the beetle through a magnifying glass. 'I certainly have not seen it before and can scarcely even guess its genus.' He gave the creature back into Martin's hand and then said, 'Oh Mr Martin, my quotation came back to me, together with the author's name: Sénac de Meilhan. I made him speak a little more emphatically than I should have done, I am afraid. What he really said was "Even the best-conducted women – les plus sages – have an aversion for the impotent," going on "and old men are despised: so one should conceal one's wounds and hide the crippling deficiencies of life – poverty, misfortune, sickness, ill-success. People begin by being touched and moved to tenderness by their friends' distress; presently this changes to pity, which has something humiliating about it; then to a masterful giving of advice; and then to scorn." Of course the later considerations have nothing to do with the subject we were discussing, but they seem to me – Lieutenant Mowett, my dear, what can I do for you?'

'I beg your pardon for bursting in upon your beetle,' said Mowett, 'but the Captain would like to know whether the human frame can support this.' He passed a mug of the rainwater collected long ago, north of the Line.

Stephen smelt to it, poured a little into a phial and looked at it with a lens. Delight dawned upon his grave, considering face and spread wide. 'Will you look at this, now?' he said, passing it to Martin. 'Perhaps the finest conferva soup I have ever seen; and I believe I make out some African forms.'

'There are also some ill-looking polyps, and some creatures no doubt close kin to the hydroblabs,' said Martin. 'I should not drink it for a deanery.'

'Pray tell the Captain that it will not do,' said Stephen, 'and that he will be obliged to bear up, bear down, bear away for that noble stream the São Francisco and fill our casks from its limpid, health-giving billows as they flow between banks covered with a luxuriant vegetation of choice exotics, echoing to the cries of the toucan, the jaguar, various apes, a hundred species of parrots, and they flying among gorgeous orchids, while huge butterflies of unparalleled splendour float over a ground strewn with Brazil nuts and boa-constrictors.'

Martin gave an involuntary skip, but Mowett replied, 'He was afraid you would say that; and if you did I was to apply to Mr Martin and ask him in a very tactful, discreet manner whether the prayers for rain we use at home could be applied to a ship at sea. Because, you know, we are most unwilling to leave our station to fetch wet, if wet can, as you might say, be induced to come to us.'

'Prayers for rain *at sea*?' said the chaplain. 'I doubt it would be orthodox. But I will look in my books and tell you what I find tomorrow.'

'I am not sure that we shall have to wait until tomorrow,' said Jack, when this message reached him. 'Look away to leeward.' There, far down the evening wind, dark clouds were gathering on the horizon, and in spite of the brilliant sun in the west lightning could be seen flickering under them. Even here the air was electrical, and the bosun's cat sprang about the forecastle rigging in a high state of excitement, its fur standing on end.

'Perhaps it would not be tempting fate, was we to lay along the clean awnings and funnels,' said Pullings.

'Fate might bear it this once,' said Jack. 'She has hardly used us very kindly so far, I believe. And what is more, I think we might be well advised to get the topgallantmasts down on deck and rig rolling-tackles; the swell is increasing.'

Pullings did these things; and when the boats returned from their distant watch he had them brought inboard and made fast to the skid-beams rather than towing astern. All this seemed labour lost until the middle watch, when Maitland, Hollom, and the larbowlines took over from Honey.

'You are a good relief, Maitland,' said Honey, and then in a formal voice, 'Here you have her: close-reefed topsails and inner jib; course east-south-east until two bells, then wear ship and west-north-west until the end of the watch. If rain falls take appropriate measures.'

'East-south-east, then wear ship: appropriate measures,' said Maitland.

'Lord, what light-balls!' cried Hollom, the mate of the watch, pointing forward to the St Elmo's fire flickering about the jibboom and spritsail yard, brilliant in the faint moonlight.

'Don't point at them, for Heaven's sake,' said Honey. 'It brings bad luck. The awnings are in the waist, the hose is stretched along, and battle-lanterns are ready under the forecastle. If there is any justice we should have something like Noah's flood before morning, from the look of things to leeward.'

'Do you think we should tell the Doctor about the fire-balls?' asked Maitland. 'They are prodigious curious.'

'Why,' said Honey, considering, 'I did think of it; but they are only electrical, you know, and I don't know he would thank us for waking him up, just to see the electrical fluid playing the fool. If they had feathers and laid eggs, I should have sent long ago.'

Stephen therefore knew nothing of St Elmo's fire: far below, swinging in an ever-widening but always peaceful arc as the swell increased, his ears blocked with balls of wax, and his mind – hitherto much harassed by thoughts of Diana and by the oppressive unbreathable air – now soothed by a judicious dose of laudanum, he knew nothing of the torrential rain that half-drowned the ship in the graveyard watch, nor of the subsequent near-tornado that flung her so violently about amidst bellowing thunder no higher than the mastheads and an almost continuous blaze of blue and orange lightning. The laudanum he had returned to at last because after mature and wholly objective consideration he had been brought to see that as a physician he was required to sleep well enough to

153

perform his duty the next day; furthermore the poppy had not been created idly, and a rejection of the natural balms provided was contumelious pride, as heretical as the notion that because a thing was pleasant it was also sinful; and in any case this was St Abdon's day. After his long abstinence it worked beautifully: but even half a pint of laudanum (and he was nowhere near his old excesses) could not have kept out the enormous crash as lightning struck the *Surprise*, melting the shank of her best bower anchor, running along the seven foremost larboard guns and setting them off, but above all rending and shattering her iron-hooped bowsprit in the most extraordinary manner.

'The French fleet is out,' thought Stephen, three parts awake. 'I must get my instruments – go to my station – God between us and evil.' Then waking a little more as his bare feet plunged into the rainwater swilling to and fro under his hanging cot, 'Nonsense. This is the New World, and we are at war with the Americans, ridiculous as it may appear.'

However, he heard no more gunfire, and after a good deal of reflexion and some unsuccessful attempts at striking a light he made his way on deck, which was lit fore and aft with lanterns. The ship lay head to wind, and the fire-engine was playing on the smoking wreckage of the bowsprit: this last enormous blast had exhausted the storm, and although the sea was still high the sky was clearing over the land. He learnt from other nightshirted figures that this was not warfare, that nobody had been hurt, and that the situation was in hand; he retired to the almost deserted quarterdeck and sat on a carronade slide. He heard the cry of 'There she goes' as the outer forty feet of the bowsprit plunged into the sea with a rending sound and a splash, followed by a good many orders; then the officers came flooding back aft. Martin was among them, and seeing Stephen he joined him and said in a low voice, 'It appears that we have lost our bowsprit: the Captain seems deeply concerned.'

'Aye,' said Stephen. 'They value it much, as essential for turning into the wind; or perhaps from it.'

'Mr Allen,' said Jack, 'the breeze is fair; you know these waters. Can you take the ship up to Penedo?'

'No, sir,' said the master, 'neither with nor without a bowsprit. The shoals in the estuary are always shifting, and the river is as much pilot-water as the Hooghly: I could not in conscience venture upon it, even if we had a compass we could rely upon, which we have not, nor even if it was clear daylight. But if I may have the launch I will run in, send off the pilot, and set Lopez's yard a-working on a new spar as fast as ever they can go. With this breeze and the turn of the tide I should be there soon after dawn; and maybe the ship could stand in, cautious, and drop anchor in say twenty fathom water about two or three mile off the bar.'

'Very good, Mr Allen,' said Jack. 'Make it so.'

Since the foremast's main support had gone with the bowsprit, it took some little time to get the swift-sailing copper-bottomed launch over the side, and while this was going on Stephen said to the master, 'Mr Allen, can I be of any use to you on shore? I am moderately fluent in Portuguese.'

'Oh dear me no, Doctor, though I thank you very kindly. I am like one of the family with the Lopezes, and with the Moreiras. But I tell you what it is: if you do not mind a little wetting, and if you like to come along with me, I think I can show you something uncommon in the botanical line, if the floods have not carried it away, which ain't likely. Parson Martin is welcome too, if so inclined: no one can call me superstitious.'

The launch was a fine boat, but she was not a dry one. She skimmed through the water, shipping large packets of it at every plunge of the long swell, two hands baling and the master at the tiller, steering by the Southern Cross. Everybody was soaked and almost cold by the time they were well into the estuary, with the bar breaking the swell and the master often letting fly the sheet as he picked out the channel, straining forward to see the rises of the land in the dim grey light, the first hint of dawn. Twice the launch grounded slightly, but a seaman on either side, no more than thigh deep, soon heaved her off; and at last, seeing a tall stake with a rag on top, Allen said, 'Here we are,' and sent the boat slanting across the stream to a long low island, brought her gently to a halt in the sand of its shore, and as Macbeth leapt out with the gang-board for Stephen and Martin he said, 'I will just run up to Penedo now to arrange with the yard, and I will tell the pilot to bring you some breakfast on his way out to the ship. Shove off, Macbeth.' And when the boat was some way out on the smooth water he called back, 'Mind the alligators, gentlemen.'

They were standing on a firm white strand and already there was light enough to see that a little way up the slope there began a grove of trees: but surely too high, too massive to be trees. The light increased, and trees they were, palms of an almost unbelievable mass and height, their enormous fan-shaped leaves bursting in a vegetable explosion well over a hundred feet above their heads, and outlined sharp against the greying sky.

'Would they be Mauritia vinifera?' asked Martin in a whisper.

'Mauritia of some kind, sure; but what I cannot tell,' said Stephen.

They walked slowly, reverently into the grove: there was no undergrowth and spring tides or perhaps floods kept the ground quite clean, so that the magnificent trees rose sheer, each some ten yards from the next, a vast grey column.

Their feet made no sound as they paced on; but very soon it was darkness that they were walking into, for the dense fronds intertwined far overhead, and except at its fringes the grove was still filled with warm silent night, the pale trunks soaring up into obscurity. They turned right-handed with one accord and as they reached the outer edge again, facing the river and the strand, the sun heaved up

156

from the eastern sea, sending an instant brilliance across the water to the other bank, no great way off. The reflected light and colour of the far bank fairly blazed upon them as they stood there in the shade of the remaining trees, a bank with a line of shining sand and then a great wall of the most intensely vivid green, an almost violent green, with palms of twenty or thirty different kinds soaring above it, all in the total silence of a dream. Martin clasped his hands as he gazed, uttering some private ejaculations; and Stephen, touching his elbow, nodded towards three trees some way up the river, three enormous cathedral-like domes that rose two hundred feet above the rest, one of them completely covered with deep red flowers.

They took a few more steps through the palms, reaching the white unshaded strand: to the left hand at the water's edge lay a twenty-foot caiman, contemplating the gentle stream, and to the right hand, full in the brilliant sun there stood a scarlet ibis.

CHAPTER FIVE

The mutilated frigate, as uncomely and as unrecognizable as a man whose nose is gone, made her way with infinite precautions through the shoals and mudbanks of the estuary with the making tide, guided by the grave pilot, who sent his men ahead to mark the turns in the channel with a pole; then she tacked painfully up the river, her head heaved round by boats at the end of each board – each short board, for by the height of Penedo the São Francisco narrowed to no more than a mile. However, they got her in at last, by torchlight, with no more than one wait in mid-channel for the ebb, and Jack found to his great satisfaction that Allen and Lopez, the owner of the shipyard, had already chosen a fine piece of timber for the new bowsprit, that the carpenters had already roughed out a splendid greenheart cap for it, and that the sheers to extract the shattered stump were to be erected first thing in the morning.

'This Lopez is a man after my own heart,' he said to Stephen. 'He understands the importance of time and the thorough leathering of a jibboom hole, and I have little doubt we shall be at sea by Sunday.'

'Only three days,' said Stephen. 'Alas for poor Martin: I told him a much longer period and he had set his heart upon seeing the boa-constrictor, the jaguar, and the owl-faced night-ape, as well as making a reasonably complete collection of the local beetles; but so much can hardly be expected in so short a time. I agree with you about Senhor Lopez, however. He is also a most amiable, hospitable man, and has invited me to stay the night and to meet a Peruvian gentleman, a great traveller, who is also a guest. This gentleman has crossed the Andes, I find, and must necessarily have seen a very great deal of the inland country.'

'I am sure he must,' said Jack. 'But I do beg of you, Stephen, not to keep Lopez long from his bed. There is not a moment to lose – think what flats we should look, was the *Norfolk* to pass by while we were sitting here – and we must start work a little before dawn; it would be the world's pity to have him stupid, sleepy and jaded. Could you not give him a hint, to the effect that you would be happy to entertain the Peruvian gentleman, if he chose to turn in?'

In the event Lopez needed no hints. He spoke Spanish only with difficulty, and seeing that both his guests were fluent, even enormously fluent, in that language and that they agreed very well, he excused himself on the grounds of early work to be done and bade them good night, leaving them on a broad veranda with a number of domesticated creatures on it, marmosets of three different kinds, an old bald toucan, a row of sleepy parrots, something hairy in the background that might have been a sloth or an ant-eater or even a doormat but that it farted from time to time, looking round censoriously on each occasion, and a strikingly elegant small blue heron that walked in and out. Two bottles of white port stood between them, two hammocks hung behind, and Lopez returned for a moment to beg them to use the mosquito-netting. 'Not that we have mosquitos in Penedo, gentlemen,' he said, 'but it must be confessed that at the change of the moon the vampires do grow a little importunate.'

They did not annoy his guests however, since the vampire really needs a sleeping prey and these two (though eyed wistfully from the rafters) never went to bed. They sat talking all night, watching the sliver of the new moon go down and the procession of great glowing stars pass across the sky: bats of a more amiable kind, two feet across, showed briefly against their light, and in the river only a few yards below could be seen the star-twinkling wake of turtles and the occasional alligator: the lion-maned marmoset in Stephen's lap snored very gently, sleeping on and on in spite of the continual flow of talk. They had surveyed the infamous career of Buonaparte (no end yet in view, alas, alas), the melancholy record of Spain as an imperial power in the New World and the almost certain liberation of her colonies – 'Though when I look at the reptiles coming to the fore in such places as Buenos Aires,' said the Peruvian, 'I sometimes fear that our last state may be even worse than our first' – and now, at the tail end of the night, they returned to the geology of the Andes, and the difficulty of crossing them.

'I should never have accomplished it but for these,' said the Peruvian, nodding toward the half-finished packet of coca leaves on the table between them. 'When we were near the top of the pass the wind increased, bringing frozen pellets of snow and cutting off one's breath, already so short at that height that every step called for two or three gasping inhalations. My companions were in much the same condition, and two of our llamas had died. I thought we should have to turn back, but the headman led us to something of a shelter among the rocks, took out his pouch of coca and his box of lime and passed them round. We each chewed a ball – an acullico, we call it – and then, resuming our burdens with the greatest ease, we walked fast up the cruel slope through the driving snow, over the top and so down into kinder weather.'

'You do not surprise me,' said Stephen. 'Ever since the first acullico that you were so good as to give me I have felt my mind glow, my mental and no doubt physical powers increase. I have little doubt that I could swim the river that lies before us. I shall not do so, however. I prefer to enjoy your conversation and my present state of remarkable well-being – no fatigue, no hunger, no perplexity of mind, but a power of apprehension and synthesis that I have rarely known before. Your coca, sir, is the most virtuous simple I have ever met with. I had read about it in Garcilasso de la Vega and in Faulkner's account, but I had no idea it was a hundredth part as efficacious.'

'This of course is the best flat-leaved mountain coca,'

160

said the Peruvian. 'It was given me by the grower, an intimate friend, and I always travel with a substantial packet of the most recent crop. Allow me to pour a glass of wine: there is some left in the other bottle.'

'You are very good, but it would be wasted on me: ever since the pleasant tingling subsided after the first ball, my sense of taste is entirely gone.'

'What, what is that outcry?' exclaimed the Peruvian, for a screech of pipes could be heard from the *Surprise*, and a roaring of 'Out or down, out or down. Rouse and bitt. Here I come with a sharp knife and a clear conscience: out or down. Bundle up, bundle up, bundle up,' as the bosun's mates roused the sleeping lower-deck and all the frigate's open ports showed golden in the darkness.

'It is only the mariners being summoned to their duty,' said Stephen. 'They like to begin cleaning the deck before daylight; the sun must not be offended with the sight of dust. It is a very superstitious ritual, I am afraid.'

A little later the stars began to pale; there was a lightening in the east; and within a few minutes the sun thrust his rim above the far edge of the sea. The briefest dawn, and it was day, full day. Captain Aubrey stepped from his cabin and Senhor Lopez from his house. They met on the quay, Lopez accompanied by an embarrassing, unnecessary spider-monkey that had to be menaced and hissed at to make it go home, and Jack by the master for the language and the bosun for any technical questions that might arise.

By mid-morning all hands were steadily at work: that is to say, all the hands there were, for Pullings in the launch and Mowett in the barge, with their respective crews, had been left far out beyond the bar to keep watch and to gather news. But there were plenty of Surprises left; the frigate had been warped alongside the sheers and the shipwrights were busy on her head; along the wharf the great smooth chips flew as the carpenters plied their adzes on the new bowsprit, cap and jibboom; the bosun, his mates and a strong party of unusually able seamen were stripping almost all her standing rigging in order to set it up again Bristol-fashion when the new spar should be in; and an army of caulkers swarmed over her decks and sides. Few of the Defenders could be of any use at these skilled tasks, but by now they could all pull an oar, more or less, and they and the Marines were sent off to complete the ship's water at a spring a little way up the river.

'I feel exceedingly guilty, watching all these men so earnestly at work and doing nothing myself,' said Martin.

'The back of my hand to guilt,' said Stephen, lively and cheerful in spite of his wholly sleepless night. 'Let us walk out and view the country. I am told that there is a path leading behind the mangrove-swamp and through the forest to an open glade where a certain palm-tree grows. Its name I forget, but it bears a round and crimson fruit. We have so little time: it would be a pity to waste it in an idle beating of one's breast.'

Little time indeed: yet it was long enough for Martin to be bitten by an owl-faced night-ape, bitten dangerously, and to the very bone. They walked behind the mangrove-swamp, along the broad forest track with vegetation rising in a brilliant green wall on either side, a wall made of trees as its powerful basis and then of uncountable twining creepers, climbers, bushes, lianas and parasites filling all the interstices so that in the thicker parts nothing but a serpent could get through. They walked with foolish smiles upon their faces, astonished by the butterflies, the innumerable butterflies of so very many different species and by the occasional humming-bird; and once the all-pervading sound of stridulating insects had lasted ten or twenty minutes it could no longer be heard and they seemed to be walking in total silence – very few birds, and these few mute. But when they came to the glade, where the trees stood fairly wide and the ground was clear, they startled a mixed flock of parrots; and there on a well-beaten path they saw a marching column of leaf-carrying ants a foot wide and so long that it vanished in either direction.

Stephen contemplated the ants, distinguishing the various soldier and worker forms; and being fond of calculation he worked out the number in a square foot and the probable weight of their burden, meaning thereby to make some estimate of all the army he could see; but his arithmetic had always been slow hesitant and poor, and he was still scratching numbers with a twig on a broad leaf when he heard a startled cry from Martin, over by a hollow tree on the far side of the glade. 'Hush,' he said, frowning. 'I write three, I carry seven.' But now the cry had anguish in it too and turning he saw that Martin's hand was streaming with blood: he ran towards him, his little penknife out and ready, crying, 'Was it a serpent, at all? Was it ever a snake?'

'No,' said Martin, with the strangest mixture of delight and pain in his face. 'It was an owl-faced night-ape. He was in here' – pointing to a hole in the hollow tree – 'peering out: such a pleasant striped round-eyed inquisitive little face, that I ventured . . .'

'To the very bone,' said Stephen. 'And you will certainly lose your nail, if you live at all. Let it bleed, soul, let it bleed: I have no doubt the ape was mad, and the flow may get rid of a little of the poison, with the blessing. There, I will bind it up now, and we will hurry back to the ship. You must certainly be cauterized as soon as possible. Where is the ape?'

'I am very sorry to say he ran off directly. I should have called you earlier.'

'Let us imitate him. There is not a moment to lose. The river-bank is quicker than the mangrove-swamp. Keep your hand in your bosom; and take notice that the handkerchief is mine.'

As they ran under the powerful sun Martin said, 'It is not every man that can show a wound inflicted by an owl-faced night-ape.'

A belt of feathery bamboos to traverse and they came on to the river-bank, broad sand now, the tide being out; and there before them stood two seamen, Awkward Davis and Fat-Arse Jenks, grasping driftwood clubs and looking grim.

'Why, it's the Doctor,' cried Davis, the brighter of the two. 'We thought you was Indians – savages – cannibals.'

'Tigers,' said Jenks. 'Theshing about in them reeds, and ravening for blood.'

'What are you doing here?' asked Stephen, since both of them belonged to the launch.

'Why, ain't you heard the news, sir?' asked Davis.

'What news?'

'He ain't heard the news,' said Davis, turning to Jenks.

'You tell him, then, mate,' said Jenks.

The news, extricated from its web of irrelevant detail and the correction of minute circumstantial points, was that the *Norfolk* had passed by, steering south-south-west under all plain sail, that Captain Pullings had instantly set off in the launch for Penedo, that they had had great difficulty in finding the channel, and that this being the lowest ebb of a spring tide or close on the launch had grounded so often in this last stretch that Davis and Jenks, being unusually heavy and not being needed to row with this leading breeze, had been told to walk the rest of the way, but to mind out for the tigers. Mr Mowett in the barge, on the other hand, had carried all away, being overset on a sandbank quite early on, and would have to wait there till the ship came down.

'The launch will have got in an hour ago,' said Davis. 'Oh my eye, they will be as busy as bees by now.'

Bees indeed, and bees under an exceptionally active taskmaster. Meals, abolished for the cabin, gunroom and midshipmen's berth, were reduced to a mere snapping ten minutes for the hands; all pretty-work was abandoned; and so many extra carpenters, hired out of Jack's pocket, were set to work on the bowsprit that they barely had room to wield their tools. Then after nightfall what could be done by the light of huge fires blazing on the quay was done, and although there was still a great deal of fine-work that must wait for the sun Jack was fairly confident that they should sail on tomorrow evening's tide.

'You will not mind its being Friday?' asked Stephen.

'Friday?' cried Jack, who had lost count in the fury of headlong work. 'God help us, so it is. But it don't signify, you know; we do not do it voluntarily; it is forced upon us. No, no. But leaving that aside – and pray don't mention it to anyone else, Stephen – there are two things in our favour: one is that the *Norfolk* was under no more than plain sail when she could easily have spread very much more canvas by far; so it is likely we may catch her by cracking on. The other is that this is a spring tide, and it will carry us down a great deal quicker than we came up.'

A third thing was the arrival of Mowett and the barge's crew, who, having accomplished prodigies of repair, appeared a little before dawn. With their help – and some of the cleverest riggers were among the bargemen – the work went forward at a splendid pace. The new bowsprit was home by half past ten, gammoned and frapped by eleven, and the new jibboom rigged out, with all stays and shrouds set up by the depth of low tide. Jack gave the order to splice the main brace, and turning to Pullings he said, 'The painting and titivating we must leave until we are at sea, and of course she don't look pretty; but I never thought we could have done so much in the time. Please ask the master to tell Mr Lopez that we should be happy to accept his invitation after all: he knows we shall have to leave him at the turn of the tide. Lord, I could do with my dinner: and with a glass of wine, by God!'

Glasses of wine were not lacking at that cheerful feast, nor excellent food (for the turtle counted as fish), nor yet song: indeed Jack thought the pilot came it a little too high with the shanties he had learnt aboard English and American merchantmen. But then Jack's mind was too much taken up with the flowing tide to take much delight in music, and as soon as the youngster he had posted by the chronometers came to tell him that the time was ripe he stood up, thanked Mr Lopez most heartily, and walked off, followed by Stephen and the master, disregarding the pilot's plea for a last toast to St Peter.

The tide, now at slack-water, was exceptionally high, so high that small waves lapped over the quay, since for most of the flood it had been a leeward tide, though now the wind had hauled conveniently into the south-west. Once this vast body of water began to ebb, reflected Jack, looking over to the far brimming bank, it would sweep the *Surprise* down to the sea at a splendid rate; and with even a little help from the breeze they should be well clear of the estuary before the turn, particularly as with so much water in the river they would not have to follow all the windings of the ebb-tide fairway. The uncommon height had another advantage too: Stephen stepped straight into the pilot's boat and sat there peaceably without having either fallen into the bottom or pitched over the far side or even barked his shins, while the pilot and his man rowed them out to the *Surprise*, which was already in the channel, holding on by two buoyed kedges belonging to the yard and only waiting for her commander to let go.

'So we are away,' said Martin, gazing at the brilliant sunlit wall of green to starboard as it glided by.

'If this had been a civilized voyage of inquiry we might have stayed for three weeks,' said Stephen. 'How is your hand?'

'It is very well, I thank you,' said Martin. 'And had it been fifty times more severe I should still have thought it nothing, for those few hours – such wealth . . . Maturin, if you direct your glass to that enormous tree upon the point and look a little to the right, do not you make out something very like a troop of monkeys?'

'I do. And take them to be howlers, black howlers.'

'Howlers, did you say? Yes, no doubt. I wish,' he added in a low voice, not to be overheard by the pilot, 'I wish that fellow would make less noise.'

'He is grown somewhat exuberant,' said Stephen. 'Let us move forward.'

But even when they were in the bows the pilot's merriment pursued them, together with his imitation of the jaguar's cry, a gruff Boo boo; and most disappointingly he moved the ship out into the middle of the river, so that neither bank could be seen in any detail. The tide had begun to ebb and she was running surprisingly fast under topsails and jib with a quartering wind. Fast, that is to say, until with a smooth but sudden check she came to a dead halt on a sandbank with her deck sloping from fore to aft and a huge cloud of mud and sand flowing away from her down the rapid stream. Hands had instantly started the sheets, and now as they were clewing up Jack came racing forward from his cabin calling out, 'Light along the lead, light along the lead there.' He leant far over the headrails, staring down into the water as it cleared: she had ploughed her way so far up the bank that the bottom was within a yard of her bridle-ports.

'Take a cast well out,' he said to the quartermaster, in the hope that the lead might show a narrow spit that she might be dragged off sideways. It showed nothing of the kind; and while the lead was whirling for the second cast to larboard he saw bushes and reeds under the frigate's forefoot. She was on a bank so high that it was rarely covered. Running aft to see how things were astern he saw that Pullings and Mowett were already getting the boats over the side. 'Cable out of the gunroom port,' he shouted as he passed.

The stern was unnaturally low in the water and the rudder was probably unshipped, but that did not matter for the moment. 'Just drop it under the counter,' he said, and the lead splashed down.

'By the mark twain, sir,' said the quartermaster in a shocked voice. 'And barely that.'

It was very bad indeed, but it was not quite hopeless. 'Best bower into the launch,' he called. 'Kedge and hawser into the red cutter.' He glanced over the taffrail to see whether the run of the current gave any hint of the bank's limits and he noticed that the pilot and his man were already two hundred yards away in their little skiff, pulling furiously. He said to the master, 'Start the water over the side,' and plunged below, to where the bosun and a gang of powerful tierers from both watches were passing one of the new fifteen-inch cables aft with rhythmic cries of 'Heave one, heave two, heave away, away and go.' All was well here and moving very fast, and as he ran on deck, calling aloud for the jolly-boat and a can-buoy, some part of his mind had time to thank God for good officers and a crew of thorough-paced seamen.

By the time he dropped into the jolly-boat the kedge had already been lowered into the red cutter, the best bower was hanging from the cathead, poised just over the launch, and fresh water was spouting over the side, lightening the ship at a great pace.

The jolly-boat cast to and fro like an eager dog, searching for depth and a good holding-ground, and at the first tolerable place Jack tossed the buoy over the gunwale and hailed the launch, now pulling as fast as it could with the anchor aboard and the cable trailing behind, pulling as fast as it could against the wind and the now much more powerful ebb, pulling so hard that the men's faces were crimson, while the oars bent dangerously at the tholes. For now there was not a moment, not a single moment to lose, now less than ever, for as every seaman knew, this tide would drop thirty feet: even in the last ten minutes five inches of precious depth had ebbed from over the shoal and round the ship, and if they did not have her off this tide there would be little hope for the next, since it would not rise so high. Furthermore there was the fear of the ship's breaking her back as the water left her. 'Stretch out, stretch out,' roared Pullings in the launch, and 'Stretch out, stretch out,' roared Mowett in the cutter.

Reaching the can-buoy the launch manhandled the perilous great anchor over the side; the cutter raced on to where the jolly-boat was signalling a reasonable bottom and dropped the kedge, thus anchoring the anchor itself. Jack stood up and hailed the ship: 'Heave away. Heave away, there,' and at once the capstan on the frigate's quarterdeck began to spin.

By the time the boats were back something like the full strain was on: the capstan was still turning, but very slowly, with the men bowed to the bars and gasping. Stephen and Martin were pushing side by side, but as the boat-crews came leaping aboard, flinging themselves at the bars, Jack plucked Stephen away and took his place, saying, 'I am heavier.' Then in a huge voice, 'Heave hearty. Heave hearty. Heave and rally.' The bars were fully manned now and the capstan went round a full turn, the iron pawls going click-click-click: the strain reached something near to breaking-point and Stephen, looking aft, saw the cable as an almost straight line. It had shrunk to less than half its size.

'Sand to the nippers,' cried Jack, now hoarse with the effort of thrusting. 'Heave and rally. Heave, oh heave.'

The capstan scarcely moved. One click – a long striving pause – another reluctant click. 'Heave and rally. Heave and rally.' Then the sound of the pawls came faster, click-click-click-click; the cook cried, 'We're off' and some of those who had not found room at the bars began to cheer: but it was the anchors that were coming home. Apart from settling a little deeper into the mud the *Surprise* had not moved, and by now the tide had dropped two feet. 'Belay,' said Jack, straightening from the bar. 'Captain Pullings,' he said, having looked at the river and its banks, 'I believe the ship will cant to starboard as the tide goes out, so we must get out some shores; at the same time we must find a hard on the nearer bank for the guns, so that she may float at the top of next high water.' 'Or,' he added to himself, 'at the top of the next spring tide: oh God send us a right full height of flood tomorrow.'

'There have been times, my dearest soul,' wrote Stephen to Diana in a letter dated 'from the shore of the São

Francisco', 'when you were not altogether pleased with Jack Aubrey, but if you had watched him this last fortnight I believe you would allow him a certain heroic quality, a certain greatness of soul. As I said, a drunken pilot ran the ship on to a sand-bank in the middle of this river at the very height of the highest tide, and although we pulled with all our might we could not get her off; nor would she shift at the next tide which, though high, was not high enough to raise her from her oozy bed. After that there was no hope until the change of the moon, which would bring another spring tide: this was a comforting reflexion, but every day that passed set another hundred or two hundred miles between us and our quarry, a quarry upon which all Jack's happiness, his professional career and his reputation depends. Furthermore it was not at all sure that the next spring tide would reach the extraordinary height of the flood that was our undoing. Yet from that moment to this I have not heard Jack complain or cry out 'Oh d—n it all', or any of those still warmer expressions that are so often used at sea and which he is so very free with on trifling occasions. Certainly he has required everybody to work very, very hard all day long, since all the cannon have had to be taken to the shore, together with countless tons of provisions and stores, and at low water a channel had to be attempted to be dug to make it easier for the ship to be plucked off when the moment came, while the rudder also had to be rehung; but with all this I do not remember an oath, scarcely a rebuke. And the curious thing is that this coolness absolutely shocks the men; they look at him nervously, and go about their duties with wonderful diligence. It was the same with Martin and me. During the first days, when the ship had to be lightened at great speed in case she should hog or break her back, being left suspended in the middle by the neap tides, all the skilled hands were employed dealing with the guns, and Martin, the purser and I were entrusted with the jolly-boat (a vile machine) to tow heavy casks ashore; and I do assure you, we were perpetually aware of that impassive, determined and authoritative eye; we felt it upon us in all our comings and goings, and we were as meek as schoolboys.

'After the first few days however we were released, with bleeding hands and no doubt permanently injured spines, since there was no more wholly unskilled work to do; and I must confess that the last week has been singularly agreeable. This is the only tropical river I know that is not infested with mosquitoes, although it has some capital marshes close at hand, with such a wealth of wading birds – imagine, my dear, a *roseate* spoonbill if you can – and of course there is an infinitely great botanical wealth on every hand. I have rarely seen a man so happy as my friend Martin: the coleoptera alone would have been worth the voyage, in his opinion, but as well as making a collection of very curious beetles he has also seen a boa, which was one of his great ambitions. We were walking in an open part of the forest, talking about jaguars, when we were both felled to the ground by what at first I took to be a heavy branch or rather liana; yet the liana writhed with great force and I quickly perceived that it was in fact an enormous serpent that had fallen from a tree. But a serpent so horribly alarmed that it had quite lost its head; and as it strove to escape threw coils in every direction. I saw that Martin was clinging to its neck with both hands and I represented to him that this was rash, heedless, imprudent. I should have gone on to remind him of the fate of Laocoön, but a coil tightening under my chin cut me short. In gasps he replied that it was a boa – boas were notoriously good-natured – he only wished to see its vestigial hind-legs – then would let it go – he was not hurting it. By this time the poor creature had recovered its wits; it darted (if the word can be used of so vast a reptile, thick, thick, and almost endless) from his grasp with a determined lunge, raced up the tree like an inverted torrent, and we saw it no more. From its brilliant appearance and its confused state of mind I think it must very recently have changed its skin.

'But the great wealth of every day is of course

botanical, and that reminds me of the cuca or coca leaves that a Peruvian traveller gave me; when they are chewed with a little lime they sharpen the mind to a wonderful degree, they induce a sense of well-being and they abolish both hunger and fatigue. I have laid in a considerable stock, because I think it will help me to throw off a somewhat troublesome habit: you may have noticed that for insomnia and a variety of other ills I take the tincture of laudanum; and this does tend to become a little too usual. I do not think there is any question of abuse, still less of addiction, yet it creates a certain need, not unlike that for tobacco; I should be glad to be set free from it, and I am confident that these valuable leaves will prove efficacious. Their powers really do surprise me, and I shall enclose a few with my letter, so that you may try them. During this period of extremely wearing toil and anxiety I have proposed them to Jack, but he said that if they did away with sleep and hunger they were not for him – in this crisis he needed his sleep and he must have his meals – in short, he would not take physic till the ship was afloat, no, not for a king's ransom.

'She is afloat now, trim, spruce, quite unharmed, having been plucked off her bank or rather island at the height of last night's spring tide; but in doing so we lost an anchor, and recovering it took up so much time that we have been obliged to wait for the next high water, when the excellent Mr Lopez (with the blessing) will guide us down to the open sea. I was about to add the proviso "if he reaches us in time", but as my pen was poised I saw his boat come round the bend of the river. He is now aboard; and when he leaves us, having taken the ship beyond the bar, I will entrust him with this letter.'

'Will I, though?' he asked aloud, having read it over. The tone was wrong, perhaps offensively wrong. It assumed that there was no difficulty between them, and the awareness that this assumption was unwarranted gave the letter a falseness, a grating artificiality. He slowly crushed the paper in his hand as he stared out over the river at the elegant little ship, swimming there in the fairway well this side of her wicked island; but then as he saw the boat pull away from her side, the boat that was to carry him aboard, with no more land perhaps until the far Pacific, he smoothed it out again and wrote 'the Dear knows when it will reach you, but early or late it brings all my love.'

The *Surprise* had sixteen days of sailing to make up; and although the *Norfolk* was probably running off her southing under no more than moderate sail, to conserve her stores, spars and canvas, she would hardly make less than five knots in the steady south-east trades, even if she double-reefed her topsails for the night: and that set her two thousand miles ahead.

The *Surprise* was therefore in a tearing hurry, and as soon as she had dropped her pilot she spread a great expanse of canvas: there was nothing unusual about this situation however; the ship and her commander had been goaded by time for nearly the whole of their career and by now hurry was almost the normal state – leisure at sea had something uneasy about it, a kind of unnatural calm. Yet in spite of the hurry Jack had no intention of pushing her to the limit of her possibilities, with everything on the very edge of carrying away, as he had often done when his chase had a ship in view or just over the horizon and when he could risk springing a topmast with a clear conscience; but he did mean to go as near to that extreme racing pace as ever he could, bearing in mind that now the far South Sea lay before him with never a ship's chandler, let alone a dockyard, on its shores; and once again he blessed the Providence that had furnished him with two officers in Pullings and Mowett who would keep her moving through the water night and day with equal determination and energy.

'Now we can get back to real sailoring again,' he said with great satisfaction as she stood out into the

173

South Atlantic, close-hauled on a north-east breeze that had no scent of land upon it, a purely maritime wind. 'And perhaps we can make the ship look a little less like something ready for the breaker's yard. How I do loathe being clapped right up tight against the land,' he added, glancing at Brazil, a dim band looming on the western horizon, but still far too near for a blue-water sailor, whose worst enemy was a lee shore. '*But sea-room, an the brine and cloudy billows kiss the moon, I care not,*' he observed, taking the words from Mowett's mouth; but then, reflecting that fate might regard this as a challenge, he grasped a belaying-pin and said, 'I am only speaking figuratively, of course.'

Jack was not one of the modern spit-and-polish captains whose idea of a crack ship was one that could shift topmasts five seconds quicker than the others in the harbour, in which great quantities of brass outshone the sun at all times and in all weathers, in which the young gentlemen wore tight white breeches, cocked hats and Hessian boots with gilt twist edging and a gold tassel, singularly well adapted for reefing topsails, and in which the round-shot in the racks and garlands was carefully blacked while the naturally black hoops of the mess-kids was sanded to a silvery whiteness. But he did like what little naked brass the *Surprise* possessed to gleam and her paintwork to look tolerably neat; his first lieutenant liked it even more, and curiously enough the men who had to do all the work thoroughly agreed with them. It was what they were used to, and they prized what they were used to, even if it called for starting the day with sand and holystones on the wet deck long before sunrise and even longer before breakfast, even if it called for painting exposed parts of the ship while she swooped and plunged, flanking across the Atlantic swell with four men at the wheel and most of the watch standing by to let all go with a run: not that this happened often, since in general the winds were no kinder to her than they had been in the early part of the voyage; and many a wry look did Hollom's back receive, the back of a wind-eating Jonah for all his successful cruising in the gunner's private waters.

The *Surprise* therefore proceeded southwards with all possible dispatch, spreading the smell of fresh paint to leeward; and as soon as the more vulnerable paint was dry, the sharp, exhilarating scent of powder-smoke too. It was rare that quarters passed without at least small-arms being fired, rarer still that the great guns were not run in and out – the fouler the weather the better the exercise, said Jack, since you could never be sure of coming up with an enemy on a smooth and placid sea, and it was as well to learn how to heave your five hundredweight a man against the slope of the wildly-heaving deck long before the knack was needed. There were two chief reasons for this steady preparation: the first was that Jack Aubrey thoroughly enjoyed life; he was of a cheerful sanguine disposition, his liver and lights were in capital order, and unless the world was treating him very roughly indeed, as it did from time to time, he generally woke up feeling pleased and filled with a lively expectation of enjoying the day. Since he took so much pleasure in life, therefore, he meant to go on living as long as ever he could, and it appeared to him that the best way of ensuring this in a naval action was to fire three broadsides for his enemy's two, and to fire them deadly straight. The second reason, closely allied to the first, was that his idea of a crack ship was one with a strong, highly-skilled crew that could out-manoeuvre and then outshoot the opponent, a taut but happy ship, an efficient man-of-war – in short a ship that was likely to win at any reasonable odds.

Southward then, degree after degree, southward with the warm Brazil current; and they had not passed under the tropic of Capricorn before the regular, accustomed nautical way of life, punctuated by bells, might have been going on time out of mind. The ship was now as pretty as paint could make her, her copper had been scrubbed during her involuntary dry-docking, she had her pale fine-weather suit of sails abroad, and she looked a most uncommonly elegant sight as she ran down and down wide-winged, leaving the sun behind her. The young gentlemen had been introduced to the first aorist, the ablative absolute, and the elements of spherical trigonometry; these they pursued with little enthusiasm until they were let out to learn horseshoe splicing with Bonden or some unusual knots with Faster Doodle, a man who never explained anything at all, being wholly inarticulate, but who showed it over and over again, with endless patience: he would turn in a dead-eye cutter-stay fashion ten times over, without a single word. They saw little of Mr Martin for the rest of the day, and sometimes it seemed that he as as eager as his pupils to abandon sines, tangents and secants: he was in fact arranging his very large collection of the Brazilian coleoptera, hastily gathered and only now revealing its full wealth of new species, new genera, and even new families. He and Stephen looked forward to several happy, tranquil months, classifying these creatures; although Stephen had not quite so great a passion for beetles, and although his duties (as well as his disinclination to miss any passing bird or whale) often called him away.

He had grown more and more dissatisfied with Higgins as a surgical assistant. The man was without any sort of doubt an excellent tooth-drawer, but he was deeply ignorant of physic and surgery, and not only ignorant but bold and rash. He also practised on the credulity of the foremast hands. There was something to be said for hocus-pocus, just as there was for placebos, but Higgins went far beyond what might be justified as useful to the patient; furthermore he was beginning to extract illicit fees (as well as eels, mice and earwigs) from those who were sick and from those who wished to malinger in the sick-bay for a while, taking their ease. Stephen therefore determined to look after all the patients himself, confining Higgins to their teeth; he knew that he would not entirely do away with the man's private or rather secret practice, sailors being what they were, but at least he could see that they were not poisoned, at least he could lock his more dangerous drugs away.

He saw the foremast-hands in the forenoon and then again when he made his rounds of the sick-bay, often accompanied by Jack, later in the day: the officers, on the other hand, usually made an appointment through the sickberth attendant, the loblolly-boy. Yet this was by no means invariable, particularly with his messmates in the gunroom, and Stephen was not at all surprised to hear a knock at his door some days out of Penedo – there were several commissioned or warranted stomachs still suffering from a surfeit of turtles and tropical fruit. But not at all: it was Mrs Horner, come at a moment when all hands were on deck, the *Surprise* having heaved to to speak a merchantman from the River Plate. When he suggested that he should examine her in the gunner's cabin with her husband present she declined; nor did she wish Mrs Lamb or the sergeant's wife to attend. Indeed no very prolonged or detailed examination was called for: Mrs Horner was pregnant, as she had known perfectly well since the last change of the moon. When Stephen told her so she said, 'Yes. And it was not Horner: you know about his trouble, Doctor; he told me so. It was not him, and when he finds out he will kill me. He is a terrible man. Unless I can get rid of it he will kill me.' In the long silence that followed she whispered, 'He will kill me,' to herself.

'I am very sorry for it,' said Stephen. 'I will not pretend not to know what you wish me to do: but it cannot be. I will do anything I can to help you, but not that. You must try to . . .' His invention failed; his voice died away and he was left looking at the ground, feeling all the weight of her bitter distress and of her present disappointment.

'I know him, yes,' said Mrs Horner in a dead voice. 'He will kill me.'

After some moments she regained at least an appearance of composure and stood up, smoothing her pinafore, looking pitifully young and ill. 'Before you go,' said Stephen,

'I must tell you two things: one is that any interference with the course of nature in these matters is extremely dangerous; and the other is that nature often interferes herself, since rather more than one pregnancy in ten ends in a natural miscarriage. I hope you will come to see me at least once a week; you may perhaps feel a little unwell, and the humours may have to be rectified.'

It was clear that she scarcely heard him, although she curtsied when he had finished speaking; and as she passed through the door she murmured to herself, 'He will kill me.'

'Perhaps he will, too,' thought Stephen some minutes later; he had gone on deck to shake off the painful impression of this interview and to hear what the merchantman had to say, and there only a few feet along the gangway from him stood the gunner, dark, angry, dangerous, liable to fly out for a nothing, a powerful man with long hanging arms.

Stephen was too late for anything but the parting civilities, exchanged over a quarter of a mile of heaving aquamarine sea all flecked with white as the ships filled on opposite tacks, but Pullings told him that the news was most disappointing: the *Norfolk* had not put into the River Plate, which might have allowed the hurrying *Surprise* to gain at least a few hundred miles, but had carried straight on. A Montevideo barque had spoken her in about forty degrees south, which almost certainly meant that she had increased her lead, having had fairer winds. 'Our only hope now,' he said, 'is meeting a ship that has seen her refitting at say Port Desire before tackling the Horn: otherwise we shall certainly have to follow her round. And God knows whether we shall ever find her.'

'But Mr Allen knows the haunts of the English whalers, and surely the *Norfolk*'s one function is to pursue them?'

'Yes, to be sure. But the fishery has spread far south and west these last years, and if we do not catch her along the coast in the waters the master knows, along by Chile, Peru, the Galapagos, Mexico and California – if she has sailed off westwards three thousand miles and more, how are we ever to find her in all that sea? No trade in those parts, no merchantmen to see her go by, no port where we can hear news of her. It would call for most uncommon luck: and luck is what we have not had much of, this goddam voyage.'

Southward and still farther south, but never a ship did they meet. Day after day, even week after week, the quiet sea was empty clean round its rim, an enormous loneliness; and all this time the winds were faint, capricious and sometimes foul: but above all faint. Three nights running Jack had his recurrent dream of riding a horse that shrank and dwindled until his feet touched the ground on either side and people looked at him with strong disapproval, even with contempt; and each time he woke up with the same sense of sweating anxiety.

Imperceptibly the air grew colder, and the sea; and every day the sun was at least a degree farther from the zenith at the noon observation. By now the young gentlemen could all take its altitude with tolerable proficiency; Jack looked at their daily workings of the ship's position south of the Line and west of Greenwich with real satisfaction, and sometimes he would call them in to hear part of a Latin ode (at present they were slowly mangling poor Horace) or the declension of a noun in Greek. 'If they are all drowned tomorrow,' he remarked to Stephen, 'their fathers cannot say I han't done my duty by them. When I was a squeaker nobody gave a tinker's curse whether my daily workings were right or wrong, and as for dashing away in Latin and Greek . . .' He also fed them almost daily, turn and turn about, often asking the youngster of the morning watch to breakfast with him and another or sometimes two to dine.

During this long slow passage there was time, ample time, for the usual invitations to resume their steady sequence and even to grow somewhat monotonous: the Captain dining with his officers in the gunroom, the members of the gunroom dining in the cabin by rotation, and the midshipmen by ones and twos with both. And the farther south the ship travelled the poorer grew the fare: both cooks did their best, but private stores were running low and although Pontius Pilate, the gunroom cock, still crowed every morning when the coops were carried up on to the quarterdeck, and although his hens still laid the occasional egg, while goat Aspasia provided milk for the cabin's holy coffee, the last sheep died a little south of the fortieth parallel – it had been shorn, nay shaved, for its own good under the equator and was now unable to endure the increasing cold – and salt pork took its place on the Captain's table on a day when the chaplain was dining with him. Jack apologized for the change, since the invitation had been 'to share his mutton' but Martin said, 'Not at all, not at all; this is the best salt pork I have ever eaten – such a very subtle combination of East India spices – yet even if it had been black penitential gruel it would still have been a feast. This morning, sir, at half past eight, I saw my first penguin! A jackass penguin, as the Doctor assures me, swimming with extraordinary speed and grace hard by the ship, flying, as it were, in the element!'

The *Surprise* was in fact on the edge of the waters where the Pacific, the Atlantic and the Indian oceans run round the world in a continuous stream common to a large number of far southern animals; the sea had quite abruptly changed its colour, temperature and even character and although it was perhaps a little too early to hope for the larger albatrosses there was a strong likelihood of mallemawks, blue petrels, whale-birds and of course many more penguins. The day after this change both he and Stephen left their warm cots as soon as they heard the familiar grinding of holystones on the deck far above their heads – a sound that was felt rather than heard, coming as a vibration through the timbers and the taut cordage – and made their way to the gunroom, where the steward gave them each a bowl of hot burgoo, a kind of liquid porridge. By this time – for Martin had washed and even shaved by the light of a purser's dip – a faint grey was showing in the east, and Honey came below, bare-footed and red legged from the cold and streaming deck, to put on his shoes and stockings in the warmth. He told them that the worst of the wet would be gone, swabbed away, in five minutes, and that the night's drizzle had lifted: 'Wind at north-east and a following sea. But it is precious cold still: will you not wait until after breakfast? It will be stockfish, judging by the smell of glue.'

No, they said, they preferred to be in the open before hammocks were piped up and stuffed into those things along the sides, sadly obstructing the view. They would go upstairs in five minutes, as soon as the decks were reasonably . . .

'Oh sir, oh sir,' cried Calamy, running barefoot down. 'A huge great enormous whale – he is just alongside.'

Alongside he was, and vast he was: a sperm whale with his great blunt squared-off head abreast of the forechains, his dark body streaming aft far along the quarterdeck, perhaps seventy-five or even eighty feet of massive creature, giving such an impression of tranquil strength the ship seemed frail beside him. He lay with the upper part of his head and the whole uneven length of his back awash, and he blew: a thick white jet that spouted up and forward while a man could count three. Then after a slight pause he deliberately sunk his head for twice that time; raised it and blew again, breathed and blew, breathed and blew, all the while keeping alongside the ship with a slight rippling motion of that huge broad horizontal tail. He was a biscuit-toss away in the grey transparent water; he could be seen above it and below; and they watched him entranced, all silent along the rail.

'That is one of your old eighty-barrel bulls,' said the master at Stephen's elbow. 'Maybe ninety. The kind we call schoolmasters, though they are usually alone.'

'He does not seem at all alarmed,' whispered Stephen.

'No. I dare say he is deaf. I have known old ones

deaf, aye, and blind of both eyes too, though they seemed to manage very well. Yet perhaps it is the company he likes; they seem to do so sometimes, the lonely ones; like dolphins. He will be going down any minute now; he has pretty well had his spoutings out, and . . .' The very shocking report of a musket in the silence cut him short. Darting a glance along the rail Stephen saw the Marine officer, still in his night-cap, with the smoking gun in his hands and a great fool's laugh upon his face. The whale's head plunged in a boil of water, his huge back arching and the tail coming clear, poised there above the surface for an instant of time before it vanished straight downwards.

Stephen looked forward to keep his extreme anger from showing, and on the gangway he saw a most unusual sight for this time of day, or any other for that matter: Mrs Lamb the carpenter's wife. She had been waiting for the silence to end and now she hurried towards him. 'Oh Doctor, if you please, can you come at once? Mrs Horner is took poorly.'

Poorly indeed, doubled up in her cot, her face yellow and sweating, her hair draggled about her cheeks and she holding her breath for the extremity of pain. The gunner stood there, distraught in a corner: the sergeant's wife knelt by the bed saying, 'There, there, my dear, there, there.' Mrs Horner had been far from Stephen's mind that morning but the moment he walked into the cabin he was as certain of what had happened as if she had told him: she had procured an abortion; Mrs Lamb knew it; the others did not, and between her fits of convulsive agony Mrs Horner's one concern was to get them out of the room.

'I must have light and air, two basins of hot water and several towels,' he said in an authoritative voice. 'Mrs Lamb will help me. There is no room for more.'

Having made a rapid inspection and dealt with the immediate problems he hurried down to the medicine-chest. On his way, far below, he met his assistant, and as there was no escape Higgins stood aside to let him pass; but Stephen took him by the elbow, led him under a grating so that some light fell on his face, and said, 'Mr Higgins, Mr Higgins, you will hang for this, if I do not save her. You are a rash wicked bungling ignorant murderous fool.' Higgins was not without bounce, confidence and resource when put to his shifts, but there was such a contained reptilian ferocity in Stephen's pale eye that now he only bowed his head, making no sort of answer.

A little later in the empty sick-bay, one of the few places in the ship where it was possible to speak without being overheard, Stephen saw the gunner, who asked him what the trouble was – what was the nature of the disease?

'It is a female disorder,' said Stephen, 'and not uncommon; but I am afraid this time it is very bad. Our great hope is the resilience of youth – how old is Mrs Horner?'

'Nineteen.'

'Yet even so you should prepare your mind: she may overcome the fever, but she may not.'

'It is not along of me?' asked the gunner in a low voice. 'It is not along of my you know what?'

'No,' said Stephen. 'It has nothing to do with you.' He looked at Horner's dark, savage face: 'Is there attachment there?' he wondered. 'Affection? Any kind of tenderness? Or only pride and concern for property?' He could not be sure; but early the next morning, when he had to tell the gunner that his wife had made no improvement at all, he had the feeling that the man's chief emotion, now that the first shock and dismay were over, was anger – anger against the world in general and anger against her too, for being ill. It did not surprise him very much: in the course of his professional career by land he had seen many and many a husband, and even some lovers, angry at a woman's sickness, impatient, full of blame: quite devoid of pity, and angry that it should be expected of them.

It was a slow dawn, with showers drifting across the

sea from the north-east; and as the light grew and the veil of rain in the south-west parted the lookout bawled, 'On deck, there. Sail on the starboard bow.'

Part of the cry reached Jack in the cabin as he was raising his first cup of coffee. He clapped it back on to the table, spilling half, and ran on deck. 'Masthead,' he called. 'Where away?'

'Can't make out nothing now, sir,' said the masthead. 'She was maybe a point on the starboard bow, hull up. Close-hauled on the larboard tack, I believe.'

'Put it on, sir,' cried Killick angrily, hurrying after him and holding out a watchcoat with a hood, a Magellan jacket. 'Put it on. Which I run it up a-purpose, ain't I? Labouring all the bleeding night, stitch, stitch, snip, snip,' – this in a discontented mutter.

'Thankee Killick,' said Jack absently, drawing the hood over his bare head. Then loud and clear, 'Hands to make sail. Topgallants and weather studdingsails.'

No more was needed. At the word the *Surprise*'s topmen raced aloft, the shrouds on either side black with men: a few cutting notes on the bosun's pipes and the sails flashed out – let fall, sheeted home, hoisted, trimmed and drawing with extraordinary rapidity. And as the *Surprise* leapt forward, her bow-wave rising fast, the lookout hailed again: the sail was there, but she had worn; she was now heading due south.

'Mr Blakeney,' said Jack to a youngster, rain-soaked but glowing pink with excitement, 'jump up to the fore-jack with a glass and tell me what you see.'

Yes, she had worn, came down the cry: Mr Blakeney could see her wake. She was going large.

Even from the quarterdeck Jack and all the rest crowding the lee-rail could see her looming far over there in the greyness, but as a pale blur, no more. 'Can you make out a crow's nest?' he asked.

'No, sir,' after a long, searching minute. 'I am sure there ain't one.'

All the officers smiled at the same moment. In these

waters any strange sail would almost certainly be a whaler or a man-of-war: but no whaler ever put to sea without a crow's nest; it was an essential and most conspicuous part of her equipment. A man-of-war, then; conceivably the *Norfolk* too had met with some accident or with very dirty weather; conceivably she had had to refit in some desolate far southern inlet; conceivably that was their quarry, just a few miles to leeward.

'On deck, there,' said the first lookout in a glum dissatisfied tone, though enormously loud, 'She's only a brig.'

The happy tension dropped at once. Of course, of course there was the packet too, the brig *Danaë*: the recollection came flooding back immediately. She too must have made extraordinarily poor progress, to be no farther on her way than this. Of course she had spun on her heel, and of course she would run as fast as ever she could until she knew who the *Surprise* might prove to be.

'Well damn her,' said Jack to Pullings. 'We shall speak her presently, no doubt. Let us hoist the short pennant with the colours as soon as they can be seen. But no sooner: there is no point in wasting valuable bunting on the desert air.' With this he returned to his coffee: and learning that Dr Maturin was engaged with a patient he moved on from his coffee to a solitary breakfast.

But there was something odd about the *Danaë*. Obviously she did not trust the *Surprise*'s colours at first sight, and it was her plain duty not to trust them; but it was strange that she should not make a satisfactory, undeniable response to the private signal either, although by now the day was reasonably clear. And it was stranger still that she kept hauling her wind a trifle, as though to get the weather-gage, while at long intervals obscure signals ran up to her mizen-peak. She was a very fast sailer indeed, as would be expected in a packet, and at present, by carrying a great press of canvas, she was drawing away from the *Surprise*.

Pullings sent to the cabin to say that he did not care

for the present appearance of things and Jack returned to the deck. He surveyed her, a piece of toast in his hand, and considered. She had made her number correctly, she was flying the right colours, and now she had broken out the signal 'Carrying dispatches' which meant that she must neither stop nor be stopped. Yet there was still that dubious private signal: it had never showed plainly, being hauled down before the entire hoist flew clear. 'Repeat it,' he said, 'And give her a windward gun.'

He put his toast carefully down on a carronade-slide and watched the *Danaë* through Mowett's telescope. Hesitation aboard her; bungling; the hoist going up and down again; the halliard jamming; and once again the essential flags vanished before the whole had been distinctly seen. He had used all these capers himself, many and many a time, to gain a few valuable minutes in a chase. In a vessel that sailed so well as the *Danaë* they were not at all convincing: they should have been combined with some wild steering, some reef-points or gaskets flying free. No, no: it would not do. She had been taken: she was in enemy hands and she meant to get away if ever she could.

Jack reflected for a moment upon the force of the breeze, the current, the bearing of the packet, and said 'Let the hands go to breakfast, and then we will turn to. If she is what I think she is, and if we catch her, you shall take her home.'

'Thank you, sir,' said Pullings, his face a great grin. From the professional point of view nothing could suit him better. There would not be the glory of a battle – the packet's armament could not possibly compete with the frigate's and would certainly not come into action – but that did not signify, since the glory always went to the credit of the captain and the first lieutenant: for a volunteer, bringing in a valuable recaptured prize would be a more evident, noteworthy testimony of his zeal, and of his good luck too, by no means a negligible quality when it came to employment.

'She will take some catching, though,' said Jack,

looking at her under his shading hand. 'You might let the Doctor know. He loves a good chase.'

'Where is the Doctor?' he asked some time later, when the *Surprise* was tearing away southwards under a perfectly astonishing show of sail with the wind on her quarter.

'Well, sir,' said Pullings. 'It seems he was up all night – the gunner's wife taken ill – and now he and the chaplain are at peace by the gunroom stove at last, spreading out their beetles. But he says that if he is given a direct order to come and enjoy himself in the cold driving rain if not sleet too as well as a tempest of wind he will of course be delighted to obey.'

Jack could easily imagine the rapid flow, the fluent run of bitter and often mutinous expressions that Pullings did not see fit to pass on. He said, 'I must ask Killick to make him a Magellan jacket too: his servant is no hand with a needle. The gunner's wife, you said? Poor woman. I dare say she had eaten something. But she could not be in better hands. You remember how he roused out Mr Day's brains on the quarterdeck of the old *Sophie*, and set them to rights directly? Forward, there: come up the forestaysail sheet half a fathom.'

The *Surprise* was now wholly given over to her chase. This was something that she, her captain and her people could do supremely well; they worked together in perfect harmony, with rarely an order needed, taking advantage of every run of the sea, every shift in the breeze, jibs and staysails continually on the move, the braces perpetually manned by keenly attentive hands. The Surprises had always dearly loved a prize; they had had more experience of taking them than most and their appetite had grown with each successive merchant ship, man-of-war or recapture, and now all the piratical side of their character was in full, intensely eager play. And though it might seem that nothing could add to the combined effect of the hunting instinct and the very strong desire of something for nothing, in this case there was also a hearty wish to do well by Captain Pullings: for Jack's promise had of course been overheard. He was very much liked aboard, and with this extra spur the men flung themselves into their work with an even greater zeal, so that although the *Danaë* was so fast and well handled that with her five miles start she might reasonably have hoped to keep ahead until the night gave her shelter, the pale sun was still well above the horizon when she was obliged to heave to and lie there with backed topsails under the frigate's lee.

'Tell the Doctor that he must come on deck and enjoy himself now whether he likes it or not,' said Jack: and when Stephen appeared, 'This is the packet we were told about. But the *Norfolk* must have taken her, since she is manned with a prize crew. This is the American officer coming across now. Have you any observations to make?'

'May we perhaps confer once you have seen him?' asked Stephen, who had no observations to make in public. 'I am happy that you should have recaptured it without any gunfire; I had no notion that the chase was going so well. Mr Martin and I had anticipated a great deal of banging and running up and down before the end.' He looked across at the *Danaë*: the smaller group of men on her forecastle slapping one another on the shoulder and calling out to the grinning Surprises were obviously prisoners who had now found a most unexpected freedom; the others, in the waist, looking desperately low and dispirited and very tired from their day-long heaving and hauling, making sail and reducing it again, were clearly her regular crew. Their captain, a youngish lieutenant, put the best face he could on it as he came up the side, saluted the quarterdeck and offered Jack his sword. 'No, sir, you must keep it,' said Jack, shaking his head. 'Upon my word, you led us an elegant dance of it.'

'I believe we might have run clear,' said the lieutenant, 'if we had not lost so much canvas south of the Horn and if we had had a heavier, more willing crew. But at least we have the satisfaction of having been taken by a famous flyer.'

'I dare say we could both do with some refreshment,' said Jack, leading him towards the cabin; and over his shoulder, 'Captain Pullings, carry on.'

Captain Pullings carried on with great effect, bringing the packet as close as she could lie so that the transfer might take place before the fading of the day and the almost certain coming of dirty weather; and for a while, before returning to their hanging stove, Stephen and Martin watched the boats going to and fro on the increasing swell, taking Surprises and Marines over and bringing back the former prisoners and the Americans, together with a long-legged midshipman and the *Danaë*'s books and papers.

'Here are her papers,' said Captain Aubrey when Stephen came for his conference. 'They do not tell us much, of course, since the English log stops when she was captured and the rest is just a bald account of her course and the weather since then: damned unpleasant weather, most of it. But the prisoners, and by that I mean the people that were captured and drafted into the *Danaë* to sail her, were more informative. Since they were taken this side of the Horn, like the packet, they do not know for a fact that the *Norfolk* is in the Pacific yet, but they do know that she took two of our homeward-bound whalers in the South Atlantic, one of them a ship that had been out more than three years and that had filled every barrel she possessed. But here is my draft of the official letter Tom Pullings will carry back with him. It will tell you the whole thing in a moment, and perhaps you would put in some style, just here and there, where you think it might fit.'

Stephen glanced at the familiar opening

Surprise at sea
(wind N by E with moderate
weather)
49°35'S., 63°11'W.

My Lord,

    I have the honour to acquaint your Lordship
that in . . .

and said, 'Listen, before I read it, tell me one thing,
will you now? Suppose there were treasure aboard that
packet, would it be safer with us or with Tom?'

'Oh, as for the treasure, I am afraid the *Norfolk* snapped
that up directly. Two iron chests full of gold, God love
us! You would hardly expect them to leave it lying about:
I am sure I should not have done so, ha, ha, ha!'

'Let it be supposed that there are documents, valuable
documents concealed in her fabric,' said Stephen patient-
ly, still in the same low tone of voice, his chair pulled up
to Jack's, 'Would they be more liable to loss with him or
with us?'

Jack cocked a considering eye at him and said, 'The
privateers are the trouble. In that craft Tom can outsail
most men-of-war except in very heavy weather, but he
will have to run the gauntlet of the privateers from the
West Indies on, both French and American. Some of them
are very fast, and he will only have a few pop-guns and
muskets and precious few men to handle them. He does
not run a very grave risk, there being such a prodigious
quantity of salt water, but even so I should say that your
hypothetical papers would be safer with us.'

'Then before it grows dark would you have the kindness
to go across into the packet with me, into the room where
the chests were found itself?'

'Very well,' said Jack. 'I wish to see her in any
case. Should we take a bag?'

'I believe not,' said Stephen, 'but an accurate yardstick
might be wise.'

His mind was uneasy. Money always had an unhealthy
effect on intelligence, often confusing the issue; and it

could sometimes prove a very dangerous substance to handle. He did not like the way he had been told about the hiding-place in the *Danaë*: a recollection of the letters in which Sir Joseph had told him of the murky, troubled atmosphere in London made him like it even less, and in these altered circumstances he was tempted to leave the whole thing alone. The instructions did not cover the present situation and whatever he did might turn out to be wrong. Yet if he did nothing and the packet were taken he would look an incompetent fool: or worse. But what if he found the cache empty? What if the rats had got at the papers? What if the captured Mr Cunningham was himself kin to the rats?

These thoughts ran through and through his head as he poked about under a long recess in the side of the cabin once inhabited by Mr Cunningham and his chests – the holes for the screws that had held them down were still to be seen – and it was not without a certain relief that he turned to Jack at last, saying, 'The mad brute-beasts have given me the wrong direction, so they have. There is nothing here. Perhaps it is just as well.'

'Should you like me to look at the paper?' asked Jack.

'By all means. But it is as plain as can be. "Press the third bolt-head under the larboard shelf-piece three foot nine inches from the bulkhead." '

'Stephen,' said Jack, 'I believe that is the starboard shelf-piece you are looking at.'

'Oh your soul to the devil, Jack,' cried Stephen. 'This is my left hand, is it not?' – holding it up – 'And what is on the left or unlucky or indeed sinister side is the larboard.'

'You are forgetting that we have turned about,' said Jack. 'We are now facing aft, you know. The third bolt-head, did you say?' He pressed, and instantly and with a surprisingly loud crash a metal box fell from the seam, striking the deck with one corner and bursting open. He bent to pick up scattered sheafs of bank-notes and other papers, putting his lantern down, and at the sight of the

191

first he cried, 'God love us! What can – ' But recollecting himself he gathered the bundles together in silence and handed them to Stephen, who gave them a cursory glance, shook his head with a worried, dissatisfied air, and put them back into their box. 'The best thing I can do is to seal this at once, and give it to you to keep in a safe place. Perhaps you had better carry it back to the *Surprise* your-self: I have slipped into the water from a boat before this.'

In the great cabin once more Stephen melted the wax, pressed his curiously engraved watch-key upon it, and handed the box over together with a small piece of paper, saying, 'This slip shows the proper recipient, if any accident should happen to me.'

'It is a damned heavy responsibility,' said Jack gravely, taking it.

'There are heavier by far, my dear,' said Stephen. 'I must be away for my rounds.'

'That reminds me,' said Jack. 'I see that the gunner's wife is on your sick-list. I hope she is better by now?'

'Better? She is not,' said Stephen emphatically.

'I am sorry for it,' said Jack. 'Would a visit be in order, or one of the chickens, or a bottle of port-wine? Or perhaps all three?'

'Listen,' said Stephen, 'I do not know that she will live.'

'Oh Lord,' cried Jack, 'I had no idea – I am extremely concerned – I hope there is something you can do for her?'

'As for that,' said Stephen, 'I set nearly all my trust in the resilience of youth. She is no more than nineteen, poor child, and at nineteen one can support hell and purgatory almost, and live. Tell me, Tom Pullings will not be leaving us at once?'

'No. He keeps company until the morning. I have a great deal of paper-work to do.'

'I must write at least one letter too,' said Stephen. 'And if I possibly can I will come and help you with the captured mail,' he added, knowing Jack's extreme reluctance to read other people's correspondence, even though it might contain priceless information. 'We shall

192

have a busy night of it.'

A busy night and a sleepless one, but in the course of it they found one letter written by an officer named Caleb Gill which gave a clear statement of the *Norfolk*'s intended movements as far as the Galapagos archipelago: from that point she was to steer westward 'to my uncle Palmer's particular Paradise, for which we have a band of colonists, who wish to be as far away from their countrymen as possible.' Uncle Palmer was obviously the captain of the *Norfolk*, and his particular Paradise might be anywhere in the South Seas; but by comparing dates and positions and what the whalers said about the *Norfolk*'s sailing qualities, Jack was reasonably confident that he should come up with her well before the Galapagos, probably at the island of Juan Fernandez, where she meant to wood and water, or in the neighbourhood of Valparaiso, where she meant to refit; and Stephen would have been quite cheerful if it had not been for two patients who weighed upon his mind, the one his old friend Joe Plaice, who had brought his head against a ring-bolt in a commonplace fall down a ladder, fracturing his skull, and the other Mrs Horner, who was not responding to his treatment in any way.

'It astonishes me that our seamen can move straight from one ship to another and sail it off with no practice,' said Martin as they stood watching the *Danaë* part company, turning in a long pure curve until her head was pointing north-north-east while the *Surprise* carried on to the west of south.

'The complexity of rigging is much the same in all, I am told,' said Stephen. 'Just as we see a clear analogy between the skeletons of vertebrates, so the mariner with his boats. In a brig I believe some ropes run forward while on a three-masted ship they run backwards, yet this is no more a source of confusion for the seaman than the ruminant's multiplicity of stomachs for the anatomist, or the howler's anomalous hyoid. Yet what I wished to say was this: I know it was your kindly intention to visit the gunner's wife, but in her present state of mental agitation and extreme physical distress I really think I should beg you not to do so until there is some improvement: I have already banished her husband. On the other hand, I should be glad of your assistance in a tolerably delicate operation as soon as there is light enough: a depressed fracture. I must trepan poor Plaice and I should like to do so today; they tell me there is dirty weather ahead, and clearly one needs a steady deck underfoot and an immobile patient. I have an improved Lavoisier's trephine, a magnificent instrument with extraordinary biting power; and if you choose, you shall turn the handle!'

The *Surprise*'s crew, like most seamen, were a hypochondriacal set of ghouls upon the whole, and they loved a surgical operation almost as much as they loved a prize. But whereas the amputation of a shipmate's arm or leg had disadvantages of which they were fully sensible, a trepanning had none: the patient had but to survive to have all his former powers restored – to be as good as new, with the glory of a silver plate and an anecdote that would last him and his friends to the grave.

It was an operation that Dr Maturin had carried out at sea before, always in the fullest possible light and therefore on deck, and many of them had seen him do so. Now they and all their mates saw him do it again: they saw Joe Plaice's scalp taken off, his skull bared, a disc of bone audibly sawn out, the handle turning solemnly; a three-shilling piece, hammered into a flattened dome by the armourer, screwed on over the hole; and the scalp replaced, neatly sewn up by the parson.

It was extremely gratifying – the Captain had been seen to go pale, and Barret Bonden too, the patient's cousin – blood running down Joe's neck regardless – brains clearly to be seen – something not to be missed for a mint of money – instructive, too – and they made the most of it. This was just as well, because it was the last gratification they had for a very long while: in some cases the last they ever had. The dirty weather, foretold by the long heavy swell from the south and west, the dropping glass and the most forbidding sky, struck them even sooner and even harder than they had expected.

Yet the *Surprise* was a well-found, weatherly ship, and she rigged preventer backstays, braces, shrouds, and of course stays throughout, as well as rolling tackles, a full suit of storm-canvas bent well in time and her topgallant masts struck down on deck. Although the gale was very heavy indeed, filled with blinding rain and sleet, and although at first it blew against the swell and cut up a wicked sea, it was not foul, and the frigate, under close-reefed topsails, raced south at a tremendous pace, half smothered in flying water, shipping green seas every other minute, so that her decks were aswim and men could never move without clinging to the life-lines stretching fore and aft.

Two days and three nights it blew, the storm-wrack as low as the mastheads, but the third day it cleared and they had a good noon observation: to his great pleasure Jack found that they were farther south than he had expected – farther south than their dead-reckoning allowed – and that they were within striking distance of Staten Island.

He and Allen had a long conference, with the charts spread out before them, charts that gave different longitudes for a good many awkward islands, reefs and headlands; and all the while they talked the decks as far aft as the taffrail were aflutter with sea-soaked clothes attempting to dry in the pale evening sun. Jack questioned the master again and again about Captain Colnett's accuracy, and again and again the master affirmed that he would take his Gospel oath on it. 'He was Captain Cook's pupil, sir, and he carried a pair of Arnold's chronometers: they lasted him all the way, always wound, never once stopping, right by observation to within ten seconds, until we were pooped south of St Helena, homeward bound.'

'A pair of Arnold's chronometers? Very well then, Mr Allen,' said Jack, satisfied at last, 'let us set course for Cape St John. And as you go forward, pray tell the Doctor that I shall be able to accompany him on his rounds this evening.'

'Well, Stephen,' he said, when the Doctor came to fetch him, 'you have a thundering long great sick-list today, I see.'

'The usual strained articulations, crushed fingers, broken bones,' said Stephen. 'I tell them, "You must have one hand for the ship, and another for yourself; and you must throw your nasty grog into the scuppers, if you are to go aloft within two hours," but they do not attend. They leap about the rigging, encouraged by the bosun, as though they were octopodes, with prehensile tails into the bargain; so of course every time there is a tempest my sick-bay fills.'

'Of course. But tell me about Mrs Horner: I thought of her often when we rolled and pitched to such an extent.'

'She was unaware of it at the time, being delirious, but in any case the hanging cot is wonderfully adapted for patients at sea. I believe I may say that she has overcome her fever – I shaved her head – and that although there is a high degree of debility the youthful resilience of which I spoke may pull her through: it may perhaps pull her through, with the blessing.'

Jack Aubrey saw very little sign of resilience when he was led without warning into the gunner's cabin, or of youth; and if it had not been for Stephen's words he would have said that her grey face, her immense dark-circled eyes, showed the marks of death. Mrs Horner had just enough strength to snatch up a scarf and wrap it round her bald head, casting a reproachful glance at Stephen as she did so, and to murmur, 'Thank you, sir,' when Jack told her that he was delighted to see her looking so much better, and that she must make haste to be quite well again for the sake of the youngsters, who missed her sadly, and of course for Mr Horner. He was about to say something about 'Juan Fernandez restoring the roses to her cheeks' when he noticed that Stephen had laid his finger to his lips, and realized that in his embarrassment he had been addressing Mrs Horner as though she were a ship some considerable distance to windward.

He felt much happier in the sick-bay, where he knew exactly what to say to each man and boy – the boy being one of his youngsters, John Nesbit, with a broken collarbone – and in his relief he said to Plaice, 'Well, Plaice, at least some good has come out of this: at least nobody will ever be able to say, "Poor old Plaice is down to his last shilling." '

'How do you make that out, sir?' asked Plaice, closing one eye and smiling in anticipation.

'Why, because there are three of 'em screwed to your head, ha, ha, ha!' said his Captain.

'You are not unlike Shakespeare,' observed Stephen, as they walked back to the cabin.

'So I am often told by those who read my letters and dispatches,' said Jack, 'but what makes you say so at this particular moment?'

'Because his clowns make quips of that bludgeoning, knock-me-down nature. You have only to add *marry, come up*, or *go to, with a pox on it*, and it is pure Gammon, or Bacon, or what you will.'

'That is only your jealousy,' said Jack. 'What do you say to some music tonight?'

'I should like it extremely. I shall not play well, being quite *fagged out*, as our American captive says.'

'But Stephen, we say fagged out too.'

'Do we? I was not aware. Still, at all events we do not say it with that touching colonial twang, like a cockle-woman's horn on Dublin Quay. He is close kin to that most amiable Captain Lawrence we met in Boston, I find.'

'Yes, the same that captured Mowett in the *Peacock* and was so good to him. I mean to pay the young fellow every attention in my power: I have asked him and his midshipman to dinner tomorrow. Stephen, you will not mind doing without our usual toasted cheese? There is only just enough to make a presentable dish for my guests.'

They played without cheese; they played far into the night, until Stephen's head bowed over his 'cello between two movements: he excused himself and crept off, still half asleep. Jack called for a glass of grog, drank it up, put on a comforter knitted by his wife, still full of warmth and love though somewhat mangled by Brazilian mice, and his Magellan jacket and went on deck. It was a little after seven bells in the first watch, a drizzling night; and Maitland had the deck. As soon as his eyes were used to the darkness Jack looked at the log- and traverse-boards. The *Surprise* had kept exactly to her course, but she had been travelling rather faster than he had expected. Somewhere out there in the darkness to leeward was Staten Island: he had seen engravings of its ironbound coast in Anson's Voyage and he had no wish to come up against it, no wish to be whirled about in the strong currents and furious tides that swept round the tip of South America and through the Straits Lemaire. 'Clew up the forecourse and pass along the deep-sea line,' he said.

A few minutes later there began the steady ritual of taking soundings: the splash of the heavy lead far forward, the cry of 'Watch, there, watch,' coming aft as each of the men along the side let go the last of his coils of deep-sea line, until it reached the quartermaster in the mizen-chains, who reported the depth to the midshipman of the watch and called, 'Ready along,' whereupon the lead passed forward and the sequence began again.

'Belay,' said Jack as eight bells struck and the pink, sleepy larbowlins and the master relieved the midnight deck. 'Good night to you, Mr Maitland. Mr Allen, I believe we should be off Cape St John. We have a little over a hundred fathom, gently shoaling. What do you say to that?'

'Why, sir,' said the master, 'I think we should arm the lead and go on casting until we strike say ninety fathom with white shelly ground.'

One bell: two bells. And then, 'Ninety-five fathom and white shelly sand, sir,' said the quartermaster at last, holding the lead to the lantern, and with a strong feeling of relief Jack gave orders to haul to the wind. With the

Surprise sailing away from that vile thing a lee-shore, but still heading south, he could go below and sleep in peace.

He was on deck again at first light: a clear day, with the wind freshening and blowing in strange, uneasy gusts, a troubled sea and sky, following no coherent pattern, but no land to leeward, no land at all. The master, having had the middle watch, ought to have been asleep, but he was not, and together they laid a course that should take the ship round the Horn with no great offing – just enough to allow their minds to rest easy yet at the same time to profit from the variable inshore winds, which were blowing at present from the north and north-east, as favourable as could be.

They were profiting from them still as the guests in the cabin finished the very last of Jack's cheese, watched by a disapproving Killick and his coal-black mate: disapproval on a black face, ordinarily lit by a white smile, is disapproval indeed. It had not been an easy party; the circumstances were obviously very much against convivial merriment in the first place, and then again the sanguine, readily-pleased, conversible Jack that his friends knew was a very different person from the tall, imposing, splendidly-uniformed Captain Aubrey, his face moulded by years of nearly absolute authority, who received the two much younger Americans – far more different than he had supposed. It was therefore with a general, though decently concealed, sense of release that they parted, the prisoners to return to the gunroom with Mowett and Martin, their fellow guests, and Jack to walk on the quarterdeck.

There he found that the *Surprise* was holding her course, though from the look of the sky it was unlikely that she should hold it very much longer. The master was also on deck, and from time to time he swept the horizon from the starboard bow to the beam with his telescope; there were several others with him, for word had gone round that the Horn itself might appear about this time if the sky stayed clear.

No false word either: Jack, pacing up and down the seventeen yards of his quarterdeck, had not travelled above three furlongs of the three miles that Stephen insisted upon to control what he termed the Captain's gross obesity, before the lookout gave the cry of land. Maitland, Howard and all the valid youngsters ran up to the maintop to see, and presently it was in sight from the deck, not so much land as the world's grim end, a tall blackness on the rim of the sea that continually flashed white as the rollers broke at its foot and dashed far up the towering rock.

More people came on deck, including the doctor and parson. 'How very like landsmen they look, poor fellows,' thought Jack, shaking his head kindly. He called them over, assured them that it was indeed Cape Horn and showed it to them through his telescope. Martin was absolutely delighted. Staring at the far deadly precipice with the foam surging up it to a preposterous height he said, 'So that spray, that breaking water, is the Pacific!'

'Some call it the Great South Sea,' said Jack, 'not allowing it to be really Pacific until the fortieth parallel; but it is all equally wet, I believe.'

'At all events, sir,' said Martin, 'what lies beyond is the far side of the world, another ocean, another hemisphere, what joy!'

Stephen said, 'Why are all the people so very earnest to double it today?'

'Because they fear the weather may change,' said Jack. 'This is west-wind country, as you remember very well from our trip in the *Leopard*; but if once we can slip round the Horn, slip round Diego Ramirez, and gain a few degrees onward, the west wind may blow great guns if it likes – we can still bear away for the Chile coast – we shall still have rounded the corner. But before we get round, do you see, a south-west or even a strong west wind would quite bar our way. We fairly dread a south-west wind at this point.'

The sun sank behind a bank of purple cloud. The

breeze entirely died. Between the changing from one wind to another the Cape Horn current seized the ship and carried her fast eastwards; and at the beginning of the graveyard watch the south-west wind came in with a shriek.

The shriek rarely lessened in the days and weeks that followed. Sometimes it rose to a maniac pitch that threatened the masts themselves, but it never dropped below a level that in ordinary times would have been thought uncommonly severe, though now it was soon taken as a matter of course.

For the first three days Jack fought as hard as he could to preserve all that could be preserved of his precious westing, flanking across the wind right down into the sixties, where the people suffered cruelly from the ice on deck, ice on the rigging, ice on the yards, the sailcloth board-hard with frozen flying spray, and the cordage seizing in the blocks. South and still farther south in spite of the danger of ice, of the mortal collision with an iceberg in the night, south in the hope of a change; but when it came the change was for the worse: the full west wind strengthened, the enormous rollers sweeping eastwards grew more monstrous still, their white, wind-torn crests a quarter of a mile apart with a deep grey-green valley between, and the *Surprise* could do no more than lie to at the best, while for one wholly outrageous day when the entire surface of the sea – mountainous waves, valleys and all – was a flying mixture of air and fragmented water and she was obliged to scud under a goose-winged foretopsail, losing an enormous distance. Each hour of that nightmare scudding meant a day of laborious beating into the wind to regain the westing lost; and although the *Surprise* and most of her people were used to the tremendous seas of the high southern latitudes, the notorious forties and the far worse fifties, they were not used to sailing or trying to sail against them. The scale of the rollers was so vast that the frigate, opposing them, behaved more like a skiff; although she was forty yards long she could not possibly

201

span two, and hers was a violently pitching, switchback path.

This very nearly caused the end of Dr Maturin. He was about to go below – reluctantly, for there were no less than seven albatrosses about the ship – when he noticed the bosun's cat washing itself on the second step: ever since it had learnt that it was not to be starved, ill-treated, flung overboard, it had abandoned all its pretty, caressing ways; it now gave him an insolent stare and went on washing. 'That is the most pretentious cat I have ever known,' he said angrily, stepping high to tread over it. The cat gave a sideways spring and at the same moment the *Surprise* ran her bows into the advancing green wall of a roller, pointed her bowsprit at the sky and flung the already unbalanced Stephen forward. Unhappily a grating in the deck below was open and he fell a great way on to a heap of coals about to be whipped up for the hanging stoves.

Nothing was broken, but he was miserably bruised, shaken, battered, strained; and this happened at a most unfortunate time. That same evening, in a lull between two storms of sleet that came driving horizontally with the force of bird-shot, Jack gave orders to hand the fore and main topsails. The two watches were on deck and they manned the clewlines, buntlines and sheets of both together; and in both cases the clewlines and buntlines parted, almost at the same moment. Since the sheets were half-flown the sails instantly split at the seams, the maintopsail shaking so furiously that the masthead must have gone had not Mowett, the bosun, Bonden, Warley the captain of the maintop and three of his men gone aloft, laid out on the ice-coated yard and cut the sail away close to the reefs. Warley was on the lee yardarm when the footrope gave way under him and he fell, plunging far clear of the side and instantly vanishing in the terrible sea. At the same time the foretopsail beat entirely to pieces, while the maincourse blew free, billowing out with horrible strength, destroying right and left. They lowered the yard a-portlast, striving harder one would have said than it was possible for men to strive, often waist-deep in swirling water; then they lowered the foreyard too, and set about securing the boats on the booms, which were on the point of breaking loose, the *Surprise* all this time lying to under a mizen. They succeeded in the end, and then they began knotting and splicing the damaged rigging: they also carried their hurt shipmates below.

Jack came down into the sick-bay when the ship was reasonably snug. 'How is Jenkins?' he asked.

'I doubt he can live,' said Stephen. 'The whole rib-cage is . . . And Rogers will probably lose his arm. What is that?' – pointing to Jack's hand, wrapped in a handkerchief.

'It is only some nails torn out. I did not notice it at the time.'

From the sailors' point of view things improved after this: at the cost of incessant toil they could make some headway, and although the wind stayed firmly in the west there were days when it allowed them to tack rather than wear, with the heartbreaking loss of distance made good that wearing entailed in such a current and such a wind. But from the medical point of view they did not. The men's clothes were permanently wet, the men themselves were horribly cold and often low-spirited, and with great concern Stephen saw the first signs of scurvy in several of them: he had only lime-juice aboard, not the far more efficient lemon, and even the lime-juice he suspected of sophistication. He nursed his sick, he amputated Rogers' shattered arm successfully, and he dealt with the many new cases that presented themselves; but although Martin, Pratt the loblolly-boy (a gentle, unpractising paederast) and Mrs Lamb were a great help to him in the nursing – Higgins far less so – he found it heavy going. He saw little of Jack, who was almost always on deck or dead asleep; and he was surprised to find how he missed the very modest gunroom dinners – all livestock but the immortal Aspasia had perished, all private stores had been eaten or destroyed, and they were down to ship's rations, eaten quickly and in discomfort: and sometimes, when the galley fires could not be lit, they dined on biscuit and thin-sliced raw salt beef alone. Heavy going, with continual pain and a continual heavy despondency about Diana – premonitions, ill dreams, foreboding. Most fortunately he had his leaves of coca, that virtuous shrub, which kept him going by day and abolished his hunger, and his laudanum by night, which made the darkness a refuge at least.

Some of his time he spent with Mrs Horner. This had been necessary to begin with, when she had to be watched almost hour by hour, and it became habitual, partly because the gunner had a swinging, rope-woven chair, the only seat in the ship that did not hurt Stephen's wrenched, bruised limbs and creaking frame, and partly because he had taken a liking to her. There were few things he admired more in a woman than courage and she had courage in a high degree, and fortitude: no self-pity at any time, no complaint, and in the worst of her pain no more than an angry gasping wholly involuntary rattle, almost a growl.

She had early confided in him, speaking of her affection for Hollom – they were going to run away together and set up a mathematical, nautical school – she would do the cooking, housekeeping, mending, as she did for the young gentlemen here – and at first, supposing her almost whispered dreaming words to be the voice of delirium, he had allowed it, replying kindly to soothe the agitation of her mind. Later, when he sternly forbade this impropriety he found that she had long since detected his liking and that his harsh words had little effect.

As for Hollom himself, he had from the first shown intense anxiety. He could not speak of it openly, but the youngsters could, and daily one or another of them would ask Stephen how Mrs Horner did, immediately relaying his words to her lover. And although he was shy of Stephen he twice reported sick in order to ask after her and perhaps to talk about her; but this did not answer. Stephen dismissed him with half a blue pill and a black draught, told him he could not discuss his patients except to say they were well, indifferent, or dead, and discouraged any approach to confidence.

Yet as time went on, and as the *Surprise* slowly worked west and north into somewhat kinder waters, and as the resilience of youth asserted itself, which after a hesitant spring it did with remarkable speed, it became clear that Hollom had established his own lines of communication. He grew far more cheerful, and sometimes he could be heard singing in the awkward little triangular berth he shared with the Captain's clerk, Higgins and the American midshipman, or playing on Honey's guitar.

On the second day that the ship could carry courses and full topsails, the gunner, a deadly hand with a harpoon and quite pitiless, killed a seal that was looking up at him out of the sea. Stephen seized upon its liver for his scorbutic patients, and having reserved a little piece he carried it to Mrs Horner, arriving somewhat before his usual evening rounds. He found them tightly clasped together, mouth to mouth, and he said in an exceedingly angry voice, 'Leave the room, sir. Leave the room at once, I say.' And to Mrs Horner, who looked like a frightened boy with her short crop of hair standing up all round her head, and pinker than he had seen her since her high fever, 'Eat that, ma'am. Eat it up directly.' He clapped the plate down on her belly and walked out. Hollom was on the other side of the door and Stephen said to him, 'The risks you choose to run are your own concern, except in so far as they affect my patient. I will not have her health endangered. I shall report this to the Captain.'

Even as the words were uttering he was ashamed of their tone of righteous indignation and surprised by their naked jealousy; and at the same time he noticed the look of pale horror that Hollom directed beyond him. Turning he saw Jack's great bulk filling the gangway – like many big powerful portly men Jack was very light on his feet. 'What shall you report to the Captain?' he asked, smiling.

'That Mrs Horner is far better, sir,' said Stephen.

'I am heartily glad of it,' said Jack. 'I was looking for you to pay her a visit. I have good news for all the invalids. We have put our head north-north-west at last; we have the breeze on the larboard quarter and we are running eleven knots right off the reel. If I cannot promise them locusts and honey at once, at least there is every likelihood of warmth and dry beds very soon.'

And in the cabin, as Stephen slowly tuned his 'cello, thinking, 'It was common jealousy I make no doubt: disapproval too – the fellow is not worth her – a poor groatsworth of a man, vox et praeterea nihil (though a very fine vox) – but sure men in general are very rarely worth their women,' Jack said, 'I did not like to raise their hopes too much, but if this goes on, and by all accounts I have read it is very likely to go on, we should raise Juan Fernandez in a fortnight. It has been a slow, rough passage, I admit; but it is not impossible that the *Norfolk* may have had it slower and rougher still. It is not impossible,' he said, trying to convince himself, 'that we may still find her lying there, refreshing her people and taking her ease.'

CHAPTER SIX

The *Surprise* lay moored head and stern in forty fathom
water on the north side of the island, in Cumberland
Bay, the only sheltered road, and Jack Aubrey sat on
his quarterdeck in an elbow chair with an awning over
his head to keep off the sun, digesting his dinner –
lobster soup, three kinds of fish, a roast shoulder of kid,
sea-elephant steak grilled to a turn – and contemplating
the now familiar shore of Juan Fernandez. No more than
two cables' lengths away began the noble sward, a sweet
smooth green with two brooks running through it upon
which his tent had been pitched until that morning, a
green theatre rimmed by green forest, and beyond the
forest wild rocky hills rising in abrupt, fantastic shapes –
black crags in general, but clothed with green wherever
greenery could take hold, and not the rank lush excessive
exuberance of the tropics either but the elegant green of
the county Clare. On one of the nearer precipices he
could see Stephen and Martin creeping up a goat-path,
anxiously shepherded by Padeen, Stephen's servant and
an intrepid cragsman whose enormous frame had been
founded on sea-birds' eggs throughout his childhood, by
Bonden, with a coil of one-inch line over his shoulder,
and by Calamy, who was obviously giving advice, begging
them to take care, to watch where he was putting his feet,
and not to look down. They had heard of a humming-bird
peculiar to the island, the cock being bright pink and the
hen bright green, and since the recovery of the invalids
they had spent what waking hours they could spare from
the Juan Fernandez ferns and epiphytes to combing the
countryside in search of a nest.

From a ravine over towards East Bay came the crackle
of gunfire: that was Howard of the Marines, the American

officers and a party of liberty-men who were roaming the island with fowling-pieces, shooting anything that moved. Only a small party, and one made up of those particularly skilled men who until now had scarcely had a free hour from the urgent task of refitting the ship. A small party, because for most of the frigate's people liberty had come to an end with yesterday's evening gun, and they had spent this forenoon striking camp – the hospital-tent had been an imposing affair with ample room for all the severe cases of scurvy and the other invalids – and carrying water, wood, dried fish and other stores aboard. There might still be a score of people on the island, apart from the look-out men he had established on the Sugar Loaf, which commanded a fine view of the Pacific, but they had only a short time left; they had to be back before the end of the afternoon watch, when he intended to weigh, run out of the sheltered anchorage on what little tide there was (for the wind was steady in the south-south-east) and steer as straight and fast as ever he could for the Galapagos Islands. They had not found the *Norfolk* at Juan Fernandez, which was perhaps just as well, with so many Surprises unfit for action; nor had they found any trace of her having been there, but that did not signify a great deal, since she might perfectly well have watered at Mas-a-Fuera, a hundred miles to the west, or have put into Valparaiso, where she meant to refit. They had not found the *Norfolk*; he had made a very slow passage and he had been obliged to spend a long while on the island to recover his invalids and patch up his ship; yet even so he was satisfied. The *Norfolk*'s obvious duty – always supposing that she was in the Pacific at all and not down in the high southern latitudes, still battling with the westerlies – was to proceed steadily along the coast of Chile and Peru, lying to at night and looking for British whalers by day; so if he were to crack on for the Galapagos there was a strong likelihood that he should get there first, or find her on the whaling grounds, or at the very least learn something of her destination.

He had other causes for satisfaction: although she had scarcely a bolt of sailcloth or a tenpenny nail to spare once she had put herself to rights, the ship was now taut and trim and beautifully dry; she was very well supplied with fresh water, fuel, stockfish and pickled seal, and her people were remarkably healthy. They had only buried two, and that was at sea, off Diego Ramirez; the others had responded wonderfully to fresh vegetables, fresh meat, warmth and plain creature comfort after the howling wet and incessant cold of the sixties. Furthermore they had been through so much together that they were now a united body of men, and the frightful passage had made something like sailors out of even the least promising Defenders. Insensibly they had taken on the tone of the Surprises – the old distinction, the old animosity had vanished – and they were not only far more efficient but also much pleasanter to command: the grating had not been rigged since the remote days of the south Atlantic. There was only one man who still stood out, and that was the silly little ventriloquial barber Compton, who would be prating. There was also the gunner. He was not a former Defender but he too was a newcomer and he too did not fit in. He drank heavily and he was probably going mad: Jack had seen a good many sea-officers go mad. Although the captain of a man-of-war had immense powers there was little he could do to prevent a man protected by a commission or a warrant from destroying himself so long as he committed no offence against the Articles of War, and this Horner never did; although he was a sombre, inhuman brute he was a conscientious one and he did his duty at all times: yet even so Jack could not like him. The reefers on the other hand – how well they were coming on, and what an agreeable set of young fellows they were; he had rarely known a pleasanter, more cheerful midshipmen's berth. Perhaps it was the Greek. They had behaved remarkably well coming round the Horn, although Boyle had had three ribs stove in, while frostbite had taken off two of Williamson's toes and the tips of his ears, and the scurvy, running to Calamy's scalp, had turned him as bald as an egg; and now they were having immense fun on Juan Fernandez, hunting goats with a troop of large feral dogs they had more or less tamed. He smiled, but his pleasant thoughts were interrupted by a musket-shot and the voice of Blakeney, the acting signal-midshipman. 'If you please, sir, Sugar Loaf is signalling. A sail, I believe.'

A sail it was, but the eddying breeze up there streamed the rest of the hoist directly away from the ship; and rather than wait for it to come fair Jack ran to the forecastle, filled his lungs and hailed the Sugar Loaf with enormous force: 'A whaler?' A combined yell of No came down, with gestures of negation, but the answer to his 'Where away?' could not be heard, though their outstretched arms pointed emphatically to leeward, and calling to Blakeney to follow him with a telescope Jack climbed to the fore crosstrees. He searched the hazy northern rim of the sea, but nothing could he find, apart from a school of whales blowing by the score some five miles away. 'Sir,' cried Blakeney, standing on the topgallant yard, 'the hoist has come straight. I can read most of it without the book. *Ship bearing north-north-east* something *leagues* – can't make out the numerals, sir – *steering west*.'

They were responsible men up there, Whately, a quartermaster, and two middle-aged able seamen: and to seamen *ship* meant only one thing, a three-masted square-rigged vessel. A frigate was of course a ship, and since this ship they were signalling somewhere beyond his range was not a whaler – and whalers could instantly be recognized from their crow's-nests – she might well be the *Norfolk*. Might very well be the *Norfolk*. 'Mr Blakeney,' he said, 'jump up to the Sugar Loaf with a glass. Take all the notice you can of what sail she is under and her course and bearing. Then bring the men and their belongings down: you may come as quick as you like, unless you choose to spend the rest of your days on this island. We shall never beat back to it in this breeze, once we have gone to leeward.' Then raising his voice and sending it aft, 'Mr Honey, there. All hands unmoor ship, if you please.'

Every man aboard and several ashore had been expecting the order ever since the Sugar Loaf answered the Captain's hail, and even before the bosun raised his call the deck was as busy as an upturned anthill. Purposefully busy however with capstan-bars hurrying to be shipped, pinned and swifted, topmen running to veer away the head-cable, forecastlemen vanishing below to the cable-tier, there to coil the stern-cable as the monstrous, wet, stiff and heavy rope came in; it took a great deal more than a sudden order to unmoor ship to make the *Surprise* lose her head, and busy though she seemed, or even to a landsman's eye distracted, she found plenty of time to break out the blue peter at the fore and fire a gun to draw attention to it.

The gun stopped Stephen and Martin dead, and before they could gather their wits and begin to reflect upon the reasons for the report they were turned about and hurried down the goat-path, losing half an hour's laborious climb in five minutes. Neither Bonden nor Calamy would attend to any speculation, any remarks about humming-birds, about reckless unnecessary haste, or the beetles left among the tree-ferns, for a moment; and although there was a long way to go through the sandal-wood trees and behind the sea-elephants' cove – 'the only place on the island where Venus mercenaria is to be found' cried Martin in anguish as he was heaved past it at a brisk trot – they brought their charges to the strand as the last three invalids (one broken leg that would not knit; one amputated forearm, gangrened after frostbite; and one perfectly irrelevant tertiary syphilis, acquired years ago behind a Hampshire hedge and now moving to its terminal general paralysis) were handed into the red cutter, attended by Higgins, and as the fife on the capstan-head died away, the *Surprise* being right over her stern anchor, having reached the point where the ritual words were spoken, 'Up and down, sir' and then, 'Thick and dry for weighing.' These were followed by an anxious period, for the anchor had dragged a little and there was danger of its being in foul ground. The fife struck up and the men heaved hearty, but the capstan moved slower and slower. The shooting-party arrived, all crammed into one boat, and the liberty-men flung themselves upon the bars. 'Heave and a-weigh,' called the bosun as he felt a yielding tremor from the depths, and the capstan began to turn with a fine click-click of its pawls, raising the best bower through a murky cloud of sediment. 'Heave and in sight.' But the best bower had moored the frigate by the stern, with the cable passing out of a gunroom port, and although the Surprises were pleased to see their anchor dangling there, they still had to pass it forward. This was a difficult task in itself, the best bower weighing thirty-one hundredweight, and it was harder now, since at the same time they had to warp the ship across the bay to heave up the second anchor, laid out ahead. A period of intense activity ensued, with the capstan turning steadily to the tune of *All Aboard for Cuckolds' Reach* and the bosun and his mates leaping to and fro, inboard and out, like so many passionate apes.

Some time passed before Jack had leisure to say, 'There you are, Doctor. There you are, Mr Martin. I am sorry to have torn you from your botanizing, but I am happy to see you aboard. We may have our enemy under our lee – we must sail directly, and with the wind so steady in the south anyone left behind is likely to stay there a great while. Mr Mowett, all the people are aboard, I believe?'

'No, sir,' said Mowett. 'The gunner, his wife, and Hollom are still ashore.'

'Mr Horner?' cried Jack. 'God's my life, I could have sworn he came in the launch. Give him another gun.'

They gave him three guns at long intervals while the *Surprise* moved steadily across the bay; but it was not until she was almost over her small bower, with the cable sloping steep, that he was reported at the landing-place, alone at the landing-place. 'What the devil does he mean? What the hell are they about? Gathering nosegays?' said Jack, glancing angrily over the pure sea, just ruffled now

212

by a most welcome breeze, blowing the way of the tide. 'Send the jolly-boat for them. Yes, Mr Hollar, what is it?'

'Beg pardon, sir,' said the bosun. 'Capstan's up to his old capers again.'

'Red hell and death,' said Jack. 'Surge the messenger.' They surged the messenger, taking the strain off the cable. and Jack crawled under the bars to the iron pawl-rim. True enough: one of the pawls had already lost its tip and the other was so distorted that it might go any minute; and if it were to go when the cable was taut any heave of the sea, any lift of the ship, would be transmitted to the bars with shocking force, spinning the capstan backwards and scattering the men like ninepins, bloody ninepins.

'Shall I have the forge set up, sir?' asked Mowett.

It would have to be done sooner or later; new pawls would have to be shaped, hammered, tempered just so and fitted; but this would take hours and they would lose not only the tide but the promising little air that was stirring the pennant. 'No,' said Jack, 'We shall weigh with a voyol to the jeer-capstan.' As he spoke he saw a horrified look spread on the bosun's face. Mr Hollar had always served in modern ships and he had never weighed with a voyol: indeed it was an antiquated practice. But as a youngster Jack had sailed under some very conservative, antiquated captains; and it also happened that his very first command, the *Sophie*, an old-fashioned brig if ever there was one, had habitually used a voyol. With scarcely a pause Jack called the midshipmen. 'I will show you how we weigh with a voyol,' he said. 'Take notice. You don't often see it done, but it may save you a tide of the first consequence.' They followed him below to the mangerboard, where he observed, 'This is a voyol with a difference: carry on *Sophie*-fashion, Bonden,' – for Bonden had already brought the big single-sheaved block. 'Watch, now. He makes it fast to the cable – he reeves the jeer-fall through it – the jeer-fall is brought to its capstan, with the standing part belayed to the bitts. So you get a direct runner-purchase instead of a dead nip, do you understand?'

They understood; but the voyol-block, so long unused, broke under the strain. It had to be replaced by various makeshifts, and by the time the cable was truly up and down and Jack on deck again the jolly-boat was lying empty alongside, its crew already busy at their various stations. As he walked aft he saw Maitland speaking to Mowett, who came forward to meet him, took off his hat and said in an odd, formal voice, 'The gunner has come aboard, sir. He came alone. He says Hollom has deserted – will not rejoin the ship – and that Mrs Horner is staying with him. He says they mean to stay on the island. He hurt his leg in the woods and has gone below.'

The atmosphere was very strange. Jack checked his first reply and glanced about the quarterdeck. Most of the officers were there: not one had a wholly natural expression on his face. Two of the jolly-boat's crew were close by, clearing away the falls, and they looked deeply perturbed, anxious, and as it were frightened. Obviously there was something known in the ship, and obviously no one was going to tell him; even Maturin's face was closed. The decision had to be made at once and he would have to make it himself. Ordinarily any deserter had to be taken up; the example was of the first importance. But this was a special case. Searching the island with all its caves and deep recesses might take a week – a week at a time when a possible enemy was in sight! While his mind was turning to and fro he was tempted to say, 'Has the gunner made no representations about pursuing them, about recovering his wife?' when he realized that the answer was implicit in Mowett's account. The question was pointless: in any case his mind was clear and settled; he said, 'Up anchor,' adding, 'We shall deal with the question of desertion at a later time, if possible. Carry on, Mr Maitland.'

'Away aloft,' cried Maitland, and the men ran up on to the yards.

'Trice up and lay out,' and they cast off the gaskets, holding the sails under their arms.

'Let fall. Sheet home.' The sails dropped: the larboard

watch sheeted home the foretopsail, the starboard watch the maintopsail, and the boys and idlers the mizen. Then, slightly ahead of the order, they manned the halliards and ran the yards up; the topgallants followed, the sails were trimmed to the breeze, and as the *Surprise*, moving easily over her small bower, plucked it up with scarcely a check, they ran back to the capstan and heaved the cable in. The hands went through these motions with the unthinking ease of very long practice but in something near dead silence; there was none of the cheerful excitement of getting to sea in great haste with the possibility of action not far ahead.

Most of them had seen the gunner come aboard, his ghastly sunken face, his blood-spattered clothes; some had heard the inhuman mechanical voice in which he reported to the officer of the watch; and the crew of the jolly-boat told how he had washed his hands and head, kneeling there at the edge of the sea.

Once the ship was clear of the island's lee she set studdingsails aloft and alow and steered a course designed to intercept the stranger: Blakeney had taken her bearing with great care and he had made out that she was on the larboard tack, at least one point free under courses and topsails. The *Surprise* was now making eight knots and Jack hoped to raise her in the evening, then, taking in all but his staysails until nightfall, and lurking under the horizon as it were, to come up with her at dawn under a press of canvas.

Up at the main crosstrees he scanned the far sea with his telescope, sweeping a twenty-degree arc from the starboard leech of the foretopgallant, and below him he heard the men in the foretop, unaware of his presence, talking in low urgent voices, little more than a whisper. They were upset; more upset than could be accounted for by a master's mate bolting with a gunner's wife on a warm and pleasant island. Whales again; a perfectly enormous school of them spouting over not much more than a mile of sea; he had never seen so many together –

certainly more than two hundred. 'Innocent blood in the sun,' said a voice in the foretop: Vincent, a West Country lay preacher.

'Innocent blood my arse,' said another, probably old Phelps.

And beyond the whales, far beyond the whales a pale flash that was certainly not a spout: he focused his glass and steadied it – the stranger, sailing steadily along, holding her course. Hull down, of course, but quite certainly there. Turning his head and leaning down he hailed the deck: an absurdly moderate hail, as though the distant ship might hear. 'On deck, there. In topgallants.'

He made his way slowly down, gave the orders that should keep the *Surprise* out of sight but still moving on a course parallel with the stranger's, and walked into his cabin. He was very much a creature of his ship and although his life was so comparatively isolated he was keenly aware of the atmosphere aboard: in tune with it too, since his intense eager looking forward to the morning was now deadened to a surprising degree. Obviously this did not prevent him from taking every proper measure; he and the master laid a very exactly calculated course: dead-lights were shipped before dark so that not a glimmer should show aboard, and half an hour after sunset the ship swung five and a half points north, increasing her speed on the regular, unvarying breeze to seven knots, with perhaps two in reserve if she needed to spread more canvas. He said to Mowett, 'It would be inhuman to harass poor Horner this evening. Let us assume that he has gone sick and ask his eldest mate to report – Wilkins, is it not? A solid man. I have no doubt about the state of the guns, but we may need some more cartridge filled, particularly if we are lucky tomorrow.'

Then as the ship sailed evenly through the moonless night with a long easy pitch and rise on the following swell and with the regular hum of her rigging transmitted to the cabin as an omnipresent comfortable sound laced through as it were with the run of the water along her side, he returned to his serial letter to Sophie. 'Although a captain is married to his ship it is with him as it is with some other husbands; there are certain things he is the last to know. There is certainly more in this than meets the eye, at least more than meets my eye. The people are shocked and I might even say grieved, and this would not have been brought about merely by what is said to have happened – a warrant officer's wife leaving him and a master's mate walking Spanish. I hate and distrust tale-bearers and I have no opinion of captains who listen to them, still less encourage them; and although I am morally certain that Mowett and Killick and Bonden, to name only three who have been shipmates with me time out of mind, know very well what is afoot I am equally certain that not one will tell me without I ask him straight out, which I shall not do. There is only one person I might decently speak to, as a friend, and that is Stephen; but whether he would tell me or not I cannot say.' He paused – a long, long pause – and then called, 'Killick. Killick, there. My compliments to the Doctor and if he should care for a little music I am at his service.' With this he took his fiddle out of its case and began tuning it, a series of pings, squeaks and groans that made a curiously satisfying pattern of their own and that began moving his mind on to another plane.

The old Scarlatti in D minor and a set of variations on a theme of Haydn's that they handed to and fro with some pleasant improvisations moved it somewhat farther; but neither was in a mood to be wholly possessed by music and when Killick came in with the wine and biscuits Jack said, 'We must turn in early: it is not impossible we may find the *Norfolk* tomorrow. Unlikely, but not impossible. But before turning in I should like to ask you something. It may be improper and I shall not take it amiss if you don't choose to reply. What do you think of this desertion?'

'Listen, my dear,' said Stephen. 'It is an awkward thing asking a ship's surgeon about any of her people, because they have nearly all of them been his patients at one time or another, and a medical man may no more discuss his

217

patients than a priest his penitents God forbid. I will not tell you what I think of this desertion, so, nor what I think of the people concerned in it; but if you wish I will tell you of what is commonly thought, though without giving you any warrant of its truth or falsity and without adding any views of my own or any private knowledge I may possess.'

'Pray do so, Stephen.'

'Well, now, it was generally supposed that Hollom has been Mrs Horner's lover for a considerable time, that Horner discovered it a week or so ago . . .'

'Enough to make any man run mad,' said Jack.

'. . . and that he took the opportunity of leading them to the far side of the island on the pretext of a private conversation and there battering them to death. He had a bludgeon with him, and he is shockingly strong. He is said to have carried their bodies to the cliff and thrown them over. The people grieve for Mrs Horner, so young; and she was good-natured, kind and uncomplaining too. They are sorry for Hollom to some degree, but above all they regret he ever came aboard, an unlucky man. Yet they feel that Horner was intolerably provoked; and although they do not like him they think he was within his rights.'

'I dare say they do,' said Jack. 'And if I know anything of the Navy they will not give him away. Not a scrap of evidence will they ever produce; an enquiry would be perfectly useless. Thank you, Stephen. That was what I wanted to know, and I dare say if I had been a little sharper I should not have had to ask. I shall have to take the thing at its face value, put an R against poor Hollom's name, and meet Horner's eye as best I can.'

In the event there was no difficulty about meeting Horner's eye. At the end of the middle watch the chase's lights were seen, a little, but only a very little, farther west than they should have been; and at first dawn there she lay, placidly holding her course under the low grey sky. Jack was on deck on his nightshirt, but Horner was there before him. The gunner was dressed in fresh white canvas trousers and new checked shirt; a wounded or twisted leg made his movements awkward but he stumped about his guns, inspecting equipment, sights and breeching with his usual surly competence. He came aft to the quarterdeck carronades, spreading intense wooden embarrassment all round but apparently feeling none himself: he touched his hat to the Captain, standing there with a lowered night-glass in his hand. Jack's whole heart and soul had been turned to the chase – he had been engaged in naval war for more than twenty years and he was very much of a sea-predator, perfectly single-minded when there was the near likelihood of violent action – and now in the most natural voice in the world he said, 'Good day to you, master gunner. I fear there will be no great chance of expending your stores this morning.'

The rising sun proved that he was right: it showed a line of figures leaning along the stranger's rail in easy attitudes, some with moustaches, some smoking cigars. The United States Navy, though easy-going and even at times verging upon the democratic, never went to such extremes as this; and indeed the chase turned out to be the *Estrella Polar*, a Spanish merchantman from Lima for the River Plate and Old Spain. She was perfectly willing to heave to and pass the time of day, and although she could not spare the *Surprise* anything but a few yards of sailcloth in exchange for bar iron she was generous with information: certainly the *Norfolk* had passed into the Pacific, and that after an easy passage of the Horn; she had watered at Valparaiso, scarcely needing to refit at all, which was just as well, since Valparaiso was notorious for possessing nothing, and that nothing of the very lowest quality as well as exorbitantly dear and delivered only after endless delay. She had sailed as soon as her water was completed and she had captured several British whalers. The *Estrella* had heard tell of one burning at sea off the Lobos rocks like an enormous torch in the night and had spoken to another, the *Acapulco* by name, which was being taken to the States by a prize-crew, a stout ship, but like most whalers a slug: the *Estrella* could give her fore and main topgallantsails and still sail two miles for her one: had met her under the tropic line, two hundred leagues north-north-east, a great way off. The *Estrella* would be happy to carry the *Surprise*'s letters to Europe and wished her a happy voyage; the two ships filled their backed topsails and drew apart, calling out civilities. The Spaniard's last audible words, over half a mile of sea, were 'Que no haya novedad.'

'What did he mean by that?' asked Captain Aubrey.

'May no new thing arise,' said Stephen. 'New things being of their nature bad.'

The Surprises were glad to have their letters carried back to the Old World; they were grateful for the half bolt of canvas; and they said good-bye to the *Estrella* with real good will. Yet after a night of the liveliest expectation and the triumph of seeing her lights in the middle watch, she could not be anything but an anticlimax, a bitter disappointment. There was also the intense mortification of the *Norfolk*'s having rounded the Horn so much before them and of her snapping up the British whalers they had been sent to protect. Many Surprises had friends or relations in the South Sea fishery, and they felt it keenly: Mr Allen most of all. He had always been a stern, unsmiling officer when he had the watch; not exactly a hard horse, since he never abused or wantonly harassed the men, but taut, very taut indeed; and now he became more so. He had the afternoon watch that day, when the sky lowered and began to weep thin rain; the breeze grew capricious, sometimes baffling, and he kept the hands perpetually on the run, making sail, trimming it, taking it in again, all in a harsh and angry bark.

He had had a long conference with Jack, and they had decided that in view of the *Estrella*'s information the best course was to bear in with the main, keeping as close to the homeward-bound whalers' path as possible; this was not the *Surprise*'s direct route for the Galapagos, but, insisted the master, they would lose little time – it was almost as broad as it was long – because of the cold current that flowed north along the coast, carrying seals and penguins right up almost as far as the equator, the whole length of Chile and Peru. Allen's reasoning and his experience of these waters seemed conclusive to Jack, and the ship was now steering as nearly east-north-east as she could, through the cheerless drizzle.

A cheerless, uneasy ship: they had got rid of one unlucky man in *poor Hollom*, as they all called him now, but they had gained a far worse, a fellow who must necessarily bring a curse upon them all. The youngsters were pitifully affected – Mrs Horner had always been very kind to them, and apart from that they had been as sensible of her good looks as grown men – Jack abruptly shifted their quarters, making them mess with Ward, his clerk, Higgins, and the tall American midshipman: Ward did not care for their company (though they were red-eyed and as quiet as mice at present) but it was intolerable that they should stay with Horner.

The gunner celebrated his freedom by getting drunk. He compelled one of his mates to sit with him and the much less reluctant barber Compton, the one person aboard who could by any stretch of the word be called his crony. Horner was well found in stores, having three breakers of Spanish brandy left, and they drank until the graveyard watch, when to their horror the hands on deck heard his thick harsh voice singing *Come it late or come it soon/I shall enjoy my rose in June*.

Day after day the *Surprise* sailed through troubled seas, with the ship labouring heavily; and every night Horner sat drinking with the barber, whose shrill ventriloquial voice could be heard going through his set pieces again and again, followed by the deep rumbling tones of the half-drunk Horner growing confidential. It shocked the men on deck; it shocked the men below. Even when she reached the cool turquoise water of the Peru current one clear day at noon and raised the jagged line of the Cordillera of the Andes, sparkling white in the clear sky far, far

221

on the starboard beam as she turned northward, the mood in the ship remained the same. The hands were oppressed and silent; they thought Compton mad to hobnob with the gunner and they were not surprised when one night there was the sound of fighting and he came racing up on deck, his face covered with blood and the gunner hard after him. Horner tripped and fell; they picked him up dead drunk and carried him below. Compton had no more than a cut mouth and a bloodied nose, but he was so frightened he could hardly stand, and to those who wiped him he said, 'I only told him she had been got with child.'

The next day the gunner sent to say that he wished to consult Dr Maturin, who received him in his cabin. The man was perfectly steady in his movements but there was no human contact with him; he was so pale that his tan showed ochre, a dull ochre, and Stephen had the impression that he was filled with an almost ungovernable rage.

'I have come to see you, Doctor,' he said. Stephen bowed, but made no reply. 'She was in kindle, when she took sick,' said the gunner suddenly.

'Listen, Mr Horner,' said Stephen. 'You are speaking of your wife, and I must tell you that I cannot discuss my patients with anyone.'

'She was in kindle, and you used an instrument on her.'

'I have nothing to say to you on this matter.'

Horner stood up, crouching under the beams, and said in a much rougher tone, 'She was in kindle, and you used an instrument on her.'

The door opened. Padeen stepped quickly in and took Horner from behind, circling his arms: Padeen was an even bigger man, and stronger by far. 'Put him down, now, Padeen,' said Stephen. 'Mr Horner, sit in that chair. Your mind is disturbed; you are upset, as well you may be, with so much emotion. You need physic. Drink this.' He poured half a wine-glass of his own tincture and passed it, saying, 'I will not pretend not to know what you mean; but you must understand that I have never used an instrument in that sense in all my life, nor ever shall.'

He spoke with an authentic kindness and this perhaps even more than the evident truth pierced through: the gunner drank his glass.

It was a dose that should have calmed a dozen men unused to the drug, but that afternoon Higgins came to see Stephen in a state not so much of alarm as of abject terror. 'He said I used an instrument on her – oh sir you must protect me – I am your assistant – I am your mate – you must protect me. He respects you: he don't respect me at all.' That was true enough: Higgins' patter had been repeated too often, his rapacity had become too naked, and he had been so foolish as to tyrannize over the loblolly-boy, a medical oracle of great standing with the lower deck, who revealed many of his capers, privately showing his shop-worn earwigs and the aged stag-beetle. And in any case Stephen's trepanning of Plaice had quite wiped out what little triumphs Higgins may have had with teeth.

'You had better keep out of his way until he has quietened,' said Stephen. 'You may stay in the sick-bay, reading to the invalids: I will ask Padeen to sit with you for a day or so. You must conciliate his good will, somewhat thoughtlessly impaired, by speaking to him civilly, perhaps by making him a small present.'

'Oh sir, I will give him half a guinea – a whole guinea – I will give him two guineas, honest fellow – and I shall never leave the sick-bay, except to turn in, and then never you fear, sir, I am surrounded by hammocks on all sides: and the big American midshipman is between me and the door.'

Yet on the Friday, that clouded, miserable day, when Stephen and Martin were dissecting a pelican, one of the many creatures that Howard the Marine had shot as the ship sailed along the fertile current, much frequented by penguins, dolphins and all kinds of seals, sea-lions and sea-bears, as well as unbelievably vast shoals of little fishes like anchovies and their attendant birds overhead, Martin said, 'What do they mean by a Jonah's lift?'

Before Stephen could answer Howard came below and

told them that a strange enormous thing rather like a sea-elephant had come within range: he had fired, but had hit only the young one that was with it, a veil of mist coming between him and his mark at the crucial moment. He wished they had seen the animal; it was prodigious like a human being, though bigger, and what he might call grey in colour. He wished very much they had seen it.

'I am sure you mean very kindly, Mr Howard,' said Stephen. 'But let me beg you not to shoot more creatures than we can collect or dissect, or than the men can eat, for all love.'

'Oh, you have never been a one for sporting, Doctor,' said Howard, with a laugh. 'Why, you could shoot all day long in these waters, was you fond of sporting; just now I had the prettiest right and left among a flight of cormorants. I shall go straight back to it; I have two men loading for me.'

'A Jonah's lift, did you say?' said Stephen. 'I believe it is a term they use when they speak of an unpopular or unlucky man having been pushed over the side.'

'Oh surely not,' said Martin, who was ignorant of these later developments, 'I heard it used of Mr Higgins.'

'Did you indeed?' said Stephen. 'Pray stretch the skin till I come back.'

Higgins was not in the sick-bay, nor in his berth; and as Stephen looked for him he caught significant glances exchanged by some of the men. He took the loblolly-boy aside and said, 'Listen, Jamie Pratt, when did you see him last?'

'Well, sir,' said Jamie, 'he dursen't go to the head, you know: he bottled himself up or used a pot. But last night he had a roaring old flux and went forwards, it being wholly dark. Which I ain't seen him since. I thought he was maybe with you, maybe in his berth, or maybe in the cable-tier. I heard tell he has a hidey-hole down there, being main frightened of a certain gent, as you might say.'

'Sure he will be in his place at quarters, if he has been hiding below,' said Stephen.

The drum beat, the bulkheads vanished, the frigate showed a clean sweep fore and aft, ready for battle, and all hands ran to their action-stations. Mowett made his rapid inspection, in order to be able to report to the Captain, 'All hands present and sober, sir, if you please.' He found the bosun on the forecastle, of course, the carpenter and his crew at the pumps and in the wings, and the gunner, his yeoman and his mates at their posts in the magazines; but when he came to the shady depths where Stephen, Martin and the loblolly-boy stood ready to attend the wounded, Stephen said, 'Sir, I have to report the absence of my assistant Mr Higgins.'

Quarters ended with no great-gun exercise; the drummer beat the retreat and Jack ordered a thorough searching of the lower platforms and the hold. Higgins might have been taken ill inside one of the great coils of cable on the tiers, or he might have fallen down a hatchway. The men lit their lanterns in the rapidly-gathering dusk – low cloud was already wafting through the upper rigging – and began going through the necessary motions. But their hearts were not in it: of course their hearts were not in it, since they knew as an evident fact that Higgins had been given a Jonah's lift: and no great loss, neither. And when the wailing started they all hurried up on deck, standing there in a huddle.

It was a wailing, a great long desperately sad O – o – o of immense volume, sometimes rising to a shriek, unlike any sound that had come from the sea in the experience of the oldest man aboard, and it circled the ship, coming quite close on either side: sometimes a form could be made out, but never clearly. In any case there were few who dared to look.

'What can it be?' asked Jack.

'I cannot tell,' said Stephen, 'but suppose it to be the creature whose young one was shot. Perhaps it was wounded, and perhaps it has now died.'

The voice grew louder still, almost intolerable before it broke off in a dying sob. 'Mr Mowett,' said Jack in a most uneasy tone, 'has the ship been thoroughly searched?'

'I am not quite sure, sir,' said Mowett, raising his voice above the wail, now on the larboard beam. 'I will find out directly.' There was the same answer to all his questions: yes, everything had been rummaged; and no, there was no good going down there again. They were responsible warrant and petty officers who spoke, sometimes lying to his face; and he knew and they knew that there would be no getting the men to return to remoter, darker, more lonely parts of the ship.

'God's my life,' cried Jack, the empty watch-glass catching his eye, the half-hour glass that was religiously turned even in the heat of battle, even when the ship was settling in the sea, her bottom pierced. 'God's my life. What the devil are you thinking of? Turn the glass and strike the bell.'

The Marine on duty turned the glass and reluctantly moved forward: eight hesitant bells, and the howling all around.

'Set the watch,' said Jack. 'Judas Priest, what are you all standing about for? Mr Mowett, lanterns will be allowed on the berth-deck tonight after lights out. Master-at-arms, take notice of that.'

He paused to see that the watch was indeed mustered. For a moment he thought it might not be accomplished, for although he had often seen sailors disturbed, alarmed, unsettled, he had never known them so frightened as this, nor so utterly cast down; but most of the officers were on deck, and the stolid, wholly unimaginative presence of Mr Adams, eagerly discussing the storage of bottled ale with Stephen and Martin, helped Maitland through his task. Once the last name was called Jack walked into his cabin, where he paced to and fro athwartships, his hands behind his back; and all the time the terrible great cry moved round the ship.

'Pass the word for the Doctor,' he said at last; and when Stephen came, 'I hear that Martin asked about a Jonah's lift: I know what is said among the people, and I have been reflecting. This cannot go on: tell me, since it is generally held that the gunner has committed monstrosities, could you certify that he is mad and must be placed under restraint?'

'I could not. Many a man has done what he is said to have done and is still reckoned sane. I could not certify a man mad on supposition no nor on the most vehement suspicion either, nor even on legal proof without examining what can be made out of his mind, to know whether he acted rationally. To know with at least that faint light of knowledge that can come from one man's fallible examination.'

'Examination?' said Jack. 'Very well.' He rang and said, 'Pass the word for the gunner.'

They sat there lost in thought as the cry went forward. The howling outside had diminished while they were speaking but now it rose to a shriek even higher than before. 'What can it be?' asked Jack again, deeply disturbed.

'Sure I cannot tell,' said Stephen, crossing himself. 'Conceivably something of the manatee kind, though the latitude is wrong entirely. God between us and evil.'

'Amen,' said Jack and the door opened – Killick appalled, could scarcely speak. 'Gunner's hanged hisself,' he brought out in a gasp.

'Have you cut him down?' cried Jack.

Stephen saw the answer in Killick's stupid look, pushed past him and ran forward, calling to Bonden and a bosun's mate as he ran.

'Lift him up till I cut the cord,' he said.

They laid him on his cot and it was there that Martin saw him, with Stephen sitting by his head. 'There is hope, is there not?' said Martin, looking at that dark, suffused, expressionless face. 'There is no question of dislocation, surely?'

227

'No drop, no dislocation,' said Stephen.

'So there is certainly hope. I have known a man hang twenty minutes and still be revived by proper measures. Why, he is still warm! Do you detect a pulse?'

'I believe I may.'

'When shall you bleed him? I do not mean to instruct you, Maturin, but should he not be let blood directly?'

'I do not think bleeding would answer in this case,' said Stephen, and after a while he went on, 'Have you ever brought a determined suicide back to life? Have you seen the despair on his face when he realizes that he has failed – that it is all to do again? It seems to me a strange thing to decide for another. Surely living or dying is a matter between a man and his Maker or Unmaker.'

'I cannot think you are right,' said Martin, and he set out the contrary view.

'Sure you speak with great authorities on your side,' said Stephen. He stood up and leant his ear to the gunner's chest, then opened his eye, gazing into it with a candle. 'But in any case he is now gone beyond my interference, God rest his soul.'

Martin shook his head and said, 'I cannot give him Christian burial, alas.' Then, after a moment, 'The wailing has stopped.'

'It stopped while you were speaking, five minutes ago,' said Stephen. 'I believe the best thing to do is to send for his mates, who will sew him up in a hammock with round-shot at his feet. I shall watch by him until the morning, when he can be slipped over first thing, without distressing the hands even further; for I must tell you, Martin, the more superstitious of them are quite capable of pining away under this kind of strain, like blacks when they have been cursed.'

But first thing in the morning or rather before it was also the time when the *Surprise* sent men to the masthead to see what the new-lit ocean might have on its surface. Rare, rare were the gifts it offered, but still the men laid aloft at a tearing pace, even in such times as these, since before now the frigate had found an opponent or a prize lying there within range of her guns. Three hundred and sixty-four mornings of the year might show nothing or only a distant fisherman but there was always the possibility of an exceptional dawn and this was one of them. The shrieking hail of 'Sail ho' cut short all the rumbling activity of holystones and bears.

'Where away?' called the master, who had the watch.

'Right in the wind's eye, sir,' said the lookout. 'Just topsails up, and a whaler, I do believe.'

A few minutes later, with the light spreading fast and the last stars dying in the west, Jack was plucked from a troubled, anxious sleep by the ship's change of course through sixty-four degrees and by young Boyle's voice loud in his ear, bringing 'Mr Allen's duty, sir, and a sail in the south-south-west, a whaler, we do believe.'

When he came on deck he found a fresh and brilliant morning, the *Surprise* close-hauled on the larboard tack, and a somewhat nervous master, who said, 'I have presumed to alter course, sir, since she may be an American or a prize of ours going home.'

'Quite right, Mr Allen,' said Jack, fixing the chase's topsails as they nicked the clear horizon. 'Quite right: there was not a moment to lose – it will be tack upon tack, as hard as ever we can pelt, to make up such a leeway.'

'Another thing, sir,' said Allen in a low voice, 'Pearce and Upjohn' – two of the Gibraltar lunatics, who had laid the hammock-shrouded gunner on the gangway – 'did not quite understand, and they launched Mr Horner over the side when the ship hauled to the wind.'

'Perhaps it was for the best,' said Jack, shaking his head. 'Perhaps it was . . . forward, there: sharp that maintop bowline. Mr Allen, I believe she will wear fore and main topgallantsails.'

With the sun a broad handsbreadth clear of the sea he was on deck again, standing there with one arm hooked round the weather mizen topmast backstay; the *Surprise* had finished her morning rituals and now all hands and her captain were settling down to the task of sailing her as fast as ever she could go without undue risk to her precious spars, sailcloth and cordage. The chase was half topsails under, thirteen or fourteen miles away, and had she been going large the frigate would probably have overhauled her by dinner-time; but they must have passed one another in the night and she was now directly to windward. The *Surprise* would therefore have to beat up against a head-sea in a stiff and freshening breeze, and she would have to make up that distance before the sun set and the moonless night hid the whaler from view. It could be done, but it called for very keen seamanship, a very close study of the ship's capabilities, and a very particular trim to carry weather-helm to a nicety.

It did not call in vain. The *Surprise* was using every possible racing manoeuvre to eat the wind out of the chase; the most expert helmsmen were at the wheel in pairs, determined not to yield an inch of leeway, perpetually watching for a smooth to edge her a little closer to the wind, while expectant hands carried out the slightest change of trim that Jack called for with the flashing perfection of long practice and the keenest zeal. For his part he felt in perfect touch with his ship: sailing on a bowline was something both he and she could do admirably well, and as he stood there, swaying to the heave of the deck, he was aware of her slightest swerve or check. He was wearing an old blue coat, for the morning was fresh although they were so near the tropic line, and the spray and even solid water that swept aft every time the *Surprise* shouldered one of the steeper seas was fresher still, turning his new-shaved face a fine bright pink. From the masthead he had seen that the whaler was British-built; he was convinced that she was an American prize, and without a word passing this conviction had communicated itself to the crew; all the old Surprises knew that if a British ship had been twenty-four hours in the enemy's possession it was not yielded up to the former owners with a polite bow and the hope of a piece of plate in acknowledgement, but became salvage, the next best thing to a prize, or in some cases even better and more direct.

When Stephen came up on to the steeply-sloping deck quite late in the day – he had been woken by the fife playing *Nancy Dawson* for the hands' noontime grog – he had an impression of all-pervading blueness: blue sky with a few high white clouds after all these days of low grey; a darker blue white-flecked sea; even blue air in the great shadowed convexities of the straining sails. 'Good afternoon to you, Doctor,' called Jack – blue coat and bright blue eyes gleaming – 'Come and take a look at our chase.'

Stephen slowly made his way aft, handed along by the jolly Marines and all the seamen who, having no immediate task in hand, were lining the weather rail so that their weight should make the ship a little stiffer, and as he went he felt the total change of mood: the people's hearts and minds were wholly set on the pursuit, intent, eager, cheerful, the past and even the events of yesterday left behind, far behind with the long-vanished wake.

'There she lays,' said Jack, nodding over the larboard beam, where the whaler could be seen standing south-east under topgallantsails with her starboard tacks aboard.

'But you are going almost directly from it,' cried Stephen. 'What kind of chase is this, at all?'

'Why, she is very much concerned with her southing, do you see,' said Jack, 'and she wears about every two hours or so: she is on the starboard tack now, as you see. Yet wearing ship takes time, and in any case I do not care to arouse her suspicions; so we do not go about – we sail as nearly south as we can, but on the other tack. I believe she is innocent as a babe unborn: takes us for a Spaniard. We put all that filth up there to encourage her to think so.' Stephen peered up, and after some searching he saw a little piece of dimity, about the size of a moderate tea-tray, fluttering at the junction of two ropes, and a few

231

untidy reef-points. 'But next time she wears we shall be on what look like parallel courses, though in fact they will be converging, since we lie much closer as well as sailing faster; and I reckon that if all goes well – if we carry nothing away – then in four more of her boards and one or perhaps two of ours we should have the weather-gage.'

'You mean to take her, I collect?'

'That is the general idea.'

'What makes you suppose she is lawful prize?'

'She is British-built to begin with, and then although her commander sails her tolerably well he does not sail her as a man who had had her for a year or so would sail her. A weak crew, too, whereas whalers' crews are strong; they take a great while wearing. You shall watch through my glass next time they make a leg. Everything points to her being a prize, probably the ship that worthy Spaniard spoke of, the *Acapulco*.'

'When do you hope to come up with her, so?'

'Come,' said Jack, 'do not let us tempt fate. I only say that if all goes well – if we carry nothing away, and the breeze is freshening, as you see . . .'

'It is already far more like a tempest than any breeze.'

'. . . then we might, with luck, speak her before dark.'

Here the drum beat for the gunroom dinner and they parted, for Jack meant to stay on deck, eating sandwiches brought by Killick. The dinner was a hurried meal, with most of the officers, including the American lieutenant, bolting their food so that they should miss not a moment of the chase: yet there was some conversation, from which it appeared that the *Surprise* did not set royals at about three bells, when the whaler spread her topgallantsails, partly from fear of losing them, but much more so that she should not appear to be chasing – that the whaler certainly had a dirty bottom: she sagged horribly to leeward – that the people who sailed her were no phoenixes – and that nothing made Mowett happier than remembering the days they had so wisely spent at Juan Fernandez, heaving the barky down as far as possible and cleaning her copper as far as ever they could reach, painful at the time but wonderfully pleasant in the recollection.

Presently the purser, the chaplain and the surgeon were left to themselves with the greater part of a long grey pudding, made with sea-elephant suet and studded with Juan Fernandez berries, and Stephen observed, 'I have seen many examples of the seaman's volatility, but none equal to this. When you recall the last week, culminating in the events of yesterday – no longer ago than yesterday itself – when you recall the silent, anxious and I might almost say haunted faces, the absence not only of the usual laughter but even of quips and small-wit, and the collective sense of impending, ineluctable doom, and when you compare that with today's brisk gaiety, the lively eye, the hop, skip and jump, why, you are tempted to ask yourself whether these are not mere irresponsible childish fribbles . . .'

'Fribble yourself,' murmured the gunroom steward the other side of the door, where he was finishing the officers' wine with Killick.

'. . . or weathercocks. But then you reflect that these same people circumnavigate the entire terraqueous globe, sometimes in trying circumstances, which argues a certain constancy.'

'I have heard their levity put down to there being no more than a nine-inch plank between them and eternity,' said Martin.

'Nine-inch?' said the purser, laughing heartily. 'Why, if you are given to levity with nine inches under you, what must you be in a little old light-built frigate? A flaming gas-balloon, no doubt. God – dear me, there are parts of *Surprise*'s bottom where you could push a penknife through with ease. Nine-inch! Oh lord, ha, ha, ha!'

'Sir, sir,' cried Calamy, running in and standing by Stephen's chair, 'the whaler's taken in her topgallantsails – we are to go about any minute now, and we'll overhaul her by the end of the watch, as sure as eggs is eggs. Please

233

sir' – with an affectionate look – 'may I have a slice of pudding? Chasing is desperate hungry work.'

As it happened the *Surprise* overhauled her well before the end of the watch. The whaler, the unlucky *Acapulco*, wholly deceived by the Spanish ensign that Jack hoisted when they were a couple of miles apart, backed her foretopsail and lay to while the captive American sailors stood in silent agony as the *Surprise* took up a raking position across the *Acapulco*'s bows, ran out her broadside guns in one brisk movement, replaced the false colours with the true, and called upon her to surrender.

There was not the least possibility of resistance, and her commander came across without any fuss, a disconsolate young man with spectacles. His name was Caleb Gill, and he was nephew to the *Norfolk*'s captain, who had captured so many whalers that in spite of having burnt several he was hard pressed for officers to take the others in.

The Surprises were very kind to Mr Gill, as well they might be, since he had done them no sort of harm, while his trusting nature had, with no great pains on their part, delivered them a prize, deep-laden with white-oil and spermaceti, mostly from other ships, that Mr Allen reckoned at a hundred thousand dollars.

'That is very fine, to be sure,' said Jack Aubrey, smiling at his report, 'and Heaven knows I am not one to fling a hundred thousand dollars in a gift-horse's teeth; yet in a way the carpenter and the bosun have even better news – the *Acapulco* is stuffed, *stuffed*, with spars, cordage and sailcloth, enough for a three-year cruise; she has only been out six months, and has hardly used anything at all.'

The gunroom was kind to Mr Gill, and the other Surprises were kind to his crew, which included some of the *Acapulco*'s men, who, anxious to avoid the accusation of foreign enlistment or comforting the King's enemies, told all they had learnt about the *Norfolk*'s movements, past and to come; but it was Caleb Gill who gave the information that relieved Jack's mind from a most gnawing anxiety. Gill was a reading man, nearer akin to Martin and Stephen than to most of the other sailors. His interests however had more to do with men, primitive men, and less with botany or brute-beasts than theirs; he was fascinated by the idea of the noble savage and had travelled far among the native Americans, learning all he could of their social order in peace and war, their laws, customs and history; and one afternoon, when the *Surprise* was still stripping the *Acapulco* of everything that could possibly be crammed between decks and Mr Lawrence was dining with Jack, the three of them lingered in the gunroom over a bottle of madeira. 'I was of course exceedingly mortified at being taken prisoner,' he observed, 'yet in a purely personal and private way I had been perhaps even more deeply mortified by being ordered to take command of that unfortunate *Acapulco*, since from the very beginning of the voyage my whole heart had been bent on beholding the Marquesas: your upas-tree, sir, your two-toed sloth, dodo, solitary-bird, were hardly more for you than the Marquesas were for me, particularly the island Huahiva, which my uncle has always represented as a Paradise.' 'As a Paradise, indeed?' asked Stephen, remembering a letter found in the *Danaë*'s packet, which used that very phrase. 'Yes, sir. Not perhaps quite an orthodox Presbyterian Paradise, but one so agreeable that he means to set up a colony upon it. Indeed he even has some colonists with him. I have heard differing and often muddle-headed accounts of the islanders' polity, but all agree that it pays great attention to various prohibitions or taboos and to relationship; and all agree that the people are most uncommonly amiable and good-looking, their only faults being cannibalism and unlimited fornication. But neither of these is erected into a religious system, oh no: the divine offerings are invariably swine, the cannibalism being simply a matter of taste or inclination; while the fornication has nothing ceremonial or compulsory about it.'

'Does your uncle mean to reform the islanders?' asked Stephen.

'Oh no, not at all,' said Gill, 'he thinks they could scarcely be improved upon. It is to be quite a utopian colony – Liberty Hall writ large – yet even so I long to see the people's way of life before it is changed in any way. And since I cannot now see it as a free man, why, I hope I shall see it as a prisoner. Captain Aubrey means to sail to the Marquesas, I take it? But perhaps my question is not quite discreet?'

'Not at all, at all,' said Stephen. 'I am not fully acquainted with his intentions, but I will ask him; and I trust that we may all three tread the shores of Huahiva before the islanders have been corrupted.'

'I hope so too. Oh yes, indeed!' cried Gill, clasping his hands with eager anticipation.

Yet when Captain Aubrey had digested his information, and when his ship had taken in all the stores she could hold, he summoned the master and said, 'Mr Allen, a little while ago you observed that Butterworth and Kyle, the *Acapulco*'s owners, had agents in Valparaiso.'

'Yes, sir; and in Pisco too, I believe. Most of the houses engaged in the South Sea fishery have agents in Chile or Peru.'

'I am very glad to hear it, because I believe they may solve one of our difficulties. I cannot afford the officers and men to take the *Acapulco* home, yet I am most unwilling to disappoint the people of their money. I therefore think of sending her into Valparaiso and delivering her up to the agents upon promise of salvage: at the same time I can liberate all our American prisoners on parole. They are decent creatures in themselves, but considered absolutely they are an infernal hell-fire nuisance, and the prospect of housing and feeding them indefinitely weighs upon me. It weighs upon Mr Adams too; and this would be killing both birds . . .' He paused, frowned, muttered 'over one stile', and went on, 'Well never mind – that would be the most seamanlike way of dealing with the situation short of making them walk the plank.'

'Very true, sir.'

'But the point is this, Mr Allen: the officer who takes her in must run the risk of being left behind. I have no intention of lying windbound in that bay; I have no intention of exchanging endless platitudes with port-admirals, generals, governors, even bishops, God forbid: but all this can be avoided by a subordinate officer on plea of urgent orders. I should therefore escort the *Acapulco* to some point within sight of land and stand off and on for a day and a night. The officer would have to take her in with no more than the prisoners and say a cutter's crew, transact the business in an expeditious manner, and instantly proceed to sea, rejoining the ship in the cutter without the slightest loss of time. From all I understand, the *Norfolk* is likely to cruise on the Galapagos whaling grounds until the end of the month, and we may catch her there by cracking on. Nevertheless I think this matter of the prize and the prisoners is worth four and twenty hours. Four and twenty hours but not a minute more: the officer would have to rejoin in that time. With your local knowledge, Mr Allen, do you think the plan feasible?'

'Yes, sir, I do. And although I not like to put myself forward you will allow me to mention that I know my way about Valparaiso, I speak the language tolerable, and I have been acquainted with Mr Metcalfe, the agent, these twenty years.'

'Very well, Mr Allen, let us make it so. Pick your men and take command of the prize at once: if we are not to reach the Galapagos the morning after the fair there is not a moment to be lost. Killick. Killick, there. My compliments to the American officers and I should like to see them directly.'

CHAPTER SEVEN

On an oppressive day and under a low and troubled sky the *Surprise* made her way along the channel between Albemarle and Narborough, the westernmost islands of the Galapagos; she was finding it uncommonly difficult, for although at present the capricious breeze was favourable she had to stem a powerful tide, setting against all reason from the north – against all reason, for as Mr Allen observed, an even stronger current beyond the Redondo Rock at the far end of the strait ran in the opposite direction at four and even five miles an hour, while the tide between Albemarle and James Island, only a little way to the east, was in full agreement with it. In her rapid, hound-like casting to and fro among the Galapagos the *Surprise* had grown used to very strong unreasonable currents and unreasonable weather – fog under the equator, for all love: penguins hooting in the fog on the very Line itself! – but this particular current showed every inclination to turn into an extremely dangerous tide-rip, and as the rock-strewn channel was one of those the master did not know Jack had taken over the deck himself.

It was the kind of navigation that he did not like at all, but this was his last chance of finding the *Norfolk* in the archipelago: she might be lying in any of the three or four sheltered bays ahead, filling up with tortoises (those from Narborough weighing between two and three hundred pounds were particularly good eating) and with what water and firewood the place could afford, and the *Surprise* might come upon her unawares. The channel therefore had to be threaded, though it was a tricky passage indeed, with a weakening, uncertain wind, a strengthening current, little room to work the ship, an iron-bound coast on either side, and – height of injustice – something very like two lee-shores, since the wind on the frigate's side urged her towards the rocks of Narborough, while the crossgrained tide and current tended to fling her upon those of Albemarle, and certainly would do so were the wind to carry out its threat of veering. The atmosphere on deck was tense, with all hands at their stations, a boat carrying a kedge and hawser out on either side, and a man in the chains continually heaving the lead and continually chanting, 'No bottom with this line: no bottom, nay, nay.'

The strait narrowed steadily and it seemed to Jack that he would almost certainly have to anchor until the height of flood, even if it meant letting the best bower go in a hundred fathoms. 'Light along the deep-sea line,' he said. For some time the shores had been less than a musket-shot apart and now they were much nearer, increasing the force of the current. All hands looked at them gravely – a wicked surf beating upon black rock on either side, and on either side a vast fissured expanse of dull black naked lava sloping up to vague mist-covered heights, the lava scattered with great heaps of volcanic clinkers, mostly black but sometimes an unhealthy red, like the waste of an enormous ironworks: here and there a crater – an inhuman landscape. Or almost all hands: the surgeon and the chaplain, either ignorant of the implications of tide-rip, unplumbed depth, uncertain breeze and want of sea-room or soaring above these things, were settled at the leeward rail, focusing their telescopes with eager, even trembling hands. They had earlier made an attempt at covering either shore, so as to miss nothing, calling their discoveries out to one another across the deck, but the officer of the watch had put a stop to this wild irregularity the moment Jack appeared, the windward side being sacred to the captain; and now they were obliged to be content with Narborough alone. Yet even so, as they confessed, there was enough to occupy a score of naturalists. They had soon discovered that the miserable sterility of the lower slopes was more apparent than real; several stunted leafless shrubs, almost certainly related to the euphorbias, could be made out standing among the natural slag-heaps, and prickly pears of an uncommon height, together with tall columnar cacti, were almost common on the upper slopes; but interesting though the land was without a doubt, the sea was even more so. As the strait grew narrower so the life in it seemed to become more concentrated: the shores on either hand – and not only the little beaches of black sand and pebbles but even the seemingly inaccessible ledges – were crowded with seals, eared seals, sea-lions and sea-bears, lying on their stomachs, on their backs, on their sides, sleeping or making love or merely barking, while others played in the crashing surf or swam by the ship, stretching their necks up and staring with intense curiosity. And where the seals left any room, the higher rocks were covered with marine iguanas, black, crested, and a good yard long. Penguins and flightless cormorants shared the water, swimming with great speed just under the surface, weaving among the shoals of silvery pilchard-like fish; and in the *Surprise*'s wake a band of female sperm whales with their calves lay blowing on the surface. Over her deck flew quantities of sea-birds, which was natural enough; but what was less so was the number that assembled in the rigging, on the hammocks in their netting and on the belfrey, maddening the hands who had to clean up their copious messes – messes that quickly ate into the metal of the guns. Many a privy blow with a swab did the larger birds receive when the Doctor was not looking; but it was no use; they remained obstinately tame, settling on the gunwhales of the boats alongside and even on their very oars. Most of these birds were boobies, masked boobies, brown boobies, spotted boobies, but above all blue-faced boobies, heavy-witted birds with a slow, expressionless stare; once, in the far Atlantic, they had been the rarities of the world, but now, although the approach of their breeding-season had quickened their minds and turned the webs of their feet an even lovelier turquoise, they were nothing in comparison with the land birds – little sooty finches or rails – that passed by; the land-birds being, as far as they could tell, of kinds unknown to the learned world. Yet in spite of the boobies being so common, one couple did fix Stephen's eye. They were perched on the back of a sleeping turtle, an amorous pair with glowing feet, and so great was their need and urgency (the day being unusually warm and propitious for boobies) that they were going through their ritual of courtship with extraordinary speed, and there was no doubt that the cock booby would have attained his end if the turtle had not submerged a moment too soon, leaving him strangely out of countenance.

The master paused behind them and pointing to Narborough Island said, 'There is Sodom and Gomorrah, gentlemen, I believe. But it is not so bad higher up the slope. Was the cloud to lift, you would see some green up there, bushes and trees all covered with a kind of Spanish moss.'

'Oh, we are quite confident,' said Martin, turning a happy face to him. 'This is the first time we have been near enough to see the land at all clearly – to see the iguanas plain.'

'I particularly admire the tall straight cactus,' said Stephen.

'We call 'em torch-thistles,' said the master, 'and they have a kind of juice, if you cut them down, that can be drank; but it gives you the wet gripes.'

The ship sailed on; the black, scaly shore moved slowly past; and amidst the cry of nautical orders, the patter of bare feet, the creak of yards and the general song of the wind in the rigging part of Stephen's mind wandered away. A small bird perched on his telescope, cocked its head, looked inquisitively at him, and then preened its black feathers for a while before flying off to the island, where it vanished against the lava. 'That was quite certainly a nondescript,' he said, and went on, 'I have been contemplating on the mating ceremonies of our own kind. Sometimes they are almost as brief as the boobies', as when two of a like inclination exchange kind looks and after a short parley retire from view: I am thinking of Herodotus' account of the Greek and Amazon warriors in the pause after their truce for dinner, when individuals from either army would wander among the bushes, and of some more recent examples that have fallen under my own observation. At other times however the evolutions of the ceremonial dance, with its feigned advances and feigned withdrawals, its ritual offerings and symbolic motions, are protracted beyond measure, lasting perhaps for years before the right true end is reached; if indeed it is reached at all and not spoilt entirely by the long delay. There are endless variations according to time and country and class, and the finding out of common factors running through them all is a fascinating pursuit.'

'Yes, indeed,' said Martin, 'and it is clearly of the first importance to the race: I wonder some writer has not made it his particular study. The ceremony, I mean, not the act itself, which is nasty, brutish and short.' He reflected for a moment and then smiling he went on, 'Yet a man-of-war is scarcely the place for your inquiries. That is to say . . .' His smile faded and his voice died away as he remembered Friday past, when according to the custom of the sea Horner's effects were put up for auction at the mast, and where some pitiful shawls and petticoats were seen: an auction at which no man thought it right to bid, not even Wilkins, now the frigate's acting gunner.

'Now, Doctor,' said Howard, passing him a hat with several small dead birds in it, 'ain't I a good boy? Not one is the same.' Under the weight of public opinion Howard had given up shooting, and apart from catching fish and harpooning turtles and dolphins, which made capital sausages when mixed with the ship's salt pork, his sport now consisted of killing the birds that settled about the rigging. The boobies, owls, frigate-birds, brown pelicans and hawks he strangled; the smaller ones he struck down with a switch. Stephen accepted them, because he disliked killing specimens himself, but with all the force at his command he had urged the Marine to be moderate, not to take more than a few of the same kind, and prevent his men from doing them any harm.

'You are most attentive, Mr Howard,' said Stephen. 'And I am particularly obliged to you for this yellow-breasted wren, a bird I have not . . .'

'Oh, oh,' cried Martin, 'I see a giant tortoise! I see two giant tortoises. Heavens, such tortoises!'

'Where? Where?'

'By the prickly pear.'

The tall prickly pear had an almost tree-like trunk: one tortoise, craning a-tiptoe, had seized a branch and was pulling with all the force of his retractile neck and huge domed body; the other had also seized it and was pulling too, though in a different direction. Martin interpreted this as an example of slightly mistaken mutual aid; Stephen as one of self-interest; but before the point could be settled the branch or rather the series of palms broke in two and each reptile walked off with his own.

'How I yearn to set foot on at least one of these islands,' said Martin. 'Such discoveries to be made in every realm! If the reptilian order can run to such extreme magnificence, what may we not expect from the cole-optera? From the butterflies, the phanerogams? But I am tormented by the thought that the ship may sail on and on, perpetually on and on.'

Here the goat Aspasia came running to Stephen for protection. Ever since the ship had reached the coast of Albemarle, small dark-grey finches with stout beaks had been persecuting her, landing on her back and plucking out hair to line their nests. She had faced the elements, thunder, lightning, two fleet actions, four between single ships; she had faced midshipmen, ship's boys, and a large variety of dogs; but this she could not bear, and every time she heard their faint twitter come aboard she hurried to Stephen. 'Come, come,' he said, 'a great goat like you, for shame,' but he flapped at the finches and went on, speaking to Martin, 'Set your heart at rest. Captain Aubrey has promised that once his search for the *Norfolk* is over, the ship shall lie up, or to, or in, and that we shall have leave to go ashore.'

'How you relieve my mind: I really could not have borne . . . see, see, another tortoise – a Goliath, and nearer still he walks down the slope. A ponderous tread!'

They focused their telescopes on Goliath, who paused in perfect view, so well turned to the light that they could even count his plates, comparing them with those of Testudo aubreii on the Indian Ocean, which Maturin had discovered, described and named, giving Jack his only likelihood of earthly immortality, and with the thin-shelled and lighter though still respectable tortoise of Rodriguez. Reflections upon insular tortoises, their origin – tortoises in general, whether deaf – their voices rarely heard – capable of a harsh cry however as well as the more usual hiss – all oviparous, careless of their young – crocodiles more diligent as parents – but tortoises more generally sympathetic – perfectly capable of attachment – instances of affection in tortoises.

'What is all this intemperate calling out?' asked Stephen without taking his eye from the telescope: a whole troop of tortoises had come into his field of vision, all walking steadily uphill on a distinctly beaten track.

'I believe they have seen a boat of some kind – there was some mention of a boat,' said Martin. 'Would this island yield a toad, do you suppose? There are few reptiles I prefer to toads, and a toad of such heroic dimensions . . .'

'If a tortoise, why not a toad? But now that I come to recollect, I found no batrachians of any kind on Rodriguez; and I could scarcely make an intelligent native understand what I meant by a frog, though I imitated his motions in a very lively manner, and his cry.'

'By your leave, sir, by your leave,' roared the captain of the afterguard, shouldering his way between them without the least ceremony as the pipes wailed for 'All hands about ship' and the seamen ran to their places.

'Why, Beckett, what's afoot?' asked Stephen.

But before Beckett could reply the *Surprise* began her smooth turn: the familiar cry of 'Helm's alee' was followed by 'Off tacks and sheets' and then by 'Mainsail haul'. She passed sweetly through stays in spite of the encumbrance of the cutters and at this point Stephen, looking ahead, saw a distant boat, a whale-boat, pulling towards them as fast as ever it could against the current.

The *Surprise* filled on the larboard tack, and although the tide was slackening, near its height, in a quarter of an hour she lost the distance she had taken three to gain. The boat came visibly nearer every minute, a whale-boat with six men aboard; but so great was their anxiety that even when they were within a hundred yards and the distance dwindling with each breath they still pulled furiously hard; they still hailed 'The ship ahoy' as loud as ever they could roar.

Their voices had almost entirely gone by the time they came grinning up the side, overflowing with happiness; but in a hoarse whisper, interspersed with throaty laughter, and wetted by the two buckets of fresh water they drank, standing there on the deck, their spokesman, the specktioneer, soon made their story plain. They belonged to the *Intrepid Fox* of London, James Holland master; she had been out just over two years, and although she had not been successful up until the time they came to the Galapagos it had then seemed that they might go home with a full hold, for there they found whales in plenty. They had killed three the first day and the boats were out after three more when the fog came down: they themselves were fast to a lively young forty-barrel bull that led them a great dance far to the north of the Redondo Rock, far from their mates, who could not see them nor yet bring fresh whale-lines. In the end he carried away lines and harpoon and all and left them a cruel night and day to pull against wind and current without a drop to drink, no, nor a morsel to bite. And when they got back, what did they see? Why, they saw the poor old *Fox* being fair pulled to pieces by an American frigate that was not only taking her new foretopmast out of her but also transferring what oil and spermaceti she had won – the forehold and perhaps half the main, no more – into another whaler, the *Amelia*, also from London river. Fortunately it was the evening and they were under land, coming down the coast, so they were not seen; the specktioneer had been in these waters before – he knew the island – and they were able to pull into a narrow inlet, hide the boat under driftwood and climb up to the old buccaneers' shelter. There was a little water up there, though it was briny and evaporating fast; there were tortoises and land-iguanas, and the boobies had started to lay, so they managed pretty well upon the whole, though parched. Presently they saw the *Amelia* set out, cheered by the American frigate; she was wearing American colours and she steered a little east of south. Then the next day the Americans brought a couple of hundred tortoises down to the beach, ferried them out to the ship, set fire to the *Fox*, won their anchor, cleared the channel, and stood away to the west. They hurried down to try to put the fire out, but it was no good; half a dozen barrels of whale-oil had been stove, with the oil running all over the deck, and the fire had such a hold there was no getting anywhere near. The Captain would see part of her blackened hull if he carried on up the strait: the *Fox* lay bilged on a reef to the north of Banks' Bay, just after the anchorage.

'When the American cleared the channel did she stand due west?' asked Jack.

'Well, sir,' said the specktioneer, 'maybe a point south of west. Moses Thomas and me, we went up to the shelter again and we watched her to the horizon, straight as a die, just a trifle south of west, topgallantsails on the fore and main.'

'For the Marquesas, specktioneer?'

'That's right, mate. There are half a dozen of us out there, and some Yankees too, now that the Sandwiches are not what they was, and New Zealand a disappointment, with the people eating you up if you so much as set foot on shore.'

'Good; very good. Mr Mowett, these men will be entered on the ship's books: capital hands, I am sure, to be rated able. Mr Adams will issue hammocks, beds, slops; and they will be excused duty for a couple of days, to recover. Mr Allen, we will clear the strait with the changing tide and lay a course for the Marquesas.'

'No tortoises, sir?' asked Mowett.

'No tortoises. We have been very economical with the ship's provisions and we can do without tortoise as a relish. No, no, she is eighteen days before us and there is not a moment to lose over tortoises or caviar or cream in our tea.' With this he went below, looking thoroughly pleased. A few minutes later Stephen hurried into the cabin. 'When are we to stop?' he cried. 'You promised we should stop.'

'The promise was subject to the requirements of the service: listen, Stephen, here I have my tide, my current and my wind all combined – my enemy with a fine head-start so that there is not a moment to be lost – could I conscientiously delay for the sake of an iguano or a beetle – interesting, no doubt, but of no immediate application in warfare? Candidly, now?'

'Banks was taken to Otaheite to observe the transit of Venus, which had no immediate practical application.'

'You forget that Banks paid for the *Endeavour*, and that we did not happen to be engaged in a war at the time: the *Endeavour* was not in pursuit of anything but knowledge.'

Stephen had not known this: it made him if any-thing angrier still, but he governed himself and said, 'As I understand it, you mean to go round the end of this long island on the left and start your voyage – take your departure – from the other side.' Jack gave a noncommittal nod. 'Well, now, were Martin and I to walk across it, we should be on the other side long before the ship. The proportions are as one to ten, so they are; and a little small boat could land us without any trouble at all,

247

and take us off. We should walk briskly, pausing only for a few important measurements and almost certainly making valuable discoveries about springs of fresh water, mineral ores, antiscorbutic vegetables and the like.'

'Stephen,' said Jack, 'if the wind and the tide had been against us, I should have said yes: they are not. I am obliged to say no.' Landing them through the surf would be difficult; getting them off again on the west side might be quite impossible; and then the 'brisk walking' of two besotted natural philosophers across a remote oceanic island filled with plants and creatures unknown to science might last until the frigate sank at her moorings or grounded on her beef bones – he had seen Maturin on shore before this with nothing more than a Madeiran woodlouse to make him lose all sense of time. But he was sorry for his friend's disappointment, so much keener than he had expected from the desperately sterile look of the islands; he was even sorrier to see a tide of anger rise in Stephen's usually impassive face, and to hear the harsh tone in which he said, 'Very well, sir; I must submit to superior force, I find. I must be content to form part of a merely belligerent expedition, hurrying past inestimable pearls, bent solely on destruction, neglecting all discovery – incapable of spending five minutes on discovery. I shall say nothing about the corruption of power or its abuse; I shall only observe that for my part I look upon a promise as binding and that until the present I must confess it had never occurred to me that you might not be of the same opinion – that you might have two words.'

'My promise was necessarily conditional,' said Jack. 'I command a King's ship, not a private yacht. You are forgetting yourself.' Then, much more kindly, and with a smile, 'But I tell you what it is, Stephen, I shall keep in as close with the shore as can be, and you shall look at the creatures with my best achromatic glass,' – reaching for a splendid five-lens Dollond, an instrument that Stephen was never allowed to use, because of his tendency to drop telescopes into the sea.

'You may take your achromatic glass and . . .' began Stephen, but he checked himself and after the slightest pause went on, 'You are very good, but I have one of my own. I shall trouble you no longer.'

He was exceedingly angry: his solution – one short side of a triangle as opposed to two of immense length – seemed to him unanswerably sound; and it made him angrier still when practically everybody aboard, and not only old friends like Bonden and Killick and the privileged Joe Plaice (who practically owned the man who had opened his skull and who lived in a state of permanent hostility with Rogers, who had only had an arm off) but Padeen, recent Defenders and the mere children of the midshipmen's berth, surrounded him with exceptional kindness and particular attention. He had always prided himself on maintaining the volto sciolto, pensieri stretti rather better than most men, and here were illiterate tarpaulins comforting him for a distress that he could have sworn was perfectly undetectable.

With a surly satisfaction he observed that in spite of the changing tide the *Surprise* did in fact make but a slow passage of her two legs, for the breeze came foul upon her twice: they slowly passed two excellent strands where a boat could have landed them and taken them off, the first in a cove beyond the reef where the blackened carcass of the whaler lay; and it was clear to him that he and Martin might have crept across the island on all fours and still have been in time. 'In half the time,' he muttered, beating the rail in an extremity of frustration.

He watched the dim, cloud-covered Galapagos vanish astern and turned in early, ending his usual prayers with one for a less rancorous mind and lying there in his cot with Boethius' *De Consolatione Philosophiae* and two measured ounces of laudanum.

Yet in spite of these he was still unusually ill-tempered at two o'clock in the morning, when Padeen roused him and very slowly and with great difficulty told him in Irish

249

and English that Mr Blakeney had swallowed a four-pound grapeshot.

'The thing is materially impossible,' said Stephen. 'The wicked little brute-beast is lying – showing away – topping it the phoenix – making himself interesting. Such a dose I shall give him – the sorrows of Munster will be nothing to his.'

But when he found the poor brute-beast, pale, frightened, apologetic and put to sit by a lantern on the half-deck, and when he learnt that the grape in question was only one of the nine that made up the charge of the launch's four-pounder, he at once had him seized up by the heels, ran for the stomach-pump and forced a large quantity of tepid salt water tinged with rum into his body, reflecting with pleasure, as among the agonized retching he heard the clang of the ball in the basin, that he had cured his patient not only of probably mortal occlusion but of any taste for spirituous liquors for some time to come.

Even so, even with this physical and moral triumph, the next day found him still thoroughly out of humour, and when Adams observed that the Captain was to be the gunroom's guest at dinner – that the dinner was to be an uncommon fine one too, quite a Lord Mayor's feast – he said, 'Oh, indeed,' in a tone that showed no kind of pleasure. 'I have known that fellow hang about in port,' he said to himself, glancing at Jack from the lee gangway as the *Surprise* ran smoothly over the vast South Sea, pure blue now from rim to unimaginably distant rim, 'I have known him hang about most shamefully when it was a question of a wench – Nelson too and many a post-captain, many an admiral when adultery was concerned – no fine-spun scruples about the King's ship then. No, no: scruples are kept for natural philosophy alone, or any useful discovery. His soul to the Devil, false, hypocritical dog; but he is probably unaware of his falsity – pravum est cor omnium, the heart is perverse above all things and unsearchable. Who shall know it?'

Yet although Stephen was of a saturnine and revengeful temperament he had been brought up to a high notion of hospitality. The Captain was the gunroom's guest, and the ship's surgeon was not to sit there in silent dogged resentment. Putting a considerable force on himself Stephen uttered four civil remarks, and after a proper interval he said, 'A glass of wine with you, sir,' bowing low.

'I must congratulate you most heartily, Doctor, on your preservation of young Blakeney,' said Jack, returning his bow. 'How I could have told our old shipmate that we had let his son perish of grapeshot I do not know. A grapeshot in these circumstances, I mean, not a French or American one.'

'How could he possibly have come to swallow such a thing?' asked Martin.

'When I was a reefer and any of the youngsters talked too much, we used to make him hold one in his mouth,' said Jack. 'We called 'em gob-stoppers. I dare say that is how it came about.'

'May I send you a piece of bonito, sir?' called Howard from the middle of the table.

'If you please. A capital fish, bonito, capital: I could eat it for ever.'

'I caught seven this morning, sir, sitting in the mizen chains and casting along the edge of the wake. I sent one to the sick-bay, one to the midshipmen's berth, three to my Marines, and kept the best for us.'

'Capital, capital,' said Jack again; and indeed it was a capital dinner altogether: best green turtle, delicate flying squid come aboard in the night, a variety of fishes, dolphin pie, and to crown all a great dish of teal, Galapagos teal, indistinguishable in taste from Christian teal, that had been netted by Howard's sergeant, a former poacher. And Stephen noticed, not without irritation, that as he ate and drank his civility was growing less artificial, his deliberately urbane expression more nearly a spontaneous smile, and that he was in danger of enjoying himself.

> '. . . behold the threaden sails
> Borne with the invisible and creeping wind,
> Draw the huge bottoms through the furrow'd sea
> Breasting the lofty surge,'

said Mowett in a momentary silence as the decanters were renewed – he and Martin had been discussing poetry for some time – 'That is the kind of thing I mean.'

'Did you write that, Mowett?' asked Jack.

'No, sir,' said Mowett. 'It was – it was another cove.'

'*The invisible and creeping wind*,' repeated Maitland. 'They say pigs can see the wind.'

'Stay, gentlemen,' cried Howard, holding up his hand and looking round with a flushed face and a gleaming eye. 'You must forgive me, but I don't often come up with a good thing at the right moment: han't done so this commission, I believe, though I came pretty close to it once off the River Plate. So by your leave, sir,' – bowing to Jack – 'there was an old woman in the Cove of Cork that lived in a cabin with just one room, no more; she bought a pig – a *pig*, eh, that's the point, that's what makes it so apposite – and they said, "What shall you do about the smell?" Because it had to live in the same room, if you follow me: the pig had to live in the same room as the old woman. "Oh, ochone," says she, "begar, he will have to get used to it," – mistaking, do you see . . .'

But Howard's explanation was drowned in a gale of laughter, led by Killick from behind Jack's chair. Jack himself said, 'he will have to get used to it', threw himself back and had his laugh out, his face scarlet and his eyes a brighter blue than usual. 'Dear me, dear me,' he said at last, wiping them with his handkerchief, 'in this vale of tears it does a man good to laugh from time to time.'

When they were quiet the purser peered round his neighbours at the first lieutenant and asked, 'Was that piece you said just now poetry? The piece before the pig.'

'Yes, it was,' said Mowett.

'It didn't rhyme,' said Adams. 'I told it over to myself, and it didn't rhyme. If Rowan were here, he would knock your poet on the head. His poetry always rhymes. I remember a piece of his as though it were only yesterday:

> *Awful the grinding noise of keel and heel*
> *With an unusual motion made the crew to reel.'*

'I believe there are almost as many kinds of poetry as there are rigs,' observed the master.

'So there are too,' said Stephen. 'Do you remember that dear Ahmed Smyth, Mr Stanhope's oriental secretary, when we were going to Kampong? He told me of a curious Malay form of verse whose name escapes me, though I have retained an example:

> *The peepul-tree grows on the edge of the forest,*
> *On the fishermen's strand nets lie in hopeless*
> *   confusion;*
> *It is true that I am sitting on your knee*
> *But you are not therefore to suppose that you may*
> *   take any other liberty at all.'*

'Did it rhyme in Malay?' asked the purser, after a silent pause.

'It did,' said Stephen. 'The first and the third . . .'

The arrival of the pudding cut him short, a most uncommonly splendid pudding brought in with conscious pride and welcomed with applause.

'What, what is this?' cried Jack.

'We thought you would be surprised, sir,' said Mowett. 'It's a floating island, or rather a floating archipelago.'

'It is the Galapagos themselves,' said Jack. 'Here's Albemarle, here's Narborough, here's Chatham and Hood . . . I had no idea there was anyone aboard capable of such a thing: a masterpiece, upon my word and honour, fit for a flagship.'

'One of the whalers made it, sir. He was a pastrycook in Danzig before he took to sea.'

'I put in the lines of longitude and latitude,' said the

master. 'They are made of spun sugar; so is the equator, but double thick and dyed with port.'

'The Galapagos,' said Jack, gazing down on them. 'The whole shooting-match: there's even the Redondo Rock and Cowly's Enchanted Isle, laid down exactly. And to think we never set foot on a single one . . . sometimes ours is a very demanding profession . . .'

'*Stern daughter of the voice of God! O Duty!*' said Mowett; but Jack, musing over the archipelago, which swayed with the heave of the ship, did not hear him, and went on, 'but I tell you what, gentlemen, if we come back this way, having done what we set out to do, we shall lie in Mr Allen's cove on James Island for a few days, and everyone shall have leave to roam to his heart's content.'

'Will you not take some Galapagos, sir, before it comes adrift?' said Mowett.

'I hesitate to spoil such a work of art,' said Jack. 'But unless we are to go without our pudding' – this with a pretty knowing look as he poised his spoon above the pastry-cook's equator – 'I believe I must cut the Line.'

The Line, the Line, day after day they sailed westwards along the Line or a little south of it. They left the penguins and the seals behind almost at once, all the inshore birds and almost all the fish; they also left the gloom, the cool water and the low-hanging cloud, and they sailed over a dark blue disk, perpetually renewed, under a pale blue dome, occasionally flecked with very high white cirrus. But they did not sail at all fast. In spite of the *Surprise*'s splendid display of light fair-weather canvas – studdingsails aloft and alow, royals and even skysails and skyscrapers – she rarely logged more than a hundred miles between one observation and the next. Almost every day the breeze dozed for two or three hours after midday, or even went fast to sleep, leaving the pyramids of sail in a dismal state of sag, while vast stretches of dead calm spread over the sea, broken only by the passage of whales, sperm whales, that would sometimes pass in wide-spaced files two and even three hundred strong, heading for

Peru. And every evening at the setting of the watch the *Surprise* snugged down to topsails: there was no trusting the sudden flurries of the night, in spite of the lamblike innocence of the day.

These were waters largely unknown to the Navy – Byron, Wallis and Cook had kept much farther south or much farther north – and this slow creeping over an apparently infinite sea would have fretted Jack to the very heart if he had not learnt, through the master, that here it was always the case when the sun began to move backwards from the tropic: and it would be as bad for the *Norfolk* or possibly worse. Allen had had many a conversation with the specktioneer, a middle-aged man named Hogg, who had made the run to the Marquesas three times and the Sandwich Islands twice: and his experience, both first- and second-hand, was a great relief to all hands aboard. They sailed on as fast as they reasonably could, but not as though they had a chase in view, not wetting the sails throughout the urgent day, since they knew that the *Norfolk* would proceed at an even more moderate pace: and when she reached the Marquesas she would spend a great while cruising among the islands in search of the British whalers fishing there. There was not a moment to spare, it was true; but then not every moment had to be flogged.

Once again, and with surprising speed, the ship settled down to a perfectly regular, self-sufficing existence; very soon it became the natural way of life once more, and the Surprises looked back to the remote and bitterly cold days far south of the Horn and even to their haunted passage up the coast of Chile and Peru as to another world.

The sun rose every morning exactly in the frigate's wake; it shone on the new-cleaned decks, but soon they were hidden from view by awnings, for although this was not Gulf of Guinea hot, with the pitch bubbling from the seams and tar dripping from on high, still less the Red Sea of infamous memory, the temperature was in the eighties and shade was grateful. Everybody walked about in duck, except for invitations to the cabin; and even for them the midshipmen were excused their thick kerseymere waistcoats.

Yet they were perhaps the only people who were not quite pleased about the return to proper blue-water sailoring with everything just so, shipshape and Bristol-fashion. Greek and Latin had never indeed been laid entirely aside except for the very worst days in the fifties and sixties, but now both came back with redoubled force; and now Captain Aubrey had time to lead them through the mazes of navigation, while at night he made them learn the name, declination and right ascension of a great many stars, and find out the angular distance between these and various planets or the moon. He and Mowett also had time to set about improving their morals, which in the naval context meant leaving their comfortable hammocks very early indeed, relieving the watch well before the stroke of the bell, never putting their hands in the pockets or leaning on the rail or resting on a carronade-slide, and always attending in the tops whenever sails were reefed. 'You are called reefers,' Mowett told them one day, 'you are given a sumptuous berth, you are fed like fighting-cocks, and all that is asked of you is to attend in the tops when the sails are being reefed. But what do I find? The maintopgallantsail being supervised from the head . . .'

'Oh sir,' cried Nesbitt, stung with the injustice. 'I was caught short just that once.'

'. . . and the foretopsail apparently reefing itself while the midshipman was rioting in swinish slumber somewhere below. I really grieve for the service if it is to be officered by such creatures as you, who think of nothing but eating and sleeping, and neglecting their duty. I have never seen the like in any ship before, and never wish to see it again.'

'These youngsters think too much of their ease,' said Jack. 'They are nothing but a parcel of helots.'

'Pray have helots a particular nautical signification, like dogs, mice, fishes and so on?' asked Stephen.

'Oh no, just the ordinary sense of idle young devils,

you know – limbs of Satan. I must stir them up, and make their lives a misery.'

Whatever his attempts may have been, they were not successful; the *Surprise* had a sprightly, high-spirited midshipmen's berth, with no real oldsters to tyrannize over the rest; and so far at least its members had plenty to eat. They had long since recovered from the hardships of the far south, although nothing would bring Williamson's toes back nor the tips of his ears, Boyle's ribs had knit perfectly, while a faint down was beginning to cover not only Calamy's bald scalp but also his girlish chin. In spite of hard duty and hard lessons, and in spite of moral improvement they remained cheerful: what is more, they learnt how to swim. In the afternoon, when the ship was becalmed, most of the people plunged over the side, most into a shallow swimming-bath made of a sunken sail but some into the open sea itself, for no sharks had been seen since they left the Galapagos, at least none that followed the ship.

This was one of the delights of their westward course; another was the competitive firing of the great guns or small-arms almost every evening at quarters; but there were many more, and the most highly prized, deeply relished, during the first weeks was the conduct of the whalers, particularly of their chief, the specktioneer Hogg. He had never been in the Royal Navy. Although the war had been going on with little interruption since his boyhood he had never been pressed; as a South Sea whaler and a harpooner he had a protection, but he had never had to use it. Neither the press-gang nor the impress officer had ever troubled him, and in fact he had never set foot on board a man-of-war before the *Surprise*. His life had been spent entirely in whalers, a particularly democratic set of vessels in which the hands worked not for wages but for shares of what the ship might earn, and in which, although there was the necessary minimum of discipline, there was little sense of hierarchy among the thirty-odd people – certainly nothing resembling that of the Navy with its far greater numbers, its different worlds afore the mast and abaft it, its different essences of humanity. He was an intelligent man – he could navigate – but he had a certain simplicity; and having spent his childhood in the heathen slums of Wapping and the rest of his life among whalers he had had little contact with civilization. Meeting the officer of the watch on his first morning, for example, he called out, 'How are you coming along, mate? Prime, I hope, prime.' And when church was rigged it was difficult to make him set down in his right place. 'Well, this is a rum go,' he said in a loud voice when at last he was settled on an upturned mess-kid; and he stared very much during the hymns, clapping when they were done. When Mr Martin put on his surplice his neighbour told him in what passed for a whisper among seamen that 'Parson was now going to preach them a sermon.' 'Is he, though?' cried Hogg, leaning forward with both hands on his knees and watching the chaplain with keen interest, 'I never heard a sermon.' Then, after a few minutes, 'You've turned over two pages. Hey, there. You've turned over two pages, master.' It was true, for Martin, an indifferent preacher, generally read from some more gifted man, such as South or Barrow, and now, flustered by his new parishioners, he had indeed made a sad and obvious blunder.

'Silence, fore and aft,' cried Mowett.

'But he's turned over two pages,' said Hogg.

'Bonden,' said Jack, in a church-going aside, 'lead Hogg forward and tell him how we do it in the Navy.'

Bonden told him, but he cannot have made the principle quite plain, for the next day, when Nesbitt, the smallest of the reefers, was bawling orders to some hands in the foretop, he used a coarse expression, and Hogg suddenly turned, held him up with one hand and slapped his buttocks with the other, telling him he should be ashamed of speaking so to men old enough to be his daddy. Any court martial sitting on Hogg's crime would have been compelled to sentence him to death, for the Twenty-Second Article of War provided no less penalty. Jack caused Mowett and

Allen to speak to him at some length, and they brought him to some sense of the enormity of his act; but even so the rest of the ship's company did not despair of seeing the whalers tell Mr Adams just what they thought of his purser's dips, for example, or trouble the Captain for a glass of his best brandy when they felt inclined for a wet; and they often urged them so to do – 'Go on, mate,' they would say, 'don't be bashful. The skipper loves a foremast jack, and will always give him a glass if he asks civil.' It was not that they disliked their new shipmates, far from it indeed, for the whalers were not only amiable but thorough-paced seamen as well; but their innocence was a standing temptation, and in principle when the Surprises were tempted they fell.

Before church was rigged again the whalers had grown wary; although they could still be made to leap half asleep from their hammocks by the cry of 'There she blows' they would no longer go to the carpenter's mate and ask for a long stand nor to the gunner's yeoman for half a fathom of firing line; yet even so they did give a great deal of innocent pleasure when an American whaler appeared at an immense distance to windward, standing east, a vessel instantly recognizable from her double-decked crow's nest on the main. Hogg and his friends rushed aft in a body, filled with passion and a wild longing for revenge; and when Honey, who had the watch, would not instantly haul to the wind they began bawling down to Jack through the skylight, and had to be removed by the Marines.

A moment's consideration showed Jack that chasing the American would mean far too great a loss of time. He sent for the specktioneer and said, 'Hogg, we have been very patient with you and your shipmates, but if you carry on like this I shall be obliged to punish you.'

'They burnt our ship,' muttered Hogg.

Jack feigned not to hear: but seeing the man's hot tears of rage and disappointment he said, 'Never mind it, man. The *Norfolk* is perhaps not so very far away, and you shall serve them out.'

259

Even if she were already in the Marquesas she would not be so very far away by now, as these things were reckoned in the prodigious expanse of the Pacific, where something in the nature of a thousand miles seemed the natural unit. Another unit might be a poem: Stephen was reading Mowett's *Iliad* and he was keeping to one book a day, no more, to make his pleasure last; he had begun a little while after leaving the Galapagos and he was now in book twelve, and he reckoned that at the present rate of sailing he would finish just before they reached the Marquesas. He did his reading in the afternoons, for now that the days were calm and untroubled, with the necessary weeks of their western passage taken out of time as it were, a self-contained whole, he and Jack filled the evenings with the music they had been obliged to forego in more demanding waters.

Night after night they played there in the great cabin with the stern-windows open and the ship's wake flowing away and away in the darkness. Few things gave them more joy; and although they were as unlike in nationality, education, religion, appearance and habit of mind as two men could well be, they were wholly at one when it came to improvising, working out variations on a theme, handing them to and fro, conversing with violin and 'cello; though this was a language in which Jack was somewhat more articulate than his friend, wittier, more original and indeed more learned. They were alike in their musical tastes, in their reasonably high degree of amateur skill, and in their untiring relish.

But on the evening of the day in which Stephen had reconciled Achilles and Agamemnon, and when the frigate's wake was rather better than two thousand miles long, they did not play at all. This was partly because the ship was passing through an immense population of phosphorescent marine organisms, and had been passing through it ever since the dark-red sun set into the misty sea, his disc neatly divided by the bowsprit, but even more because the hands had been turned up to sing and dance on the forecastle and they were making much more noise than usual. The order was purely formal, since the hands were already there, dancing and singing as they always did on fine evenings when the ship was sailing easy, and its only function was to let them know that they might keep it up, this being the whalers' particular feast-day.

'I am glad I cancelled the youngsters' lesson,' said Jack, looking up through the open skylight. 'There is scarcely a star to be seen. Jupiter is no more than a blur, and I do not suppose that even he will last another five minutes.'

'Perhaps it was on Wednesday,' replied Stephen at the stern-window, leaning far out and down.

'I said Jupiter will not last another five minutes,' said Jack in a voice calculated to drown the merriment afore: but it was badly calculated, not having taken the whalers into account, and they had just begun *Away my boys, away my boys, 'tis time for us to go* in voices that would have suited the whales themselves; Stephen answered, 'Probably Wednesday, I said,' in a rather impatient tone. 'Will you not pass me the long-handled net, now? I have asked you three times, and there is a creature I just cannot reach with this miserable . . .'

Jack found the long-handled net quite soon, but when he came to pass it there was no Stephen in the stern-window, only a strangled voice from the wake: 'A rope, a rope.'

'Clap on to the cutter,' cried Jack and he dived straight in. He did not hail the ship on coming to the surface because he knew the red cutter was towing astern: Stephen would either seize it or be towed towards it, and then they could regain the stern-window without the ship's way being checked or her surgeon being still further exposed for what in fact he was, the most hopeless lubber yet born.

No cutter: someone must have hauled the boat alongside. No Stephen either; but at that moment he saw and heard a gasping boil that rose and sank in the troubled, phosphorescent water. He dived again, swimming deeper and deeper until he saw his friend against the luminous

261

surface. Stephen had become strangely entangled in his own net, his head and one elbow tight in its meshes, its handle down the back of his shirt. Jack got him out; but breaking the stout handle, ripping off the shirt, and at the same time holding Stephen so that his head was above water took some while, and when at last he drew breath and shouted, '*Surprise*, ahoy,' the hail coincided with the roaring chorus *There she blows, there she blows, there she blows*, taken up by the whole ship's company. He had set Stephen to float on his back, which he could do tolerably well when the sea was calm; but an unfortunate ripple, washing over his face just as he breathed in, sank him again; again he had to be brought up, and now Jack's '*Surprise* ahoy' coming at the full pitch of his powerful voice, had an edge of anxiety to it, for although the ship was not sailing fast, every minute she moved more than a hundred yards, and already her lights were dimming in the mist.

Hail after hail after hail, enough to startle the dead: but when she was no more than the blur of the planet earlier in the night he fell silent, and Stephen said, 'I am extremely concerned, Jack, that my awkwardness should have brought you into such very grave danger.'

'Bless you,' said Jack, 'it ain't so very grave as all that. Killick is bound to come into the cabin in half an hour or so, and Mowett will put the ship about directly.'

'But do you think they will ever see us, with this fog, and no moon, no moon at all?'

'They may find it a little difficult, though it is amazing how something that floats shows up on the night sea, when you are looking for it. In any case I shall hail every so often, like a minute gun, to help them. But, you know, it would be no very great harm, were we to have to wait until day. The water is as warm as milk, there is no kind of a sea apart from the swell, and if you stretch out your arms, stick out your belly and throw your head back till your ears are awash you will find you float as easy as kiss my hand.'

The minute-gun hails succeeded one another in a long, long series; Stephen floated easy; and they drifted westwards on the equatorial current, westwards and probably a little north. Jack reflected upon the relativity of motion, upon the difficulty of measuring the speed or set of a current if your ship is moving with it and you can neither anchor nor observe any fixed point of land; and he wondered how Mowett would set about searching once the alarm was raised. If the observations were conscientiously made and the log accurately heaved, read and recorded, then it would not be very hard for him to run back close-hauled or even with the wind one point free, always provided that the breeze remained steady at south-east by south and that his estimate of the current was correct: each degree of error in that would, in the course of an hour's sailing at four and a half knots, amount to . . . In the midst of his calculations he became aware that Stephen, lying there as stiff as a board, was becoming distressed. 'Stephen,' he said, pushing him, for Stephen's head was thrown back so far that he could not easily hear, 'Stephen, turn over, put your arms round my neck, and we will swim for a little.' Then as he felt Stephen's feet on the back of his legs, 'You have not kicked off your shoes. Do not you know you must kick off your shoes? What a fellow you are, Stephen.'

So they went on, sometimes swimming gently, sometimes floating in the luke-warm sea, rising and falling on the very long, regular swell. They did not talk much, though Stephen did observe that it was all very much easier, now that he was allowed to change position from time to time; even the act of floating came to him more naturally with use – 'I believe I may set up as a Triton.' And on another occasion he said, 'I am very deeply indebted to you, Jack, for supporting me in this way.'

Once Jack found that he must have slept awhile; and once they were rocked by a sudden upsurge of water quite close at hand, a looming on the swell, and they were in the enormous presence of a whale. As far as they could make out in the phosphorescence he was an old bull, rather better than eighty feet long: he lay there for perhaps ten minutes, spouting at steady intervals – they could see the white jet and faintly hear it – and then with a great inward sigh he put down his head, raised his flukes clear of the sea, and silently vanished.

Shortly after this the mist began to clear; the stars showed through, at first dimly and then brilliantly clear, and to his relief Jack saw that the dawn was closer than he had supposed. It was not that he had much hope of being rescued now. That had depended on Killick's looking into the cabin before going to bed; there was no particular reason why he should have looked in and clearly he had not done so, otherwise Mowett would have turned well before the end of the first watch. He would have cracked on with all the sail she could bear, and with all the boats strung out within hailing distance on either side he would have combed a broad stretch of sea, picking them up some time early in the middle watch: and the middle watch was already over. But if Mowett did not hear of their absence till the morning, clearly the dear *Surprise* would have sailed that much farther west, and she could not be brought back much before the evening. The probability of error from the current would be very, very much greater, and in any case he did not think they could hold out much beyond dawn – almost certainly not until the late afternoon. Although the sea had seemed so warm to begin with they were both of them shivering convulsively by now; they were waterlogged; Jack for one was overcome with an enormous hunger; and both of them were haunted by the fear of sharks. Neither had spoken for a long time, apart from the brief words when they changed position and when Jack towed Stephen on his shoulders for a while.

There was very little hope now, he admitted, yet he did long for the light. The heat of the sun might revive them wonderfully, and it was not wholly inconceivable that a coral island might appear: although the charts showed none for another three or four hundred miles, these were largely uncharted waters. Hogg had spoken of islands known to whalers and sandalwood cutters alone, their observed positions kept private. But what he really hoped for was a piece of driftwood: palm-trunks were almost indestructible and in the course of the last few days he had seen several drifting on the current, borne, perhaps, from the Guatemalan shore; and with one of those to buoy them up they could last all day and more, much more. He turned it over in his mind – the ways of dealing with a palm-trunk, and how to give it some kind of stability with an outrigger in the South Seas fashion. Almost wholly useless reflection, but even so better than the piercing, sterile, pointless regrets that had tormented him for the last few hours, regrets about leaving Sophie surrounded with law-suits, regrets for not having managed things more cleverly, bitter regret at having to leave life behind and all those he loved.

The earth turned and the ocean with it; the water in which they swam turned towards the sun. Over in the west there was the last of the night, and in the east, to windward, the first of the day; and there, clear against the lightening sky, lay a vessel, already quite near, a very large two-masted double-hulled canoe with a broad platform or deck overlapping the hulls with a thatched house upon it; and the vessel had two towering fore and aft sails, each with a curved crest reaching forwards. These however were details that Jack did not consciously observe until he had uttered a great roaring hail: it roused Stephen, who had been in something not far from a coma.

'A South Sea craft,' said Jack, pointing; and he hailed again. The vessel was very like what Captain Cook called a pahi.

'Will they take us up, do you suppose?' asked Stephen.

'Oh surely,' said Jack, and he saw a narrow outrigger canoe put off from the vessel's side, hoist a triangular sail and come racing down towards them. One young woman sat in the stern steering; another straddled the booms connecting the slender hull and the outrigger, balancing with wonderful grace. She held a spear in her hand and as the other girl let fly the sheet, bringing the canoe almost to a halt three yards from them, she was all poised to throw. But seeing what they were she paused, frowning, quite amazed; the other one laughed, a fine flash of white teeth. They were both strikingly good-looking young women, brown, long-legged, dressed in little kilts and no more. Ordinarily Jack was attentive to an elegant form, an elegant bosom, a well-rounded shape, but now he would not have cared if they had been old man baboon, so long as they took him and Stephen aboard. He lifted up his hands and uttered a supplicatory croak; Stephen did the same; but the girls, laughing, filled and ran back the way they had come, sailing with extraordinary skill and speed, unbelievably close to the wind. Yet as they swept off they smiled and they made motions signifying, perhaps, that the outrigger was too frail for any more weight, and that Jack and Stephen might swim to the two-master.

That was how Jack's willing mind interpreted them; and in fact when they reached the double canoe, which in any case was bearing down upon them, these same girls and several others helped them up on to the mat-covered deck. There appeared to be a positive crowd of young women and a good many older and stouter; but this was not time for fine observation. Jack said, 'Thank you, thank you, ma'am,' very earnestly to the cheerful helmswoman, who had given him a particularly hearty hand, and looked all his gratitude at the rest, while Stephen said, 'Ladies, I am obliged beyond measure.' Then they sat down with hanging heads, scarcely aware of their pleasure, and dripped upon the deck, shivering uncontrollably. There was a great deal of talk above them; they were certainly addressed at length by two or three of the older women, and questioned, and sometimes brown hands plucked at their hair and clothes, but little notice did they take until Jack felt the power of the sun warming him through and through as it mounted. His trembling stopped; hunger

266

and thirst came upon him with redoubled force, and turning to the women, who were still watching with close attention, he made gestures begging for food and drink. There was some discussion, and two of the middle-aged women seemed to disapprove, but some of the younger ones stepped down into the starboard hull and brought up green coconuts, a small bundle of dried fishes, and two baskets, one containing sour breadfruit pap and the other dried bananas.

How quickly humanity and pleasure in being alive flowed back with food and drink and the warmth of the sun! They looked about them, and smiled, and renewed their thanks. The stern broad-shouldered spear-girl and her jollier companion seemed to think them to some degree their property. The one opened the drinking-coconuts and passed them, the other handed the dried fishes, one by one. But not very valuable property: the spear-girl, whose name appeared to be Taio, looked at the white, hairy, waterlogged, water-wrinkled skin of Jack's leg where his trousers were rolled back, and uttered a sound of sincere and candid disgust, while the other one, Manu, took hold of a lock of his long yellow hair, now untied and hanging down his back, plucked out a few strands, turned them in her fingers and tossed them over the side, shaking her head and then carefully washing her hands.

By now the scene changed, almost as it might have done in a man-of-war, though there was no evident signal, no pipe, no bell. Part of the crew began washing most scrupulously, first hanging over the water, then diving in and swimming like dolphins: they paid no attention whatsoever to nakedness. Others took up the mats covering the platform, shook them to leeward, lashed them down again in a seamanlike manner, and heaved on the forestays, now slackening with the heat of the sun, while a third party brought up small pigs, edible dogs and fowls, in baskets, mostly from the larboard hull, and arranged them on the forward part of the deck where they sat good and quiet, as ship-borne animals so often do.

During all this activity no one had much time to stare at them, and Stephen, whose spirits had recovered wonderfully, grew less discreet in looking about. He considered first the hurrying crew, which seemed to consist of about a score of young women and nine or ten between old and young, together with an indefinite number heard but not seen in the deckhouse aft. A dozen of the young women were cheerful, unaffected creatures, good looking though often heavily tattooed, full of curiosity, talk and laughter, and reasonably friendly, though it was clear that they considered Jack and Stephen physically unattractive, if not worse. The young women and most of those of thirty or forty were more reserved if not downright inimical; Stephen suspected that they did not approve of the rescue, still less of the feeding of those saved from the sea. But whatever their opinion, all the women talked all the time, in a mellifluous language that he took to be that of Polynesia in general: all the women, that is to say, except four of the youngest who sat industriously chewing the root from which kava was made and spitting the fibrous pulp into a bowl: Stephen knew that once coconut milk had been stirred in and the mixture had stood for a while it would be ready to drink. He had read a few accounts of the islands, but since he had had no idea of visiting them this commission he had learnt nothing of their language and he retained no more than a word or two from his books, of which kava was one. He therefore sat uncomprehending in the babble and presently his mind wandered from this curious community – a sea-going convent? – to their vessel. It was obviously stocked for a long voyage, one of those very long Polynesian voyages of which he had heard, and it certainly seemed capable of undertaking one: he much admired the two smooth hulls upon which the platform and its house reposed, the windward hull acting as a counterpoise in a side-breeze, so that there was a much greater lateral stability as well as much less friction, an improvement that might well be introduced into the Navy. The idea of the Navy's considering a man-of-war with two hulls for a moment, after the terrible outcry it had raised about a slight change in the traditional stern made him smile, and his eye ran along the tall rising stems in which these particular hulls ended, their prows, as it were, or figureheads. And here some indistinct recollections of that black though ingenious Cromwellian thief Sir William Petty and his double-bottomed vessel were driven clear out of his mind, for lashed to the starboard stem was a carving some six feet high, a very lively carving of three men: the first had the second standing on his shoulders and the second the third; and these three were connected by the huge penis which rose from the loins of the first, towering past the second to a point above the third man's head and held by all three as it mounted. It was coloured red and purple and it had no doubt reached higher still, but it had been much gashed and mutilated and now there was no telling whether it was common to them all, though this seemed probable. All the figures had been castrated, and judging by the freshness and the rough texture of the splintered wood this had been done quite recently, and with a coarse instrument. 'Dear me,' he murmured, and turned his attention to the other stem. This bore a tall piece of wood, adze-flattened on its two faces with the side indented or crenellated in regular squares; it had something of the air and presence of a totem-pole and it was topped by a skull. The skull did not surprise Stephen very much – he had already noticed one rolling about among the coconut bailers and he knew they had no great significance in the South Seas – but it was with real concern that he saw and after a moment recognized the little wizened purselike objects pinned to the slab, as vermin might be to a European gamekeeper's door.

He was about to tell Jack of his discovery and his conclusions, to caution him against the least ill-humour and to advise submission, meekness, a deferential bearing and above all no hint of gallantry however innocent, when he found that he was alone. Jack had left him when the second part of the crew started their washing and the first set about arranging their hair, all this on the windward side of the platform. He walked aft along to the other side, taking great notice of the shaped planks, sewn together edge to edge and caulked with what he took to be coconut fibre mixed with something sticky, of the cordage and the sails, made of fine matting with an immensely long piece of creeper or supple-jack as a bolt-rope; and skirting the deck-house, in which several women were all talking at once in loud contentious voices, he came to the helm. It was a large paddle, but to his astonishment he found that it was not moved from side to side, rudder-fashion, but thrust down to turn from the wind and raised to luff it up. The woman who held it had a sensible, manly look as far as could be seen through the complex lines and spirals of her tattoo; she understood him quite readily, demonstrated the use of the paddle and showed him that the vessel could come tolerably close to the wind, though of course you had to reckon on a good deal of leeway – she showed the angle with her parted fingers and blew to indicate the increasing force of the wind. But she could make nothing of his other inquiries, to do with the stars, navigation by night, and the vessel's destination, even though he illustrated them with gestures.

He was trying to make himself plainer when three stout middle-aged women like bosun's mates came round the corner from the deck-house, gasped with indignation and hustled him forward at a great pace, one helping him on his way with a flying kick that would have done credit to a Spithead nightingale. All three, and some of the other women, seemed very angry; they railed and scolded for a quarter of an hour, and then Jack was given a mortar with some dried roots in it and a heavy pestle, while Stephen was put to mind a young hog. Like most of the animals on deck it was in a basket, but unlike the others it was restless, and in poor health. It had to be nursed and it would not keep still.

For some time the bosun's mates stood just behind, pinching and slapping them if the hog complained or

270

the roots skipped out of the mortar, and sometimes for no reason at all. But presently other duties called them away and in a low voice Jack said, 'I should never have gone aft. We are clearly foremast hands, no more, and must never move from here unless we are told.'

Stephen was about to agree, and to add his recommendations about their behaviour, his hypothesis on the nature of this community and the purpose of its voyage, and some remarks on the prevalence of cannibalism in the South Seas, when Jack interrupted, saying, 'Ain't you hellfire thirsty, Stephen? I am. I believe it was those dried fish. But, you know, they don't seem to like the look of me; whereas you are almost as brown as they are.'

'This I attribute to my practice of aprication,' said Stephen, looking at his bare belly with some complacency. It was true: Stephen regularly sat in the tops with nothing on and he had none of the dank, corpselike pallor of naked Europeans. 'I have little doubt that to them you resemble a leper; or at any rate something diseased, unwholesome. The colour of your hair is disgusting. To those who are not used to it, I mean.'

'Yes,' said Jack, 'so pray be a good fellow and sing out to the girl forward there, among the coconuts.'

Stephen's first gentle call, accompanied by a timid gesture of drinking, was unsuccessful; she pursed her lips and looked coldly away, with a righteous expression. His second had more luck. Manu was passing by and she brought four nuts across and opened the shells with a shark's tooth set in a handle; and as they drank the exquisite milk she spoke to them rather severely, no doubt telling them something for their own good. At one time she put her hands together, as though in prayer, and looked emphatically aft; they could make nothing of it at all, but they both nodded gravely and said, 'Yes indeed, ma'am. Certainly. We are most obliged to you.'

Once again Stephen was about to tell Jack of his intimate conviction, derived not only from the figureheads but from many little signs, forms of behaviour, caresses, quarrels and reconciliations, that they were aboard a vessel belonging to women who did not like men, who had revolted from the tyranny of men, and who were sailing away to some island, perhaps a great way off, to set up a female commonwealth; and to say that he dreaded the possibility of Jack's being gelded, knocked on the head, and eaten. But before he could do so his hog grew restless, squealed and fouled the deck; at the same time Jack was seen to be idling with his pestle, and the bosun's mates stepped in. When the mess was cleaned, and Stephen's trousers too – this they insisted upon, having an exceedingly high standard of cleanliness: they made him take them off and wring them out again and again before they were satisfied – and when all the shouting, cuffing, pinching, slapping and reproof had died down, Jack said, 'Here comes the captain, I believe; and the officers.'

She was a broad, squat woman, much darker than most, with a long trunk and short legs; she had a handsome, high-nosed, but exceedingly cross and authoritarian face; and as she made her tour of the vessel she was accompanied by two taller women, obviously stupid and obviously devoted to her. They both carried the same weapons, a three-foot palm-rib topped with a hardwood knob with mother-of-pearl eyes on either side of an obsidian beak, possibly a mark of rank, since they held them with a certain amount of pomp. She had no mark of rank – far from it: she was casually nibbling at something she held – but as she came forward the members of the crew stood with their hands clasped and their heads bowed.

'Perhaps we should adopt a respectful submissive attitude,' murmured Stephen; and as the captain came nearer he saw that what she was gnawing was a hand, a smoked or pickled hand. She looked at Jack and Stephen without any pleasure or interest and without making any reply to their bows or their 'Your most humble devoted servant, ma'am,' and 'Most honoured and happy to be aboard you, ma'am.' And having looked at them she entered into a long, displeased conversation with Taio and Manu, who in spite of their clasped hands spoke up very freely in their clear young voices: Stephen suspected that they belonged to a privileged class – they were taller, lighter in colour, and their tatooing was quite different; and the captain's attitude towards Manu in particular was civiller than it was to the others.

The captain and her officers went by walking aft along the larboard side; and a little later Jack, having turned the mortar so that he could see, said, 'I believe they are rigging church.' Indeed something very like an altar appeared in the middle of the platform and six mother-of-pearl disks and an obsidian knife were laid upon it, with a variety of weapons ranged in front. Again Jack and Stephen slackened a little in their attention to work and again some sort of ship's corporal brought them back to a sense of duty with a furious roar; she then harangued them at length, with gestures, and although no single word had any meaning it was clear from her intonation that sometimes she was describing the conduct of the virtuous, sometimes that of the worthless. And behind her Taio, Manu and half a dozen of the jollier girls imitated her gestures and her expressions with such perfection that at last Jack could not contain but burst out into a strangled horse-laugh. The ship's corporal darted to the row of weapons and came at him with just such a beaked club as the officers carried, a tool designed to peck through a skull at a single blow; but in fact she only kicked him in the stomach. She had scarcely done so before the whole thing was over: everybody was shrieking and pointing over the side, where Manu had sighted a shark close on the starboard beam.

It was a medium-sized brute, twelve or thirteen feet long, though of what species Stephen could not tell; nor had he any time for deliberation, for Manu, catching up the obsidian knife from the altar, slipped into the sea between the two hulls. What happened next he could not make out, but there was a furious threshing convulsion a few yards out to starboard and there were the girls and the ship's corporal laughing heartily as Manu came dripping aboard and the shark dropped astern, disembowelled but still lashing with enormous force.

Clearly no one but Jack and Stephen thought it out of the way; the others carried on with their preparations for church as though nothing of importance had happened, except that two of them helped Manu rearrange her wet hair. A bosun's mate, now dressed in a striped garment with tags, had just time to throw Jack more roots to grind and to give him a passing swipe with a rope's end and drums started to beat.

The ceremony began with a dance: two lines of women facing the captain, rhythmically advancing, retiring, waving their weapons while she chanted, and at the end of each verse they all cried *Wahu*. Their weapons were spears, the hardwood skull-splitter called pattoo-pattoo, a name that came to Stephen the moment he saw it, and clubs, some studded with human teeth, some with those of sharks; and all the women, even the kava-chewing girls, handled them most convincingly.

The dance went on and on and on, the drum-beat acquiring a hypnotic quality. 'Stephen,' whispered Jack, 'I must go to the head.'

'Very well,' said Stephen, calming his hog. 'I have seen the women do so repeatedly. They mostly go over the side.'

'But I shall have to take off my trousers,' said Jack.

'Then no doubt it would be more seemly to dip between the two floaters, holding on to the platform; for although they seem to be innocent as Eve before the apple, at least as far as nakedness is concerned, they may not view the shameful parts of a man in quite the same light.'

'I believe it was that dried fish,' said Jack. 'But perhaps I can wait. To tell you the truth, that ill-looking bitch' – lowering his voice and nodding towards the captain – 'quite daunts me. I do not know what she would be at.'

'Go on, Jack – go on while you may – it may be worse

later – go on directly – I believe they are reaching their climax.'

Rarely had Stephen given better advice. Jack had not been back to his pestle five minutes, with a look of profound relief on his face, before the dancing stopped and the ill-looking bitch delivered a long address, during which she often pointed at the men, growing steadily more passionate.

The address came to an end and the congregation got up and moved about; but this was only the beginning of the real ceremony. The fire that Jack had noticed on his way aft was brought forward – embers in a bowl that floated in another – and set down before the altar. Presently the smell of grilling flesh came forward, together with ritual cries; but glancing discreetly round Stephen observed that the captain and her officers were in fact drinking the kava prepared that morning. The flesh was only formal at this stage.

'Some say that kava is not truly intoxicating,' remarked Stephen, 'that it contains no alcohol. I wish they may be right.'

Alcohol or no, the captain, her officers and the big middle-aged women were obviously affected when at last they came forward, dancing heavily behind their leader, who held the obsidian knife in her hand. The effect would have been grotesque but for the fact that the jaw-bones they had now hung round their necks were in most cases quite fresh and that drunk or not they handled their weapons with great dexterity.

The captain's mood had been disagreeable in the first place; it was now very much worse, much more fierce and aggressive. She stood in front of the men with her knees bent, her head thrust forward, pouring out words that sounded full of blame, indeed of intense hatred. Yet she did not carry the whole crew with her; the older women were clearly on her side and they often repeated her last words when she paused for breath, but several of the younger were not. They seemed uneasy, unwilling, displeased, and Manu and the spear-girl obviously spoke for them when they broke in during the pauses or even frankly interrupted the full flow, so that on occasion at least three were talking at the same time. Manu was the chief interrupter and Stephen became even more convinced that there was a special relation between her and the captain that gave her more than usual confidence. She kept pointing away over the starboard bow towards a little patch of white unmoving cloud but every time the captain brushed her words aside with the same set of phrases and a sweep of the obsidian knife. Yet in spite of the captain's vehemence – vehemence that increased with the last few interruptions – Stephen felt that she knew she was no longer in full control, that she had gone on too long, that the climax was slipping away from her; and he was afraid she would do something exceptionally violent to re-establish the situation. Indeed she did call out some orders and the biggest of the women moved closer, some with cords, some with clubs; but once again Manu interrupted and before the captain could reply Stephen stepped forward, and pointing at Jack's loins he said, 'Bah, bah, bah. Taboo,' his third Polynesian word.

It had an instant effect. 'Taboo?' they said 'Taboo!' in every tone of affirmation, astonishment, and concern, every tone but that of scepticism. The tension fell at once: the club-bearers moved away, and Stephen sat down again with his hog, which had begun to whimper. He paid little attention to the subsequent discussion, which went on in a more normal tone, though he did notice accusations, tears and reproaches.

For a great while Jack and Stephen had thought it more prudent, more discreet, not to speak, but now Jack whispered, 'They have altered course,' and Stephen observed that the vessel was heading for the patch of white cloud.

Presently the talking died away. The captain and the officers retired to the deckhouse. Stephen's hog was taken from him and Jack's mortar; they were put to sit in the starboard hull among the drinking-coconuts, and there, towards the middle of the afternoon, they were fed with little separate baskets of raw fish, breadfruit pap and taro. But there was no cheerfulness, no merriment, no curiosity. A flatness and gloom had come over the pahi's company, so lively before; and in spite of their enormous relief it affected even Jack and Stephen as they sat there, watching the clouds and then the little island under them come closer. When Manu brought the outrigger round to take them ashore she had clearly been crying.

It was a charming little island, not ten acres in an infinity of sea, green in the middle with a grove of palm-trees, a brilliant white strand all round, and surrounding the whole a broad coral reef, two hundred yards out. Manu obviously knew the island; she put the canoe through a gap in the reef so narrow that the outrigger clipped weed from the far side. She rounded to a few yards from the shore, and as Jack stood there up to his middle, turning the canoe, she gave him two mother-of-pearl fish-hooks and a length of fine line. Then she hauled in the sheet, Jack shoved her off, and the canoe raced back for the gap with the strong breeze abeam and Manu standing up braced against it, as lovely a sight as could be imagined. They waved until she was far out at sea, but she never replied.

CHAPTER EIGHT

The sea increased during the night, so that by dawn the reef surrounding the little island was whiter still with broken water flying high, particularly on the windward side, and the solemn, measured boom of rollers filled the air. Jack was conscious of this before he opened his eyes, he was also pretty sure that the breeze had strengthened too, backing perhaps as much as a whole point, and this was confirmed when he walked quietly from their shelter under the palm-trees, leaving Stephen curled in sleep, and sat on the white strand, yawning and stretching himself.

The scene before him was one of extraordinary beauty: the sun was not yet high enough to make the coral sand blaze and glare but it did bring out the bright green of the lagoon in all its glory, the whiteness of the breakers, the ocean-blue beyond them, and the various purities of the sky, ranging by imperceptible gradations from violet in the extreme west to something wholly celestial where the sun was rising. He was aware of it, and together with the lively freshness of the day it delighted all that part of his mind which was not taken up with trying to estimate the course of the pahi while they were aboard her and their present position with regard to the *Surprise*'s probable line of return.

He had made attempts before this of course, and many of them; but at that time his wits were too harrassed to supply him with any convincing answer. He had merely assured Stephen that all was well – capital – quite in order – and had gone to sleep, far down into sleep, with waves of figures rising and falling in his head.

So many things had happened yesterday that he had not paid as much attention as he should have done to the pahi's speed or direction, but he did remember that she kept the wind between two and three points abaft the beam, apart from the last leg, and as for her speed he doubted whether it would have exceeded four knots at any time. 'An uncommon ingenious well-contrived craft,' he reflected, 'but necessarily frail, and happier on a wind than sailing large: I should not be surprised if she lay to during the night, when the sea began to get up – I should not be surprised if she were still lying a-try at present, some few hours to leeward.'

Four miles in each hour, then, and the course, allowing for leeway and the last leg to northward, probably within half a point of west-north-west. He drew two lines in the sand, the one marking the pahi's voyage from where she took them aboard to the island, the other the *Surprise*'s westward continuation and her return close-hauled. She should now be sailing westward once again, having lain-to during the darkness at some point to the east of where they had been lost, and at present she should be somewhere near the right meridian. He dropped a perpendicular from the island to this second line and looked very grave; he checked his figures, and looked graver still. Even with all her boats spread to the utmost limit it was scarcely possible that she should see this low island so far to the north, a speck of land in such an immensity of sea, a speck shown on no chart, so that no one would expect it.

'Scarcely possible,' he said; but then with a sudden jet of hope he remembered that the pahi's sheets had been slackened off during church, almost to the point of flapping. That shortened his perpendicular: not by a great deal – perhaps a mile and a half or even two miles for every hour of dancing and harangue – but enough to loosen the cold grip round his heart a little.

The question was, how long would Mowett persist in his search, with all the boats strung out and the frigate moving slowly, perhaps steering a zigzag course to cover more of the ocean? Jack was known to be a very good swimmer, but no man could stay afloat indefinitely.

With a proper regard for the frigate's duty, for her pursuit of the *Norfolk*, how long could Mowett go on combing the apparently empty sea? Had he already abandoned it? There were Hogg's words about unmarked islands, but even so . . .

'Good morning to you, Jack,' said Stephen. 'Is it not the elegant day? How I hope you slept as well as I did: a most profound restoring plunge into comfortable darkness. Have you seen the ship yet?'

'No, not yet. Tell me, Stephen, how long do you think their ceremonies lasted yesterday? Their church, as you might say.'

'Oh, no great time at all, I am sure.'

'But surely, Stephen, the sermon went on for hours.'

'It was boredom and dread that made it seem so long.'

'Nonsense,' said Jack.

'Why, brother,' said Stephen, 'you look quite furious – you dash out your drawing in the sand. Are you vexed at not seeing the ship? It will soon appear, I am sure; your explanation last night convinced me entirely. Nothing could have been more reasonable, nor more cogently expressed.' He scratched himself for a short while. 'You have not yet swum, I find. Might it not set you up, and rectify the humours?'

'It might,' said Jack, smiling, 'but truly I have had enough of swimming for a while; I am still sodden through and through, like a soused pig's face.'

'Then in that case,' said Stephen, 'I trust you will not think it improper if I suggest that you climb up a coconut-tree for our breakfast. I have made repeated and earnest attempts, but I have never ascended higher than six feet, or perhaps seven, before falling, often with painful and perhaps dangerous abrasions; there are some parts of the mariner's art in which I am still a little deficient, whereas you are the complete sailorman.'

Complete he was, but Jack Aubrey had not climbed a coconut-tree since he was a slim nimble reefer in the West Indies; he was still tolerably nimble, but he now weighed rather more than sixteen stone, and he looked thoughtfully at the towering palms. The thickest stem was not much above eighteen inches across, yet it shot up a hundred feet; there was not one that stood straight even in a dead calm and now that a fine topsail breeze was blowing they swayed far over in a most graceful and elastic fashion. It was not the swaying that made Jack pensive – wild irregular motion was after all reasonably familiar to him – but rather the thought of what sixteen stone might do at the top end of such a lever, its motion unconstrained by shrouds, forestays or backstays, and the immense force that it would exert upon the lower part of the trunk and upon roots sunk in little more than coral sand and a trifle of vegetable debris.

He padded about the sparse grove, looking for the stoutest of them all. 'At least,' he observed, gazing up at the outburst of green high above, 'at least the spreading top will break the fall if it does come down.' And there were times during his long and arduous upward journey when it seemed that the palm must come down, must yield under the great and increasing mechanical advantage of his body heaving upon it, sometimes at an angle of forty-five degrees when the wind brought the tree far over; but no, after every plunge the palm swept up again, so fast and so far beyond the vertical that he had to cling tight, and eventually there he was among the great fronds, firmly wedged and breathing easy after his climb, he and the palm-top speeding to and fro on the now familiar trajectory, a kind of inverted swing, quite exhilarating in a way, even for one who was intensely anxious, hungry and thirsty. And as the palm came upright on its tenth backward heave, far out there to leeward he saw the pahi, lying-to. 'Stephen,' he called.

'Hallo?'

'I see the pahi, perhaps twelve miles to leeward, lying-to.'

'Is that so? Listen, Jack, are you privately eating a

nut up there, and drinking, while I perish here for mere want, the shame of it?'

The palm bowed to a gust, then rose again, slower and slower to its height, and Jack, now perched higher still among the fronds, let out a great bellowing roar, 'There she lays, there she lays, there she lays!' for clear on the horizon, farther than the double canoe and well to the south, he saw the *Surprise*'s topsails and her lower yards. She had her starboard tacks aboard and she was steering for the pahi with the wind almost on her beam. He explained this to Stephen at some length as the palm swayed to and fro. 'Is there anything you must do at this point?' asked Stephen in a moderate shout above the thunder of the sea, the sound of the wind and the high clatter of the palms themselves.

'Why no,' said Jack, in the same strong voice. 'She must be seven or eight leagues away. There is nothing I can do for quite a while, until she can see a signal.'

'Then I do beg you will cease springing about in that reckless inconsiderate way. Throw down some coconuts now, will you, and let us have our breakfast at last, for all love.'

'Stand from under, then,' said Jack, sending down a deadly rain of nuts. And setting foot on the ground some minutes later, 'No huzzay? No capers?'

'Why should I cry huzzay, or cut capers?'

'Because of the ship, of course.'

'But you always said it would be there. Why did you not choose green coconuts? These are as hard as cannon-balls; old hairy things. Cannot you tell one from another, good from bad, God and Mary preserve you? But will I open you one, to be drinking?'

'Pray do. I am fairly clemmed, with climbing and hallooing – Stephen, you have a knife!'

'Not at all: it is my pocket-lancet. I had taken it to deal with a damnable knot in my shoe-string – the valuable shoes you made me kick off – and had forgot it until last night, when it dug into my side as I lay. This I regret: had I remembered we could have made some slight acknowledgement of that dear broad-shouldered young woman's kindness. I think of her with great affection.'

Jack heartily agreed, saying all that was proper with great warmth, and adding, 'But, however, it does open an old coconut finely, and it will be most uncommon useful for boring holes, when I set about rigging up some kind of signal later on.'

This signal took him all the morning and rather more. It was a tripod made from the long ribs of palm-fronds lashed together with yarn worked from the leaves and passed through lancet-holes, the whole made fast to the topmost growth of the tallest tree and flying Captain Aubrey's shirt. It stood on its elastic base quite well, making a strange sharp conspicuous angular shape among all those billowing curves; but by the time it was finished and he had made the last of his countless journeys down that lofty stem, his heart was very low. He had in fact little or no faith in his tripod or his shirt. Throughout the morning, at intervals between spells of fine-work, he had observed that the sky was spoiling from the east, the wind strengthening and backing still more, and the great swell increasing; but much more than that he had watched the movements of the frigate and the pahi with passionate intensity: to his astonishment he had seen the pahi strike her deck-house and put before the wind goose-winged, with a square mat sail set between the masts, a rig he did not know she was capable of and one that carried her away westwards at a spanking pace. The *Surprise* had borne up to intercept her, and so both ran fast and far on converging courses a great way to the leeward of the island: they were now at such a distance that under the clouded sky he could only now and then catch the flash of the frigate's sails on the rise, while the pahi had practically vanished. He could not tell whether the frigate had spoken the pahi or not: all he knew was that both wind and sea had strengthened and that even if by some extraordinarily lucky chance the *Surprise* gained any information from the pahi, it must be fragmentary, uncertain, totally unreliable. With this wind, this head-sea and this current a square-rigged ship might beat up for the island a week on end and gain no eastward distance at all, a waste of time that could not be justified by the vague pointing of a crew of monoglot and largely hostile women, even supposing they pointed at all. Duty would require Mowett to carry on to the Marquesas.

'Never look so care-worn, brother,' said Stephen. 'Sit comfortably on the ground and listen to the noble booming of the sea, how it thunders.'

'Aye, so it does,' said Jack. 'It has certainly been blowing very hard somewhere, to raise this almighty swell. But I tell you what, Stephen, I am afraid the weather must be breaking up in these parts too; and even if it don't, perhaps we should make up our minds to staying on this island for quite a considerable time – capital fishing, I dare say, and winkles for relish, once we can get on to the reef.'

Stephen objected that the ship was just at hand; Jack replied that she had run far to the lee; Stephen said that in that case she must ply diligently to windward; and once again Jack was about to explain the increasing degree of leeway that even the most weatherly ship must make as the increasing force of the wind obliged the sails to be reefed or taken in when he reflected that his explanation would do no good. Invincible ignorance could not be enlightened; and although no doubt he might succeed in making Stephen anxious and unhappy this would not really advance them very much. He therefore listened quietly to his friend's assurance that 'Mowett would certainly find some means of overcoming these difficulties – impossible was not a word he connected with the Navy – nothing could exceed the zeal of the mariners – and should there be a little delay, it would enable him to complete his study of the island's flora and fauna – only a brief delay was required however, so pitifully meagre was the tale by land.'

'But,' said Stephen, after these comfortable words, 'I have been contemplating on coral, and my mind is staggered amazed confounded at the thought of these countless myriads of animalcula industriously sifting the lime from the sea-water for so vast a sequence of generations and in such prodigious quantities that they have formed this island, this reef, to say nothing of the countless others that do exist. And all founded upon what? Upon the skeletons of other coral-polyps, the calcareous external skeletons of other coral-polyps, in quantities that run far beyond conception, that is what. For I do assure you, Jack, that everything here, apart from these trifling adventitious vegetables' – waving towards the palms – 'is coral, living or dead, coral sand or solid coralline accumulation. There is no subjacent rock at all. How can it have begun, in this deep tempestuous sea? The force of these waves is very great: the animalculum is miserably frail. How do these islands come about? I cannot tell at all: I cannot form the beginning of a hypothesis.'

'No underlying rock, you say?'

'None whatsoever, brother. Coral, all coral, and nothing but coral.' He paused, shaking his head, and sank deep into thought while Jack looked out over the green lagoon to the leaping wall of white water on the far side of the reef, reflecting that presently he should try to find something in the way of bait and then wade out with Manu's line on the end of a palm-rib. He had gone on to think about ways of making fire when Stephen said, 'And these things being so, I become convinced that the large rounded object about the size of a moderate turtle but more lumpish there on the strand to your right, where the water is lapping it, could not be a boulder. No. I have more than half persuaded myself that it is an enormous piece of ambergris, washed up by the sea.'

'Have you not been to look at it?'

'I have not. The association of rarity, wealth and so on instantly brought that unfortunate brass box to my mind, that most unwelcome box from the *Danaë* packet which is now aboard the *Surprise*; and as the recollection came to me, so I grew perfectly convinced, as by a revelation, that rats or cockroaches or book-worms or various moulds were eating its contents, to our utter ruin – eating them with tropical avidity, a million of money. The thought fairly cut my legs from under me, and I have sat here ever since.'

'It is a thousand to one we shall never have any need of the brass box, nor of the ambergris unless it can be eaten,' said Jack to himself. 'And if the weather goes on breaking up like this – if it really comes on to blow and *Surprise* is driven a great way to leeward, then it is ten thousand to one or more, much more.' But aloud, giving Stephen a hand up, he said, 'Let us go and have a look. If it is ambergris, we are made men: we have but to go to the nearest dealer and change it for its weight in gold, ha, ha, ha!'

It was not ambergris: it was a piece of crystalline limestone, mottled and in part translucent, and it fairly stupefied Maturin. 'How can such things be?' he asked, gazing out into the offing. 'There is no question of glaciers, icebergs . . . How can such things possibly come about? There is the boat. I have it,' he cried. 'This rock was brought tangled in the roots of a tree, a great tree swept away by some remote flood or tornado, cast up after the Dear knows how many thousand miles of drifting, and here decaying, leaving its incorruptible burden. Come, Jack, help me turn it – see,' he cried with a shining face as it heaved over, 'in these anfractuosities there are still traces of my roots. What a discovery!'

'What did you mean when you said boat?'

'Why, our boat, of course. The big one, the launch, come to fetch us, as you always said it would. Lord, Jack,' he said, looking up with an entirely different expression, 'how in God's name shall I ever face them, at all?'

He was still there, sitting by his rock, when the *Surprise*'s launch, following her Captain's directions from the height of his palm-tree, dashed through the perilous gap in the reef, crossed the lagoon and ran nose-up on to the shore. 'Oh, sir,' cried Honey, leaping from the bows and very nearly clasping his Captain in his arms, 'how glad I am to see you! We caught sight of the signal a couple of hours ago, but scarcely dared hope it was you. How are you, sir? And the Doctor?' – this last with a very anxious doubtful cock of his head.

'He is prime, I thank you, Honey, and so am I,' said Jack, shaking his hand; and then louder, to the crew of the boat who were staring round, on their thwarts, nodding, becking and grinning, against all decent naval order, 'Well fare ye, shipmates. You are most heartily welcome. A long pull?'

'About eight hours, sir,' said Bonden, laughing as though this were a really brilliant witticism.

'Then haul her up a couple of foot and come ashore. I dare say we shall have to push off with the turn of the tide, but you will have time to wet your whistles with a coconut or two. Mr Calamy, you will find the Doctor sitting by a rock on the other side of the island, at low-water mark: tell him – is there anything to eat or drink in the boat?'

'Which Killick put up some milk-punch and pickled seal, sir, in case you wasn't dead,' said Bonden. 'And we have our rations.'

'Tell him punch and seal, then. Tell him we are going to have a sup and a bite if he chooses to join us; but in any case he should hold himself in readiness to leave quite soon, as I fear it may come on to blow. Now, Mr Honey, pray let me know what happened.'

They had been missed a little before dawn, when a swabber of the afterguard saw the stern-windows wide open. On being told, Mowett instantly cried, 'It's the Doctor,' and put the ship about. All the officers worked out a course that should take the ship back to the point where the Captain was last known to be aboard. This course they followed for several hours, seeing driftwood four times, until they reached the position they had determined upon, which they did with an excellent observation to check it but with their hearts in their boots and their eyes fairly destroyed with having stared so long quite in vain; they then lay to for the night, taking very great care to forereach a trifle to counteract the current. All the officers were on deck or in the tops, and the atmosphere was like that of an undertaker's barge with a crew of mutes. Before dawn they spread the boats out as before and at first light they began their westward sweep. Almost at once they were cheered by the sight of two more tree-trunks, battered but not water-logged, floating quite high, which renewed their hope; and shortly after this the northernmost boat, one of the cutters . . .

'The blue cutter: seven bells in the morning watch: beg pardon, your honour,' said Bonden.

. . . signalled something very likely, and they bore up; it proved to be only an empty barrel, but it was a United States Navy beef-barrel, and quite fresh.

'A beef-barrel, eh?' said Jack with intense satisfaction. 'Carry on, Mr Honey.'

Then at the changing of the watch Hogg, the whaler's specktioneer, came aft and said there was an island away to the north: asked how he knew, pointed out a patch of white cloud and a green reflection in the sky. He was supported by the other South Sea whalers, who said the islanders always navigated by such signs. Asked how far, he said it depended on the size: about twenty miles for a small one, much more for a large. There were plenty of islands not laid down on charts.

If the castaways had found a piece of driftwood, could they have reached it? What was the true set of the current? Might it have carried them so far north? Those were the questions that tormented the quarterdeck. Would it be right to leave their known course? It was decided that the distance was too great to warrant a change unless the island's existence were quite certain, but the blue cutter was ordered away north-north-east for an hour under all possible sail while the ship and the other boats carried on their sweep: this on the reasoning that if the island existed it would cause an indraught, attracting driftwood from a great way off. Time went by slowly, but at last the cutter was seen racing back; her signals were hard to make out, because now that the *Surprise* had moved farther westward she could only see the flags end-on and what was more cloud was coming up, spoiling the light. It was not until the boat was almost within hailing distance that they understood she had seen not only a low island but also a two-masted vessel far to the west-north-west of it. By this time the wind was freshening and backing east or even north of east, the sea was getting up, and greasy weather was surely on the way: Hogg and the other whalers said they had known a very heavy blow indeed in these waters after just such a swell. This was probably their last chance, they thought, so they called the boats in and altered course, 'feeling almighty queer'. They cracked on and presently the lookout on the jacks caught sight of the sail.

'That was me, sir,' cried Calamy. 'With old Boyle's spyglass, ha, ha, ha!'

Hogg went aloft and declared the sail to be a native craft, a double canoe, very like a Tuamotu pahi, though not quite the same in some particulars; and while he was considering it he also saw the island, farther off and to the east.

Mowett at once manned and provisioned the launch and told Honey to proceed to the island with all possible dispatch: for his part he was going to see whether the pahi had picked them up or whether its people could give any information – Hogg understood the language of the islands – and then to lie to until the launch should rejoin. He fixed a rendezvous in the Marquesas in case of dirty weather.

The launch was rigged as a schooner and she was a fine weatherly boat; but it had been clear from the start that beating up would never do, and they had taken to their oars, thus becoming practically invisible from the island in such a sea. After a few hours the people had grown quite tired and jaded, pulling against what was now a head-sea or close on; but then, standing up with his glass, Honey had seen Jack's shirt flying from the palm-tree and after

that they had stretched out like heroes – both Davis and
Padeen Colman, Stephen's servant, had broken their oars.

'Remind me to stop it out of their pay, Mr Honey,'
said Jack; and when the mirth had died away (for this
was perhaps his most deeply relished stroke of wit since
Gibraltar), 'At least sore hands will have a rest once we
are out of the lagoon. I saw the barky right to leeward,
and with this breeze we should rejoin before sunset, never
touching an oar. Bonden, cut along to the Doctor' – for
Stephen had sent back a message by Calamy to the effect
that he was not hungry – had some last investigations to
make – would come presently – 'and tell him we are off
and help him into the stern-sheets while the masts are
stepping. It would be as well,' raising his voice – 'for
nobody to wish him joy or ask him how he does. He has
been taken a little poorly, what with soaking so long and
drinking salt water.'

Jack need not have spoken, at least not to the seamen:
in their delicacy they would never have taken the least
notice of Stephen's misfortune, nor have made him feel
the enormous amount of trouble he had caused; and in
fact when he came sidling awkwardly down the strand
they showed what might have been taken for a brutal
indifference, relieved only by the singular gentleness with
which he was lifted in and settled with a sailcloth apron
over his knees and somebody's old blue jacket about his
shoulders.

In the course of their flying voyage westwards with
the launch impelled by following seas and an ever more
powerful wind Stephen's spirits recovered a little, particularly when Jack gave an account of their time aboard
the pahi. He could not have had a more attentive or
more appreciative audience – how they laughed at his
near-castration and the Doctor's terror when his pig mis-
behaved and the bosun's mates stood behind him – and
after a while Stephen added a few details, feeling much
more at his ease. Yet when the ship came in sight – when
she came so close that people could be seen against the

low sunset sky, running about the deck and waving their hats – he lapsed into silence again.

But the hearty unfeigned affectionate welcome and the underlying kindness so characteristic of the service, brutal though it was at times, would have dealt with a temperament far more morose than Stephen's. In any case his professional skill was called upon at once: the boarding-party sent to the pahi had been repelled with shocking ferocity. Martin and Hogg, leading the way with presents and kind words, had almost instantly been clubbed, and the seamen who dragged them back to the boat speared, beaten with heavy wooden blades, and stabbed with bamboo skewers, all in a terrible yelling screaming uproar. Five men were in the sickbay with wounds far beyond the loblolly-boy's competence, all inflicted within a few moments of the attempted boarding, while the hail of sling-stones and darts delivered as the pahi sheered off accounted for another half dozen less serious casualties.

'They did not give a damn for gunfire,' said Mowett, in the cabin. 'I don't believe they knew what it was. Every time we sent a shot near or over their heads they jumped up and down and waved their spears. I could have knocked away a spar or two, of course, but in such a sea . . . and in any case we could see you was not aboard. And as for information, they would never have given us any, I am sure.'

'You did very well, Mowett,' said Jack. 'In your place I should have been terrified they might attack the ship.'

'I have the villain,' said Stephen in the sickbay, where he was operating by the last of the daylight and seventeen purser's dips. 'I have him in my crow's-bill. A shark's tooth, as I had supposed, detached from the club and driven into the gluteus maximus to a most surprising depth. The question is, what shark?'

'May I see it?' asked Martin in a reasonably firm voice. He had already had thirty-six stitches in his scalp, while a square foot of court plaster covered his lacerated shoulders, but he was a man of some fortitude and above all a natural philosopher. 'A shark without a doubt,' he said, holding the tooth down towards the deck, for he was lying on his belly – most of the Surprises had been wounded ingloriously from behind, running away as fast as ever they could – 'But what shark I cannot tell. However, I shall keep it in my snuff-box, and look at it whenever I think about matrimony. Whenever I think about women, indeed. Dear me, I shall never pull off my hat to one again without remembering today. Do you know, Maturin, as I set foot on that floating thing, that pahi, I saluted the woman confronting me, bowing and baring my head, and she instantly took advantage of it to strike me down.'

'This is the far side of the world,' said Stephen. 'Now your calf, if you please. I am afraid we shall have to cut it bodily out. I had hoped to push it through, but the tibia is in the way.'

'Perhaps we could wait until tomorrow,' said Martin, whose fortitude had its limits.

'A barbed spearhead cannot wait,' said Stephen. 'I wish to see no proud flesh, no black mortification, no gangrene spreading upwards. Pratt, I believe Mr Martin would like to be attached; otherwise he might give an involuntary start and there I should be in an artery.' With quick practised fingers he passed a leather-covered chain round Martin's ankle and another behind his knee; Pratt made them fast to ring-bolts effectually pinning the limb and its owner. These were motions Stephen had made again and again and they were as familiar to him as his patients' unwillingness to be operated upon and all their transparent shifts.

He was very much at home in this place, with his familiar instruments, the smell of tallow, bilgewater, tow, lint, the rum and tincture of laudanum with which he deadened those whom he would be obliged to cut deep; and when he had finished bandaging the leg – Martin was silent now, having drifted away on his drug at last – he felt quite part of the ship once more.

He stood up, threw his operating coat into its usual corner, washed his hands, and walked into the cabin. Jack was writing in a book: he glanced up, said, 'There you are, Stephen,' with a smile, and wrote on, his pen scratching busily.

Stephen sat down in his particular chair and looked about the beautiful room. Everything was in its place, Jack's telescopes in their rack, his sword hanging by the barometer, the 'cello and fiddle cases lying where they always lay, and the particularly magnificent gold-mounted dressing-case cum music-stand – Diana's present to her husband – standing where it always stood, and the unlucky brass box from the *Danaë*, its seals intact, was hidden behind the foot-waling as he knew very well; but there was something amiss, and all at once he noticed that dead-lights had been fitted to the stern-windows: no one could possibly fall out of them.

'No, it is not that,' said Jack, catching his look. 'That would be locking the horse after the stable door is gone, a very foolish thing to do.'

'Still and all, there are some horses that are obliged to be controlled, I am afraid.'

'No, it was just that I think we may have a blow, and I do not choose to lose the window-glasses again.'

'Is that right? I had supposed the sea was calmer.'

'So it is, but the barometer has dropped in a very horrid manner . . . forgive me, Stephen, I must just finish this page.'

The ship rose and fell, rose and fell, a pure long following sea with never a hint of roll in it. Jack's pen squeaked on. At some distance Killick's disagreeable voice could be heard singing *Heave and ho; rumbelow*, and presently the smell of toasted cheese reached the cabin.

This was their particular delight in the evening, but there had been no cheese, toasted or otherwise, in the great cabin for some thousands of miles. Could there be such things as olfactory illusions, wondered Stephen, blinking at the lantern as it swung fore and aft, fore and aft. Conceivably. There was after all no limit at all to error. But then again, he reflected, Killick's notion of his perquisites had a right naval breadth to it: he stole as steadily and conscientiously as the bosun, but whereas the bosun, by immemorial custom, might sell his winnings without being thought the worse of so long as he was not caught or unless he criminally weakened the ship, the same did not apply to the Captain's steward, and Killick never passed anything over the side. His perquisites were for himself and his friends, and it was possible that he had preserved a piece of the almost imperishable manchego or parmesan for some private feast of his own: physical, material, objective cheese was certainly toasting no very great way off. Stephen was aware that his mouth was watering, but that at the same time his eyes were closing. 'A curious combination, truly.' He heard Jack say that it was certainly going to blow, and with that he went fast to sleep.

CHAPTER NINE

Jack Aubrey lay in his cot, savouring his resurrection; this was Sunday morning and according to ancient naval custom the day's life began half an hour earlier than usual – hammocks were piped up at six bells rather than seven – so that the ship's people could wash, shave and make themselves fine for divisions and church. Ordinarily he was up and about with the rest, but today he deliberately took his ease, indulging in perfectly relaxed sloth and in the comfort of his bed, infinitely soft and well-moulded compared with harsh, scaly palm-fronds, and infinitely warm and dry compared with the open sea. The usual swabs and holystones scouring the deck a few feet above his head had not woken him, because Mowett had allowed nothing but silent, largely symbolic sweeping abaft the mainmast. But for all Mowett's care Jack was pretty well aware of the time of the day: the intensity of the light and the smell of roasting coffee were in themselves a clock; yet still he lay, taking conscious pleasure in being alive.

At last the scent of coffee died away, giving place to the everyday smell of fresh sea, tar, warm wood and cordage, and distant bilge, and his ear caught the click-click of Killick's mate's pestle grinding the beans in the brass mortar belonging to the sick-bay; for Stephen was even more particular about his coffee than Jack, and having learnt the true Arabian way of preparing it when they were in the Red Sea (an otherwise profitless voyage) he had banished the commonplace mill. Jack's ear also caught Killick's shrill abuse as his mate let some of the beans skip out; it had just the same tone of righteous indignation as the dreadful bosun's mates aboard the pahi or Sophie's mother, Mrs Williams. He smiled again. How pleasant it was to be alive. Mrs Williams had come to stay with them; his old and horribly energetic father, General Aubrey, a member of parliament in the extreme Radical interest, seemed bent on destroying Jack's career; even apart from political considerations the Admiralty had treated him with striking injustice ever since he was a master and commander, promising him ships and then giving them elsewhere, failing to promote his subordinates, though infinitely deserving, frequently questioning some one or another of the horribly intricate accounts he was required to keep, and regularly threatening him with unemployment, with being thrown on the shore, there to live in wretched idleness on half pay. Yet how utterly trifling these things were, and the law-suits too, in comparison with being alive! Stephen, a Catholic, had already performed his action of grace; Jack's happy, thankful mind now did much the same, though in a less formal manner, revelling and delighting in what he had been given back.

Light pittering hooves could be heard overhead: Aspasia, fresh from her milking. It was even later than he had thought, he observed, and he sat up. Killick had obviously been listening outside the door of the sleeping-cabin, for it opened straight away, letting in a flood of eastern light.

'Good morning, Killick,' said Jack.

'Good morning, sir,' said Killick, holding up a towel. 'Are you going to take a dip?'

In these waters Jack usually swam before breakfast, even if it were only a plunge from the forechains and a return by the stern-ladder so as not to check the ship's way, but now he said no, he would prefer a pot of hot water. His skin and particularly the rolls of fat round his belly were still strangely waterlogged, and at present sea-bathing had no attraction for him.

'Is the Doctor about yet?' he called, stropping his razor.

'No, sir,' said Killick from the great cabin, where he was laying the breakfast-table. 'He was called up in the night, which Mr Adams had a fit of the strong fives in consequence of eating and drinking too much by way of wishing the Doctor joy of his return. But a clyster soon settled his hash. Don't I wish I had given it to him myself, the b - - r,' added Killick in a low voice when he was sure that Jack could not hear, for the purser objected to Killick's way of robbing the foremast hands, the Marines, the warrant officers, the midshipmen's berth and the gunroom mess in order to keep the cabin well supplied.

With their voices diminished by the distance and the following wind Hollar and his mates could be heard calling down the hatchways, 'D'ye hear there, fore and aft? Clean shirt for muster at five bells. Duck frocks and white trousers.' 'D'ye hear there? Clean shirt and shave for muster at five bells.'

'Clean shirt, sir,' said Killick, passing it.

'Thankee, Killick,' said Jack. He pulled on his second-best white breeches, observing with regret that in spite of his soaking and his privations they were still so tight round his waist that the topmost hook had to be left undone: his long waistcoat would cover the gap, however.

'Not far from three bells, sir,' said Killick. 'Too late to ask anyone else to breakfast, which is just as well, seeing as how Aspasia was precious near with her milk this morning.'

Soft tack and therefore toast was as much a thing of the past as eggs and bacon or beefsteak and onions, but Jack's cook had turned out a highly spiced and savoury dish of Juan Fernandez stockfish, crisp on top, and Killick had produced one of the few remaining pots of Ashgrove Cottage marmalade, which went very well with ship's bread. 'How I wish Sophie were here,' he said aloud, looking at the label she had written such a great way off.

Three bells sounded. He drank the last of the coffee, stood up, looped his sword-belt over his shoulder and put on the splendid blue coat that Killick held out for him, a coat of singular elegance with its massive golden epaulettes and the ribbon of the Nile medal in a buttonhole, but one made of a stout broadcloth more calculated for the English Channel in winter than the equator. 'But, however,' he reflected, as his temperature rose, 'I do not have to do it up. It is worse for the others,' and in the gaiety of his heart he added, 'Il faut souffrir pour être beau' as he clapped on his cocked hat.

'Good morning, Oakes,' he said to the Marine sentry at his door, and 'Good morning, gentlemen,' as he stepped on to the quarterdeck. In the general chorus of 'Good morning, sir,' hats flew off, and immediately afterwards a dozen waistcoats partly vanished under close-buttoned coats.

Automatically Jack looked up at the sails, the rigging and the sky; all was just as he could wish – a whole topsail breeze in which she could carry the fore topgallantsail if she were pressed. But the sea was not all he could wish by any means. The heavy blow that made him ship deadlights yesterday evening had not come about, but the following swell had not subsided – indeed, the pitching made it difficult for the hands to arrange their bags, brought up so that the 'tween decks could be cleaned, in the usual pyramid on the booms, and it was traversed by a curious diagonal cross-swell that cut up the surface in an uneasy, fretful way: an ugly sea, and one that he was not used to, in spite of all his experience. The forthcoming ceremony however was one that he knew by heart; it was performed in all well-regulated men-of-war once a week except in a very heavy weather and he must have seen it at least a thousand times.

The subdued conversation on the lee side of the quarter-deck died away. The quartermaster at the con cleared his throat, and as the last grain of sand fell into the lower part of the half-hour glass he cried, 'Turn the glass and strike the bell.' The Marine on duty moved forward, very careful of his step with such a pitch and with the whole ship's company watching him, and struck five bells.

'Mr Boyle,' said Maitland, the officer of the watch, to the young gentleman acting as mate of the watch, 'beat to divisions.'

Boyle turned to the Marine drummer, who stood there

with his sticks poised, said 'Beat to divisions,' and the drum instantly roared out the generale.

The seamen, who had been standing about in amorphous groups, taking great care of their best, beautifully washed, ironed and often embroidered clothes, now hurried to form lines according to their various divisions – forecastlemen, topmen, gunners and afterguard only, for the *Surprise* had no waisters – toeing well-known seams on either side of the quarterdeck, on the gangways and the forecastle. The Marines were already drawn up far aft, near the taffrail. The midshipmen inspected the hands in their division, tried to make them stand up straight and soldierly and stop talking and then reported to the lieutenants and the master; the lieutenants and the master inspected them again, tried to make them stop staring about and hitching up their trousers, and reported that the men were 'present, properly dressed and clean' to Mowett, who stepped across the deck to Captain Aubrey, took off his hat and said, 'All the officers have reported, sir.'

'Then we will go round the ship, Mr Mowett, if you please,' said Jack, and first he turned aft, to where the Marines were standing as straight as ramrods in their scarlet coats: their cross-belts were brilliant with pipeclay, their muskets and side-arms shone again, their hair was powdered to a turn, their leather stocks were as tight as stocks could well be and allow a little circulation of the blood; and although awnings had been rigged, the eastern sun, not yet at its height, beat on their backs with shocking force. They might not be beautiful, but they were certainly suffering. Accompanied by Howard, his sword drawn, and by Mowett, he passed along the rows of faces, many of them nameless to him even now and all of them impersonal, gazing out beyond him, wholly without expression.

'Very creditable, Mr Howard,' said Jack. 'I believe you may dismiss your men now. They may put on their duck jackets and wait quietly under the forecastle until church.' Then, still with Mowett and with each of the divisional officers in turn, he went round the rest of the ship.

This was quite a different ceremony. Here he knew every man, many of them – indeed most of them – intimately well, knew their virtues, vices, particular skills, particular failings. And here there was no remote impassive gaze, no eyes trained to avoid the charge of familiarity or dumb insolence. Far from it: they were very pleased to see him and they smiled and nodded as he came by – Davis even laughed aloud. Furthermore it was perfectly obvious to all concerned that a rescued captain, just returned to his ship by a combination of extraordinary luck and extraordinary exertions, could not decently find fault with his ship's company. As an inspection his tour was therefore a matter of pure though amiable form; and it very nearly turned into a farce when the bosun's cat joined them and marched steadily in front of the Captain, its tail in the air.

Far below, under the grateful freshness of a windsail, Stephen was sitting with his patient Martin. They were not exactly bickering, but in both the spirit of contradiction was distinctly present and active: present in the chaplain because of his wounds and in Stephen because of a more than usually wretched night on top of two really trying days. 'That may be so,' said he, 'yet in the public mind the service is often associated with drunkenness, sodomy and brutal punishment.'

'I was at a great English public school,' said Martin, 'and the vices to which you refer were by no means uncommon there; they are I believe fairly usual whenever a large number of men are gathered together. But what is unusual in the service, and what I have not encountered elsewhere, is the essential good-nature. I do not speak of the seamen's courage and altruism, which need no comments of mine, though I shall never forget those noble fellows who dragged me back into the boat from the pahi . . .'

Stephen, cross-grained though he was that morning, really could not disagree. He waited until Martin had finished and then said, 'You did not happen to notice a tall slim broad-shouldered young woman with a spear, very like an undraped Athene?'

'No,' said Martin, 'I saw nothing but a swarthy crew of ill-looking female savages, full of malignant fury, a disgrace to their sex.'

'I dare say they had been ill-used, the creatures,' said Stephen.

'Perhaps they had,' said Martin. 'But to carry resentment to the point of the emasculation you described seems to me inhuman, and profoundly wicked.'

'Oh, as far as unsexing is concerned, who are we to throw stones? With us any girl that cannot find a husband is unsexed. If she is very high or very low she may go her own way, with the risks entailed therein, but otherwise she must either have no sex or be disgraced. She burns, and she is ridiculed for burning. To say nothing of male tyranny – a wife or a daughter being a mere chattel in most codes of law or custom – and brute force – to say nothing of that, hundreds of thousands of girls are in effect unsexed every generation: and barren women are as much despised as eunuchs. I do assure you, Martin, that if I were a woman I should march out with a flaming torch and a sword; I should emasculate right and left. As for the women of the pahi, I am astonished at their moderation.'

'You would have been still more astonished at the force of their blows.'

'It is the black shame of the world that they should be deprived of the joys of love – Tiresias said they were ten times as great as those enjoyed by men, or was it thirty? – leaving aside the far more dubious pleasures of motherhood and keeping house.'

'Tiresias represents no more than the warm imaginings of Homer: decent women take no pleasure in the act, but only seek to – '

301

'Nonsense.'

'I quite agree with you in your dislike of interruptions, Maturin,' said Martin.

'I beg your pardon.' Stephen cocked his ear to the mouth of the wind-sail and said, 'What is all that huzzaying on deck?'

'No doubt they have taken the pahi, and now you will be able to carry your charitable theories into practice,' said Martin, but without any real ill-humour.

They both listened attentively, and while they were listening feet came running aft. Padeen opened the door and stood there making inarticulate sounds, pointing a thumb over his shoulder. 'Himself, is it?' asked Stephen. Padeen smiled and nodded and passed Stephen his coat. Stephen put it on, buttoned it, and stood up as the Captain and the first lieutenant came in.

'Good morning, Doctor,' said Jack. 'How are your patients?'

'Good morning, sir,' said Stephen. 'Some are a little contradictory and fractious, but a comfortable slime-draught at noon will deal with that. The others do tolerably well, and are looking forward to their Sunday duff.'

'I am heartily glad to hear it. And I believe you will be glad to hear that we have picked up another of the *Norfolk*'s barrels. A pork-barrel this time, fresh and floating high, marked Boston in December of last year.'

'Does that mean we are close to her?'

'There is no telling within a week or so, but it does mean that we are probably in the same ocean.'

After some more remarks about barrels, their drifting and signs of wear, Martin said, 'I believe, sir, that you mean to read one of Dean Donne's sermons this morning. I have told Killick just where to find it.'

'Yes, sir, I thank you, and he did find it. But now that I have looked it over I feel that it would come better from a learned man, from a real parson. I shall confine myself to the Articles of War, which I do

302

understand and which in any case are obliged to be read once a month.'

This he did: in the pause that followed the singing of the *Old Hundredth*, Ward, who on these occasions acted as parish clerk as well as captain's clerk, stepped forward, took the slim folio of the Articles from beneath the Bible and passed it to Jack, who began in a strong, minatory voice (though not without a certain relish), 'For the regulating and better government of his Majesty's navies, ships of war, and forces by sea, whereon, under the good providence of God, the wealth, safety, and strength of this kingdom chiefly depend, be it enacted by the King's most excellent Majesty, by and with the advice and consent of the lords spiritual and temporal, and commons, in this present parliament assembled . . .'

His words came down the wind-sail in snatches as the breeze strengthened on the top of the swell and diminished when the *Surprise* sank into the trough, and fragments of the Articles mingled with Stephen's and Martin's conversation, which now moved off, by way of the phalarope, to the less dangerous ground of birds.

'Did you ever see a phalarope, at all?' asked Stephen.

'Never a live one, alas; only in the pages of a book, and that a most indifferent cut.'

'Will I describe him to you?'

'If you please.'

'All flag officers, and all persons in or belonging to his Majesty's ships or vessels of war, being guilty of profane oaths, cursings, execrations, drunkenness, uncleanness, or other scandalous actions in derogation of God's honour, and corruption of good manners . . .'

'But the hen bird is much larger and much brighter; and she is a creature that does not believe that a hen's duty is merely to tend her nest, brood her eggs, and nourish her chicks. I once had the happiness of watching a pair from a fisherman's cabin on the far far tip of the County Mayo; there was a group of them in the neighbourhood,

303

but it was this particular pair I watched, so close to the cabin they were.'

'If any ship or vessel shall be taken as prize, none of the officers, mariners, or other persons on board her, shall be stripped of their clothes, or in any sort pillaged, beaten, or evil-intreated . . .'

'The evening she had laid the last of her clutch – '

'Forgive me,' said Martin, laying his hand upon Stephen's knee, 'but how many?'

'Four: snipe-shaped and much the same colours. That same evening, then, she was away and the poor cock had to look after them himself. I was afraid some harm had come to her, but not at all, there she was – and I knew her well from her face and the odd white streak on the side of her bosom – swimming about on the sea and the little lough this side of it and playing with the other hens and the unattached cocks. And all the while the poor fellow brooded the eggs there not fifteen yards from me under a turf-stack, covering them as well as he could from the rain and never eating but five minutes or so in the day. It was worse when they hatched, because clearly they had to be fed single-handed, the four of them bawling and screeching all the day long; and he was not very handy at cleaning up after them either. He grew anxious and thin and partially bald, and there she was on the lough, chasing the other phalaropes and being chased by them, crying pleep, pleep, pleep and never doing a beak's turn by way of labour or toil. There was a fowl that knew how to live a life of her own, I believe.'

'But surely, Maturin, as a married man you cannot approve the phalarope hen?'

'Why, as to that,' said Stephen, with a sudden vivid image of Diana dancing a quadrille, 'perhaps she may carry things a little far; but it does go some way towards redressing a balance that is so shamefully down on the one side alone.'

'Any person in the fleet who shall unlawfully burn or set fire to any magazine or store of powder, or ship, boat, ketch, hoy, or vessel, tackle or furniture thereunto belonging, not then appertaining to an enemy, pirate, or rebel . . . shall suffer death.'

These words came down the ventilator with unusual force, and after a rather solemn pause Martin asked, 'Just how does one define a hoy, Maturin?'

'As this is a Sunday, I will tell you candidly that I do not know,' said Stephen. 'But I have heard it used by way of reproach, as "You infernal two-masted Dutch hoy" or "The place was all ahoo, like the deck of the Gravesend hoy." '

Only a very little later Jack used these same words, *as this is a Sunday*, when he refused a request submitted by the hands through the captains of the tops to the bosun, by him to the first lieutenant, and by Mowett to the Captain. The idea was that as the Doctor was very curious to see a prize-fight, his return to the ship might be celebrated by a series of contests on the forecastle that evening, the more so as the Marines and even the whalers had long been prating of their extraordinary skill and courage in the ring. 'No,' said Jack, 'as this is a Sunday, I am afraid I cannot countenance prize-fighting. I am sure Mr Martin would agree that Sunday is no day for semi-slaughter, for real fighting, bare-knuckle fighting. But if they choose to ask Sails to run up properly padded gloves, and if they like to set to, sparring and boxing like Christians, with nothing on the murdering lay, no wrestling, no cross-buttock falls or gouging or strangling, no head in chancery or catching hold of pigtails, why, I cannot see that the Archbishop of Canterbury himself could object.' Then turning to Stephen, 'I never knew you were interested in prize-fighting.'

'You never asked,' said Stephen. 'I have seen many a squalid scuffle, of course, many a Donnybrook Fair, but as I was telling Bonden the other day although it is so much a part of modern life, I have never seen the peculiarly English prize-fighting. I was very near to it once. I met a particularly amiable young man in a stage-coach, a pugilist named Henry Pearce – '

'The Game Chicken?' cried Jack and Mowett together.

'I dare say: they told me he was a famous man. And he invited me to see him fight some other hero – Thomas Cribb, was it? – but at the last moment I was disappointed of my treat.'

'So you met the Game Chicken,' said Mowett, looking at Stephen with a new respect. 'I saw him fight the Wapping Slasher on Epsom Downs until they were both of them groggy and very nearly blind with blood, and after an hour and seventeen minutes and forty-one rounds Pearce was the only one who could come up to the scratch, although he had had five knockdown blows and the Slasher had fallen on him twice, squelch with all his weight, the way some bruisers do when there is a big purse.'

'How you have missed seeing one in all this time I cannot tell,' said Jack, who had often travelled fifty miles to see Mendoza or Belcher or Dutch Sam, who had frequented Gentleman Jackson's establishment, and who had himself lost two teeth in friendly encounters. 'But at least that can be repaired this evening. We have some capital bruisers aboard: Bonden won the belt at Pompey, with eight ships of the line and three frigates competing; Davis is a smiter that will stand like a Trojan until his legs are cut from under him, and one of the whalers is said to be very dangerous. Mowett, the hide we use for covering the laniards would be better than sailcloth, if we have any that is supple enough.'

'I will go and see, sir.'

'Lord, Stephen,' said Jack when they were alone, 'how pleasant it is to be aboard again, don't you find?'

'Certainly,' said Stephen.

'Only this morning I was thinking how right they were to say it was better to be a dead horse than a live lion.' He gazed out of the scuttle, obviously going over

306

the words in his mind. 'No. I mean better to flog a dead horse than a live lion.'

'I quite agree.'

'Yet even that's not quite right, neither. I know there is a dead horse in it somewhere; but I am afraid I'm brought by the lee this time, though I rather pride myself on proverbs, bringing them in aptly, you know, and to the point.'

'Never distress yourself, brother; there is no mistake, I am sure. It is a valuable saying, and one that admonishes us never to underestimate our enemy, for whereas flogging a dead horse is child's play, doing the same to a lion is potentially dangerous, even though one may take a long spoon.'

In this case the enemy was the swell, and in their eagerness for the entertainment all those concerned had underestimated it and continued to do so in spite of the evidence of their senses up to and indeed beyond the last possible moment: even when it had increased to such an extent that the ship was pitching headrails under and a man could scarcely keep his feet without holding on there were those who swore it was all a mere flurry – it would die away well before sunset – they should certainly have their fight, and any ugly Dutch-built bugger that spoke to the contrary was a croaker, a goddam crow, a fool and no seaman.

'I am afraid you will be disappointed of your treat again,' said Jack. 'But if this sea dies down, and if the work of the ship allows, you shall have it tomorrow.'

The swell, in so far as it was a vast, regular up and down, certainly diminished, yet Stephen, lying there awake in the morning, felt a strange uneasy motion that was neither a strong pitching nor a heavy roll but a quick sudden kind of lurching with no decided direction, unlike anything he had known before. This lurching caused the ship's timbers to work and it had obviously been going on for some considerable time, since there was a good deal of water washing to and fro in his cabin, and his shoes were afloat.

'Padeen,' he called several times; and after a listening pause, 'Where is that black thief, his soul to the Devil?'

'God and Mary be with you, gentleman,' said Padeen, opening the door and letting more water in.

'God and Mary be with you,' said Stephen, 'and Patrick.'

Padeen pointed upwards through the decks and after some gasps he said in English, 'The Devil's abroad.'

'I dare say he is,' said Stephen. 'Listen, Padeen, just reach me those dry shoes from the little net on the wall, will you now?'

His cabin was not far from the ship's centre of gravity and as he made his way up the ladders the motion increased, so that twice he was nearly flung off, once sideways and once backwards. The only person in the gun room was Howard's Marine servant, who said, with a frightened look, 'All the gentlemen are on deck, your honour.'

So they were, even the purser and even Honey, who had had the graveyard watch and who should have been fast asleep; but in spite of the gathering there was little talk and apart from good mornings Stephen himself said not a word. The horizon all round was of a blackish purple and over the whole sky there rolled great masses of cloud of a deep copper colour, moving in every direction with a strange unnatural speed; lightning flashed almost continually in every part and the air was filled with the tremble of enormous thunder, far astern but travelling nearer. There was a steep, irregular sea, bursting with a tremendous surf as though under the impulsion of a very hard gale: in fact the breeze was no more than moderate. Yet in spite of its moderation it was strikingly cold and it whistled through the rigging with a singularly keen and shrilling note.

The topgallantmasts had already been struck down on deck and all hands were now busy securing the boats on the booms with double gripes, sending up preventer stays, shrouds, braces and backstays, clapping double-breechings on to the guns, covering the forehatch and scuttles with tarpaulins and battening them down. Aspasia came and nuzzled his hand, pressing against his leg like an anxious dog: a sudden jerk nearly had him over, but he saved himself by grasping her horns.

'Hold on, Doctor,' called Jack from the windward rail. 'The barky is skittish today.'

'Pray what does all this signify?' asked Stephen.

'Something of a blow,' said Jack. 'Forecastle, there: Mr Boyle, guy it to the cathead. I will tell you at breakfast. Have you seen the bird?'

'I have not. No bird these many days. What kind of a bird?'

'A sort of albatross, I believe, or perhaps a prodigious great mew. He has been following the ship since – there he is, crossing the wake – he comes up the side.'

Stephen caught a glimpse of wings, huge wings, and he ran forward along the gangway to get a clear view from the bows. The fall from the gangway into the waist of the ship was not much above six feet, but Stephen was flung off with unusual force, and he hit his head on the iron breech of a gun.

They carried him aft and laid him on Jack's cot, dead apart from a just perceptible breathing and a very faint pulse. It was here that Martin found him, having crawled up from the depths.

'How good of you to come, Mr Martin,' cried Jack. 'But surely you should not be about, with your leg . . . I only sent to ask whether you thought he should be let blood, since you understand physic. We cannot bring him round.'

'I cannot advise letting blood,' said Martin, having felt Stephen's unresisting, impassive head. 'Nor brandy,' – glancing at the two bottles, one from the cabin, one from the gunroom. 'I do know something of physic, and am persuaded this is a cerebral commotion – not a full coma, since there is no stertor – which must be treated by rest, quiet, darkness. I will consult the Doctor's books, if

I may, but I do not think they will contradict me in this; nor when I say that he would be far better downstairs, where the sideways motion is so much less.'

'You are quite right, I am sure,' said Jack, and to Killick, 'Pass the word for Bonden. Bonden, can you and Colman and say Davis carry the Doctor below without jerking him, or should you be happier with a tackle?'

'A tackle too, sir, if you please. I would not slip with him, no not for a world of gold.'

'Make it so then, Bonden,' said Jack; and while the tackles were being set up, 'What do you think, Mr Martin? Is he bad? Is he in danger?'

'My opinion is not worth a great deal, but this is obviously much more than an ordinary stunning fall. I have read of comatose states of such a kind lasting for days, sometimes growing deeper and ending in death, sometimes giving way and dispersing like natural sleep. When there is no bone broken I believe internal haemorrhage is often the deciding factor.'

'All ready, sir,' said Bonden. The strongest men in the ship were with him, and between them, wedged against stanchions and bulkheads, they lowered Stephen inch by inch, as though his skin were made of eggshell, until he was back in his own cot, with Padeen by to curb its swinging. The cabin was small and somewhat airless, but it was dark, it was quiet, it was in the least agitated part of the ship, and here the hours passed over him in black silence.

On deck all hell broke loose as they were striking the maintopmast half an hour later; the preventer top-rope reeved through the fid-hole parted at the very moment a deluge of warm rain beat down on the ship, so thick they could scarcely breathe, much less see. From that time on until full darkness and beyond it was an incessant battle with mad blasts of wind from every direction, thunder and lightning right overhead, unbelievably steep seas that made no sense at all, bursting with such force that they threatened to engulf the ship – bursting as though they were over a reef, although there was no bottom to be found with any line the ship possessed. All this and such freaks as a waterspout that collapsed on their astonished heads, bringing the maindeck level with the surface for several minutes; and without a pause thunder bellowed about them, while St Elmo's fire flickered and blazed on the bowsprit and catheads. It was a time or rather – since ordinary time was gone by the board – a series of instant shifts and expedients, of surviving from one stunning thunderclap and invasion of water to the next and between them making fast such things as the jollyboat, the binnacle itself and the booms that had carried away. And all the while the pumps turned like fury, flinging out tons of water that the sea or the sky flung right back again. Yet even so it was the hands at the pumps who were the least harassed; although they had to work until they could hardly stand, often up to their middles in water, often half-choked with flying spray or still more rain, immeasurable quantities of rain, at least they knew exactly what to do. For the others it was a perpetually renewed state of emergency in which anything might happen – unheard of, shockingly dangerous accidents such as the seventy-foot palm-trunk that a freakish sea flung bodily aboard so that its far end wedged in the mainshrouds while the rest lashed murderously to and fro, sweeping the gangways and the forecastle just as an equally freakish squall took what little storm-canvas the ship dared show full aback, checking her as though she had run on to a reef and laying her so far over that many thought she was gone at last. Indeed, if a windward gun had broken loose at this point of utmost strain it would certainly have plunged right through her side.

It was not until sunset that the weather began to have a direction and some sort of a meaning. The whirling turning formless blasts passed north and westwards and they were succeeded by the pent-up south-east wind, which, though full of flaws and slanting squalls, blew with enormous force, eventually bringing up a swell which rivalled that they had known in the fifties, so very far south.

It was a hard blow, a very, very hard blow, with a dangerous following sea; but it was what they were used to in their calling, and compared with the maniac day it was positive relief. The hands were piped by half-watch and half-watch to their very late supper; Jack ordered the splicing of the mainbrace and made his way below. He went first to the sick-bay, where he knew there would be some injured men, and there he found Martin splinting Hogg's broken arm in a most workmanlike fashion: Pratt was standing by with bandages and lint and it was clear that Martin had taken over. 'This is very good of you, Mr Martin,' he cried. 'I hope you are not in too much pain yourself. There is blood on your bandage.'

'Not at all,' said the parson, 'I took Maturin's potion, the tincture – pray hold this end for a moment – and feel very little. I have just come from him: I found no change. Mrs Lamb is with him at present.'

'I will look at your other patients and then, if it would do no harm, I will go and see him.' Considering the extraordinary severity of the day there were surprisingly few casualties, and apart from the broken arm none very serious: he felt encouraged as he went down the ladder and quite hopeful as he opened the cabin door. But there under the swinging lantern Stephen looked like a dead man: his temples were sunk, his nostrils pinched, his lips were colourless: he was lying on his back and his grey closed utterly motionless face had an inhuman lack of expression. 'I thought he was gone not five minutes ago,' said Mrs Lamb. 'Perhaps with the turning of the tide . . .'

There was no change at two bells in the middle watch, when Jack came down to sit with him for a while before turning in. There was no change when Martin hobbled up to take a first breath of morning air on the ravaged quarterdeck, desolation fore and aft, and stood for a while watching the ship tearing along under no more than close-reefed topsail and jib over a dark indigo sea laced with white streams of foam and broken water, tearing along with fag-ends of rope flying, broken spars at every turn, and the rigging giving out a general note two full tones lower than usual, tearing along just ahead of great following seas that rose to the height of the mizentop.

'What shall you do now?' he asked at breakfast in the gunroom, after he had answered all their questions about Stephen.

'Do?' said Mowett, 'Why, what any ship must do in such a blow – scud and pray we are not pooped and that we may not run into anything by night. Scud, knotting and splicing as we go.'

There was no change when Martin came to a makeshift dinner in the cabin. Jack said, 'I am not to teach you anything about medicine, Mr Martin, but it occurred to me that as the injury was much the same as Plaice's, perhaps the same operation might answer.'

'I too have been thinking of that,' said Martin, 'and now I have had time to read in some of his books on the subject. Although I find no depressed fracture in this case, which is the usual reason for trepanning, I fear that there may be a clot of extravasated blood under the point of impact which is having the same effect.'

'Should you not try the operation, then? Would it not relieve the brain?'

'I should not dare to do so.'

'You turned the handle when Plaice was done.'

'Yes, but I had an expert by me. No, no, there are many other considerations – I have a great deal more to read – much of it is dark to me. In any case no amateur could possibly operate with the ship in such a state of violent motion.'

Jack was obliged to admit the truth of this; but his face grew stern and he tapped his biscuit on the table for a few moments before forcing a smile and saying, 'I promised to tell you about the weather when we had time to draw breath: it seems that we were on the southern side and near the tail of a typhoon that has travelled off north-westerly. That would account for the whirlwinds and the seas from every quarter, do not you agree, Mowett?'

'Yes, sir,' said Mowett. 'And we are certainly in quite different waters now. Have you noticed the quantities of long thin pale sharks around the ship? One of them took the bullock's hide we had towing under the mainchains to soften it. When I went below to ask Hogg how he did he said he had often seen them, approaching the Marquesas; he also said he did not think the weather had blown itself out yet, no, not by a chalk as long as your arm.'

Dinner ended on that note. As Martin took his leave he said he would pass the afternoon reading, very attentively watching the patient's symptoms, and perhaps practising with the trephine on some of the seal's skulls he and Maturin possessed.

Late that night he said he was becoming more and more nearly convinced that the operation was called for, above all since Stephen's breathing had now become slightly stertorous; and he showed passages in Pott and La Faye supporting his view. But what, he asked, was the use of his growing conviction with the ship plunging about like this? In so delicate an operation the slightest lurch, the slightest want of balance and exact control might mean the patient's death. Would it be possible to heave the ship to?

'That would make no difference to the absolute motion,' said Jack. 'Indeed, it would make the heave and roll come quicker. No, the only hope is that this sea should go down, which, bar a miracle, it cannot do in less than three or four days, or that we should lie to under the lee of some reef or island. But there is no reef or island laid down on the chart until we reach the Marquesas. Of course there is the alternative that you should – how shall I put it? – that you should steel yourself to the act. After all, naval surgeons cannot wait for calm weather; and if I remember right, Plaice was operated on in a close-reefed topsail breeze.'

'Very true, though the sea was fairly calm. Yet we

must distinguish between timidity and temerity; and in any case, even if I were quite certain it was right, in view of my inexperience and remaining doubts, I certainly could not operate without the full light of day.'

But even when the full light of day came it did not bring full conviction: Martin was still torn with uncertainty.

'I cannot bear the sight of Maturin just fading away like this for want of care – for want of a bold stroke,' said Jack: the pulse under his attentive fingers was now so faint that it was not above once in five minutes that he could be sure of it.

'I cannot bear the thought of Maturin being killed by my want of skill or by some wretched jerk of the deck under me,' said Martin, whose improvised Lavoisier trephine had made some shocking plunges right through the practice skulls. 'Fools rush in where angels fear to tread.'

The *Surprise* raced westwards over the same dark-blue enormously heaving sea, under a brilliant sky filled with high white clouds, re-rigging, re-reeving, fishing the sprung mizenmast. Her mainshrouds on the weather side, shattered by the palm-trunk, had already been replaced, set up and rattled down, and her Captain had his usual walk restored. The quarterdeck was just fifty feet long and by stepping short at a particular ring-bolt, now worn thin and silver-bright, he could make fifty of his turns fore and aft amount to a measured mile by land. Up and down he went amid the busy noise of the ship and the steady, omnipresent great voice of the wind and the very powerful sea; with his bowed head and his stern expression he seemed so absorbed that the other people on the quarterdeck spoke very quietly and kept well over to leeward, but he was in fact perfectly aware of what was going forward and at the first cry of 'Land ho' from the maintop he sprang into the shrouds. It was a furious hard climb with the huge wind tearing him sideways and his shirt-tail out, billowing round his ears, and he was glad

315

the lookout had been sent no higher. 'Where away, Sims?' he asked, coming into the top through the lubber-hole.

'Three points on the starboard bow, sir,' said Sims, pointing; and there indeed, as the ship rose on the swell, was land, quite high land with a hint of green, an island some eleven or twelve leagues away.

'Well done, Sims,' said Jack, and he slipped down through the hole again. Even before he reached the deck he began roaring for the bosun, who was busy on the forecastle. 'Leave that for the moment, Mr Hollar,' he said, 'and get me light hawsers to the mastheads.'

'Aye aye sir,' said Hollar, smiling. This was an old trick of the Captain's, horrible in appearance but wonderfully effective. The hairy, brutish hawsers and cablets allowed him to carry sail that would otherwise tear the masts out of the ship, and this had won the frigate many a charming prize before now, or had allowed her to run clear away from much superior force.

'Mr Mowett,' he said, 'four good men to the wheel, and let them be relieved every glass. We are going to crack on. Mr Allen, please to con the ship: course north-west by west a half west.'

Then, half an hour later, catching sight of Hogg supported by his mates on the gangway he stepped forward and said, 'Well, specktioneer, do you make it out?'

'Yes, mate, I do,' said Hogg. 'If you look under them clouds not moving, under their floor, like, don't you see a bright round, and dark in the middle?'

'I believe I do. Yes, certainly I do.'

'The bright is surf and coral sand, and the dark is trees: there ain't much lagoon.'

'How do you know that?'

'Why, because lagoon shows green, in course. Quite a high island, from the amount of cloud. I wonder you never saw it, Bill,' – this to his supporter. ''Tis as plain as plain.'

'All stretched along and a-tanto, sir,' said the bosun.

316

'Very good, Mr Hollar,' said Jack, and raising his voice, 'All hands to make sail.'

The new course brought the great wind almost on to the frigate's quarter, and methodically he began spreading her canvas. They had long since swayed up the topmasts, though not of course the topgallants, and he gave her a little high storm-jib first, then the main staysail, then instead of the close-reefed maintopsail the maintopmast staysail. Each time he paused for the *Surprise* to take up the full force of the new thrust: this she did with immense spirit, with the buoyant living grace which so moved his heart – never was such a ship – and when she was moving perhaps as fast as she had ever moved, with her lee cathead well under the foam of her bow-wave, he laid one hand on the hances, feeling the deep note of her hull as he might have felt the vibrations of his fiddle, and the other on a backstay, gauging the exact degree of strain.

They were used to the Captain; they had nearly all of them seen him cracking on like smoke and oakum and they were pretty nearly sure he had not finished. But no man had expected his call for the forecourse itself and it was with grave, anxious faces that they jumped to their task. It took fifty-seven men to haul the foresheet aft, to tally and belay; and as the strain increased so the *Surprise* heeled another strake, another and yet another, until she showed a broad streak of copper on her windward side, while the howl in the rigging rose shriller and shriller, almost to the breaking-note. And there she steadied, racing through the sea and flinging a bow-wave so high to leeward that the sun sent back a double rainbow. Discreet cheering started forward and spread aft: everybody on the quarterdeck was grinning.

'Watch your dog-vane,' said Jack to the helmsman. 'If you once let her be brought by the lee, you will never see Portsmouth Point again. Mr Howard, pray let your men line the weather gangway.'

Four bells. Boyle walked cautiously down the sloping

deck with the log and reel under his arm, followed by a quartermaster with the little sand-glass.

'Double the stray-line,' called Jack, who wanted an accurate measurement, with the log-ship well clear of the wake before the knots were counted.

'Double the stray-line it is, sir,' replied Boyle in as deep a voice as his puny frame could manage. When the red tuft had been shifted fifteen fathoms he took up his station by the rail, asked, 'Is your glass clear?' and on being told, 'Glass clear, sir,' heaved the log well out, holding the reel high in his left hand. 'Turn,' he cried as the end of the stray-line went by. The sand streamed down, the reel whirred, the knots fleeted by, intently watched by all hands who had an eye to spare. The quartermaster opened his mouth to cry 'Nip', but before the last grains had run through Boyle uttered a screech and the reel shot from his hand.

'I am very sorry, sir,' he said to Mowett after a moment's confusion. 'I let the reel go.'

Mowett stepped across to Jack and said, 'Boyle is very sorry, sir, but he let the reel go. The line ran clean out and I suppose the pin was stiff: it took him unawares.'

'Never mind,' said Jack, who in spite of his intense underlying anxiety was deeply moved by this splendid measurement of flying speed. 'Let him try with a fourteen-second glass at six bells.'

By six bells the upper part of the island was clear to those on the deck, a hilly little island, with clouds just above it; and from the maintop could be seen the tremendous surf beating against its shore. No lagoon on this windward side, but there seemed to be reefs running out some way on the north-east and south-west with lighter-coloured water beyond them.

The wind had diminished by now and the *Surprise* logged no astonishing number of knots, but there was that ineffaceable memory, dear to all the people, of a whole 150 fathoms being run straight off the reel before the glass was out; and in any case she was still bringing the land a mile closer every four or five minutes.

'Mr Martin,' said Jack in the sick-bay, 'we have raised an island, as I dare say you know, and in an hour's time we should be under its lee: or it may be possible to land. In either case I beg you will hold yourself in readiness to operate.'

'Let us go and look at him,' said Martin. Padeen Colman was sitting there, his beads in his hand: he shook his head without a word, meaning 'No change'.

'It is an awful decision,' said Martin as they stood swaying with the motion of the ship, looking down at that stern mask. 'Above all because the symptoms do not quite agree with any of the books.' Once again and this time at greater length he explained what he understood to be the nature of the case.

He was still doing so when Mowett came and said softly, 'I beg your pardon, sir, but there is a signal flying from the island.'

The island had come very much closer during Jack's time below and the signal was quite clear in his glass: a torn blue and white flag on a high-standing rock. Jack climbed into the foretop with his first lieutenant and from there the shore line was as plain as could be: cliffs with rollers bursting high on them on this eastern side and then a reef tending away southward and west. He called down the orders that put the ship before the wind under a close-reefed main topsail and forecourse: she skirted the end of the reef and hauled up round it, coming to the verge of the island's lee. Here the reef enclosed a considerable lagoon, and on its landward shore, intensely white under this brilliant sky, he saw a number of men, probably white men, from the trousers and occasional shirt: some were running to and fro but more were making emphatic gestures northwards.

The *Surprise*, with little more than steerage-way on her now, moved cautiously along the outside of the reef: quite close, but still in such deep water that the man in the chains perpetually cried, 'No bottom with this line; no bottom, nay, nay.'

Although there was still a powerful swell, the wind was very, very much less here, and its near silence gave their slow gliding the feeling of a dream. The reef slipped by, sometimes with little palm-grown islands on it, coconut-palms, often laid flat or broken off short, and beyond the reef the calm lagoon; beyond that the shining strand, backed first by palms and then by a rising general greenery whose wind-ravaged state could be seen only in a glass; and on the strand the white men ran and capered and pointed. They were not much more than a mile away, but the shifting airs under the island's lee did not carry their voices, which were reduced to an occasional faint 'Ahoy, the ship ahoy,' or a confused babbling.

'I believe that is a gap, sir,' said Mowett, pointing along the broad reef: and just beyond an island with three uprooted palms and three still standing, there was indeed a channel through into the lagoon.

'Flat in forward, there,' cried Jack, staring intently; and as the *Surprise* edged nearer to the gap, he heard a concerted howl from the strand, no doubt a warning, for a sunken ship lay clean across the fairway. An unnecessary warning however; in this clear water and with the ebbing tide she was clear from her stem, which was wedged just below the surface in the coral of the little island, to her stern far down in the rocks of the other side. Her bowsprit and masts had gone by the board, her back was broken, her midship gunports had been stove in, and there was a gaping hole from her starboard mainchains to her quarter-gallery, a hole through which passed long pale-grey sharks, blurred by the ripple and the swell; but she was perfectly recognizable as the *Norfolk*, and Jack at once called out, 'Hoist the short pennant and the colours.'

This seemed to cause some consternation on shore. Most of the men ran off northwards; a few still stood staring; the capering stopped and there were no more gestures. Jack returned to the quarterdeck and the ship sailed gently on, following the reef. The shore turned inward, opening a little cove in which there stood a cluster of tents and shelters where a stream ran out of the woods over the sand. Here there were more people, more distant now that the lagoon was wider and quite inaudible; but now, evidently by command, they all pointed their right arms northwards to the place where the stream flowed through a long winding channel in the reef, quarter of a mile broad at this point.

There were no breakers here, on this most sheltered part of the coast, but even so the swell still rose high on the glistening coral and receded with an enormous sigh. 'I will be damned if I venture the ship in there, on an ebbing tide, without sounding,' said Jack, looking at the light-green channel, and he ordered a boat away.

It could just be done, said Honey, returning, but it would be nip and tuck until the flood; and the coral rocks on either side and on the bottom were razor-sharp. There was no great current now, near slack-water; but the tide must scour through at a great rate, to keep the bottom so clean, unless indeed that was the effect of the heavy blow. If the ship were to go through, perhaps he had better buoy one or two of the worst places.

'No,' said Jack. 'It don't signify. We are in forty fathom water with a good clean ground; we could anchor if we chose. Mr Mowett, while I stand off and on take my barge and a proper guard of Marines, proceed to the shore – flag of truce and ensign of course – present my compliments to the captain of the *Norfolk* and desire him to repair aboard without delay and surrender himself prisoner.'

The barge had not been painted since they were off the River Plate; the bargemen had not had time to renew their broad-brimmed sennit hats; the uniforms of the lieutenant, the midshipman and the Marines were not as fresh as they had been before undergoing antarctic cold and equatorial heat; but even so the Surprises were quite proud of their turn-out, so very far from home and after such an uncommon savage blow. They watched the barge thread the channel and cross the broad, smooth lagoon, and during the long pull many of the watch below passed a small private telescope from hand to hand, looking for women on the shore: in spite of their shocking experience with the pahi they still looked for women, looked very eagerly indeed. Those who had been in the South Sea before had attentive, silent listeners: 'As free and kind she was as kiss my hand,' said Hogg, speaking of the first he had known, in the island of Oahua. 'And so were the rest. Some of the men had to be tied, and carried aboard slung on a pole: they would have jumped ship else, though they had forty and fifty pound due to them in shares.'

'There ain't no women,' said Plaice to a young main-topman after a long and searching stare. 'Nor no men neither. It is a desert island, apart from those Boston beans walking up and down. But that there, sheltering the biggest tent by the stream, that's a breadfruit-tree, I dare say.'

'You can —— your breadfruit-tree,' said the young top-man bitterly.

'That's no way to talk to a man old enough to be your dad, Ned Harris,' said the captain of the forecastle.

'Saucy young bugger,' said two others.

'I only meant it by way of a joke,' said Harris, reddening. 'I was talking lighthearted.'

'You want your arse tanned,' observed the yeoman of the signals.

'There's a precious lot of sharks about,' said Harris, by way of changing the subject. 'Uncommon long thin grey ones.'

'Never you mind if they are grey or pink with orange stripes,' said the captain of the forecastle. 'You just keep a civil tongue in your head, Ned Harris, that's all.'

'They're putting off with the American captain, sir,' said Killick, in the cabin.

'Undo this damned hook for me, will you, Killick?' said Jack, who was getting into his uniform. 'I must be growing fat.'

He looked into his dining-cabin, where a cold collation

had been spread to welcome the captain of the *Norfolk*, ate one of the little salt biscuits and then buckled on his sword. He did not wish to appear too eager, strutting about on his quarterdeck throughout his prisoner's approach – it was a damned unpleasant thing having to surrender in any case, as he knew from experience, without having people crow over you – but on the other hand he did not wish to appear casual, as though the surrender of a post-captain were of no great importance.

He waited until it seemed to him that the moment was as nearly right as possible, put on his cocked hat, and went on deck. A quick look showed him that Honey had everything in hand: midshipmen quite respectable, sideboys washed and holding their white gloves ready – rather hairy, big-boned sideboys now – Marines at hand, and the ship, which had been toing and froing, now standing gently in, just stemming the tide, to receive the barge.

He began his usual pacing; but at the third turn a glance at the short figure sitting there between Calamy and Mowett in the stern-sheets made him look again, look much harder. It was too late to start staring with a spyglass, but from his time as a prisoner of war in Boston he was very well acquainted with American naval uniforms, and there was something amiss.

When the barge was a little nearer he said to the Marine sentry, 'Trollope, hail that boat.'

The Marine was on the point of saying, 'But it's our own barge, sir,' when a glazed, disciplined look came over his eyes: he shut his mouth, drew a deep breath and called, 'The boat ahoy.'

'No, no,' came Bonden's answer, very loud and clear, meaning that no commissioned officer was coming to the *Surprise*.

'Carry on, Mr Honey,' said Jack, withdrawing to the taffrail: the sideboys stuffed their gloves into their pockets, the midshipmen abandoned their reverential looks, and Howard dismissed his men. The barge hooked on and

Mowett bounded up the side. His face was quite aghast as he came hurrying aft to Jack. 'I am very sorry, sir,' he cried, 'but the war is over.'

He was immediately followed by a cheerful short thick round-headed man in a plain uniform coat who brushed past Honey and approached Jack with a beaming smile, his hand held out. 'My dear Captain Aubrey, give you joy of the peace,' he said. 'I am delighted to see you again, and how is your arm? Very well, I see, and much the same length as the other, according to my prediction. You do not remember me, sir, though without boasting I may say you owe me your right arm. Mr Evans was actually filing the teeth of his saw, but I said No, let us give it another day – Butcher, formerly assistant surgeon in *Constitution* and now surgeon of *Norfolk*.'

'Of course I remember you, Mr Butcher,' said Jack, his mind filled with the recollection of that painful voyage to Boston as a wounded prisoner after the American *Constitution* had taken the British *Java*. 'But where is Captain Palmer? Did he survive the wreck of the *Norfolk*?'

'Oh yes, yes. He was battered, but not drowned. We did not lose a very great many people compared with what it might have been. All our clothes went, however, and I am the only man with a respectable coat. That is why I was sent – Captain Palmer could not bear the idea of going aboard a British man-of-war in a torn shirt and no hat – he desires his best compliments, of course – had the pleasure of meeting you in Boston with Captain Lawrence – and hope you and your officers will dine with him on what the island affords tomorrow at three o'clock.'

'You spoke of a peace, Mr Butcher?'

'Oh yes, and he will tell you about that in more detail than I can. We first had the news from a British whaler – how blank we looked when we had to let her go, a splendid prize – and then from a ship out of Nantucket. But tell me, sir, what is this I hear about Dr Maturin, that you wish to open his head?'

'He had an ugly fall, and our chaplain, who understands physic, thinks it might save him.'

'If it is a question of trepanning, I am your man. It is an operation I have performed scores, nay hundreds of times without losing a patient. That is to say except in a very few cases of vicious cachexy, where it was only done to please the relations. I trepanned Mrs Butcher for a persistent migraine, and she has never complained since. I have the greatest faith in the operation; it has brought many men back from the edge of the grave, and not only for depressed fractures, either. May I see the patient?'

'A very fine instrument indeed,' said Butcher to Martin, turning Stephen's trephine over and over in his hands. 'With many improvements unknown to me. French, I believe? I remember our friend' – nodding towards Maturin – 'saying he had studied in France. A trifle of snuff, sir?'

'Thank you, but I do not take it.'

'It is my only indulgence,' said Butcher. 'A very fine instrument; but I do not wonder you hesitated to use it. I should hesitate myself, even in a swell as moderate as this, let alone the sea you describe. Let us get him ashore at once: this pressure must not be allowed to continue another night, or I will not answer for the consequences.'

'Can he safely be moved?'

'Of course he can. Wrapped in blankets, made fast to a padded six by two plank with cingulum bandages – a crosspiece for his feet, of course – and raised and lowered vertically by tackles, he will come to no harm, no harm at all. And if Captain Aubrey could send his carpenter to knock up a hut a little more solid than our canvas, why, the patient will be as well off as in any naval hospital.'

'Mr Mowett,' said Jack, 'I am going ashore with the Doctor. It will be too dark by the height of flood for you to try the channel, so you will anchor the ship, gackling your cables a good twenty fathom. In all probability I shall rejoin when things are well in hand, but if I do not, you will come in tomorrow evening. Do not forget to gackle your cables, Mowett.'

Stephen, more corpse-like still with his face shrouded from the sun, was lowered into the boat – the launch this time, as being more roomy than the barge – and it pushed off, loaded deep with the carpenter, his crew, a working-party, a good deal of material, and some stores that Jack thought might be welcome to castaways.

Captain Palmer had hobbled down to greet him at the landing-place, a little hard on the left-hand side of the stream, away from the tents. He had done what he could to improve his appearance, but he was an unusually hairy man by nature, and a grizzled beard, together with his ragged clothes and bare feet, gave him the look of a vagrant: he had also been miserably bruised and scraped at the time of the wreck and he was covered with makeshift plasters and bandages where the coral rock had rasped him to the bone. The hair and the plasters made the expression on his face difficult to interpret, but his words were both polite and obliging. 'I hope, sir,' he said, 'that you will come and drink what we have to offer while everything is being fixed; for I conclude the gentleman on the plank under the awning is your surgeon, come ashore to be opened by Mr Butcher.'

'Just so: Mr Butcher was so very kind as to offer his services. But if you will forgive me, sir, I must see to some kind of a shelter first, while there is still light. Do not stir, I beg,' he said as Palmer made a move to accompany him. 'On our way in I noticed a glade that will probably answer very well.'

'I shall look forward to your visit, as soon as you have settled on your place and given your orders,' said Palmer with a courtly bow.

This bow was almost the only acknowledgement between the two sides. The small group of men behind Palmer, presumably his remaining officers, uttered no word, while the surviving Norfolks, some eighty or ninety of them, stood at some distance on the right-hand side of the stream; the Surprises stood on the left, and they stared heavily at one another across the water like two unacquainted, potentially hostile bands of cattle. Jack was surprised. In this absurd, unnecessary war there had been little real ill-feeling except on the part of the civilians, and he had expected much more spontaneous pleasure, much more calling out between the hands. He had little time for these reflections, however; the well-drained, open, light, airy place he wanted for his shelter was by no means as easy to find as he had imagined. The hurricane had littered the ground with branches, some of them huge; there were great trees uprooted and others dangerously unsteady; and it was not until late twilight, after driving hard work, that the roof was on and the patient laid out on the solid, sweet-smelling table, newly cut from fresh sandal-wood.

'I hope the want of light will not trouble you, Mr Butcher,' said Jack.

'Not at all,' said Butcher. 'I am so used to operating between decks that I really prefer a lantern. Mr Martin, sir, if you will place one there, by the beam, while I set the other here, I believe we shall have the benefit of the converging rays. Captain Aubrey, was you to sit on the barrel by the door, you would have an excellent view. You will not have long to wait: as soon as I have put the last edge on this scalpel I shall make the first incision.'

'No,' said Jack. 'I shall go to see Captain Palmer, and then I must get back to the ship. Please to let me know the moment the operation is over. Colman here will wait outside to bring me word.'

'Certainly,' said Butcher. 'But as for your going back to the ship tonight, never think of it, sir. The flood-tide comes in through that channel like a mill-race; a boat could not possibly row against it, and the wind is foul.'

'Come along, Blakeney,' said Jack to his midshipman: he closed the door and walked quickly away: his stomach was strong enough for most purposes, but not for seeing Stephen's scalp turned down over his face, inside out, and a trephine deliberately cutting into his living bone.

At the bottom of the glade they could see the Surprises eating their supper in the lee of the launch, a noble fire burning before them. 'Cut along and have a bite,' said Jack. 'Tell them that everything is in train; and when they have finished their supper let Bonden bring the stores I put up for the Americans.'

He walked slowly on, listened to the sea on the distant reef and sometimes glanced up at the moon, just past the full. He liked neither the sound of the one nor the look of the other. Nor did he like the atmosphere on the island.

He crossed the stream, still deep in reflection. 'Halt,' cried a sentry. 'Who goes there?'

'Friend,' replied Jack.

'Pass friend,' said the sentry.

'There you are, sir,' said Palmer, ushering him into his tent, lit with a rescued top-light turned very low. 'You look anxious: I hope all is well?'

'I hope so,' said Jack. 'They are operating now. They will send me word as soon as it is over.'

'I am sure all will be well. I have never known Butcher miss his stroke; he is as clever as any surgeon in the service.'

'I am very happy to hear you say so,' said Jack. 'It should not take long, I believe.' His ear was already cocked for approaching footsteps.

'Do you understand tides, Mr Martin?' asked Butcher, slowly shaving hairs off his forearm with the scalpel.

'Not I,' said Martin.

'A fascinating study,' said Butcher. 'Here they are particularly curious, being neither semi-diurnal nor quite diurnal. There is an immense reef to the west of this island and I believe it is that which pens up the current and causes the anomaly: but whether it is that or a whole raft of other factors, a spring tide, like tonight's, comes in with great force, torrential force, and the flow lasts nine hours or more. It will not be high water till morning, and your captain is as one might say marooned for the night, ha, ha! Will you take snuff, sir?'

'Thank you, sir,' said Martin. 'I never do.'

'Mine was a waterproof box, glory be,' said Butcher, turning Stephen's head and considering it with pursed lips. 'I always fortify myself before operating. Some gentlemen smoke a cigar. I prefer snuff.' He opened his box and took so vast a pinch that a good deal fell down his shirt-front and more on his patient; he flapped it off both with his handkerchief and Stephen gave a tiny sneeze. Then painfully he drew a deeper breath, sneezed like a Christian, muttered something about spoonbills and brought his hand up to cover his eyes, saying, 'Jesus, Mary, and Joseph,' in his usual harsh, grating voice, though very low.

'Pin him,' cried Butcher, 'or he will be sitting up.' And through the door to Padeen, 'Hey there, go fetch a rope.'

'Maturin,' said Martin, bending over him, 'you have come to yourself! How happy I am. I have prayed for this. You had a great fall, but are now recovered.'

'Put out that goddam light,' said Stephen.

'Come, sir, lie back and set your mind at ease,' said Butcher. 'We must relieve the pressure on your brain — just a little discomfort, a little restraint — it will soon be over . . .' But he spoke without much hope, and when Stephen did sit up, desiring Padeen not to stand there in the door like a great dumb ox but to fetch him a draught of good fresh water for the love of God, he put down his scalpel, saying quietly, 'Now I shall never have a chance of using the new French trephine.'

After a silent pause, Captain Palmer said, 'Well, sir, and how did your ship come through this blow?'

'Pretty well, I thank you, upon the whole, apart from some lost spars and a sprung mizen; but most of the storm had already passed over, somewhat to the

329

north, I believe. We only caught the southern skirt, or the tail.'

'We were in the heart of it, or rather the forefront, since we had no warning; and it hit us at night. A sad time we had of it, as you may imagine, particularly as we were shorthanded, having sent so many men away – ' Palmer hardly liked to say 'in prizes' so he repeated 'having sent so many men away', merely changing the stress. It was evident from his account that the typhoon had struck the *Norfolk* much earlier than the *Surprise*: it had also set her far north of her reckoning, so that on the Thursday morning, when they were driving before an enormous sea with no more than a scrap of sail on the stump of the foremast, to their surprise and horror they saw Old Sodbury's Island fine on the starboard bow.

'This island, sir?' Palmer nodded. 'So you knew it, then?'

'I knew *of* it, sir. The whalers sometimes come here – indeed, it is named for Reuben Sodbury of Nantucket – but they usually avoid it because of the very long and dangerous shoals a few miles to the west – shoals that were right under our lee. So rather than run plumb on to them, with no hope at all, we bore up for Old Sodbury. Two of my men, whalers from New Bedford, had been there before and they knew the pass.' He shook his head, and then went on, 'Still, we did at least strike at the very tail of the ebb, so most of us could scramble from the bows to the little island and so along the reef to the shore. But we saved nothing – no boats, no stores, no clothes, almost no tools, no tobacco . . .'

'Have you not been able to dive for anything?'

'No, sir. No. The place is alive with sharks, the grey kind, Old Sodbury's sharks. My second and a midshipman tried, at low water: they didn't leave us enough to bury, though they were not big fish.'

They heard the sentry's 'Halt. Who goes there?' followed by a strangled gasp, then the sound of blows, and Bonden's strong, 'Now then, mate, who are you a shoving of? Don't you know he's dumb?'

'Why didn't he say so, then?' said the sentry in a faint voice. 'Let me up.'

Padeen burst in and touched his forehead with a bleeding knuckle; he brought out no clear word, but his message was plain on his shining face, and in any case Bonden was there to interpret: 'He means the Doctor was not opened at all, sir – recovered by himself, sprang up like a fairy, damned everyone all round, called for water, called for coconut-milk, and is now asleep, no visitors allowed. Which I brought the stores, sir. And sir, it may be turning dirty outside.'

'Thank you, both of you: you could not have brought better news. I shall be with you presently, Bonden. Now here, sir,' – opening the chest – 'are some little things we brought along: no caviar or champagne, I am afraid, but this is smoked seal, and this salt pork and dolphin sausage . . .'

'Rum, port wine and tobacco!' cried Palmer. 'Bless you, Captain Aubrey! I sometimes thought I should never see them again. Allow me to freshen your coconut-milk with some of this excellent rum. And then if I may I will call in my officers, the few I still have, and introduce them.'

Jack smiled while Palmer was uncorking the bottle; it was not what he was about to say that made him so cheerful but rather the thought of Stephen sitting up and cursing. The rum was poured, the mixture stirred. Composing his face Jack said, 'There is something one might almost say sacred about wine or grog or even perhaps beer that water or coconut-milk does not possess; so before I drink with you, it is but right that I should say you must consider yourself a prisoner of war. Of course I shall not proceed to extremes. I shall not insist upon your coming back to the ship with me tonight, for example, or anything of that kind. No manacles, no irons or bilboes' – this with a smile, although in fact the *Constitution* had handcuffed the captured seamen from the *Java*. 'Yet I thought I should make the position clear.'

'But, my dear sir, the war is over,' cried Palmer.

'So I hear,' said Jack after a slight pause, in a less cordial voice. 'But I have no official knowledge of it, and your sources may be mistaken. And as you know, hostilities continue until they are countermanded by one's superior officers.'

Once again Palmer spoke of the British whaler, the *Vega* of London, that had lain to for him and had told him of the peace – had shown him a newspaper bought in Acapulco, fresh from New York with an account of the treaty; and he spoke of the Nantucket ship, whose officers and men all talked about it as a matter of course. He spoke in great detail, and most earnestly.

'Obviously,' he said, 'I cannot argue with twenty-eight great guns; but I hope I can reason with the officer who commands them, unless he is only concerned with bloodshed and destruction.'

'Certainly,' said Jack. 'But you must know that even the most humane of officers is required to do his duty, and that his duty may sometimes be very disagreeable to his feelings.'

'He is also required to use discretion,' said Palmer. 'Everyone has heard of those miserable killings in the remote parts of the world long after peace has been signed, deaths that every decent man must regret. Ships sunk or burnt too, or taken only to be given back after endless delay and loss. Aubrey, do you not see that if you use your superior strength to carry us back to Europe, just at a time when this wretched, unhappy war has been patched up, your action will be as bitterly resented in the States as the *Leopard*'s when she fired into the *Chesapeake*?'

This was a shrewd blow. At one time Jack had commanded that unlucky ship, a two-decker carrying fifty guns, and he knew very well that one of his predecessors, Salusbury Humphreys, had been ordered to recover some deserters from the Royal Navy from the American *Chesapeake*, a thirty-six gun frigate; the American commander was unwilling to have his ship searched, and the *Leopard* fired three broadsides into her, killing or wounding twenty-one of her people. She succeeded in recovering some of the deserters, but the incident very nearly caused a war and did in fact close all United States ports to British men-of-war. It also meant the shore for most of the officers concerned, including the Admiral.

'Conceivably Captain Humphreys was just within his legal right, firing upon the *Chesapeake*,' said Palmer. 'I do not know: I am no lawyer. And conceivably you would be within the strict letter of yours if you were to carry us to Europe as prisoners. But I cannot think that such a cheap victory over unarmed, shipwrecked men would be much to the honour of your service or would give you much satisfaction. No, sir, what I hope you will do is use your wide powers of discretion and carry us to Huahiva in the Marquesas, not a hundred leagues away, where I have friends and can shift for myself and my men; or if you do not like that, then I hope you will at least leave us here and let our friends know where they can find us. For I presume you will now go home by the Cape, passing close by the Marquesas. We can hold out here for a month or two, although food is short because of the hurricane. Think it over, sir; sleep on it, I beg. And in the meantime let us drink a health to Dr Maturin.' At these words a most enormous lightning-flash lit up his anxious face.

'With all my heart,' said Jack, draining his coconut-shell and standing up. 'I must get back to the ship.'

Long and vehement thunder drowned the beginning of Palmer's reply but Jack did catch the words '. . . should have told you before . . . nine- or ten-hour flood, impossible to pull against in the channel. Pray accept of this bed,' – pointing to a heap of leaves covered with sailcloth.

'Thank you, but I shall go and ask for news of Maturin,' said Jack.

On leaving the trees he looked out beyond the white

line of the reef for the *Surprise*'s riding-light, and when his eyes grew used to the darkness he made it out, low in the west, like a setting star. 'I am sure Mowett will have gackled his cables,' he said.

The launch had been hauled well above the high-water mark and turned bottom-up on broken palm-trunks so that it formed a low but commodious house; its copper could be seen gleaming in the moon, and from beneath the gunnel the acrid smoke of a dozen pipes drifted to leeward. Bonden was walking up and down at some distance, waiting for him. 'Dirty weather, sir,' he said.

'Yes,' said Jack, and they both stared up at the moon, peering now and then through racing, whirling cloud, though down here there was no more than a shifting, uneasy breeze. 'It looks very like the mixture as before. You have heard about the nine-hour tide, I collect.'

'Yes, sir. A very nasty piece of work caught me up when I was coming back from the tent. An Englishman: he told me. Also said he was a Hermione, and there was several more in the *Norfolk*, a score or so apart from other deserters. Said he would point them out if you would hold him safe and guarantee he would get the reward. They were main terrified at the sight of *Surprise* – thought she was a Russian ship at first, and cheered, then grew main terrified when they saw what she really was.'

'I am sure they did. What did you say to this Hermione?'

'Told him I'd tell you, sir.'

The heavens lit from rim to rim, showing a vast solid blackness rushing across the sky from the south-east. Both ran for shelter, but before Jack could reach his the wall of rain caught him and soaked him through. With ludicrous precaution he silently opened and closed the door and stood dripping there in the hut, while the hissing roar of falling water and the crash of thunder filled the outside world; with equal absurdity Martin, reading a book by a shaded lantern, put his fingers to his lips and pointed at Stephen, lying there curled on his side sleeping peacefully, naturally, and occasionally smiling.

All night he slept, though a rough night it was, as rough as Jack had known, and noisier. For when the wind really began, which it did with a sudden shriek at one in the morning, it had not only the masts and rigging of a ship to howl through but all the island's remaining trees and bushes; while the tremendous surf, coming more from the south than it had before, produced a ground-bass of equal enormity, more to be felt with one's whole being than really heard through the screaming wind and the headlong crash of trees.

'What was that?' asked Martin, when the hut reverberated with hammer-blows during a particularly violent blast.

'Coconuts,' said Jack. 'Thank God Lamb made such a good job of the roof: they are mortal in a breeze like this.'

Stephen slept through the coconuts, slept through the first bleary light of dawn, but he opened an eye during the lull that came with the sunrise, said, 'Good morning to you, now, Jack,' and closed it again.

With the same precautions as before Jack crept out of the door into the streaming wind-wrecked landscape. He hurried ankle-deep down to the shore, where he observed that the launch had not moved, and there, standing on the broad bole of a fallen tree and bracing himself against a still unbroken palm, he searched the white, torn ocean with his pocket glass. To and fro he swept the horizon, watching until every trough in the swell became a rise; near and far, north and south; but there was never a ship on the sea.

CHAPTER TEN

'Two thoughts occur to me,' said Jack Aubrey without taking his eye from the hole in the wall that commanded the western approaches to the island, the rainswept waters in which the *Surprise* might eventually appear. 'The one is that by and large, taking one thing with another, I have never known any commission with so much weather in it.'

'Not even in the horrible old *Leopard*?' asked Stephen. 'I seem to recall such gusts, such immeasurable billows . . .' He also remembered a remote landlocked antarctic bay where they had lain refitting for weeks and weeks among albatrosses, whale-birds, giant petrels, blue-eyed shags and a variety of penguins, all of them hand-tame.

'The *Leopard* was pretty severe,' said Jack, 'and so it was when I was a mid in the *Namur* and we were escorting the Archangel trade. I had just washed my hair in fresh water that my tie-mate and I had melted from ice, and we had each plaited the other's pigtail – we used to wear them long like the seamen in those days, you know, not clubbed except in action – when all hands were called to shorten sail. It was blowing hard from the north-north-east with ice-crystals driving thick and hard: I laid aloft to help close-reef the maintopsail, and a devil of a time we had with it, the bunt perpetually blowing out to leeward, one of the lines having parted – I was on the windward yardarm. However we did manage it in the end and we were about to lay in when my hat flew off and I heard a great crack just behind my ear: it was my pigtail, flung up against the lift. It was frozen stiff and it had snapped off short in the middle; upon my word, Stephen, it had absolutely snapped off short like a dry stick. They picked it up on deck and I kept it for a girl I was fond of at that time, at the Keppel's Knob in

Pompey, thinking she would like it; but, however, she did not.' A pause. 'It was wet through, do you see, and so it froze.'

'I believe I understand,' said Stephen. 'But, my dear, are you not wandering from your subject a little?'

'What I mean is, that although other bouts may have been more extreme while they lasted, for sheer weather, for sheer quantity and I might almost say *mass* of weather, this commission bears the bell away. The other thing that occurred to me,' he said, turning round, 'is that it is extremely awkward talking to a man with hair all over his face; you cannot tell what he is thinking, what he really means, whether he is false or not. Sometimes people wear blue spectacles, and it is much the same.'

'You refer to Captain Palmer, I make no doubt.'

'Just so. This last spell, crammed in here with Martin and Colman, and with you so indifferent, I have not liked to speak about him.' By this last spell he meant the three days of excessively violent storm that had kept them in the hut with scarcely an hour's intermission; the wind had now diminished to a fresh gale and although the rain had started again it no longer had the choking, blinding quality of the earlier deluge and people were already creeping about the island picking up battered breadfruit, particularly the sort with large chestnut-like seeds, and coconuts, many of them broken in spite of their thick husks. 'Just so. I really could not tell what to make of him. My first notion was that what Butcher had said and what Palmer said was true – that the war was over. It did not occur to me that an officer would tell a direct lie.'

'Oh come, Jack, for all love! You are an officer and I have known you lie times without number, like Ulysses. I have seen you hang out flags stating that you were a Dutchman, a French merchant, a Spanish man-of-war – that you were a friend, an ally – anything to deceive. Why, the earthly paradise would soon be with us, if government, monarchical or republican, had but to give a man a commission to preserve him from lying – from

337

pride, envy, sloth, gule, avarice, ire and incontinence.'

Jack's face, which had darkened at the word lie, cleared at that of incontinence. 'Oh,' cried he, 'those are just ruses de guerre, and perfectly legitimate: they are not direct lies like saying it is peace when you know damned well it is war. That would be like approaching an enemy under false colours, which is perfectly proper, and then firing before hauling them down and hoisting your own at the last moment, which is profoundly dishonourable, the act of a mere pirate, and one for which any man can be hanged. Perhaps it is a distinction too nice for a civilian, but I do assure you it is perfectly clear to sailors. Anyhow, I did not think Palmer would lie and my first idea was to carry them all to the Marquesas and set them free, the officers on parole not to serve again until exchanged if there had been a mistake – if the treaty had not been ratified, or something of that kind. Yet although the capture as I saw it was no more than a formality, I wished to make the point right away; I did not like to go on doing the civil thing, dining to and fro and drinking together, and then saying, "By the by, I must trouble you for your sword." So at this first meeting I told him he was a prisoner of war. I said it not exactly with levity – apart from anything else he is a much older man, a greybeard – but with a certain obvious exaggeration: I said he should not be compelled to go back with me to the ship that very night, and that his people should not be handcuffed. To my astonishment he took this seriously, and that made me begin to think perhaps there was something amiss; I remembered that when I first came ashore I had thought it strange the Norfolks were not more pleased to see us, the war being over and we being as it were their rescuers: and I felt the whole thing was somehow out of tune, badly out of tune.'

'Tell me, Jack, just how would you have expected him to reply to your statement that he was a prisoner?'

'As I made it, I should have expected any sea-officer to have replied by damning my eyes, in a civil way of course, or by clasping his hands and begging me not to confine them all in the hold nor to flog them more than twice a day. That is to say, if he really believed it was peace.'

'Perhaps the cetacean facetiousness I have so often noticed in the Royal Navy may not have crossed the Atlantic. And then again, if there is deceit, may it not originate in the English whaler? The *Vega*, after all, had every inducement to elude capture.'

'The *Vega* may have tried it too, of course. However by this time I felt so doubtful that I did not speak to Palmer about parole or the Marquesas or anything of that kind; because if in fact the war was still carrying on I should certainly have to pen them all up. It would be gross neglect of duty not to do so. It was not just his solemnity that made me so doubtful, but a hundred little nameless things, indeed the whole atmosphere; though his full motive escaped me. And then on my way back to the hut I learnt that Palmer had some Hermiones on board, quite apart from several ordinary deserters. Surely I must have told you about the *Hermione*?' he said, seeing Stephen's blank expression.

'I believe not, brother.'

'Well, perhaps I have not. It was the ugliest thing in my time, apart from the glorious end. Very briefly it was this: a man who should never have been made post – who should never have been an officer at all – was given the *Hermione*, a thirty-two-gun frigate, and he turned her into a hell afloat. In the West Indies her crew mutinied and killed him, which some people might say was fair enough; but they also murdered the three lieutenants and the Marine officer quite horribly, the purser, the surgeon, the clerk, the bosun and a reefer, hunting him right through the ship; then they carried her into La Guayra and gave her up to the Spaniards, with whom we were then at war. A hideous business from beginning to end. But some time later the Spaniards sailed her to Puerto Cabello, and there Ned Hamilton, who had the dear *Surprise* at that time, and a damned good crew as well, took the boats in at night and cut her out, although she was moored head and stern between two very powerful batteries and although the Spaniards were rowing guard. His surgeon, I remember, commanded a gig, a splendid man named M'Mullen. The Surprises killed a great many Spaniards, but most of the mutineers escaped; and when Spain joined us against the French a good many of them removed to the States. Some shipped in merchantmen, which was foolish, because merchantmen are often searched and whenever one was found he was taken out and hanged without a hope: their exact descriptions, tattoo-marks and everything, had been circulated to all the stations and there was a thumping price on their heads.'

'And there are some of these unfortunate men among the *Norfolk*'s crew?'

'Yes. One of them has offered to point out the rest if he is allowed to turn King's evidence and have the reward.'

'Informers – Lord, the world is full of them, so it is.'

'Well, now, this puts quite a different face upon it. Palmer has a score or so of Hermiones as well as other deserters aboard: the other deserters are liable to be hanged if they are taken, though they may be let off with five hundred lashes if they are foreigners, but for the Hermiones it is certain death; and although they are no doubt a pretty worthless set it is Palmer's clear duty to protect them: they are his men. Even as nominal prisoners of war they would have to be mustered and inspected and entered on the ship's books, and they would almost certainly be recognized and laid in irons, there to rot till they hang; but if they were merely rescued as castaways in time of peace they could be shuffled aboard with the rest. That seems to me his reasoning.'

'Perhaps these men are the band referred to in the ingenuous Mr Gill's letter that we captured in the packet. I quote from memory, "My Uncle Palmer's Paradise, for which we have some colonists, men who wish to live as far from their countrymen as ever can be." '

'May I come in?' asked Martin at the door: he had on a tarpaulin jacket, and in one streaming hand he held a barrel-hoop, also covered with tarpaulin, that served as a primitive umbrella, while with the other he kept the upper part of his shirt together, his bosom being stuffed with coconuts and breadfruit. 'Pray take these nuts before they fall,' he said; and as Jack turned from the hole, 'You have not seen the ship yet, sir, I suppose?'

'Oh no,' said Jack. 'She could not possibly be here today: I am only arranging my tube so as to sweep as much of the north-western horizon as possible when the time comes.'

'Would it be possible to form an estimate of how long she will take to come back?' asked Stephen.

'There are so many factors,' said Jack, 'but if they were able to make just a little northing towards the end of the first day, when the extreme force of the storm had dropped, and then to have brought the wind say two points on the quarter, so as to diminish the leeway as much as possible until they could shape a course for the island after the third day, why, then I think we might start looking for them in a week. Mr Martin, may I ask you for the jacket? I am going to see the men.'

'I met Mr Butcher during my walk or rather scramble,' said Martin as Captain Aubrey's steps went splashing away down the rain-soaked glade. 'He too possesses shoes and he too had made his way up the stream almost to its source. He inquired for you most earnestly, said that he was delighted with my account and that he would attend at a moment's notice if there were any renewed pressure or discomfort. But he also spoke of the ship in a way that made me very uneasy indeed. It appears that there is a chain of reefs and submerged islands a little to the west, a chain of great length, extending perhaps a hundred miles, and that it is almost impossible that the *Surprise* should not have been driven on some part of it.'

'Mr Butcher may be an excellent surgeon, but he is not a sailor.'

'Perhaps not, but he reported this as the considered opinion of the *Norfolk*'s officers.'

'I should not prefer their opinion to Captain Aubrey's. He knows of these reefs – he mentioned them when we were discussing the curious tide – and yet he spoke quite confidently of the ship's return.'

'Oh, I was not aware he knew of them. That is a great comfort to my mind, a very great comfort. I am quite easy again. Let me tell you about my walk. I did succeed in reaching the higher denuded ground; it was there, where the stream can be crossed as it flows over an uncomfortable bed of shattered obsidian and trachyte, that I met Mr Butcher, who agrees that the island is obviously volcanic; and it was there that I saw what I took to be a flightless rail, though perhaps it was only wet.'

Wet: the whole island was soaking wet, saturated with water; where the trees, great ferns and undergrowth stood on very steep slopes there had been landslides, leaving the dark rock bare, and the stream that came out at the landing-place was now a broad river, pouring thick mud and débris into the lagoon.

Jack's path took him along its left bank, strewn with tree-trunks and tangled, wrecked vegetation, and on the far side he saw Captain Palmer: Jack took off his hat and called out, 'Good day to you, sir,' and Palmer bowed and said something about 'the wind backing – more rain, maybe.'

These acknowledgements, repeated sometimes twice a day, were all the communication they had for the ensuing week. It was a dismal week upon the whole, with a good deal of rain, which kept the stream full; a week in which their hopes of fishing were disappointed. The vegetable food within easy reach had already been gathered; most of the broken coconuts and bruised breadfruits were rapidly going bad in the damp heat, and the Surprises had taken great pains to unlay cordage and spin fishing-lines as quickly as they could. But the lagoon was in a state of unexampled filth and most of its inhabitants had deserted it, though some, indeed, had been cast up dead in stinking swathes on the highwater-mark. The lean grey sharks were still there, however, and they made wading and casting surprisingly dangerous, they having a way of coming in to very shallow water; but in any case casting produced nothing but floating logs. Even when they righted the launch – a very heavy task – and rowed out things were not much better: most of the fish they caught were snatched hook and all by the sharks, and those they managed to preserve were ill-looking bloated purple creatures with livid spines that Edwards, one of the whalers and an old South Sea hand, said were poisonous – the spines were poisonous, the fish unwholesome. Fishing from the reef at low tide was a little more rewarding, but this too had its drawbacks: there were broad patches of stinging coral and many sea-urchins with wicked spines that broke off short when trodden upon, piercing bare feet deep and turning bad; two men were attacked and bitten by moray eels as they groped for clams, and a harmless-looking fish not unlike the rock-cod of Juan Fernandez brought all those who ate him out in a scarlet rash, accompanied by black vomit and the temporary loss of sight; while lame seamen were ten a penny, for although they were used to running about on deck barefoot, the smooth wood did not give their soles any great toughness – they usually put on shoes to go aloft, for example – and thorns, volcanic glass and coral rock soon wounded them.

In spite of the rain, the tangled and sometimes almost impenetrable vegetation, and the spiny creeper that made walking barefoot so unpleasant, men did move about the island, however, impelled by hunger or in one case by fear. On Thursday Bonden said to Jack, 'That fellow Haines, sir, the Hermione as wanted to peach on his mates, he's afraid they know and are going to scrag him: says, may he come over to our side?'

Jack checked his first violent reply, reflected, and said, 'There is nothing to prevent him making himself a shelter in the woods somewhere behind us, shifting for himself and hiding until the ship comes in.'

For those who had shoes walking was less painful, of course, and Martin and Butcher met quite often; Butcher was a friendly, rather loquacious man and during these meetings the chaplain learnt that the Norfolks had hoped for the visit of a Russian man-of-war, known to be on a cruise of exploration in the central Pacific, or for that of one or another of the half dozen New Bedford or Nantucket whalers fishing in these waters or passing through them. Yet since these hopes, though lively, were necessarily indefinite, they had also intended to make a boat from the wood of the wreck, a boat in which an officer and two or three of the best seamen would sail to Huahiva for help: once the trade-wind had returned to its usual steadiness the journey, even with the long dog-leg to avoid the dreaded western reefs, would be only about four hundred miles, nothing in comparison with Captain Bligh's four thousand in this same ocean. But they had very little in the way of tools – only a small box that some freakish wave had flung on the reef – and the wreck had scarcely begun to break up; so far it had yielded no more than the hatches from which they had made their almost useless fishing-raft.

Towards the end of the week the rain diminished; crossing the upper part of the stream became easier and more men from either side came into contact with one another. This led to the first trouble. Like all the other whalers Edwards had most bitterly resented the burning of the *Intrepid Fox* and when he met an American he called him a whoreson longshoreman and no seaman, a poxed nigger's bastard, and gave him a blow with the stick he was carrying; the American made no reply but instantly kicked him in the private parts. They were separated in time by the carpenter and one of his mates and the American withdrew, followed by cries of 'Yankee poodle' and 'Keep your side of the bloody stream,' for the Surprises felt it to be a self-evident truth that all the territory this side was theirs. It must have seemed a natural limit, since the same day, a little lower down, Blakeney was chased back across the

344

water by a tall American midshipman with a red beard, who told him that if he were found poaching on their preserves again he should be cut up for bait.

But these incidents excited no great attention, all minds being turned to Sunday, the earliest day upon which the Captain had said the ship might be seen: most of the week's weather, though wet overhead and underfoot, had been favourable for her return, with the wind moderating and hanging a little south of south-east, and the great all-shaking crash of the swell on the outer reef dropping to a steady, half-heard thunder.

Sunday, and Jack's razor made the round of the officers, while the two surgical instruments trimmed the foremast hands, trimmed and scraped them painfully, none being an expert shaver – that was the ship's barber's job – but the pain was endured gladly, there being a pagan notion abroad that the more they suffered the more certainly they should see the ship. Church was rigged in the lee of the launch, with an awning spread and a reading-desk run up from stretchers and a thwart, lashed rather than nailed. Jack sent a note to Captain Palmer saying that if he, his officers and men chose to attend, they would be welcome; but Palmer declined on the grounds that few of his people belonged to the Anglican communion and none was in a state to appear at a public ceremony. His reply was civil and well-turned, however: it was necessarily verbal, since the Norfolks were as destitute of paper and pen as they were of everything else, and it was delivered by Mr Butcher; he remained for the service, which in spite of the lack of books was carried through creditably to the end. The Surprises ashore included five of the ship's truest and most determined singers, and the others followed them through the familiar hymns and psalms in a fine convincing volume of sound that carried out over the lagoon and far beyond the reef. Mr Martin did not venture upon a sermon of his own but turned once again to Dean Donne, quoting directly where he could rely on his memory and paraphrasing where he could not. All those present, apart from the score or so of Americans who sat here and there on the farther bank, had heard the matter before, a very real advantage for so intensely conservative a congregation. They approved of it; they admired it, and they listened with something of that same earnestness with which their eyes searched the horizon, straining for the slightest fleck of topsails against the pure blue sky.

It was odd, among so many seafaring men, accustomed to the uncertainty of the ocean and the unpredictability of anything to do with a voyage, that such importance should have been attributed to this first day of Jack's forecast, as though it possessed some magical quality; yet such was the case on both sides of the stream, and when the frigate was not seen that Sunday the Surprises, at least, were strangely cast down.

She was not seen on Monday, nor Tuesday, nor Wednesday, although the weather was so good; and as the week wore on Jack noticed that Palmer's bow grew daily less profound until by Friday it was little more than a casual nod. A great deal can be conveyed by a salute and no great perspicacity was called for to see that the Norfolks were perfectly aware that they outnumbered the Surprises by four to one, that every day increased their confidence and spirits, and that it would be difficult to oblige Palmer to deal with his people's share of the increasing hostility, with the isolated fights and scuffles that threatened to develop into general violence.

Jack blamed himself extremely. He should have stayed in his ship: his presence on shore had done nothing more towards furthering Stephen's operation than that of any of the other officers. He had behaved like an anxious old woman. Or if he had felt absolutely obliged to go ashore to deal with Palmer he should in the very first place have attended to the tide, for in spite of their partial obliteration by the hurricane an intelligent seaman's eye could have detected the signs of its unusual period and great force in the channel; and in the second place he should certainly have brought a party of Marines; even perhaps the launch's carronade. As it was, all the weapons the Surprises possessed were his sword, Blakeney's dirk and pocket-pistol, and the boat-hook; the seamen all had their knives, of course, but then so did most of the Norfolks.

'I fear you are grieving for the *Surprise*, brother,' said Stephen as they sat alone outside the hut, looking down to the evening sea. 'I trust you do not despair of our friends?'

'Despair? Oh Lord, no,' cried Jack. 'She is a sound, well-found, weatherly ship, and Mowett has a crew of thorough-paced seamen. Even though he may not have known of that damned reef, I am sure that when her cables parted his first instinct would have been to keep her from going away to leeward as much as ever he could; and from what I remember of the changing direction of the wind and from all I can learn of the position of the shoal, he must have weathered its northern end. No, what I am afraid for is that wretched fished mizen. Mr Lamb is of the same opinion. How he regrets not having clapped on a double woulding while there was yet time!'

'Would the loss of the mizen be very grave, at all?'

'Not for going before the wind, since with the breeze right aft it wears no sails; but for beating up, for turning to windward – in short for getting back to this island – it is absolutely essential. If the fished mizen went, then clearly the *Surprise* would have to bear away. She would necessarily go away to the westward, and Mowett would steer for Huahiva.'

'He could then return, however, having found a new mast?'

'Yes. But it would take some finding, and with Lamb and his mates all here it would take some assembling, fitting and stepping; but above all he would be compelled to beat up against the trade-wind and the current day after day. He could not be here for a month.'

'Oh, oh,' said Stephen, with a significant look.

'Just so. The situation here is not going to remain steady for a month, nor anything like so long.' There were voices behind the hut, and although Captain Aubrey had the highest opinion of the launch's crew as shipmates and seamen, he knew they were very much given to eaves-dropping – the theoretically watertight compartments of a man-of-war were pierced through and through by this universal practice and most schemes were known to the men who were to carry them out long before the order was given, while most people's domestic affairs were also the subject of informed discussion. Certainly this had its uses and it gave the ship something of a family quality; but in the present case Jack did not wish to have his views widely known, for the contacts between the two sides were not solely hostile by any means, and the more peacable men from either ship, meeting in the higher woods, the vague no-man's land beyond the rising of the stream, would often fall into conversation, particularly if they happened to be neutrals. It was a Finn, for example, who told the *Surprise*'s Pole, Jackruski, that there was a strong party led by two sea-lawyers, who maintained that the *Norfolk*'s officers, having lost both their ship and their commissions, had at the same time lost their authority, and that this made discipline hard to maintain, particularly as the *Norfolk*'s bosun and her hard-horse first lieutenant, dreaded by all, had both been drowned.

These particular voices in fact belonged to Martin and Butcher, who were walking down the path together. Butcher had come to call on Dr Maturin and to convey a message to Captain Aubrey from Captain Palmer. Captain Palmer presented his best compliments, and begged to remind Captain Aubrey of the agreement that the stream should mark the boundary between their territories, with the exception of the fore-shore on the Surprises' side of the water, which the Norfolks might traverse without let or hindrance to reach the beginning of the eastern reef: Captain Palmer was however concerned to report that a small group of his men had been turned back that morning, jeered at and pelted with seaweed; and he trusted that Captain Aubrey would at once take the proper measures. 'Pray tell Captain Palmer, with my compliments,' said Jack, 'that if this was not mere horseplay the culprits shall be dealt with, and if he wishes he may attend or send an officer to witness punishment: in any event you will present my expressions of regret and assurance that it will not occur again.'

'Now, Stephen,' he said when they were alone, 'let me give you an arm up towards the top of the island. There is a flat place over the black cliff that gives a splendid visto. You have not been there yet.'

'By all means,' said Stephen. 'And on the way we may possibly catch a glimpse of Martin's flightless rail. But perhaps you will have to bring me down on your back; my legs are still miserably weak.'

The flightless rail crept silently into a bush at the sound of Captain Aubrey's heavy-footed gasping approach, but the bare volcanic platform they eventually reached did provide them with a stretch of some thirty miles of white-flecked ocean westwards and on either side, with two separate schools of whales, one to the north, the other to the south, and with a plunging view of the entire leeward side of the island with the stream running dark and troubled into the still turbid lagoon, the white line of the reefs, and foreshortened people walking about on the sand.

Mr Lamb and two of his mates were putting the finishing touches to a little house they had begun making for themselves the very day after that ominous Sunday when the ship did not appear.

To them, from among the trees, entered the young carpenter of the *Norfolk*, who called out an affable greeting: 'What cheer, mates.'

'What cheer,' they replied in noncommittal voices, putting down their tools and looking at him with a studious lack of expression.

'It might come on to blow tonight, but we have had a fine clear day so far, and must not complain.' The Surprises did not choose to commit themselves on that either,

349

and after a pause the Norfolk went on, 'You wouldn't lend a man a saw-sett, I suppose? Mine went down with the barky.'

'No, mate, I wouldn't,' said Mr Lamb. 'Because why? Because firsto I never lend tools anyhow, and secondo because that would be comforting the King's enemies, which is death at the yardarm and may God have mercy on your soul, amen.'

'But the war's over,' cried the Norfolk.

'You tell that to the Marines, cully,' said Mr Lamb, laying his right forefinger along the side of his nose. 'I wasn't born yesterday.'

'I met your mate in the woods Thursday,' said the Norfolk, pointing at Henry Choles, carpenter's crew, 'under a breadfruit tree.'

'Under a breadfruit tree it was,' said Choles, nodding solemnly. 'Which it had lost three branches as thick as the mainmast. I passed the remark at the time.'

'And we wished one another joy of the peace. So he believes it's peace. Of course it's peace.'

'Henry Choles is a tolerable good craftsman, and he is as honest as the day is long,' said Mr Lamb, gazing at him objectively. 'But the trouble with him is, he was born on the Surrey side, and not so very long ago neither. No, young chap,' – this to the Norfolk, quite kindly – 'I was out of my time before you stopped shitting yellow, and I never seen any set of men behave like your mates in time of peace. I reckon it is all a pack of lies to get sent home free, gratis and for nothing, and to do us out of our head-money.'

'Stephen,' said Jack, passing his little pocket-glass, 'if you look steadily just this side of the horizon, where I am pointing, I believe you will see a steadier line of white water trending away to the right. I take it to be the shoals they spoke of. A damned awkward thing to find under your lee by night. From here you would have to steer almost due north for half a day on a breeze like this.' The 'breeze like this' was the warm steady trade, eddying about them on this sheltered platform but singing steadily over the high ridge behind, a fine topgallantsail wind. 'However, what I really meant to say was this: I intend to lengthen the launch to take her to Huahiva. It must be done fairly soon, or we shall have no launch left to lengthen; ill-feeling is growing stronger and when the island is stripped bare of food it will obviously grow stronger still. I do not think Palmer has a strong hold over his men, and the Hermiones have an even greater motive for knocking us on the head than the others, above all now that Haines has deserted them and they know they are detected. And every day the *Surprise* does not appear makes them bolder.'

'Why must you lengthen the launch?'

'To get everybody in. She was loaded to the gunnels when we brought you ashore. She must be lengthened if she is to face the open sea.'

'A long task would it be, at all?'

'Inside a week, I believe.'

'I will not ask, have you thought they may take it away from us when it is done, or even before? I know they wish to be away to Huahiva themselves, to bring a whaler back for their friends, God forbid.'

'It had occurred to me. I do not think their spirits are high enough to make the attempt before we start work; and then I think that if we are brisk enough we can find means to dissuade 'em when it is done. No, my chief concern is victualling, victualling for what may be quite a long voyage, since I have no instruments. As for water, we have barrels enough for a fortnight at short measure and I hope we can still find a few hundred sound drinking-coconuts; but the question is food. Now that fishing has failed us – and I had banked on drying them as we did at Juan Fernandez – I should like to know whether there is anything you can suggest. The pith of the tree-ferns? Roots? Bark? Pounded leaves?'

'Sure we did pass a little dwarvish sorts of yam on the way up, an undoubted Dioscorea – I called out to you, but you were far ahead, snorting, and did not attend – yet they do not really thrive here, any more than the land-crab, alas, and I should place my chief reliance upon the shark. He may not be very palatable; his appearance cannot recommend him anywhere; but his flesh, like that of most selachians, is reasonably wholesome and nourishing. He is easily taken; and I recommend that his upper flanks should be cut in long thin strips, dried and smoked.'

'But Stephen,' said Jack, glancing towards the wreck of the *Norfolk*, 'think what they must have been feeding on.'

'Never let us be missish, my dear: all earthly plants to some degree partake of the countless dead since Adam's time, and all the fishes of the sea share at first or second or hundredth hand in all the drowned. In any case,' he added, seeing Jack's look of distaste, 'sharks are very like robins, you know; they defend their territory with equal jealousy, and if we take ours over by the far channel no one will be able to reproach us with anthropophagy, even at one remove.'

'Well,' said Jack, 'I am too fat anyway. Please to show me your yams.'

The yams sprawled down a scree descending from the island's highest point: the path to the platform skirted the lower edge of the fall and here Stephen showed the climbing stems and typical leaf and a single misshapen tuber that he found by turning a few stones. 'They are not happy here, poor stunted things; it is not a scree they want at all but deep damp earth. Yet if you were to climb there is a fair possibility that you might find the parents of these dwarfs, a fine prosperous stock with great stout roots growing in a long-filled crater at the top of this scree, a territory from which these miseries have overflowed. I shall wait for you here, being but feeble. If you should chance upon any beetles on your way up, put them gently in your handkerchief, if you please.'

Stephen sat; and presently, with a beating heart and that very particular lively fresh happiness that had not changed since his boyhood, he saw the flightless rail walk out on to a bare patch of ground, stretch one useless though decorative wing, scratch itself, yawn, and eventually pass on, allowing him to breathe again.

Jack climbed, travelling along the edge of the scree and sampling yams every now and then; they began if anything even more dwarvish and misshapen, not unlike the potatoes he grew himself at home; but stimulated by the hope of Stephen's crater and the recollection of the monstrous tubers he had seen in former times, insipid great things that would feed a boat's crew for a day, he climbed on. The top was much farther than he had thought, and a recent deluge, blocking the crater's outlet, had turned it into a lake, with the no doubt enormous yams rotting under ten feet of putrid water. But the greater height gave him an even greater expanse of ocean and as he sat there recovering his breath he gazed at the far western reef, or chain of sunken islands. The horizon lay far beyond it now and he had a much clearer view of its length and breadth: a most formidable shoal indeed, with never a gap or channel that he could make out. And obliging his mind to be as cold, objective and analytical as it could be, he gauged the *Surprise*'s chances of having weathered it, in the exact circumstances of that wicked night. Not as much as one in three was the answer, and his eyes filled with tears.

A series of atolls far to the north was the most dangerous place, he reflected; and while he stared at it, taking in the whole naked-eye field of vision, it seemed to him that he saw something dark beyond and he reached for his glass. Dark it was: a ship it was. He lay flat, resting his telescope on a rock and covering his head with his coat against all outside light. He had known at once that she was not the *Surprise* but it took him ten minutes, a quarter of an hour, of very careful focusing and staring to be certain that she was an American whaler, steering south.

She was on the western side of that immensely long shoal: if she meant to call at this island she would have to work clean round it and then beat up; but unless the wind increased she could easily do so in a week. He fixed the bearings in his mind and ran down the scree. 'Forgive me, Stephen,' he said, 'I must hurry down to the camp: there is not a moment to be lost. Follow me at your own pace.'

'Mr Lamb,' he said in an even voice, having recovered his wind, 'a word with you.' They walked along the highwater-mark. 'I wish you to lengthen the launch by eight feet so that she may take us to Huahiva, there probably to rejoin the ship. Can you do that with the tools and materials at your disposition?'

'Oh Lord, yes, sir. We could cut some lovely natural aprons and timber-heads not fifty yards from the shore.'

'I meant at once, with the wood you have. There is not a moment to lose.'

'Why, sir, I reckon I could; but it would mean pulling down the Doctor's place straight away.'

'He shall have a tent. But before we lengthen the boat we must be armed: what can you turn into hangers or boarding-pikes without jeopardizing your work?'

The carpenter reflected. 'For hangars or cutlasses I can't do much, seeing as how I must keep my saws; but for boarding-pikes, Lord love you, sir,' – laughing very cheerfully – 'I could arm the hosts of Midian, if so desired. I tossed a whole keg of ten-inch spikes into the boat, and Henry Choles, thinking I had forgot, tossed in another. And your ten-inch spike, with its head flattened and given a curl on the bick of the anvil, its body shaped just so, and the whole tempered at cherry-pink in loo-warm seawater, gives a very serviceable pike. Not Tower of London work, they may say; but when they have six inches of converted spike in their weams, there's little odds whether it's London work or local.'

'Have you your forge and anvil here?'

'No, sir, but I can soon fudge up a pair of bellows, and there are all these old black stones for our anvil.

Sam Johnson, the armourer's mate that rows bow oar is just the man; he served his time to a cutler, and is uncommon neat.'

'Capital, capital. Then let that be put in hand at once, together with the shaping of the staves. Twenty will answer very well: I have my sword, Mr Blakeney has his dirk and a pistol – in any case he could scarcely manage a pike – and I do not suppose Mr Martin would think it right. We shall also need three shark-hooks, fast to as much of the bridlechain as we can spare: indeed, they had better precede the pikes, and they will give colour to the lighting of the forge. But, Mr Lamb, let the whole thing be done as privately as possible, among the trees. The launch will go a-fishing as soon as the hooks are ready and some sort of a light frame will be required for drying and smoking about thirty stone of shark in strips. At the same time it would be as well to make sure our casks are water-tight. And I cannot impress upon you too strongly, Mr Lamb, that there is not a moment to lose: all hands will work double tides.'

All hands were much shocked at this. During their weeks ashore on Old Sodbury, with little more than the formal skeleton of ship's routine maintained and with a great deal of wandering about by themselves in the woods or on the reef in search of food or fishing with a line from the rocks, they had lost the habit of brisk motion and instant unquestioning obedience; they were also still fractious from the absence of tobacco and grog, and it was with indignation and a sense of outrage that they heard their Captain 'roaring like a bull in a bush' as Plaice put it, insisting that everything should be done at the double if not triple and even wielding a rope's end – a weapon very few had ever seen him use except on his midshipmen in the privacy of the cabin – with horrible force and accuracy.

'It is like being in a prison-ship,' said George Abel, bow-oar in Johnson's absence, 'only worse. "Jump to it, you idle lubber. Quick's the word and sharp's the action, damn your eyes." What has come over him, topping it the slave-driver?'

'Perhaps this will pacimollify him,' said Plaice, spitting towards the moderate-sized shark towing behind, pursued by its kin.

'Rowed off all!' cried Bonden, and the launch ran crunching up the strand. Abel instantly leapt out and seized not the painter but the stout line hitched round the shark's tail, with which he and half a dozen others hauled the creature from the sea, its followers rushing in so close for a last bite that they were only just awash.

Abel and his mates cut the shark's head off with the carpenter's axe and looked up for approval – a fish just the size required, and hardly bitten at all. This was no time for idle gaping, they were told; this was not Bartholomew Fair; they might join Mr Blakeney's party and run, *run*, not waddle, to the north-east point of the island, where there were still coconuts to be found. Any man that did not bring back twenty would curse the day he was born.

They left at the double, passing the forge among the trees, where the bellows wheezed and the sweating armourer hammered, naked but for an apron; and they met files of worried-looking men running down from the ruins of the hut with loads of timber, while others, equally anxious, brought in faggots of pike-staves as straight and knot-free as they could find.

So they spent the day, never sitting down, never merely walking; but that was not enough. They were divided into watches as though they were on board, and each watch spent part of the night turning the long strips of shark's flesh on the framework by the fire and teasing coconut-fibre into oakum for caulking the lengthened boat; and it was striking to see how much their sleeping minds returned to shipboard time and its four-hour rhythm – each watch relieved the other almost as regularly as though the bell had been struck throughout the night. It was as well that there was a watch on deck as it were, for at two in the morning a curious wind got up and for three or four hours it blew hard from the north-west, working up a heavy short sea against the swell and endangering the fire, the unsavoury, glue-smelling food, and the new pitched tents.

It was a sea that drove straight into the lagoon through the two channels; it came on the flood-tide, hissing far up the beach, and there was not a sailor who did not know that it must work upon the wrecked frigate. The Norfolks themselves were not very early risers in general but a little after sunrise, when the Surprises were at their breakfast, a small part of them crossed the stream and hurried along the tide-line, on their way to the beginning of the reef. Although it was understood on both sides that they had a right of way they did not care to go by in the presence of many of the Surprises and their officers and most pretended not to notice them, though two of the more friendly, the more conversable, uttered a discreet howl and gave a jerk of the thumb.

Although in fact the wreck had not yet opened to any significant extent and although the red-bearded midshipman reported this to Captain Palmer, more men went by in the course of the morning; but it was not until half past eleven that they came back, twenty-five or thirty of them, dragging the *Norfolk*'s larboard headrails and some of her forecastle planking. By this time most of the Surprises were scattered about the island, engaged on various urgent tasks, and the carpenters were almost alone, busily sawing the launch in two: though Mr Lamb himself had retired privately into the bushes. The only other man on the beach was Haines, a cooper by trade, who had won a kind of half-acceptance by making himself useful to Mr Martin, and who was now attending to the very troublesome barrels. He ran away as soon as he saw the Norfolks, pursued by shouts of 'Judas'; but there were no former Hermiones among the band and they did not pursue him for any distance – a few made as if to catch him, but only for the fun. Another group came up to the carpenters and asked them what they were doing – commended their tools, their workmanship – said they too would presently be building their own boat, now the wreck was breaking up – and talked on at some length in spite of surly answers or none at all. Then suddenly their leader cried 'Look! Look!' pointing inland. The carpenters turned their heads. The Norfolks seized a compass-saw, a sheet of the launch's copper, a handful of spikes, a pair of pincers, a small auger and a rasp and ran away laughing. It was a laughing matter for a hundred yards or so: one man tripped and lost his rasp, and another threw down his awkward sheet of copper to run faster; but by the time Choles overtook the man with the compass-saw he was already among his fellow Norfolks. Choles tried to snatch the saw, but they flung him down: Choles' friends came to his help, one hitting out with a carpenter's maul, breaking an arm directly, and Mr Lamb came running from the wood with a dozen Surprises. At this the Norfolks all drew together, wielding pieces of wood, and withdrew steadily across the water into their own territory, leaving most of their timber on the bank. The Surprises had two carpenter's axes and an adze and they would have gone on to recover the tools if they had not been stopped this side of the water by an enormous roar of 'Belay, there' from Captain Aubrey, some way up the hill.

They hurried back to him, the carpenters all talking together, calling for an instant raid with the pikemen to recover the tools.

'Mr Lamb,' he asked, 'how necessary are the lost tools for the immediate work in hand?' But he was obliged to shake the carpenter by the shoulder before Lamb's face, pale with fury, showed much sense, and shake him again before he made a coherent reply to the effect that the compass-saw would be needed tomorrow.

'Well then,' said Jack, 'get on with your work until dinner-time. I shall attend to the matter in the afternoon.'

He ate his own dinner – a discouraging piece of shark, grilled, and coconut for pudding – in company with

Stephen and Martin. They talked in a general way about flightless birds and the colonization of remote oceanic islands, and he followed fairly well; but by far the greater part of his mind was taken up with his forthcoming interview with Palmer.

This morning's incident had to be dealt with, of that there was no doubt. Anything more of this kind would lead to open bloody battle, and although with his pikemen and axes he could probably sustain it, continual open violence would delay the launching of the boat intolerably and even perhaps make it impossible. There was not only the lengthening but the re-rigging, the caulking, the victualling and a thousand other things. A final attack, an attempt at taking the launch once it was ready – that was another matter, and if it could not be avoided by the various stratagems he had in mind he was reasonable confident that it could be dealt with by main force, particularly if the pikes could be kept in reserve, for the full daunting effect of surprise. What he must aim at was comparative tranquillity for three days, and then, before she was obviously ready, they could run her down to the beach before moonrise on Thursday night, pull out into the lagoon, lie there at a grapnel, step the masts, complete the re-rigging and the half-deck, out of reach from the shore, and sail on the evening tide. The question was, how much command did Palmer have over his men? He had lost almost all his officers either by drowning or by being sent away in prizes – no doubt many of his best seamen too – and he was very much alone, unseconded. How much were the former Hermiones an integral part of the *Norfolk*'s crew? Could they draw many of the others with them? How much was Palmer influenced by his remaining officers, the surgeon and the shadowy master or lieutenant who kept so very much out of sight? These were questions whose answers he should have to read on Palmer's hairy enigmatic face that afternoon.

When dinner was finished he took a few turns on the level sward in front of the tent and then called his coxswain. 'Bonden,' he said, 'I am going to see the captain of the *Norfolk*. Give my hat and coat a shake over the side, will you?'

'Yes, sir,' said Bonden, who was perfectly prepared for the visit. 'Which I have put a shaving edge on your sword, taken Mr Blakeney's pistol, drawn and dried the charges, and knapped the flints.'

'Just the thing for a cutting-out expedition, Bonden,' said Jack, 'but this is a genteel morning call.'

'Morning call my arse,' muttered Bonden, shaking the Captain's coat vehemently, some way to leeward. 'How I wish we had the carronade.' He slipped the pistol into his pocket – there was already a long thin dangerous blade of the kind called a gully inside his belt and a jacknife on a laniard round his neck – passed the hat and followed his Captain.

It was indeed the air of a social call that Jack gave his visit, and Palmer, a man of breeding, responded with trivialities of much the same kind; but while the small-talk was running its smooth insipid course Jack observed that the man he was speaking to had changed very much since their last interview: Palmer was obviously ill; he looked much older; he had shrunk; he was under great tension and Jack had the impression that he had been quarrelling furiously within the last few hours.

'Now, sir,' said Jack at last, 'it seems that some of our men got into a foolish scrape this morning. I do not believe that any real harm was meant, but it was the kind of horse-play that might have turned very ugly.'

'It did turn very ugly. John Adams' arm was broke: Mr Butcher is setting it now.'

'I am sorry for that; but what I meant by ugly was half a dozen men stretched out dead for a miserable compass-saw – for a foolish young seaman's prank. I did manage to call my carpenters off – they had axes, you know – but it was not easy and I should not like to have to do it again. Perhaps you may have noticed that men ashore, if the ship is not just at hand, are never so easy to control.'

'I have noticed nothing of the kind,' said Palmer sharply, darting a suspicious look from under his bushy eyebrows.

'Well I have,' said Jack. 'And it appears to me, Captain Palmer, that there is such a state of hostility between our men that it is like sitting in a powder-magazine with a naked light. The least thing may cause an explosion. So I must beg you will give very strict orders that this dangerous sort of caper should never be repeated: and incidentally I must have my compass-saw again. I do not suppose there was ever any intention of really stealing it.'

The tent wall bulged slightly in and it was fairly clear that Palmer was in contact, either by whispering or nudging, with someone outside. 'You shall have your compass-saw,' he said. 'But I must tell you, Captain Aubrey, that I was on the point of sending for you . . .'

'Sending for me?' said Jack, laughing. 'Oh no, no, no. Nonsense. Post-captains do not send for one another, my dear sir. And even if they did so far forget themselves, I must remind you that you are at least *de jure* my prisoner.'

'Of desiring you to come, then, so that I might officially acquaint you that this island is American territory, by right of first discovery, and direct you to remove to the far side of the northern reef, where your men will not hinder the recovery of the *Norfolk*'s timbers and stores.'

'I cannot accept your contention about sovereignty for a moment,' said Jack. 'In any event it is a political question quite outside my competence. But as to your notion of putting a greater distance between our men, I entirely agree. You have noticed, I am sure, that we are lengthening our boat. When the work is finished I shall take my people so far that there will be very little likelihood of trouble. But for that I must have my tools again.'

'You shall have them,' said Palmer, and he uttered a hail that began well but died in a most pitiful quaver. 'You shall have them,' he muttered again, passing his hand over his eyes. They came in a piece of sailcloth, the spikes, pincers and compass-saw, brought by the red-haired midshipman, and while Jack was making some civil remarks about his satisfaction Palmer broke out in a strong voice, 'Finally, Captain Aubrey, since you maintain that a state of war still subsists, you must be prepared to take the logical consequences of your words.'

'I do not understand you, sir,' said Jack: but Palmer, obviously unwell, replied only with a choking excuse and hurried out of the tent. Jack stood there for a moment in the opening and then, asking the midshipman to send word if Mr Butcher would like to consult Dr Maturin, handed the tools to Bonden and took his leave.

The path from the tent to the stream was bordered with close-packed tree-ferns, and in their deep shade stood men, a dozen or so on either side and more to be guessed behind the trunks; they were silent as Jack approached but when he passed their voices could be heard, low and urgent, arguing – English voices. 'Scrag the bugger now,' cried one and a stone hit Jack's shoulder. Almost immediately the strong metallic Boston shouting of the midshipman echoed through the trees and Jack walked on, crossing the stream in the usual place.

'Mr Lamb,' he said, coming up to the dismantled launch, 'here are your tools. Ply them like a hero and I believe we may still be afloat the day I had reckoned on. You may have every man-jack you want to hold a plank or shape a treenail.'

That evening and the next day the launch began to take shape again, and on the Wednesday it was fairly covered with men fitting, joining, faying, rasping and hammering under their Captain's immediate eye, for by now the victualling, such as it was, had been completed: net after net of coconuts stood ready to be loaded; the strong-smelling parched shark lay there in flat sailcloth bales; and only the water-casks stood apart, still leaking badly. The boat was screened from public view by casually draped sails and Jack thought it unlikely that the Norfolks knew just what stage they had reached. He had told Martin that although the launch would probably be ready late on

Friday he would not put to sea until the next day, because of the foremast jacks' superstition; and this Martin had handed on in perfect good faith to Butcher. And quite apart from that Jack felt reasonable confident that there would be no attempt at seizing the boat until dawn on Friday at the earliest, if indeed there was an attempt at all; and by then she would already have been floating out on the lagoon for some hours. But by way of precaution he had the pikes stowed close at hand, and he took a casual shot or two with the pistol, to show that ammunition was there in plenty.

The entire period since his remote sighting of the American whaler had been one of the most intense driving activity, but this Wednesday outdid all the rest. Although for the purpose of deceit the launch's masts were not to be stepped, a great deal of rigging could be prepared in advance; so on this afternoon there was not a skilled hand but was hard at work – carpenters, riggers, sailmakers, caulkers, ropemakers, stripped to the waist and labouring under the shade of the palm fronds with such concentration that they rarely spoke.

In this connection neither the chaplain nor the surgeon could be looked upon as skilled hands, and they had been sent with net bags to gather yams. They had most conscientiously filled their bags, but they had spent even more of their time persecuting the rail, creeping after it through bushes until it made a dash across the open part of the scree, running as fast as a partridge and leaping down a ten-foot drop with a despairing cry. Now, before going down to call on Mr Butcher and inquire for Captain Palmer, they were resting on the high platform, lying on their backs with their heads on the yams, gazing up at the cloud that hung over the island, perpetually torn away to leeward and perpetually renewed from the south-east.

'Gmelin says that the Siberian rail sleeps buried in the snow,' observed Martin.

'Where did you find that?'

'In Darwin. Speaking of the early spring flowering of Muschus corallinus he says

Down the white hills dissolving torrents pour,
Green springs the turf, and purple blows the flower;
His torpid wing the Rail exulting tries,
Mounts the soft gale, and wantons in the skies –

and this he justifies in a note, citing John George Gmelin as his authority.'

'Sure, I honour the Gmelins; but there is something about rails that excites credulity. In my part of Ireland it is said that the land-rail, the corncrake, changes into a water-rail at the approach of autumn and then turns back again in spring. I trust Dr Darwin did not really believe in this hibernation: he is a respectable man.'

'Did you ever look into his *Zoonomia*?'

'I did not. But I do recall some lines of his *Origin of Society* that a lewd cousin of mine used often to recite:

"Behold!" he cries "Earth! Ocean! Air above,
And hail the Deities of Sexual Love!
All forms of life shall this fond pair delight,
And sex to sex the willing world unite."

Do you suppose, Martin, that that is what they are doing, down there on the strand? Hailing the deities, I mean. Seafaring men are wonderfully devoted to them, according to my experience.'

'Certainly they are making a most prodigious outcry.'

'Joyful, they sound.'

'Demented.'

'I shall look over the edge,' said Stephen, getting up. 'Oh my God,' he cried, for there on his left hand, not two miles from the shore, was an American whaler. She had rounded the southern headland and she was in full view of the shore, which was crowded with Norfolks, roaring and cheering, quite beside themselves. The red-headed midshipman and another youth had already raced out along the reef with incredible speed to warn her of the dangerous passage with the wreck across it. Some were running aimlessly up and down, bellowing and waving, but a score of men, a tight, eager pack, were after Haines in his red checked shirt; he dodged among the barrels, among the heaps of firewood, among the stores; he was headed off from the shelter of the trees, headed off from the launch, and hunted fast along the sea. They brought him down at the edge of the stream, disembowelled him and threw him into the water. Yet far the greater number swarmed round the boat, which the Surprises were desperately trying to push down to the hard sand and the sea. Some snatched away the slides, others flung her precious stores about or staved the water-casks with great stones in a mad destruction, and others, perfectly without fear of the pikes or anything else, tripped up the men who were shoving or threw whatever came to hand on the highwater-mark – seaweed, driftwood, lumps of coral – or even pushed in the other direction. Some had been put out of action – Jack's sword-arm was red to the elbow – but it had no effect; and presently the launch was hopelessly deep in dry sand. Once this was so, once escape was impossible, the attackers drew off, to line the sea and cheer their long-awaited whaler. All the Surprises were now inside the boat, which bristled with pikes, an impregnable stronghold for the time being. But for how long a time?

Stephen's heart was big to bursting with the violence of his grief, yet even as he looked distractedly from side to side his mind told him that there was something amiss, the more so as the cheering had now almost entirely died away. The whaler had a huge spread of canvas aboard, far too great a press of sail for her possibly to enter the lagoon: she was tearing along with a great bow-wave and she sped past the mouth of the farther channel. A cable's length beyond the opening her main and fore topgallantmasts carried clean away, as though brought down by a shot, and she instantly hauled to the wind, striking her colours as she did so. Her pursuer came racing into sight round

H.M.S. *Surprise*
Patrick O'Brian

'I don't see that anyone could wish for anything better than Mr O'Brian's sea stories.'   Julian Symonds, *Sunday Times*

H.M.S. *Surprise* follows the variable fortunes of Captain Jack Aubrey's career in Nelson's navy as he attempts to hold his ground against admirals, colleagues and the enemy, accepting a commission to convey a British ambassador to the East Indies. The voyage takes him and his friend Stephen Maturin to the strange sights and smells of the Indian subcontinent, and through the archipelago of spice islands where the French have a near-overwhelming local superiority.

Rarely has a novel managed to convey more vividly the fragility of a sailing ship in a wild sea. Rarely has a historical novelist combined action and lyricism of style in the way that O'Brian does. His superb sense of place, brilliant characterization and a vigour and joy of writing lifts O'Brian above any but the most exalted of comparisons.

'Few, very few books have made my heart thump with excitement. H.M.S. *Surprise* managed it. [O'Brian's] erudition is phenomenal, as is his capacity for creating another completely believable world. I might have given a better idea of this book if I had simply written 600 times the word "superb".'   Helen Lucy Burke, *Irish Times*

ISBN 0 00 614181 1

The Works of Patrick O'Brian

All these books are available from your local bookseller or can be ordered direct from the publishers.

To order direct just tick the titles you want and fill in the form below:

Name: _____

Address: _____

Postcode: _____

Send to HarperCollins Paperbacks Mail Order, Dept 8, HarperCollins *Publishers*, Westerhill Road, Bishopbriggs, Glasgow G64 2QT.

Please enclose a cheque made payable to HarperCollins Publishers, or a postal order or your authority to debit your Visa/Access account –

Credit card no: _____

Expiry date: _____

Signature: _____

to the value of the cover price plus:

UK & BFPO: Add £1.00 for the first book and 25p for each additional book ordered.

Overseas orders including Eire: Please add £2.95 service charge.

Books will be sent by surface mail but quotes for airmail despatches will be given on request.

24 HOUR TELEPHONE ORDERING SERVICE FOR ACCESS/VISA CARDHOLDERS –

TEL: GLASGOW 0141 772 2281 or LONDON 0181 307 4052